Praise for the early novels of
George R. R. Martin

DREAMSONGS

"A collection that achieves its aim in highlighting the true challenge
creative writing presents and the magic that can appear if we attempt
it. . . . From 'The Fortress' forwards, the reader will find nothing
that could be described as less than excellent, whilst occasionally
encountering a piece that is truly breathtaking. . . . George R. R.
Martin's *Dreamsongs* will fill the world with their sound for some
time to come and what better to follow a song than a Dance?"
—SF Crowsnest.com

WINDHAVEN
WITH LISA TUTTLE

"The pace never slackens, shifting easily from moments of almost
unbearable tension to others of sheer poetry and exhilaration.
Martin and Tuttle make wonderful professional music together."
—*Fort Worth Star-Telegram*

"I didn't mean to stay up all night to finish *Windhaven* but I had to!"
—Anne McCaffrey

"It's romance. It's science fantasy. It's beautiful."
—A. E. van Vogt

FEVRE DREAM

"Reads more like a strongly themed historical novel than gothic horror . . . far more engaging and meaningful than the usual flip-page violence that passes for horror fiction nowadays."
—*The Washington Post Book World*

"Grace, suspense, and just good old-fashioned knockout storytelling make it the kind of chiller one reads with unabated enthusiasm . . . and rereads with the rare commitment accorded only to the best tale-spinners."
—*Los Angeles Herald Examiner*

"A chilling vampire novel that will have those little hairs on the back of your neck standing at constant attention. A five star beauty [and one of] the best two books of the season."
—*Boston News Digest*

"[Here] solid characters, vivid descriptions of an opulent world, a plausible explanation of vampirism and some genuinely chilling scenes create one of the best. . . . The most satisfying and frightening novel of its kind since Stephen King's *Salem's Lot*."
—*Roanoke Times & World Herald*

"Spectacular, simply one of the best frighteners to appear in years . . . inventive, lucid, and genuinely scary—I'd recommend this to anyone who scoffs at genre writing."
—*Time Out*

"Skillfully balances historical realism and flights into fantasy and obsession. Its characters linger in the mind, along with the beauty of the great boats and the greater river." —*Locus*

"A skillful blend of adventure, supernatural horror, and accurate historical settings . . . Exceptionally good, this deserves superlatives in almost every respect."
—*Science Fiction Chronicle*

"Will delight fans of both Stephen King and Mark Twain . . . Darkly romantic, chilling and rousing by turns, moody and memorable, Martin's novel is a thundering success."
—Roger Zelazny

THE ARMAGEDDON RAG

"The best novel concerning the American pop music culture of the '60s I've ever read."
—Stephen King

"George R. R. Martin takes us on a wild, melodramatic, mystical hallucinatory voyage through the last two decades. Beautifully written. I couldn't put it down."
—Timothy Leary

"Moving . . . comic . . . eerie . . . really and truly a walk down memory lane." —*The Washington Post*

"A knowing, wistful appraisal of . . . a crucial American generation . . . poetic, nostalgic, daring."
—*Chicago Sun-Times*

"The wilder aspects of the '60s—the frenzied idealism, the cultism, the orgiastic rock music—roar back to life in this hallucinatory story by a master of chilling suspense."
—*Publishers Weekly*

"Vivid, perceptive, and passionate, *The Armageddon Rag* is George R. R. Martin's best book so far. . . . A must for anyone who mourns the '60s—or who loved good, old-fashioned rock 'n' roll."
—Stephen R. Donaldson

"What a story, full of nostalgia and endless excitement for everyone! It's taut, tense, moves like lightning and it proves George Martin is . . . a master."
—Tony Hillerman

"Martin builds a never-been time in musical history in all its glory; the only thing the book lacks, to my mind, is a soundtrack album."
—SFSite.com

"Like a 'road movie' blended with amateur detective mixed with heavy rock and is one of the best goddamn books that I've ever read. Although originally released in 1983, it is a master class in how to write characters and develop them, set mood, etc. It even tells a story. . . . This book has a hearty recommendation for anyone with a liking for rock, old lyrics and a stonking good story."
—SF Crowsnest.com

DYING OF THE LIGHT

"I read *Dying of the Light* for the first time when I was fourteen, and it blew the doors off of my idea of what fiction could be and could do, what a work of unbridled imagination could make a reader feel and believe. Almost thirty years later I find that it reminds me of all that with as much power as ever, and that its heartbroken universe feels even more like home."
—Michael Chabon

"The Wild West in outer space, complete with a chase that will keep you awake. Slick science fiction."
—*Los Angeles Times*

"The kind of imagination that makes science fiction worth reading . . . An effective, affecting story."
—*Galaxy* magazine

"George R. R. Martin has the voice of a poet and a mind like a steel trap."
—Algis Budrys

"By turns thrilling, funny, scary, emotionally devastating, oddly inspirational, and just plain grand . . . This is top-notch kitchen-sink storytelling—part straightforward pulp, part high fantasy—that will leave you thirsty for more. Luckily, Martin has two more books on the way. But let's not rush the man, people: When the writing is this good, it's worth the wait."
—*Entertainment Weekly* (Grade: A)

A FEAST FOR CROWS

"Of those who work in the grand epic-fantasy tradition, Martin is by far the best. In fact . . . this is as good a time as any to proclaim him the American Tolkien. . . . *A Feast for Crows* isn't pretty elves against gnarly orcs. It's men and women slugging it out in the muck, for money and power and lust and love." —*Time*

"A Song of Ice and Fire is firmly at the top of the bestseller lists, probably because it's the best fantasy series out there."
—*Detroit Free Press*

"George R. R. Martin has created the unlikely gene of the realpolitik fantasy novel. Complete with warring kings, noble heroes and backroom dealings, it's addictive reading and reflects our current world a lot better than *The Lord of the Rings*."
—*Rolling Stone*

A STORM OF SWORDS

"George R. R. Martin continues to take epic fantasy to new levels of insight and sophistication, resonant with the turmoils and stress of the world we call our own."
—*Locus*

"Like a cross between a complicated game of chess, a quirky Stephen King tale and *Braveheart*, Martin's epic advances his series with gritty characterizations, bold plot moves and plenty of action."
—*St. Louis Post-Dispatch*

DREAMSONGS

❖

VOLUME I

George R. R. Martin

BANTAM BOOKS TRADE PAPERBACKS
NEW YORK

2012 Bantam Books Trade Paperback Edition

Illustrations by Michael Wm. Kaluta

Published in the United States of America by Bantam Books, an imprint of the
Random House Publishing Group, a division of Random House, Inc., New York.

Bantam Books and the rooster colophon are registered trademarks of Random House, Inc.

Originally published in one volume as *GRRM: A RRetrospective* by Subterranean Press in 2003.
Later republished in hardcover by Bantam Books in November 2007.

Library of Congress Cataloging-in-Publication Data
Martin, George R. R.
[GRRM]
Dreamsongs / George R. R. Martin.
p. cm.
Originally published in one volume as: GRRM : a rretrospective.
Burton, MI : Subterranean Press, c2003.
ISBN 978-0-553-38568-7 (v. I)
ISBN 978-0-553-38569-4 (v. II)
eBook 978-0-553-90432-1 (v. I)
eBook 978-0-553-90434-5 (v. II)
1. Fantasy fiction, American.   I. Title.
PS3563.A7239G7   2007
813'.54—dc22   2007017681

Printed in the United States of America

www.bantamdell.com

10 9 8 7 6 5 4 3 2

Book design by Susan Turner

CONTENTS

for Phipps, of course,

there is a road, no simple highway,
between the dawn and the dark of night.

I'm glad you're here to walk it with me.

ONE

A FOUR-COLOR FANBOY

GEORGE R. R. MARTIN

BY GARDNER DOZOIS

ALTHOUGH HE'S BEEN A MAJOR PLAYER IN SEVERAL DIFFERENT GENRES FOR MORE THAN thirty years, has won Hugo Awards, Nebula Awards, and World Fantasy Awards, George R. R. Martin has finally *made it,* beyond the shadow of a doubt.

The sure and certain sign of this is that someone else's book was recently advertised as being "In the tradition of George R. R. Martin!" When you're successful enough, when your books *sell* well enough that publishers try to entice customers to buy someone *else's* book by saying that it's *like* yours, then you've made it, you're a *really* Big Name Author, and no argument is possible.

If you doubt me, think of the *other* writers whose names are invoked with the phrase "in the tradition of" to sell books: J. R. R. Tolkien, Robert E. Howard, H. P. Lovecraft, Stephen King, J. K. Rowling. That's pretty heady and high-powered company, but there's little doubt that George—who, with his epic *A Song of Ice and Fire* novel sequence has become one of the best-selling, and, at the same time, most critically acclaimed of modern fantasists—belongs there... although if you'd told young George, the unpublished eager novice, that one day his name would be ranked in such august company, I'm sure he wouldn't have believed you... wouldn't have dared to *let* himself believe you, believe such an obvious wish-fulfillment fantasy.

Another thing the young George might not have believed, and something that many of his legions of present-day fans might not even *know* (and one thing that this collection is designed to demonstrate), is that George would become prominent in several *different* fields of endeavor. George has had respectable careers as a science fiction writer, a horror writer, a fantasy writer, a writer and producer for the television industry, and as an editor/compiler/concept-originator for the long-running *Wild Cards* series of stories and novels by many different hands, which has now reached its sixteenth volume, with the seventeenth on the way. What George has accomplished in each of these fields would satisfy many another professional as a life's work—one to be bragged about, in fact.

Not *George*, though, the greedy swine—he had to go and reach well-deserved prominence in *all* of them!

Born in Bayonne, New Jersey, George R. R. Martin made his first sale in 1971, and soon established himself as a mainstay of the Ben Bova *Analog* with vivid, evocative, and emotionally powerful stories such as "With Morning Comes Mistfall," "And Seven Times Never Kill Man," "The Second Kind of Loneliness," "The Storms of Windhaven" (in collaboration with Lisa Tuttle, and later expanded by them into the novel *Windhaven*), "Override," and others, although he was also selling to *Amazing, Fantastic, Galaxy, Orbit,* and other markets during this period. One of his *Analog* stories, the striking novella "A Song for Lya," won him his first Hugo Award, in 1974.

By the end of the '70s, he had reached the height of his influence as a science fiction writer, and was producing his best work in that category—and some of the best work by anyone in that period—with stories such as the famous "Sandkings," perhaps his single best-known story, which won both the Nebula and the Hugo in 1980, "The Way of Cross and Dragon," which won a Hugo Award in the same year (making George the first author ever to receive *two* Hugo Awards for fiction in the same year), "Bitterblooms," "The Stone City," "Starlady," and others. These stories would be initially collected in *Sandkings,* one of the strongest collections of the period. By now, he had mostly moved away from *Analog,* although he would have a long sequence of stories about the droll interstellar adventures of Haviland Tuf (later collected in *Tuf Voyaging*) running throughout the '80s in the Stanley Schmidt *Analog,* as well as a few strong individual pieces such as the novella "Nightflyers"—most of his major work of the late '70s and early '80s, though, would appear in *Omni,* at the time the best-paying market in science fiction, the top of the SF short-fiction food chain. (The late '70s also saw the publication of his memorable novel *Dying of the Light,* his only solo SF novel.)

By the early middle years of the '80s, though, George's career was turning in other directions, directions that would take him far from the kind of career-path that you might have forecast for him in the '70s. Horror was starting to burgeon then as a separate publishing category, in the early and middle '80s, and George would produce two of the most original and distinctive novels of the Great Horror Boom period of the '80s: 1982's *Fevre Dream*, an intelligent and suspenseful horror novel set in a vividly realized historical *milieu*, still one of the best of modern vampire novels, and 1983's big, ambitious, "rock 'n' roll horror apocalypse," *Armageddon Rag*. Although still considered a cult classic by some, *Armageddon Rag* was a severe commercial disappointment, and would pretty much bring George's career as a horror novelist to an end, although he'd continue to write horror at short lengths for a while, later winning the Bram Stoker Award for his horror story "The Pear-Shaped Man" and the World Fantasy Award for his werewolf novella "The Skin Trade." (Although most of George's horror was supernatural horror, he'd also do some interesting work during this period with science fiction/horror hybrids, including the above-mentioned "Sandkings" and "Nightflyers," two of the best such stories ever produced, perfectly valid both as science fiction *and* as horror at the same time.)

The fact that the Great Horror Boom of the '80s was itself beginning to run out of steam by this point, with stores pulling *out* the separate shelves for horror they'd put *in* a few years before and publishers folding their horror imprints, probably helped George with his decision to turn away from the horror genre. Increasingly, though, he'd turn away from the print world *altogether,* and move into the world of television instead, becoming a story editor on the new *Twilight Zone* series in the mid '80s, and later becoming a producer on the hugely popular fantasy series *Beauty and the Beast*.

Highly successful as a writer/story editor/producer in the television world, George had little contact with the print world throughout the mid-'80s (although he did win another Nebula in 1985 for his story "Portraits of His Children") and throughout most of the decade of the '90s, except as editor of the long-running *Wild Cards* shared-world anthologies, which reached fifteen volumes before the series faltered to a stop in the late '90s (it has made a resurgence in the new century, though, after a seven-year hiatus, so that *Wild Cards* is back in business as I write these words). By then, soured on the television business by the failure of his stillborn series *Doorways* to make it onto the air, Martin returned to the print world with the publication in

1996 of the immensely popular and successful fantasy novel *A Game of Thrones*, one of that year's best-selling genre titles.

The rest, as they say, is history. Genre fantasy history, but history nevertheless.

The novels and stories in the *A Song of Ice and Fire* sequence have maintained their popularity throughout the rest of the '90s and into the first years of the new century, and even built on it. All three volumes to date have won the Locus Award for Best Fantasy Novel in their respective years, and all three have been on the Final Nebula Ballot. *A Game of Thrones* was also a finalist for the World Fantasy Award, and *A Storm of Swords* was a finalist for the Hugo Award. A free-standing novella taken from *A Game of Thrones* and published in *Asimov's Science Fiction*, "Blood of the Dragon," won Martin another Hugo Award in 1997.

What is it that has enabled George to captivate readers in so many different fields? What qualities are there about George's work that ensnare readers, no matter *what* kind of story he's telling?

For one thing, George has always been a richly *romantic* writer. Dry minimalism or the cooly ironic games of postmodernism so beloved by many modern writers and critics are *not* what you're going to get when you open something by George R. R. Martin. What you're going to get instead is a strongly-plotted story driven by emotional conflict and crafted by someone who's a natural-born storyteller, a story that grabs you on the first page and refuses to let go. You're going to get adventure, action, conflict, romance, and lush, vivid human emotion: obsessive, doomed love, stark undying hatred, unquenchable desire, dedication to duty even in the face of death, unexpected veins of rich humor . . . and something that's rare even in science fiction and fantasy these days (let alone the mainstream)—a love of adventure for adventure's sake, a delighting in the strange and colorful, bizarre plants and animals, exotic scenery, strange lands, strange customs, stranger people, backed by the inexhaustible desire to see what's over the next hill, or waiting on the next world.

George is clearly a direct descendant of the old *Planet Stories* tradition, probably influenced by Jack Vance and Leigh Brackett in particular, although you can see strong traces of writers such as Poul Anderson and Roger Zelazny in his work as well. In spite of having long been a mainstay of *Analog*, science and technology play little real part in his work, where the emphasis is on color, adventure, exoticism, and lush romance, in a universe crowded and jostling both with alien races and human societies that have evolved toward strangeness in isolation, and where the drama is often generated by the inability of one of these cultures to clearly understand the psychology and values and motivations of another. "Color" is a word that can't be used too much in describing George's worlds, and, if you let him sweep you away with him, he'll take you to some of the most evocative places in recent SF and fantasy: to Mistfall at Castle Cloud on Wraithworld, to the endless windswept grasslands known as "the Dothraki Sea," to the cold ancient maze of the Stone City, to the bristlingly deadly oceans of Namor, to dusk over the High Lakes at Kabaraijian....

The most important reason, though, why so many readers are affected so strongly by George's work is the *people*. George has created a gallery of vivid characters—sometimes touching, sometimes grotesque, sometimes touching *and* grotesque—unmatched by most other writers, one rich and various enough to be reminiscent of Dickens: Damien Har Veris, the conflicted and tormented Inquisitor of the Order Militant of the Knights of Jesus Christ, in "The Way of Cross and Dragon," and his boss, the immense, aquatic, four-armed Grand Inquisitor, Torgathon Nine-Klariis Tûn, in the same tale; Shawn, the desperate survivor fleeing from icewolves and vampires across a bleak landscape of eternal winter, toward a stranger and more subtle danger, in "Bitterblooms;" Tyrion Lannister, the machiavellian dwarf who comes to shape the destiny of nations, in *A Clash of Kings;* the obsessed and ruthless games-player, Simon Kress, in "Sandkings;" the wistful ghost in "Remembering Melody;" the grotesque, creepy, unforgettable Pear-Shaped Man in the story of the same name; Lya and Robb, the doomed telepathic lovers in "A Song for Lya;" Haviland Tuf, the neurotic but clever albino ecological engineer with the power of a god at his command, in the stories collected in *Tuf Voyaging;* Daenerys Stormborn, daughter of kings and reluctant khaleesi of a khalasar of Dothraki horselords, on her way to face her destiny as the future Mother of Dragons . . . and dozens more.

George cares deeply about all of his people, even the spearcarriers, even the villains—and by caring so deeply, he makes *you* care for them as well.

Once you've mastered this magic trick, you don't really need another. That above all else is the thing that has earned George his place among all those other "in the Tradition of . . ." folk listed above. And it is the thing that ensures that, no matter what field he chooses to work in, people will read him—and want to read him again.

DREAMSONGS

VOLUME I

IN THE BEGINNING, I TOLD MY TALES TO NO ONE BUT MYSELF.

Most of them existed only in my head, but once I learned to read and write I would sometimes put down bits on paper. The oldest surviving example of my writing, which looks like something I might have done in kindergarten or first grade, is an encyclopedia of outer space, block-printed in one of those school tablets with the marbled black and white covers. Each page has a drawing of a planet or a moon, and a few lines about its climate and its people. Real planets like Mars and Venus co-exist happily with ones I'd swiped from *Flash Gordon* and *Rocky Jones,* and others that I made up myself.

It's pretty cool, my encyclopedia, but it isn't finished. I was a lot better at starting stories than I was at finishing them. They were only things I made up to amuse myself.

Amusing myself was something I'd learned to do at a very early age. I was born on September 20, 1948, in Bayonne, New Jersey, the firstborn child of Raymond Collins Martin and Margaret Brady Martin. I don't recall having any playmates my own age until we moved into the projects when I was four.

Before that, my parents lived in my great grandmother's house with my great grandmother, her sister, my grandmother, her brother, my parents, and me. Until my sister Darleen was born two years later, I was the only child. We had no kids next door either. Grandma Jones was a stubborn woman who refused to sell her house even after the rest of Broadway had gone commercial, so ours was the only residence for twenty blocks.

When I was four and Darleen was two and Janet was three years shy of being born, my parents finally moved into an apartment of their own in the new federal housing projects down on First Street. The word "projects" conjures up images of decaying high-rises set amongst grim concrete wastelands, but the LaTourette Gardens were not Cabrini-Green. The buildings stood three stories high, with six apartments on each floor. We had playgrounds and basketball courts, and across the street a park ran beside the oily waters of the Kill van Kull. It wasn't a bad place to grow up . . . and unlike Grandma Jones' house, there were other children around.

We swung on swings and slid down slides, went wading in the summer and had snowball fights in the winter, climbed trees and roller-skated, played stickball in the streets. When the other kids weren't around, I had comic books and television and toys to pass the time. Green plastic army men, cowboys with hats and vests and guns that you could swap around, knights and dinosaurs and spacemen. Like every red-blooded American kid, I knew the proper names of all the different dinosaurs (*Brontosaurus,* damn it, don't tell me any different). I made up the names for the knights and the spacemen.

At Mary Jane Donohoe School on Fifth Street, I learned to read with Dick and Jane and Sally and their dog, Spot. Run, Spot, run. See Spot run. Did you ever wonder why Spot runs so much? He's running away from Dick and Jane and Sally, the dullest family in the world. I wanted to run away from them as well, right back to my comic books . . . or "funny books," as we called them. My first exposure to the seminal works of western literature came through *Classics Illustrated* comics. I read *Archie* too, and *Uncle Scrooge,* and *Cosmo the Merry Martian.* But the Superman and Batman titles were my favorites . . . especially *World's Finest Comics,* where the two of them teamed up every month.

The first stories I can remember finishing were written on pages torn from my school tablets. They were scary stories about a monster hunter, and

I sold them to the other kids in my building for a penny a page. The first story was a page long, and I got a penny. The next was two pages long, and went for two cents. A free dramatic reading was part of the deal; I was the best reader in the projects, renowned for my werewolf howls. The last story in my monster hunter series was five pages long and sold for a nickel, the price of a Milky Way, my favorite candy bar. I remember thinking I had it made. Write a story, buy a Milky Way. Life was sweet . . .

. . . until my best customer started having bad dreams, and told his mother about my monster stories. She came to my mother, who talked to my father, and that was that. I switched from monsters to spacemen (Jarn of Mars and his gang, I'll talk about them later), and stopped showing my stories to anyone.

But I kept reading comics. I saved them in a bookcase made from an orange crate, and over time my collection grew big enough to fill both shelves. When I was ten years old I read my first science fiction novel, and began buying paperbacks too. That stretched my budget thin. Caught in a financial crunch, at eleven I reached the momentous decision that I had grown "too old" for comics. They were fine for little kids, but I was almost a teenager. So I cleared out my orange crate, and my mother donated all my comics to Bayonne Hospital, for the kids in the sick ward to read.

(Dirty rotten sick kids. *I want my comics back!*)

My too-old-for-comics phase lasted perhaps a year. Every time I went into the candy store on Kelly Parkway to buy an Ace Double, the new comics were right there. I couldn't help but see the covers, and some of them looked so *interesting* . . . there were new stories, new heroes, whole new companies . . .

It was the first issue of *Justice League of America* that destroyed my year-old maturity. I had always loved *World's Finest Comics,* where Superman and Batman teamed up, but JLA brought together all the major DC heroes. The cover of that first issue showed the Flash playing chess against a three-eyed alien. The pieces were shaped like the members of the JLA, and whenever one was captured, the real hero disappeared. I had to have it.

Next thing I knew, the orange crate was filling up once more. And a good thing too. Otherwise I might not have been at the comics rack in 1962, to stumble on the fourth issue of some weird-looking funny book that had the temerity to call itself "the World's Greatest Comic Magazine." It wasn't a DC. It was from an obscure, third-rate company best known for their not-very-scary monster comics . . . but it did seem to be a superhero team, which was my favorite thing. I bought it, even though it cost *twelve cents* (comics were meant to be a dime!), and thereby changed my life.

It was the World's Greatest Comic Magazine, actually. Stan Lee and Jack Kirby were about to remake the world of funny books. The *Fantastic Four* broke all the rules. Their identities were not secret. One of them was a *monster* (the Thing, who at once became my favorite), at a time when all heroes were required to be handsome. They were a family, rather than a league or a society or a team. And like real families, they squabbled endlessly with one another. The DC heroes in the *Justice League* could only be told apart by their costumes and their hair colors (okay, the Atom was short, the Martian Manhunter was green, and Wonder Woman had breasts, but aside from that they were the same), but the Fantastic Four had *personalities*. Characterization had come to comics, and in 1961 that was a revelation and a revolution.

The first words of mine ever to appear in print were "Dear Stan and Jack."

They appeared in *Fantastic Four* #20, dated August 1963, in the letter column. My letter of comment was insightful, intelligent, analytical—the main thrust of it was that Shakespeare had better move on over now that Stan Lee had arrived. At the end of my words of approbation, Stan and Jack printed my name and address.

Soon after, a chain letter turned up in my mailbox.

Mail for *me*? That was astonishing. It was the summer between my freshman and sophomore years at Marist High School, and everyone I knew lived in either Bayonne or Jersey City. Nobody wrote me letters. But here was this list of names, and it said that if I sent a quarter to the name at the top of the list, removed the top name and added mine at the bottom, then sent out four copies, in a few weeks I'd get $64 in quarters. That was enough to keep me in funny books and Milky Ways for years to come. So I scotch-taped a quarter to an index card, put it in an envelope, mailed it off to the name at the top of the list, and sat back to await my riches.

I never got a single quarter, damn it.

Instead I got something much more interesting. It so happened that the guy at the top of the list published a comic fanzine, priced at twenty-five cents. No doubt he mistook my quarter for an order. The 'zine he sent me was printed in faded purple (that was "ditto," I would learn later), badly written and crudely drawn, but I didn't care. It had articles and editorials and letters and pinups and even amateur comic strips, starring heroes I had never heard of. And there were reviews of other fanzines too, some of which sounded even cooler. I mailed off more sticky quarters, and before long I was up to my neck in the infant comics fandom of the '60s.

Today, comics are big business. The San Diego Comicon has grown into a mammoth trade show that draws crowds ten times the size of science fiction's annual WorldCon. Some small independent comics are still coming out, and comicdom has its trade journals and adzines as well, but no true fanzines as they were in days of yore. The moneychangers long ago took over the temple. In the ultimate act of obscenity, Golden Age comics are bought and sold inside slabs of Mylar to ensure that their owners can never actually *read* them, and risk decreasing their value as collectibles (whoever thought of that should be sealed inside a slab of Mylar himself, if you ask me). No one calls them "funny books" anymore.

Forty years ago it was very different. Comics fandom was in its infancy. Comicons were just starting up (I was at the first one in 1964, held in one room in Manhattan, and organized by a fan named Len Wein, who went on to run both DC and Marvel and create Wolverine), but there were hundreds of fanzines. A few, like *Alter Ego,* were published by actual adults with jobs and lives and wives, but most were written, drawn, and edited by kids no older than myself. The best were professionally printed by photo-offset or letterpress, but those were few. The second tier were done on mimeograph machines, like most of the science fiction fanzines of the day. The majority relied on spirit duplicators, hektographs, or xerox. (*The Rocket's Blast,* which went on to become one of comicdom's largest fanzines, was reproduced by *carbon paper* when it began, which gives you some idea of how large a circulation it had.)

Almost all the fanzines included a page or two of ads, where the readers could offer back issues for sale and list the comics they wanted to buy. In one such ad, I saw that some guy from Arlington, Texas, was selling *The Brave and the Bold* #28, the issue that introduced the JLA. I mailed off a sticky quarter, and the guy in Texas sent the funny book with a cardboard stiffener on which he'd drawn a rather good barbarian warrior. That was how my lifelong friendship with Howard Waldrop began. How long ago? Well, John F. Kennedy flew down to Dallas not long after.

My involvement in this strange and wondrous world did not end with reading fanzines. Having been published in the *Fantastic Four,* it was no challenge to get my letters printed by fanzines. Before long I was seeing my name in print all over the place. Stan and Jack published more of my LOCs as well. Down the slippery slope I went, from letters to short articles, and then a regular column in a fanzine called *The Comic World News*, where I offered suggestions on how comics I did not like could be "saved." I did some art for *TCWN* as well, despite the handicap of not being able to draw. I even had one cover published: a picture of the Human Torch spelling out the fanzine's name in fiery letters. Since the Torch was a vague human outline surrounded by flames, he was easier to draw than characters who had noses and mouths and fingers and muscles and stuff.

When I was a freshman at Marist, my dream was still to be an astronaut . . . and not just your regular old astronaut, but the first man on the moon. I still recall the day one of the brothers asked each of us what we wanted to be, and the entire class burst into raucous laughter at my answer. By junior year, a different brother assigned us to research our chosen careers, and I researched fiction writing (and learned that the average fiction writer made $1200 a year from his stories, a discovery almost as appalling as that laughter two years earlier). Something profound had happened to me in between, to change my dreams for good and all. That something was comics fandom. It was during my sophomore and junior years at Marist that I first began to write actual stories for the fanzines.

I had an ancient manual typewriter that I'd found in Aunt Gladys' attic, and had fooled around on it enough to become a real one-finger wonder. The black half of the black-and-red ribbon was so worn you could hardly read the type, but I made up for that by pounding the keys so hard they incised the letters into the paper. The inner parts of the "e" and "o" often fell right out, leaving holes. The red half of the ribbon was comparatively fresh; I used red for emphasis, since I didn't know anything about italics. I didn't know about margins, doublespacing, or carbon paper either.

My first stories starred a superhero come to Earth from outer space, like Superman. Unlike Superman, however, my guy did not have a super physique. In fact, he had no physique at all, since he lacked a body. He was a brain in a goldfish bowl. Not the most original of notions; brains in jars were a staple of both print SF and comics, although usually they were the villains. Making my brain-in-a-jar the good guy seemed a terrific twist to me.

Of course, my hero had a robot body he could put on to fight crime. In fact, he had a whole *bunch* of robot bodies. Some had jets so he could fly, some had tank treads so he could roll, some had jointed robot legs so he could walk. He had arms ending in fingers, arms ending in tentacles, arms ending in big nasty metal pincers, arms ending in ray guns. In each story my space brain would don a different body, and if he got smashed up by the villain, there were always spares back in his spaceship.

I called him Garizan, the Mechanical Warrior.

I wrote three stories about Garizan; all very short, but *complete*. I even did the art. A brain in a goldfish bowl is almost as easy to draw as a guy made of fire.

When I shipped off the Garizan stories, I chose one of the lesser fanzines of the day, figuring they stood a better chance of being accepted there. I was right. The editor snapped them up with shouts of glee. This was less of an accomplishment than it might seem. Many of those early fanzines were perpetually desperate for material to fill their dittoed pages, and would have accepted anything anyone cared to send them, even stories about a brain in a goldfish bowl. I could scarcely wait to see my stories in print.

Alas. The fanzine and its editor promptly vanished, before publishing even one of my Garizan stories. The manuscripts were not returned, and since I had not yet mastered the complexities of carbon paper, I had no file copies.

You would think that might have discouraged me, but in fact the acceptance of my stories had done such wonders for my confidence that I hardly noticed their subsequent disappearance. I went back to my typewriter, and invented a new hero. This one I named Manta Ray. A Batman wannabee, Manta Ray was a masked avenger of the night who fought crime with a bullwhip. In his first adventure I pitted him against a villain named the Executioner who had a special gun that shot tiny little guillotine blades instead of bullets.

"Meet the Executioner" turned out much better than any of the Garizan stories, so when it was done I raised my sights and sent it to a higher-quality fanzine. *Ymir*, edited by Johnny Chambers, was one of a number of 'zines coming out of the San Francisco Bay Area, a hotbed of early comics fandom.

Chambers accepted my story . . . and what's more, he *published* it! It appeared in *Ymir* #2, dated February 1965; nine pages of superheroics in glorious purple ditto. Don Fowler, one of the leading fan artists of the time (actually a pseudonym for Buddy Saunders), provided a dramatic title page showing the Executioner shooting little guillotines at Manta Ray. He added some nice spot illoes as well. Fowler's art was so much better than anything I could have done that I gave up my own feeble attempts at drawing after that, and settled for telling my stories in prose. "Text stories," they were called in those early days of comicdom, to distinguish them from fully-illustrated comic strips (which were much more popular with my fellow fanboys).

Manta Ray later returned for a second story, this one so long (twenty single-spaced pages or so) that Chambers decided to serialize it. The first half of "The Isle of Death" appeared in *Ymir* #5, and ended with a "To Be Continued." Only it wasn't. *Ymir* never had another issue, and the second half of Manta Ray's second adventure went the same way as the three lost Garizan stories.

Meanwhile, I had raised my sights still higher. The most prestigious fanzine in early comics fandom was *Alter Ego,* but that was largely given over to articles, critiques, interviews. For text stories and amateur strips, the place to be was *Star-Studded Comics,* published by three Texas fans named Larry Herndon, Buddy Saunders, and Howard Keltner, who called themselves the Texas Trio.

When *SSC* was launched in '63, it featured a full-color, printed cover glorious to behold, compared to most other fanzines of the day. The inside of the first few issues was the usual faded ditto, but with their fourth issue the Texas Trio went to photo-offset for the interiors as well, making *SSC* far and away the best-looking fanzine of its time. Just like Marvel and DC, the Trio had their own stable of superheroes; Powerman, the Defender, Changling, Dr. Weird, the Eye, the Human Cat, the Astral Man, and more. Don Fowler, Grass Green, Biljo White, Ronn Foss, and most of the other top fan artists were doing strips for them, and Howard Waldrop was writing text stories (Howard was sort of the fourth member of the Texas Trio, kind of like being the fifth Beatle). So far as comics fandom was concerned in 1964, *Star-Studded Comics* was the big time.

I wanted to be part of it, and I had a terrific *original* idea. Brains in jars like Garizan and masked crimefighters like Manta Ray were old hat, but no one had ever put a superhero on *skis.* (I had never skiied. Still haven't.) My hero had one ski pole that was also a flamethrower, while the other doubled as a machine gun. Instead of fighting some stupid supervillain, I pitted him against the Commies to be "realistic." But the best part of my story was the ending, where the White Raider met a shocking, tragic end. *That* would make the Texas Trio sit up and take notice, I was certain.

I called the story "The Strange Saga of the White Raider," and sent it off to Larry Herndon. As well as being one-third of *SSC*'s august editorial triad, Larry had been one of the first people I'd struck up a correspondence with on entering comicdom. I was sure that he would like the story.

He did . . . but not for *SSC*. He explained to me that the Trio's flagship fanzine had a full slate of characters. Rather than adding more, he and Howard and Buddy wanted to develop the heroes they had already introduced. They all liked my writing, though. They would be glad to have me write for *Star-Studded Comics* . . . so long as I wrote stories about their existing characters.

That was how it happened that "The Strange Saga of the White Raider" ran in *Batwing,* Larry Herndon's solo fanzine, while I went on to appear in *SSC* with text stories about two of Howard Keltner's creations. The Powerman story came first. "Powerman Vs. The Blue Barrier!" was published in SSC #7, in August 1965, and was well-received . . . but it was "Only Kids Are Afraid of the Dark," my Dr. Weird story in *SSC* #10, that really made my name in comicdom.

Dr. Weird was a mystic avenger who fought ghosts, werewolves, and other supernatural menaces. Despite the similarity of their names, he had little in common with Marvel's Dr. Strange. Keltner had modeled him on a Golden Age hero called Mr. Justice. Doc Weird went my White Raider one better, dying halfway through his first story instead of at the end. A time traveler from the future, he had stepped out of his time machine right into the middle of a robbery, and was immediately shot and killed. By dying before he was born, however, he had unbalanced the cosmos, so now he had to walk the earth righting wrongs until his birth came round.

I soon found I had an affinity for Doc Weird. Keltner liked what I did with him and encouraged me to do more stories, so when he spun the character off into his own fanzine, I wrote a script called "The Sword and the Spider" that a new, unknown artist illustrated handsomely. Jim Starlin also adapted "Only Kids Are Afraid of the Dark" to comic form . . . but the text story came first.

Comicdom had established its own awards by then. The Alley Awards were named after Alley Oop, "the oldest comic character of all" (the Yellow Kid might have disagreed). Like the Hugo Awards, the Alleys had categories for both professional and fan work; Golden Alleys for the pros, Silver Alleys for the fans. "Only Kids Are Afraid of the Dark" was nominated for a Silver Alley for best text story...and to my shock and delight, it *won* (quite undeservedly, as Howard Waldrop and Paul Moslander were writing rings around me). Visions of gleaming silver trophies danced briefly in my head, but I never received a thing. The sponsoring organization soon collapsed, and that was the end of the Alley Awards...but the recognition did wonders for my confidence, and helped to keep me writing.

By the time my Dr. Weird stories appeared in print, however, my life had undergone some profound changes. I graduated Marist High in June of 1966. That September I left home for the first time in my life, and rode the Greyhound out to Illinois to attend the Medill School of Journalism at Northwestern University.

College was a strange new world, as exciting as it was scary. I lived in a freshman dorm called Bobb Hall (my mother kept getting confused and thinking Bob was my roommate), in this strange midwestern land where the news came on too early and no one knew how to make a decent pizza pie. The coursework was challenging, there were new friends to make, new assholes to contend with, new vices to acquire (hearts my freshman year, beer when I was a junior)...and there were *girls* in my classes. I still bought comics when I saw them, but soon I was missing issues, and my fanac dropped off precipitously. With so much newness to contend with, it was hard to find the time to write. I finished only one story my freshman year—a straight science fiction story called "The Coach and the Computer," which was published in the first (and only) issue of an obscure fanzine called *In-Depth*.

My major was journalism, but I took a minor in history. My sophomore year I signed up for the History of Scandinavia, thinking it would be cool to study Vikings. Professor Franklin D. Scott was an enthusiastic teacher who invited the class to his home for Scandinavian food and *glug* (a mulled wine with raisins and nuts floating in it). We read Norse sagas, Icelandic eddas, and the poems of the Finnish patriotic poet Johan Ludvig Runeberg.

I loved the sagas and the eddas, which reminded me of Tolkien and Howard, and was much taken with Runeberg's poem "Sveaborg," a rousing lament for the great Helsinki fortress "Gibraltar of the North," which surrendered inexplicably during the Russo-Swedish War of 1808. When it came time to write term papers, I chose "Sveaborg" for my topic. Then I had an off-the-wall idea. I asked Professor Scott if he would allow me to submit a *story* about "Sveaborg" rather than a conventional paper. To my delight, he agreed.

"The Fortress" got me an A . . . but more than that, Professor Scott was so pleased with the story that he sent it off to *The American-Scandinavian Review* for possible publication.

The first rejection letter I ever received was not from Damon Knight, nor Frederik Pohl, nor John Wood Campbell, Jr., but from Erik J. Friis, editor of *The American-Scandinavian Review,* who regretted "very much" having to return "The Fortress" to me. "It is a very good article," he wrote in a letter dated June 14, 1968, "but unfortunately too long for our purpose."

Seldom has a writer been so thrilled by a rejection. A real editor had seen one of my stories, and liked it well enough to send a letter instead of a rejection slip. I felt as though a door had opened. The next fall, when I returned for my junior year at Northwestern, I signed up for creative writing . . . and soon found myself surrounded by would-be modern poets writing free verse and prose poems. I loved poetry, but not that sort. I had no idea what to say about my classmates' poems, and they had no idea what to say about my stories. Where I dreamed of selling stories to *Analog* and *Galaxy,* and maybe *Playboy,* my classmates hoped to place a poem with *TriQuarterly,* Northwestern's prestigious literary magazine.

A few of the other writers did submit the occasional short story; plotless character pieces, for the most part, many written in the present tense, some in the second person, a few without the benefit of capitalization. (To be fair, there were exceptions. I remember one, a creepy little horror story set in an old department store, almost Lovecraftian in tone. I liked that story best of all those I read that year; the rest of the class hated it, of course.)

Nonetheless, I managed to complete four short stories (and no poems) for creative writing. "The Added Safety Factor" and "The Hero" were science fiction. "And Death His Legacy" and "Protector" were mainstream stories with a political slant (it was 1968, and revolution was in the air). The former grew out of a character I'd first envisioned back at Marist, after developing an enthusiasm for James Bond (Ursula Andress had nothing to do with it, no sir, and neither did those sex scenes in the books, nope, nope). Maximilian de Laurier was intended to be an "elegant assassin," who would jaunt about the world killing evil dictators in exotic locations. His big gimmick would be a pipe that doubled as a blowgun.

By the time I got around to putting him on paper, only the name remained. My politics had changed, and assassination no longer seemed so sexy after 1968. The story never sold, but you can read it here, only thirty-five short years after it was written.

The class liked the mainstream stories better than the SF stories, but didn't like any of them very much. Our prof, a hip young instructor who drove a classic Porsche and wore corduroy jackets with leather patches on the elbows, was similarly tepid . . . but he also thought that grades were bullshit, so I was able to escape with high marks and four finished stories.

Though the class hadn't liked my stories, I remained hopeful that some editors might. I would send my stories out, and see what happened. I knew the process: find the addresses in *Writer's Market,* put a crisp new ribbon in my Smith-Corona, type up a clean doublespaced manuscript, ship it off with a brief cover letter and a stamped, self-addressed return envelope, and wait. I could do that.

As my junior year at Northwestern was winding down, I began to market the four stories I'd written for creative writing. Whenever a story was returned by one magazine, I'd ship it off to another that same day. I started with the best-paying markets and worked my way down the pay scale, as the writers' magazines all recommended. And I made a solemn vow that *I would not give up.*

Good thing. "The Added Safety Factor" alone collected thirty-seven rejection slips before I finally ran out of places to send it. Nine years after I'd written it, when I was living in Iowa and teaching classes instead of attending them, a fellow teacher named George Guthridge read the story and said he knew how to fix it. I gave him my blessing, and Guthridge rewrote "The Added Safety Factor" into "Warship" and sent it forth as a collaboration. As "Warship" it collected another five rejections before finally finding a home at *F&SF.* Those forty-two rejections remain my personal record, one that I am in no rush to break.

The other stories were all gathering rejections as well, though at a lesser clip. I soon discovered that most magazines did not share the enthusiasm of *The American-Scandinavian Review* for stories about the Russo-Swedish War of 1808, and returned "The Fortress" to the drawer. "Protector" was revised and retitled "The Protectors," but that didn't help. And "The Hero" came back from *Playboy* and *Analog,* went off to *Galaxy* . . .

. . . and vanished. I'll tell you what became of it in my second commentary. Meanwhile, have a look at my apprentice work, if you dare.

Only Kids Are Afraid
of the Dark

❖

Through the silent, shifting shadows
Grotesque forms go drifting by;
Phantom shapes prowl o'er the darkness;
Great winged hellions stalk the sky.
In the ghostly, ghastly grayness
Soul-less horrors make their home.
Know they well this land of evil—
Corlos is the world they roam.

    —found in a Central European cavern,
      once the temple of a dark sect;
      author unknown.

DARKNESS. EVERYWHERE THERE WAS DARKNESS. GRIM, FOREBODING, omnipresent; it hung over the plain like a great stifling mantle. No moonlight sifted down; no stars shone from above; only night, sinister and eternal, and the swirling, choking gray mists that shifted and stirred with every movement. Something screeched in the distance, but its form could not be seen. The mists and the shadows cloaked all.

But no. One object was visible. In the middle of the plain, rising to challenge the grim black mountains in the distance, a smooth, needle-like tower thrust up into the dead sky. Miles it rose, up to where the crackling crimson lightnings played eternally on the polished black rock. A dull scarlet light gleamed from the lone tower window, one single isle in a sea of night.

In the swirling mists below things stirred uneasily, and the rustles of strange movements and scramblings broke the deathly silence. The unholy denizens of Corlos were uneasy, for when the light shone in the tower, it meant that its owner was at home. And even demons can know fear.

High in the summit of the black tower, a grim entity looked out of the single window at the yawning darkness of the plains and cursed them solemnly. Raging, the being turned from the swirling mist of the eternal night toward the well-lighted interior of its citadel. A whimper broke the silence. Chained helplessly to the marble wall, a hideous shape twisted in vain against its bonds. The entity was displeased. Raising one hand, it unleashed a bolt of black power toward the straining horror on the wall.

A shriek of agony cut the endless night, and the bonds went limp. The chained demon was gone. No sound disturbed the solitude of the tower or its grim occupant. The entity rested on a great batlike throne carved from some glowing black rock. It stared across the room and out the window, at the half-seen somethings churning through the dark clouds.

At last the being cried aloud, and its shout echoed and re-echoed down the miles and miles of the sinister tower. Even in the black pit of the dungeons far below it was heard, and the demons imprisoned there shuddered in expectation of even greater agony, for the cry was the epitome of rage.

A bolt of black power shot from an upraised fist into the night. Something screamed outside, and an unseen shape fell writhing from the skies. The entity snarled.

"Feeble sport. There is better to be had in the realm of mortals, where once I reigned, and where I would roam once more, to hunt again for human souls! When will the commandment be fulfilled, and the sacrifice be made that will release me from this eternal exile?"

Thunder rumbled through the darkness. Crimson lightnings played among the black mountains. And the denizens of Corlos cringed in fear. Saagael, Prince of Demons, Lord of Corlos, King of the Netherworld, was angry and restless once more. And when the

Lord of Darkness was displeased, his subjects were sent scrambling in terror through the mists.

———

FOR LONG AGES THE GREAT TEMPLE HAD LAIN HIDDEN BY SAND AND jungle, alone and deserted. The dust of centuries had gathered on its floor, and the silence of eons brooded in the grim, dark recesses. Dark and evil it was, so generations of natives declared it taboo, and it stood alone through the ages.

But now, after timeless solitude, the great black doors carved with their hideous and forgotten symbols creaked open once more. Footsteps stirred the dust of three thousand years, and echoes disturbed the silence of the dark places. Slowly, nervously, with cautious glances into the darkness, two men sneaked into the ancient temple.

They were dirty men, unwashed and unshaven, and their faces were masks of greed and brutality. Their clothes were in rags, and they each carried long, keen knives next to their empty, useless revolvers. They were hunted men, coming to the temple with blood on their hands and fear in their hearts.

The larger of the two, the tall, lean one called Jasper, surveyed the dark, empty temple with a cold and cynical eye. It was a grim place, even by his standards. Darkness prevailed everywhere, in spite of the burning jungle sun outside, for the few windows there were had been stained a deep purple hue through which little light could pass. The rest was stone, a grim ebony stone carved centuries ago. There were strange, hideous murals on the walls, and the air was dank and stale with the smell of death. Of the furnishings, all had long decayed into dust save the huge black altar at the far end of the room. Once there had been stairs leading to a higher level, but they were gone now, rotted into nothingness.

Jasper unslung his knapsack from his back and turned to his short, fat companion. "Guess this is it, Willie," he said, his voice a low guttural rumble. "Here's where we spend the night."

Willie's eyes moved nervously in their sockets, and his tongue flicked over dry lips. "I don't like it," he said. "This place gives me th' creeps. It's too dark and spooky. And lookit them things on the walls." He pointed toward one of the more bizarre of the murals.

Jasper laughed, a snarling, bitter, cruel laugh from deep in his throat. "We got to stay some place, and the natives will kill us if they find us out in the open. They know we've got those sacred rubies of theirs. C'mon, Willie, there's nothing wrong with this joint, and the natives are scared to come near it. So it's a little dark . . . big deal. Only kids are afraid of the dark."

"Yeah, I . . . I guess yer right," Willie said hesitantly. Removing his knapsack, he squatted down in the dust next to Jasper and began removing the makings of a meal. Jasper went back out into the jungle and returned minutes later, his arms laden with wood. A small fire was started, and the two squatted in silence and hastily consumed their small meal. Afterward they sat around the fire and spoke in whispers of what they would do in civilization with the sudden wealth they had come upon.

Time passed, slowly but inexorably. Outside, the sun sank behind the mountains in the west. Night came to the jungle.

The temple's interior was even more foreboding by night. The creeping darkness that spread from the walls put a damper on conversation. Yawning, Jasper spread his sleeping bag out on the dust-covered floor and stretched out. He looked up at Willie. "I'm gonna call it a day," he said. "How about you?"

Willie nodded. "Yeah," he said. "Guess so." He hesitated. "But not on the floor. All that dust . . . could be bugs . . . spiders, mebbe. Nightcrawlers. I ain't gonna be bit all night in my sleep."

Jasper frowned. "Where, then? Ain't no furniture left in the place."

Willie's hard dark eyes traveled around the room, searching. "There," he exclaimed. "That thing looks wide enough to hold me. And the bugs won't be able to get at me up there."

Jasper shrugged. "Suit yourself," he said. He turned over and soon was asleep. Willie waddled over to the great carven rock, spread his sleeping bag open on it, and clambered up noisily. He stretched out and closed his eyes, shuddering as he beheld the carving on the ceiling. Within minutes his stout frame was heaving regularly, and he was snoring.

Across the length of the dark room Jasper stirred, sat up, and peered through the gloom at his sleeping companion. Thoughts were running feverishly through his head. The natives were hot on their trail, and one man could move much faster than two, especially if the second was a fat, slow cow like Willie. And then there were the rubies—gleaming wealth, greater than any he had ever dreamed of. They could be his—*all* his.

Silently Jasper rose, and crept wolflike through the blackness toward Willie. His hand went to his waist, and extracted a slim, gleaming knife. Reaching the dais, he stood a moment and looked down on his comrade. Willie heaved and tossed in his sleep. The thought of those gleaming red rubies in Willie's knapsack ran again through Jasper's brain. The blade flashed up, then down.

The fat one groaned once, briefly, and blood was spilled on the ancient sacrificial altar.

Outside, lightning flashed from a clear sky, and thunder rumbled ominously over the hills. The darkness inside the temple seemed to deepen, and a low, howling noise filled the room. Probably the wind whistling through the ancient steeple, thought Jasper, as he fumbled for the jewels in Willie's knapsack. But it was strange how the wind seemed to be whispering a word, lowly and beckoningly. "Saagael," it seemed to call softly. "Saaaaagael . . ."

The noise grew, from a whisper to a shout to a roar, until it filled the ancient temple. Jasper looked around in annoyance. He could not understand what was going on. Above the altar, a large crack appeared, and beyond it mist swirled and things moved. Darkness flowed from the crack, darkness blacker and denser and colder than anything Jasper had ever witnessed. Swirling, shifting, it gathered itself into a pocket of absolute black in one corner of the room. It seemed to grow, to change shape, to harden, and to coalesce.

And quickly it was gone. In its place stood something vaguely humanoid; a large, powerful frame clad in garments of a soft, dark gray. It wore a belt and a cape, leathery things made from the hide of some unholy creature never before seen on earth. A hood of the cape covered its head, and underneath it only blackness stared out, marked by two pits of final night darker and deeper than the rest. A great batlike clasp of some dark, glowing rock fastened the cape in place.

Jasper's voice was a whisper. "W-w-who are you?"

A low, hollow, haunting laughter filled the recesses of the temple and spread out through the night. "I? I am War, and Plague, and Blood. I am Death, and Darkness, and Fear." The laughter again. "I am

Saagael, Prince of Demons, Lord of Darkness, King of Corlos, unquestioned Sovereign of the Netherworld. I am Saagael, he whom your ancestors called the Soul-Destroyer. And you have called me."

Jasper's eyes were wide with fear, and the rubies, forgotten, lay in the dust. The apparition had raised a hand, and blackness and night gathered around it. Evil power coursed through the air. Then, for Jasper, there was only darkness, final and eternal.

———

HALFWAY AROUND THE WORLD A SPECTRAL FIGURE IN GOLD AND GREEN stiffened suddenly in mid-flight, its body growing tense and alert. Across the death-white features spread a look of intense concern, as the fathomless phantom-mind once again became in tune with the very essence of its being. Doctor Weird recognized the strange sensations; they were telling him of the presence of a supernatural evil somewhere on the earth. All he had to do was to follow the eerie emanations drawing him like a magnet to the source of the abominable activities.

With the speed of thought the spectral figure flashed away toward the east, led swiftly and unwaveringly to the source of evil; mountains, valleys, rivers, woodlands zipped under him with eye-blurring speed. Great seacoast cities appeared on the horizon, their skyscrapers leaning on the heavens. Then they, too, vanished behind him, and angry, rolling waves moved below. In a wink a continent had been spanned; in another an ocean was crossed. Earthly limits of speed and matter are of no consequence to a spirit; and suddenly it was night.

Thick, clutching jungles appeared below the Golden Ghost, their foliage all the more sinister by night. There was a patch of desert, a great roaring river, more desert. Then the jungle again. Human settlements popped up and vanished in the blink of an eye. The night parted in front of the streaking figure.

Doctor Weird stopped. Huge and ominous, the ancient temple appeared suddenly in front of him, its great walls hiding grim and evil secrets. He approached cautiously. There was an aura of intense evil here, and the darkness clung to the temple thicker and denser than to the jungle around it.

Slowly and warily the Astral Avenger approached a huge black wall. His substance seemed to waver and fade as he passed effortlessly through it into the blackened inside.

Doctor Weird shuddered as he beheld the interior of that dread sanctum; it was horribly familiar to him now. The dark, hideous murals, the row on row of felted, ebony benches, and the huge statue that stared down from above the altar marked this unclean place as a temple of a long-forgotten sect; those who had worshipped one of the black deities that lurk Beyond. The earth had been cleaner when the last such had died out.

And yet—Doctor Weird paused and pondered. Everywhere, everything looked new and unused and—a sense of horror gripped him—there was fresh blood on the sacrificial altar! Could it be that the cult had been revived? That the dwellers in the shadows were worshipped again?

There was a slight noise from a recess near the altar. Instantly, Doctor Weird whirled and searched for its source. Something barely moved in the darkness; and in a flash the Golden Ghost was upon it.

It was a man—or what remained of one. Tall, lean, and muscular, it lay unmoving on the floor and stared from unseeing eyes. A heart beat, and lungs inhaled, but there was no other motion. No will stirred this creature; no instincts prompted it. It lay still and silent, eyes focused vacantly on the ceiling; a discarded, empty shell.

It was a thing without a mind—or a soul.

Anger and horror raged through the breast of the Astral Avenger as he whirled, searching the shadows for the thing of evil whose presence now overwhelmed him. Never had he encountered such an engulfing aura of raw, stark wickedness.

"All right!" he shouted. "I know you are here somewhere. I sense your evil presence. Show yourself . . . if you dare!"

A hollow, haunting laughter issued from the great dark walls and echoed through the hall. "And who might *you* be?"

But Doctor Weird did not move. His spectral eyes swept the length and breadth of the temple, searching for the source of the eerie laughter.

And again it came, deep, booming, and full of malevolence. "But what does it matter? Rash mortal, you presume to challenge forces you cannot begin to comprehend! Yet, I shall fulfill your request—I shall reveal myself!" The laughter grew louder. "You shall soon rue your foolhardy words!"

From above, where polished ebony steps wound upward into the highest reaches of the black temple's tower and steeple, a viscous, fluid, living darkness seemed to ooze down the winding staircase. Like a great cloud of absolute black from the nightmare of a madman it descended until, halfway down, it solidified and took shape. The thing that stood on the stairs was vaguely manlike, but the resemblance only made it even more horrible. Its laughter filled the temple again. "Doth my visage please you, mortal? Why do you not answer? Can it be you know—fear?"

The answer rang back instantly, loud, clear, and defiant. "Never, dark one! You call me mortal and expect me to tremble at the sight of you. But you are wrong, for I am as eternal as you. I, who have battled werewolves, vampires, and sorcerers in the past have no qualms about subduing a demon of your ilk!" With this, Doctor Weird shot forward toward the grotesque apparition on the stairs.

Underneath the dark hood, the two great pits of blackness blazed scarlet for an instant, and the laughter began again, wilder than ever. "So then, spirit, you would fight a demon? Very well! You shall have a demon! We will see who survives!" The dark shape gestured impatiently with its hand.

Doctor Weird had gotten halfway to the staircase when the crack above the altar suddenly opened in front of him and something huge and evil blocked his path. It stood well over twice his height, its mouth a mass of gleaming fangs, the eyes two baleful pinpoints of red. There was a musty odor of death in the air surrounding the monstrous entity.

Barely pausing long enough to size up the situation, the Golden Ghost lashed out at the hideous newcomer, fist burying itself in the cold, clammy flesh. In spite of himself, Doctor Weird shuddered. The flesh of the monster was like soft, yet superstrong dough; foul and filthy, so repulsive as to make the skin crawl.

The being shrugged off the blow. Demoniac talons raked painfully and with stunning force across the shoulder of the Mystic Marauder, leaving a trail of agony in their wake. With sudden alarm, Doctor

Weird realized that this was no creature of the ordinary realm, against which he was invulnerable; this horror was of the netherworld, and was as fully capable of inflicting pain upon him as he was on it.

A great arm flashed out, catching him across the chest and sending him staggering backward. Gibbering and drooling horribly, the demon leaped after him, its great clawed hands reaching. Doctor Weird was caught squarely, thrown off balance, and slammed backward onto the cold stone floor. The thing landed on top of him. Gleaming yellow fangs flashed for his throat.

In desperation, Doctor Weird swung his left arm around and up into the face of the demon as it descended upon him. Spectral muscles strained, and his right fist connected with brutal force, smashing into the horrid visage like a pile driver. The thing gave a sickening squeal of pain, rolled to the side, and scrambled to its feet. In an instant the Golden Ghost had regained his footing.

Eyes blazing hungrily at him, the demon rushed the Super Spirit once again, arms spread wide to grab him. Neatly sidestepping the charge and ducking under the outstretched arms, Doctor Weird took to the air as the creature's speed carried it past him. The demon stopped and whirled quickly, and the airborne wraith smashed into him feet first. The thing roared in anger as it toppled and lay flat. With all of the force he could muster, Doctor Weird brought the heel of his boot down squarely onto the demon's neck.

Like a watermelon hit by a battering ram, the monster's head bulged, then smashed under the impact. Thick dark blood formed a great pool on the stone floor, and the hulklike demon did not stir. Doctor Weird staggered to one side in exhaustion.

Devilish laughter rang about him, snapping him instantly to attention. "Very good, spirit! You have entertained me! You *have* overcome a demon!" Scarlet flashed again under the hood of the thing on the stairway. "But I, you see, am no ordinary demon. I am Saagael, the Demon Prince, the Lord of Darkness! That subject of mine you disposed of with such difficulty is as nothing against *my* power!"

Saagael raised a hand and gestured at the fallen demon. "You have shown me your might, so I will tell you of mine. That shell you found was my work, for I am he they called the Soul-Destroyer, and it is long since I have exercised my power. That mortal shall know no afterlife, no bliss nor damnation, no Immortality. He is gone, as if he had never been, completely nonexistent. I have eradicated his soul, and that is a fate far worse than death."

The Golden Ghost stared up at him unbelievingly, and a cold chill went through him. "You mean . . ."

The voice of the Demon Prince was raised in triumph. "Yes! I perceive you know what I mean. So think, and *now* tremble! You are but a spirit, a discorporate entity. I cannot affect the physical shell of one of mortal birth, but you, a spirit, I could destroy utterly. But it will amuse me to have you stand by helpless and fearful while I enslave your world, so I shall spare you for now. Stand, and behold the fate of the planet where I reigned once, before history began, and now shall reign again!"

The Lord of Darkness gestured expansively, and all light in the temple vanished. A thick darkness prevailed everywhere, and a vision slowly took shape before the awestruck eyes of Doctor Weird.

He saw men turn against other men in anger and hatred. He witnessed wars and holocaust and blood. Death, grinning and horrible, was everywhere. The world was bathed in chaos and destruction. And then, in the aftermath, he beheld flood and fire and plague, and famine upon the land. Fear and superstition reached new heights. There was a vision of churches being torn down, and of crosses burning against the night sky. Awesome statues were raised in their stead, bearing the hideous likeness of the Demon Prince. Everywhere men bowed before the great dark altars, and gave their daughters to the priests of Saagael. And, lo, the creatures of the night burst forth again in new strength, walking the earth and lusting for blood. Locked doors were no protection. The servants of Saagael ruled supreme on earth, and their dark lord hunted for men's souls. The gates of Corlos were opened, and a great shadow descended over the land. Not in a thousand generations would it be lifted.

As suddenly as it had come the vision was gone, and there was only the thick blackness and the hideous ringing laughter, more cruel now, coming from everywhere and nowhere, echoing and re-echoing in the confines of the huge temple. "Go now, spirit, before I tire of you. I have preparations to make abroad, and I do not wish to find you in my temple when I return. Hark you this—it is morning now, yet all is still dark outside. From this day forth, night shall be eternal on earth!"

The darkness cleared and Doctor Weird could see again. He stood alone in the empty temple. Saagael was gone, as were the remains of the vanquished demon. Only he and the thing that had once been a man called Jasper remained amongst the silence, and the darkness, and the dust.

————

THEY CAME FROM ALL OVER, FROM THE HOT NEARBY JUNGLES, FROM the burning desert beyond, from the great cities of Europe, from the frigid north of Asia. They were the hard ones, the brutal ones, the cruel ones, those who had long waited the coming of one like the Demon Prince and welcomed him now. They were students of the occult; they had studied those black arts and ancient scrolls that sane men do not believe in, and they knew the dark secrets others spoke of in whispers. Saagael was no mystery to them, for their lore went back to the dim forgotten eras before history had begun when the Lord of Darkness had held dominion over the earth.

And now, from all the corners of the globe, they flocked to his temple and bowed before his statue. Even a dark god needs priests and they were eager to strain in his service in return for forbidden knowledge. When the long night had come over the earth, and the Demon Prince had roamed abroad and feasted, they knew their hour had arrived. So the unclean ones, the dark ones, the evil ones, jammed the great temple even as in the days of yore and formed again the dreaded Sect of Saagael. There they sang their songs of worship, and read their black tomes, and waited for the coming of their lord, for Saagael was still abroad. It was long since he had hunted men's souls, and his hunger was insatiable.

But his servants grew impatient, and so they made for to summon him back. Torches lit the black hall, and hundreds sat moaning a hymn of praise. They read aloud from the unholy texts, as they had not dared to do for many a year, and they sang his name. "Saagael," the call went up and echoed in the depths of the temple. "Saagael," it beckoned, louder and louder, until the hall rang with it. "Saagael," it demanded, a roar now, shrieking out into the night and filling the land and the air with the awful call.

A young girl was strapped to the sacrificial altar, straining and tugging at her bonds, a look of horror in her wide staring eyes. Now the chief of priests, a huge monster of a man with a brutal red slash for a mouth and two dark, piglike eyes, approached her. A long, gleaming, silver knife was in his hand, flashing with reflected torch-light.

He halted and raised his eyes to the huge, towering image of the Demon Prince that loomed above the altar. "Saagael," he intoned, his voice a deep, eerie whisper that chilled the blood. "Prince of Demons, Lord of Darkness, Monarch of the Netherworld, we summon thee. Soul-Destroyer, we, your followers, call. Hear us and appear. Accept our offer of the soul and spirit of this maiden!"

He lowered his eyes. The blade lifted slowly, began to descend. A hush came over the assemblage. The blade flashed silver. The girl screamed.

Then something caught the sleeve of the priest's robe, bent his arm back with a wrench, and snapped it. A spectral figure glowed in front of the altar, and the night paled in the illumination of the green and gold interloper. Pale white fingers grasped the knife as it fell from the hand of the priest. Wordlessly, they lifted the slim blade and drove it down into the heart of the huge man. Blood flowed, a gasp shocked the silence, and the body fell to the floor.

As the intruder turned and calmly slit the bonds of the now fainted girl, everywhere cries of rage and fear went up among the people, followed by cries of "sacrilege," and "Saagael, protect us!"

Then, as if a heavy cloud had drifted overhead, a great darkness came over the hall and, one by one, the torches winked out. Utter blackness flowed through the air, shimmered, and took shape. A cry of relief and triumph went up from the mortals present.

Scarlet fires flamed under the blackness inside the hood. "You have gone too far, spirit," boomed the voice of the Demon Prince. "You attack the mortals who wisely choose to serve me, and for that you shall pay with your very soul!" The dark aura that surrounded the Lord of Corlos grew in strength, and pushed back the light that emanated from the muscular figure in green and gold.

"Shall I?" Doctor Weird replied. "I think not. You have witnessed but a small part of my power—I have more I have never shown you! You were born of darkness and death and blood, Saagael. You stand for all that is evil and foul-made-flesh. But I was created by the Will of Powers that dwarf you, that could destroy you with but a mere thought. I stand in defiance of you, those like you, and the vermin that serve you!"

The light that surrounded the Golden Ghost blazed once more and filled the hall like a small sun, driving the inky blackness of the Demon Prince before it. It was as if, suddenly, the Lord of Corlos had felt his first twinge of doubt. But he rallied himself and, without deigning the use of further talk, raised a gloved hand. To it flowed the powers of darkness and death and fear. Then a massive bolt of black pulsating power streaked through the air, evil and unclean. Straight it flew, and fast.

The Golden Ghost stood his ground, hands on hips. The bolt struck him squarely, and light and darkness flashed for a moment. Then the light went out, and the figure fell quickly and soundlessly.

A horrible, mocking laughter filled the room, and Saagael turned to his worshippers. "Thus perish those who would defy the dark power, those who would oppose the will of . . ." He stopped. There was a look of total, awesome fear on the faces of his disciples, as they stared at something behind him. The Demon Prince whirled.

The golden figure was rising to his feet. The light blazed forth once more, and momentary fear smote the Lord of Corlos. But again he overcame his doubt, and again an awesome bolt of black power shot through the air, smashing into the advancing Doctor Weird. Again the Astral Avenger keeled over. An instant later, as Saagael watched in mounting horror, the figure rose once more. Silently, wordlessly, it strode toward him.

Panicking, Saagael smashed down the figure a third time. A third time it rose. A gurgle of horror went up from the crowd. The Golden

Ghost advanced again toward the Demon Prince. Raising a glowing arm, at last he spoke. "Too bad, Saagael. I have withstood the best you could throw at me, and I still live. But now, Dark One, you shall feel *my* power!"

"N-NOOOOoooo," a hideous shriek went through the hall. The figure of the Lord of Darkness shuddered, paled, and melted away into a great black cloud. The crack opened again above the ebony altar. Beyond it mists swirled, and things moved in an eternal night. The black cloud expanded, flowed to the crack, and was gone. An instant later the crack vanished.

Doctor Weird turned to the mortals who filled the room, the shocked and broken servants of Saagael. A howl of fear went up and they fled screaming from the temple. Then the figure turned to the altar, shuddered, and fell. Something fluttered in the air above it, streaked across the room, and vanished into the shadows.

An instant later, a second Astral Avenger strode from the dark recesses, walked to the altar, and bent over the first. A spectral hand wiped a layer of white makeup from the fallen figure's face. An eerie voice broke the silence. "He called you a shell—an empty thing—and he was right. By reverting to my ectoplasmic form and hiding my physical self in the shadows, I was able to wear you like a suit of clothing. He could not affect your corporeal body, so I left you just before his bolts struck, and got back in afterward. And it worked. Even he could be fooled, and frightened."

Outside the sun was coming up in the east. In the interior of the grim sanctum, ebony benches and carved stairways rotted, decayed swiftly, and gave way to piles of dust. One thing, now, remained.

Doctor Weird rose and approached the black altar. Mighty hands gripped the great legs of the statue of Saagael, and rippling muscles strained. The statue toppled, and shattered. It fell, broken and smashed, near the empty hulk of the thing called Jasper, clad in a green and gold costume.

Doctor Weird surveyed the scene with an ironic smile flicking over his dead-white features. "Even after he had destroyed your mind and soul, it was a man who brought about the downfall of the Lord of Darkness."

He lifted his eyes to the girl on the altar, now beginning to stir from the terror that had taken her consciousness. He approached her and said, "Do not be afraid of me. I will take you home now."

It was day outside. The shadow had lifted. The eternal night was over.

NEXT ISSUE: DR. WEIRD MEETS THE DEMON

THE FORTRESS

---❖---

Have you beheld her gray form rise
Superb o'er bay and sea
With menace in her granite eyes:
Come try your strength on me?
My very look, so grim and dread,
Can strike the impious foeman dead.

Whatever course the war may take
In forest or on plain,
Rouse not the ocean's queen to break
The calm of her disdain.
A thousand cannon, tongued with fire,
Will whelm you with their savage ire!

—*The Tales of Ensign Stål,*
   Johan Ludvig Runeberg

ALONE AND SILENT IN THE NIGHT, SVEABORG WAITED.

Dark shapes in a sea of ice, the six island citadels of the fortress threw shadows in the moonlight—waiting. Jagged granite walls rose from the islands, and bristled with row on row of silent cannon—waiting. And behind the walls, grim and determined men sat by the guns day and night—waiting.

From the northwest, a bitter wind brought the sounds and smells of the city in the distance to Sveaborg as it shrieked about the fortress walls. And high on the parapets of Vargön, largest of the six islands, Colonel Bengt Anttonen shivered with the cold as he stared morosely into the distance. His uniform hanging loosely from his hard, lean frame, Anttonen's gray eyes were cloudy and troubled.

"Colonel?" The voice came from just behind the brooding officer. Anttonen half turned, and grinned. Captain Carl Bannersson saluted briskly and stepped up to the battlements beside the colonel. "I hope I'm not disturbing you," he asked.

Anttonen snorted. "Not at all, Carl. Just thinking."

There was a moment of silence. "The Russian barrage was fairly heavy today," began Bannersson. "Several men were wounded out on the ice, and we had to put out two fires."

Anttonen's eyes roamed over the ice beyond the walls. He seemed almost unmindful of the tall, youthful Swedish captain, and lost in thought. "The men should never have been out on the ice," he said, absently.

Bannersson's blue eyes probed the colonel's face questioningly. He hesitated. "Why do you say that?" he asked. There was no answer from the older officer. Anttonen stared into the night, and was silent.

After a long minute, Anttonen stirred, and turned to face the captain. His face was tense and worried. "There's something wrong, Carl. Something very wrong."

Bannersson looked puzzled. "What are you talking about?"

"Admiral Cronstedt," replied the colonel. "I don't like the way he's been acting lately. He worries me."

"In what way?"

Anttonen shook his head. "His orders. The way he talks." The tall, lean Finn gestured towards the city in the distance. "Remember when the Russian siege began in early March? Their first battery was dragged to Sveaborg on a sledge and mounted on a rock in Helsinki harbor. When we replied to their shelling, every shot told on the city."

"True. What of it?"

"So the Russians ran up a truce flag, and negotiated, and Admiral Cronstedt agreed that Helsinki should be neutral ground, and neither side should build fortifications near it." Anttonen pulled a piece of paper from his pocket, and waved it at Bannersson. "General Suchtelen allows officers' wives from the city to visit us at times, and through them I got this report. It seems the Russians have moved their guns all right, but have established barracks, hospitals, and magazines in Helsinki. And we can't touch them!"

Bannersson frowned. "I see what you mean. Does the admiral know of this report?"

"Of course," said Anttonen impatiently. "But he will not act. Jägerhorn and the others have persuaded him that the report is unreliable. So the Russians hide in the city, in perfect safety." He crumpled the report savagely, and jammed it into his pocket in disgust.

Bannersson did not reply, and the colonel turned to stare out over the walls again, mumbling under his breath.

There were several moments of strained silence. Captain Bannersson shifted his weight uneasily, and coughed. "Sir?" he said at last. "You don't think we're in any real danger, do you?"

Anttonen looked at him blankly. "Danger?" he said, "No, not really. The fortress is too strong, and the Russians too weak. They need much more artillery and many more men before they would dare an assault. And we have enough food to outlast their siege. Once the ice melts Sweden can easily reinforce by sea."

He paused a moment, then continued. "Still, I'm worried. Admiral Cronstedt finds new vulnerable spots every day, and every day more men die trying to break up the ice in front of them. Cronstedt's family is trapped here with all the other refugees, and he worries about them to excess. He sees weakness everywhere. The men are loyal and ready to die in defense of Sveaborg, but the officers—"

Anttonen sighed and shook his head. After a moment of silence he straightened and turned from the ramparts. "It's damn cold out here," he said. "We had better be getting inside."

Bannersson smiled. "True. Perhaps Suchtelen will attack tomorrow, and solve all of our problems."

The colonel laughed, and clapped him on the back. Together they left the battlements.

And at midnight, March became April. And still Sveaborg waited.

"Iꜰ ᴛʜᴇ ᴀᴅᴍɪʀᴀʟ ᴘʟᴇᴀꜱᴇꜱ, I ᴡᴏᴜʟᴅ ʟɪᴋᴇ ᴛᴏ ᴅɪꜱᴀɢʀᴇᴇ. I ꜱᴇᴇ ɴᴏ ʀᴇᴀꜱᴏɴ to negotiate at this time. Sveaborg is secure against assault, and our supplies are adequate. General Suchtelen can offer us nothing."

Colonel Anttonen's face was stiff and formal as he spoke, but his knuckles were white where his hand curled around his sword hilt.

"Absurd!" Colonel F. A. Jägerhorn twisted his aristocratic features into a sneer of contempt. "Our situation is highly dangerous. As the admiral well knows, our defenses are flawed, and are made even more imperfect by the ice that makes them accessible from all sides. Our powder is running low. The Russians ring us with guns, and their numbers swell daily."

Behind the commandant's desk, Vice-Admiral Carl Olof Cronstedt nodded gravely. "Colonel Jägerhorn is right, Bengt. We have many reasons to meet with General Suchtelen. Sveaborg is far from secure."

"But, Admiral." Anttonen waved the sheaf of papers clutched in his hands. "My reports indicate no such thing. The Russians have only about forty guns, and we still outnumber them. They cannot attack."

Jägerhorn laughed. "If your reports say that, Colonel Anttonen, they are in error. Lieutenant Klick is in Helsinki, and he informs me that the enemy greatly outnumber us. And they have well over forty guns!"

Anttonen whirled towards his fellow officer furiously. "Klick! You listen to Klick! Klick is a fool and a damned Anjala traitor; if he is in Helsinki it is because he is working for the Russians!"

The two officers eyed each other angrily, Jägerhorn cold and haughty, Anttonen flushed and impassioned. "I had relatives in the Anjala League," began the young aristocrat. "They were not traitors, nor is Klick. They are loyal Finns."

Anttonen snarled something unintelligible, and turned back to Cronstedt. "Admiral, I swear to you, my reports are accurate. We have nothing to fear if we can hold out until the ice melts, and we can easily do that. Once the sea is open, Sweden will send help."

Cronstedt rose slowly from his chair, his face drawn and tired,

"No, Bengt. We cannot refuse to negotiate." He shook his head, and smiled. "You are too eager for a fight. We cannot be rash."

"Sir," said Anttonen. "If you must, then, negotiate. But give up nothing. Sweden and Finland depend on us. In the spring, General Klingspor and the Swedish fleet will launch their counteroffensive to drive the Russians from Finland; but control of Sveaborg is vital to the plan. The army's morale would be smashed if we should fall. A few months, sir—hold out a few months and Sweden can win the war."

Cronstedt's face was a mask of despair. "Colonel, you have not been reading the news. Everywhere Sweden is being routed; her armies are defeated on all fronts. We cannot hope to triumph."

"But, sir. That news is from the papers that General Suchtelen sends you; they are largely Russian papers. Don't you see, sir, that news is slanted. We cannot rely on it." Anttonen's eyes were wide with horror; he spoke like a desperate man.

Jägerhorn laughed, coldly and cynically. "What matters it if the news is true or false? Do you really think Sweden will win, Anttonen? A small, poor state in the far north hold off Russia? Russia, which extends from the Baltic to the Pacific, from the Black Sea to the Arctic Ocean? Russia, the ally of Napoleon, who has trod upon the crowned heads of Europe?" He laughed again. "We are beaten, Bengt, beaten. It only remains to see what terms we can get."

Anttonen stared at Jägerhorn in silence for a moment, and when he spoke his voice was harsh and strained. "Jägerhorn, you are a defeatist, a coward, and a traitor. You are a disgrace to the uniform you wear."

The aristocrat's eyes blazed, and his hand sped to his sword hilt. He stepped forward aggressively.

"Gentlemen, gentlemen." Cronstedt was suddenly between the two officers, holding Jägerhorn at bay. "We are besieged by the enemy, our country is in flames, and our armies are being routed. This is no time to fight among ourselves." His face grew stern and hard. "Colonel Jägerhorn, return to your quarters at once."

"Yes, sir." Jägerhorn saluted, whirled, and left the room. Admiral Cronstedt turned back to Anttonen.

He shook his head sadly. "Bengt, Bengt. Why can't you under-stand? Jägerhorn is right, Bengt; the other officers agree with him to a man. If we negotiate now we can save the fleet, and much Finnish blood."

Colonel Anttonen stood stiffly at attention. His eyes were cold, and looked past his admiral as if he were not there. "Admiral," he said sternly. "What if you had felt this way before Ruotsinsalmi? What would have become of your victory then, sir? Defeatism wins no battles."

Cronstedt's face became harsh, and there was anger in his voice. "That is enough, Colonel. I will not tolerate insubordination. I am compelled by circumstance to negotiate for the surrender of Sveaborg. The meeting between Suchtelen and myself has been arranged for April sixth; I will be there. And in the future, you will not question this decision. That is an order!"

Anttonen was silent.

Admiral Cronstedt stared at the colonel for a brief moment, his eyes still mirroring anger. Then he turned with a snort, and gestured impatiently towards the door. "You are dismissed, Colonel. Return to quarters at once."

Captain Bannersson's face masked his shock and disbelief. "It can't be true, sir. Surrendering? But why would the admiral do such a thing? The men, at least, are ready and willing to fight."

Anttonen laughed, but it was a hollow, bitter laugh, totally without humor. His eyes held a wild despair, and his hands flexed the blade of his rapier nervously. He was leaning against an elaborately carved tomb, in the shadow of two trees within one of the central courtyards of the Vargön citadel. Bannersson stood a few feet away in the dark-ness, on the steps that led up to the memorial.

"All the men are willing to fight," said Anttonen. "Only the offi-cers are not." He laughed again. "Admiral Cronstedt—the hero of our victory at Ruotsinsalmi—reduced to a doubting, fear-wracked old man. General Suchtelen has played upon him well; the newspapers from France and Russia he sent him, the rumors from Helsinki carried here by the officers' wives, all served to plant the seed of defeatism. And then Colonel Jägerhorn helped it to grow."

Bannersson was still stunned, and puzzled. "But—but what does the admiral fear?"

"Everything. He sees weak points in our defenses no one else can see. He fears for his family. He fears for the fleet he once led to victory. He claims Sveaborg is helpless in the winter. He is weak and apprehensive, and every time he doubts, Jägerhorn and his cronies are there to tell him he is right."

Anttonen's face was distorted with rage. He was nearly shouting now. "The cowards! The traitors! Admiral Cronstedt wavers and trembles, but if *they* would only be resolute, *he* would find his courage and his mind also."

"Sir, please, not so loudly," cautioned Bannersson. "If what you said is true, what can we do about it?"

Anttonen's eyes lifted, and focused on the Swedish captain below. He considered him coldly. "The parley is set for tomorrow. Cronstedt may not yield, but if he does, we must be prepared. Get all the loyal men you can, and tell them to be ready. Call it mutiny if you will, but Sveaborg will not capitulate without a fight so long as there is a single man of honor to fire her guns." The Finnish officer straightened and sheathed his sword. "Meanwhile, I will speak with Colonel Jägerhorn. Perhaps I can stop this madness yet."

Bannersson, his face dead white, nodded slowly and turned to leave. Anttonen strode down the steps, then halted. "Carl?" he called. The departing Swedish officer turned. "You understand that my life, and perhaps the future of Finland, are in your hands, don't you?"

"Yes, sir," replied Bannersson. "You can trust us." He turned again, and a few seconds later was gone.

Anttonen stood alone in the dark, staring absently at his hand. It was bleeding from where it had gripped the sword blade. Laughing, the officer looked up at the tomb. "You designed your fortress well, Ehrensvard," he said, his voice a soft whisper in the night. "Let's hope the men who guard her are equal to her strength."

JÄGERHORN SCOWLED WHEN HE SAW WHO WAS AT THE DOOR. "You, Anttonen? After this afternoon? You have courage. What do you want?"

Anttonen stepped inside the room, and closed the door. "I want to talk to you. I want to change your mind. Cronstedt listens to you; if you advise against it, he will not capitulate. Sveaborg will not fall."

Jägerhorn grinned and sank back into a chair. "Perhaps. I am a relative. The admiral respects my opinion. But it is only a matter of time. Sweden cannot win this war, and the more we prolong it, the more Finns will die in battle."

The aristocrat stared at his fellow officer calmly. "Sweden is lost," he continued, "but Finland need not be. We have assurances from Czar Alexander that Finland will be an autonomous state under his protection. We will have more freedom than we ever had under Sweden."

"We are Swedes," said Anttonen. "We have a duty to defend our king and our homeland." His voice was brittle with disdain.

A thin smile played across Jägerhorn's lips. "Swedes? Bah! We are Finns. What did Sweden ever do for us? She taxed us. She took our boys and left them dying in the mud of Poland, and Germany, and Denmark. She made our countryside a battleground for her wars. For this we owe Sweden loyalty?"

"Sweden will aid us when the ice melts," answered Anttonen. "We need only hold out till spring, and wait for her fleet."

Jägerhorn was on his feet, and his words rang with bitterness and scorn. "I would not count on Swedish aid, Colonel. A look at their history would teach you better than that. Where was Carl XII during the Great Wrath? All over Europe he rode, but could not spare an army for suffering Finland. Where is Marshal Klingspor now, while the Russians lay waste to our land and burn our towns? Did he even fight for Finland? No! He retreated—to save Sweden from attack."

"So for the Swedes who do not aid us fast enough, you would trade the Russians? The butchers of the Great Wrath? The people who pillage our nation even now? That seems a sorry trade."

"No. The Russians treat us now as enemies; when we are on

their side things will be different. No longer will we have to fight a war every twenty years to please a Swedish king. No longer will the ambitions of a Carl XII or a Gustav III cost thousands of Finnish lives. Once the Czar rules in Finland, we will have peace and freedom."

Jägerhorn's voice was hot with excitement and conviction, but Anttonen remained cold and formal. He looked at Jägerhorn sadly, almost wistfully, and sighed. "It was better when I thought you were a traitor. You're not. An idealist, a dreamer, yes. But not a traitor."

"Me? A dreamer?" Jägerhorn's eyebrows arched in surprise. "No, Bengt. You're the dreamer. You're the man who deludes himself with hopes of a Swedish victory. I look at the world the way it is, and deal with it on its own terms."

Anttonen shook his head. "We've fought Russia over and over through the years; we've been foes for centuries. And you think we can live together peacefully. It won't work, Colonel. Finland knows Russia too well. And she does not forget. This will not be our last war with Russia. Not by any means."

He turned away slowly, and opened the door to leave. Then, almost as an afterthought, he paused and looked back. "You're just a misguided dreamer, and Cronstedt's only a weak old man." He laughed softly. "There's no one left to hate, Jägerhorn. There's no one left to hate."

The door closed softly, and Colonel Bengt Anttonen was alone in the darkened, silent hallway. Leaning against the cold stone wall in exhaustion, he sobbed, and covered his face with his hands.

His voice was a hoarse, choking whisper, his body gray and shaken. "My God, my God. A fool's dreams and an old man's doubts. And between them they'll topple the Gibraltar of the North."

He laughed a broken, sobbing laugh, straightened, and walked out into the night.

———

"——SHALL BE ALLOWED TO DISPATCH TWO COURIERS TO THE KING, THE one by the northern, the other by the southern road. They shall be furnished with passports and safeguards, and every possible facility shall be given them for accomplishing their journey. Done at the island of Lonan, 6 April, 1808."

The droning voice of the officer reading the agreement stopped suddenly, and the large meeting room was deathly quiet. There were mumblings from the back of the room, and a few of the Swedish officers stirred uneasily in their seats, but no one spoke.

From the commandant's desk in front of the gathering of Sveaborg's senior officers, Admiral Cronstedt rose slowly. His face was old beyond its years, his eyes weary and bloodshot. And those in the front could see his gnarled hands trembling slightly.

"That is the agreement," he began. "Considering the position of Sveaborg, it is better than we could have hoped for. We have used a third of our powder already; our defenses are exposed to attack from all sides because of the ice; we are outnumbered and forced to support a large number of fugitives, who rapidly consume our provisions. Considering all this, General Suchtelen was in a position to demand our immediate surrender."

He paused and ran tired fingers through his hair. His eyes searched the faces of the Finnish and Swedish officers who sat before him.

"He did not demand that surrender," continued Cronstedt. "Instead, we have been allowed to retain three of Sveaborg's six islands, and will regain two of the others if five Swedish ships-of-the-line arrive to aid us before the third of May. If not, we must surrender. But in either case the fleet shall be restored to Sweden after the war, and the truce between now and then will prevent the loss of any more lives."

Admiral Cronstedt halted, and looked to the side. Instantly Colonel Jägerhorn, sitting beside him, was on his feet. "I assisted the admiral in negotiating this agreement. It is a good one, a very good one. General Suchtelen has given us very generous terms. However, in case the Swedish aid does not arrive in time, we must make provisions for surrendering the garrison. That is the purpose of this meeting. We—"

"NO!" The shout rang through the large room and echoed from its walls, cutting off Jägerhorn abruptly. At once there was a shocked silence. All eyes turned towards the rear of the room, where Colonel

Bengt Anttonen stood among his fellow officers, white-faced and smoldering with anger.

"Generous terms? Hah! What generous terms?" His voice was sharp with derision. "Immediate surrender of Wester-Svartö, Oster-Lilla-Svartö, and Langorn; the rest of Sveaborg to come later. *These* are generous terms? NO! Never! It is little more than surrender postponed for a month. And there is no need to surrender. We are NOT out-numbered. We are NOT weak. Sveaborg does not need provisions— it needs only a little courage, and a little faith."

The atmosphere in the council room had suddenly grown very cold, as Admiral Cronstedt regarded the dissident with frigid distaste. When he spoke, there was a hint of his old authority in his voice. "Colonel, I remind you of the orders I gave you the other day. I am tired of you questioning each of my actions. True, I have made small concessions, but I have given us a chance of retaining everything for Sweden. It is our only chance! Now SIT DOWN, Colonel!"

There was a murmur of agreement from the officers around the room. Anttonen regarded them with disgust, then turned his gaze back to the admiral. "Yes, sir," he said. "But, sir, this chance you have given us is no chance at all, no chance whatsoever. You see, sir, Sweden can't get ships here fast enough. The ice will not melt in time."

Cronstedt ignored his words. "I gave you an order, Colonel," he said, with iron in his voice. "Sit down!"

Anttonen stared at him coldly, his eyes burning, his hands clench-ing and unclenching spasmodically at his sides. There was a long mo-ment of tense silence. Then he sat down.

Colonel Jägerhorn coughed, and rattled the sheaf of papers he was holding in his hands. "To continue with the business at hand," he said, "we must first dispatch the messengers to Stockholm. Speed is essential here. The Russians will provide the necessary papers."

His eyes combed the room. "If the admiral agrees," he said, "I would suggest Lieutenant Eriksson and—and—"

He paused a second, and a slow smile spread across his features.

"—and Captain Bannersson," he concluded.

Cronstedt nodded.

THE MORNING AIR WAS CRISP AND COLD, AND THE SUN WAS RISING IN the east. But no one watched. All eyes in Sveaborg were fixed on the dark and cloudy western horizon. For hours on end officer and soldier, Swede and Finn, sailor and artilleryman all searched the empty sea, and hoped. They looked to Sweden, and prayed for the sails they knew would never come.

And among those who prayed was Colonel Bengt Anttonen. High atop the battlements of Vargön, he scanned the seas with a small telescope, like so many others in Sveaborg. And like the others, he found nothing.

Folding his telescope, Anttonen turned from the ramparts with a frown to address the young ensign who stood by his side. "Useless," he said. "I'm wasting valuable time."

The ensign looked scared and nervous. "There's always the chance, sir. Suchtelen's deadline is not until noon. A few hours, but we can hope, can't we?"

Anttonen was grim, sober. "I wish we could, but we're just deluding ourselves. The armistice agreement provides that the ships must not merely be in sight by noon, but must have entered Sveaborg's harbor."

The ensign looked puzzled. "What of it?" he asked.

Anttonen pointed out over the walls, towards an island dimly visible in the distance. "Look there," he said. His arm moved to indicate a second island. "And there. Russian fortifications. They've used the truce to gain command of the sea approaches. Any ship attempting to reach Sveaborg will come under heavy attack."

The colonel sighed. "Besides, the sea is dogged with ice. No ship will be able to reach us for weeks. The winter and the Russians have combined to kill our hopes."

Glumly, ensign and colonel walked from the ramparts into the interior of the fortress together. The corridors were dim and depressing; silence reigned everywhere.

At last, Anttonen spoke. "We've delayed long enough, Ensign. Vain hopes will no longer suffice; we must strike." He looked into his companion's eyes as they walked. "Gather the men. The time has come. I shall meet you near my quarters in two hours."

The ensign hesitated. "Sir," he asked. "Do you think we have a chance? We have so few men. We're a handful against a fortress."

In the dim light, Anttonen's face was tired and troubled. "I don't know," he said. "I just don't know. Captain Bannersson had contacts; if he had remained, our numbers would be greater. But I don't know the enlisted men like Carl did. I don't know who we can trust."

The colonel halted, and clasped the ensign firmly on the shoulder. "But, regardless, we've got to try. Finland's army has starved and been frozen and watched their homeland burn all winter. The only thing that has kept them going is the dream of winning it back. And without Sveaborg, that dream will die." He shook his head sadly. "We can't let that happen. With that dream dies Finland."

The ensign nodded. "Two hours, sir. You can count on us. We'll put some fight in Admiral Cronstedt yet." He grinned, and hurried on his way.

Alone in the silent corridor, Colonel Bengt Anttonen drew his sword, and held it up to where the dim light played along its blade. He gazed at it sadly, and wondered in silence how many Finns he'd have to kill in order to save Finland.

But there was no answer.

————

THE TWO GUARDS FIDGETED UNEASILY. "I DON'T KNOW, COLONEL," said one. "Our orders are to admit no one to the armory without authorization."

"I should think my rank would be sufficient authorization," snapped back Anttonen. "I am giving you a direct order to let us pass."

The first guard looked at his companion doubtfully. "Well," he said. "In that case perhaps we—"

"No, sir," said the second guard. "Colonel Jägerhorn ordered us not to admit anyone without authorization from Admiral Cronstedt. I'm afraid that includes you, too, sir."

Anttonen regarded him coldly. "Perhaps we should see Admiral Cronstedt about this," he said. "I think he might like to hear how you disobeyed a direct order."

The first guard winced. Both of them were squirming with unease, and had focused all their attention on the angry Finnish colonel. Anttonen scowled at them. "Come along," he said. "Now."

The pistol shots that rang out from the nearby corridor at that word took the guards completely by surprise. There was a cry of pain as one clutched his bleeding arm, his gun clattering to the floor. The second whirled towards the sound, and simultaneously Anttonen leaped forward to seize his musket in an iron grip. Before the guard had quite grasped what was happening, the colonel had wrenched his gun from startled fingers. From the corridor on the right issued a group of armed men, most bearing muskets, a few holding still-smoking pistols.

"What shall we do with these two?" asked a gruff, burly corporal at the head of the group. He leveled his bayonet suggestively at the chest of the guard still standing. The other had fallen to his knees, holding his wounded arm tenderly.

Handing the guard's musket to one of the men standing beside him, Anttonen regarded his prisoners coldly. He reached forward and yanked a ring of keys from the belt of the chief guard. "Tie them up," he said. "And watch them. We don't want any more bloodshed than can be helped."

The corporal nodded and, gesturing with his bayonet, herded the guards away from the door. Stepping forward with the keys, Anttonen worked intently for a moment, then opened the heavy wooden door on the fortress armory.

Instantly there was a rush of men through the doorway. They had prepared for this moment for some time, and they worked quickly and efficiently. Heavy wooden boxes creaked in protest as they were forced open, and there was the rasp of metal on metal as the muskets were lifted from the boxes and passed around.

Standing just inside the door, Anttonen surveyed the scene nervously. "Hurry up," he ordered. "And be sure to take plenty of powder and ammunition. We'll have to leave a good number of men to hold the armory against counterattacks, and—"

Suddenly the colonel whirled. From the hall outside came the sounds of musket fire, and the echo of running footsteps. Fingering his sword hilt apprehensively, Anttonen stepped back outside of the door.

And froze.

The guards he had posted outside of the armory were huddled against the far wall of the corridor, their weapons thrown in a heap at their feet. And facing him was a body of men twice as numerous as his insurgents, their guns trained on him and the armory door behind him. At their head, smiling confidently, was the lean, aristocratic form of Colonel F. A. Jägerhorn, a pistol cradled in his right hand.

"It's all over, Bengt," he said. "We figured you'd try something like this, and we've been watching every move you made since the armistice was signed. Your mutiny is finished."

"I wouldn't be so sure of that," said Anttonen, shaken but still resolute. "By now a group of my men have taken Admiral Cronstedt's office, and with him as prisoner are fanning out to seize the main batteries."

Jägerhorn threw back his head, and laughed. "Don't be a fool. Our men captured the ensign and his squad before they even got near Admiral Cronstedt. You never had a chance."

Anttonen's face went white. Horror and despair flickered across his eyes, and were replaced by a coldly burning anger. "NO!" he cried from behind clenched teeth. "NO!" His sword leaped from its sheath and flashed silver in the light as he sprang forward towards Jägerhorn.

He had taken but three steps when the first bullet caught him in the shoulder and sent his sword skittering from his grasp. The second and third ripped into his stomach and doubled him up. He took another halting step, and sank slowly to the floor.

Jägerhorn's eyes swept over him indifferently. "You men in the armory," he shouted, his voice ringing clearly through the hall. "Put down your guns and come out slowly. You are outnumbered and surrounded. The revolt is over. Don't make us spill any more blood."

There was no answer. From the side, where he was being held under guard, the veteran corporal shouted out, "Do as he says, men. He's got too many men to fight." He looked towards his commander. "Sir, tell them to give up. We have no chance now. Tell them, sir."

But the silence mocked his words, and the colonel lay quite still.

For Colonel Bengt Anttonen was dead.

A few short minutes after it had begun, the mutiny was over. And soon thereafter, the flag of Russia flew from the parapets of Vargön.

And as it flew above Sveaborg, soon it flew above Finland.

EPILOG

The old man propped himself up in the bed painfully, and stared with open curiosity at the visitor who stood in the doorway. The man was tall and powerfully built, with cold blue eyes and dirty blond hair. He wore the uniform of a major in the Swedish army, and carried himself with the confident air of a hardened warrior.

The visitor moved forward, and leaned against the foot of the old man's bed. "So you don't recognize me?" he said. "I can see why. I imagine that you've tried to forget Sveaborg and everything connected with it, Admiral Cronstedt."

The old man coughed violently. "Sveaborg?" he said weakly, trying to place the stranger who stood before him. "Were you at Sveaborg?"

The visitor laughed. "Yes, Admiral. For a good while at any rate. My name is Bannersson, Carl Bannersson. I was a captain then."

Cronstedt blinked. "Yes, yes. Bannersson. I remember you now. But you've changed since then."

"True. You sent me back to Stockholm, and in the years that followed I fought with Carl Johan against Napoleon. I've seen a lot of battles and a lot of sieges since then, sir. But I never forgot Sveaborg. Never."

The admiral doubled over suddenly with a fit of uncontrollable coughing. "W-what do you want?" he managed to gasp out at last. "I'm sorry if I'm rude, but I'm a sick man. Talking is a great strain." He coughed again. "I hope you'll forgive me."

Bannersson's eyes wandered around the small, dirty bedchamber. He straightened and reached into the breast pocket of his uniform, withdrawing a thick sealed envelope.

"Admiral," he said, tapping the envelope gently against the palm of his hand for emphasis. "Admiral, do you know what day this is?"

Cronstedt frowned. "The sixth of April," he replied.

"Yes. April 6, 1820. Exactly twelve years since that day you met with General Suchtelen on Lonan, and gave Sveaborg to the Russians."

The old man shook his head slowly from side to side. "Please, Major. You're awakening memories I had sealed up long ago. I don't want to talk about Sveaborg."

Bannersson's eyes blazed, and the lines of his mouth grew hard and angry. "No? Well, that's too bad. You'd rather talk about Ruotsinsalmi, I suppose. But we won't. We're going to talk about Sveaborg, old man, whether you like it or not."

Cronstedt shuddered at the violence in his voice. "Alright, Major. I had to surrender. Once surrounded by ice, Sveaborg is very weak. Our fleet was in danger. And our powder was low."

The Swedish officer considered him scornfully. "I have documents here," he said, holding up the envelope, "to show just how wrong you were. Facts, Admiral. Cold historical facts."

He ripped the end of the envelope off violently, and tossed the papers inside it onto Cronstedt's bed. "Twelve years ago you said we were outnumbered," he began, his voice hard and emotionless as he recited the facts. "We were not. The Russians barely had enough men to take over the fortress after it was surrendered to them. We had 7,386 enlisted men and 208 officers. Many more than the Russians.

"Twelve years ago you said Sveaborg could not be defended in winter due to the ice. That's hogwash. I have letters from all the finest military minds of the Swedish, Finnish, and Russian armies testifying to the strength of Sveaborg, summer or winter.

"Twelve years ago you spoke of the formidable Russian artillery that ringed us. It did not exist. At no time did Suchtelen have more than forty-six pieces of cannon, sixteen of which were mortars. We had ten times that number.

"Twelve years ago you said our provisions were running low, and our store of powder was dangerously depleted. It was not so. We had 9,535 cannon cartridges, 10,000 cartouches, 2 frigates, and over 130 smaller ships, magnificent naval stores, enough food to last for months, and over 3,000 barrels of powder. We could easily have waited for Swedish relief."

The old man shrieked. "Stop it, stop it!" He put his hands to his ears. "I won't hear any more. Why are you torturing me? Can't you let an old man rest in peace?"

Bannersson looked at him contemptuously. "I won't continue," he said. "But I'll leave the papers. You can read it all yourself."

Cronstedt was choking and gasping for breath. "It was a chance," he replied. "It was a chance to save everything for Sweden."

Bannersson laughed, a hard, cruel, bitter laugh. "A chance? I was one of your messengers, Admiral; I know what sort of a chance the Russians gave you. They detained us for weeks. You know when I got to Stockholm, Admiral? When I delivered your message?"

The old man's head lifted slowly, and his eyes looked into Bannersson's. His face was pale and sickly, his hands trembling.

"May 3, 1808," said Bannersson. And Cronstedt winced as if struck.

The tall Swedish major turned and walked to the door. There, knob in hand, he turned and looked back.

"You know," he said, "history will forget Bengt and what he tried to do, and will remember Colonel Jägerhorn only as one of the first Finnish nationalists. But you I don't know about. You live in Russian Finland on your thirty pieces of silver, yet Bengt said you were only weak." He shook his head. "Which is it, Admiral? What will history have to say about you?"

There was no answer. Count Carl Olof Cronstedt, Vice-Admiral of the Fleet, hero of Ruotsinsalmi, Commandant of Sveaborg, was weeping softly into his pillow.

AND A DAY LATER, HE WAS DEAD.

Call him the arm we trusted in
That shrank in time of stress,
Call him Affliction, Scorn and Sin
And Death and Bitterness

But mention not his former name,
Lest they should blush who bear the same.

Take all that's dismal in the tomb,
Take all in life that's base,
To form one name of guilt and gloom
For that one man's disgrace,
Twill rouse less grief in Finland's men
Than his at Sveaborg did them.

—*The Tales of Ensign Stål,*
  JOHAN LUDVIG RUNEBERG

AND DEATH HIS LEGACY

❖

THE PROPHET CAME OUT OF THE SOUTH WITH A FLAG IN HIS RIGHT hand and an ax handle in his left, to preach the creed of Americanism. He spoke to the poor and the angry, to the confused and to the fearful, and in them he woke a new determination. For his words were like a fire in the land, and wherever he stopped to speak, there the multitudes arose to march behind him.

His name was Norvel Arlington Beauregard, and he had been a governor before he became a Prophet. He was a big, stocky man, with round black eyes and a square face that flushed blood red when he got excited. His heavy, bushy eyebrows were perpetually crinkled down in suspicion, while his full lips seemed frozen in a sneering half-smile.

But his disciples did not care what he looked like. For Norvel Arlington Beauregard was a Prophet, and Prophets are not to be questioned. He did no miracles, but still they gathered to him, North and South, poor and affluent, steelworkers and factory owners. And soon their numbers were like unto an army.

And the army marched to the music of a military band.

"MAXIMILIAN DE LAURIER IS DEAD," SAID MAXIMILIAN DE LAURIER aloud to himself as he sat alone in a darkened, book-lined study.

He laughed a low, soft laugh. A match flared briefly in the darkness, flickered momentarily as he touched it to his pipe, and winked out. Maxim de Laurier leaned back in the plush leather armchair, and puffed slowly.

No, he thought. It doesn't work. The words just don't sound right. They've got a hollow ring to them. I'm Maxim de Laurier, and I'm alive.

Yes, answered another part of him, but not for long. Quit fooling yourself. They all say the same thing now. Cancer. Terminal. A year at most. Probably not even that long.

I'm a dead man, then, he told himself. Funny. I don't feel like a dead man. I can't imagine being dead. Not me. Not Maxim de Laurier.

He tried it again. "Maximilian de Laurier is dead," he said firmly to the silence.

Then he shook his head. It still doesn't work, he thought. I've got everything to live for. Money. Position. Influence. All that, and more. Everything.

The answer rang ruthless and cold through his head. It doesn't matter, it said. Nothing matters anymore, nothing except that cancer. You're dead. A living dead man.

In the dark, silent room, his hand trembled suddenly, and the pipe flew from his grasp and spilled ashes on the expensive carpet. His fists clenched, and his knuckles began to whiten.

Maximilian de Laurier rose slowly from the chair and walked across the room, brushing a light switch as he passed it. He stopped before the full-length mirror on the door, and surveyed the tall, gray-haired reflection that stared back from the glass. There was a curious whiteness about the face, he noted, and the hands were still trembling slightly.

"And my life?" he said to the reflection. "What have I done with my life? Read a few books. Driven a few sports cars. Made a few fortunes. A blast, one long, wild blast. Playboy of the Western World."

He laughed softly, but the reflection still looked grim and shaken. "But what have I accomplished? In a year, will there be anything to show that Maxim de Laurier has lived?"

He turned from the mirror with a snarl, a bitter, dying man with eyes like the gray ash of a fire that has long since gone out. As he turned, those eyes drank in the gathered remains of a life, sweeping over the rich, heavy furniture, the polished wooden bookcases with their rows of heavy, leather-bound volumes, the cold, sooty fireplace, and the imported hunting rifles mounted in a rack above the mantelpiece.

Suddenly the fire burned again. With quick strides, de Laurier crossed the room and yanked one of the rifles from its mounting. He stroked the stock softly with a trembling hand, but his voice when he spoke was cold and hard and determined.

"Damn it," he said. "I'm not dead yet."

He laughed a wild, snarling laugh as he sat down to oil the gun.

Through the Far West the Prophet stormed, spreading the Word from a private jet. Everywhere the crowds gathered to cheer him, and husky steelworkers lifted up their children on their shoulders so they could hear him speak. The long-haired hecklers who dared to mock his cause were put down, shouted down, and sometimes beaten down.

"Ah'm for the little man," he said in San Diego. "Ah'm for the good patriotic Americans who get forgotten today. This is a free country and I don't mind dissent, but Ah'm not about to let the Commies and the anarchists take over. Let's let'em know they can't fly the Communist flag in this country if there are any red-blooded Americans left around. And if we have to bust a few heads to teach 'em, well, that's okay too."

And they flocked to him, the patriots and the superpatriots, the vets and the GIs, the angry and the frightened. They flew their flags by day, and read their bibles by night, and pasted "Beauregard" stickers on the bumpers of their cars.

"Any man has got a right to dissent," the Prophet shouted from a platform in Los Angeles, "but when these long-haired anarchists try to impede the progress of the war, why, that's not dissent, that's treason.

"And when these traitors try to block troop trains carrying vital war materials to our boys overseas, Ah say it's time to give our policemen some good stout clubs, untie their hands, and let 'em spill a little Commie blood. That'll teach those anarchists to respect the law!"

And all the people cheered and cheered, and the noise all but drowned out the faint echo of jackboots in the distance.

———

RECLINING IN THE DECK CHAIR, THE TALL, GRAY-HAIRED MAN GLANCED at the copy of the *New York Times* lying across his lap. He was a nondescript sort of fellow, with a worn off-the-rack sports jacket and a pair of cheap plastic sunglasses. Few would notice him in a crowd. Fewer still would look closely enough to recognize the dead man who once had been Maximilian de Laurier.

A half smile flickered across the dead man's lips as he read one of the first-page stories. The headline read "De Laurier Fortune Liquidated" in prim gray type. Below, in smaller print, a somber subhead observed that "English Millionaire Vanishes; Friends Believe Money Deposited in Swiss Banks."

Yes, he thought. How appropriate. The man vanishes, but the money gets the headlines. I wonder what the papers will say a year from now? Something like "Heirs Await Reading of Will," perhaps?

His eyes left the article and wandered upward across the page, coming to rest on the lead story. He stared at the headline in silence, a frown set across his features. Then, slowly and carefully, he read the article.

When he finished, de Laurier rose from the chair, folded the paper carefully, and dropped it over the rail into the murky green water that churned lustily in the liner's wake. Then he shoved his hands into his jacket pockets and walked slowly back to his stateroom in the economy section of the ship. Below, the newspaper tumbled over and over in the turbulence caused by the great liner's passing until it finally became waterlogged and sank. It came to rest at last on the muddy, rock-strewn bottom, where the silence and the darkness were eternal.

And the crabs scuttled to and fro across the fading front-page photo of a stocky, square-faced man with bushy eyebrows and a crooked sneer.

———

THE PROPHET SWUNG EAST WITH A VENGEANCE, FOR HERE WAS THE homeland of the false seers who had led his people astray, here was the stronghold of those who opposed him. No matter. Here his crowds were even greater, and the sons and the grandsons of the immigrants of the last century were his to a man. So here Norvel Arlington Beauregard chose to attack his enemies in their own lair.

"Ah'm for the little man," he said in New York City. "Ah support the right of every American to rent his house or sell his goods to whoever he so chooses, without any interference by briefcase-toting bureaucrats and egghead professors who sit up in their ivory towers and decide how you and me have to live."

And the people cheered and cheered, and they waved their flags and said the Pledge of Allegiance, and chanted "Beauregard—Beauregard—Beauregard" over and over again until the arena rocked with the noise. And the Prophet grinned and waved happily, and the Eastern reporters who covered him shook their heads in disbelief and muttered dire things about "charisma" and "irony."

"Ah'm for the working man," the Prophet told a great labor convention in Philadelphia. "And Ah say all these anarchists and demonstrators better damn well quit their yappin' and go out and get jobs just like everybody else! You and me had to work for what we had, so why should they get pampered by the government? Why should you good folks have to pay taxes to support a bunch of lazy, ignorant bums who don't want to work anyway?"

The crowd roared its approval, and the Prophet clenched his fist and shook it above his head in triumph. For the Word had touched the souls of the workers and the laborers, the strainers and the sweaters, the just-haves of a nation. And they were his. They would follow false gods no longer.

So they all stood up and sang "The Star-Spangled Banner" together.

———

In New York, Maxim de Laurier caught the first bus from customs to the heart of Manhattan. He carried only one small suitcase packed with clothing, so he did not bother to stop at a hotel. Instead, he went straight towards the financial district, to one of the city's largest banks.

"I'd like to cash a check," he said to a teller. "On my bank in

Switzerland." He scribbled in his checkbook sloppily, ripped the page loose, and shoved it across the counter.

The teller's eyebrows shot up slightly as he noticed the figure. "Mmmm," he said. "I'll have to check this out, sir. I hope you don't mind waiting a few moments. You do have identification, of course, Mister——?"

He glanced at the check again. "Mister Lawrence," he concluded.

De Laurier smiled amiably. "Of course," he said. "I'd hardly try to cash a check of this size without proper identification."

Twenty minutes later he left the bank, walking with measured confidence down the avenue. He made several stops that day, before he finally checked into a cheap hotel for the night.

He bought some clothing, several newspapers, a large number of maps, a battered used car, and a collection of rifles and pistols. He took plenty of ammo, and made sure every rifle had a telescopic sight.

Maximilian de Laurier stayed up late that night, bent over a cheap card table in his hotel room. First he read the newspapers he had purchased. He read them slowly, and carefully, and over and over again. Several times he got up and placed phone calls to the papers' information services, and took down careful notes of what they told him.

And then he spread out his maps, and studied them intently, far into the morning. Selecting those he wanted, he traced a heavy black line across them, constantly referring back to his papers as he worked.

Finally, near dawn, he picked up a red pencil and circled the name of a medium-sized city in Ohio.

Afterward, he sat down and oiled his guns.

THE PROPHET RETURNED TO THE MIDWEST WITH A FURY, FOR HERE, more than anywhere except in his homeland, he had found his people. The high priests who had fanned out before him sent back their reports, and they all read the same way. Illinois was going to be good, they said. Indiana was even better. He'd really clean up in Indiana. And Ohio—Ohio was great, Ohio was fantastic.

And so the Prophet crisscrossed the Midwest, bringing the Word to those who were ripe for it, preaching the creed of Americanism in the heartland of America.

"Chicago is my kind of town," he said repeatedly as he stumped through Illinois, "You people know how to handle anarchists and Communists in Chicago. There's a lot of good, sensible, patriotic folks in Chicago. You're not about to let those terrorists take over the streets from good, law-abiding citizens in Chicago."

And all the people cheered and cheered, and Beauregard led them in a salute to the police of Chicago. One long-haired heckler yelled out "Nazi," but his lone shout was lost in the roar of the applause. Except, at the back of the hall, two burly security guards noted him, nodded to each other, and began to move swiftly and silently through the crowd.

"Ah'm not a racist," the Prophet said as he crossed the border to speak in northern Indiana. "Ah stand for the rights of all good Americans, regardless of race, creed, or color. However, Ah support your right to sell or rent your property to whoever you choose. And Ah say every person ought to work like you and me, without being allowed to live in dirt and ignorance and immorality on a government handout. And Ah say that looters and anarchists ought to be shot."

And all the people cheered and cheered, and then went out to spread the Word to their friends, their relatives, and their neighbors. "I'm no racist and Beauregard's not one either," they'd tell each other, "but would you want one to marry your sister?" And the crowds grew larger and larger each week.

And as the Prophet moved east into Ohio, a dead man drove west to meet him.

———

"IS THIS ROOM SATISFACTORY, MR. LAUREL?" ASKED THE THIN, ELDERLY landlady, holding the door open for his inspection.

Maxim de Laurier brushed past her and deposited his suitcases on the sagging double bed that stood against one wall. He smiled amiably as he surveyed the dingy cold-water flat. Crossing the room, he lifted the shade and glanced out the window.

"Oh, dear," said the landlady, fumbling with her keys. "I hope you won't mind the stadium being located right next door. There's going to be a game next Saturday, and those boys do make a dreadful lot of noise." She punctuated her sentence with a sharp stomp as her foot came down to crush a cockroach that had crawled out from under the carpet.

De Laurier brushed aside her fears with a wave of his hand. "The room will be just fine," he said, "I rather enjoy football anyway, and from here I'll have a fine view of the game."

The landlady smiled weakly. "Very well," she said, holding out the key. "I'll take the week's rent in advance, if you don't mind."

When she left, de Laurier carefully locked the door, and then pulled up a chair in front of the window.

Yes, he thought. A fine view. A perfect view. Of course, the stands are on the other side, so they'll probably have the platform facing that way. But that shouldn't pose any problems. He's a big man, a stocky man, probably quite distinctive even from behind. And those arc lights will be a big help.

Nodding in satisfaction, he rose and returned the chair to its normal place. Then he sat down to oil his guns.

———

IT WAS QUITE COLD OUT, BUT THE STADIUM WAS PACKED NONETHELESS. The grandstands were crammed with people, and an overflow crowd had been permitted to drift out onto the field and squat in the grass at the foot of the platform.

The platform itself, draped in red, white, and blue, had been erected on the 50-yard line. American flags flew from staffs at both ends of the platform, with the speaker's podium situated between them. Two harsh white spotlights converged on the rostrum, adding to the garish brilliance of the stadium's own arc lights. The microphones had been carefully hooked up to the stadium's loudspeaker system, and tested over and over again.

It was lucky that they were working, for the roar was deafening when the Prophet stepped up to the podium, and subsided only when he began to speak. And then the hush was sudden and complete, and the call of the Prophet rang out unchallenged through the night.

Time had not dimmed the fire that burned in the soul of the Prophet, and his words were white-hot with his anger and his conviction. They came loud and defiant from the platform, and echoed back and forth through the grandstands. They carried far in the clear, cold night air.

They carried to a dingy cold-water flat where Maxim de Laurier sat alone in the darkness, staring out his window. Leaning against his chair was a high-caliber rifle, well oiled and equipped with a telescopic sight.

On the platform, the Prophet preached the faith to the patriots and to the frightened. He spoke of Americanism, and his whiplike words flailed the Communists, the anarchists, and the long-haired terrorists who were haunting the streets of the nation.

Ah yes, thought de Laurier. I can hear the echoes. Oh, how I can hear the echoes. There was another who attacked the Communists and the anarchists. There was another who said he would save his nation from their clutches.

"—and Ah say to you good folks of Ohio that when Ah'm in charge, the streets of this country are going to be safe to walk on. Ah'm going to untie the hands of our policemen, and see that they enforce the laws and teach these criminals and terrorists a few lessons."

A few lessons, thought de Laurier. Yes, yes. It fits, it fits. The police and the army teaching lessons. And such effective teachers. With clubs and guns as study aids. Oh, Mister Beauregard, how well it all fits.

"—and Ah say that when our boys, our fine boys from Mississippi and Ohio and everywhere else, are fighting and dying for our flag overseas, that we've got to give them all the support we can here at home. And that includes busting the heads of a few of these traitors who defile the flag and call for an enemy victory and obstruct the progress of the war. Ah say that it's time to let 'em know how a patriotic, red-blooded American takes care of treason!"

Treason, thought de Laurier. Yes, treason was what he called it too, that other one so long ago. He said he would get rid of the traitors in the government, the traitors who had caused the nation's defeat and humiliation.

De Laurier slid the chair back slowly. He dropped to one knee, and lifted the rifle to his shoulder.

"—Ah'm no racist, but Ah say that these people oughta—"

De Laurier's face was chalk white, and the gun was unsteady in his hands. "So sick," he whispered hoarsely to himself, "so very, very sick. But do I have the right? If he is what they want, *can* I have the right, alone, to overrule them in the name of sanity?"

He was trembling badly now, and his body was cold and wet with his sweat, despite the chilling wind from outside.

The Prophet's words rang all around him, but he heard them no longer. His mind flashed back, to the visions of another Prophet, and the promised land to which he led his people. He remembered the echo of great armies on the march. He remembered the shriek of the rockets and the bombers in the night. He remembered the terror of the knock on the door. He remembered the charnel smell of the battlefield.

He remembered the gas chambers prepared for the inferior race.

And he wondered, and he listened, and his hands grew steady.

"If he had died early," said Maximilian de Laurier alone to himself in the darkness, "how would they have known what horror they had averted?"

He centered the crosshairs on the back of the Prophet's head, and his finger tightened on the trigger.

And the gun spoke death.

Norvel Arlington Beauregard, his fist shaking in the air, jerked suddenly and pitched forward from the platform into the crowd below. And then the screaming started, while the Secret Service men swore and rushed towards the fallen Prophet.

By the time they reached him, Maximilian de Laurier was turning the ignition key in his car and heading for the turnpike.

———

THE NEWS OF THE PROPHET'S DEATH ROCKED A NATION, AND THE WAIL went up from all parts of the land.

"They killed him," they said. "Those damn Commies knew that he was the man who could lick them, so they killed him."

Or, sometimes, they said, "It was the niggers, the damn niggers. They knew that Beauregard was going to keep them in their places, so they killed him."

Or, sometimes, "It was those demonstrators. Goddam traitors.

Beau had 'em pegged for what they were, a bunch of anarchists and terrorists. So they killed him, the filthy scum."

Crosses burned across the land that night, and all the polls turned sharply upward. The Prophet had become a Martyr.

And, three weeks later, Beauregard's vice-presidential candidate announced on a nationwide television address that he was carrying on. "Our cause is not dead," he said. "I promise to fight on for Beau and all that he stood for. And we will fight to victory!"

And all the people cheered and cheered.

———

A FEW HUNDRED MILES AWAY, MAXIM DE LAURIER SAT IN A HOTEL room and watched, his face a milk-white mask. "No," he whispered, choking on the words. "Not this. This wasn't supposed to happen. It's wrong, all wrong."

And he buried his head in his hands, and sobbed, "My God, my God, what have I done?" And then he was still and silent for a long time. When he rose at last his face was still pale and twisted, but a single dying ember burned still in the ashes of his eyes. "Maybe," he said. "Maybe I can still—"

And he sat down to oil his gun.

TWO

THE FILTHY PRO

You never forget the first time you do it for money.

I became a filthy pro in 1970, during the summer between my senior and graduate years at Northwestern University. The story that turned the trick for me was "The Hero," which I'd originally written for creative writing my junior year, and had been trying to sell ever since. *Playboy* had seen it first, and returned it with a form rejection slip. *Analog* sent it back with a pithy letter of rejection from John W. Campbell, Jr., the first, last, and only time I got a personal response from that legendary editor. After that "The Hero" went to Fred Pohl at *Galaxy* . . .

. . .where it vanished.

It was a year before I realized that Pohl was no longer the editor at *Galaxy*, that the magazine had changed both publisher and address. When I did, I retyped the story from my carbon—yes, I had finally started to use the stuff, hurrah—and sent it out to *Galaxy*'s new editor, Ejler Jakobsson, at *Galaxy*'s new address . . .

. . .where it vanished *again*!

Meanwhile, I had celebrated my graduation from Northwestern, though I still had a year of post-graduate study looming ahead of me. Medill offered a five-year program in journalism; at the end of the fourth year you received a

Bachelor's degree, but you were encouraged to return for the fifth year, which included a quarter's internship doing political reporting in Washington, D.C. At the end of the fifth year, you received a Master's.

After graduation I returned to Bayonne, and my summer job as a sports-writer/public relations man for the Department of Parks and Recreation. The city sponsored several summer baseball leagues, and my job was to write up the games for the local papers, the *Bayonne Times* and *Jersey Journal*. There were half a dozen leagues, for different age groups, with several games going on every day at different fields around the city, so there was no way for me to actually cover the action. Instead I spent my days in the office, and after every game the umps would bring me a box score. I'd use those as the basis for my stories. So I spent four summers working as a baseball writer, and never saw a game.

By that August, "The Hero" had been at *Galaxy* for a year. I decided, instead of writing a query letter, to phone the magazine's offices in New York City and inquire about my lost story. The woman who answered was brusque and unfriendly at first, and when I mumbled something about inquiring after a manuscript that had been there for a long time, she told me *Galaxy* could not possibly keep track of all the stories it rejected. I might have given up right there, but somehow I managed to blurt out the title of the story.

There was a pregnant pause. "Wait a minute," the woman said. "We bought that story." (Years later, I discovered that the woman I was speaking to was Judy-Lynn Benjamin, later Judy-Lynn del Rey, who went on to found the Del Rey imprint for Ballatine Books). The story had been purchased *months* ago, she told me, but somehow the manuscript and purchase order had fallen behind a filing cabinet, and had only recently turned up again. (In some alternate universe, no one ever looked behind those files, and I'm a journalist today.)

I hung up the phone with a dazed look on my face, before heading off to my summer job. I must have floated, since I was far too high for my feet to touch the ground. Afterward, when neither contract nor check appeared, I began to wonder if the woman on the phone had misremembered. Perhaps there was some other story called "The Hero." I developed a paranoid fear that *Galaxy* might go out of business before publishing my story, a fear that was inflamed when summer ended and I headed back to Chicago, still without a check.

It turned out that *Galaxy* had mailed the check and contract to the North Shore Hotel, the dorm I had vacated on graduating Northwestern that June. By the time it was finally forwarded to my summer address, I was back at school, but in a *different* dorm.

There was a check, though, and I did get my hands on it at last. It proved to be for $94, not an inconsiderable sum of money in 1970. "The Hero" appeared in the February 1971 issue of *Galaxy*, in the winter of my graduate year at Medill. Since I did not own a car, I made one of my friends drive me around to half the newsstands on the north shore, so I could buy up all the copies I could find.

Meanwhile, my college years were winding down. I breezed through the first two quarters of my graduate year in Evanston, then packed my bags for Washington and my internship on Capitol Hill. In a few months my real life would begin. I had been doing interviews and sending out job applications, and was looking forward to sorting through all the offers and deciding which of them I'd take. After all, I had graduated *magna cum laude* from the finest journalism school in the country, and would soon have a Master's degree and a prestigious internship under my belt as well. I had lost a lot of weight my graduate year and bought new clothes to suit, so I arrived in D.C. the very picture of a hippie journalist, with my shoulder-length hair, bell bottoms, aviator glasses, and double-breasted pin-striped mustard-yellow sports jacket.

My internship was demanding, but exciting. The nation was in turmoil in the spring of 1971, and I was at the center of it all, walking the corridors of power, reporting on congressmen and senators, sitting in the Senate press gallery with real reporters. The Medill News Service had client newspapers all over the country, so a number of my stories actually saw print. The program was run by Neil McNeil, a hardnosed political reporter of the green-eyeshade school who would sit in his cubicle reading your copy, and roar your name whenever he came on something he didn't like. My own name was roared frequently. "Too cute," McNeil would scrawl atop my stories, and I'd have to rewrite them and take out everything but the facts before he'd pass them on. I hated it, but I learned a lot.

It was also in Washington that I attended my first actual *science fiction* convention, almost seven years after that first comicon. When I walked into the Sheraton Park Hotel in my burgundy bell bottoms and double-breasted pin-striped mustard-yellow sports jacket, the fellow behind the registration table was this bone-thin hippie writer, with a scraggy beard and long orange hair. He recognized my name [no one forgets the R.R.] and told me that he was *Galaxy*'s slush reader, the very fellow who'd fished "The Hero" out of the slush pile and pushed it on Ejler Jakobsson. So I suppose Gardner Dozois made me a pro and a fan both (though I have since wondered whether he was actually working on registration, or whether he just saw the table unattended and realized that if he sat there people would hand him money. Reading slush for *Galaxy* didn't pay much, after all).

By that time I had a second sale under my belt. Just a few weeks before, Ted White, the new editor at *Amazing* and *Fantastic,* had informed me that he was buying "The Exit to San Breta," a futuristic fantasy that I'd written during the spring break of my senior year of college. (Yes, sad to say, when all my friends were down in Florida drinking beer with bikini-clad coeds on the beaches of Ft. Lauderdale, I was back in Bayonne, writing.) The story of my second sale was eerily similar to that of my first. Relying on the listings in *Writer's Market,* I'd sent the story off to Harry Harrison at the address given for *Fantastic,* never to see it again. Only later did I learn that both the editor and address had changed, requiring me to retype the manuscript all over again and, well . . . I was starting to wonder if having your story lost in the mail was somehow a necessary prerequisite to selling it.

Galaxy had paid me my $94 on acceptance for "The Hero," but Fantastic paid on publication, so I would not actually see the money for "The Exit to San Breta" until October. And when the check did come, it was only for $50. A sale is a sale, however, and your second time is almost as exciting as your first, in writing as in sex. One sale might be a fluke, but *two* sales to two different editors suggested that maybe I had some talent after all.

"The Exit to San Breta" was set in the Southwest, where I live at present, but at the time I wrote it I had never been west of Chicago. The story is all about driving and takes place entirely on highways, but at the time I wrote it I had never been behind the wheel of an automobile. (Our family never owned a car.) Despite its futuristic setting, "Exit" is a fantasy, which is why it appeared in *Fantastic* and not *Amazing,* and why I had not even bothered to send it to *Analog* or *Galaxy.* Inspired by example of Fritz Leiber's "Smoke Ghost," I wanted to take the ghost out of his mouldering old Victorian mansion and put him where a proper twentieth century ghost belonged . . . in a car.

Though the most horrible thing that happens in it is an auto accident, "The Exit to San Breta" might even be classified as a horror story. If so, my first two sales prefigured my entire career to come, by including all three of the genres I would write in.

Gardner Dozois was not the only writer at that Disclave. I met Joe Haldeman and his brother Jack as well, and George Alec Effinger (still called Piglet at that time), Ted White, Bob Toomey. All of them were talking about stories they were writing, stories they had written, stories that they meant to write. Terry Carr was the Guest of Honor; a fine writer himself, Carr was also the editor of *Ace Specials* and the original anthology *Universe*, and went out of his way to be friendly and helpful to all the young writers swarming about him, including me. No convention ever had a warmer or more accessible guest.

I left Disclave resolved to attend more science fiction conventions . . . and to sell more stories. Before I could do that, of course, I would need to *write* more stories. Talking with Gardner and Piglet and the Haldemans had made me realize how little I had actually produced, compared to any of them. If I was serious about wanting to be a writer, I would need to finish more stories.

Of course, that was the summer when my real life was supposed to begin. I would soon be moving somewhere, working at my first real job, living in an apartment of my own. For months I had been dreaming of paychecks, cars, and girlfriends, and wondering where life would take me. Would I have *time* to write fiction? That was hard to say.

Well, life took me back to my old room in Bayonne. Despite all those interviews, letters, and applications, despite my degree and my internship and *magna cum laude*, I had no job.

It did look for a while as if I were going to get an offer from a newspaper in Boca Raton, Florida, and another from *Women's Wear Daily*, but in the end neither place came through. I don't know, maybe I shouldn't have worn the double-breasted pin-striped mustard-yellow sports jacket to that follow-up interview. Even Marvel Comics turned me down, as seemingly unimpressed by my Master's as they were by my old Alley Award.

I did get an offer of sorts from my hometown paper, the *Bayonne Times*, but it was withdrawn when I asked about salary and benefits. "A beginner should get a job and experience," the editor scolded me. "That should have been your first consideration." (I got my revenge. The *Bayonne Times* ceased publishing that very summer, and both the editor and the guy he hired in place of me found themselves out of work. If I had taken the job, my "experience" would have lasted all of two weeks.)

Far from starting my real life in some exotic new city, with a salary and an apartment of my own, I found myself covering summer baseball for the Bayonne Department of Parks and Recreation once more. As if that were not wound enough, the Department of Parks had some nice salt to rub in. Because of budget cuts, they could only afford to hire me half-time. However, there were just as many games to write up as last summer, so I would be expected to do the same amount of work in half the time for half the pay.

There were black days that summer when I felt as if my five years of college had been a total waste, that I would be forever trapped in Bayonne and might end up running the Tubs o' Fun again at Uncle Milty's down on 1st Street, as I had my first summer out of high school. Vietnam also loomed. My number had come up in the draft lottery, and by losing all that weight over the past year I had also managed to lose my 4-F exemption. I was opposed to the war in Vietnam, and had applied for conscientious objector status with my local draft board, but everyone told me that my chances of receiving it were small to none. More likely, I'd be drafted. I might only have a month or two of civilian life remaining.

I had that much, however . . . and since I only had a part-time job, I had half of every day as well. I decided to use that time for writing fiction, as I'd resolved to do at Disclave. To work at it *every day,* and see how much I could produce before Uncle Sam called me up. My Parks Department job began in the afternoon, so the mornings became my time to write. Every day after breakfast I would drag out my Smith-Corona portable electric, set it up on my mother's kitchen table, plug it in, flick on the switch that made it *hummmmm,* and set to writing. Nor would I allow myself to put a story aside until I'd finished it. I wanted finished stories I could sell, not fragments and half-developed notions.

That summer I finished a story every two weeks, on the average. I wrote "Night Shift" and "Dark, Dark Were the Tunnels." I wrote "The Last Super Bowl," though my title was "The Final Touchdown Drive." I wrote "A Peripheral Affair" and "Nobody Leaves New Pittsburg," both of them intended as the first story of a series. And I wrote "With Morning Comes Mistfall" and "The Second Kind of Loneliness," which follow. Seven stories, all

in all. Maybe it was the spectre of Vietnam that goaded me, or my accumu-
lated frustration at having neither a job, a girl, nor a life. ("Nobody Leaves
New Pittsburg," though perhaps the weakest story I produced that summer,
reflects my state of mind most clearly. For "New Pittsburg," read "Bayonne."
For "corpse," read me.)

Whatever the cause, the words came pouring out of me as they never
had before. Ultimately, all seven of the stories that I wrote that summer
would go on to sell, though for some it would require four or five years
and a score of rejections. Two of the seven, however, proved to be important milestones in my career, and those are the two that I've included
here.

They were the two best. I knew that when I wrote them, and said as
much in the letters I sent to Howard Waldrop that summer. "With Morning
Comes Mistfall" was the finest thing that I had ever written, *ever* . . . until I
wrote "The Second Kind of Loneliness" a few weeks later. "Mistfall" seemed to
me to be the more polished of the two, a wistful mood piece with little in the
way of traditional "action," yet evocative and, I hoped, effective. "Loneliness,"
on the other hand, was an open wound of a story, painful to write, painful to
read. It represented a real breakthrough for my writing. My earlier stories had
come wholly from the head, but this one came from the heart and the balls
as well. It was the first story I ever wrote that truly left me feeling vulnerable,
the first story that ever made me ask myself, "Do I *really* want to let people
read this?"

"The Second Kind of Loneliness" and "With Morning Comes Mistfall"
were the stories that would make or break my career, I was convinced. For
the next half-year, *break* looked more likely than *make*. Neither story sold
its first time out. Or its second. Or its third. My other "summer stories"
were getting bounced around as well, but it was the rejections for "Mistfall"
and "Loneliness" that hurt the most. These were *strong* stories, I was convinced, the best work that I was capable of. If the editors did not want
them, maybe I did not understand what makes a good story after all . . . or
maybe my best work was just not good enough. It was a dark day each time
one of these two came straggling home, and a dark night of doubt that followed.

But in the end my faith was vindicated. Both stories sold, and when
they did it was to *Analog*, which boasted the highest circulation and best
rates of any magazine in the field. John W. Campbell, Jr., had died that

spring, and after a hiatus of several months Ben Bova had been named to take his place as editor of SF's most respected magazine. Campbell would never have touched either of these stories, I am convinced, but Bova intended to take *Analog* in new directions. He bought them both, after some minor rewrites.

"The Second Kind of Loneliness" appeared first, as the cover story of the December 1972 issue. Frank Kelly Freas did the cover, a gorgeous depiction of my protagonist floating above the whorl of the nullspace vortex. (It was my first cover and I wanted to buy the painting. Freas offered it to me for $200 . . . but I had only received $250 for the story, so I flinched, and bought the two-page interior spread and a cover rough instead. They're both swell, but I wish that I'd gone ahead and bought the painting. The last time I inquired, its current owner was willing to sell for $20,000.)

"With Morning Comes Mistfall" followed "Loneliness" into print, in the issue for May 1973. Two stories appearing in the field's top magazine so close together attracted attention, and "Mistfall" was nominated for both the Nebula and Hugo Awards, the first of my works to contend for either honor. It lost the Nebula to James Tiptree's "Love Is the Plan, the Plan Is Death," and the Hugo to Ursula K. Le Guin's "The Ones Who Walk Away from Omelas," but I received a handsome certificate suitable for framing and Gardner Dozois inducted me into the Hugo-and-Nebula Losers Club, chanting *One of us, one of us, one of us.* I can't complain.

That summer of 1971 proved to be a turning point in my life. If I had been able to find an entry-level job in journalism, I might very well have taken the road more traveled by, the one that came with a salary and health insurance. I suspect I would have continued to write the occasional short story, but with a full-time job to fill my days they would have been few and far between. Today I might be a foreign correspondent for the *New York Times,* an entertainment reporter for *Variety,* a columnist appearing daily in three hundred newspapers coast to coast . . . or more likely, a sour, disgruntled rewrite man on the *Jersey Journal.*

Instead circumstances forced me to do what I loved best.

That summer ended happily in other ways as well. To the vast surprise of all, my draft board granted me my conscientious objector status. (Perhaps "The Hero" had a bit to do with that. I'd sent it in as part of my application.) With my low lottery number, I was still called up to serve at the end of the summer . . . but now, instead of flying off to Vietnam, I was returning to Chicago for two years of alternative service with VISTA.

During the next decade I would find myself directing chess tournaments and teaching college . . . but those were only things I *did,* to pay the rent. After the summer of '71, when people asked me what I was, I always said, "A writer."

THE HERO

❖

THE CITY WAS DEAD AND THE FLAMES OF ITS PASSING SPREAD A RED stain across the green-gray sky.

It had been a long time dying. Resistance had lasted almost a week and the fighting had been bitter for a while. But in the end the invaders had broken the defenders, as they had broken so many others in the past. The alien sky with its double sun did not bother them. They had fought and won under skies of azure blue and speckled gold and inky black.

The Weather Control boys had hit first, while the main force was still hundreds of miles to the east. Storm after storm had flailed at the streets of the city, to slow defensive preparations and smash the spirit of resistance.

When they were closer the invaders had sent up howlers. Unending high-pitched shrieks had echoed back and forth both day and night and before long most of the populace had fled in demoralized panic. By then the attackers' main force was in range and launched plague bombs on a steady westward wind.

Even then the natives had tried to fight back. From their defensive emplacements ringing the city the survivors had sent up a hail of atomics, managing to vaporize one whole company whose defensive screens were overloaded by the sudden assault. But the gesture was a feeble one at best. By that time incendiary bombs were raining down steadily upon the city and great clouds of acid-gas were blowing across the plains.

And behind the gas, the dreaded assault squads of the Terran Expeditionary Force moved on the last defenses.

———

KAGEN SCOWLED AT THE DENTED PLASTOID HELMET AT HIS FEET AND cursed his luck. A routine mopping-up detail, he thought. A perfectly routine operation—and some damned automatic interceptor emplacement somewhere had lobbed a low-grade atomic at him.

It had been only a near miss but the shock waves had damaged his hip rockets and knocked him out of the sky, landing him in this god-forsaken little ravine east of the city. His light plastoid battle armor had protected him from the impact but his helmet had taken a good whack.

Kagen squatted and picked up the dented helmet to examine it. His long-range com and all of his sensory equipment were out. With his rockets gone, too, he was crippled, deaf, dumb, and half-blind. He swore.

A flicker of movement along the top of the shallow ravine caught his attention. Five natives came suddenly into view, each carrying a hair-trigger submachine gun. They carried them at the ready, trained on Kagen. They were fanned out in line, covering him from both right and left. One began to speak.

He never finished. One instant, Kagen's screech gun lay on the rocks at his feet. Quite suddenly it was in his hand.

Five men will hesitate where one alone will not. During the brief flickering instant before the natives' fingers began to tighten on their triggers, Kagen did not pause, Kagen did not hesitate, Kagen did not think.

Kagen killed.

The screech gun emitted a loud, ear-piercing shriek. The enemy squad leader shuddered as the invisible beam of concentrated high-frequency sound ripped into him. Then his flesh began to liquify. By then Kagen's gun had found two more targets.

The guns of the two remaining natives finally began to chatter. A rain of bullets enveloped Kagen as he whirled to his right and he grunted under the impact as the shots caromed off his battle armor. His screech gun leveled—and a random shot sent it spinning from his grasp.

Kagen did not hesitate or pause as the gun was wrenched from his grip. He bounded to the top of the shallow ravine with one leap, directly toward one of the soldiers.

The man wavered briefly and brought up his gun. The instant was all Kagen needed. With all the momentum of his leap behind it, his right hand smashed the gun butt into the enemy's face and his left, backed by fifteen hundred pounds of force, hammered into the native's body right under the breastbone.

Kagen seized the corpse and heaved it toward the second native, who had ceased fire briefly as his comrade came between himself and Kagen. Now his bullets tore into the airborne body. He took a quick step back, his gun level and firing.

And then Kagen was on him. Kagen knew a searing flash of pain as a shot bruised his temple. He ignored it, drove the edge of his hand into the native's throat. The man toppled, lay still.

Kagen spun, still reacting, searching for the next foe.

He was alone.

Kagen bent and wiped the blood from his hand with a piece of the native's uniform. He frowned in disgust. It was going to be a long trek back to camp, he thought, tossing the blood-soaked rag casually to the ground.

Today was definitely not his lucky day.

He grunted dismally, then scrambled back down into the ravine to recover his screech gun and helmet for the hike.

On the horizon, the city was still burning.

———

RAGELLI'S VOICE WAS LOUD AND CHEERFUL AS IT CAME CRACKLING over the short-range communicator nestled in Kagen's fist.

"So it's you, Kagen," he said, laughing. "You signaled just in time. My sensors were starting to pick up something. Little closer and I would've screeched you down."

"My helmet's busted and the sensors are out," Kagen replied. "Damn hard to judge distance. Long-range com is busted, too."

"The brass was wondering what happened to you," Ragelli cut in. "Made 'em sweat a little. But I figured you'd turn up sooner or later."

"Right," Kagen said. "One of these mudworms zapped the hell out of my rockets and it took me a while to get back. But I'm coming in now."

He emerged slowly from the crater he had crouched in, coming in sight of the guard in the distance. He took it slow and easy.

Outlined against the outpost barrier, Ragelli lifted a ponderous silver-gray arm in greeting. He was armored completely in a full duralloy battlesuit that made Kagen's plastoid armor look like tissue paper, and sat in the trigger-seat of a swiveling screech-gun battery. A bubble of defensive screens enveloped him, turning his massive figure into an indistinct blur.

Kagen waved back and began to eat up the distance between them with long, loping strides. He stopped just in front of the barrier, at the foot of Ragelli's emplacement.

"You look damned battered," said Ragelli, appraising him from behind a plastoid visor, aided by his sensory devices. "That light armor doesn't buy you a nickel's worth of protection. Any farm boy with a pea shooter can plug you."

Kagen laughed. "At least I can move. You may be able to stand off an assault squad in that duralloy monkey suit, but I'd like to see you do anything on offense, chum. And defense doesn't win wars."

"Your pot," Ragelli said. "This sentry duty is boring as hell." He flicked a switch on his control panel and a section of the barrier winked out. Kagen was through it at once. A split second later it came back on again.

Kagen strode quickly to his squad barracks. The door slid open automatically as he approached it and he stepped inside gratefully. It felt good to be home again and back at his normal weight. These light gravity mudholes made him queasy after a while. The barracks were artificially maintained at Wellington-normal gravity, twice Earth-normal. It was expensive but the brass kept saying that nothing was too good for the comfort of our fighting men.

Kagen stripped off his plastoid armor in the squad ready room and tossed it into the replacement bin. He headed straight for his cubicle and sprawled across the bed.

Reaching over to the plain metal table alongside his bed, he yanked open a drawer and took out a fat greenish capsule. He swallowed it hastily, and lay back to relax as it took hold throughout his system. The regulations prohibited taking synthastim between meals, he knew, but the rule was never enforced. Like most troopers, Kagen took it almost continuously to maintain his speed and endurance at maximum.

He was dozing comfortably a few minutes later when the com box mounted on the wall above his bed came to sudden life.

"Kagen."

Kagen sat up instantly, wide awake.

"Acknowledged," he said.

"Report to Major Grady at once."

Kagen grinned broadly. His request was being acted on quickly, he thought. And by a high officer, no less. Dressing quickly in loose-fitting brown fatigues, he set off across the base.

The high officers' quarters were at the center of the outpost. They consisted of a brightly lit, three-story building, blanketed overhead by defensive screens and ringed by guardsmen in light battle armor. One of the guards recognized Kagen and he was admitted on orders.

Immediately beyond the door he halted briefly as a bank of sensors scanned him for weapons. Troopers, of course, were not allowed to bear arms in the presence of high officers. Had he been carrying a screech gun alarms would have gone off all over the building while the tractor beams hidden in the walls and ceilings immobilized him completely.

But he passed the inspection and continued down the long corridor toward Major Grady's office. A third of the way down, the first set of tractor beams locked firmly onto his wrists. He struggled the instant he felt the invisible touch against his skin—but the tractors held him steady. Others, triggered automatically by his passing, came on as he continued down the corridor.

Kagen cursed under his breath and fought with his impulse to resist. He hated being pinned by tractor beams, but those were the rules if you wanted to see a high officer.

The door opened before him and he stepped through. A full bank of tractor beams seized him instantly and immobilized him. A few adjusted slightly and he was snapped to rigid attention, although his muscles screamed resistance.

Major Carl Grady was working at a cluttered wooden desk a few feet away, scribbling something on a sheet of paper. A large stack of papers rested at his elbow, an old-fashioned laser pistol sitting on top of them as a paperweight.

Kagen recognized the laser. It was some sort of heirloom, passed down in Grady's family for generations. The story was that some ancestor of his had used it back on Earth, in the Fire Wars of the early twenty-first century. Despite its age, the thing was still supposed to be in working order.

After several minutes of silence Grady finally set down his pen and looked up at Kagen. He was unusually young for a high officer but his unruly gray hair made him look older than he was. Like all high officers, he was Earth-born; frail and slow before the assault squad troopers from the dense, heavy gravity War Worlds of Wellington and Rommel.

"Report your presence," Grady said curtly. As always, his lean, pale face mirrored immense boredom.

"Field Officer John Kagen, assault squads, Terran Expeditionary Force."

Grady nodded, not really listening. He opened one of his desk drawers and extracted a sheet of paper.

"Kagen," he said, fiddling with the paper, "I think you know why you're here." He tapped the paper with his finger. "What's the meaning of this?"

"Just what it says, Major," Kagen replied. He tried to shift his weight but the tractor beams held him rigid.

Grady noticed and gestured impatiently. "At rest," he said. Most of the tractor beams snapped off, leaving Kagen free to move, if only at half his normal speed. He flexed in relief and grinned.

"My term of enlistment is up within two weeks, Major. I don't plan to reenlist. So I've requested transportation to Earth. That's all there is to it."

Grady's eyebrows arched a fraction of an inch but the dark eyes beneath them remained bored.

"Really?" he asked. "You've been a soldier for almost twenty years now, Kagen. Why retire? I'm afraid I don't understand."

Kagen shrugged. "I don't know. I'm getting old. Maybe I'm just getting tired of camp life. It's all starting to get boring, taking one damn mudhole after another. I want something different. Some excitement."

Grady nodded. "I see. But I don't think I agree with you, Kagen." His voice was soft and persuasive. "I think you're underselling the T.E.F. There is excitement ahead, if you'll only give us a chance." He leaned back in his chair, toying with a pencil he had picked up. "I'll tell you something, Kagen. You know, we've been at war with the Hrangan Empire for nearly three decades now. Direct clashes between us and the enemy have been few and far between up to now. Do you know why?"

"Sure," Kagen said.

Grady ignored him. "I'll tell you why," he continued. "So far each of us has been struggling to consolidate his position by grabbing these little worlds in the border regions. These mudholes, as you call them. But they're very important mudholes. We need them for bases, for their raw materials, for their industrial capacity, and for the conscript labor they provide. That's why we try to minimize damage in our campaigns. And that's why we use psychwar tactics like the howlers. To frighten away as many natives as possible before each attack. To preserve labor."

"I know all that," Kagen interrupted with typical Wellington bluntness. "What of it? I didn't come here for a lecture."

Grady looked up from the pencil. "No," he said. "No, you didn't. So I'll tell you, Kagen. The prelims are over. It's time for the main event. There are only a handful of unclaimed worlds left. Soon now, we'll be coming into direct conflict with the Hrangan Conquest Corps. Within a year we'll be attacking their bases."

The major stared at Kagen expectantly, waiting for a reply. When none came, a puzzled look flickered across his face. He leaned forward again.

"Don't you understand, Kagen?" he asked. "What more excitement could you want? No more fighting these piddling civilians in uniform, with their dirty little atomics and their primitive projectile guns. The Hrangans are a real enemy. Like us, they've had a professional army for generations upon generations. They're soldiers, born and bred. Good ones, too. They've got screens and modem weapons. They'll be foes to give our assault squads a real test."

"Maybe," Kagen said doubtfully. "But that kind of excitement isn't what I had in mind. I'm getting old. I've noticed that I'm definitely slower lately—even synthastim isn't keeping up my speed."

Grady shook his head. "You've got one of the best records in the whole T.E.F., Kagen. You've received the Stellar Cross twice and the World Congress Decoration three times. Every com station on Earth carried the story when you saved the landing party on Torego. Why should you doubt your effectiveness now? We're going to need men like you against the Hrangans. Reenlist."

"No," said Kagen emphatically. "The regs say you're entitled to your pension after twenty years and those medals have earned me a nice bunch of retirement bonuses. Now I want to enjoy them." He grinned broadly. "As you say, everyone on Earth must know me. I'm a hero. With that reputation, I figure I can have a real screechout."

Grady frowned and drummed on the desk impatiently. "I know what the regulations say, Kagen. But no one ever really retires—you must know that. Most troopers prefer to stay with the front. That's their job. That's what the War Worlds are all about."

"I don't really care, Major," Kagen replied. "I know the regs and I know I have a right to retire on full pension. You can't stop me."

Grady considered the statement calmly, his eyes dark with thought.

"All right," he said after a long pause. "Let's be reasonable about this. You'll retire with full pension and bonuses. We'll set you down on Wellington in a place of your own. Or Rommel if you like. We'll make you a youth barracks director—any age group you like. Or a training camp director. With your record you can start right at the top."

"Uh-uh," Kagen said firmly. "Not Wellington. Not Rommel. Earth."

"But why? You were born and raised on Wellington—in one of the hill barracks, I believe. You've never seen Earth."

"True," said Kagen. "But I've seen it in camp telecasts and flicks. I like what I've seen. I've been reading about Earth a lot lately, too. So now I want to see what it's like." He paused, then grinned again. "Let's just say I want to see what I've been fighting for."

Grady's frown reflected his displeasure. "I'm from Earth, Kagen," he said. "I tell you, you won't like it. You won't fit in. The gravity is too low—and there are no artificial heavy gravity barracks to take shelter in. Synthastim is illegal, strictly prohibited. But War Worlders need it, so you'll have to pay exorbitant prices to get the stuff. Earthers aren't reaction trained, either. They're a different kind of people. Go back to Wellington. You'll be among your own kind."

"Maybe that's one of the reasons I want Earth," Kagen said stubbornly. "On Wellington I'm just one of hundreds of old vets. Hell, every one of the troopers who *does* retire heads back to his old barracks. But on Earth I'll be a celebrity. Why, I'll be the fastest, strongest guy on the whole damn planet. That's got to have some advantages."

Grady was starting to look agitated. "What about the gravity?" he demanded. "The synthastim?"

"I'll get used to light gravity after a while, that's no problem. And I won't be needing that much speed and endurance, so I figure I can kick the synthastim habit."

Grady ran his fingers through his unkempt hair and shook his head doubtfully. There was a long, awkward silence. He leaned across the desk.

And, suddenly, his hand darted toward the laser pistol.

Kagen reacted. He dove forward, delayed only slightly by the few tractor beams that still held him. His hand flashed toward Grady's wrist in a crippling arc.

And suddenly wrenched to a halt as the tractor beams seized Kagen roughly, held him rigid, and then smashed him to the floor.

Grady, his hand frozen halfway to the pistol, leaned back in the chair. His face was white and shaken. He raised his hand and the tractor beams let up a bit. Kagen climbed slowly to his feet.

"You see, Kagen," said Grady. "That little test proves you're as fit as ever. You'd have gotten me if I hadn't kept a few tractors on you to slow you down. I tell you, we need men with your training and experience. We need you against the Hrangans. Reenlist."

Kagen's cold blue eyes still seethed with anger. "Damn the Hrangans," he said. "I'm not reenlisting and no goddamn little tricks of yours are going to make me change my mind. I'm going to Earth. You can't stop me."

Grady buried his face in his hands and sighed.

"All right, Kagen," he said at last. "You win. I'll put through your request."

He looked up one more time, and his dark eyes looked strangely troubled.

"You've been a great soldier, Kagen. We'll miss you. I tell you that you'll regret this decision. Are you sure you won't reconsider?"

"Absolutely sure," Kagen snapped.

The strange look suddenly vanished from Grady's eyes. His face once more took on the mask of bored indifference.

"Very well," he said curtly. "You are dismissed."

The tractors stayed on Kagen as he turned. They guided him—very firmly—from the building.

————

"You ready, Kagen?" Ragelli asked, leaning casually against the door of the cubicle.

Kagen picked up his small travel bag and threw one last glance around to make sure he hadn't forgotten anything. He hadn't. The room was quite bare.

"Guess so," he said, stepping through the door.

Ragelli slipped on the plastoid helmet that had been cradled under his arm and hurried to catch up as Kagen strode down the corridor.

"I guess this is it," he said as he matched strides.

"Yeah," Kagen replied. "A week from now I'll be taking it easy back on Earth while you're getting blisters on your tail sitting around in that damned duralloy tuxedo of yours."

Ragelli laughed. "Maybe," he said. "But I still say you're nuts to go to Earth of all places, when you could command a whole damned training camp on Wellington. Assuming you wanted to quit at all, which is also crazy—"

The barracks door slid open before them and they stepped through, Ragelli still talking. A second guard flanked Kagen on the other side. Like Ragelli, he was wearing light battle armor.

Kagen himself was in full dress whites, trimmed with gold braid. A ceremonial laser, deactivated, was slung in a black leather holster at his side. Matching leather boots and a polished steel helmet set off the uniform. Azure blue bars on his shoulder signified field officer rank. His medals jangled against his chest as he walked.

Kagen's entire third assault squad was drawn up at attention on the spacefield behind the barracks in honor of his retirement. Alongside the ramp to the shuttlecraft, a group of high officers stood by, cordoned off by defensive screens. Major Grady was in the front row, his bored expression blurred somewhat by the screens.

Flanked by the two guards, Kagen walked across the concrete slowly, grinning under his helmet. Piped music welled out over the field, and Kagen recognized the T.E.F. battle hymn and the Wellington anthem.

At the foot of the ramp he turned and looked back. The company spread out before him saluted in unison on a command from the high officers and held position until Kagen returned the salute. Then one of the squad's other field officers stepped forward, and presented him with his discharge papers.

Jamming them into his belt, Kagen threw a quick, casual wave to Ragelli, then hurried up the ramp. It lifted slowly behind him.

Inside the ship, a crewman greeted him with a curt nod. "Got special quarters prepared for you," he said. "Follow me. Trip should only take about fifteen minutes. Then we'll transfer you to a starship for the Earth trip."

Kagen nodded and followed the man to his quarters. They turned out to be a plain, empty room, reinforced with duralloy plates. A viewscreen covered one wall. An acceleration couch faced it.

Alone, Kagen sprawled out on the acceleration couch, clipping his helmet to a holder on the side. Tractor beams pressed down gently, holding him firmly in place for the liftoff.

A few minutes later a dull roar came from deep within the ship and Kagen felt several gravities press down upon him as the shuttlecraft took off. The viewscreen, suddenly coming to life, showed the planet dwindling below.

The viewer blinked off when they reached orbit. Kagen started to sit up but found he still could not move. The tractor beams held him pinned to the couch.

He frowned. There was no need for him to stay in the couch once the craft was in orbit. Some idiot had forgotten to release him.

"Hey," he shouted, figuring there would be a com box somewhere in the room. "These tractors are still on. Loosen the damned things so I can move a little."

No one answered.

He strained against the beams. Their pressure seemed to increase. The blasted things were starting to pinch a little, he thought. Now those morons were turning the knob the wrong way.

He cursed under his breath. "No," he shouted. "Now the tractors are getting heavier. You're adjusting them the wrong way."

But the pressure continued to climb and he felt more beams locking on him, until they covered his body like an invisible blanket. The damned things were really starting to hurt now.

"You idiots," he yelled. "You morons. Cut it out, you bastards." With a surge of anger he strained against the beams, cursing. But even Wellington-bred muscle was no match for tractors. He was held tightly to the couch.

One of the beams was trained on his chest pocket. Its pressure was driving his Stellar Cross painfully into his skin. The sharp edge of the polished medal had already sliced through the uniform and he could see a red stain spreading slowly through the white.

The pressure continued to mount and Kagen writhed in pain, squirming against his invisible shackles. It did no good. The pressure still went higher and more and more beams came on.

"Cut it out!" he screeched. "You bastards, I'll rip you apart when I get out of here. You're killing me, dammit!"

He heard the sharp snap of a bone suddenly breaking under the strain. Kagen felt a stab of intense pain in his right wrist. An instant later there was another snap.

"Cut it out!" he cried, his voice shrill with pain. "You're killing me. Damn you, you're killing me!"

And suddenly he realized he was right.

———

Grady looked up with a scowl at the aide who entered the office.

"Yes? What is it?"

The aide, a young Earther in training for high officer rank, saluted briskly. "We just got the report from the shuttlecraft, sir. It's all over. They want to know what to do with the body."

"Space it," Grady replied. "Good as anything." A thin smile flickered across his face and he shook his head. "Too bad. Kagen was a good man in combat but his psych training must have slipped somewhere. We should send a strong note back to his barracks conditioner. Though it's funny it didn't show up until now."

He shook his head again. "Earth," he said. "For a moment he even had me wondering if it was possible. But when I tested him with my laser, I knew. No way, no way." He shuddered a little. "As if we'd ever let a War Worlder loose on Earth." Then he turned back to his paperwork.

As the aide turned to leave Grady looked up again.

"One other thing," he said. "Don't forget to send that PR release back to Earth. Make it War-Hero-Dies-When-Hrangans-Blast-Ship. Jazz it up good. Some of the big com networks should pick it up and it'll make good publicity. And forward his medals to Wellington. They'll want them for his barracks museum."

The aide nodded and Grady returned to his work. He still looked quite bored.

THE EXIT TO SAN BRETA

❖

IT WAS THE HIGHWAY THAT FIRST CAUGHT MY ATTENTION. UP TO
that night, it had been a perfectly normal trip. It was my vacation, and
I was driving to L.A. through the Southwest, taking my own sweet
time about it. That was nothing new; I'd done it several times before.

Driving is my hobby. Or cars in general, to be precise. Not many
people take the time to drive anymore. It's just too slow for most. The
automobile's been pretty much obsolete since they started mass-
producing cheap copters back in '93. And whatever life it had left in it
was knocked out by the invention of the personal gravpak.

But it was different when I was a kid. Back then, everybody had a
car, and you were considered some sort of a social freak if you didn't
get your driver's license as soon as you were old enough. I got interested in cars when I was in my late teens, and have stayed interested
ever since.

Anyway, when my vacation rolled around, I figured it was a
chance to try out my latest find. It was a great car, an English sports
model from the late '70s. Jaguar XKL. Not one of the classics, true, but
a nice car all the same. It handled beautifully.

I was doing most of my traveling at night, as usual. There's something special about night driving. The old, deserted highways have an
atmosphere about them in the starlight, and you can almost see them as

they once were—vital and crowded and full of life, with cars jammed bumper to bumper as far as the eye could see.

Today, there's none of that. Only the roads themselves are left, and most of them are cracked and overgrown with weeds. The states can't bother taking care of them anymore—too many people objected to the waste of tax money. But ripping them up would be too expensive. So they just sit, year after year, slowly falling apart. Most of them are still drivable, though; they built their roads well back in the old days.

There's still some traffic. Car nuts like me, of course. And the hovertrucks. They can ride over just about anything, but they can go faster over flat surfaces. So they stick to the old highways pretty much.

It's kind of awesome whenever a hovertruck passes you at night. They do about two hundred or so, and no sooner do you spot one in your rearview mirror then it's on top of you. You don't see much—just a long silver blur, and a shriek as it goes by. And then you're alone again.

Anyway, I was in the middle of Arizona, just outside San Breta, when I first noticed the highway. I didn't think much of it then. Oh, it was unusual all right, but not that unusual.

The highway itself was quite ordinary. It was an eight-lane freeway, with a good, fast surface, and it ran straight from horizon to horizon. At night, it was like a gleaming black ribbon running across the white sands of the desert.

No, it wasn't the highway that was unusual. It was its condition. At first, I didn't really notice. I was enjoying myself too much. It was a clear, cold night, and the stars were out, and the Jag was riding beautifully.

Riding *too* beautifully. That's when it first dawned on me. There were no bumps, no cracks, no potholes. The road was in prime condition, almost as if it had just been built. Oh, I'd been on good roads before. Some of them just stood up better than others. There's a section outside Baltimore that's superb, and parts of the L.A. freeway system are quite good.

But I'd never been on one this good. It was hard to believe a road could be in such good shape, after all those years without repair.

And then there were the lights. They were all on, all bright and clear. None of them were busted. None of them were out, or blinking. Hell, none of them were even dim. The road was beautifully lighted.

After that, I began to notice other things. Like the traffic signs. Most places, the traffic signs are long gone, removed by souvenir hunters or antique collectors as a reminder of an older, slower America. No one replaces them—they aren't needed. Once in a while you'll come across one that's been missed, but there's never anything left but an oddly shaped, rusted hunk of metal.

But this highway had traffic signs. Real traffic signs. I mean, ones you could read. Speed limit signs, when no one's observed a speed limit in years. Yield signs, when there's seldom any other traffic to yield to. Turn signs, exit signs, caution signs—all kinds of signs. And all as good as new.

But the biggest shock was the lines. Paint fades fast, and I doubt that there's a highway in America where you could still make out the white lines in a speeding car. But you could on this one. The lines were sharp and clear, the paint fresh, the eight lanes clearly marked.

Oh, it was a beautiful highway all right. The kind they had back in the old days. But it didn't make sense. No road could stay in this condition all these years. Which meant someone had to be maintaining it. But who? Who would bother to maintain a highway that only a handful of people used each year? The cost would be enormous, with no return at all.

I was still trying to puzzle it out when I saw the other car.

I had just flashed by a big red sign marking Exit 76, the exit to San Breta, when I saw it. Just a white speck on the horizon, but I knew it had to be another motorist. It couldn't be a hovertruck, since I was plainly gaining on it. And that meant another car, and a fellow aficionado.

It was a rare occasion. It's damn seldom you meet another car on the open road. Oh, there are regular conventions, like the Fresno Festival on Wheels and the American Motoring Association's Annual Trafficjam. But they're too artificial for my tastes. Coming across another motorist on the highway is something else indeed.

I hit the gas, and speeded up to around one-twenty. The Jag could do better, but I'm not a nut on speed like some of my fellow drivers. And I was picking up ground fast. From the way I was gaining, the other car couldn't have been doing better than seventy.

When I got within range, I let go with a blast on my horn, trying to attract his attention. But he didn't seem to hear me. Or at least he didn't show any sign. I honked again.

And then, suddenly, I recognized the make.

It was an Edsel.

I could hardly believe it. The Edsel is one of the real classics, right up there with the Stanley Steamer and the Model T.

The few that are left sell for a rather large fortune nowadays.

And this was one of the rarest, one of those original models with the funny noses. There were only three or four like it left in the world, and those were not for sale at any price. An automotive legend, and here it was on the highway in front of me, as classically ugly as the day it came off the Ford assembly line.

I pulled alongside, and slowed down to keep even with it. I couldn't say that I thought much of the way the thing had been kept up. The white paint was chipped, the car was dirty, and there were signs of body rust on the lower part of the doors. But it was still an Edsel, and it could easily be restored. I honked again to get the attention of the driver, but he ignored me. There were five people in the car from what I could see, evidently a family on an outing. In the back, a heavy-set woman was trying to control two small kids who seemed to be fighting. Her husband appeared to be soundly asleep in the front seat, while a younger man, probably his son, was behind the wheel.

That burned me. The driver was very young, probably only in his late teens, and it irked me that a kid that age should have the chance to drive such a treasure. I wanted to be in his place.

I had read a lot about the Edsel; books of auto lore were full of it. There was never anything quite like it. It was the greatest disaster the field had ever known. The myths and legends that had grown up around its name were beyond number.

All over the nation, in the scattered dingy garages and gas depots where car nuts gather to tinker and talk, the tales of the Edsel are told to this day. They say they built the car too big to fit in most garages. They say it was all horsepower, and no brake. They call it the ugliest machine ever designed by man. They retell the old jokes about its name. And there's one famous legend that when you got it going fast enough, the wind made a funny whistling noise as it rushed around that hood.

All the romance and mystery and tragedy of the old automobile was wrapped up in the Edsel. And the stories about it are remembered and retold long after its glittering contemporaries are so much scrap metal in the junkyards.

As I drove along beside it, all the old legends about the Edsel came flooding back to me, and I was lost in my own nostalgia. I tried a few more blasts on my horn, but the driver seemed intent on ignoring me, so I soon gave up. Besides, I was listening to see if the hood really did whistle in the wind.

I should have realized by then how peculiar the whole thing was— the road, the Edsel, the way they were ignoring me. But I was too enraptured to do much thinking. I was barely able to keep my eyes on the road.

I wanted to talk to the owners, of course. Maybe even borrow it for a little while. Since they were being so damned unfriendly about stopping, I decided to follow them for a bit, until they pulled in for gas or food. So I slowed and began to tail them. I wanted to stay fairly close without tailgating, so I kept to the lane on their immediate left.

As I trailed them, I remember thinking what a thorough collector the owner must be. Why, he had even taken the time to hunt up some rare, old-style license plates. The kind that haven't been used in years. I was still mulling over that when we passed the sign announcing Exit 77.

The kid driving the Edsel suddenly looked agitated. He turned in his seat and looked back over his shoulder, almost as if he was trying to get another look at the sign we had already left behind. And then, with no warning, the Edsel swerved right into my lane.

I hit the brakes, but it was hopeless, of course. Everything seemed to happen at once. There was a horrible squealing noise, and I remember getting a brief glimpse of the kid's terrified face just before the two cars made impact. Then came the shock of the crash.

The Jag hit the Edsel broadside, smashing into the driver's compartment at seventy. Then it spun away into the guard rail, and came to a stop. The Edsel, hit straight on, flipped over on its back in the center of the road. I don't recall unfastening my seat belt or scrambling out of my car, but I must have done so, because the next thing I remember I was crawling on the roadway, dazed but unhurt.

I should have tried to do something right away, to answer the cries for help that were coming from the Edsel. But I didn't. I was still shaken, in shock. I don't know how long I lay there before the Edsel exploded and began to burn. The cries suddenly became screams. And then there were no cries.

By the time I climbed to my feet, the fire had burned itself out, and it was too late to do anything. But I still wasn't thinking very clearly. I could see lights in the distance, down the road that led from the exit ramp. I began to walk towards them.

That walk seemed to take forever. I couldn't seem to get my bearings, and I kept stumbling. The road was very poorly lighted, and I could hardly see where I was going. My hands were scraped badly once when I fell down. It was the only injury I suffered in the entire accident.

The lights were from a small café, a dingy place that had marked off a section of the abandoned highway as its airlot. There were only three customers inside when I stumbled through the door, but one of them was a local cop.

"There's been an accident," I said from the doorway. "Somebody's got to help them."

The cop drained his coffee cup in a gulp, and rose from his chair. "A copter crash, mister?" he said. "Where is it?"

I shook my head. "N-no. No. Cars. A crash, a highway accident. Out on the old interstate." I pointed vaguely in the direction I had come.

Halfway across the room, the cop stopped suddenly and frowned. Everybody else laughed. "Hell, no one's used that road in twenty years, you sot," a fat man yelled from the corner of the room. "It's got so many potholes we use it for a golf course," he added, laughing loudly at his own joke.

The cop looked at me doubtfully. "Go home and sober up, mister," he said. "I don't want to have to run you in." He started back towards his chair.

I took a step into the room. "Dammit, I'm telling the truth," I said, angry now more than dazed. "And I'm not drunk. There's been a collision on the interstate, and there's people trapped up there in. . . ." My voice trailed off as it finally struck me that any help I could bring would be far too late.

The cop still looked dubious. "Maybe you ought to go check it out," the waitress suggested from behind the counter. "He might be telling the truth. There was a highway accident last year, in Ohio somewhere. I remember seeing a story about it on 3V."

"Yeah, I guess so," the cop said at last. "Let's go, buddy. And you better be telling the truth."

We walked across the airlot in silence, and climbed into the four-man police copter. As he started up the blades, the cop looked at me and said, "You know, if you're on the level, you and that other guy should get some kind of medal."

I stared at him blankly.

"What I mean is, you're probably the only two cars to use that road in ten years. And you still manage to collide. Now, that had to take some doing, didn't it?" He shook his head ruefully. "Not every-body could pull off a stunt like that. Like I said, they ought to give you a medal."

The interstate wasn't nearly as far from the café as it had seemed when I was walking. Once airborne, we covered the distance in less than five minutes. But there was something wrong. The highway looked somehow different from the air.

And suddenly I realized why. It was darker. Much darker.

Most of the lights were out, and those that weren't were dim and flickering.

As I sat there stunned, the copter came down with a thud in the middle of a pool of sickly yellow light thrown out by one of the fading lamps. I climbed out in a daze, and tripped as I accidentally stepped into one of the potholes that pockmarked the road. There was a big clump of weeds growing in the bottom of this one, and a lot more rooted in the jagged network of cracks that ran across the highway.

My head was starting to pound. This didn't make sense. None of it made sense. I didn't know what the hell was going on.

The cop came around from the other side of the copter, a portable med sensor slung over one shoulder on a leather strap. "Let's move it," he said. "Where's this accident of yours?"

"Down the road, I think," I mumbled, unsure of myself. There was no sign of my car, and I was beginning to think we might be on the wrong road altogether, although I didn't see how that could be.

It was the right road, though. We found my car a few minutes later, sitting by the guard rail on a pitch black section of highway where all the lights had burnt out. Yes, we found my car all right.

Only there wasn't a scratch on it. And there was no Edsel.

I remembered the Jaguar as I had left it. The windshield shattered. The entire front of the car in ruins. The right fender smashed up where it had scraped along the guard rail. And here it was, in mint condition.

The cop, scowling, played the med sensor over me as I stood there staring at my car. "Well, you're not drunk," he said at last, looking up. "So I'm not going to run you in, even though I should. Here's what you're going to do, mister—you're going to get in that relic, and turn around, and get out of here as fast as you can. 'Cause if I *ever* see you around here again, you might have a real accident. Understand?"

I wanted to protest, but I couldn't find the words. What could I say that would possibly make sense? Instead, I nodded weakly. The cop turned with disgust, muttering something about practical jokes, and stalked back to his copter.

When he was gone, I walked up to the Jaguar and felt the front of it incredulously, feeling like a fool. But it was real. And when I climbed in and turned the key in the ignition, the engine rumbled reassuringly, and the headlights speared out into the darkness. I sat there for a long time before I finally swung the car out into the middle of the road, and made a U-turn.

The drive back to San Breta was long and rough. I was constantly bouncing in and out of potholes. And thanks to the poor lighting and the treacherous road conditions, I had to keep my speed at a minimum.

The road was lousy. There was no doubt about that. Usually I went out of my way to avoid roads that were this bad. There was too much chance of blowing a tire.

I managed to make it to San Breta without incident, taking it slow and easy. It was two A.M. before I pulled into town. The exit ramp, like the rest of the road, was cracked and darkened. And there was no sign to mark it.

I recalled from previous trips through the area that San Breta boasted a large hobbyist garage and gas depot, so I headed there and checked my car with a bored young night attendant. Then I went straight to the nearest motel. A night's sleep, I thought, would make everything make sense.

But it didn't. I was every bit as confused when I woke up in the morning. More so, even. Now something in the back of my head kept telling me the whole thing had been a bad dream. I swatted down that tempting thought out of hand, and tried to puzzle it out.

I kept puzzling through a shower and breakfast, and the short walk back to the gas depot. But I wasn't making any progress. Either my mind had been playing tricks on me, or something mighty funny had been going on last night. I didn't want to believe the former, so I made up my mind to investigate the latter.

The owner, a spry old man in his eighties, was on duty at the gas depot when I returned. He was wearing an old-fashioned mechanic's coverall, a quaint touch. He nodded amiably when I checked out the Jaguar.

"Good to see you again," he said. "Where you headed this time?"

"L.A. I'm taking the interstate this time."

His eyebrows rose a trifle at that. "The interstate? I thought you had more sense than that. That road's a disaster. No way to treat a fine piece of machinery like that Jaguar of yours."

I didn't have the courage to try to explain, so I just grinned weakly and let him go get the car. The Jag had been washed, checked over, and gassed up. It was in prime shape.

I took a quick look for dents, but there were none to be found.

"How many regular customers you get around here?" I asked the old man as I was paying him. "Local collectors, I mean, not guys passing through."

He shrugged. "Must be about a hundred in the state. We get most of their business. Got the best gas and the only decent service facilities in these parts."

"Any decent collections?"

"Some," he said. "One guy comes in all the time with a Pierce-Arrow. Another fellow specializes in the forties. He's got a really fine collection. In good shape, too."

I nodded. "Anybody around here own an Edsel?" I asked.

"Hardly," he replied. "None of my customers have that kind of money. Why do you ask?"

I decided to throw caution on the road, so to speak. "I saw one last night on the road. Didn't get to speak to the owner, though. Figured it might be somebody local."

The old man's expression was blank, so I turned to get into the Jag. "Nobody from around here," he said as I shut the door. "Must've been another guy driving through. Funny meeting him on the road like that, though. Don't often get—"

Then, just as I was turning the key in the ignition, his jaw dropped about six feet. "Wait a minute!" he yelled. "You said you were driving on the old interstate. You saw an Edsel on the interstate?"

I turned the motor off again. "That's right," I said.

"Christ," he said. "I'd almost forgotten, it's been so long. Was it a white Edsel? Five people in it?"

I opened the door and got out again. "Yeah," I said. "Do you know something about it?"

The old man grabbed my shoulders with both hands. There was a funny look in his eyes. "You just saw it?" he said, shaking me. "Are you sure that's all that happened?"

I hesitated a moment, feeling foolish. "No," I finally admitted. "I had a collision with it. That is, I thought I had a collision with it. But then—" I gestured limply towards the Jaguar.

The old man took his hands off me, and laughed. "Again," he muttered. "After all these years."

"What do you know about this?" I demanded. "What the hell went on out there last night?"

He sighed. "C'mon," he said. "I'll tell you all about it."

———

"It was over forty years ago," he told me over a cup of coffee in a café across the street. "Back in the '70s. They were a family on a vacation outing. The kid and his father were taking shifts behind the wheel. Anyway, they had hotel reservations at San Breta. But the kid was driving, and it was late at night, and somehow he missed his exit. Didn't even notice it.

"Until he hit Exit 77, that is. He must've been really scared when he saw that sign. According to people who knew them, his father was a real bastard. The kind who'd give him a real hard time over something like that. We don't know what happened, but they figure the kid panicked. He'd only had his license about two weeks. Of all things, he tried to make a U-turn and head back towards San Breta.

"The other car hit him broadside. The driver of that car didn't have his seat belt on. He went through the windshield, hit the road, and was killed instantly. The people in the Edsel weren't so lucky. The Edsel turned over and exploded, with them trapped inside. All five were burned to death."

I shuddered a little as I remembered the screams from the burning car. "But that was forty years ago, you said. How does that explain what happened to me last night?"

"I'm getting to that," the old man said. He picked up a donut, dunked it into his coffee, and chewed on it thoughtfully. "Next thing was about two years later," he said at last. "Guy reported a collision to the cops. Collision with an Edsel. Late at night. On the interstate. The way he described it, it was an instant replay of the other crash. Only, when they got there, his car wasn't even dented. And there was no sign of the other car.

"Well, that guy was a local boy, so it was dismissed as a publicity stunt of some sort. But then, a year later, still another guy came in with the same story. This time he was from the East, couldn't possibly have heard of the first accident. The cops didn't know what to make of it.

"Over the years it happened again and again. There were a few things common to all the incidents. Each time it was late at night. Each time the man involved was alone in his car, with no other cars in sight. There were never any witnesses, as there had been for the first crash, the real one. All the collisions took place just beyond Exit 77, when the Edsel swerved and tried to make a U-turn.

"Lots of people tried to explain it. Hallucinations, somebody said. Highway hypnosis, claimed somebody else. Hoaxes, one guy argued. But only one explanation ever made sense, and that was the simplest. The Edsel was a ghost. The papers made the most of that. 'The haunted highway,' they called the interstate."

The old man stopped to drain his coffee, and then stared into the cup moodily. "Well, the crashes continued right up through the years whenever the conditions were right. Until '93. And then traffic began slacking off. Fewer and fewer people were using the interstate. And there were fewer and fewer incidents." He looked up at me. "You were the first one in more than twenty years. I'd almost forgotten." Then he looked down again, and fell silent.

I considered what he had said for a few minutes. "I don't know," I said finally, shaking my head. "It all fits. But a ghost? I don't think I believe in ghosts. And it all seems so out of place."

"Not really," said the old man, looking up. "Think back on all the ghost stories you read as a kid. What did they all have in common?"

I frowned. "Don't know."

"Violent death, that's what. Ghosts were the products of murders and of executions, debris of blood and violence. Haunted houses were all places where someone had met a grisly end a hundred years before. But in twentieth century America, you didn't find the violent death in mansions and castles. You found it on the highways, the bloodstained highways where thousands died each year. A modern ghost wouldn't live in a castle or wield an axe. He'd haunt a highway, and drive a car. What could be more logical?"

It made a certain amount of sense. I nodded. "But why this highway? Why this car? So many people died on the roads. Why is this case special?"

The old man shrugged. "I don't know. What made one murder different from another? Why did only some produce ghosts? Who's to say? But I've heard theories. Some said the Edsel is doomed to haunt the highway forever because it is, in a sense, a murderer. It caused the accident, caused those deaths. This is a punishment."

"Maybe," I said doubtfully. "But the whole family? You could make a case that it was the kid's fault. Or even the father's, for letting him drive with so little experience. But what about the rest of the family? Why should they be punished?"

"True, true," the old man said. "I never bought that theory myself. I've got my own explanation." He looked me straight in the eye.

"I think they're lost," he said.

"Lost?" I repeated, and he nodded.

"Yes," he said. "In the old days, when the roads were crowded, you couldn't just turn around when you missed an exit. You had to keep going, sometimes for miles and miles, before you could find a way to get off the road and then get back on. Some of the cloverleaves they designed were so complicated you might never find your way back to your exit.

"And that's what happened to the Edsel, I think. They missed their exit, and now they can't find it. They've got to keep going. Forever." He sighed. Then he turned, and ordered another cup of coffee.

We drank in silence, then walked back to the gas depot. From there, I drove straight to the town library. It was all there, in the old newspapers on file. The details of the original accident, the first incident two years later, and the others, in irregular sequence. The same story, the same crash, over and over. Everything was identical, right down to the screams.

The old highway was dark and unlit that night when I resumed my trip. There were no traffic signs or white lines, but there were plenty of cracks and potholes. I drove slowly, lost in thought.

A few miles beyond San Breta I stopped and got out of the car. I sat there in the starlight until it was nearly dawn, looking and listening. But the lights stayed out, and I saw nothing.

Yet, around midnight, there was a peculiar whistling sound in the distance. It built quickly, until it was right on top of me, and then faded away equally fast.

It could have been a hovertruck off over the horizon somewhere, I suppose. I've never heard a hovertruck make that sort of noise, but still, it might have been a hovertruck.

But I don't think so.

I think it was the wind whistling through the nose of a rusty white ghost car, driving on a haunted highway you won't find on any road maps. I think it was the cry of a little lost Edsel, searching forever for the exit to San Breta.

THE SECOND KIND OF
LONELINESS

◈

JUNE 18 — My relief left Earth today.

It will be at least three months before he gets here, of course. But he's on his way.

Today he lifted off from the Cape, just as I did, four long years ago. Out at Komarov Station he'll switch to a moon boat, then switch again in orbit around Luna, at Deepspace Station. There his voyage will really begin. Up to then he's still been in his own backyard.

Not until the *Charon* casts loose from Deepspace Station and sets out into the night will he feel it, *really* feel it, as I felt it four years ago. Not until Earth and Luna vanish behind him will it hit. He's known from the first that there's no turning back, of course. But there's a difference between knowing it and feeling it. Now he'll feel it.

There will be an orbital stopover around Mars, to send supplies down to Burroughs City. And more stops in the belt. But then the *Charon* will begin to gather speed. It will be going very fast when it reaches Jupiter. And much faster after it whips by, using the gravity of the giant planet like a slingshot to boost its acceleration.

After that there are no stops for the *Charon*. No stops at all until it reaches me, out here at the Cerberus Star Ring, six million miles beyond Pluto.

My relief will have a long time to brood. As I did.

I'm still brooding now, today, four years later. But then, there's not much else to do out here. Ringships are infrequent, and you get pretty weary of films and tapes and books after a time. So you brood. You think about your past, and dream about your future. And you try to keep the loneliness and the boredom from driving you out of your skull.

It's been a long four years. But it's almost over now. And it will be nice to get back. I want to walk on grass again, and see clouds, and eat an ice cream sundae.

Still, for all that, I don't regret coming. These four years alone in the darkness have done me good, I think. It's not as if I had left much. My days on Earth seem remote to me now, but I can still remember them if I try. The memories aren't all that pleasant. I was pretty screwed up back then.

I needed time to think, and that's one thing you get out here. The man who goes back on the *Charon* won't be the same one who came out here four years ago. I'll build a whole new life back on Earth. I know I will.

JUNE 20 — Ship today.

I didn't know it was coming, of course. I never do. The ringships are irregular, and the kind of energies I'm playing with out here turn radio signals into crackling chaos. By the time the ship finally punched through the static, the station's scanners had already picked it up and notified me.

It was clearly a ringship. Much bigger than the old system rust-buckets like the *Charon,* and heavily armored to withstand the stresses of the nullspace vortex. It came straight on, with no attempt to decelerate.

While I was heading down to the control room to strap in, a thought hit me. This might be the last. Probably not, of course. There's still three months to go, and that's time enough for a dozen ships. But you can never tell. The ringships are irregular, like I said.

Somehow the thought disturbed me. The ships have been part of my life for four years now. An important part. And the one today might have been the last. If so, I want it all down here. I want to re-member it. With good reason, I think. When the ships come, that makes everything else worthwhile.

The control room is in the heart of my quarters. It's the center of everything, where the nerves and the tendons and the muscles of the station are gathered. But it's not very impressive. The room is very small, and once the door slides shut the walls and floor and ceiling are all a featureless white.

There's only one thing in the room: a horseshoe-shaped console that surrounds a single padded chair.

I sat down in that chair today for what might be the last time. I strapped myself in, and put on the earphones, and lowered the helmet. I reached for the controls and touched them and turned them on.

And the room vanished.

It's all done with holographs, of course. I *know* that. But that doesn't make a bit of difference when I'm sitting in that chair. Then, as far as I'm concerned, I'm not inside anymore. I'm out *there,* in the void. The control console is still there, and the chair. But the rest has gone. Instead, the aching darkness is everywhere, above me, below me, all around me. The distant sun is only one star among many, and all the stars are terribly far away.

That's the way it always is. That's the way it was today. When I threw that switch I was alone in the universe with the cold stars and the ring. The Cerberus Star Ring.

I saw the ring as if from outside, looking down on it. It's a vast structure, really. But from out here, it's nothing. It's swallowed by the immensity of it all, a slim silver thread lost in the blackness.

But I know better. The ring is huge. My living quarters take up but a single degree in the circle it forms, a circle whose diameter is more than a hundred miles. The rest is circuitry and scanners and power banks. And the engines, the waiting nullspace engines.

The ring turned silent beneath me, its far side stretching away into nothingness. I touched a switch on my console. Below me, the null-space engines woke.

In the center of the ring, a new star was born.

It was a tiny dot amid the dark at first. Green today, bright green. But not always, and not for long. Nullspace has many colors.

I could see the far side of the ring then, if I'd wanted to. It was glowing with a light of its own. Alive and awake, the nullspace engines were pouring unimaginable amounts of energy inward, to rip wide a hole in space itself.

The hole had been there long before Cerberus, long before man. Men found it, quite by accident, when they reached Pluto. They built the ring around it. Later they found two other holes, and built other star rings.

The holes were small, too small. But they could be enlarged. Temporarily, at the expense of vast amounts of power, they could be ripped open. Raw energy could be pumped through that tiny, unseen hole in the universe until the placid surface of nullspace roiled and lashed back, and the nullspace vortex formed.

And now it happened.

The star in the center of the ring grew and flattened. It was a pulsing disc, not a globe. But it was still the brightest thing in the heavens. And it swelled visibly. From the spinning green disc, flame-like orange spears lanced out, and fell back, and smoky bluish tendrils uncoiled. Specks of red danced and flashed among the green, grew and blended. The colors all began to run together.

The flat, spinning, multi-colored star doubled in size, doubled again, again. A few minutes before it had not been. Now it filled the ring, lapped against the silver walls, seared them with its awful energy. It began to spin faster and faster, a whirlpool in space, a maelstrom of flame and light.

The vortex. The nullspace vortex. The howling storm that is not a storm and does not howl, for there is no sound in space.

To it came the ringship. A moving star at first, it took on visible form and shape almost faster than my human eyes could follow. It became a dark silver bullet in the blackness, a bullet fired at the vortex.

The aim was good. The ship hit very close to the center of the ring. The swirling colors closed over it.

I hit my controls. Even more suddenly than it had come, the vortex was gone. The ship was gone too, of course. Once more there was only me, and the ring, and the stars.

Then I touched another switch, and I was back in the blank white control room, unstrapping. Unstrapping for what might be the last time, ever.

Somehow I hope not. I never thought I'd miss anything about this place. But I will. I'll miss the ringships. I'll miss moments like today.

I hope I get a few more chances at it before I give it up forever. I want to feel the nullspace engines wake again under my hands, and watch the vortex boil and churn while I float alone between the stars. Once more, at least. Before I go.

JUNE 23 — That ringship has set me to thinking. Even more than usual.

It's funny that with all the ships I've seen pass through the vortex, I've never even given a thought to riding one. There's a whole new world on the other side of nullspace; Second Chance, a rich green planet of a star so far away that astronomers are still unsure whether it shares the same galaxy with us. That's the funny thing about the holes—you can't be sure where they lead until you go through.

When I was a kid, I read a lot about star travel. Most people didn't think it was possible. But those that did always mentioned Alpha Centauri as the first system we'd explore and colonize. Closest, and all that. Funny how wrong they were. Instead, our colonies orbit suns we can't even see. And I don't think we'll ever get to Alpha Centauri—

Somehow I never thought of the colonies in personal terms. Still can't. Earth is where I failed before. That's got to be where I succeed now. The colonies would be just another escape.

Like Cerberus?

JUNE 26 — Ship today. So the other wasn't the last, after all. But what about this one?

JUNE 29 — Why does a man volunteer for a job like this? Why does a man run to a silver ring six million miles beyond Pluto, to guard a hole in space? Why throw away four years of life alone in the darkness?

Why?

I used to ask myself that, in the early days. I couldn't answer it then. Now I think I can. I bitterly regretted the impulse that drove me out here, then. Now I think I understand it.

And it wasn't really an impulse. I ran to Cerberus. Ran. Ran to escape from loneliness.

That doesn't make sense?

Yet it does. I know about loneliness. It's been the theme of my life. I've been alone for as long as I can remember.

But there are two kinds of loneliness.

Most people don't realize the difference. I do. I've sampled both kinds.

They talk and write about the loneliness of the men who man the star rings. The lighthouses of space, and all that. And they're right.

There are times, out here at Cerberus, when I think I'm the only man in the universe. Earth was just a fever dream. The people I remember were just creations of my own mind.

There are times, out here, when I want someone to talk to so badly that I scream, and start pounding on the walls. There are times when the boredom crawls under my skin and all but drives me mad.

But there are *other* times, too. When the ringships come. When I go outside to make repairs. Or when I just sit in the control chair, imaging myself out into the darkness to watch the stars.

Lonely? Yes. But a solemn, brooding, tragic loneliness that a man hates with a passion—and yet loves so much he craves for more.

And then there is the second kind of loneliness.

You don't need the Cerberus Star Ring for that kind. You can find it anywhere on Earth. I know. I did. I found it everywhere I went, in everything I did.

It's the loneliness of people trapped within themselves. The loneliness of people who have said the wrong thing so often that they don't have the courage to say anything anymore.

The loneliness, not of distance, but of fear.

The loneliness of people who sit alone in furnished rooms in crowded cities, because they've got nowhere to go and no one to talk to. The loneliness of guys who go to bars to meet someone, only to discover they don't know how to strike up a conversation, and wouldn't have the courage to do so if they did.

There's no grandeur to that kind of loneliness. No purpose and no poetry. It's loneliness without meaning. It's sad and squalid and pathetic, and it stinks of self-pity.

Oh yes, it hurts at times to be alone among the stars.

But it hurts a lot more to be alone at a party. A lot more.

JUNE 30 — Reading yesterday's entry. Talk about self-pity—

JULY 1 — Reading *yesterday's* entry. My flippant mask. After four years, I still fight back whenever I try to be honest with myself. That's not good. If things are going to be any different this time, I have to understand myself.

So why do I have to ridicule myself when I admit that I'm lonely and vulnerable? Why do I have to struggle to admit that I was scared of life? No one's ever going to read this thing. I'm talking to myself, about myself.

So why are there so many things I can't bring myself to say?

JULY 4 — No ringship today. Too bad. Earth ain't never *had* no fireworks that could match the nullspace vortex, and I felt like celebrating.

But why do I keep Earth calendar out here, where the years are centuries and the seasons a dim memory? July is just like December. So what's the use?

JULY 10 — I dreamed of Karen last night. And now I can't get her out of my skull.

I thought I buried her long ago. It was all a fantasy anyway. Oh, she liked me well enough. Loved me, maybe. But no more than a half-dozen other guys. I wasn't really *special* to her, and she never realized just how special she was to me.

Nor how much I wanted to be special to her—how much I needed to be special to someone, somewhere.

So I elected her. But it was all a fantasy. And I knew it was, in my more rational moments. I had no right to be so hurt. I had no special claim on her.

But I thought I did, in my daydreams. And I was hurt. It was my fault, though, not hers.

Karen would never hurt anyone willingly. She just never realized how fragile I was.

Even out here, in the early years, I kept dreaming. I dreamed of how she'd change her mind. How she'd be waiting for me. Etc.

But that was more wish fulfillment. It was before I came to terms with myself out here. I know now that she won't be waiting. She doesn't need me, and never did. I was just a friend.

So I don't much like dreaming about her. That's bad. Whatever I do, I must *not* look up Karen when I get back. I have to start all over again. I have to find someone who *does* need me. And I won't find her if I try to slip back into my old life.

JULY 18 — A month since my relief left Earth. The *Charon* should be in the belt by now. Two months to go.

JULY 23 — Nightmares. God help me.

I'm dreaming of Earth again. And Karen. I can't stop. Every night it's the same.

It's funny, calling Karen a nightmare. Up to now she's always been a dream. A beautiful dream, with her long, soft hair, and her laugh, and that funny way she had of grinning. But those dreams were always wish fulfillments. In the dreams Karen needed me and wanted me and loved me.

The nightmares have the bite of truth to them. They're all the same. It's always a replay of me and Karen, together on that last night.

It was a good night, as nights went for me. We ate at one of my favorite restaurants, and went to a show. We talked together easily, about many things. We laughed together, too.

Only later, back at her place, I reverted to form. When I tried to tell her how much she meant to me, I remember how awkward and stupid I felt, how I struggled to get things out, how I stumbled over my own words. So much came out wrong.

I remember how she looked at me then. Strangely. How she tried to disillusion me. Gently. She was always gentle. And I looked into her eyes and listened to her voice. But I didn't find love, or need. Just— just pity, I guess.

Pity for an inarticulate jerk who'd been letting life pass him by without touching it. Not because he didn't want to. But because he was afraid to and didn't know how. She'd found that jerk, and loved him, in her way—she loved everybody. She'd tried to help, to give him some of her self-confidence, some of the courage and bounce that she faced life with. And, to an extent, she had.

Not enough, though. The jerk liked to make fantasies about the day he wouldn't be lonely anymore. And when Karen tried to help him, he thought she was his fantasy come to life. Or deluded himself into thinking that. The jerk suspected the truth all along, of course, but he lied to himself about it.

And when the day came that he couldn't lie any longer, he was still vulnerable enough to be hurt. He wasn't the type to grow scar tissue easily. He didn't have the courage to try again with someone else. So he ran.

I hope the nightmares stop. I can't take them, night after night. I can't take reliving that hour in Karen's apartment.

I've had four years out here. I've looked at myself hard. I've changed what I didn't like, or tried to. I've tried to cultivate that scar tissue, to gather the confidence I need to face the new rejections I'm going to meet before I find acceptance. But I know myself damn well now, and I know it's only been a partial success. There will always be things that will hurt, things that I'll never be able to face the way I'd like to.

Memories of that last hour with Karen are among those things. *God,* I hope the nightmares end.

JULY 26 — More nightmares. Please, Karen. I loved you. Leave me alone. Please.

JULY 29 — There was a ringship yesterday, thank God. I needed one. It helped take my mind off Earth, off Karen. And there was no nightmare last night, for the first time in a week. Instead I dreamed of the nullspace vortex. The raging silent storm.

AUGUST 1 — The nightmares have returned. Not always Karen now. Older memories, too. Infinitely less meaningful, but still painful. All the stupid things I've said, all the girls I never met, all the things I never did.

Bad. Bad. I have to keep reminding myself. I'm not like that anymore. There's a new me, a me I built out here, six million miles beyond Pluto. Made of steel and stars and nullspace, hard and confident and self-assured. And not afraid of life.

The past is behind me. But it still hurts.

AUGUST 2 — Ship today. The nightmares continue. Damn.

AUGUST 3 — No nightmare last night. Second time for that, that I've rested easy after opening the hole for a ringship during the day. (Day? Night? Nonsense out here—but I still write as if they had meaning. Four years haven't even touched the Earth in me.) Maybe the vortex is scaring Karen away. But I never wanted to scare Karen away before. Besides, I shouldn't need crutches.

AUGUST 13 — Another ship came through a few nights ago. No dream afterward. A pattern!

I'm fighting the memories. I'm thinking of other things about Earth. The good times. There were a lot of them, really, and there will be lots more when I get back. I'm going to make sure of that. These nightmares are stupid. I won't permit them to continue. There was so much else I shared with Karen, so much I'd like to recall. Why can't I?

AUGUST 18 — The *Charon* is about a month away. I wonder who my relief will be. I wonder what drove *him* out here?

Earth dreams continue. No. Call them Karen dreams. Am I even afraid to write her name now?

AUGUST 20 — Ship today. After it was through I stayed out and looked at stars. For several hours, it seems. Didn't seem as long at the time.

It's beautiful out here. Lonely, yes. But such a loneliness! You're alone with the universe, the stars spread out at your feet and scattered around your head.

Each one is a sun. Yet they still look cold to me. I find myself shivering, lost in the vastness of it all, wondering how it got there and what it means.

My relief, whoever it is, I hope he can appreciate this, as it should be appreciated. There are so many who can't, or won't. Men who walk at night, and never look up at the sky. I hope my relief isn't like that.

AUGUST 24 — When I get back to Earth, I *will* look up Karen. I must. How can I pretend that things are going to be different this time if I can't even work up the courage to do that? And they *are* going to be different. So I *must* face Karen, and prove that I've changed. Really changed.

AUGUST 25 — The nonsense of yesterday. *How* could I face Karen? What would I say to her? I'd only start deluding myself again, and wind up getting burned all over again. No. I must *not* see Karen. Hell, I can't even take the dreams.

AUGUST 30 — I've been going down to the control room and flipping myself out regularly of late. No ringships. But I find that going outside makes the memories of Earth dim. More and more I know I'll miss Cerberus. A year from now, I'll be back on Earth, looking up at the night sky, and remembering how the ring shone silver in the starlight. I know I will.

And the vortex. I'll remember the vortex, and the ways the colors swirled and mixed. Different every time.

Too bad I was never a holo buff. You could make a fortune back on Earth with a tape of the way the vortex looks when it spins. The ballet of the void. I'm surprised no one's ever thought of it.

Maybe I'll suggest it to my relief. Something to do to fill the hours, if he's interested. I hope he is. Earth would be richer if someone brought back a record.

I'd do it myself, but the equipment isn't right, and I don't have the time to modify it.

SEPTEMBER 4 — I've gone outside every day for the last week, I find. No nightmares. Just dreams of the darkness, laced with the colors of nullspace.

SEPTEMBER 9 — Continue to go outside, and drink it all in. Soon, soon now, all this will be lost to me. Forever. I feel as though I must take advantage of every second. I must memorize the way things are out here at Cerberus, so I can keep the awe and the wonder and the beauty fresh inside me when I return to Earth.

SEPTEMBER 10 — There hasn't been a ship in a long time. Is it over, then? Have I seen my last?

SEPTEMBER 12 — No ship today. But I went outside and woke the engines and let the vortex roar.

Why do I always write about the vortex roaring and howling? There is no sound in space. I hear nothing. But I watch it. And it does roar. It does.

The sounds of silence. But not the way the poets meant.

SEPTEMBER 13 — I've watched the vortex again today, though there was no ship.

I've never done that before. Now I've done it twice. It's forbidden. The costs in terms of power are enormous, and Cerberus lives on power. So why?

It's almost as though I don't want to give up the vortex. But I have to. Soon.

SEPTEMBER 14 — Idiot, idiot, idiot. What have I been doing? The *Charon* is less than a week away, and I've been gawking at the stars as if I'd never seen them before. I haven't even started to pack, and I've got to clean up my records for my relief, and get the station in order.

Idiot! Why am I wasting time writing in this damn *book!*

September 15 — Packing almost done. I've uncovered some weird things, too. Things I tried to hide in the early years. Like my novel. I wrote it in the first six months, and thought it was great. I could hardly wait to get back to Earth, and sell it, and become an author. Ah, yes. Read it over a year later. It stinks.

Also, I found a picture of Karen.

September 16 — Today I took a bottle of scotch and a glass down to the control room, set them down on the console, and strapped myself in. Drank a toast to the blackness and the stars and the vortex. I'll miss them.

September 17 — A day, by my calculations. A day. Then I'm on my way home, to a fresh start and a new life. If I have the courage to live it.

September 18 — Nearly midnight. No sign of the *Charon*. What's wrong?

Nothing, probably. These schedules are never precise. Sometimes as much as a week off. So why do I worry? Hell, I was late getting here myself. I wonder what the poor guy I replaced was thinking then?

September 20 — The *Charon* didn't come yesterday, either. After I got tired of waiting, I took that bottle of scotch and went back to the control room. And out. To drink another toast to the stars. And the vortex. I woke the vortex and let it flame, and toasted it.

A lot of toasts. I finished the bottle. And today I've got such a hangover I think I'll never make it back to Earth.

It was a stupid thing to do. The crew of the *Charon* might have seen the vortex colors. If they report me, I'll get docked a small fortune from the pile of money that's waiting back on Earth.

SEPTEMBER 21 — *Where* is the *Charon!* Did something happen to it? Is it coming?

SEPTEMBER 22 — I went outside again.

God, so beautiful, so lonely, so vast. Haunting, that's the word I want. The beauty out there is haunting. Sometimes I think I'm a fool to go back. I'm giving up all of eternity for a pizza and a lay and a kind word.

NO! What the hell am I writing! No. I'm going back, of course I am. I need Earth, I miss Earth, I want Earth. And this time it *will* be different.

I'll find another Karen, and this time I won't blow it.

SEPTEMBER 23 — I'm sick. God, but I'm sick. The things I've been thinking. I thought I had changed, but now I don't know. I find myself actually thinking about staying, about signing on for another term. I don't want to. No. But I think I'm still afraid of life, of Earth, of every-thing.

Hurry, *Charon.* Hurry, before I change my mind.

SEPTEMBER 24 — Karen or the vortex? Earth or eternity?

Dammit, how can I *think* that! Karen! Earth! I have to have courage, I have to risk pain, I have to taste life.

I am not a rock. Or an island. Or a star.

SEPTEMBER 25 — No sign of the *Charon.* A full week late. That hap-pens sometimes. But not very often. It will arrive soon. I know it.

SEPTEMBER 30 — Nothing. Each day I watch, and wait. I listen to my scanners, and go outside to look, and pace back and forth through the ring. But nothing. It's never been this late. What's wrong?

OCTOBER 3 — Ship today. Not the *Charon.* I thought it was at first, when the scanners picked it up. I yelled loud enough to wake the vortex. But then I looked, and my heart sank. It was too big, and it was coming straight on without decelerating.

I went outside and let it through. And stayed out for a long time afterward.

OCTOBER 4 — I want to go home. Where are they? I don't understand. I don't understand.

They can't just leave me here. They can't. They won't.

OCTOBER 5 — Ship today. Ringship again. I used to look forward to them. Now I hate them, because they're not the *Charon*. But I let it through.

OCTOBER 7 — I unpacked. It's silly for me to live out of suitcases when I don't know if the *Charon* is coming, or when.

I still look for it, though. I wait. It's coming, I know. Just delayed somewhere. An emergency in the belt maybe. There are lots of explanations.

Meanwhile, I'm doing odd jobs around the ring. I never did get it in proper shape for my relief. Too busy star watching at the time to do what I should have been doing.

OCTOBER 8(OR THEREABOUTS) — Darkness and despair.

I know why the *Charon* hasn't arrived. It isn't due. The calendar was all screwed up. It's January, not October. And I've been living on the wrong time for months. Even celebrated the Fourth of July on the wrong day.

I discovered it yesterday when I was doing those chores around the ring. I wanted to make sure everything was running right. For my relief.

Only there won't be any relief.

The *Charon* arrived three months ago. I—I destroyed it.

Sick. It was sick. I was sick, mad. As soon as it was done, it hit me. What I'd done. Oh, God. I screamed for hours.

And then I set back the wall calendar. And forgot. Maybe deliberately.

Maybe I couldn't bear to remember. I don't know. All I know is that I forgot.

But now I remember. Now I remember it all.

The scanners had warned me of the *Charon*'s approach. I was outside, waiting. Watching. Trying to get enough of the stars and the darkness to last me forever.

Through that darkness, *Charon* came. It seemed so slow compared to the ringships. And so small. It was my salvation, my relief, but it looked fragile, and silly, and somehow ugly. Squalid. It reminded me of Earth.

It moved towards docking, dropping into the ring from above, groping towards the locks in the habitable section of Cerberus. So very slow. I watched it come. Suddenly I wondered what I'd say to the crewmen, and my relief. I wondered what they'd think of me. Somewhere in my gut, a fist clenched.

And suddenly I couldn't stand it. Suddenly I was afraid of it. Suddenly I hated it.

So I woke the vortex.

A red flare, branching into yellow tongues, growing quickly, shooting off blue-green bolts. One passed near the *Charon*. And the ship shuddered.

I tell myself, now, that I didn't realize what I was doing. Yet I knew the *Charon* was unarmored. I knew it couldn't take vortex energies. I knew.

The *Charon* was so slow, the vortex so fast. In two heartbeats the maelstrom was brushing against the ship. In three it had swallowed it.

It was gone so fast. I don't know if the ship melted, or burst asunder, or crumpled. But I know it couldn't have survived. There's no blood on my star ring, though. The debris is somewhere on the other side of nullspace. If there is any debris.

The ring and the darkness looked the same as ever.

That made it so easy to forget. And I must have wanted to forget very much.

And now? What do I do *now*? Will Earth find out? Will there ever be relief? I want to go home.

Karen, I—

JUNE 18 — My relief left Earth today.

At least I think he did. Somehow the wall calendar was broken, so I'm not precisely sure of the date. But I've got it back into working order.

Anyway, it can't have been off for more than a few hours, or I would have noticed. So my relief *is* on the way. It will take him three months to get here, of course.

But at least he's coming.

WITH MORNING
COMES MISTFALL

❖

I WAS EARLY TO BREAKFAST THAT MORNING, THE FIRST DAY AFTER landing. But Sanders was already out on the dining balcony when I got there. He was standing alone by the edge, looking out over the mountains and the mists.

I walked up behind him and muttered hello. He didn't bother to reply. "It's beautiful, isn't it?" he said, without turning.

And it was.

Only a few feet below balcony level the mists rolled, sending ghostly breakers to crash against the stones of Sanders' castle. A thick white blanket extended from horizon to horizon, cloaking everything. We could see the summit of the Red Ghost, off to the north; a barbed dagger of scarlet rock jabbing into the sky. But that was all. The other mountains were still below mist level.

But we were above the mists. Sanders had built his hotel atop the tallest mountain in the chain. We were floating alone in a swirling white ocean, on a flying castle amid a sea of clouds.

Castle Cloud, in fact. That was what Sanders had named the place. It was easy to see why.

"Is it always like this?" I asked Sanders, after drinking it all in for a while.

"Every mistfall," he replied, turning toward me with a wistful smile. He was a fat man, with a jovial red face. Not the sort who should smile wistfully. But he did.

He gestured toward the east, where Wraithworld's sun rising above the mists made a crimson and orange spectacle out of the dawn sky.

"The sun," he said. "As it rises, the heat drives the mists back into the valleys, forces them to surrender the mountains they've conquered during the night. The mists sink, and one by one the peaks come into view. By noon the whole range is visible for miles and miles. There's nothing like it on Earth, or anywhere else."

He smiled again, and led me over to one of the tables scattered around the balcony. "And then, at sunset, it's all reversed. You must watch mistrise tonight," he said.

We sat down, and a sleek robowaiter came rolling out to serve us as the chairs registered our presence. Sanders ignored it. "It's war, you know," he continued. "Eternal war between the sun and the mists. And the mists have the better of it. They have the valleys, and the plains, and the seacoasts. The sun has only a few mountaintops. And them only by day."

He turned to the robowaiter and ordered coffee for both of us, to keep us occupied until the others arrived. It would be fresh-brewed, of course. Sanders didn't tolerate instants or synthetics on his planet.

"You like it here," I said, while we waited for the coffee.

Sanders laughed. "What's not to like? Castle Cloud has everything. Good food, entertainment, gambling, and all the other comforts of home. Plus this planet. I've got the best of both worlds, don't I?"

"I suppose so. But most people don't think in those terms. Nobody comes to Wraithworld for the gambling, or the food."

Sanders nodded. "But we do get some hunters. Out after rockcats and plains devils. And once in a while someone will come to look at the ruins."

"Maybe," I said. "But those are your exceptions. Not your rule. Most of your guests are here for one reason."

"Sure," he admitted, grinning. "The wraiths."

"The wraiths," I echoed. "You've got beauty here, and hunting and fishing and mountaineering. But none of that brings the tourists here. It's the wraiths they come for."

The coffee arrived then, two big steaming mugs accompanied by a pitcher of thick cream. It was very strong, and very hot, and very good. After weeks of spaceship synthetic, it was an awakening.

Sanders sipped at his coffee with care, his eyes studying me over the mug. He set it down thoughtfully. "And it's the wraiths you've come for, too," he said.

I shrugged. "Of course. My readers aren't interested in scenery, no matter how spectacular. Dubowski and his men are here to find wraiths, and I'm here to cover the search."

Sanders was about to answer, but he never got the chance. A sharp, precise voice cut in suddenly. "If there are any wraiths to find," the voice said.

We turned to face the balcony entrance. Dr. Charles Dubowski, head of the Wraithworld Research Team, was standing in the doorway, squinting at the light. He had managed to shake the gaggle of research assistants who usually trailed him everywhere.

Dubowski paused for a second, then walked over to our table, pulled out a chair, and sat down. The robowaiter came rolling out again.

Sanders eyed the thin scientist with unconcealed distaste. "What makes you think the wraiths aren't there, Doctor?" he asked.

Dubowski shrugged, and smiled lightly. "I just don't feel there's enough evidence," he said. "But don't worry. I never let my feelings interfere with my work. I want the truth as much as anyone. So I'll run an impartial expedition. If your wraiths *are* out there, I'll find them."

"Or they'll find you," Sanders said. He looked grave. "And that might not be too pleasant."

Dubowski laughed. "Oh, come now, Sanders. Just because you live in a castle doesn't mean you have to be so melodramatic."

"Don't laugh, Doctor. The wraiths have killed people before, you know."

"No proof of that," said Dubowski. "No proof at all. Just as there's no proof of the wraiths themselves. But that's why we're here. To find proof. Or disproof. But come, I'm famished." He turned to our robowaiter, who had been standing by and humming impatiently.

Dubowski and I ordered rockcat steaks, with a basket of hot, freshly baked biscuits. Sanders took advantage of the Earth supplies our ship had brought in last night, and got a massive slab of ham with a half dozen eggs.

Rockcat has a flavor that Earth meat hasn't had in centuries. I loved it, although Dubowski left much of his steak uneaten. He was too busy talking to eat.

"You shouldn't dismiss the wraiths so lightly," Sanders said after the robowaiter had stalked off with our orders. "There is evidence. Plenty of it. Twenty-two deaths since this planet was discovered. And eyewitness accounts of wraiths by the dozens."

"True," Dubowski said. "But I wouldn't call that real evidence. Deaths? Yes. Most are simple disappearances, however. Probably people who fell off a mountain, or got eaten by a rockcat, or something. It's impossible to find the bodies in the mists.

"More people vanish every day on Earth, and nothing is thought of it. But here, every time someone disappears, people claim the wraiths got him. No, I'm sorry. It's not enough."

"Bodies have been found, Doctor," Sanders said quietly. "Slain horribly. And not by falls or rockcats, either."

It was my turn to cut in. "Only four bodies have been recovered that I know of," I said. "And I've backgrounded myself pretty thoroughly on the wraiths."

Sanders frowned. "All right," he admitted. "But what about those four cases? Pretty convincing evidence, if you ask me."

The food showed up about then, but Sanders continued as we ate. "The first sighting, for example. That's never been explained satisfactorily. The Gregor Expedition."

I nodded. Dave Gregor had captained the ship that had discovered Wraithworld, nearly seventy-five years earlier. He had probed through the mists with his sensors, and set his ship down on the seacoast plains. Then he sent teams out to explore.

There were two men in each team, both well armed. But in one case, only a single man came back, and he was in hysteria. He and his partner had gotten separated in the mists, and suddenly he heard a bloodcurdling scream. When he found his friend, he was quite dead. And something was standing over the body.

The survivor described the killer as manlike, eight feet tall, and somehow insubstantial. He claimed that when he fired at it, the blaster bolt went right through it. Then the creature had wavered, and vanished in the mists.

Gregor sent other teams out to search for the thing. They recovered the body, but that was all. Without special instruments, it was difficult to find the same place twice in the mists. Let alone something like the creature that had been described.

So the story was never confirmed. But nonetheless, it caused a sensation when Gregor returned to Earth. Another ship was sent to conduct a more thorough search. It found nothing. But one of its search teams disappeared without a trace.

And the legend of the mist wraiths was born, and began to grow. Other ships came to Wraithworld, and a trickle of colonists came and went, and Paul Sanders landed one day and erected the Castle Cloud so the public might safely visit the mysterious planet of the wraiths.

And there were other deaths, and other disappearances, and many people claimed to catch brief glimpses of wraiths prowling through the mists. And then someone found the ruins. Just tumbled stone blocks now. But once, structures of some sort. The homes of the wraiths, people said.

There was evidence, I thought. And some of it was hard to deny. But Dubowski was shaking his head vigorously.

"The Gregor affair proves nothing," he said. "You know as well as I this planet has never been explored thoroughly. Especially the plains area, where Gregor's ship put down. It was probably some sort of animal that killed that man. A rare animal of some sort native to that area."

"What about the testimony of his partner?" Sanders asked.

"Hysteria, pure and simple."

"The other sightings? There have been an awful lot of them. And the witnesses weren't always hysterical."

"Proves nothing," Dubowski said, shaking his head. "Back on Earth, plenty of people still claim to have seen ghosts and flying saucers. And here, with those damned mists, mistakes and hallucinations are naturally even easier."

He jabbed at Sanders with the knife he was using to butter a biscuit. "It's these mists that foul up everything. The wraith myth would have died long ago without the mists. Up to now, no one has had the equipment or the money to conduct a really thorough investigation. But we do. And we will. We'll get the truth once and for all."

Sanders grimaced. "If you don't get yourself killed first. The wraiths may not like being investigated."

"I don't understand you, Sanders," Dubowski said. "If you're so afraid of the wraiths and so convinced that they're down there prowling about, why have you lived here so long?"

"Castle Cloud was built with safeguards," Sanders said. "The brochure we send prospective guests describes them. No one is in any danger here. For one thing, the wraiths won't come out of the mists. And we're in sunlight most of the day. But it's a different story down in the valleys."

"That's superstitious nonsense. If I had to guess, I'd say these mist wraiths of yours were nothing but transplanted Earth ghosts. Phantoms of someone's imagination. But I won't guess—I'll wait until the results are in. Then we'll see. If they are real, they won't be able to hide from us."

Sanders looked over at me. "What about you? Do you agree with him?"

"I'm a journalist," I said carefully. "I'm just here to cover what happens. The wraiths are famous, and my readers are interested. So I've got no opinions. Or none that I'd care to broadcast, anyway."

Sanders lapsed into a disgruntled silence, and attacked his ham and eggs with a renewed vigor. Dubowski took over for him, and steered the conversation over to the details of the investigation he was planning. The rest of the meal was a montage of eager talk about wraith traps, and search plans, and roboprobes, and sensors. I listened carefully and took mental notes for a column on the subject.

Sanders listened carefully, too. But you could tell from his face that he was far from pleased by what he heard.

———

NOTHING MUCH ELSE HAPPENED THAT DAY. DUBOWSKI SPENT HIS TIME at the spacefield, built on a small plateau below the castle, and supervised the unloading of his equipment. I wrote a column on his plans for the expedition, and beamed it back to Earth. Sanders tended to his other guests, and did whatever else a hotel manager does, I guess.

I went out to the balcony again at sunset, to watch the mists rise.

It was war, like Sanders had said. At mistfall, I had seen the sun victorious in the first of the daily battles. But now the conflict was renewed. The mists began to creep back to the heights as the temperature fell. Wispy gray-white tendrils stole up silently from the valleys, and curled around the jagged mountain peaks like ghostly fingers. Then the fingers began to grow thicker and stronger, and after a while they pulled the mists up after them.

One by one the stark, wind-carved summits were swallowed up for another night. The Red Ghost, the giant to the north, was the last mountain to vanish in the lapping white ocean. And then the mists began to pour in over the balcony ledge and close around Castle Cloud itself.

I went back inside. Sanders was standing there, just inside the doors. He had been watching me.

"You were right," I said. "It was beautiful."

He nodded. "You know, I don't think Dubowski has bothered to look yet," he said.

"Busy, I guess."

Sanders sighed. "Too damn busy. C'mon. I'll buy you a drink."

The hotel bar was quiet and dark, with the kind of mood that promotes good talk and serious drinking. The more I saw of Sanders' castle, the more I liked the man. Our tastes were in remarkable accord.

We found a table in the darkest and most secluded part of the room, and ordered drinks from a stock that included liquors from a dozen worlds. And we talked.

"You don't seem very happy to have Dubowski here," I said after the drinks came. "Why not? He's filling up your hotel."

Sanders looked up from his drink and smiled. "True. It is the slow season. But I don't like what he's trying to do."

"So you try to scare him away?"

Sanders' smile vanished. "Was I that transparent?"

I nodded.

He sighed. "Didn't think it would work," he said. He sipped thoughtfully at his drink. "But I had to try something."

"Why?"

"Because. Because he's going to destroy this world, if I let him. By the time he and his kind get through, there won't be a mystery left in the universe."

"He's just trying to find some answers. Do the wraiths exist? What about the ruins? Who built them? Didn't you ever want to know those things, Sanders?"

He drained his drink, looked around, and caught the waiter's eye to order another. No robowaiters in here. Only human help. Sanders was particular about atmosphere.

"Of course," he said when he had his drink. "Everyone's wondered about those questions. That's why people come here to Wraithworld, to the Castle Cloud. Each guy who touches down here is secretly hoping he'll have an adventure with the wraiths, and find out all the answers personally.

"So he doesn't. So he slaps on a blaster and wanders around the mist forests for a few days, or a few weeks, and finds nothing. So what? He can come back and search again. The dream is still there, and the romance, and the mystery.

"And who knows? Maybe one trip he glimpses a wraith drifting through the mists. Or something he thinks is a wraith. And then he'll go home happy, 'cause he's been part of a legend. He's touched a little bit of creation that hasn't had all the awe and the wonder ripped from it yet by Dubowski's sort."

He fell silent and stared morosely into his drink. Finally, after a long pause, he continued. "Dubowski! Bah! He makes me boil. He comes here with his ship full of lackeys and his million credit grant and all his gadgets, to hunt for wraiths. Oh, he'll get them all right. That's what frightens me. Either he'll prove they don't exist, or he'll find them, and they'll turn out to be some kind of submen or animal or something."

He emptied his glass again, savagely. "And that will ruin it. Ruin it, you hear! He'll answer all the questions with his gadgets, and there'll be nothing left for anyone else. It isn't fair."

I sat there and sipped quietly at my drink and said nothing. Sanders ordered another. A foul thought was running around in my head. Finally I had to say it aloud.

"If Dubowski answers all the questions," I said, "then there will be no reason to come here anymore. And you'll be put out of business. Are you sure that's not why you're so worried?"

Sanders glared at me, and I thought he was going to hit me for a second. But he didn't. "I thought you were different. You looked at mistfall, and understood. I thought you did, anyway. But I guess I was wrong." He jerked his head toward the door. "Get out of here," he said.

I rose. "All right," I said. "I'm sorry, Sanders. But it's my job to ask nasty questions like that."

He ignored me, and I left the table. When I reached the door, I turned and looked back across the room. Sanders was staring into his drink again, and talking loudly to himself.

"Answers," he said. He made it sound obscene. "Answers. Always they have to have answers. But the questions are so much finer. Why can't they leave them alone?"

I left him alone then. Alone with his drinks.

THE NEXT FEW WEEKS WERE HECTIC ONES, FOR THE EXPEDITION AND FOR me. Dubowski went about things thoroughly, you had to give him that. He had planned his assault on Wraithworld with meticulous precision.

Mapping came first. Thanks to the mists, what maps there were of Wraithworld were very crude by modern standards. So Dubowski sent out a whole fleet of roboprobes, to skim above the mists and steal their secrets with sophisticated sensory devices. From the information that came pouring in, a detailed topography of the region was pieced together.

That done, Dubowski and his assistants then used the maps to carefully plot every recorded wraith sighting since the Gregor Expedition. Considerable data on the sightings had been compiled and analyzed long before we left Earth, of course. Heavy use of the matchless collection on wraiths in the Castle Cloud library filled in the gaps that remained. As expected, sightings were most common in the valleys around the hotel, the only permanent human habitation on the planet.

When the plotting was completed, Dubowski set out his wraith traps, scattering most of them in the areas where wraiths had been reported most frequently. He also put a few in distant, outlying regions, however, including the seacoast plain where Gregor's ship had made the initial contact.

The traps weren't really traps, of course. They were squat duralloy pillars, packed with most every type of sensing and recording equipment known to Earth science. To the traps, the mists were all but nonexistent. If some unfortunate wraith wandered into survey range, there would be no way it could avoid detection.

Meanwhile, the mapping roboprobes were pulled in to be overhauled and reprogrammed, and then sent out again. With the topography known in detail, the probes could be sent through the mists on low-level patrols without fear of banging into a concealed mountain. The sensing equipment carried by the probes was not the equal of that in the wraith traps, of course. But the probes had a much greater range, and could cover thousands of square miles each day.

Finally, when the wraith traps were deployed and the roboprobes were in the air, Dubowski and his men took to the mist forests themselves. Each carried a heavy backpack of sensors and detection devices. The human search teams had more mobility than the wraith traps, and more sophisticated equipment than the probes. They covered a different area each day, in painstaking detail.

I went along on a few of those trips, with a backpack of my own. It made for some interesting copy, even though we never found anything. And while on search, I fell in love with the mist forests.

The tourist literature likes to call them "the ghastly mist forests of haunted Wraithworld." But they're not ghastly. Not really. There's a strange sort of beauty there, for those who can appreciate it.

The trees are thin and very tall, with white bark and pale gray leaves. But the forests are not without color. There's a parasite, a hanging moss of some sort, that's very common, and it drips from the overhanging branches in cascades of dark green and scarlet. And there are rocks, and vines, and low bushes choked with misshapen purplish fruits.

But there's no sun, of course. The mists hide everything. They swirl and slide around you as you walk, caressing you with unseen hands, clutching at your feet.

Once in a while, the mists play games with you. Most of the time you walk through a thick fog, unable to see more than a few feet in any direction, your own shoes lost in the mist carpet below. Sometimes, though, the fog closes in suddenly. And then you can't see at all. I blundered into more than one tree when that happened.

At other times, though, the mists—for no apparent reason—will roll back suddenly, and leave you standing alone in a clear pocket within a cloud. That's when you can see the forest in all its grotesque beauty. It's a brief, breathtaking glimpse of never-never land. Moments like that are few and short-lived. But they stay with you.

They stay with you.

In those early weeks, I didn't have much time for walking in the forests, except when I joined a search team to get the feel of it. Mostly I was busy writing. I did a series on the history of the planet, highlighted by the stories of the most famous sightings. I did feature profiles on some of the more colorful members of the expedition. I did a piece on Sanders, and the problems he encountered and overcame in building Castle Cloud. I did science pieces on the little known about the planet's ecology. I did mood pieces about the forests and the mountains. I did speculative thought pieces about the ruins. I wrote about rockcat hunting, and mountain climbing, and the huge and dangerous swamp lizards native to some offshore islands.

And, of course, I wrote about Dubowski and his search. On that I wrote reams.

Finally, however, the search began to settle down into dull routine, and I began to exhaust the myriad other topics Wraithworld offered. My output began to decline. I started to have time on my hands.

That's when I really began to enjoy Wraithworld. I began to take daily walks through the forests, ranging wider each day. I visited the ruins, and flew half a continent away to see the swamp lizards firsthand instead of by holo. I befriended a group of hunters passing through, and shot myself a rockcat. I accompanied some other hunters to the western seacoast, and nearly got myself killed by a plains devil.

And I began to talk to Sanders again.

Through all of this, Sanders had pretty well ignored me and Dubowski and everyone else connected with the wraith research. He spoke to us grudgingly, if at all, greeted us curtly, and spent all his free time with his other guests.

At first, after the way he had talked in the bar that night, I worried about what he might do. I had visions of him murdering someone out in the mists, and trying to make it look like a wraith killing. Or maybe just sabotaging the wraith traps. But I was sure he would try something to scare off Dubowski or otherwise undermine the expedition.

Comes of watching too much holovision, I guess. Sanders did nothing of the sort. He merely sulked, glared at us in the castle corridors, and gave us less than full cooperation at all times.

After a while, though, he began to warm up again. Not toward Dubowski and his men.

Just toward me.

I guess that was because of my walks in the forests. Dubowski never went out into the mists unless he had to. And then he went out reluctantly, and came back quickly. His men followed their chief's example. I was the only joker in the deck. But then, I wasn't really part of the same deck.

Sanders noticed, of course. He didn't miss much of what went on in his castle. And he began to speak to me again. Civilly. One day, finally, he even invited me for drinks again.

It was about two months into the expedition. Winter was coming to Wraithworld and Castle Cloud, and the air was getting cold and crisp. Dubowski and I were out on the dining balcony, lingering over coffee after another superb meal. Sanders sat at a nearby table, talking to some tourists.

I forget what Dubowski and I were discussing. Whatever it was, Dubowski interrupted me with a shiver at one point. "It's getting cold out here," he complained. "Why don't we move inside?" Dubowski never liked the dining balcony very much.

I sort of frowned. "It's not that bad," I said. "Besides, it's nearly sunset. One of the best parts of the day."

Dubowski shivered again, and stood up. "Suit yourself," he said. "But I'm going in. I don't feel like catching a cold just so you can watch another mistfall."

He started to walk off. But he hadn't taken three steps before Sanders was up out of his seat, howling like a wounded rockcat.

"Mistfall," he bellowed. *"Mistfall!"* He launched into a long, incoherent string of obscenities. I had never seen Sanders so angry, not even when he threw me out of the bar that first night. He stood there, literally trembling with rage, his face flushed, his fat fists clenching and unclenching at his sides.

I got up in a hurry, and got between them. Dubowski turned to me, looking baffled and scared. "Wha—" he started.

"Get inside," I interrupted. "Get up to your room. Get to the lounge. Get somewhere. Get anywhere. But get out of here before he kills you."

"But—but—what's wrong? What happened? I don't—"

"Mistfall is in the morning," I told him. "At night, at sunset, it's mistrise. Now go."

"That's *all*? Why should that get him so—so—"

"GO!"

Dubowski shook his head, as if to say he still didn't understand what was going on. But he went.

I turned to Sanders. "Calm down," I said. "Calm down."

He stopped trembling, but his eyes threw blaster bolts at Dubowski's back. "Mistfall," he muttered. "Two months that bastard has been here, and he doesn't know the difference between mistfall and mistrise."

"He's never bothered to watch either one," I said. "Things like that don't interest him. That's his loss, though. No reason for you to get upset about it."

He looked at me, frowning. Finally he nodded. "Yeah," he said. "Maybe you're right." He sighed. "But *mistfall!* Hell." There was a short silence, then, "I need a drink. Join me?"

I nodded.

We wound up in the same dark corner as the first night, at what must have been Sanders' favorite table. He put away three drinks before I had finished my first. Big drinks. Everything in Castle Cloud was big.

There were no arguments this time. We talked about mistfall, and the forests, and the ruins. We talked about the wraiths, and Sanders lovingly told me the stories of the great sightings. I knew them all already, of course. But not the way Sanders told them.

At one point, I mentioned that I'd been born in Bradbury when my parents were spending a short vacation on Mars. Sanders' eyes lit up at that, and he spent the next hour or so regaling me with Earthman jokes. I'd heard them all before, too. But I was getting more than a little drunk, and somehow they all seemed hilarious.

After that night, I spent more time with Sanders than with anyone else in the hotel. I thought I knew Wraithworld pretty well by that time. But that was an empty conceit, and Sanders proved it. He showed me hidden spots in the forests that have haunted me ever since. He took me to island swamps, where the trees are of a very different sort and sway horridly without a wind. We flew to the far north, to another mountain range where the peaks are higher and sheathed in ice, and to a southern plateau where the mists pour eternally over the edge in a ghostly imitation of a waterfall.

I continued to write about Dubowski and his wraith hunt, of course. But there was little new to write about, so most of my time was spent with Sanders. I didn't worry too much about my output. My Wraithworld series had gotten excellent play on Earth and most of the colony worlds, so I thought I had it made.

Not so.

I'd been on Wraithworld just a little over three months when my syndicate beamed me. A few systems away, a civil war had broken out on a planet called New Refuge. They wanted me to cover it. No news was coming out of Wraithworld anyway, they said, since Dubowski's expedition still had over a year to run.

Much as I liked Wraithworld, I jumped at the chance. My stories had been getting a little stale, and I was running out of ideas, and the New Refuge thing sounded like it could be very big.

So I said goodbye to Sanders and Dubowski and Castle Cloud, and took a last walk through the mist forests, and booked passage on the next ship through.

———

THE NEW REFUGE CIVIL WAR WAS A FIRECRACKER. I SPENT LESS THAN a month on the planet, but it was a dreary month. The place had been colonized by religious fanatics, but the original cult had schismed, and both sides accused the other of heresy. It was all very dingy. The planet itself had all the charm of a Martian suburb.

I moved on as quickly as I could, hopping from planet to planet, from story to story. In six months, I had worked myself back to Earth. Elections were coming up, so I got slapped onto a political beat. That was fine by me. It was a lively campaign, and there was a ton of good stories to be mined.

But throughout it all, I kept myself up on the little news that came out of Wraithworld. And finally, as I'd expected, Dubowski announced a press conference. As the syndicate's resident wraith, I got myself assigned to cover it, and headed out on the fastest starship I could find.

I got there a week before the conference, ahead of everyone else. I had beamed Sanders before taking ship, and he met me at the spaceport. We adjourned to the dining balcony, and had our drinks served out there.

"Well?" I asked him, after we had traded amenities. "You know what Dubowski's going to announce?"

Sanders looked very glum. "I can guess," he said. "He called in all his damn gadgets a month ago, and he's been cross-checking findings on a computer. We've had a couple of wraith sightings since you left. Dubowski moved in hours after each sighting, and went over the areas with a fine-tooth comb. Nothing. That's what he's going to announce, I think. Nothing."

I nodded. "Is that so bad, though? Gregor found nothing."

"Not the same," Sanders said. "Gregor didn't look the way Dubowski has. People will believe him, whatever he says."

I wasn't so sure of that, and was about to say so, when Dubowski arrived. Someone must have told him I was there. He came striding out on the balcony, smiling, spied me, and came over to sit down.

Sanders glared at him and studied his drink. Dubowski trained all of his attention on me. He seemed very pleased with himself. He asked what I'd been doing since I left, and I told him, and he said that was nice.

Finally I got to ask him about his results. "No comment," he said. "That's what I've called the press conference for."

"C'mon," I said. "I covered you for months when everybody else was ignoring the expedition. You can give me some kind of beat. What have you got?"

He hesitated. "Well, okay," he said doubtfully. "But don't release it yet. You can beam it out a few hours ahead of the conference. That should be enough time for a beat."

I nodded agreement. "What do you have?"

"The wraiths," he said. "I have the wraiths, bagged neatly. They don't exist. I've got enough evidence to prove it beyond a shadow of a doubt." He smiled broadly.

"Just because you didn't find anything?" I started. "Maybe they were avoiding you. If they're sentient, they might be smart enough. Or maybe they're beyond the ability of your sensors to detect."

"Come now," Dubowski said. "You don't believe that. Our wraith traps had every kind of sensor we could come up with. If the wraiths existed, they would have registered on something. But they didn't. We had the traps planted in the areas where three of Sanders' so-called sightings took place. Nothing. Absolutely nothing. Conclusive proof that those people were seeing things. Sightings, indeed."

"What about the deaths, the vanishings?" I asked. "What about the Gregor Expedition and the other classic cases?"

His smile spread. "Couldn't disprove all the deaths, of course. But our probes and our searches turned up four skeletons." He ticked them off on his fingers. "Two were killed by a rockslide, and one had rock-cat claw marks on the bones."

"The fourth?"

"Murder," he said. "The body was buried in a shallow grave, clearly by human hands. A flood of some sort had exposed it. It was down in the records as a disappearance. I'm sure all the other bodies could be found, if we searched long enough. And we'd find that all died perfectly normal deaths."

Sanders raised his eyes from his drink. They were bitter eyes. "Gregor," he said stubbornly. "Gregor and the other classics."

Dubowski's smile became a smirk. "Ah, yes. We searched that area quite thoroughly. My theory was right. We found a tribe of apes nearby. Big brutes. Like giant baboons, with dirty white fur. Not a very successful species, either. We found only one small tribe, and they were dying out. But clearly, that was what Gregor's man sighted. And exaggerated all out of proportion."

There was silence. Then Sanders spoke, but his voice was beaten. "Just one question," he said softly. "Why?"

That brought Dubowski up short, and his smile faded. "You never have understood, have you, Sanders?" he said. "It was for truth. To free this planet from ignorance and superstition."

"Free Wraithworld?" Sanders said. "Was it enslaved?"

"Yes," Dubowski answered. "Enslaved by foolish myth. By fear. Now this planet will be free, and open. We can find out the truth behind those ruins now, without murky legends about half-human wraiths to fog the facts. We can open this planet for colonization.

People won't be afraid to come here, and live, and farm. We've conquered the fear."

"A colony world? Here?" Sanders looked amused. "Are you going to bring big fans to blow away the mists, or what? Colonists have come before. And left. The soil's all wrong. You can't farm here, with all these mountains. At least not on a commercial scale. There's no way you can make a profit growing things on Wraithworld.

"Besides, there are hundreds of colony worlds crying for people. Did you need another so badly? Must Wraithworld become yet another Earth?"

He shook his head sadly, drained his drink, and continued. "You're the one who doesn't understand, Doctor. Don't kid yourself. You haven't freed Wraithworld. You've destroyed it. You've stolen its wraiths, and left an empty planet."

Dubowski shook his head. "I think you're wrong. They'll find plenty of good, profitable ways to exploit this planet. But even if you were correct, well, it's just too bad. Knowledge is what man is all about. People like you have tried to hold back progress since the beginning of time. But they failed, and you failed. Man needs to know."

"Maybe," Sanders said. "But is that the *only* thing man needs? I don't think so. I think he also needs mystery, and poetry, and romance. I think he needs a few unanswered questions to make him brood and wonder."

Dubowski stood up abruptly, and frowned. "This conversation is as pointless as your philosophy, Sanders. There's no room in my universe for unanswered questions."

"Then you live in a very drab universe, Doctor."

"And you, Sanders, live in the stink of your own ignorance. Find some new superstitions if you must. But don't try to foist them off on me with your tales and legends. I've got no time for wraiths." He looked at me. "I'll see you at the press conference," he said. Then he turned and walked briskly from the balcony.

Sanders watched him depart in silence, then swiveled in his chair to look out over the mountains. "The mists are rising," he said.

SANDERS WAS WRONG ABOUT THE COLONY TOO, AS IT TURNED OUT. They did establish one, although it wasn't much to boast of. Some vineyards, some factories, and a few thousand people; all belonging to a couple of big companies.

Commercial farming did turn out to be unprofitable, you see. With one exception—a native grape, a fat gray thing the size of a lemon. So Wraithworld has only one export, a smoky white wine with a mellow, lingering flavor.

They call it mistwine, of course. I've grown fond of it over the years. The taste reminds me of mistfall somehow, and makes me dream. But that's probably me, not the wine. Most people don't care for it much.

Still, in a very minor way, it's a profitable item. So Wraithworld is still a regular stop on the spacelanes. For freighters, at least.

The tourists are long gone, though. Sanders was right about that. Scenery they can get closer to home, and cheaper. The wraiths were why they came.

Sanders is long gone, too. He was too stubborn and too impractical to buy in on the mistwine operations when he had the chance. So he stayed behind his ramparts at Castle Cloud until the last. I don't know what happened to him afterward, when the hotel finally went out of business.

The castle itself is still there. I saw it a few years ago, when I stopped for a day en route to a story on New Refuge. It's already crumbling, though. Too expensive to maintain. In a few years, you won't be able to tell it from those other, older ruins.

Otherwise the planet hasn't changed much. The mists still rise at sunset, and fall at dawn. The Red Ghost is still stark and beautiful in the early morning light. The forests are still there, and the rockcats still prowl.

Only the wraiths are missing.

Only the wraiths.

THREE

The Light of Distant Stars

HERE'S THE THING OF IT. I WAS BORN AND RAISED IN BAYONNE, NEW JERSEY, AND NEVER went *anywhere* . . . not till college, at any rate.

Bayonne is a peninsula, part of New York City's metropolitan area, but when I was growing up it was a world unto itself. An industrial city dominated by its oil refineries and its navy base, it was small, three miles long and only one mile wide. Bayonne adjoins Jersey City on the north; elsewise it is entirely surrounded by water, with Newark Bay to the west, New York Bay to the east, and the narrow deepwater channel that connects them, the Kill van Kull, to the south. Big oceangoing freighters travel along the Kill by night and day, on their way to and from Elizabeth and Port Newark.

When I was four years old, my family moved into the new projects on First Street, facing the dark, polluted waters of the Kill. Across the channel the lights of Staten Island glimmered by night, far off and magical. Aside from a trip to the Staten Island Zoo every three or four years, we never crossed the Kill.

You could get to Staten Island easily enough by driving across the Bayonne Bridge, but my family did not own a car, and neither of my parents drove. You could cross by ferry too. The terminal was only a few blocks from the projects, next to Uncle Milty's amusement park. There was a secret "cove" a kid could get to by walking along the oil-slick rocks during low tide and slipping around the fence, a grassy little ledge hidden from both the ferry and the street. I liked to go there sometimes, to sit on the grass above the water with a candy bar and some funny books, reading and watching the ferries go back and forth between Bayonne and Staten Island.

The boats made frequent crossings. Often one would be coming as the other one was going, and they would pass each other in the middle of the channel. The ferry line operated three boats, named the *Deneb,* the *Altair,* and the *Vega.* For me, no tramp steamer or clipper ship could have been any more romantic than those little ferries. The fact that they were all named after stars was part of their magic, I think. Although the three boats were identical, so far as I could tell, the *Altair* was always my favorite. Maybe that had something to do with *Forbidden Planet.*

Sometimes, after supper, our apartment could seem crowded and noisy, even if it was just me and my parents and my two sisters. If my parents had friends over, the kitchen would grow hazy with cigarette smoke and loud with voices. Sometimes I would retreat to my own room and close the door. Sometimes I'd stay in the living room, watching TV with my sisters. And sometimes I'd go outside.

Just across the street was Brady's Dock and a long, narrow park that ran beside the Kill van Kull. I would sit on a bench there and watch the big ships go by, or I'd stretch out in the grass and look up at the stars, whose lights were even farther off than those of Staten Island. Even on the hottest, muggiest summer nights, the stars always gave me a thrill. Orion was the first constellation that I learned to recognize. I would gaze up at its two bright stars, blue Rigel and red Betelgeuse, and wonder if there was anyone up there looking back down at me.

Fans write of a "sense of wonder," and argue over how to define it. To me, a sense of wonder is the feeling I got while lying in the grass beside the Kill van Kull, pondering the light of distant stars. They always made me feel very large and very small. It was a sad feeling, but strange and sweet as well.

Science fiction can give me that same feeling.

My earliest exposure to SF came from television. Mine was the first generation weaned on the tube. We might not have had *Sesame Street,* but we had *Ding Dong School* during the week, *Howdy Doody* on Saturday mornings, and cartoons every day of the week. On *Andy's Gang* Froggy the Gremlin plunked his magic twanger. Though I watched Gene Autry, Roy Rogers, and

Hopalong Cassidy, cowboys were more my father's passion than my own. I preferred knights: *Robin Hood* and *Ivanhoe* and *Sir Lancelot*. But nothing could match the space shows.

I must have seen *Captain Video* on the Dumont network, since I have a vague memory of his nemesis, Tobor ("Robot" spelled backward, of course). I don't recall *Space Cadet,* though; my memories of Tom Corbett derive from the books by Carey Rockwell that I read later. I did catch *Flash Gordon,* for certain . . . the TV show, not the movie serial. In one episode Flash visits a planet whose people are good by day and bad by night, a concept that I thought was so cool that I used it in some of my own earliest attempts at stories.

All of these paled, however, before *Rocky Jones, Space Ranger,* the crème de la crème of the SF shows of the early '50s. Rocky had the best-looking spaceship on the tube, the sleek, silvery *Orbit Jet.* I was devastated when the *Orbit Jet* got destroyed one episode, but fortunately it was soon replaced by the *Silver Moon,* which looked exactly the same. His crew included the usual comic co-pilot, simpering girlfriend, pompous professor, and annoying little kid, but he also had Pinto Vortando. (Anyone who thinks Gene Roddenberry brought anything fresh to television should take a look at *Rocky Jones.* It's all there, but for Spock, who owes more to D. C. Fontana than to Roddenberry. Harry Mudd is just Pinto Vortando with the accent toned down.)

When I wasn't watching spacemen and aliens on television, I was playing with them at home. Along with the usual cowboys, knights, and green army men, I had all the space toys, the ray guns and rocket ships and hard plastic spacemen with the removable clear plastic helmets that were always getting lost. Best of all were the colored plastic aliens I bought for a nickel apiece from bins in Woolworth's and Kresge's. Some had big swollen brains and some had four arms, and some were spiders with faces or snakes with arms and heads. My favorite guy had a tiny little head and chest on top of a gigantic, hairy lower body. I gave them all names, and decided they were a gang of space pirates, led by the malignant big-brained Martian I called Jarn, who was not *nearly* as nice as Pinto Vortando. And of course I dreamed up endless stories of their adventures, and even made some halting attempts at writing one or two of them down.

Science fiction could be found in the movies as well. I saw *Them* and *War of the Worlds* and *The Day the Earth Stood Still* and *This Island Earth* and *Destination Moon.* And *Forbidden Planet,* which put all of them to shame.

Little did I suspect that I was getting my first taste of Shakespeare there in the DeWitt Theater, courtesy of Dr. Morbius and Robby the Robot.

Most of my beloved funny books were science fiction of a sort as well. Superman was from another planet, wasn't he? He came to Earth in a *space-ship*, how scientific could you get? The Martian Manhunter came from Mars, Green Lantern was given his ring by a crashed alien, and the Flash and the Atom got their powers in a lab. The comics offered pure space opera as well. There was Space Ranger (my favorite), Adam Strange (everybody else's favorite), Tommy Tomorrow (nobody's favorite), and this guy who drove a space cab along the space freeways . . . There were the Atomic Knights, post-holocaust heroes who patrolled a radioactive wasteland in suits of lead-lined armor, riding giant mutant Dalmations . . . and on a somewhat more elevated plane, there were the wonderful *Classics Illustrated* adaptions of *War of the Worlds* and *The Time Machine*, which gave me my first introduction to the works of H. G. Wells.

All that was only prelude, though. When I was ten years old, my mother's childhood friend Lucy Antonsson gave me a book for Christmas. Not a comic book, but a *book* book, a hardcover of *Have Space Suit, Will Travel,* by Robert A. Heinlein.

I was a little dubious at first, but I liked Paladin on TV, and the title suggested this might be about some kind of space Paladin, so I took it home and began to read about this kid named Kip, who lived in a small town and never went anywhere, just like me. Some critics have suggested that *Citizen of the Galaxy* is the best of the Heinlein juveniles. *Citizen of the Galaxy* is a fine book. So too are *Tunnel Through the Sky, Starman Jones, Time for the Stars,* and many of the others . . . but *Have Space Suit, Will Travel* towers above them all. Kip and PeeWee, Ace and the malt shop, the old used spacesuit (I could *smell* it), the Mother Thing, the wormfaces, the trek across the moon, the trial in the Lesser Magellanic Cloud with the fate of humanity at stake. "Die trying is the proudest human thing." What could compare with that?

Nothing.

To a ten-year-old boy in 1958, *Have Space Suit, Will Travel* was crack with an Ed Emshwiller cover. I had to have more.

There was no way I could afford hardcovers, of course. *Have Space Suit, Will Travel* had cost $2.95, according to the price inside the dustwrapper . . . but the paperbacks on the spinner rack in the candy store on Kelly Parkway only went for 35¢, the price of three-and-a-half funny books. If I didn't buy so many comics and skipped a Milky Way from time to time, I could scrape together the price of one of those. So I saved my dimes and nickels, stopped reading some comics I didn't like all that much to begin with, played a few less games of Skee-Ball, avoided the Good Humor truck and Mister Softee when they came by, and started buying paperbacks.

Worlds and universes opened wide before me. I bought every Heinlein that I found; his "adult" books like *The Man Who Sold the Moon* and *Revolt in 2100,* since the other juveniles were not to be found. RAH was "the dean of science fiction," it said so right on the back of his books. If he was the dean, he must be the best. He remained my favorite writer for years to come, and *Have Space Suit, Will Travel* remained my favorite book . . . until the day when I read *The Puppet Masters.*

But I tried other authors too, and found that I enjoyed some of them almost as much as RAH. I loved Andrew North, who turned out to be Andre Norton. What's in a name? Andrew's *Plague Ship* and Andre's *Star Guard* both thrilled me. A. E. van Vogt's stuff had tremendous energy, especially *Slan,* although I never could quite figure out who was doing what to whom, or why. I became enamored of *One Against Herculum,* by Jerry Sohl, which took me to a world where you registered your crimes with the police before you committed them. Eric Frank Russell rocketed to the top of my list when I chanced upon *The Space Willies,* the funniest thing I'd ever read.

Though I bought books from Signet, Gold Medal, and all the other publishers, the Ace Doubles were my mainstay. *Two* "complete novels," printed back-to-back and upside down, with *two* covers, all for the price of one. Wilson Tucker, Alan Nourse, John Brunner, Robert Silverberg, Poul Anderson (*The War of the Wing-Men* was so good it threatened the supremacy of *Have Space Suit, Will Travel*), Damon Knight, Philip K. Dick, Edmond Hamilton, and the magnificent Jack Vance; I met them all in the pages of those stubby paperbacks with the blue-and-red spines. Tommy Tomorrow and Rocky Jones could not compare with this. This was the real stuff, and I drank it straight, with another for a chaser.

(Eventually my reading would lead me to Robert E. Howard, H. P. Lovecraft, and J.R.R. Tolkien as well, but I'll save those discoveries for my other commentaries.)

I sampled different *kinds* of science fiction along with different authors: "aliens among us" stories, "if this goes on" stories, time travel yarns, "sideways in time" alternate histories, post-holocaust tales, utopias and dystopias. Later, as a writer, I would revisit many of these subgenres . . . but there was one type of science fiction that I loved above all others, both as a reader and later as a writer. I was born and raised in Bayonne and never went *anywhere,* and my favorite books and stories were those that took me over the hills and far away, to lands undreamed of, where I might walk beneath the light of distant stars.

The six stories I've chosen here all belong to that category. I wrote a great deal of science fiction in the '70s and '80s, but these stories are among my favorites. They also share a common universe; all six are part of the loose "future history" that formed the backdrop for much of my SF.

(Though not all of it. "Run to Starlight" and "A Peripheral Affair" are part of a different continuity, the two star ring stories are set in yet another, the corpse stories in a third. "Fast-Friend" stands by itself, as do a number of my other stories. I have no intention of trying to cram these orphans into my future history by retroactive backfill either. That's always a mistake.)

What I thought of as my "main" future history began with "The Hero" and reached its fullest development in my first novel, *Dying of the Light.* I never had a name for it, at least not one that stuck. In "The Stone City" I coined the word "manrealm" and for a while tried using that as an overall term for the history, analogous to Larry Niven's "Known Space." Later, I hit on the "Thousand Worlds," which had a nicer ring to it, and would have given me plenty of room to add new planets as I needed them . . . not to mention putting me nine hundred and ninety-two worlds up on John Varley and his "Eight Worlds." By that time my writing was taking me in other directions, however, so the name became moot.

"A Song for Lya" is the oldest of the six stories in this section. It was written in 1973, during my days in VISTA, when I was living on Margate Terrace in Chicago's Uptown, sharing a third-floor walk-up with some of my college chess cronies, and working at the Cook County Legal Assistance Foundation. I was also in the midst of the first serious romance of my life; it was not the first time I had ever been in love, but it was certainly the first time my feelings had been reciprocated. That relationship gave "Lya" its emotional core; without it, I would have been the proverbial blind man describing a sunset. "A Song for Lya" was also my longest story to date, my first novella. When I finished it, I knew that I had finally surpassed "With Morning Comes Mistfall" and "The Second Kind of Loneliness," written two years earlier. *This* was the best thing I'd ever done.

Analog had become my major market, so I sent it off to Ben Bova and he bought it straightaway. Terry Carr and Donald A. Wollheim both selected "Lya" for their competing "Best of the Year" anthologies, and it was nominated for the Nebula and the Hugo. Robert A. Silverberg had a powerful novella entitled "Born with the Dead" out that year as well, and we ended up splitting the honors. Silverberg defeated me for the Nebula, but at the 1975 worldcon in Melbourne, Australia, Ben Bova accepted the Hugo on behalf of "A Song for Lya." I was in Chicago, sound asleep. Flying to Australia was way beyond my budget at that point in my life. Besides, Silverberg had already won the Nebula and the Locus Poll, and I was dead certain he was going to make it three-for-three.

It took months for me to get my hands on the actual rocket. Bova passed through Minneapolis on the way home, and handed it off to Gordon R. Dickson, who gave it Joe Haldeman the next time he saw him, who took it to Iowa City for a while and finally delivered it to me at a con in Chicago. The next time Gardner Dozois saw me, he threw me out of the Hugo Losers Club. Robert Silverberg announced his retirement from writing science fiction. I felt guilty about that, since I was a huge fan of the work he was doing at that time ... but not so guilty that I contemplated sending him my Hugo, once I'd finally pried the damn thing away from Joe Haldeman.

By the time I wrote "This Tower of Ashes" in 1974, my life had changed markedly from what it had been a year and a half before, when I'd written "Lya." My alternative service with VISTA had come to an end, and I was directing chess tournaments on the weekends to supplement my writing income. I had started the novel that would become *Dying of the Light*, but had put it aside; it would be two years before I felt I was ready to return to it. My great love affair had ended badly, when my girlfriend dumped me in favor of one of my best friends. With that wound still raw and bleeding, I promptly fell in love again, this time with a woman with whom I had so much in common that I felt as though I'd known her all my life. Yet that relationship had only begun to bloom when it ended, almost overnight, as she fell head-over-heels for someone else.

"This Tower of Ashes" came out of all that. Ben Bova bought it for *Analog*, but ended up publishing it in the *Analog Annual*, an original anthology from Pyramid. The idea of the *Annual* was to try and reach book readers and get them interested in the magazine. Whether it did or not, I couldn't say ... but I would sooner my story had remained in *Analog* itself. One lesson I learned early in my career remains as true today as it was then: the best place for a story to get noticed is in the *magazines*. If anyone ever read "This Tower of Ashes" besides Ben Bova, you couldn't prove it by me.

"And Seven Times Never Kill Man" was written in 1974 and published in 1975. It got me my second *Analog* cover for that year (a few months earlier, a gorgeous Jack Gaughan painting had adorned the issue featuring "The Storms of Windhaven," a collaboration between me and Lisa Tuttle), this one a stunning John Schoenherr that I wish I'd bought. The Steel Angels were created as my answer to Gordy Dickson's Dorsai, although the term "Steel Angel" came from a song by Kris Kristofferson. Their god, the pale child with a sword, had an older and more dubious pedigree: he was one of the seven dark gods of the mythos I'd designed for Dr. Weird, as glimpsed in "Only Kids Are Afraid of the Dark." The title is from Kipling's *The Jungle Book,* of course, and got me almost as much praise as the story. Afterward several other writers, all Kipling fans, announced that they were annoyed they hadn't thought of it first.

"And Seven Times Never Kill Man" was nominated for a Hugo as the Best Novelette of 1974. "The Storms of Windhaven" was also up that year for Best Novella. At "Big Mac," the 1976 worldcon in Kansas City, the two stories both lost within minutes of each other (the former to Larry Niven, who promptly dropped and broke his Hugo, the latter to Roger Zelazny). The following night, aided and abetted by Gardner Dozois and armed with a jug of cheap white wine left over from someone else's party, I threw the very first Hugo Losers Party in my room at the Muehlebach Hotel. It was the best party at the convention, and in later years would become a worldcon tradition, although recently some irony-challenged smofs have insisted on renaming it "the Hugo Nominees Party."

"The Stone City" was first published in *New Voices in Science Fiction,* a hardcover anthology I edited for Macmillan in 1977, but its roots went all the way to the 1973 worldcon in Toronto. John W. Campbell, Jr., the longtime editor of *Analog* and *Astounding,* had died in 1971, and *Analog*'s publisher, Conde Nast, had established a new award in his honor, for the best new writer to enter the field during the previous two years. The first time the award was given, I was one of the finalists, along with Lisa Tuttle, George Alec Effinger, Ruth Berman, and Jerry Pournelle. The Campbell was voted by the fans and would be given out at the Toronto worldcon, with the Hugos. If not quite a Hugo itself, it was the next best thing.

My nomination took me utterly by surprise, but it thrilled and delighted me, even though I knew I had no hope of winning. Nor did I. Pournelle took home that first Campbell Award, although Effinger finished so close in the balloting that Torcon awarded him a plaque for second place, the only time I've seen that done. I have no idea where I finished, but for me, at that time, the old cliche was true: it really was an honor just to be nominated.

Afterward, at some of the parties, I told a couple of editors named Dave that there needed to be an anthology devoted to the new award, as there were for the Hugo and the Nebula. I was angling for a *sale,* of course; in 1973, I was still at the point where every one was precious. I got more than I bargained for; both editors named Dave agreed that a Campbell Awards anthology was a fine idea, but they said I had to put it together. "I've never edited an anthology," I argued. "So this will be your first," they replied.

It was. It took me a year to sell *New Voices* (to an editor named Ellen), and a couple more before all my authors delivered their promised stories, which is why the anthology showcasing the 1973 John W. Campbell Award nominees was published in 1977.

One of my writers gave me no trouble whatsoever, though. Since I was one of the finalists, I got to sell a story to myself.

There is a certain freedom that comes from knowing that the editor is not likely to reject your submission, no matter what you do. On the other hand, there is a certain amount of pressure as well. You don't want the readers thinking you just pulled some sorry old turkey out of the trunk, after all.

"The Stone City" was the story that grew from that freedom and that pressure. Though one of the core stories of my future history, this one is also a bit subversive. I wanted to season it with a little Lovecraft and a pinch of Kafka, and plant the suggestion that, when we go far enough from home, rationality, causality, and the physical laws of the universe itself begin to break down. And yet, of all the stories that I've ever written, "The Stone City" is the one that comes closest to capturing the yearnings of that boy stretched out in the summer grass beside the Kill van Kull, staring up at Orion. I don't know that I ever evoked the vastness of space or that elusive "sense of wonder" any better than I did here.

In 1977 a new science fiction magazine named *Cosmos* was launched, edited by David G. Hartwell. David asked me for a story, and I was pleased to oblige. If "Bitterblooms" has a certain chill to it, that may be because it was one of the first things I wrote after moving to Dubuque, Iowa, where the winters were even more brutal than those I'd weathered in Chicago. Over the years I have done a number of stories inspired by songs. "Bitterblooms" is one of those as well. (Anyone who can tell me the name of the song that inspired it will win... absolutely nothing.) Hartwell liked the story well enough to feature it on the cover of the fourth issue of *Cosmos*. Unfortunately the fourth issue of *Cosmos* also proved to be the last issue of *Cosmos*. (It wasn't my fault.) I had headed for Dubuque in the spring of 1976, to take a job teaching journalism at a small Catholic woman's college. Though my writing was going well, I was still wasn't earning enough from my fiction to support myself as a full-time writer, and the chess tournaments had all dried up. Also, I had married in 1975, and had a wife to put through college. The position at Clarke College seemed the perfect answer. I would only be teaching two or three hours a day, after all. Four at the most. That would leave me half of every day to write my stories. Wouldn't it?

Anyone who has ever taught is laughing very loudly right now. The truth is, the demands on a teacher's time are much greater than they appear. You are only in the classroom a few hours a day, true... but there are always lessons to be prepared, lectures to be written, papers to read, tests to grade, committees to attend, textbooks to review, students to counsel. As the journalism teacher, I was also expected to serve as faculty advisor to the school newspaper, the *Courier,* which was great fun but got me in no end of trouble with the nuns, since I refused to be a censor.

I soon found that I had neither the time nor the energy to devote to my fiction while Clarke was in session. If I wanted to get any writing done, I had to take advantage of the long summer vacation, and the shorter breaks at Christmas and Easter.

The Christmas break in the winter of 1978-79 was the most productive period I ever had during my years at Clarke. In a few short weeks, I completed three very different stories. "The Way of Cross and Dragon" was science fiction, "The Ice Dragon" was a fairy tale fantasy, and "Sandkings" married an SF background to a horror plot. All three stories are included in this retrospective. I will discuss "Sandkings" and "The Ice Dragon" when we reach them.

As for "The Way of Cross and Dragon," it is certainly my most *Catholic* story. Though I'd been raised Roman Catholic and had attended a Catholic prep school, I'd stopped practicing during my sophomore year at Northwestern. At Clarke, however, surrounded by nuns and Catholic girls, I found myself wondering what the Church might become, out among the stars.

Ben Bova had recently left *Analog* to become fiction editor for a slick new magazine called *Omni,* that published science fact as well as science fiction. "The Way of Cross and Dragon" became my first sale to this new market. The story was nominated for both the Hugo and the Nebula, lost the latter to Edward Bryant's "giAnts," but won the former as the Best Short Story of 1979 ... on the same night that "Sandkings" won for Best Novelette, at Noreascon 2 in Boston.

They were my second and third Hugos ... and since Boston was a good deal closer than Australia, I was actually present for these two. That night, I walked into the Hugo Losers Party with a rocket in each hand, grinning ear to ear, and Gardner Dozois sprayed whipped cream in my hair. I partied with my friends for half the night, and afterward went upstairs with a beautiful woman. (I was happily divorced by that time.) We made love as stars shone through the window, and bathed us in their light.

Nights don't come much better than that.

A Song for Lya

THE CITIES OF THE SHKEEN ARE OLD, OLDER FAR THAN MAN'S, AND the great rust-red metropolis that rose from their sacred hill country had proved to be the oldest of them all. The Shkeen city had no name. It needed none. Though they built cities and towns by the hundreds and the thousands, the hill city had no rivals. It was the largest in size and population, and it was alone in the sacred hills. It was their Rome, Mecca, Jerusalem; all in one. It was *the* city, and all Shkeen came to it at last, in the final days before Union.

That city had been ancient in the days before Rome fell, had been huge and sprawling when Babylon was still a dream. But there was no feel of age to it. The human eye saw only miles and miles of low, red-brick domes; small hummocks of dried mud that covered the rolling hills like a rash. Inside they were dim and nearly airless. The rooms were small and the furniture crude.

Yet it was not a grim city. Day after day it squatted in those scrubby hills, broiling under a hot sun that sat in the sky like a weary orange melon; but the city teemed with life: smells of cooking, the sounds of laughter and talk and children running, the bustle and sweat of brickmen repairing the domes, the bells of the Joined ringing in the streets. The Shkeen were a lusty and exuberant people, almost childlike. Certainly there was nothing about them that told of great age or ancient wisdom. This is a young race, said the signs, this is a culture in its infancy.

But that infancy had lasted more than fourteen thousand years.

The human city was the real infant, less than ten Earth years old. It was built on the edge of the hills, between the Shkeen metropolis and the dusty brown plains where the spaceport had gone up. In human terms, it was a beautiful city; open and airy, full of graceful archways and glistening fountains and wide boulevards lined by trees. The buildings were wrought of metal and colored plastic and native woods, and most of them were low in deference to Shkeen architecture. Most of them . . . the Administration Tower was the exception, a polished blue steel needle that split a crystal sky.

You could see it for miles in all directions. Lyanna spied it even before we landed, and we admired it from the air. The gaunt skyscrapers of Old Earth and Baldur were taller, and the fantastic webbed cities of Arachne were far more beautiful—but that slim blue Tower was still imposing enough as it rose unrivaled to its lonely dominance above the sacred hills.

The spaceport was in the shadow of the tower, easy walking distance. But they met us anyway. A low-slung scarlet aircar sat purring at the base of the ramp as we disembarked, with a driver lounging against the stick. Dino Valcarenghi stood next to it, leaning on the door and talking to an aide.

Valcarenghi was the planetary administrator, the boy wonder of the sector. Young, of course, but I'd known that. Short, and good-looking, in a dark, intense way, with black hair that curled thickly against his head and an easy, genial smile.

He flashed us that smile then, when we stepped off the ramp, and reached to shake hands. "Hi," he began, "I'm glad to see you." There was no nonsense with formal introductions. He knew who we were, and we knew who he was, and Valcarenghi wasn't the kind of man who put much stock in ritual.

Lyanna took his hand lightly in hers, and gave him her vampire look: big, dark eyes opened wide and staring, thin mouth lifted in a tiny faint smile. She's a small girl, almost waiflike, with short brown hair and a child's figure. She can look very fragile, very helpless. When she wants to. But she rattles people with that look. If they know Lya's a telepath they figure she's poking around amid their innermost secrets. Actually she's playing with them. When Lyanna is *really* reading, her whole body goes stiff and you can almost see her tremble. And those big, soul-sucking eyes get narrow and hard and opaque.

But not many people know that, so they squirm under her vampire eyes and look the other way and hurry to release her hand. Not Valcarenghi, though. He just smiled and stared back, then moved on to me.

I was reading when I took his hand—my standard operating procedure. Also a bad habit, I guess, since it's put some promising friendships into an early grave. My talent isn't equal to Lya's. But it's not as demanding either. I reach emotions. Valcarenghi's geniality came through strong and genuine. With nothing behind it, or at least nothing that was close enough to the surface for me to catch.

We also shook hands with the aide, a middle-aged blond stork named Nelson Gourlay. Then Valcarenghi ushered everybody into the aircar and we took off. "I imagine you're tired," he said after we were airborne, "so we'll save the tour of the city and head straight for the Tower. Nelse will show you your quarters, then you can join us for a drink, and we'll talk over the problem. You've read the materials we sent?"

"Yes," I said. Lya nodded. "Interesting background, but I'm not sure why we're here."

"We'll get to that soon enough," Valcarenghi replied. "I ought to be letting you enjoy the scenery." He gestured toward the window, smiled, and fell silent.

So Lya and I enjoyed the scenery, or as much as we could enjoy during the five-minute flight from spaceport to Tower. The aircar was whisking down the main street at treetop level, stirring up a breeze that whipped the thin branches as we went by. It was cool and dark in the interior of the car, but outside the Shkeen sun was riding toward noon, and you could see the heat waves shimmering from the pavement. The population must have been inside huddled around their air conditioners, because we saw very little traffic.

We got out near the main entrance to the Tower and walked through a huge, sparkling-clean lobby. Valcarenghi left us then to talk to some underlings. Gourlay led us into one of the tubes and we shot up fifty floors. Then we waltzed past a secretary into another, private tube, and climbed some more.

Our rooms were lovely, carpeted in cool green and paneled with wood. There was a complete library there, mostly Earth classics bound in synthaleather, with a few novels from Baldur, our home world. Somebody had been researching our tastes. One of the walls of the bedroom was tinted glass, giving a panoramic view of the city far below us, with a control that could darken it for sleeping.

Gourlay showed it to us dutifully, like a dour bellhop. I read him briefly though, and found no resentment. He was nervous, but only slightly. There was honest affection there for someone. Us? Valcarenghi?

Lya sat down on one of the twin beds. "Is someone bringing our luggage?" she asked.

Gourlay nodded. "You'll be well taken care of," he said. "Anything you want, ask."

"Don't worry, we will," I said. I dropped to the second bed, and gestured Gourlay to a chair. "How long have you been here?"

"Six years," he said, taking the chair gratefully and sprawling out all over it. "I'm one of the veterans. I've worked under four administrators now. Dino, and Stuart before him, and Gustaffson before him. I was even under Rockwood a few months."

Lya perked up, crossing her legs under her and leaning forward. "That was all Rockwood lasted, wasn't it?"

"Right," Gourlay said. "He didn't like the planet, took a quick demotion to assistant administrator someplace else. I didn't care much, to tell the truth. He was the nervous type, always giving orders to prove who was boss."

"And Valcarenghi?" I asked.

Gourlay made a smile look like a yawn. "Dino? Dino's OK, the best of the lot. He's good, knows he's good. He's only been here two months, but he's gotten a lot done, and he's made a lot of friends. He treats the staff like people, calls everybody by his first name, all that stuff. People like that."

I was reading, and I read sincerity. It was Valcarenghi that Gourlay was affectionate toward, then. He believed what he was saying.

I had more questions, but I didn't get to ask them. Gourlay got up suddenly. "I really shouldn't stay," he said. "You want to rest, right? Come up to the top in about two hours and we'll go over things with you. You know where the tube is?"

We nodded, and Gourlay left. I turned to Lyanna. "What do you think?"

She lay back on the bed and considered the ceiling. "I don't know," she said. "I wasn't reading. I wonder why they've had so many administrators. And why they wanted us."

"We're Talented," I said, smiling. With the capital, yes. Lyanna and I have been tested and registered as psi Talents, and we have the licenses to prove it.

"Uh-huh," she said, turning on her side and smiling back at me. Not her vampire half-smile this time. Her sexy little girl smile.

"Valcarenghi wants us to get some rest," I said. "It's probably not a bad idea."

Lya bounced out of bed. "OK," she said, "but these twins have got to go."

"We could push them together."

She smiled again. We pushed them together.

And we *did* get some sleep. Eventually.

Our luggage was outside the door when we woke. We changed into fresh clothes, old casual stuff, counting on Valcarenghi's notorious lack of pomp. The tube took us to the top of the Tower.

THE OFFICE OF THE PLANETARY ADMINISTRATOR WAS HARDLY AN OFFICE. There was no desk, none of the usual trappings. Just a bar and lush blue carpets that swallowed us ankle-high, and six or seven scattered chairs. Plus lots of space and sunlight, with Shkea laid out at our feet beyond the tinted glass. All four walls this time.

Valcarenghi and Gourlay were waiting for us, and Valcarenghi did the bartending chores personally. I didn't recognize the beverage, but it was cool and spicy and aromatic, with a real sting to it. I sipped it gratefully. For some reason I felt I needed a lift.

"Shkeen wine," Valcarenghi said, smiling, in answer to an unasked question. "They've got a name for it, but I can't pronounce it yet. But give me time. I've only been here two months, and the language is rough."

"You're learning Shkeen?" Lya asked, surprised. I knew why. Shkeen is rough on human tongues, but the natives learned Terran with stunning ease. Most people accept that happily, and just forgot about the difficulties of cracking the alien language.

"It gives me an insight into the way they think," Valcarenghi said. "At least that's the theory." He smiled.

I read him again, although it was more difficult. Physical contact makes things sharper. Again, I got a simple emotion, close to the surface—pride this time. With pleasure mixed in. I chalked that up to the wine. Nothing beneath.

"However you pronounce the drink, I like it," I said.

"The Shkeen produce a wide variety of liquors and foodstuffs," Gourlay put in. "We've cleared many for export already, and we're checking others. Market should be good."

"You'll have a chance to sample more of the local produce this evening." Valcarenghi said. "I've set up a tour of the city, with a stop or two in Shkeentown. For a settlement of our size, our nightlife is fairly interesting. I'll be your guide."

"Sounds good," I said. Lya was smiling too. A tour was unusually considerate. Most Normals feel uneasy around Talents, so they rush us in to do whatever they want done, then rush us out again as quickly as possible. They certainly don't socialize with us.

"Now—the problem," Valcarenghi said, lowering his drink and leaning forward in the chair. "You read about the Cult of the Union?"

"A Shkeen religion," Lya said.

"*The* Shkeen religion," corrected Valcarenghi. "Every one of them is a believer. This is a planet without heretics."

"We read the materials you sent on it," Lya said. "Along with everything else."

"What do you think?"

I shrugged. "Grim. Primitive. But no more than any number of others I've read about. The Shkeen aren't very advanced, after all. There were religions on Old Earth that included human sacrifice."

Valcarenghi shook his head, and looked toward Gourlay.

"No, you don't understand," Gourlay started, putting his drink down on the carpet. "I've been studying their religion for six years. It's like no other in history. Nothing on Old Earth like it, no sir. Nor in any other race we've encountered.

"And Union, well, it's wrong to compare it to human sacrifice, just wrong. The Old Earth religions sacrificed one or two unwilling victims to appease their gods. Killed a handful to get mercy for the millions. And the handful generally protested. The Shkeen don't work it that way. The Greeshka takes *everyone*. And they go willingly. Like lemmings they march off to the caves to be eaten alive by those parasites. *Every* Shkeen is Joined at forty, and goes to Final Union before he's fifty."

I was confused. "All right," I said. "I see the distinction, I guess. But so what? Is this the problem? I imagine that Union is rough on the Shkeen, but that's their business. Their religion is no worse than the ritual cannibalism of the Hrangans, is it?"

Valcarenghi finished his drink and got up, heading for the bar. As he poured himself a refill, he said, almost casually, "As far as I know, Hrangan cannibalism has claimed no human converts."

Lya looked startled. I felt startled. I sat up and stared. "What?"

Valcarenghi headed back to his seat, glass in hand. "Human converts have been joining the Cult of the Union. Dozens of them are already Joined. None of them has achieved full Union yet, but that's only a question of time." He sat down, and looked at Gourlay. So did we.

The gangling blond aide picked up the narrative. "The first convert was about seven years ago. Nearly a year before I got here, two and a half after Shkea was discovered and the settlement built. Guy named Magly. Psipsych, worked closely with the Shkeen. He was it for two years. Then another in '08, more the next year. And the rate's been climbing ever since. There was one big one. Phil Gustaffson."

Lya blinked. "The planetary administrator?"

"The same," said Gourlay. "We've had a lot of administrators. Gustaffson came in after Rockwood couldn't stand it. He was a big, gruff old guy. Everybody loved him. He'd lost his wife and kids on his last assignment, but you'd never have known it. He was always hearty, full of fun. Well, he got interested in the Shkeen religion, started talking to them. Talked to Magly and some of the other converts too. Even went to see a Greeshka. That shook him up real bad for a while. But finally he got over it, went back to his researches. I worked with him, but I never guessed what he had in mind. A little over a year ago, he converted. He's Joined now. Nobody's ever been accepted that fast. I hear talk in Shkeentown that he may even be admitted to Final Union, rushed right in. Well, Phil was administrator here longer than anybody else. People liked him, and when he went over, a lot of his friends followed. The rate's way up now."

"Not quite one percent, and rising," Valcarenghi said. "That seems low, but remember what it means. One percent of the people in my settlement are choosing a religion that includes a very unpleasant form of suicide."

Lya looked from him to Gourlay and back again. "Why hasn't this been reported?"

"It should have been," Valcarenghi said, "but Stuart succeeded Gustaffson, and he was scared stiff of a scandal. There's no law against humans adopting an alien religion, so Stuart defined it as a nonproblem. He reported the conversion rate routinely, and nobody higher up ever bothered to make the correlation and remember just what all these people were converting *to*."

I finished my drink, set it down. "Go on," I said to Valcarenghi.

"I define the situation as a problem," he said. "I don't care how few people are involved, the idea that human beings would allow the Greeshka to consume them alarms me. I've had a team of psychs on it since I took over, but they're getting nowhere. I needed Talent. I want you two to find out why these people are converting. Then I'll be able to deal with the situation."

The problem was strange, but the assignment seemed straightforward enough. I read Valcarenghi to be sure. His emotions were a bit more complex this time, but not much.

Confidence above all: he was sure we could handle the problem. There was honest concern there, but no fear, and not even a hint of deception. Again, I couldn't catch anything below the surface. Valcarenghi kept his hidden turmoil well hidden, if he had any.

I glanced at Lyanna. She was sitting awkwardly in her chair, and her fingers were wrapped very tightly around her wine glass. Reading. Then she loosened up and looked my way and nodded.

"All right," I said. "I think we can do it."

Valcarenghi smiled. "That I never doubted," he said. "It was only a question of whether you *would*. But enough of business for tonight. I've promised you a night on the town, and I always try to deliver on my promises. I'll meet you downstairs in the lobby in a half hour."

LYA AND I CHANGED INTO SOMETHING MORE FORMAL BACK IN OUR room. I picked a dark blue tunic, with white slacks and a matching mesh scarf. Not the height of fashion, but I was hoping that Shkea would be several months behind the times. Lya slipped into a silky white skintight with a tracery of thin blue lines that flowed over her in sensuous patterns in response to her body heat. The lines were definitely lecherous, accentuating her thin figure with a singleminded determination. A blue raincape completed the outfit.

"Valcarenghi's funny," she said as she fastened it.

"Oh?" I was struggling with the sealseam on my tunic, which refused to seal. "You catch something when you read him?"

"No," she said. She finished attaching the cape and admired herself in the mirror. Then she spun toward me, the cape swirling behind her. "That's it. He was thinking what he was saying. Oh, variations in the wording, of course, but nothing important. His mind was on what we were discussing, and behind that there was only a wall." She smiled. "Didn't get a single one of his deep dark secrets."

I finally conquered the sealseam. "Tsk," I said. "Well, you get another chance tonight."

That got me a grimace. "The hell I do. I don't read people on off-time. It isn't fair. Besides, it's such a strain. I wish I could catch thoughts as easily as you do feelings."

"The price of Talent," I said. "You're more Talented, your price is higher." I rummaged in our luggage for a raincape, but I didn't find anything that went well, so I decided not to wear one. Capes were out, anyway. "I didn't get much on Valcarenghi either. You could have told as much by watching his face. He must be a very disciplined mind. But I'll forgive him. He serves good wine."

Lya nodded. "Right! That stuff did me good. Got rid of the headache I woke up with."

"The altitude," I suggested. We headed for the door.

The lobby was deserted, but Valcarenghi didn't keep us waiting long. This time he drove his own aircar, a battered black job that had evidently been with him for a while. Gourlay wasn't the sociable type, but Valcarenghi had a woman with him, a stunning auburn-haired vision named Laurie Blackburn. She was even younger than Valcarenghi—mid-twenties, by the look of her.

It was sunset when we took off. The whole far horizon was a gorgeous tapestry in red and orange, and a cool breeze was blowing in from the plains. Valcarenghi left the coolers off and opened the car windows, and we watched the city darken into twilight as we drove.

Dinner was at a plush restaurant with Baldurian decor—to make us feel comfortable, I guessed. The food, however, was very cosmopolitan. The spices, the herbs, the *style* of cooking were all Baldur. The meats and vegetables were native. It made for an interesting combination. Valcarenghi ordered for all four of us, and we wound up sampling about a dozen different dishes. My favorite was a tiny Shkeen bird that they cooked in sourtang sauce. There wasn't very much of it, but what there was tasted great. We also polished off three bottles of wine during the meal: more of the Shkeen stuff we'd sampled that afternoon, a flask of chilled Veltaar from Baldur, and some real Old Earth Burgundy.

The talk warmed up quickly; Valcarenghi was a born storyteller and an equally good listener. Eventually, of course, the conversation got around to Shkea and Shkeen. Laurie led it there. She'd been on Shkea for about six months, working toward an advanced degree in extee anthropology. She was trying to discover why the Shkeen civilization had remained frozen for so many millennia.

"They're older than we are, you know," she told us. "They had cities before men were using tools. It should have been space-traveling Shkeen that stumbled on primitive men, not the other way around."

"Aren't there theories on that already?" I asked.

"Yes, but none of them are universally accepted," she said. "Cullen cites a lack of heavy metals, for example. A factor, but is it the *whole* answer? Von Hamrin claims the Shkeen didn't get enough competition. No big carnivores on the planet, so there was nothing to breed aggressiveness into the race. But he's come under a lot of fire. Shkea isn't all *that* idyllic; if it were, the Shkeen never would have reached their present level. Besides, what's the Greeshka if not a carnivore? It *eats* them, doesn't it?"

"What do you think?" Lya asked.

"I think it had something to do with the religion, but I haven't worked it all out yet. Dino's helping me talk to people and the Shkeen are open enough, but research isn't easy." She stopped suddenly and looked at Lya hard. "For me, anyway. I imagine it'd be easier for you."

We'd heard that before. Normals often figure that Talents have unfair advantages, which is perfectly understandable. We do. But Laurie wasn't resentful. She delivered her statement in a wistful, speculative tone, instead of etching it in verbal acid.

Valcarenghi leaned over and put an arm around her. "Hey," he said. "Enough shoptalk. Robb and Lya shouldn't be worrying about the Shkeen until tomorrow."

Laurie looked at him, and smiled tentatively. "OK," she said lightly. "I get carried away. Sorry."

"That's OK," I told her. "It's an interesting subject. Give us a day and we'll probably be getting enthusiastic too."

Lya nodded agreement, and added that Laurie would be the first to know if our work turned up anything that would support her theory. I was hardly listening. I know it's not polite to read Normals when you're out with them socially, but there are times I can't resist. Valcarenghi had his arm around Laurie and had pulled her toward him gently. I was curious.

So I took a quick, guilty reading. He was very high—slightly drunk, I guess, and feeling very confident and protective. The master of the situation. But Laurie was a jumble—uncertainty, repressed anger, a vague fading hint of fright. And love, confused but very strong. I doubted that it was for me or Lya. She loved Valcarenghi.

I reached under the table, searching for Lya's hand, and found her knee. I squeezed it gently and she looked at me and smiled. She wasn't reading, which was good. It bothered me that Laurie loved Valcarenghi, though I didn't know why, and I was just as glad that Lya didn't see my discontent.

We finished off the last of the wine in short order, and Valcarenghi took care of the whole bill. Then he rose. "Onward!" he announced. "The night is fresh, and we've got visits to make."

So we made visits. No holoshows or anything that drab, although the city had its share of theaters. A casino was next on the list. Gambling was legal on Shkea, of course, and Valcarenghi would have legalized it if it weren't. He supplied the chips and I lost some for him, as did Laurie. Lya was barred from playing; her Talent was too strong. Valcarenghi won big; he was a superb mindspin player, and pretty good at the traditional games too.

Then came a bar. More drinks, plus local entertainment which was better than I would have expected.

It was pitch-black when we got out, and I assumed that the expedition was nearing its end. Valcarenghi surprised us. When we got back to the car, he reached under the controls, pulled out a box of sober-ups, and passed them around.

"Hey," I said. "You're driving. Why do I need this? I just barely got up here."

"I'm about to take you to a genuine Shkeen cultural event, Robb," he said. "I don't want you making rude comments or throwing up on the natives. Take your pill."

I took my pill, and the buzz in my head began to fade. Valcarenghi already had the car airborne. I leaned back and put my arm around Lya, and she rested her head on my shoulder. "Where are we going?" I asked.

"Shkeentown," he replied, never looking back, "to their Great Hall. There's a Gathering tonight, and I figured you'd be interested."

"It will be in Shkeen, of course," Laurie said, "but Dino can translate for you. I know a little of the language too, and I'll fill in whatever he misses."

Lya looked excited. We'd read about Gatherings, of course, but we hardly expected go see one on our first day on Shkea. The Gatherings were a species of religious rite; a mass confessional of sorts for pilgrims who were about to be admitted to the ranks of the Joined. Pilgrims swelled the hill city daily, but Gatherings were conducted only three or four times a year when the numbers of those-about-to-be-Joined climbed high enough.

The aircar streaked almost soundlessly through the brightly lit settlement, passing huge fountains that danced with a dozen colors and pretty ornamental arches that flowed like liquid fire. A few other cars were airborne, and here and there we flew above pedestrians strolling the city's broad malls. But most people were inside, and light and music flooded from many of the homes we passed.

Then, abruptly, the character of the city began to change. The level ground began to roll and heave, hills rose before us and then behind us, and the lights vanished. Below, the malls gave way to unlit roads of crushed stone and dust, and the domes of glass and metal done in fashionable mock-Shkeen yielded to their older brick brothers. The Shkeen city was quieter than its human counterpart; most of the houses were darkly silent.

Then, ahead of us, a hummock appeared that was larger than the others—almost a hill in itself, with a big arched door and a series of slitlike windows. And light leaked from this one, and noise, and there were Shkeen outside.

I suddenly realized that, although I'd been on Shkea for nearly a day, this was the first sight I'd caught of the Shkeen. Not that I could see them all that clearly from an aircar at night. But I did see them. They were smaller than men—the tallest was around five feet—with big eyes and long arms. That was all I could tell from above.

Valcarenghi put the car down alongside the Great Hall, and we piled out. Shkeen were trickling through the arch from several directions, but most of them were already inside. We joined the trickle, and nobody even looked twice at us, except for one character who hailed Valcarenghi in a thin, squeaky voice and called him Dino. He had friends even here.

The interior was one huge room, with a great crude platform built in the center and an immense crowd of Shkeen circling it. The only light was from torches that were stuck in grooves along the walls and on high poles surrounding the platform. Someone was speaking, and every one of those great, bulging eyes was turned his way. We four were the only humans in the Hall.

The speaker, outlined brightly by the torches, was a fat, middle-aged Shkeen who moved his arms slowly, almost hypnotically, as he talked. His speech was a series of whistles, wheezes, and grunts, so I didn't listen very closely. He was much too far away to read. I was reduced to studying his appearance, and that of other Shkeen near me. All of them were hairless, as far as I could see, with softish-looking orange skin that was creased by a thousand tiny wrinkles. They wore simple shifts of crude, multicolored cloth, and I had difficulty telling male from female.

Valcarenghi leaned over toward me and whispered, careful to keep his voice low. "The speaker is a farmer," he said. "He's telling the crowd how far he's come, and some of the hardships of his life."

I looked around. Valcarenghi's whisper was the only sound in the place. Everyone else was dead quiet, eyes riveted on the platform, scarcely breathing. "He's saying that he has four brothers," Valcarenghi told me. "Two have gone on to Final Union, one is among the Joined. The other is younger than himself, and now owns the farm." He frowned. "The speaker will never see his farm again," he said, more loudly, "but he's happy about it."

"Bad crops?" asked Lya, smiling irreverently. She'd been listening to the same whisper. I gave her a stern look.

The Shkeen went on. Valcarenghi stumbled after him. "Now he's telling his crimes, all the things he's done that he's ashamed of, his blackest soul-secrets. He's had a sharp tongue at times, he's vain, once he actually struck his younger brother. Now he speaks of his wife, and the other women he has known. He has betrayed her many times, copulating with others. As a boy, he mated with animals for he feared females. In recent years he has grown incapable, and his brother has serviced his wife."

On and on and on it went, in incredible detail, detail that was both startling and frightening. No intimacy went untold, no secret was left undisturbed. I stood and listened to Valcarenghi's whispers, shocked at first, finally growing bored with the squalor of it all. I began to get restless. I wondered briefly if I knew any human half so well as I now knew this great fat Shkeen. Then I wondered whether Lyanna, with her Talent, knew anyone half so well. It was almost as if the speaker wanted all of us to live through his life right here and now.

His speech lasted for what seemed hours, but finally it began to wind up. "He speaks now of Union," Valcarenghi whispered. "He will be Joined, he is joyful about it, he has craved it for so long. His misery is at an end, his aloneness will cease, soon he shall walk the streets of the sacred city and peal his joy with the bells. And then Final Union, in the years to come. He will be with his brothers in the afterlife."

"No, Dino." This whisper was Laurie. "Quit wrapping human phrases around what he says. He will be his brothers, he says. The phrase also implies they will be him."

Valcarenghi smiled. "OK, Laurie. If you say so . . ."

Suddenly the fat farmer was gone from the platform. The crowd rustled, and another figure took his place: much shorter, wrinkled excessively, one eye a great gaping hole. He began to speak, haltingly at first, then with greater skill.

"This one is a brickman, he has worked many domes, he lives in the sacred city. His eye was lost many years ago, when he fell from a dome and a sharp stick poked into him. The pain was very great, but he returned to work within a year, he did not beg for premature Union, he was very brave, he is proud of his courage. He has a wife, but they have never had offspring, he is sad of that, he cannot talk to his wife easily, they are apart even when together and she weeps at night, he is sad of that too, but he has never hurt her and . . ."

It went on for hours again. My restlessness stirred again, but I cracked down on it—this was too important. I let myself get lost in Valcarenghi's narration, and the story of the one-eyed Shkeen. Before long, I was riveted as closely to the tale as the aliens around me. It was hot and stuffy and all but airless in the dome, and my tunic was getting sooty and soaked by sweat, some of it from the creatures who pressed around me. But I hardly noticed.

The second speaker ended as had the first, with a long praise of the joy of being Joined and the coming of Final Union. Toward the end, I hardly even needed Valcarenghi's translation—I could hear the happiness in the voice of the Shkeen, and see it in his trembling figure. Or maybe I was reading, unconsciously. But I can't read at that distance—unless the target is emoting very hard.

A third speaker ascended the platform, and spoke in a voice louder than the others. Valcarenghi kept pace. "A woman this time," he said. "She has carried eight children for her man, she has four sisters and three brothers, she has farmed all her life, she . . ."

Suddenly her speech seemed to peak, and she ended a long sequence with several sharp, high whistles. Then she fell silent. The crowd, as one, began to respond with whistles of their own. An eerie, echoing music filled the Great Hall, and the Shkeen around us all began to sway and whistle. The woman looked out at the scene from a bent and broken position.

Valcarenghi started to translate, but he stumbled over something. Laurie cut in before he could backtrack. "She has now told them of great tragedy," she whispered. "They whistle to show their grief, their oneness with her pain."

"Sympathy, yes," said Valcarenghi, taking over again. "When she was young, her brother grew ill, and seemed to be dying. Her parents told her to take him to the sacred hills, for they could not leave the younger children. But she shattered a wheel on her cart through careless driving, and her brother died upon the plains. He perished without Union. She blames herself."

The Shkeen had begun again. Laurie began to translate, leaning close to us and using a soft whisper. "Her brother died, she is saying again. She faulted him, denied him Union, now he is sundered and alone and gone without . . . without . . ."

"Afterlife," said Valcarenghi. "Without afterlife."

"I'm not sure that's entirely right," Laurie said. "That concept is . . ."

Valcarenghi waved her silent. "Listen," he said. He continued to translate.

We listened to her story, told in Valcarenghi's increasingly hoarse whisper. She spoke longest of all, and her story was the grimmest of the three. When she finished, she too was replaced. But Valcarenghi put a hand on my shoulder and beckoned toward the exit.

The cool night air hit like ice water, and I suddenly realized that I was drenched with sweat. Valcarenghi walked quickly toward the car. Behind us, the speaking was still in progress, and the Shkeen showed no signs of tiring.

"Gatherings go on for days, sometimes weeks," Laurie told us as we climbed inside the aircar. "The Shkeen listen in shifts, more or less—they try terribly to hear every word, but exhaustion gets to them sooner or later and they retire for brief rests, then return for more. It is a great honor to last through an entire Gathering without sleep."

Valcarenghi shot us aloft. "I'm going to try that someday," he said. "I've never attended for more than a couple of hours, but I think I could make it if I fortified myself with drugs. We'll get more understanding between human and Shkeen if we participate more fully in their rituals."

"Oh," I said. "Maybe Gustaffson felt the same way."

Valcarenghi laughed lightly. "Yes, well, I don't intend to participate *that* fully."

The trip home was a tired silence. I'd lost track of time but my body insisted that it was almost dawn. Lya, curled up under my arm, looked drained and empty and only half-awake. I felt the same way.

We left the aircar in front of the Tower and took the tubes up. I was past thinking. Sleep came very, very quickly.

I dreamed that night. A good dream, I think, but it faded with the coming of the light, leaving me empty and feeling cheated. I lay there, after waking, with my arm around Lya and my eyes on the ceiling, trying to recall what the dream had been about. But nothing came.

Instead, I found myself thinking about the Gathering, running it through again in my head. Finally I disentangled myself and climbed out of bed. We'd darkened the glass, so the room was still pitch-black. But I found the controls easily enough, and let through a trickle of late morning light.

Lya mumbled some sort of sleepy protest and rolled over, but made no effort to get up. I left her alone in the bedroom and went out to our library, looking for a book on the Shkeen—something with a little more detail than the material we'd been sent. No luck. The library was meant for recreation, not research.

I found a viewscreen and punched up to Valcarenghi's office. Gourlay answered. "Hello," he said. "Dino figured you'd be calling. He's not here right now. He's out arbitrating a trade contract. What do you need?"

"Books," I said, my voice still a little sleepy. "Something on the Shkeen."

"That I can't do," Gourlay said. "Are none, really. Lots of papers and studies and monographs, but no full-fledged books. I'm going to write one, but I haven't gotten to it yet. Dino figured I could be your resource, I guess."

"Oh."

"Got any questions?"

I searched for a question, found none. "Not really," I said, shrugging. "I just wanted general background, maybe some more information on Gatherings."

"I can talk to you about that later," Gourlay said. "Dino figured you'd want to get to work today. We can bring people to the Tower, if you'd like, or you can get out to them."

"We'll go out," I said quickly. "Bringing subjects in for interviews fouls up everything. They get all anxious, and that covers up any emotions I might want to read, and they think on different things too, so Lyanna has trouble."

"Fine," said Gourlay. "Dino put an aircar at your disposal. Pick it up down in the lobby. Also, they'll have some keys for you, so you can come straight up here in the office without bothering with the secretaries and all."

"Thanks," I said. "Talk to you later." I flicked off the viewscreen and walked back to the bedroom.

Lya was sitting up, the covers around her waist. I sat down next to her and kissed her. She smiled, but didn't respond. "Hey," I said. "What's wrong?"

"Headache," she replied. "I thought sober-ups were supposed to get rid of hangovers."

"That's the theory. Mine worked pretty well." I went to the closet and began looking for something to wear. "We should have headache pills around here someplace. I'm sure Dino wouldn't forget anything that obvious."

"Umpf. Yes. Throw me some clothes."

I grabbed one of her coveralls and tossed it across the room. Lya stood up and slipped into it while I dressed, then went off to the washroom.

"Better," she said. "You're right, he didn't forget medicines."

"He's the thorough sort."

She smiled. "I guess. Laurie knows the language better, though. I read her. Dino made a couple of mistakes in that translation last night."

I'd guessed at something like that. No discredit to Valcarenghi; he was working on a four-month handicap, from what they said. I nodded. "Read anything else?"

"No. I tried to get those speakers, but the distance was too much." She came up and took my hand. "Where are we going today?"

"Shkeentown," I said. "Let's try to find some of these Joined. I didn't notice any at the Gathering."

"No. Those things are for Shkeen about-to-be-Joined."

"So I hear. Let's go."

We went. We stopped at the fourth level for a late breakfast in the

Tower cafeteria, then got our aircar pointed out to us by a man in the lobby. A sporty green four-seater, very common, very inconspicuous.

I didn't take the aircar all the way into the Shkeen city, figuring we'd get more of the feel of the place if we went through on foot. So I dropped down just beyond the first range of hills, and we walked.

———

THE HUMAN CITY HAD SEEMED ALMOST EMPTY, BUT SHKEENTOWN lived. The crushed-rock streets were full of aliens, hustling back and forth busily, carrying loads of bricks and baskets of fruit and clothing. There were children everywhere, most of them naked; fat balls of orange energy that ran around us in circles, whistling and grunting and grinning, tugging at us every once in a while. The kids looked different from the adults. They had a few patches of reddish hair, for one thing, and their skins were still smooth and unwrinkled. They were the only ones who really paid any attention to us. The adult Shkeen just went about their business, and gave us an occasional friendly smile. Humans were obviously not all that uncommon in the streets of Shkeentown.

Most of the traffic was on foot, but small wooden carts were also common. The Shkeen draft animal looked like a big green dog that was about to be sick. They were strapped to the carts in pairs, and they whined constantly as they pulled. So, naturally, men called them whiners. In addition to whining, they also defecated constantly. That, with odors from the food peddled in baskets and the Shkeen themselves, gave the city a definite pungency.

There was noise too, a constant clamor. Kids whistling. Shkeen talking loudly with grunts and whimpers and squeaks, whiners whining, and their carts rattling over the rocks. Lya and I walked through it all silently, hand in hand, watching and listening and smelling and . . . reading.

I was wide open when I entered Shkeentown, letting everything wash over me as I walked, unfocused but receptive. I was the center of a small bubble of emotion—feelings rushed up at me as Shkeen approached, faded as they walked away, circled around and around with the dancing children. I swam in a sea of impressions. And it startled me.

It startled me because it was all so familiar. I'd read aliens before.

Sometimes it was difficult, sometimes it was easy, but it was never pleasant. The Hrangans have sour minds, rank with hate and bitterness, and I feel unclean when I come out. The Fyndii feel emotions so palely that I can scarcely read them at all. The Damoosh are . . . *different*. I read them strongly, but I can't find names for the feelings I read.

But the Shkeen—it was like walking down a street on Baldur. No, wait—more like one of the Lost Colonies, when a human settlement has fallen back into barbarism and forgotten its origins. Human emotions rage there, primal and strong and real, but less sophisticated than on Old Earth or Baldur. The Shkeen were like that: primitive, maybe, but very understandable. I read joy and sorrow, envy, anger, whimsy, bitterness, yearning, pain. The same heady mixture that engulfs me everywhere, when I open myself to it.

Lya was reading too. I felt her hand tense in mine. After a while, it softened again. I turned to her, and she saw the question in my eyes.

"They're people," she said. "They're like us."

I nodded. "Parallel evolution, maybe. Shkea might be an older Earth, with a few minor differences. But you're right. They're more human than any other race we've encountered in space." I considered that. "Does that answer Dino's question? If they're like us, it follows that their religion would be more appealing than a *really* alien one."

"No, Robb," Lya said. "I don't think so. Just the reverse. If they're like us, it doesn't make sense that *they'd* go off so willingly to die. See?"

She was right, of course. There was nothing suicidal in the emotions I'd read, nothing unstable, nothing really abnormal. Yet every one of the Shkeen went off to Final Union in the end.

"We should focus on somebody," I said. "This blend of thought isn't getting us anywhere." I looked around to find a subject, but just then I heard the bells begin.

They were off to the left somewhere, nearly lost in the city's gentle roar. I tugged Lya by the hand, and we ran down the street to find them, turning left at the first gap in the orderly row of domes.

The bells were still ahead, and we kept running, cutting through what must have been somebody's yard, and climbing over a low bush-fence that bristled with sweethorns. Beyond that was another yard, a dung-pit, more domes, and finally a street. It was there we found the bell-ringers.

There were four of them, all Joined, wearing long gowns of bright red fabric that trailed in the dust, with great bronze bells in either hand. They rang the bells constantly, their long arms swinging back and forth, the sharp, clanging notes filling the street. All four were elderly, as Shkeen go—hairless and pinched up with a million tiny wrinkles. But they smiled very widely, and the younger Shkeen that passed smiled at them.

On their heads rode the Greeshka.

I'd expected to find the sight hideous. I didn't. It was faintly disquieting, but only because I knew what it meant. The parasites were bright blobs of crimson goo, ranging in size from a pulsing wart on the back of one Shkeen skull to a great sheet of dripping, moving red that covered the head and shoulders of the smallest like a living cowl. The Greeshka lived by sharing the nutrients in the Shkeen bloodstream, I knew.

And also by slowly—oh so slowly—consuming its host.

Lya and I stopped a few yards from them, and watched them ring. Her face was solemn, and I think mine was. All of the others were smiling, and the songs that the bells sang were songs of joy. I squeezed Lyanna's hand tightly. "Read," I whispered.

We read.

Me: I read bells. Not the sound of bells, no, no, but the *feel* of bells, the *emotion* of bells, the bright clanging joy, the hooting-shouting-ringing loudness, the song of the Joined, the togetherness and the sharing of it all. I read what the Joined felt as they pealed their bells, their happiness and anticipation, their ecstasy in telling others of their clamorous contentment. And I read love, coming from them in great hot waves, passionate possessive love of a man and woman together, not the weak watery affection of the human who "loves" his brothers. This was real and fervent and it burned almost as it washed over me and surrounded me. They loved themselves, and they loved all Shkeen, and they loved the Greeshka, and they loved each other, and they loved us. They loved us. They loved *me*, as hotly and wildly as Lya loved me. And with love I read belonging, and sharing. They four were all apart, all distinct, but they thought as one almost, and they belonged to each other, and they belonged to the Greeshka, and they were all *together* and linked although each was still himself and none could read the others as I read them.

And Lyanna? I reeled back from them, and shut myself off, and looked at Lya. She was white-faced, but smiling. "They're beautiful," she said, her voice very small and soft and wondering. Drenched in love, I still remembered how much I loved *her,* and how I was a part of her and her of me.

"What—what did you read?" I asked, my voice fighting the continued clangor of the bells.

She shook her head, as if to clear it. "They love us," she said. "You must know that, but oh, I felt it, they *do* love us. And it's so *deep.* Below that love there's more love, and below that more, and on and on forever. Their minds are so deep, so open. I don't think I've ever read a human that deeply. Everything is right at the surface, right there, their whole lives and all their dreams and feelings and memories and oh—I just took it in, swept it up with a reading, a glance. With men, with humans, it's so much work, I have to dig, I have to fight, and even then I don't get down very far. You know, Robb, you know. Oh, *Robb!*" And she came to me and pressed tight against me, and I held her in my arms. The torrent of feeling that had washed over me must have been a tidal wave for her. Her Talent was broader and deeper than mine, and now she was shaken. I read her as she clutched me, and I read love, great love, and wonder and happiness, but also fear, nervous fear swirling through it all.

Around us, the ringing suddenly stopped. The bells, one by one, ceased to swing, and the four Joined stood in silence for a brief second. One of the other Shkeen nearby came up to them with a huge, cloth-covered basket. The smallest of the Joined threw back the cloth, and the aroma of hot meatrolls rose in the street. Each of the Joined took several from the basket, and before long they were all crunching away happily, and the owner of the rolls was grinning at them. Another Shkeen, a small nude girl, ran up and offered them a flask of water, and they passed it around without comment.

"What's going on?" I asked Lya. Then, even before she told me, I remembered. Something from the literature that Valcarenghi had sent. The Joined did no work. Forty Earth-years they lived and toiled, but from First Joining to Final Union there was only joy and music, and they wandered the streets and rang their bells and talked and sang, and other Shkeen gave them food and drink. It was an honor to feed a

Joined, and the Shkeen who had given up his meatrolls was radiating pride and pleasure.

"Lya," I whispered, "can you read them now?"

She nodded against my chest and pulled away and stared at the Joined, her eyes going hard and then softening again. She looked back at me. "It's different," she said, curious.

"How?"

She squinted in puzzlement. "I don't know. I mean, they still love us, and all. But now their thoughts are, well, sort of more human. There are levels, you know, and digging isn't easy, and there are hidden things, things they hide even from themselves. It's not all open like it was. They're thinking about the food now and how good it tastes. It's all very vivid. I could taste the rolls myself. But it's not the same."

I had an inspiration. "How many minds are there?"

"Four," she said. "Linked somehow, I think. But not really." She stopped, confused, and shook her head. "I mean, they sort of feel one another's emotions, like you do, I guess. But not thoughts, not the detail. I can read them, but they don't read one another. Each one is distinct. They were closer before, when they were ringing, but they were always individuals."

I was slightly disappointed. "Four minds, then, not one?"

"Umpf, yes. Four."

"And the Greeshka?" My other bright idea. If the Greeshka had minds of their own . . .

"Nothing," Lya said. "Like reading a plant, or a piece of clothing. Not even yes-I-live."

That was disturbing. Even lower animals had some vague consciousness of life—the feeling Talents called yes-I-live—usually only a dim spark that it took a major Talent to see. But Lya *was* a major Talent.

"Let's talk to them," I said. She nodded, and we walked up to where the Joined were munching their meatrolls. "Hello," I said awkwardly, wondering how to address them. "Can you speak Terran?"

Three of them looked at me without comprehension. But the fourth one, the little one whose Greeshka was a rippling red cape, bobbed his head up and down. "Yesh," he said, in a piping-thin voice.

I suddenly forgot what I was going to ask, but Lyanna came to my rescue. "Do you know of human Joined?" she said.

He grinned. "All Joined are one," he said.

"Oh," I said. "Well, yes, but do you know any who look like us? Tall, you know, with hair and skin that's pink or brown or something?" I came to another awkward halt, wondering just how *much* Terran the old Shkeen knew, and eyeing his Greeshka a little apprehensively.

His head hobbled from side to side. "Joined are all different, but all are one, all are same. Shome look ash you. Would you Join?"

"No, thanks," I said. "Where can I find a human Joined?"

He bobbed his head some more. "Joined shing and ring and walk the shacred city."

Lya had been reading. "He doesn't know," she told me. "The Joined just wander and play their bells. There's no pattern to it, no-body keeps track. It's all random. Some travel in groups, some alone, and new groups form every time two bunches meet."

"We'll have to search," I said.

"Eat," the Shkeen told us. He reached into the basket on the ground and his hands came out with two steaming meatrolls. He pressed one into my hand, one in Lya's.

I looked at it dubiously. "Thank you," I told him. I pulled at Lya with my free hand and we walked off together. The Joined grinned at us as we left, and started ringing once more before we were halfway down the street.

The meatroll was still in my hand, its crust burning my fingers. "Should I eat this?" I asked Lya.

She took a bite out of hers. "Why not? We had them last night in the restaurant, right? And I'm sure Valcarenghi would've warned us if the native food was poisonous."

That made sense, so I lifted the roll to my mouth and took a bite as I walked. It was hot, and also *hot,* and it wasn't a bit like the meatrolls we'd sampled the previous night. Those had been golden, flaky things, seasoned gently with orangespice from Baldur. The Shkeen version was crunchy, and the meat inside dripped grease and burned my mouth. But it was good, and I was hungry, and the roll didn't last long.

"Get anything else when you read the small guy?" I asked Lya around a mouthful of hot roll.

She swallowed, and nodded. "Yes, I did. He was happy, even more than the rest. He's older. He's near Final Union, and he's very thrilled about it." She spoke with her old easy manner; the aftereffects of reading the Joined seemed to have faded.

"Why?" I was musing out loud. "He's going to die. Why is he so happy about it?"

Lya shrugged. "He wasn't thinking in any great analytical detail, I'm afraid."

I licked my fingers to get rid of the last of the grease. We were at a crossroads, with Shkeen bustling by us in all directions, and now we could hear more bells on the wind. "More Joined," I said. "Want to look them up?"

"What would we find out? That we don't already know? We need a *human* Joined."

"Maybe one of this batch *will* be human."

I got Lya's withering look. "Ha. What are the odds?"

"All right," I conceded. It was now late afternoon. "Maybe we'd better head back. Get an earlier start tomorrow. Besides, Dino is probably expecting us for dinner."

———

DINNER, THIS TIME, WAS SERVED IN VALCARENGHI'S OFFICE, AFTER A little additional furniture had been dragged in. His quarters, it turned out, were on the level below, but he preferred to entertain upstairs where his guests could enjoy the spectacular Tower view.

There were five of us, all told: me and Lya, Valcarenghi and Laurie, plus Gourlay. Laurie did the cooking, supervised by master chef Valcarenghi. We had beefsteaks, bred on Shkea from Old Earth stock, plus a fascinating blend of vegetables that included mushrooms from Old Earth, ground-pips from Baldur, and Shkeen sweethorns. Dino liked to experiment and the dish was one of his inventions.

Lya and I gave a full report on the day's adventures, interrupted only by Valcarenghi's sharp, perceptive questioning. After dinner, we got rid of tables and dishes and sat around drinking Veltaar and talking. This time Lya and I asked the questions, with Gourlay supplying the biggest chunk of the answers. Valcarenghi listened from a cushion on the floor, one arm around Laurie, the other holding his wine glass. We were not the first Talents to visit Shkea, he told us. Nor the first to claim the Shkeen were manlike.

"Suppose that means something," he said. "But I don't know. They're *not* men, you know. No, sir. They're much more social, for one thing. Great little city builders from way back, always in towns, always surrounding themselves with others. And they're more communal than man too. Cooperate in all sorts of things, and they're big on sharing. Trade, for instance—they see that as mutual-sharing."

Valcarenghi laughed. "You can say that again. I just spent the whole day trying to work out a trade contract with a group of farmers who hadn't dealt with us before. It's not easy, believe me. They give us as much of their stuff as we ask for, if they don't need it themselves and no one else has asked for it earlier. But then they want to get whatever they ask for in the future. They expect it, in fact. So every time we deal we've got a choice; hand them a blank check, or go through an incredible round of talks that ends with them convinced that we're totally selfish."

Lya wasn't satisfied. "What about sex?" she demanded. "From the stuff you were translating last night, I got the impression they're monogamous."

"They're confused about sex relationships," Gourlay said. "It's very strange. Sex is sharing, you see, and it's good to share with everyone. But the sharing has to be real and meaningful. That creates problems."

Laurie sat up, attentive. "I've studied the point," she said quickly. "Shkeen morality insists they love *everybody*. But they can't do it, they're too human, too possessive. They wind up in monogamous relationships, because a really deep sex-sharing with one person is better than a million shallow physical things, in their culture. The ideal Shkeen would sex-share with everyone, with each of the unions being just as deep, but they can't achieve that ideal."

I frowned. "Wasn't somebody guilty last night over betraying his wife?"

Laurie nodded eagerly. "Yes, but the guilt was because his other relationships caused his sharing with his wife to diminish. *That* was the betrayal. If he'd been able to manage it without hurting his older relationship, the sex would have been meaningless. And, if all of the relationships have been real love-sharing, it would have been a plus. His wife would have been proud of him. It's quite an achievement for a Shkeen to be in a multiple union that works."

"And one of the greatest Shkeen crimes is to leave another alone," Gourlay said. "Emotionally alone. Without sharing."

I mulled over that, while Gourlay went on. The Shkeen had little crime, he told us. Especially no violent crime. No murders, no beatings, no prisons, no wars in their long, empty history.

"They're a race without murderers," Valcarenghi said, "which may explain something. On Old Earth, the same cultures that had the highest suicide rates often had the lowest murder rates too. And the Shkeen suicide rate is one hundred percent."

"They kill animals," I said.

"Not part of the Union," Gourlay replied. "The Union embraces all that thinks, and its creatures may not be killed. They do not kill Shkeen, or humans, or Greeshka."

Lya looked at me, then at Gourlay. "The Greeshka don't think," she said. "I tried to read them this morning and got nothing but the minds of the Shkeen they rode. Not even a yes-I-live."

"We've known that, but the point's always puzzled me," Valcarenghi said, climbing to his feet. He went to the bar for more wine, brought out a bottle, and filled our glasses. "A truly mindless parasite, but an intelligent race like the Shkeen are enslaved by it. Why?"

The new wine was good and chilled, a cold trail down my throat. I drank it, and nodded, remembering the flood of euphoria that had swept over us earlier that day. "Drugs," I said, speculatively. "The Greeshka must produce an organic pleasure-drug. The Shkeen submit to it willingly and die happy. The joy is real, believe me. We felt it."

Lyanna looked doubtful, though, and Gourlay shook his head adamantly. "No, Robb. Not so. We've experimented on the Greeshka, and . . ."

He must have noticed my raised eyebrows. He stopped.

"How did the Shkeen feel about that?" I asked.

"Didn't tell them. They wouldn't have liked it, not at all. Greeshka's just an animal, but it's their god. Don't fool around with God, you know. We refrained for a long time, but when Gustaffson went over, old Stuart had to know. His orders. We didn't get anywhere, though. No extracts that might be a drug, no secretions, nothing. In fact, the Shkeen are the *only* native life that submits so easily. We caught a whiner, you see, and strapped it down, and let a Greeshka link up. Then, couple hours later, we yanked the straps. Damn whiner was furious, screeching and yelping, attacking the thing on its head. Nearly clawed its own skull to ribbons before it got it off."

"Maybe only the Shkeen are susceptible?" I said. A feeble rescue attempt.

"Not quite," said Valcarenghi, with a small, thin smile. "There's us."

———

Lya was strangely silent in the tube, almost withdrawn. I assumed she was thinking about the conversation. But the door to our suite had barely slid shut behind us when she turned toward me and wrapped her arms around me.

I reached up and stroked her soft brown hair, slightly startled by the hug. "Hey," I muttered, "what's wrong?"

She gave me her vampire look, big-eyed and fragile. "Make love to me, Robb," she said with a soft sudden urgency. "Please. Make love to me now."

I smiled, but it was a puzzled smile, not my usual lecherous bedroom grin. Lya generally comes on impish and wicked when she's horny, but now she was all troubled and vulnerable. I didn't quite get it.

But it wasn't a time for questions, and I didn't ask any. I just pulled her to me wordlessly and kissed her hard, and we walked together to the bedroom.

And we made love, *really* made love, more than poor Normals can do. We joined our bodies as one, and I felt Lya stiffen as her mind reached out to mine. And as we moved together I was opening myself to her, drowning myself in the flood of love and need and fear that was pouring from her.

Then, quickly as it had begun, it ended. Her pleasure washed over me in a raw red wave. And I joined her on the crest, and Lya clutched me tightly, her eyes shrunk up small as she drank it all in.

Afterward, we lay there in the darkness and let the stars of Shkea pour their radiance through the window. Lya huddled against me, her head on my chest, while I stroked her. "That was good," I said in a drowsy-dreamy voice, smiling in the star-filled darkness.

"Yes," she replied. Her voice was soft and small, so small I barely heard it. "I love you, Robb," she whispered.

"Uh-huh," I said. "And I love you."

She pulled loose of my arm and rolled over, propping her head on a hand to stare at me and smile. "You do," she said. "I read it. I know it. And you know how much I love you too, don't you?"

I nodded, smiling. "Sure."

"We're lucky, you know. The Normals have only words. Poor little Normals. How can they *tell,* with just words? How can they *know*? They're always apart from each other, trying to reach each other and failing. Even when they make love, even when they come, they're always apart. They must be very lonely."

There was something . . . disturbing . . . in that. I looked at Lya, into her bright happy eyes, and thought about it. "Maybe," I said, finally. "But it's not that bad for them. They don't know any other way. And they try, they love too. They bridge the gap sometimes."

" 'Only a look and a voice, then darkness again and a silence,' " Lya quoted, her voice sad and tender. "We're luckier, aren't we? We have so much more."

"We're luckier," I echoed. And I reached out to read her too. Her mind was a haze of satisfaction, with a gentle scent of wistful, lonely longing. But there was something else, way down, almost gone now, but still faintly detectable.

I sat up slowly. "Hey," I said. "You're worried about something. And before, when we came in, you were scared. What's the matter?"

"I don't know, really," she said. She sounded puzzled and she *was* puzzled; I read it there. "I *was* scared, but I don't know why. The Joined, I think. I kept thinking about how much they loved me. They didn't even *know* me, but they loved me so much, and they understood—it was almost like what we have. It—I don't know. It bothered me. I mean, I didn't think I could ever be loved that way, except by you. And they were so close, so together. I felt kind of lonely, just holding hands and talking. I wanted to be close to you that way. After the way they were all sharing and everything, being alone just seemed empty. And frightening. You know?"

"I know," I said, touching her lightly again, with hand and mind. "I understand. We do understand each other. We're together almost as they are, as Normals can't ever be."

Lya nodded, and smiled, and hugged me. We went to sleep in each other's arms.

———

Dreams again. But again, at dawn, the memory stole away from me. It was all very annoying. The dream had been pleasant, comfortable. I wanted it back, and I couldn't even remember what it was. Our bedroom, washed by harsh daylight, seemed drab compared to the splendors of my lost vision.

Lya woke after me, with another headache. This time she had the pills on hand, by the bedstand. She grimaced and took one.

"It must be the Shkeen wine," I told her. "Something about it takes a dim view of your metabolism."

She pulled on a fresh coverall and scowled at me. "Ha. We were drinking Veltaar last night, remember? My father gave me my first glass of Veltaar when I was nine. It never gave me headaches before."

"A first!" I said, smiling.

"It's not funny," she said. "It hurts."

I quit kidding, and tried to read her. She was right. It *did* hurt. Her whole forehead throbbed with pain. I withdrew quickly before I caught it too.

"All right," I said. "I'm sorry. The pills will take care of it, though. Meanwhile, we've got work to do."

Lya nodded. She'd never let anything interfere with work yet.

The second day was a day of manhunt. We got off to a much earlier start, had a quick breakfast with Gourlay, then picked up our aircar outside the Tower. This time we didn't drop down when we hit Shkeentown. We wanted a human Joined, which meant we had to cover a lot of ground. The city was the biggest I'd ever seen, in area at any rate, and the thousand-odd human cultists were lost among millions of Shkeen. And, of those humans, only about half were actually Joined yet.

So we kept the aircar low, and buzzed up and down the dome-dotted hills like a floating roller coaster, causing quite a stir in the streets below us. The Shkeen had seen aircars before, of course, but it still had some novelty value, particularly to the kids, who tried to run after us whenever we flashed by. We also panicked a whiner, causing him to upset the cart full of fruit he was dragging. I felt guilty about that, so I kept the car higher afterward.

We spotted Joined all over the city, singing, eating, walking—and ringing those bells, those eternal bronze bells. But for the first three hours, all we found were Shkeen Joined. Lya and I took turns driving and watching. After the excitement of the previous day, the search was tedious and tiring.

Finally, however, we found something: a large group of Joined, ten of them, clustered around a bread cart behind one of the steeper hills. Two were taller than the rest.

We landed on the other side of the hill and walked around to meet them, leaving our aircar surrounded by a crowd of Shkeen children. The Joined were still eating when we arrived. Eight of them were Shkeen of various sizes and hues, Greeshka pulsing atop their skulls. The other two were human.

They wore the same long red gowns as the Shkeen, and they carried the same bells. One of them was a big man, with loose skin that hung in flaps, as if he'd lost a lot of weight recently. His hair was white and curly, his face marked by a broad smile and laugh wrinkles around the eyes. The other was a thin, dark weasel of a man with a big hooked nose.

Both of them had Greeshka sucking at their skulls. The parasite riding the weasel was barely a pimple, but the older man had a lordly specimen that dripped down beyond his shoulders and into the back of the gown.

Somehow, this time, it *did* look hideous.

Lyanna and I walked up to them, trying hard to smile, not reading—at least at first. They smiled at us as we approached. Then they waved.

"Hello," the weasel said cheerily when we got there. "I've never seen you. Are you new on Shkea?"

That took me slightly by surprise. I'd been expecting some sort of garbled mystic greeting, or maybe no greeting at all. I was assuming that somehow the human converts would have abandoned their humanity to become mock-Shkeen. I was wrong.

"More or less," I replied. And I read the weasel. He was genuinely pleased to see us, and just bubbled with contentment and good cheer.

"We've been hired to talk to people like you." I'd decided to be honest about it.

The weasel stretched his grin further than I thought it would go. "I am Joined, and happy," he said. "I'll be glad to talk to you. My name is Lester Kamenz. What do you want to know, brother?"

Lya, next to me, was going tense. I decided I'd let her read in depth while I asked questions. "When did you convert to the Cult?"

"Cult?" Kamenz said.

"The Union."

He nodded, and I was struck by the grotesque similarity of his bobbing head and that of the elderly Shkeen we'd seen yesterday. "I have always been in the Union. You are in the Union. All that thinks is in the Union."

"Some of us weren't told," I said. "How about you? When did you realize you were in the Union?"

"A year ago, Old Earth time. I was admitted to the ranks of the Joined only a few weeks ago. The First Joining is a joyful time. I am joyful. Now I will walk the streets and ring my bells until the Final Union."

"What did you do before?"

"Before?" A short vague look. "I ran machines once. I ran computers, in the Tower. But my life was empty, brother. I did not know I was in the Union, and I was alone. I had only machines, cold machines. Now I am Joined. Now I am"—again he searched—"not alone."

I reached into him, and found the happiness still there, with love. But now there was an ache too, a vague recollection of past pain, the stink of unwelcome memories. Did these fade? Maybe the gift the Greeshka gave its victims was oblivion, sweet mindless rest and end of struggle. Maybe.

I decided to try something. "That thing on your head," I said, sharply. "It's a parasite. It's drinking your blood right now, feeding on it. As it grows, it will take more and more of the things *you* need to live. Finally it will start to eat your tissue. Understand? It will *eat* you. I don't know how painful it will be, but however it feels, at the end you'll be *dead*. Unless you come back to the Tower now, and have the surgeons remove it. Or maybe you could remove it yourself. Why don't you try? Just reach up and pull it off. Go ahead."

I'd expected—what? Rage? Horror? Disgust? I got none of these. Kamenz just stuffed bread in his mouth and smiled at me, and all I read was his love and joy and a little pity.

"The Greeshka does not kill," he said finally. "The Greeshka gives joy and happy Union. Only those who have no Greeshka die. They are . . . alone. Oh, forever alone." Something in his mind trembled with sudden fear, but it faded quickly.

I glanced at Lya. She was stiff and hard-eyed, still reading. I looked back and began to phrase another question. But suddenly the Joined began to ring. One of the Shkeen started it off, swinging his bell up and down to produce a single sharp clang. Then his other hand swung, then the first again, then the second, then another Joined began to ring, then still another, and then they were all swinging and clanging and the noise of their bells was smashing against my ears as the joy and the love and the feel of the bells assaulted my mind once again.

I lingered to savor it. The love there was breathtaking, awesome, almost frightening in its heat and intensity, and there was so much sharing to frolic in and wonder at, such a soothing-calming-exhilarating tapestry of good feeling. Something happened to the Joined when they rang, something touched them and lifted them and gave them a glow, something strange and glorious that mere Normals could not hear in their harsh clanging music. I was no Normal, though. I could hear it.

I withdrew reluctantly, slowly. Kamenz and the other human were both ringing vigorously now, with broad smiles and glowing twinkling eyes that transfigured their faces. Lyanna was still tense, still reading. Her mouth was slightly open, and she trembled where she stood.

I put an arm around her and waited, listening to the music, patient. Lya continued to read. Finally, after minutes, I shook her gently. She turned and studied me with hard, distant eyes. Then blinked. And her eyes widened and she came back, shaking her head and frowning.

Puzzled, I looked into her head. Strange and stranger. It was a swirling fog of emotion, a dense moving blend of more feelings than I'd care to put a name to. No sooner had I entered than I was lost, lost and uneasy. Somewhere in the fog there was a bottomless abyss lurking to engulf me. At least it felt that way.

"Lya," I said. "What's wrong?"

She shook her head again, and looked at the Joined with a look that was equal parts fear and longing. I repeated my question.

"I—I don't know," she said. "Robb, let's not talk now. Let's go. I want time to think."

"OK," I said. What was going on here? I took her hand and we walked slowly around the hill to the slope where we'd left the car. Shkeen kids were climbing all over it. I chased them, laughing. Lya just stood there, her eyes gone all faraway on me. I wanted to read her again, but somehow I felt it would be an invasion of privacy.

Airborne, we streaked back toward the Tower, riding higher and faster this time. I drove, while Lya sat beside me and stared out into the distance.

"Did you get anything useful?" I asked her, trying to get her mind back on the assignment.

"Yes. No. Maybe." Her voice sounded distracted, as if only part of her was talking to me. "I read their lives, both of them. Kamenz was a computer programmer, as he said. But he wasn't very good. An ugly little man with an ugly little personality, no friends, no sex, no nothing. Lived by himself, avoided the Shkeen, didn't like them at all. Didn't even like people, really. But Gustaffson got through to him, somehow. He ignored Kamenz' coldness, his bitter little cuts, his cruel jokes. He didn't retaliate, you know? After a while, Kamenz came to like Gustaffson, to admire him. They were never really friends in any normal sense, but still Gustaffson was the nearest thing to a friend that Kamenz had."

She stopped suddenly. "So he went over with Gustaffson?" I prompted, glancing at her quickly. Her eyes still wandered.

"No, not at first. He was still afraid, still scared of the Shkeen and terrified of the Greeshka. But later, with Gustaffson gone, he began to realize how empty his life was. He worked all day with people who despised him and machines that didn't care, then sat alone at night reading and watching holoshows. Not life, really. He hardly touched the people around him. Finally he went to find Gustaffson, and wound up converted. Now . . ."

"Now . . . ?"

She hesitated. "He's happy, Robb," she said. "He really is. For the first time in his life, he's happy. He'd never known love before. Now it fills him."

"You got a lot," I said.

"Yes." Still the distracted voice, the lost eyes. "He was open, sort of. There were levels, but digging wasn't as hard as it usually is—as if his barriers were weakening, coming down almost. . . ."

"How about the other guy?"

She stroked the instrument panel, staring only at her hand. "Him? That was Gustaffson. . . ."

And that, suddenly, seemed to wake her, to restore her to the Lya I knew and loved. She shook her head and looked at me, and the aimless voice became an animated torrent of words. "Robb, listen, that was *Gustaffson,* he's been Joined over a year now, and he's going on to Final Union within a week. The Greeshka has accepted him, and he wants it, you know? He really does, and—and—oh Robb, he's *dying!*"

"Within a week, according to what you just said."

"No. I mean yes, but that's not what I mean. Final Union isn't death, to him. He believes it, all of it, the whole religion. The Greeshka is his god, and he's going to join it. But before, and now, he was dying. He's got the Slow Plague, Robb. A terminal case. It's been eating at him from inside for over fifteen years now. He got it back on Nightmare, in the swamps, when his family died. That's no world for people, but he was there, the administrator over a research base, a short-term thing. They lived on Thor; it was only a visit, but the ship crashed. Gustaffson got all wild and tried to reach them before the end, but he grabbed a faulty pair of skinthins, and the spores got through. And they were all dead when he got there. He had an awful lot of pain, Robb. From the Slow Plague, but more from the loss. He really loved them, and it was never the same after. They gave him Shkea as a reward, kind of, to take his mind off the crash, but he still thought of it all the time. I could see the picture, Robb. It was vivid. He couldn't forget it. The kids were inside the ship, safe behind the walls, but the life system failed and choked them to death. But his wife—oh, Robb—she took some skinthins and tried to go for help, and outside those *things,* those big wrigglers they have on Nightmare—?"

I swallowed hard, feeling a little sick. "The eater-worms," I said, dully. I'd read about them, and seen holos. I could imagine the picture that Lya'd seen in Gustaffson's memory, and it wasn't at all pretty. I was glad I didn't have her Talent.

"They were still—still—when Gustaffson got there. You know. He killed them all with a screechgun."

I shook my head. "I didn't think things like that really went on."

"No," Lya said. "Neither did Gustaffson. They'd been so—so *happy* before that, before the thing on Nightmare. He loved her, and they were really close, and his career had been almost charmed. He didn't have to go to Nightmare, you know. He took it because it was a challenge, because nobody else could handle it. That gnaws at him too. And he remembers all the time. He—they—" Her voice faltered. "They thought they were *lucky*," she said, before falling into silence.

There was nothing to say to that. I just kept quiet and drove, thinking, feeling a blurred, watered-down version of what Gustaffson's pain must have been like. After a while, Lya began to speak again.

"It was all there, Robb," she said, her voice softer and slower and more thoughtful once again. "But he was at peace. He still remembered it all, and the way it had hurt, but it didn't bother him as it had. Only now he was sorry they weren't with him. He was sorry that they died without Final Union. Almost like the Shkeen woman, remember? The one at the Gathering? With her brother?"

"I remember," I said.

"Like that. And his mind was open too. More than Kamenz', much more. When he rang, the levels all vanished, and everything was right at the surface, all the love and pain and everything. His whole life, Robb. I shared his whole life with him, in an instant. And all his thoughts too . . . he's seen the caves of Union . . . he went down once, before he converted. I . . ."

More silence, settling over us and darkening the car. We were close to the end of Shkeentown. The Tower slashed the sky ahead of us, shining in the sun. And the lower domes and archways of the glittering human city were coming into view.

"Robb," Lya said. "Land here. I have to think awhile, you know? Go back without me. I want to walk among the Shkeen a little."

I glanced at her, frowning. "Walk? It's a long way back to the Tower, Lya."

"I'll be all right. Please. Just let me think a bit."

I read her. The thought fog had returned, denser than ever, laced through with the colors of fear. "Are you sure?" I said. "You're scared, Lyanna. Why? What's wrong? The eater-worms are a long way off."

She just looked at me, troubled. "Please, Robb," she repeated.

I didn't know what else to do, so I landed.

AND I TOO THOUGHT, AS I GUIDED THE AIRCAR HOME. OF WHAT Lyanna had said, and read—of Kamenz and Gustaffson. I kept my mind on the problem we'd been assigned to crack. I tried to keep it off Lya, and whatever was bothering her. That would solve itself, I thought.

Back at the Tower, I wasted no time. I went straight up to Valcarenghi's office. He was there, alone, dictating into a machine. He shut it off when I entered.

"Hi, Robb," he began. "Where's Lya?"

"Out walking. She wanted to think. I've been thinking too. And I believe I've got your answer."

He raised his eyebrows, waiting.

I sat down. "We found Gustaffson this afternoon, and Lya read him. I think it's clear why he went over. He was a broken man, inside, however much he smiled. The Greeshka gave him an end to his pain. And there was another convert with him, a Lester Kamenz. He'd been miserable too, a pathetic lonely man with nothing to live for. Why *shouldn't* he convert? Check out the other converts, and I bet you'll find a pattern. The most lost and vulnerable, the failures, the isolated—those will be the ones that turned to Union."

Valcarenghi nodded. "OK, I'll buy that," he said. "But our psychs guessed that long ago, Robb. Only it's no answer, not really. Sure, the converts on the whole have been a messed-up crew, I won't dispute that. But why turn to the Cult of the Union? The psychs can't answer that. Take Gustaffson, now. He was a strong man, believe me. I never knew him personally, but I knew his career. He took some rough assignments, generally for the hell of it, and beat them. He could have had the cushy jobs, but he wasn't interested. I've heard about the incident on Nightmare. It's famous, in a warped sort of way. But Phil Gustaffson wasn't the sort of man to be beaten, even by something like that. He snapped out of it very quickly, from what Nelse tells me. He came to Shkea and really set the place in order, cleaning up the mess that Rockwood had left. He pushed through the first real trade contract we ever got, *and* he made the Shkeen understand what it meant, which isn't easy.

"So here he is, this competent, talented man, who's made a career of beating tough jobs and handling men. He's gone through a personal nightmare, but it hasn't destroyed him. He's as tough as ever. And suddenly he turns to the Cult of the Union, signs up for a grotesque suicide. Why? For an end to his pain, you say? An interesting theory, but there are other ways to end pain. Gustaffson had years between Nightmare and the Greeshka. He never ran away from pain then. He didn't turn to drink, or drugs, or any of the usual outs. He didn't head back to Old Earth to have a psipsych clean up his memories—and believe me, he could've gotten it paid for, if he'd wanted it. The colonial office would have done anything for him, after Nightmare. He went on, swallowed his pain, rebuilt. Until suddenly he converts.

"His pain made him more vulnerable, yes, no doubt of it. But something else brought him over—something that Union offered, something he couldn't get from wine or memory wipe. The same's true of Kamenz, and the others. They had other outs, other ways to vote no on life. They passed them up. But they chose Union. You see what I'm getting at?"

I did, of course. My answer was no answer at all, and I realized it. But Valcarenghi was wrong too, in parts.

"Yes," I said. "I guess we've still got some reading to do." I smiled wanly. "One thing, though. Gustaffson hadn't really beaten his pain, not ever. Lya was very clear on that. It was inside him all the time, tormenting him. He just never let it come out."

"That's victory, isn't it?" Valcarenghi said. "If you bury your hurts so deep that no one can tell you have them?"

"I don't know. I don't think so. But . . . anyway, there was more. Gustaffson has the Slow Plague. He's dying. He's been dying for years."

Valcarenghi's expression flickered briefly. "That I didn't know, but it just bolsters my point. I've read that some eighty percent of Slow Plague victims opt for euthanasia, if they happen to be on a planet where it's legal. Gustaffson was a planetary administrator. He could have *made* it legal. If he passed up suicide for all those years, why choose it now?"

I didn't have an answer for that. Lyanna hadn't given me one, if she had one. I didn't know where we could find one, either, unless . . .

"The caves," I said suddenly. "The caves of Union. We've got to witness a Final Union. There must be something about it, something that accounts for the conversions. Give us a chance to find out what it is."

Valcarenghi smiled. "All right," he said. "I can arrange it. I expected it would come to that. It's not pleasant, though, I'll warn you. I've gone down myself, so I know what I'm talking about."

"That's OK," I told him. "If you think reading Gustaffson was any fun, you should have seen Lya when she was through. She's out now trying to walk it off." That, I'd decided, must have been what was bothering her. "Final Union won't be any worse than those memories of Nightmare, I'm sure."

"Fine, then. I'll set it up for tomorrow. I'm going with you, of course. I don't want to take any chances on anything happening to you."

I nodded. Valcarenghi rose. "Good enough," he said. "Meanwhile, let's think about more interesting things. You have any plans for dinner?"

We wound up eating at a mock-Shkeen restaurant run by humans, in the company of Gourlay and Laurie Blackburn. The talk was mostly social noises—sports, politics, art, old jokes, that sort of thing. I don't think there was a mention of the Shkeen or the Greeshka all evening.

Afterwards, when I got back to our suite, I found Lyanna waiting for me. She was in bed, reading one of the handsome volumes from our library, a book of Old Earth poetry. She looked up when I entered.

"Hi," I said. "How was your walk?"

"Long." A smile creased her pale, small face, then faded. "But I had time to think. About this afternoon, and yesterday, and about the Joined. And us."

"Us?"

"Robb, do you love me?" The question was delivered almost

matter-of-factly, in a voice full of question. As if she didn't know. As if she really didn't know.

I sat down on the bed and took her hand and tried to smile. "Sure," I said. "You know that, Lya."

"I did. I do. You love me, Robb, really you do. As much as a human can love. But . . ." She stopped. She shook her head and closed her book and sighed. "But we're still apart, Robb. We're still apart."

"What *are* you talking about?"

"This afternoon. I was so confused afterwards, and scared. I wasn't sure why, but I've thought about it. When I was reading, Robb—I was in there, with the Joined, sharing them and their love. I really was. And I didn't want to come out. I didn't want to leave them, Robb. When I did, I felt so isolated, so cut off."

"That's your fault," I said. "I tried to talk to you. You were too busy thinking."

"Talking? What good is talking? It's communication, I guess, but is it *really?* I used to think so, before they trained my Talent. After that, reading seemed to be the real communication, the real way to reach somebody else, somebody like you. But now I don't know. The Joined—when they ring—they're so *together,* Robb. All linked. Like us when we make love, almost. And they love each other too. And they love us, so intensely. I felt—I don't know. But Gustaffson loves me as much as you do. No. He loves me more."

Her face was white as she said that, her eyes wide, lost, lonely. And me, I felt a sudden chill, like a cold wind blowing through my soul. I didn't say anything. I only looked at her, and wet my lips. And bled.

She saw the hurt in my eyes, I guess. Or read it. Her hand pulled at mine, caressed it. "Oh, Robb. Please. I don't mean to hurt you. It's not you. It's all of us. What do *we* have, compared to *them?*"

"I don't know what you're talking about, Lya." Half of me suddenly wanted to cry. The other half wanted to shout. I stifled both halves, and kept my voice steady. But inside I wasn't steady, I wasn't steady at all.

"Do you love me, Robb?" Again. Wondering.

"Yes!" Fiercely. A challenge.

"What does that mean?" she said.

"You know what it means," I said. "Dammit, Lya, *think!* Remember all we've had, all we've shared together. *That's* love, Lya. It is. We're the lucky ones, remember? You said that yourself. The Normals have only a touch and a voice, then back to their darkness. They can barely find each other. They're alone. Always. Groping. Trying, over and over, to climb out of their isolation booths, and failing, over and over. But not us, we found the way, we know each other as much as any human beings ever can. There's nothing I wouldn't tell you, or share with you. I've said that before, and you know it's true, you can read it in me. *That's* love, dammit. *Isn't it?*"

"I don't know," she said, in a voice so sadly baffled. Soundlessly, without even a sob, she began to cry. And while the tears ran in lonely paths down her cheeks, she talked. "Maybe that's love. I always thought it was. But now I don't know. If what we have is love, what was it I felt this afternoon, what was it I touched and shared in? Oh, Robb. I love you too. You know that. I try to share with you. I want to share what I read, what it was like. But I can't. We're cut off. I can't make you understand. I'm here and you're there and we can touch and make love and talk, but we're still apart. You see? You see? I'm alone. And this afternoon, I wasn't."

"You're not alone, dammit," I said suddenly. "I'm here." I clutched her hand tightly. "Feel? Hear? You're not alone!"

She shook her head, and the tears flowed on. "You don't understand, see? And there's no way I can make you. You said we know each other as much as any human beings ever can. You're right. But how much can human beings know each other? Aren't all of them cut off, really? Each alone in a big dark empty universe? We only trick ourselves when we think that someone else is there. In the end, in the cold lonely end, it's only us, by ourselves, in the blackness. Are you there, Robb? How do I know? Will you die with me, Robb? Will we be together then? Are we together now? You say we're luckier than the Normals. I've said it too. They have only a touch and voice, right? How many times have I quoted that? But what do we have? A touch and two voices, maybe. It's not enough anymore. I'm scared. Suddenly I'm scared."

She began to sob. Instinctively I reached out to her, wrapped her in my arms, stroked her. We lay back together, and she wept against my chest. I read her, briefly, and I read her pain, her sudden loneliness, her hunger, all aswirl in a darkening mindstorm of fear. And, though I touched her and caressed her and whispered—over and over—that it would be all right, that I was here, that she wasn't alone, I knew that it would not be enough. Suddenly there was a gulf between us, a great dark yawning thing that grew and grew, and I didn't know how to bridge it. And Lya, my Lya, was crying, and she needed me. And I needed her, but I couldn't get to her.

Then I realized that I was crying too.

We held each other, in silent tears, for what must have been an hour. But finally the tears ran out. Lya clutched her body to me so tightly I could hardly breathe, and I held her just as tightly.

"Robb," she whispered. "You said—you said we really know each other. All those times you've said it. And you say, sometimes, that I'm *right* for you, that I'm perfect."

I nodded, wanting to believe. "Yes. You are."

"No," she said, choking out the word, forcing it into the air, fighting herself to say it. "It's not *so*. I read you, yes. I can hear the words rattling around in your head as you fit a sentence together before saying it. And I listen to you scold yourself when you've done something stupid. And I see memories, some memories, and live through them with you. But it's all on the surface, Robb, all on the top. Below it, there's more, more of *you*. Drifting half-thoughts I don't quite catch. Feelings I can't put a name to. Passions you suppress, and memories even you don't know you have. Sometimes I can get to that level. Sometimes. If I really fight, if I drain myself to exhaustion. But when I get there, I know—I *know*—that there's another level below *that*. And more and more, on and on, down and down. I can't reach them, Robb, though they're part of you. I don't know you, I can't know you. You don't even know yourself, see? And me, do you know me? No. Even less. You know what I tell you, and I tell you the truth, but maybe not all. And you read my feelings, my surface feelings—the pain of a stubbed toe, a quick flash of annoyance, the pleasure I get when you're in me. Does that mean you know me? What of *my* levels, and levels? What about the things I don't even know myself? Do *you* know them? How, Robb, how?"

She shook her head again, with that funny little gesture she had whenever she was confused. "And you say I'm perfect, and that you love me. I'm so right for you. But *am* I? Robb, *I read your thoughts.* I know when you want me to be sexy, so I'm sexy. I see what turns you on, so I do it. I know when you want me to be serious, and when you want me to joke. I know what kind of jokes to tell too. Never the cutting kind, you don't like that, to hurt or see people hurt. You laugh *with* people not *at* them, and I laugh with you, and love you for your tastes. I know when you want me to talk, and when to keep quiet. I know when you want me to be your proud tigress, your tawny telepath, and when you want a little girl to shelter in your arms. And I *am* those things, Robb, because you want me to be, because I love you, because I can feel the joy in your mind at every *right* thing that I do. I never set out to do it that way, but it happened. I didn't mind, I don't mind. Most of the time it wasn't even conscious. You do the same thing too. I read it in you. You can't read as I do, so sometimes you guess wrong—you come on witty when I want silent understanding, or you act the strong man when I need a boy to mother. But you get it right sometimes too. And you *try,* you always try.

"But is it really *you?* Is it really *me?* What if I wasn't perfect, you see, if I was just myself, with all my faults and the things you don't like out in the open? Would you love me *then?* I don't know. But Gustaffson would, and Kamenz. I know that, Robb. I saw it. I know *them.* Their levels . . . vanished. I *KNOW* them, and if I went back I could share with them, more than with you. And they know me, the real me, all of me, I think. And they love me. *You see? You see?*"

Did I see? I don't know. I was confused. Would I love Lya if she was "herself"? But what was "herself"? How was it different from the Lya I knew? I thought I loved Lya and would always love Lya—but what if the real Lya wasn't like my Lya? *What* did I love? The strange abstract concept of a human being, or the flesh and voice and personality that I thought of as Lya? I didn't know. I didn't know who Lya was, or who I was, or what the hell it all meant. And I was scared. Maybe I couldn't feel what she had felt that afternoon. But I knew what she was feeling then. I was alone, and I needed someone.

"Lya," I called. "Lya, let's try. We don't have to give up. We can reach each other. There's a way, our way. We've done it before. Come, Lya, come with me, come to me."

As I spoke, I undressed her, and she responded and her hands joined mine. When we were nude, I began to stroke her, slowly, and she me. Our minds reached out to each other. Reached and probed as never before. I could feel her, inside my head, digging. Deeper and deeper. Down. And I opened myself to her, I surrendered, all the petty little secrets I had kept even from her, or tried to, now I yielded up to her, everything I could remember, my triumphs and shames, the good moments and the pain, the times I'd hurt someone, the times I'd been hurt, the long crying sessions by myself, the fears I wouldn't admit, the prejudices I fought, the vanities I battled when the time struck, the silly boyish sins. All. Everything. I buried nothing. I hid nothing. I gave myself to her, to Lya, to *my* Lya. She had to know me.

And so too she yielded. Her mind was a forest through which I roamed, hunting down wisps of emotion, the fear and the need and the love at the top, the fainter things beneath, the half-formed whims and passions still deeper into the woods. I don't have Lya's Talent, I read only feelings, never thoughts. But I read thoughts then, for the first and only time, thoughts she threw at me because I'd never seen them before. I couldn't read much, but some I got.

And as her mind opened to mine, so did her body. I entered her, and we moved together, bodies one, minds entwined, as close as human beings can join. I felt pleasure washing over me in great glorious waves, my pleasure, her pleasure, both together building on each other, and I rode the crest for an eternity as it approached a far distant shore. And finally as it smashed into that beach, we came together, and for a second—for a tiny, fleeting second—I could not tell which orgasm was mine, and which was hers.

But then it passed. We lay, bodies locked together, on the bed. In the starlight. But it was not a bed. It was the beach, the flat black beach, and there were no stars above. A thought touched me, a vagrant thought that was not mine. Lya's thought. We were on a plain, she was thinking, and I saw that she was right. The waters that had carried us here were gone, receded. There was only a vast flat blackness stretching away in all directions, with dim ominous shapes moving on either horizon. *We are here as on a darkling plain,* Lya thought. And suddenly I knew what those shapes were, and what poem she had been reading. We slept.

I WOKE, ALONE.

The room was dark. Lya lay on the other side of the bed, curled up, still asleep. It was late, near dawn, I thought. But I wasn't sure. I was restless.

I got up and dressed in silence. I needed to walk somewhere, to think, to work things out. Where, though?

There was a key in my pocket. I touched it when I pulled on my tunic, and remembered. Valcarenghi's office. It would be locked and deserted at this time of night. And the view might help me think.

I left, found the tubes, and shot up, up, up to the apex of the Tower, the top of man's steel challenge to the Shkeen. The office was unlit, the furniture dark shapes in the shadows. There was only the starlight. Shkea is closer to the galactic center than Old Earth, or Baldur. The stars are a fiery canopy across the night sky. Some of them are very close, and they burn like red and blue-white fires in the awesome blackness above. In Valcarenghi's office, all the walls are glass; I went to one, and looked out. I wasn't thinking. Just feeling. And I felt cold and lost and little.

Then there was a soft voice behind me saying hello. I barely heard it.

I turned away from the window, but other stars leaped at me from the far walls. Laurie Blackburn sat in one of the low chairs, concealed by the darkness.

"Hello," I said. "I didn't mean to intrude. I thought no one would be here."

She smiled. A radiant smile in a radiant face, but there was no humor in it. Her hair fell in sweeping auburn waves past her shoulders, and she was dressed in something long and gauzy. I could see her gentle curves through its folds, and she made no effort to hide herself.

"I come up here a lot," she said. "At night, usually. When Dino's asleep. It's a good place to think."

"Yes," I said, smiling. "My thoughts too."

"The stars are pretty, aren't they?"

"Yes."

"I think so. I—" Hesitation. Then she rose and came to me. "Do you love Lya?" she said.

A hammer of a question. Timed terribly. But I handled it well, I think. My mind was still on my talk with Lya. "Yes," I said. "Very much. Why?"

She was standing close to me, looking at my face, and past me, out to the stars. "I don't know. I wonder about love, sometimes. I love Dino, you know. He came here two months ago, so we haven't known each other long. But I love him already. I've never known anybody like him. He's kind, and considerate, and he does everything well. I've never seen him fail at anything he tried. Yet he doesn't seem driven, like some men. He wins so easily. He believes in himself a lot, and that's attractive. He's given me anything I could ask for, everything."

I read her, caught her love and worry, and guessed. "Except himself," I said.

She looked at me, startled. Then she smiled. "I forgot. You're a Talent. Of course you know. You're right. I don't know what I worry about, but I do worry. Dino is so perfect, you know. I've told him— well, everything. All about me and my life. And he listens and understands. He's always receptive, he's there when I need him. But—"

"It's all one way," I said. It was a statement. I knew.

She nodded. "It's not that he keeps secrets. He doesn't. He'll answer any question I ask. But the answers mean nothing. I ask him what he fears, and he says nothing, and makes me believe it. He's very rational, very calm. He never gets angry, he never has. I asked him. He doesn't hate people, he thinks hate is bad. He's never felt pain, either, or he says he hasn't. Emotional pain, I mean. Yet he understands me when I talk about my life. Once he said his biggest fault was laziness. But he's not lazy at all, I know that. Is he really that perfect? He tells me he's always sure of himself, because he *knows* he's good, but he smiles when he says it, so I can't even accuse him of being vain. He says he believes in God, but he never talks about it. If you try to talk seriously, he'll listen patiently, or joke with you, or lead the conversation away. He says he loves me, but—"

I nodded. I knew what was coming.

It came. She looked up at me, eyes begging. "You're a Talent," she said. "You've read him, haven't you? You know him? Tell me. Please tell me."

I was reading her. I could see how much she needed to know, how much she worried and feared, how much she loved. I couldn't lie to her. Yet it was hard to give her the answer I had to.

"I've read him," I said. Slowly. Carefully. Measuring out my words like precious fluids. "And you, you too. I saw your love, on that first night, when we ate together."

"And Dino?"

My words caught in my throat. "He's—funny, Lya said once. I can read his surface emotions easily enough. Below that, nothing. He's very self-contained, walled off. Almost as if his only emotions are the ones he—*allows* himself to feel. I've felt his confidence, his pleasure. I've felt worry too, but never real fear. He's very affectionate toward you, very protective. He enjoys feeling protective."

"Is that all?" So hopeful. It hurt.

"I'm afraid it is. He's walled off, Laurie. He needs himself, only himself. If there's love in him, it's behind that wall, hidden. I can't read it. He thinks a lot of you, Laurie. But love—well, it's different. It's stronger and more unreasoning and it comes in crashing floods. And Dino's not like that, at least not out where I can read."

"Closed," she said. "He's closed to me. I opened myself to him, totally. But he didn't. I was always afraid—even when he was with me, I felt sometimes that he wasn't there at all—"

She sighed. I read her despair, her welling loneliness. I didn't know what to do. "Cry if you like," I told her, inanely. "Sometimes it helps. I know. I've cried enough in my time."

She didn't cry. She looked up, and laughed lightly. "No," she said. "I can't. Dino taught me never to cry. He said tears never solve anything."

A sad philosophy. Tears don't solve anything, maybe, but they're part of being human. I wanted to tell her so, but instead I just smiled at her.

She smiled back, and cocked her head. "You cry," she said suddenly, in a voice strangely delighted. "That's funny. That's more of an admission than I ever heard from Dino, in a way. Thank you, Robb. Thank you."

And Laurie stood on her toes and looked up, expectant. And I could read what she expected. So I took her and kissed her, and she pressed her body hard against mine. And all the while I thought of Lya, telling myself that she wouldn't mind, that she'd be proud of me, that she'd understand.

Afterwards, I stayed up in the office alone to watch the dawn come up. I was drained, but somehow content. The light that crept over the horizon was chasing the shadows before it, and suddenly all the fears that had seemed so threatening in the night were silly, unreasoning. We'd bridged it, I thought—Lya and I. Whatever it was, we'd handled it, and today we'd handle the Greeshka with the same ease, together.

When I got back to our room, Lya was gone.

"WE FOUND THE AIRCAR IN THE MIDDLE OF SHKEENTOWN," VALCARENGHI was saying. He was cool, precise, reassuring. His voice told me, without words, that there was nothing to worry about. "I've got men out looking for her. But Shkeentown's a big place. Do you have any idea where she might have gone?"

"No," I said, dully. "Not really. Maybe to see some more Joined. She seemed—well, almost obsessed by them. I don't know."

"Well, we've got a good police force. We'll find her. I'm certain of that. But it may take a while. Did you two have a fight?"

"Yes. No. Sort of, but it wasn't a real fight. It was strange."

"I see," he said. But he didn't. "Laurie tells me you came up here last night, alone."

"Yes. I needed to think."

"All right," said Valcarenghi. "So let's say Lya woke up, decided she wanted to think too. You came up here. She took a ride. Maybe she just wants a day off to wander around Shkeentown. She did something like that yesterday, didn't she?"

"Yes."

"So she's doing it again. No problem. She'll probably be back well before dinner." He smiled.

"Why did she go without telling me, then? Or leaving a note, or *something*?"

"I don't know. It's not important."

Wasn't it, though? *Wasn't it?* I sat in the chair, head in my hands and a scowl on my face, and I was sweating. Suddenly I was very much afraid, of what I didn't know. I should never have left her alone, I was telling myself. While I was up here with Laurie, Lyanna woke alone in a darkened room, and—and—and *what?* And left.

"Meanwhile, though," Valcarenghi said, "we've got work to do. The trip to the caves is all set."

I looked up, disbelieving. "The caves? I can't go there, not now, not alone."

He gave a sigh of exasperation, exaggerated for effect. "Oh, come now, Robb. It's not the end of the world. Lya will be all right. She seemed to be a perfectly sensible girl, and I'm sure she can take care of herself. Right?"

I nodded.

"Meanwhile, we'll cover the caves. I still want to get to the bottom of this."

"It won't do any good," I protested. "Not without Lya. She's the major Talent. I—I just read emotions. I can't get down deep, as she can. I won't solve anything for you."

He shrugged. "Maybe not. But the trip is on, and we've got nothing to lose. We can always make a second run after Lya comes back. Besides, this should do you good, get your mind off this other business. There's nothing you can do for Lya now. I've got every available man out searching for her, and if they don't find her you certainly won't. So there's no sense dwelling on it. Just get back into action, keep busy." He turned, headed for the tube. "Come. There's an aircar waiting for us. Nelse will go too."

Reluctantly, I stood. I was in no mood to consider the problems of the Shkeen, but Valcarenghi's arguments made a certain amount of sense. Besides which, he'd hired Lyanna and me, and we still had obligations to him. I could try anyway, I thought.

On the ride out, Valcarenghi sat in the front with the driver, a hulking police sergeant with a face chiseled out of granite. He'd selected a police car this time so we could keep posted on the search for Lya. Gourlay and I were in the backseat together. Gourlay had covered our laps with a big map, and he was telling me about the caves of Final Union.

"Theory is the caves are the original home of the Greeshka," he said. "Probably true, makes sense. Greeshka are a lot bigger there. You'll see. The caves are all through the hills, away from our part of

Shkeentown, where the country gets wilder. A regular little honey-comb. Greeshka in every one too. Or so I've heard. Been in a few my-self, Greeshka in all of them. So I believe what they say about the rest. The city, the sacred city, well, it was probably built *because* of the caves. Shkeen come here from all over the continent, you know, for Final Union. Here, this is the cave region." He took out a pen, and made a big circle in red near the center of the map. It was meaningless to me. The map was getting me down. I hadn't realized that the Shkeen city was so *huge*. How the hell could they find anyone who didn't want to be found?

Valcarenghi looked back from the front seat. "The cave we're go-ing to is a big one, as these places go. I've been there before. There's no formality about Final Union, you understand. The Shkeen just pick a cave, and walk in, and lie down on top of the Greeshka. They'll use whatever entrance is most convenient. Some of them are no bigger than sewer pipes, but if you went in far enough, theory says you'd run into a Greeshka, setting back in the dark and pulsing away. The biggest caves are lighted with torches, like the Great Hall, but that's just a frill. It doesn't play any real part in the Union."

"I take it we're going to one of them?" I said.

Valcarenghi nodded. "Right. I figured you'd want to see what a mature Greeshka is like. It's not pretty, but it's educational. So we need lighting."

Gourlay resumed his narrative then, but I tuned him out. I felt I knew quite enough about the Shkeen and the Greeshka, and I was still worried about Lyanna. After a while he wound down, and the rest of the trip was in silence. We covered more ground than we ever had be-fore. Even the Tower—our shining steel landmark—had been swal-lowed by the hills behind us.

The terrain got rougher, rockier, and more overgrown, and the hills rose higher and wilder. But the domes went on and on and on, and there were Shkeen everywhere. Lya could be down there, I thought, lost among those teeming millions. Looking for what? Thinking what?

Finally we landed, in a wooded valley between two massive, rock-studded hills. Even here there were Shkeen, the red-brick domes ris-ing from the undergrowth among the stubby trees. I had no trouble spotting the cave. It was halfway up one of the slopes, a dark yawn in the rock face, with a dusty road winding up to it.

We set down in the valley and climbed that road. Gourlay ate up the distance with long, gawky strides, while Valcarenghi moved with an easy, untiring grace, and the policeman plodded on stolidly. I was the straggler. I dragged myself up, and I was half-winded by the time we got to the cave mouth.

If I'd expected cave paintings, or an altar, or some kind of nature temple, I was sadly disappointed. It was an ordinary cave, with damp stone walls and low ceilings and cold, wet air. Cooler than most of Shkea, and less dusty, but that was about it. There was one long, winding passage through the rock, wide enough for the four of us to walk abreast yet low enough so Gourlay had to stoop. Torches were set along the walls at regular intervals, but only every fourth one or so was lit. They burned with an oily smoke that seemed to cling to the top of the cave and drift down into the depths before us. I wondered what was sucking it in.

After about ten minutes of walking, most of it down a barely perceptible incline, the passage led us out into a high, brightly lit room, with a vaulting stone roof that was stained sooty by torch smoke. In the room, the Greeshka.

Its color was a dull brownish-red, like old blood, not the bright near-translucent crimson of the small creatures that clung to the skulls of the Joined. There were spots of black too, like burns or soot stains on the vast body. I could barely see the far side of the cave; the Greeshka was too huge, it towered above us so that there was only a thin crack between it and the roof. But it sloped down abruptly halfway across the chamber, like an immense jellied hill, and ended a good twenty feet from where we stood. Between us and the great bulk of the Greeshka was a forest of hanging, dangling red strands, a living cobweb of Greeshka tissue that came almost to our faces.

And it pulsed. As one organism. Even the strands kept time, widening and then contracting again, moving to a silent beat that was one with the great Greeshka behind them.

My stomach churned, but my companions seemed unmoved. They'd seen this before. "Come," Valcarenghi said, switching on a flashlight he'd brought to augment the torchlight. The light, twisting around the pulsing web, gave the illusion of some weird haunted forest. Valcarenghi stepped into that forest. Lightly. Swinging the light and brushing aside the Greeshka.

Gourlay followed him, but I recoiled. Valcarenghi looked back and smiled. "Don't worry," he said. "The Greeshka takes hours to attach itself, and it's easily removed. It won't grab you if you stumble against it."

I screwed up my courage, reached out, and touched one of the living strands. It was soft and wet, and there was a slimy feel to it. But that was all. It broke easily enough. I walked through it, reaching before me and bending and breaking the web to clear my path. The policeman walked silently behind me.

Then we stood on the far side of the web, at the front of the great Greeshka. Valcarenghi studied it for a second, then pointed with his flashlight. "Look," he said. "Final Union."

I looked. His beam had thrown a pool of light around one of the dark spots, a blemish on the reddish hulk. I looked closer. There was a head in the blemish. Centered in the dark spot, with just the face showing, and even that covered by a thin reddish film. But the features were unmistakable. An elderly Shkeen, wrinkled and big-eyed, his eyes closed now. But smiling. Smiling.

I moved closer. A little lower and to the right, a few fingertips hung out of the mass. But that was all. Most of the body was already gone, sunken into the Greeshka, dissolved or dissolving. The old Shkeen was dead, and the parasite was digesting his corpse.

"Every one of the dark spots is a recent Union," Valcarenghi was saying, moving his light around like a pointer. "The spots fade in time, of course. The Greeshka is growing steadily. In another hundred years it will fill this chamber, and start up the passageway."

Then there was a rustle of movement behind us. I looked back. Someone else was coming through the web.

She reached us soon, and smiled. A Shkeen woman, old, naked, breasts hanging past her waist. Joined, of course. Her Greeshka covered most of her head and hung lower than her breasts. It was still bright and translucent from its time in the sun. You could see through it, to where it was eating the skin off her back.

"A candidate for Final Union," Gourlay said.

"This is a popular cave," Valcarenghi added in a low, sardonic voice.

The woman did not speak to us, nor us to her. Smiling, she walked past us. And lay down on the Greeshka.

The little Greeshka, the one that rode her back, seemed almost to dissolve on contact, melting away into the great cave creature, so the Shkeen woman and the great Greeshka were joined as one. After that, nothing. She just closed her eyes, and lay peacefully, seemingly asleep.

"What's happening?" I asked.

"Union," said Valcarenghi. "It'll be an hour before you'd notice anything, but the Greeshka is closing over her even now, swallowing her. A response to her body heat, I'm told. In a day she'll be buried in it. In two, like him—" The flash found the half-dissolved face above us.

"Can you read her?" Gourlay suggested. "Maybe that'd tell us something."

"All right," I said, repelled but curious. I opened myself. And the mindstorm hit.

But it's wrong to call it a mindstorm. It was immense and awesome and intense, searing and blinding and choking. But it was peaceful too, and gentle with a gentleness that was more violent than human hate. It shrieked soft shrieks and siren calls and pulled at me seductively, and it washed over me in crimson waves of passion, and drew me to it. It filled me and emptied me all at once. And I heard the bells somewhere, clanging a harsh bronze song, a song of love and surrender and togetherness, of Joining and Union and never being alone.

Storm, mindstorm, yes, it was that. But it was to an ordinary mindstorm as a supernova is to a hurricane, and its violence was the violence of love. It loved me, that mindstorm, and it wanted me, and its bells called to me, and sang its love, and I reached to it and touched, wanting to be with it, wanting to link, wanting never to be alone again. And suddenly I was on the crest of a great wave once again, a wave of fire that washed across the stars forever, and this time I knew the wave would never end, this time I would not be alone afterwards upon my darkling plain.

But with that phrase I thought of Lya.

And suddenly I was struggling, fighting it, battling back against the sea of sucking love. I ran, ran, *ran, RAN* . . . and closed my minddoor and hammered shut the latch and let the storm flail and howl against it while I held it with all my strength, resisting. Yet the door began to buckle and crack.

I screamed. The door smashed open, and the storm whipped in and clutched at me, whirled me out and around and around. I sailed up to the cold stars but they were cold no longer, and I grew bigger and bigger until I *was* the stars and they were me, and I was Union, and for a single solitary glittering instant I was the universe.

Then nothing.

———

I WOKE UP BACK IN MY ROOM, WITH A HEADACHE THAT WAS TRYING TO tear my skull apart. Gourlay was sitting on a chair reading one of our books. He looked up when I groaned.

Lya's headache pills were still on the bedstand. I took one hastily, then struggled to sit up in bed.

"You all right?" Gourlay asked.

"Headache," I said, rubbing my forehead. It *throbbed,* as if it was about to burst. Worse than the time I'd peered into Lya's pain. "What happened?"

He stood up. "You scared the hell out of us. After you began to read, all of a sudden you started trembling. Then you walked right into the goddamn Greeshka. And you screamed. Dino and the sergeant had to drag you out. You were stepping right in the thing, and it was up to your knees. Twitching too. Weird. Dino hit you, knocked you out."

He shook his head, started for the door. "Where are you going?" I said.

"To sleep," he said. "You've been out for eight hours or so. Dino asked me to watch you till you came to. OK, you came to. Now get some rest, and I will too. We'll talk about it tomorrow."

"I want to talk about it now."

"It's late," he said, as he closed the bedroom door. I listened to his footsteps on the way out. And I'm sure I heard the outer door lock. Somebody was clearly afraid of Talents who steal away into the night. I wasn't going anywhere.

I got up and went out for a drink. There was Veltaar chilling. I put away a couple of glasses quick, and ate a light snack. The headache began to fade. Then I went back to the bedroom, turned off the light, and cleared the glass, so the stars would all shine through. Then back to sleep.

————

BUT I DIDN'T SLEEP, NOT RIGHT AWAY. TOO MUCH HAD HAPPENED. I had to think about it. The headache first, the incredible headache that ripped at my skull. Like Lya's. But Lya hadn't been through what I had. Or had she? Lya was a major Talent, much more sensitive than I was, with a greater range. Could that mindstorm have reached *this* far, over miles and miles? Late at night, when humans and Shkeen were sleeping and their thoughts dim? Maybe. And maybe my half-remembered dreams were pale reflections of whatever she had felt the same nights. But my dreams had been pleasant. It was waking that bothered me, waking and not remembering.

But again, had I had this headache when I slept? Or when I woke?

What the hell had happened? What was that thing, that reached me there in the cave, and pulled me to it? The Greeshka? It had to be. I hadn't even time to focus on the Shkeen woman, it *had* to be the Greeshka. But Lyanna had said that Greeshka had no minds, not even a yes-I-live. . . .

It all swirled around me, questions on questions on questions, and I had no answers. I began to think of Lya then, to wonder where she was and why she'd left me. Was this what she had been going through? Why hadn't I understood? I missed her then. I needed her beside me, and she wasn't there. I was alone, and very aware of it.

I slept.

Long darkness then, but finally a dream, and finally I remembered. I was back on the plain again, the infinite darkling plain with its starless sky and black shapes in the distance, the plain Lya had spoken of so often. It was from one of her favorite poems. I was alone, forever alone, and I knew it. That was the nature of things. I was the only reality in the universe, and I was cold and hungry and frightened, and the shapes were moving toward me, inhuman and inexorable. And there was no one to call to, no one to turn to, no one to hear my cries. There never had been anyone. There never would be anyone.

Then Lya came to me.

She floated down from the starless sky, pale and thin and fragile, and stood beside me on the plain. She brushed her hair back with her hand, and looked at me with glowing wide eyes, and smiled. And I knew it was no dream. She was with me, somehow. We talked.

Hi, Robb.

Lya? Hi, Lya. Where are you? You left me.

I'm sorry. I had to. You understand, Robb. You have to. I didn't want to be here anymore, ever, in this place, this awful place. I would have been, Robb. Men are always here, but for brief moments.

A touch and a voice?

Yes, Robb. Then darkness again, and a silence. And the darkling plain.

You're mixing two poems, Lya. But it's OK. You know them better than I do. But aren't you leaving out something? The earlier part. "Ah love, let us be true. . . ."

Oh, Robb.

Where are you?

I'm—everywhere. But mostly in a cave. I was ready, Robb. I was already more open than the rest. I could skip the Gathering, and the Joining. My Talent made me used to sharing. It took me.

Final Union?

Yes.

Oh, Lya.

Robb. Please. Join us, join me. It's happiness, you know? Forever and for-ever, and belonging and sharing and being together. I'm in love, Robb, I'm in love with a billion billion people, and I know all of them better than I ever knew you, and they know me, all of me, and they love me. And it will last forever. Me. Us. The Union. I'm still me, but I'm them too, you see? And they're me. The Joined, the reading, opened me, and the Union called to me every night, because it loved me, you see? Oh, Robb, join us, join us. I love you.

The Union. The Greeshka, you mean. I love you, Lya. Please come back. It can't have absorbed you already. Tell me where you are. I'll come to you.

Yes, come to me. Come anywhere, Robb. The Greeshka is all one, the caves all connect under the hills, the little Greeshka are all part of the Union. Come to me and join me. Love me as you said you did. Join me. You're so far away, I can hardly reach you, even with the Union. Come and be one with us.

No. I will not be eaten. Please, Lya, tell me where you are.

Poor Robb. Don't worry, love. The body isn't important. The Greeshka needs it for nourishment, and we need the Greeshka. But, oh Robb, the Union isn't just the Greeshka, you see? The Greeshka isn't important, it doesn't even have a mind, it's just the link, the medium, the Union is the Shkeen. A million billion billion Shkeen, all the Shkeen that have lived and Joined in fourteen thousand years, all together and loving and belonging, immortal. It's beautiful, Robb, it's more than we had, much more, and we were the lucky ones, remember? We were! But this is better.

Lya. My Lya. I loved you. This isn't for you, this isn't for humans. Come back to me.

This isn't for humans? Oh, it IS! It's what humans have always been look-ing for, searching for, crying for on lonely nights. It's love, Robb, real love, and hu-man love is only a pale imitation. You see?

No.

Come, Robb. Join. Or you'll be alone forever, alone on the plain, with only a voice and a touch to keep you going. And in the end when your body dies, you won't even have that. Just an eternity of empty blackness. The plain, Robb, forever and ever. And I won't be able to reach you, not ever. But it doesn't have to be. . . .

No.

Oh, Robb. I'm fading. Please come.

No. Lya, don't go. I love you, Lya. Don't leave me.

I love you, Robb. I did. I really did. . . .

And then she was gone. I was alone on the plain again. A wind was blowing from somewhere, and it whipped her fading words away from me, out into the cold vastness of infinity.

IN THE CHEERLESS MORNING, THE OUTER DOOR WAS UNLOCKED. I ascended the tower and found Valcarenghi alone in his office. "Do you believe in God?" I asked him.

He looked up, smiled. "Sure." Said lightly. I was reading him. It was a subject he'd never thought about.

"I don't," I said. "Neither did Lya. Most Talents are atheists, you know. There was an experiment tried back on Old Earth fifty years ago. It was organized by a major Talent named Linnel, who was also devoutly religious. He thought that by using drugs, and linking to-gether the minds of the world's most potent Talents, he could reach something he called the Universal Yes-I-Live. Also known as God. The experiment was a dismal failure, but *something* happened. Linnel went mad, and the others came away with only a vision of a vast, dark, uncaring nothingness, a void without reason or form or meaning. Other Talents have felt the same way, and Normals too. Centuries ago there was a poet named Arnold, who wrote of a darkling plain. The poem's in one of the old languages, but it's worth reading. It shows— fear, I think. Something basic in man, some dread of being alone in the cosmos. Maybe it's just fear of death, maybe it's more. I don't know. But it's primal. All men are forever alone, but they don't want to be. They're always searching, trying to make contact, trying to reach others across the void. Some people never succeed, some break through occasionally. Lya and I were lucky. But it's never permanent. In the end you're alone again, back on the darkling plain. You see, Dino? *Do you see?*"

He smiled an amused little smile. Not derisive—that wasn't his style—just surprised and disbelieving. "No," he said.

"Look again, then. Always people are reaching for something, for someone, searching. Talk, Talent, love, sex, it's all part of the same thing, the same search. And gods too. Man invents gods because he's afraid of being alone, scared of an empty universe, scared of the darkling plain. That's why your men are converting, Dino, that's why people are going over. They've found God, or as much of a God as they're ever likely to find. The Union is a mass-mind, an immortal mass-mind, many in one, all love. The Shkeen don't die, dammit. No wonder they don't have the concept of an afterlife. They *know* there's a God. Maybe it didn't create the universe, but it's love, pure love, and they say that God is love, don't they? Or maybe what we call love is a tiny piece of God. I don't care, whatever it is, the Union is it. The end of the search for the Shkeen, and for Man too. We're alike after all, we're so alike it hurts."

Valcarenghi gave his exaggerated sigh. "Robb, you're overwrought. You sound like one of the Joined."

"Maybe that's just what I should be. Lya is. She's part of the Union now."

He blinked. "How do you know that?"

"She came to me last night, in a dream."

"Oh. A dream."

"It was *true,* dammit. It's all true."

Valcarenghi stood, and smiled. "I believe you," he said. "That is, I believe that the Greeshka uses a psi-lure, a love lure if you will, to draw in its prey, something so powerful that it convinces men—even you—that it's God. Dangerous, of course. I'll have to think about this before taking action. We could guard the caves to keep humans out, but there are too many caves. And sealing off the Greeshka wouldn't help our relations with the Shkeen. But now it's my problem. You've done your job."

I waited until he was through. "You're wrong, Dino. This is real, no trick, no illusion. I *felt* it, and Lya too. The Greeshka hasn't even a yes–I–live, let alone a psi-lure strong enough to bring in Shkeen and men."

"You expect me to believe that God is an animal who lives in the caves of Shkea?"

"Yes."

"Robb, that's absurd, and you know it. You think the Shkeen have found the answer to the mysteries of creation. But look at them. The oldest civilized race in known space, but they've been stuck in the Bronze Age for fourteen thousand years. We came to *them.* Where are their spaceships? Where are their Towers?"

"Where are our bells?" I said. "And our joy? They're happy, Dino. Are we? Maybe they've found what we're still looking for. Why the hell is man so driven, anyway? Why is he out to conquer the galaxy, the universe, whatever? Looking for God, maybe . . . ? Maybe. He can't find him anywhere, though, so on he goes, on and on, always looking. But always back to the same darkling plain in the end."

"Compare the accomplishments. I'll take humanity's record."

"Is it worth it?"

"I think so." He went to the window, and looked out. "We've got the only Tower on their world," he said, smiling, as he looked down through the clouds.

"They've got the only God in our universe," I told him. But he only smiled.

"All right, Robb," he said, when he finally turned from the window. "I'll keep all this in mind. And we'll find Lyanna for you."

My voice softened. "Lya is lost," I said. "I know that now. I will be too, if I wait. I'm leaving tonight. I'll book passage on the first ship out to Baldur."

He nodded. "If you like. I'll have your money ready." He grinned. "And we'll send Lya after you, when we find her. I imagine she'll be a little miffed, but that's your worry."

I didn't answer. Instead I shrugged, and headed for the tube. I was almost there when he stopped me.

"Wait," he said. "How about dinner tonight? You've done a good job for us. We're having a farewell party anyway, Laurie and me. She's leaving too."

"I'm sorry," I said.

His turn to shrug. "What for? Laurie's a beautiful person, and I'll miss her. But it's no tragedy. There are other beautiful people. I think she was getting restless with Shkea, anyway."

I'd almost forgotten my Talent, in my heat and the pain of my loss. I remembered it now. I read him. There was no sorrow, no pain, just a vague disappointment. And below that, his wall. Always the wall, keeping him apart, this man who was a first-name friend to everyone and an intimate to none. And on it, it was almost as if there were a sign that read, THIS FAR YOU GO, and no further.

"Come up," he said. "It should be fun." I nodded.

I asked myself, when my ship lifted off, why I was leaving.

Maybe to return home. We have a house on Baldur, away from the cities, on one of the undeveloped continents with only wilderness for a neighbor. It stands on a cliff, above a high waterfall that tumbles endlessly down into a shaded green pool. Lya and I swam there often, in the sunlit days between assignments. And afterwards we'd lie down nude in the shade of the orangespice trees, and make love on a carpet of silver moss. Maybe I'm returning to that. But it won't be the same without Lya, lost Lya. . . .

Lya whom I still could have. Whom I could have now. It would be easy, so easy. A slow stroll into a darkened cave, a short sleep. Then Lya with me for eternity, in me, sharing me, being me, and I her. Loving and knowing more of each other than men can ever do. Union and joy, and no darkness again, ever. God. If I believed that, what I told Valcarenghi, then why did I tell Lya no?

Maybe because I'm not sure. Maybe I still hope, for something still greater and more loving than the Union, for the God they told me of so long ago. Maybe I'm taking a risk, because part of me still believes. But if I'm wrong . . . then the darkness, and the plain . . .

But maybe it's something else, something I saw in Valcarenghi, something that made me doubt what I had said.

For man is more than Shkeen, somehow; there are men like Dino and Gourlay as well as Lya and Gustaffson, men who fear love and Union as much as they crave it. A dichotomy, then. Man has two primal urges, and the Shkeen only one? If so, perhaps there is a human answer, to reach and join and not be alone, and yet to still be men.

I do not envy Valcarenghi. He cries behind his wall, I think, and no one knows, not even he. And no one will ever know, and in the end he'll always be alone in smiling pain. No, I do not envy Dino.

Yet there is something of him in me, Lya, as well as much of you. And that is why I ran, though I loved you.

Laurie Blackburn was on the ship with me. I ate with her after liftoff, and we spent the evening talking over wine. Not a happy conversation, maybe, but a human one. Both of us needed someone, and we reached out.

Afterwards, I took her back to my cabin, and made love to her as fiercely as I could. Then, the darkness softened, we held each other and talked away the night.

This Tower of Ashes

MY TOWER IS BUILT OF BRICKS, SMALL SOOT-GRAY BRICKS MORTARED together with a shiny black substance that looks strangely like obsidian to my untrained eye, though it clearly cannot be obsidian. It sits by an arm of the Skinny Sea, twenty feet tall and sagging, the edge of the forest only a few feet away.

I found the tower nearly four years ago, when Squirrel and I left Port Jamison in the silver aircar that now lies gutted and overgrown in the weeds outside my doorstep. To this day I know almost nothing about the structure, but I have my theories.

I do not think it was built by men, for one. It clearly predates Port Jamison, and I often suspect it predates human spaceflight. The bricks (which are curiously small, less than a quarter the size of normal bricks) are tired and weathered and old, and they crumble visibly beneath my feet. Dust is everywhere and I know its source, for more than once I have pried loose a brick from the parapet on the roof and crushed it idly to fine dark powder in my naked fist. When the salt wind blows from the east, the tower flies a plume of ashes.

Inside, the bricks are in better condition, since the wind and the rain have not touched them quite so much, but the tower is still far from pleasant. The interior is a single room full of dust and echoes, without windows; the only light comes from the circular opening in the center of the roof. A spiral stair, built of the same ancient brick as the rest, is part of the wall; around and around it circles, like the threading on a screw, before it reaches roof level. Squirrel, who is quite small as cats go, finds the stairs easy climbing, but for human feet they are narrow and awkward.

But I still climb them. Each night I return from the cool forests, my arrows black with the caked blood of the dream-spiders and my bag heavy with their poison sacs, and I set aside my bow and wash my hands and then climb up to the roof to spend the last few hours before dawn. Across the narrow salt channel, the lights of Port Jamison burn on the island, and from up there it is not the city I remember. The square black buildings wear a bright romantic glow at night; the lights, all smoky orange and muted blue, speak of mystery and silent song and more than a little loneliness, while the starships rise and fall against the stars like the tireless wandering fireflies of my boyhood on Old Earth.

"There are stories over there," I told Korbec once, before I had learned better. "There are people behind every light, and each person has a life, a story. Only they lead those lives without ever touching us, so we'll never know the stories." I think I gestured then; I was, of course, quite drunk.

Korbec answered with a toothy smile and a shake of his head. He was a great dark fleshy man, with a beard like knotted wire. Each month he came out from the city in his pitted black aircar to drop off my supplies and take the venom I had collected, and each month we went up to the roof and got drunk together. A track driver, that was all Korbec was, a seller of cut-rate dreams and secondhand rainbows. But he fancied himself a philosopher and a student of man.

"Don't fool yourself," he said to me then, his face flush with wine and darkness, "you're not missing nothin'. Lives are rotten stories, y'know. Real stories, now, they usually got a plot to 'em. They start and they go on a bit and when they end they're over, unless the guy's got a series goin'. People's lives don't do that no-how, they just kinda wander around and ramble and go on and on. Nothin' ever finishes."

"People die," I said. "That's enough of a finish, I'd think."

Korbec made a loud noise. "Sure, but have you ever known anybody to die at the right time? No, don't happen that way. Some guys fall over before their lives have properly gotten started, some right in the middle of the best part. Others kinda linger on after everything is really over."

Often when I sit up there alone, with Squirrel warm in my lap and a glass of wine by my side, I remember Korbec's words and the heavy way he said them, his coarse voice oddly gentle. He is not a smart man, Korbec, but that night I think he spoke the truth, maybe never realizing it himself. But the weary realism that he offered me then is the only antidote there is for the dreams that spiders weave.

But I am not Korbec, nor can I be, and while I recognize his truth, I cannot live it.

————

I WAS OUTSIDE TAKING TARGET PRACTICE IN THE LATE AFTERNOON, wearing nothing but my quiver and a pair of cut-offs, when they came. It was closing on dusk and I was loosening up for my nightly foray into the forest—even in those early days I lived from twilight to dawn, as the dream-spiders do. The grass felt good under my bare feet, the double-curved silverwood bow felt even better in my hand, and I was shooting well.

Then I heard them coming. I glanced over my shoulder toward the beach, and saw the dark blue aircar swelling rapidly against the eastern sky. Gerry, of course; I knew that from the sound; his aircar had been making noises as long as I had known him.

I turned my back on them, drew another arrow—quite steady—and notched my first bull's-eye of the day.

Gerry set his aircar down in the weeds near the base of the tower, just a few feet from my own. Crystal was with him, slim and grave, her long gold hair full of red glints from the afternoon sun. They climbed out and started toward me.

"Don't stand near the target," I told them, as I slipped another arrow into place and bent the bow. "How did you find me?" The twang of the arrow vibrating in the target punctuated my question.

They circled well around my line of fire. "You'd mentioned spotting this place from the air once," Gerry said, "and we knew you weren't anywhere in Port Jamison. Figured it was worth a chance." He stopped a few feet from me, with his hands on his hips, looking just as

I remembered him: big, dark-haired, and very fit. Crystal came up beside him and put one hand lightly on his arm.

I lowered my bow and turned to face them. "So. Well, you found me. Why?"

"I was worried about you, Johnny," Crystal said softly. But she avoided my eyes when I looked at her.

Gerry put a hand around her waist, very possessively, and something flared within me. "Running away never solves anything," he told me, his voice full of the strange mixture of friendly concern and patronizing arrogance he had been using on me for months.

"I did *not* run away," I said, my voice strained. "Damn it. You should never have come."

Crystal glanced at Gerry, looking very sad, and it was clear that suddenly she was thinking the same thing. Gerry just frowned. I don't think he ever once understood why I said the things I said, or did the things I did; whenever we discussed the subject, which was infrequently, he would only tell me with vague puzzlement what he would have done if our roles had been reversed. It seemed infinitely strange to him that anyone could possibly do anything differently in the same position.

His frown did not touch me, but he'd already done his damage. For the month I'd been in my self-imposed exile at the tower, I had been trying to come to terms with my actions and my moods, and it had been far from easy. Crystal and I had been together for a long time—nearly four years—when we came to Jamison's World, trying to track down some unique silver and obsidian artifacts that we'd picked up on Baldur. I had loved her all that time, and I still loved her, even now, after she had left me for Gerry. When I was feeling good about myself, it seemed to me that the impulse that had driven me out of Port Jamison was a noble and unselfish one. I wanted Crys to be happy, simply, and she could not be happy with me there. My wounds were too deep, and I wasn't good at hiding them; my presence put the damper of guilt on the newborn joy she'd found with Gerry. And since she could not bear to cut me off completely, I felt compelled to cut myself off. For them. For her.

Or so I liked to tell myself. But there were hours when that bright rationalization broke down, dark hours of self-loathing. Were those the real reasons? Or was I simply out to hurt myself in a fit of angry immaturity, and by doing so, punish them—like a willful child who plays with thoughts of suicide as a form of revenge?

I honestly didn't know. For a month I'd fluctuated from one belief to the other while I tried to understand myself and decide what I'd do next. I wanted to think myself a hero, willing to make a sacrifice for the happiness of the woman I loved. But Gerry's words made it clear that he didn't see it that way at all.

"Why do you have to be so damned dramatic about everything?" he said, looking stubborn. He had been determined all along to be very civilized, and seemed perpetually annoyed at me because I wouldn't shape up and heal my wounds so that everybody could be friends. Nothing annoyed me quite so much as his annoyance; I thought I was handling the situation pretty well, all things considered, and I resented the inference that I wasn't.

But Gerry was determined to convert me, and my best withering look was wasted on him. "We're going to stay here and talk things out until you agree to fly back to Port Jamison with us," he told me, in his most forceful now-I'm-getting-tough tone.

"Like shit," I said, turning sharply away from them and yanking an arrow from my quiver. I slid it into place, pulled, and released, all too quickly. The arrow missed the target by a good foot and buried itself in the soft dark brick of my crumbling tower.

"What *is* this place, anyway?" Crys asked, looking at the tower as if she'd just seen it for the first time. It's possible that she had—that it took the incongruous sight of my arrow lodging in stone to make her notice the ancient structure. More likely, though, it was a premeditated change of subject, designed to cool the argument that was building between Gerry and me.

I lowered my bow again and walked up to the target to recover the arrows I'd expended. "I'm really not sure," I said, somewhat mollified and anxious to pick up the cue she'd thrown me. "A watchtower, I think, of nonhuman origin. Jamison's World has never been thoroughly explored. It may have had a sentient race once." I walked

222 GEORGE R. R. MARTIN

around the target to the tower, and yanked loose the final arrow from the crumbling brick. "It still may, actually. We know very little of what goes on on the mainland."

"A damn gloomy place to live, if you ask me," Gerry put in, looking over the tower. "Could fall in any moment, from the way it looks."

I gave him a bemused smile. "The thought had occurred to me. But when I first came out here, I was past caring." As soon as the words were out, I regretted saying them; Crys winced visibly. That had been the whole story of my final weeks in Port Jamison. Try as I might, it had seemed that I had only two choices; I could lie, or I could hurt her. Neither appealed to me, so here I was. But here they were too, so the whole impossible situation was back.

Gerry had another comment ready, but he never got to say it. Just then Squirrel came bounding out from between the weeds, straight at Crystal.

She smiled at him and knelt, and an instant later he was at her feet, licking her hand and chewing on her fingers. Squirrel was in a good mood, clearly. He liked life near the tower. Back in Port Jamison, his life had been constrained by Crystal's fears that he'd be eaten by alleysnarls or chased by dogs or strung up by local children. Out here I let him run free, which was much more to his liking. The brush around the tower was overrun by whipping-mice, a native rodent with a hairless tail three times its own body length. The tail packed a mild sting, but Squirrel didn't care, even though he swelled up and got grouchy every time a tail connected. He liked stalking whipping-mice all day. Squirrel always fancied himself a great hunter, and there's no skill involved in chasing down a bowl of cat-food.

He'd been with me even longer than Crys had, but she'd become suitably fond of him during our time together. I often suspected that Crystal would have gone with Gerry even sooner than she did, except that she was upset at the idea of leaving Squirrel. Not that he was any great beauty. He was a small, thin, scuffy-looking cat, with ears like a fox and fur a scroungy gray-brown color, and a big bushy tail two sizes too big for him. The friend who gave him to me back on Avalon informed me gravely that Squirrel was the illegitimate offspring of a genetically-engineered psicat and a mangy alley tom.

But if Squirrel could read his owner's mind, he didn't pay much attention. When he wanted affection, he'd do things like climb right up on the book I was reading and knock it away and begin biting my chin: when he wanted to be let alone, it was dangerous folly to try to pet him.

As Crystal knelt by him and stroked him and Squirrel nuzzled up to her hand, she seemed very much the woman I'd traveled with and loved and talked to at endless length and slept with every night, and I suddenly realized how I'd missed her. I think I smiled; the sight of her, even under these conditions, still gave me a cloud-shadowed joy. Maybe I was being silly and stupid and vindictive to send them away, I thought, after they had come so far to see me. Crys was still Crys, and Gerry could hardly be so bad, since she loved him.

Watching her, wordless, I made a sudden decision; I would let them stay. And we could see what happened. "It's close to dusk," I heard myself saying. "Are you folks hungry?"

Crys looked up, still petting Squirrel, and smiled. Gerry nodded. "Sure."

"All right," I said. I walked past them, turned and paused in the doorway, and gestured them inside. "Welcome to my ruin."

I turned on the electric torches and set about making dinner. My lockers were well stocked back in those days; I had not yet started living off the forests. I thawed three big sandragons, the silver-shelled crustacean that Jamie fishermen dragged for relentlessly, and served them up with bread and cheese and white wine.

Mealtime conversation was polite and guarded. We talked of mutual friends in Port Jamison, Crystal told me about a letter she'd received from a couple we had known on Baldur, Gerry held forth on politics and the efforts of the Port police to crack down on the traffic in dreaming venom. "The Council is sponsoring research on some sort of super-pesticide that would wipe out the dream-spiders," he told me. "A saturation spraying of the near coast would cut off most of the supply, I'd think."

"Certainly," I said, a bit high on the wine and a bit piqued at Gerry's stupidity. Once again, listening to him, I had found myself questioning Crystal's taste. "Never mind what other effects it might have on the ecology, right?"

Gerry shrugged. "Mainland," he said simply. He was Jamie through-and-through, and the comment translated to, "Who cares?" The accidents of history had given the residents of Jamison's World a singularly cavalier attitude toward their planet's one large continent. Most of the original settlers had come from Old Poseidon, where the sea had been a way of life for generations. The rich, teeming oceans and peaceful archipelagoes of their new world had attracted them far more than the dark forests of the mainland. Their children grew up to the same attitudes, except for a handful who found an illegal profit selling dreams.

"Don't shrug it all off so easy," I said.

"Be realistic," he replied. "The mainland's no use to anyone, except the spidermen. Who would it hurt?"

"Damn it, Gerry, look at this tower! Where did it come from, tell me that! I tell *you,* there might be intelligence out there, in those forests. The Jamies have never even been bothered to look."

Crystal was nodding over her wine. "Johnny could be right," she said, glancing at Gerry. "That was why I came here, remember. The artifacts. The shop on Baldur said they were shipped out of Port Jamison. He couldn't trace them back any farther than that. And the workmanship—I've handled alien art for years, Gerry. I know Fyndii work, and Damoosh, and I've seen all the others. This was *different.*"

Gerry only smiled. "Proves nothing. There are other races, millions of them, farther in toward the core. The distances are too great, so we don't hear of them very often, except maybe third-hand, but it isn't impossible that every so often a piece of their art would trickle through." He shook his head. "No, I'd bet this tower was put up by some early settler. Who knows? Could be there was another discoverer, before Jamison, who never reported his find. Maybe he built the place. But I'm not going to buy mainland sentients."

"At least not until you fumigate the damned forests and they all come out waving their spears," I said sourly. Gerry laughed and Crystal smiled at me. And suddenly, suddenly, I had an overpowering desire to win this argument. My thoughts had the hazy clarity that only wine can give, and it seemed so logical. I was so clearly *right,* and here was my chance to show up Gerry like the provincial he was and make points with Crys.

I leaned forward. "If you Jamies would ever look, you might find sentients," I said. "I've only been on the mainland a month, and already I've found a great deal. You've no damned concept of the kind of beauty you talk so blithely of wiping out. A whole ecology is out there, different from the islands, species upon species, a lot probably not even discovered yet. But what do you know about it? Any of you?"

Gerry nodded. "So, show me." He stood up suddenly. "I'm always willing to learn, Bowen. Why don't you take us out and show us all the wonders of the mainland?"

I think Gerry was trying to make points, too. He probably never thought I'd take up his offer, but it was exactly what I'd wanted. It was dark outside now, and we had been talking by the light of my torches. Above, stars shone through the hole in my roof. The forest would be alive now, eerie and beautiful, and I was suddenly eager to be out there, bow in hand, in a world where I was a force and a friend, Gerry a bumbling tourist.

"Crystal?" I said.

She looked interested. "Sounds like fun. If it's safe."

"It will be," I said. "I'll take my bow." We both rose, and Crys looked happy. I remembered the times we tackled Baldurian wilderness together, and suddenly I felt very happy, certain that everything would work out well. Gerry was just part of a bad dream. She couldn't possibly be in love with him.

First I found the sober-ups; I was feeling good, but not good enough to head out into the forest when I was still dizzy from wine. Crystal and I flipped ours down immediately, and seconds after, my alcoholic glow began to fade. Gerry, however, waved away the pill I offered him. "I haven't had that much," he insisted. "Don't need it."

I shrugged, thinking that things were getting better and better. If Gerry went crashing drunkenly through the woods, it couldn't help but turn Crys away from him. "Suit yourself," I said.

Neither of them was really dressed for wilderness, but I hoped that wouldn't be a problem, since I didn't really plan on taking them very deep in the forest. It would be a quick trip, I thought; wander down my trail a bit, show them the dust pile and the spider-chasm, maybe nail a dream-spider for them. Nothing to it, out and back again.

I put on a dark coverall, heavy trail boots, and my quiver, handed Crystal a flash in case we wandered away from the bluemoss regions, and picked up my bow. "You really need that?" Gerry asked, with sarcasm.

"Protection," I said.

"Can't be that dangerous."

It isn't, if you know what you're doing, but I didn't tell him that. "Then why do you Jamies stay on your islands?"

He smiled. "I'd rather trust a laser."

"I'm cultivating a deathwish. A bow gives the prey a chance, of sorts."

Crys gave me a smile of shared memories. "He only hunts predators," she told Gerry. I bowed.

Squirrel agreed to guard my castle. Steady and very sure of myself, I belted on a knife and led my ex-wife and her lover out into the forests of Jamison's World.

We walked in single file, close together, me up front with the bow, Crys following, Gerry behind her. Crys used the flashlight when we first set out, playing it over the trail as we wound our way through the thick grove of spikearrows that stood like a wall against the sea. Tall and very straight, crusty gray of bark and some as big around as my tower, they climbed to a ridiculous height before sprouting their meager load of branches. Here and there they crowded together and squeezed the path between them, and more than one seemingly impassable fence of wood confronted us suddenly in the dark. But Crys could always pick out the way, with me a foot ahead of her to point her flash when it paused.

Ten minutes out from the tower, the character of the forest began to change. The ground and the very air were drier here, the wind cool but without the snap of salt; the water-hungry spikearrows had drained most of the moisture from the air. They began to grow smaller and less frequent, the spaces between them larger and easier to find. Other species of plant began to appear: stunted little goblin trees, sprawling mockoaks, graceful ebonfires whose red veins pulsed brilliantly in the dark wood when caught by Crystal's wandering flash.

And bluemoss.

Just a little at first; here a ropy web dangling from a goblin's arm, there a small patch on the ground, frequently chewing its way up the back of an ebonfire or a withering solitary spikearrow. Then more and more; thick carpets underfoot, mossy blankets on the leaves above, heavy trailers that dangled from the branches and danced around in the wind. Crystal sent the flash darting about, finding bigger and better bunches of the soft blue fungus, and peripherally I began to see the glow.

"Enough," I said, and Crys turned off the light.

Darkness lasted only for a moment, till our eyes adjusted to a dimmer light. Around us, the forest was suffused by a gentle radiance, as the bluemoss drenched us in its ghostly phosphorescence. We were standing near one side of a small clearing, below a shiny black ebonfire, but even the flames of its red-veined wood seemed cool in the faint blue light. The moss had taken over the undergrowth, supplanting all the local grasses and making nearby shrubs into fuzzy blue beachballs. It climbed the sides of most of the trees, and when we looked up through the branches at the stars, we saw that other colonies had set upon the woods a glowing crown.

I laid my bow carefully against the dark flank of the ebonfire, bent, and offered a handful of light to Crystal. When I held it under her chin, she smiled at me again, her features softened by the cool magic in my hand. I remember feeling very good, to have led them to this beauty.

But Gerry only grinned at me. "Is this what we're going to endanger, Bowen?" he asked. "A forest full of bluemoss?"

I dropped the moss. "You don't think it's pretty?"

Gerry shrugged. "Sure, it's pretty. It is also a fungus, a parasite with a dangerous tendency to overrun and crowd out all other forms of plantlife. Bluemoss was very thick on Jolostar and the Barbis Archipelago once, you know. We rooted it all out; it can eat its way through a good corn crop in a month." He shook his head.

And Crystal nodded. "He's right, you know," she said.

I looked at her for a long time, suddenly feeling very sober indeed, the last memory of the wine long gone. Abruptly it dawned on me that I had, all unthinking, built myself another fantasy. Out here, in a world I had started to make my own, a world of dream-spiders and magic moss, somehow I had thought that I could recapture my own dream long fled, my smiling crystalline soulmate. In the timeless wilderness of the mainland, she would see us both in fresh light and would realize once again that it was me she loved.

So I'd spun a pretty web, bright and alluring as the trap of any dream-spider, and Crys had shattered the flimsy filaments with a word. She was his; mine no longer, not now, not ever. And if Gerry seemed to me stupid or insensitive or overpractical, well, perhaps it was those very qualities that made Crys choose him. And perhaps not—I had no right to second-guess her love, and possibly I would never understand it.

I brushed the last flakes of glowing moss from my hands while Gerry took the heavy flash from Crystal and flicked it on again. My blue fairyland dissolved, burned away by the bright white reality of his flashlight beam. "What now?" he asked, smiling. He was not so very drunk after all.

I lifted my bow from where I'd set it down. "Follow me," I said, quickly, curtly. Both of them looked eager and interested, but my own mood had shifted dramatically. Suddenly the whole trip seemed point-less. I wished that they were gone, that I was back at my tower with Squirrel. I was down . . .

. . . and sinking. Deeper in the moss-heavy woods, we came upon a dark swift stream, and the brilliance of the flashlight speared a solitary ironhorn that had come to drink. It looked up quickly, pale and star-tled, then bounded away through the trees, for a fleeting instant look-ing a bit like the unicorn of Old Earth legend. Long habit made me glance at Crystal, but her eyes sought Gerry's when she laughed.

Later, as we climbed a rocky incline, a cave loomed near at hand; from the smell, a woodsnarl lair.

I turned to warn them around it, only to discover that I'd lost my audience. They were ten steps behind me, at the bottom of the rocks, walking very slowly and talking quietly, holding hands.

Dark and angry, wordless, I turned away again and continued on over the hill. We did not speak again until I'd found the dust pile.

I paused on its edge, my boots an inch deep in the fine gray powder, and they came straggling up behind me. "Go ahead, Gerry," I said. "Use your flash here."

The light roamed. The hill was at our back, rocky and lit here and there with the blurred cold fire of bluemoss-choked vegetation. But in front of us was only desolation; a wide vacant plain, black and blasted and lifeless, open to the stars. Back and forth Gerry moved the flashlight, pushing at the borders of the dust nearby, fading as he shone it straight out into the gray distance. The only sound was the wind.

"So?" he said at last.

"Feel the dust," I told him. I was not going to stoop this time. "And when you're back at the tower, crush one of my bricks and feel that. It's the same thing, a sort of powdery ash." I made an expansive gesture. "I'd guess there was a city here once, but now it's all crumbled into dust. Maybe my tower was an outpost of the people who built it, you see?"

"The vanished sentients of the forests," Gerry said, still smiling. "Well, I'll admit there's nothing like this on the islands. For a good reason. We don't let forest fires rage unchecked."

"*Forest fire!* Don't give me that. Forest fires don't reduce everything to a fine powder, you always get a few blackened stumps or something."

"Oh? You're probably right. But all the ruined cities I know have at least a few bricks still piled on top of one another for the tourists to take pictures of," Gerry said. The flash beam flicked to and fro over the dust pile, dismissing it. "All you have is a mound of rubbish."

Crystal said nothing.

I began walking back, while they followed in silence. I was losing points every minute; it had been idiocy to bring them out here. At that moment nothing more was on my mind than getting back to my tower as quickly as possible, packing them off to Port Jamison together, and resuming my exile.

Crystal stopped me, after we'd come back over the hill into the bluemoss forest.

"Johnny," she said. I stopped, they caught up, Crys pointed.

"Turn off the light," I told Gerry. In the fainter illumination of the moss, it was easier to spot: the intricate iridescent web of a dreamspider, slanting groundward from the low branches of a mockoak. The patches of moss that shone softly all around us were nothing to this; each web strand was as thick as my little finger, oily and brilliant, running with the colors of the rainbow.

Crys took a step toward it, but I took her by the arm and stopped her. "The spiders are around someplace," I said. "Don't go too close. Papa spider never leaves the web, and Mama ranges around in the trees at night."

Gerry glanced upward a little apprehensively. His flash was dark, and suddenly he didn't seem to have all the answers. The dream-spiders are dangerous predators, and I suppose he'd never seen one outside of a display case. They weren't native to the islands. "Pretty big web," he said. "Spiders must be a fair size."

"Fair," I said, and at once I was inspired. I could discomfort him a lot more if an ordinary web like this got to him. And he had been discomforting me all night. "Follow me. I'll show you a real dream-spider." We circled around the web carefully, never seeing either of its guardians. I led them to the spider-chasm.

It was a great V in the sandy earth, once a creekbed perhaps, but dry and overgrown now. The chasm is hardly very deep by daylight, but at night it looks formidable enough, as you stare down into it from the wooded hills on either side. The bottom is a dark tangle of shrubbery, alive with little flickering phantom lights; higher up, trees of all kinds lean into the chasm, almost meeting in the center. One of them, in fact, does cross the gap. An ancient, rotting spikearrow, withered by lack of moisture, had fallen long ago to provide a natural bridge. The bridge hangs with bluemoss, and glows. The three of us walked out on that dim-lit, curving trunk, and I gestured down.

Yards below us, a glittering multihued net hung from hill to hill, each strand of the web thick as a cable and aglisten with sticky oils. It tied all the lower trees together in a twisting intricate embrace, and it was a shining fairy-roof above the chasm. Very pretty; it made you want to reach out and touch it.

That, of course, was why the dream-spiders spun it. They were nocturnal predators, and the bright colors of their webs afire in the night made a potent lure.

"Look," Crystal said, "the spider." She pointed. In one of the darker corners of the web, half-hidden by the tangle of a goblin tree that grew out of the rock, it was sitting. I could see it dimly, by the webfire and moss light, a great eight-legged white thing the size of a large pumpkin. Unmoving. Waiting.

Gerry glanced around uneasily again, up into the branches of a crooked mockoak that hung partially above us. "The mate's around somewhere, isn't it?"

I nodded. The dream-spiders of Jamison's World are not quite twins to the arachnids of Old Earth. The female is indeed the deadlier of the species, but far from eating the male, she takes him for life in a permanent specialized partnership. For it is the sluggish, great-bodied male who wears the spinnerets, who weaves the shining-fire web and makes it sticky with his oils, who binds and ties the prey snared by light and color. Meanwhile, the smaller female roams the dark branches, her poison sac full of the viscous dreaming-venom that grants bright visions and ecstasy and final blackness. Creatures many times her own size she stings, and drags limp back to the web to add to the larder.

The dream-spiders are soft, merciful hunters for all that. If they prefer live food, no matter; the captive probably enjoys being eaten. Popular Jamie wisdom says a spider's prey moans with joy as it is consumed. Like all popular wisdoms, it is vastly exaggerated. But the truth is, the captives never struggle.

Except that night, something was struggling in the web below us.

"What's that?" I said, blinking. The iridescent web was not even close to empty—the half-eaten corpse of an ironhorn lay close at hand below us, and some great dark bat was bound in bright strands just slightly farther away—but these were not what I watched. In the corner opposite the male spider, near the western trees, something was caught and fluttering. I remember a brief glimpse of thrashing pale limbs, wide luminous eyes, and something like wings. But I did not see it clearly.

That was when Gerry slipped.

Maybe it was the wine that made him unsteady, or maybe the moss under our feet, or the curve of the trunk on which we stood. Maybe he was just trying to step around me to see whatever it was I was staring at. But, in any case, he slipped and lost his balance, let out a yelp, and suddenly he was five yards below us, caught in the web. The whole thing shook to the impact of his fall, but it didn't come close to breaking—dream-spider webs are strong enough to catch ironhorns and wood-snarls, after all.

"Damn," Gerry yelled. He looked ridiculous; one leg plunged right down through the fibers of the web, his arms half-sunk and tangled hopelessly, only his head and shoulders really free of the mess. "This stuff is sticky. I can hardly move."

"Don't try," I told him. "It'll just get worse. I'll figure out a way to climb down and cut you loose. I've got my knife." I looked around, searching for a tree limb to shimmy out on.

"John." Crystal's voice was tense, on edge.

The male spider had left his lurking place behind the goblin tree. He was moving toward Gerry with a heavy deliberate gait; a gross white shape clamoring over the preternatural beauty of his web.

"Damn," I said. I wasn't seriously alarmed, but it was a bother. The great male was the biggest spider I'd ever seen, and it seemed a shame to kill him. But I didn't see that I had much choice. The male dream-spider has no venom, but he is a carnivore, and his bite can be most final, especially when he's the size of this one. I couldn't let him get within biting distance of Gerry.

Steadily, carefully, I drew a long gray arrow out of my quiver and fitted it to my bowstring. It was night, of course, but I wasn't really worried. I was a good shot, and my target was outlined clearly by the glowing strands of his web.

Crystal screamed.

I stopped briefly, annoyed that she'd panic when everything was under control. But I knew all along that she would not, of course. It was something else. For an instant I couldn't imagine what it could be.

Then I saw, as I followed Crys' eyes with my own. A fat white spider the size of a big man's fist had dropped down from the mockoak to the bridge we were standing on, not ten feet away. Crystal, thank God, was safe behind me.

I stood there—how long? I don't know. If I had just acted, without stopping, without thought, I could have handled everything. I should have taken care of the male first, with the arrow I had ready. There would have been plenty of time to pull a second arrow for the female.

But I froze instead, caught in that dark bright moment, for an instant timeless, my bow in my hand yet unable to act. It was all so complicated, suddenly. The female was scuttling toward me, faster than I would have believed, and it seemed so much quicker and deadlier than the slow white thing below. Perhaps I should take it out first. I might miss, and then I would need time to go for my knife or a second arrow.

Except that would leave Gerry tangled and helpless under the jaws of the male that moved toward him inexorably. He could die. He could die. Crystal could never blame me. I had to save myself, and her, she would understand that. And I'd have her back again.

Yes.

NO!

Crystal was screaming, screaming, and suddenly everything was clear and I knew what it had all meant and why I was here in this forest and what I had to do. There was a moment of glorious transcendence. I had lost the gift of making her happy, my Crystal, but now for a moment suspended in time that power had returned to me, and I could give or withhold happiness forever. With an arrow, I could prove a love that Gerry would never match.

I think I smiled. I'm sure I did.

And my arrow flew darkly through the cool night, and found its mark in the bloated white spider that raced across a web of light.

The female was on me, and I made no move to kick it away or crush it beneath my heel. There was a sharp stabbing pain in my ankle.

Bright and many-colored are the webs the dream-spiders weave.

At night, when I return from the forests, I clean my arrows carefully and open my great knife, with its slim barbed blade, to cut apart the poison sacs I've collected. I slit them open, each in turn, as I have earlier cut them from the still white bodies of the dream-spiders, and then I drain the venom off into a bottle, to wait for the day when Korbec flies out to collect it.

Afterwards I set out the miniature goblet, exquisitely wrought in silver and obsidian and bright with spider motifs, and pour it full of the heavy black wine they bring me from the city. I stir the cup with my knife, around and around until the blade is shiny clean again and the wine a trifle darker than before. And I ascend to the roof.

Often Korbec's words will return to me then, and with them my story. Crystal my love, and Gerry, and a night of lights and spiders. It all seemed so very right for that brief moment, when I stood upon the moss-covered bridge with an arrow in my hand, and decided. And it has all gone so very very *wrong* . . .

. . . from the moment I awoke, after a month of fever and visions, to find myself in the tower where Crys and Gerry had taken me to nurse me back to health. My decision, my transcendent choice, was not so final as I would have thought.

At times I wonder if it *was* a choice. We talked about it, often, while I regained my strength, and the tale that Crystal tells me is not the one that I remember. She says that we never saw the female at all, until it was too late, that it dropped silently onto my neck just as I released the arrow that killed the male. Then, she says, she smashed it with the flashlight that Gerry had given her to hold, and I went tumbling into the web.

In fact, there *is* a wound on my neck, and none on my ankle. And her story has a ring of truth. For I have come to know the dream-spiders in the slow-flowing years since that night, and I know that the females are stealthy killers that drop down on their prey unawares. They do not charge across fallen trees like berserk ironhorns; it is not the spiders' way.

And neither Crystal nor Gerry has any memory of a pale winged thing flapping in the web.

Yet *I* remember it clearly . . . as I remember the female spider that scuttled toward me during the endless years that I stood frozen . . . but then . . . they say the bite of a dream-spider does strange things to your mind.

That could be it, of course.

Sometimes when Squirrel comes behind me up the stairs, scraping the sooty bricks with his eight white legs, the wrongness of it all hits me, and I know I've dwelt with dreams too long.

Yet the dreams are often better than the waking, the stories so much finer than the lives.

Crystal did not come back to me, then or ever. They left when I was healthy. And the happiness I'd brought her with the choice that was not a choice and the sacrifice not a sacrifice, my gift to her forever—it lasted less than a year. Korbec tells me that she and Gerry broke up violently, and that she has since left Jamison's World.

I suppose that's truth enough, if you can believe a man like Korbec. I don't worry about it overmuch.

I just kill dream-spiders, drink wine, pet Squirrel. And each night I climb this tower of ashes to gaze at distant lights.

AND SEVEN TIMES
NEVER KILL MAN

———— ✦ ————

Ye may kill for yourselves,
and your mates,
and your cubs as they need,
and ye can;

But kill not for pleasure of killing,
and seven times never kill Man!

—Rudyard Kipling

OUTSIDE THE WALLS THE JAENSHI CHILDREN HUNG, A ROW OF SMALL gray-furred bodies still and motionless at the ends of long ropes. The oldest among them, obviously, had been slaughtered before hanging; here a headless male swung upside down, the noose around the feet, while there dangled the blast-burned carcass of a female. But most of them, the dark hairy infants with the wide golden eyes, most of them had simply been hanged. Toward dusk, when the wind came swirling down out of the ragged hills, the bodies of the lighter children would twist at the ends of their ropes and bang against the city walls, as if they were alive and pounding for admission.

But the guards on the walls paid the thumping no mind as they walked their relentless rounds, and the rust-streaked metal gates did not open.

"Do you believe in evil?" Arik neKrol asked Jannis Ryther as they looked down on the City of the Steel Angels from the crest of a nearby hill. Anger was written across every line of his flat yellow-brown face, as he squatted among the broken shards of what once had been a Jaenshi worship pyramid.

"Evil?" Ryther murmured in a distracted way. Her eyes never left the redstone walls below, where the dark bodies of the children were outlined starkly. The sun was going down, the fat red globe that the Steel Angels called the Heart of Bakkalon, and the valley beneath them seemed to swim in bloody mists.

"Evil," neKrol repeated. The trader was a short, pudgy man, his features decidedly mongoloid except for the flame-red hair that fell nearly to his waist. "It is a religious concept, and I am not a religious man. Long ago, when I was a very child growing up on ai-Emerel, I decided that there was no good or evil, only different ways of thinking." His small, soft hands felt around in the dust until he had a large, jagged shard that filled his fist. He stood and offered it to Ryther. "The Steel Angels have made me believe in evil again," he said.

She took the fragment from him wordlessly and turned it over in her hands. Ryther was much taller than neKrol, and much tinier; a hard bony woman with a long face, short black hair, and eyes without expression. The sweat-stained coveralls she wore hung loosely on her spare frame.

"Interesting," she said finally, after studying the shard for several minutes. It was as hard and smooth as glass, but stronger; colored a translucent red, yet so very dark it was almost black. "A plastic?" she asked, throwing it back to the ground.

NeKrol shrugged. "That was my very guess, but of course it is impossible. The Jaenshi work in bone and wood and sometimes metal, but plastic is centuries beyond them."

"Or behind them," Ryther said. "You say these worship pyramids are scattered all through the forest?"

"Yes, as far as I have ranged. But the Angels have smashed all those close to their valley to drive the Jaenshi away. As they expand, and they *will* expand, they will smash others."

Ryther nodded. She looked down into the valley again, and as she did the last sliver of the Heart of Bakkalon slid below the western mountains and the city lights began to come on. The Jaenshi children swung in pools of soft blue illumination, and just above the city gates two stick figures could be seen working. Shortly they heaved something outward, a rope uncoiled, and then another small dark shadow jerked and twitched against the wall. "Why?" Ryther said, in a cool voice, watching.

NeKrol was anything but cool. "The Jaenshi tried to defend one of their pyramids. Spears and knives and rocks against the Steel Angels with lasers and blasters and screechguns. But they caught them unaware, killed a man. The Proctor announced it would not happen again." He spat. "Evil. The children trust them, you see."

"Interesting," Ryther said.

"Can you do anything?" neKrol asked, his voice agitated. "You have your ship, your crew. The Jaenshi need a protector, Jannis. They are helpless before the Angels."

"I have four men in my crew," Ryther said evenly. "Perhaps four hunting lasers as well." That was all the answer she gave.

NeKrol looked at her helplessly. *"Nothing?"*

"Tomorrow, perhaps, the Proctor will call on us. He has surely seen the *Lights* descend. Perhaps the Angels wish to trade." She glanced again into the valley. "Come, Arik, we must go back to your base. The trade goods must be loaded."

Wyatt, Proctor of the Children of Bakkalon on the World of Corlos, was tall and red and skeletal, and the muscles stood out clearly on his bare arms. His blue-black hair was cropped very short, his carriage was stiff and erect. Like all the Steel Angels, he wore a uniform of chameleon cloth (a pale brown now, as he stood in the full light of day on the edge of the small, crude spacefield), a mesh-steel belt with hand-laser and communicator and screechgun, and a stiff red Roman collar. The tiny figurine that hung on a chain about his neck—the pale child Bakkalon, nude and innocent and bright-eyed, but holding a great black sword in one small fist—was the only sign of Wyatt's rank.

Four other Angels stood behind him: two men, two women, all dressed identically. There was a sameness about their faces, too; the hair always cropped tightly, whether it was blond or red or brown, the eyes alert and cold and a little fanatic, the upright posture that seemed to characterize members of the military-religious sect, the bodies hard and fit. NeKrol, who was soft and slouching and sloppy, disliked everything about the Angels.

Proctor Wyatt had arrived shortly after dawn, sending one of his squad to pound on the door of the small gray prefab bubble that was neKrol's trading base and home. Sleepy and angry, but with a guarded politeness, the trader had risen to greet the Angels, and had escorted them out to the center of the spacefield, where the scarred metal teardrop of the *Lights of Jolostar* squatted on three retractable legs.

The cargo ports were all sealed now; Ryther's crew had spent most of the evening unloading neKrol's trade goods and replacing them in the ship's hold with crates of Jaenshi artifacts that might bring good prices from collectors of extraterrestrial art. No way of knowing until a dealer looked over the goods; Ryther had dropped neKrol only a year ago, and this was the first pickup.

"I am an independent trader, and Arik is my agent on this world," Ryther told the proctor when she met him on the edge of the field. "You must deal through him."

"I see," Proctor Wyatt said. He still held the list he had offered Ryther, of goods the Angels wanted from the industrialized colonies on Avalon and Jamison's World. "But neKrol will not deal with us."

Ryther looked at him blankly.

"With good reason," neKrol said. "I trade with the Jaenshi, you slaughter them."

The Proctor had spoken to neKrol often in the months since the Steel Angels had established their city-colony, and the talks had all ended in arguments; now he ignored him. "The steps we took were needed," Wyatt said to Ryther. "When an animal kills a man, the animal must be punished, and other animals must see and learn, so that beasts may know that man, the seed of Earth and child of Bakkalon, is the lord and master of them all."

NeKrol snorted. "The Jaenshi are not beasts, Proctor, they are an intelligent race, with their own religion and art and customs, and they . . ."

Wyatt looked at him. "They have no soul. Only the children of Bakkalon have souls, only the seed of Earth. What mind they may have is relevant only to you, and perhaps them. Soulless, they are beasts."

"Arik has shown me the worship pyramids they build," Ryther said. "Surely creatures that build such shrines must have souls."

The Proctor shook his head. "You are in error in your belief. It is written clearly in the Book. We, the seed of Earth, are truly the children of Bakkalon, and no others. The rest are animals, and in Bakkalon's name we must assert our dominion over them."

"Very well," Ryther said. "But you will have to assert your dominion without aid from the *Lights of Jolostar,* I'm afraid. And I must inform you, Proctor, that I find your actions seriously disturbing, and intend to report them when I return to Jamison's World."

"I expected no less," Wyatt said. "Perhaps by next year you will burn with love of Bakkalon, and we may talk again. Until then, the world of Corlos will survive." He saluted her, and walked briskly from the field, followed by the four Steel Angels.

"What good will it do to report them?" neKrol said bitterly, after they had gone.

"None," Ryther said, looking off toward the forest. The wind was kicking up the dust around her, and her shoulders slumped, as if she were very tired. "The Jamies won't care, and if they did, what could they do?"

NeKrol remembered the heavy red-bound book that Wyatt had given him months ago. "And Bakkalon the pale child fashioned his children out of steel," he quoted, "for the stars will break those of softer flesh. And in the hand of each new-made infant He placed a beaten sword, telling them, 'This is the Truth and the Way.'" He spat in disgust. "That is their very creed. And we can do nothing?"

Her face was empty of expression now. "I will leave you two lasers. In a year, make sure the Jaenshi know how to use them. I believe I know what sort of trade goods I should bring."

———

THE JAENSHI LIVED IN CLANS (AS NEKROL THOUGHT OF THEM) OF twenty to thirty, each clan divided equally between adults and children, each having its own home-forest and worship pyramid. They did not build; they slept curled up in trees around their pyramid. For food, they foraged; juicy blue-black fruits grew everywhere, and there were three varieties of edible berries, a hallucinogenic leaf, and a soapy yellow root the Jaenshi dug for. NeKrol had found them to be hunters as well, though infrequently. A clan would go for months without meat, while the snuffling brown bushogs multiplied all around them, digging up roots and playing with the children. Then suddenly, when the bushog population had reached some critical point, the Jaenshi spearmen would walk among them calmly, killing two out of every three, and that week great hog roasts would be held each night around the pyramid. Similar patterns could be discerned with the white-bodied tree slugs that sometimes covered the fruit trees like a plague, until the Jaenshi gathered them for a stew, and with the fruit-stealing pseudomonks that haunted the higher limbs.

So far as neKrol could tell, there were no predators in the forests of the Jaenshi. In his early months on their world, he had worn a long force-knife and a hand-laser as he walked from pyramid to pyramid on his trade route. But he had never encountered anything even remotely hostile, and now the knife lay broken in his kitchen, while the laser was long lost.

The day after the *Lights of Jolostar* departed, neKrol went armed into the forest again, with one of Ryther's hunting lasers slung over his shoulder.

Less than two kilometers from his base, neKrol found the camp of the Jaenshi he called the waterfall folk. They lived up against the side of a heavy-wooded hill, where a stream of tumbling blue-white water came sliding and bouncing down, dividing and rejoining itself over and over, so the whole hillside was an intricate glittering web of water-falls and rapids and shallow pools and spraying wet curtains. The clan's worship pyramid sat in the bottommost pool, on a flat gray stone in the middle of the eddies: taller than most Jaenshi, coming up to neKrol's chin, looking infinitely heavy and solid and immovable, a three-sided block of dark, dark red.

NeKrol was not fooled. He had seen other pyramids sliced to pieces by the lasers of the Steel Angels and shattered by the flames of their blasters; whatever powers the pyramids might have in Jaenshi myth, whatever mysteries might lie behind their origin, it was not enough to stay the swords of Bakkalon.

The glade around the pyramid-pool was alive with sunlight when neKrol entered, and the long grasses swayed in the light breeze, but most of the waterfall folk were elsewhere. In the trees perhaps, climbing and coupling and pulling down fruits, or ranging through the forests on their hill. The trader found only a few small children riding on a bushog in the clearing when he arrived. He sat down to wait, warm in the sunlight.

Soon the old talker appeared.

He sat down next to neKrol, a tiny shriveled Jaenshi with only a few patches of dirty gray-white fur left to hide the wrinkles in his skin. He was toothless, clawless, feeble; but his eyes, wide and golden and pupil-less as those of any Jaenshi, were still alert, alive. He was the talker of the waterfall folk, the one in closest communication with the worship pyramid. Every clan had a talker.

"I have something new to trade," neKrol said, in the soft slurred speech of the Jaenshi. He had learned the tongue before coming here, back on Avalon. Tomas Chung, the legendary Avalonian linguist, had broken it centuries before, when the Kleronomas Survey brushed by this world. No other human had visited the Jaenshi since, but the maps of Kleronomas and Chung's language-pattern analysis both remained alive in the computers at the Avalon Institute for the Study of Non-Human Intelligence.

"We have made you more statues, have fashioned new woods," the old talker said. "What have you brought? Salt?"

NeKrol undid his knapsack, laid it out, and opened it. He took out one of the bricks of salt he carried, and laid it before the old talker. "Salt," he said. "And more." He laid the hunting rifle before the Jaenshi.

"What is this?" the old talker asked.

"Do you know of the Steel Angels?" neKrol asked.

The other nodded, a gesture neKrol had taught him. "The godless who run from the dead valley speak of them. They are the ones who make the gods grow silent, the pyramid breakers."

"This is a tool like the Steel Angels use to break your pyramids," neKrol said. "I am offering it to you in trade."

The old talker sat very still. "But we do not wish to break pyramids," he said.

"This tool can be used for other things," neKrol said. "In time, the Steel Angels may come here, to break the pyramid of the waterfall folk. If by then you have tools like this, you can stop them. The people of the pyramid in the ring-of-stone tried to stop the Steel Angels with spears and knives, and now they are scattered and wild and their children hang dead from the walls of the City of the Steel Angels. Other clans of the Jaenshi were unresisting, yet now they too are godless and landless. The time will come when the waterfall folk will need this tool, old talker."

The Jaenshi elder lifted the laser and turned it curiously in his small withered hands. "We must pray on this," he said. "Stay, Arik. Tonight we shall tell you, when the god looks down on us. Until then, we shall trade." He rose abruptly, gave a swift glance at the pyramid across the pool, and faded into the forest, still holding the laser.

NeKrol sighed. He had a long wait before him; the prayer assemblies never came until sundown. He moved to the edge of the pool and unlaced his heavy boots to soak his sweaty, calloused feet in the crisp cold waters.

When he looked up, the first of the carvers had arrived; a lithe young Jaenshi female with a touch of auburn in her body fur. Silent (they were all silent in neKrol's presence, all save the talker), she offered him her work.

It was a statuette no larger than his fist, a heavy-breasted fertility goddess fashioned out of the fragrant, thin-veined blue wood of the fruit trees. She sat cross-legged on a triangular base, and three thin slivers of bone rose from each corner of the triangle to meet above her head in a blob of clay.

NeKrol took the carving, turned it this way and that, and nodded his approval. The Jaenshi smiled and vanished, taking the salt brick with her. Long after she was gone, neKrol continued to admire his acquisition. He had traded all his life, spending ten years among the squid-faced gethsoids of Aath and four with the stick-thin Fyndii, traveling a trader's circuit to a half-dozen Stone Age planets that had once been slaveworlds of the broken Hrangan Empire; but nowhere had he found artists like the Jaenshi. Not for the first time, he wondered why neither Kleronomas nor Chung had mentioned the native carvings. He was glad they hadn't, though, and fairly certain that once the dealers saw the crates of wooden gods he had sent back with Ryther, the world would be overrun by traders. As it was, he had been sent here entirely on speculation, in hopes of finding a Jaenshi drug or herb or liquor that might move well in stellar trade. Instead he'd found the art, like an answer to a prayer.

Other workmen came and went as the morning turned to afternoon and the afternoon to dusk, setting their craft before him. He looked over each piece carefully, taking some and declining others, paying for what he took in salt. Before full darkness had descended, a small pile of goods sat by his right hand; a matched set of redstone knives, a gray deathcloth woven from the fur of an elderly Jaenshi by his widow and friends (with his face wrought upon it in the silky golden hairs of a pseudomonk), a bone spear with tracings that reminded neKrol of the runes of Old Earth legend; and statues. The statues were his favorites, always; so often alien art was alien beyond comprehension, but the Jaenshi workmen touched emotional chords in him. The gods they carved, each sitting in a bone pyramid, wore Jaenshi faces, yet at the same time seemed archetypically human: stern-faced war gods, things that looked oddly like satyrs, fertility goddesses like the one he had bought, almost-manlike warriors and nymphs. Often neKrol had wished that he had a formal education in extee anthropology, so that he might write a book on the universals of myth. The Jaenshi surely had a rich mythology, though the talkers never spoke of it; nothing else could explain the carvings. Perhaps the old gods were no longer worshipped, but they were still remembered.

By the time the Heart of Bakkalon went down and the last reddish rays ceased to filter through the looming trees, neKrol had gathered as much as he could carry, and his salt was all but exhausted. He laced up his boots again, packed his acquisitions with painstaking care, and sat patiently in the poolside grass, waiting. One by one, the waterfall folk joined him. Finally the old talker returned.

The prayers began.

The old talker, with the laser still in his hand, waded carefully across the night-dark waters, to squat by the black bulk of the pyramid. The others, adults and children together, now some forty strong, chose spots in the grass near the banks, behind neKrol and around him. Like him, they looked out over the pool, at the pyramid and the talker outlined clearly in the light of a new-risen, oversized moon. Setting the laser down on the stone, the old talker pressed both palms flat against the side of the pyramid, and his body seemed to go stiff, while all the other Jaenshi also tensed and grew very quiet.

NeKrol shifted restlessly and fought a yawn. It was not the first time he'd sat through a prayer ritual, and he knew the routine. A good hour of boredom lay before him; the Jaenshi did silent worship, and there was nothing to be heard but their steady breathing, nothing to be seen but forty impassive faces. Sighing, the trader tried to relax, closing his eyes and concentrating on the soft grass beneath him and the warm breeze that tossed his wild mane of hair. Here, briefly, he found peace. How long would it last, he mused, should the Steel Angels leave their valley. . . .

The hour passed, but neKrol, lost in meditation, scarce felt the flow of time. Until suddenly he heard the rustlings and chatter around him, as the waterfall folk rose and went back into the forest. And then the old talker stood in front of him, and laid the laser at his feet.

"No," he said simply.

NeKrol started. "What? But you *must*. Let me show you what it can do. . . ."

"I have had a vision, Arik. The god has shown me. But also he has shown me that it would not be a good thing to take this in trade."

"Old Talker, the Steel Angels will come. . . ."

"If they come, our god shall speak to them," the Jaenshi elder said, in his purring speech, but there was finality in the gentle voice, and no appeal in the vast liquid eyes.

———

"FOR OUR FOOD, WE THANK OURSELVES, NONE OTHER. IT IS OURS BE-cause we worked for it, ours because we fought for it, ours by the only right that is: the right of the strong. But for that strength—for the might of our arms and the steel of our swords and the fire in our hearts—we thank Bakkalon, the pale child, who gave us life and taught us how to keep it."

The Proctor stood stiffly at the centermost of the five long wooden tables that stretched the length of the great mess hall, pro-nouncing each word of the grace with solemn dignity. His large veined hands pressed tightly together as he spoke, against the flat of the upward-jutting sword, and the dim lights had faded his uniform to an almost-black. Around him, the Steel Angels sat at attention, their food untouched before them: fat boiled tubers, steaming chunks of bushog meat, black bread, bowls of crunchy green neograss. Children below the fighting age of ten, in smocks of starchy white and the omnipresent mesh-steel belts, filled the two outermost tables beneath the slitlike windows; toddlers struggled to sit still under the watchful eyes of stern nine-year-old houseparents with hardwood batons in their belts. Farther in, the fighting brotherhood sat, fully armed, at two equally long tables, men and women alternating, leather-skinned veterans sitting next to ten-year-olds who had barely moved from the children's dorm to the barracks. All of them wore the same chameleon cloth as Wyatt, though without his collar, and a few had buttons of rank. The center table, less than half the length of the others, held the cadre of the Steel Angels; the squadfathers and squadmothers, the weaponsmasters, the healers, the four fieldbishops, all those who wore the high, stiff crimson collar. And the Proctor, at its head.

"Let us eat," Wyatt said at last. His sword moved above his table with a whoosh, describing the slash of blessing, and he sat to his meal. The Proctor, like all the others, had stood single-file in the line that wound past the kitchen to the mess hall, and his portions were no larger than the least of the brotherhood.

There was a clink of knives and forks, and the infrequent clatter of a plate, and from time to time the thwack of a baton, as a houseparent punished some transgression of discipline by one of his charges; other than that, the hall was silent. The Steel Angels did not speak at meals, but rather meditated on the lessons of the day as they consumed their spartan fare.

Afterwards, the children—still silent—marched out of the hall, back to their dormitory. The fighting brotherhood followed, some to chapel, most to the barracks, a few to guard duty on the walls. The men they were relieving would find late meals still warm in the kitchen.

The officer corp remained; after the plates were cleared away, the meal became a staff meeting.

"At ease," Wyatt said, but the figures along the table relaxed little, if at all. Relaxation had been bred out of them by now. The Proctor found one of them with his eyes. "Dhallis," he said, "you have the report I requested?"

Fieldbishop Dhallis nodded. She was a husky middle-aged woman with thick muscles and skin the color of brown leather. On her collar was a small steel insignia, an ornamental memory-chip that meant Computer Services. "Yes, Proctor," she said, in a hard, precise voice. "Jamison's World is a fourth-generation colony, settled mostly from Old Poseidon. One large continent, almost entirely unexplored, and more than twelve thousand islands of various sizes. The human population is concentrated almost entirely on the islands, and makes its living by farming sea and land, aquatic husbandry, and heavy industry. The oceans are rich in food and metal. The total population is about seventy-nine million. There are two large cities, both with spaceports: Port Jamison and Jolostar." She looked down at the computer printout on the table. "Jamison's World was not even charted at the time of the Double War. It has never known military action, and the only Jamie armed forces are their planetary police. It has no colonial program and has never attempted to claim political jurisdiction beyond its own atmosphere."

The Proctor nodded. "Excellent. Then the trader's threat to report us is essentially an empty one. We can proceed. Squadfather Walman?"

"Four Jaenshi were taken today, Proctor, and are now on the walls," Walman reported. He was a ruddy young man with a blond crewcut and large ears. "If I might, sir, I would request discussion of possible termination of the campaign. Each day we search harder for less. We have virtually wiped out every Jaenshi youngling of the clans who originally inhabited Sword Valley."

Wyatt nodded. "Other opinions?"

Fieldbishop Lyon, blue-eyed and gaunt, indicated dissent. "The adults remain alive. The mature beast is more dangerous than the youngling, Squadfather."

"Not in this case," Weaponsmaster C'ara DaHan said. DaHan was a giant of a man, bald and bronze-colored, the chief of Psychological Weaponry and Enemy Intelligence. "Our studies show that once the pyramid is destroyed, neither full-grown Jaenshi nor the immature pose any threat whatsoever to the children of Bakkalon. Their social structure virtually disintegrates. The adults either flee, hoping to join some other clan, or revert to near-animal savagery. They abandon the younglings, most of whom fend for themselves in a confused sort of way and offer no resistance when we take them. Considering the number of Jaenshi on our walls, and those reported slain by predators or each other, I strongly feel that Sword Valley is virtually clean of the animals. Winter is coming, Proctor, and much must be done. Squadfather Walman and his men should be set to other tasks."

There was more discussion, but the tone had been set; most of the speakers backed DaHan. Wyatt listened carefully, and all the while prayed to Bakkalon for guidance. Finally he motioned for quiet.

"Squadfather," he said to Walman, "tomorrow collect all the Jaenshi—both adults and children—that you can, but do not hang them if they are unresisting. Instead, take them to the city, and show them their clanmates on our walls. Then cast them from the valley, one in each direction of the compass." He bowed his head. "It is my hope that they will carry a message, to all the Jaenshi, of the price that must be paid when a beast raises hand or claw or blade against the seed of Earth. Then, when the spring comes and the children of Bakkalon move beyond Sword Valley, the Jaenshi will peacefully abandon their pyramids and quit whatever lands men may require, so the glory of the pale child might be spread."

Lyon and DaHan both nodded, among others. "Speak wisdom to us," Fieldbishop Dhallis said then.

Proctor Wyatt agreed. One of the lesser-ranking squadmothers brought him the Book, and he opened it to the Chapter of Teachings.

"In those days much evil had come upon the seed of Earth," the Proctor read, "for the children of Bakkalon had abandoned Him to bow to softer gods. So their skies grew dark and upon them from above came the Sons of Hranga with red eyes and demon teeth, and upon them from below came the vast Horde of Fyndii like a cloud of locusts that blotted out the stars. And the worlds flamed, and the children cried out, 'Save us! Save us!'

"And the pale child came and stood before them, with His great sword in His hand, and in a voice like thunder He rebuked them. 'You have been weak children,' He told them, 'for you have disobeyed. Where are your swords? Did I not set swords in your hands?'

"And the children cried out, 'We have beaten them into plowshares, oh Bakkalon!'

"And He was sore angry. 'With plowshares, then, shall you face the Sons of Hranga! With plowshares shall you slay the Horde of Fyndii?' And He left them, and heard no more their weeping, for the Heart of Bakkalon is a Heart of Fire.

"But then one among the seed of Earth dried his tears, for the skies did burn so bright that they ran scalding on his cheeks. And the blood-lust rose in him and he beat his plowshare back into a sword, and charged the Sons of Hranga, slaying as he went. The others saw, and followed, and a great battle cry rang across the worlds.

"And the pale child heard, and came again, for the sound of battle is more pleasing to his ears than the sound of wails. And when He saw, He smiled. 'Now you are my children again,' He said to the seed of Earth. 'For you had turned against me to worship a god who calls himself a lamb, but did you not know that lambs go only to the slaughter? Yet now your eyes have cleared, and again you are the Wolves of God!'

"And Bakkalon gave them all swords again, all His children and all the seed of Earth, and He lifted his great black blade, the Demon-Reaver that slays the soulless, and swung it. And the Sons of Hranga fell before His might, and the great Horde that was the Fyndii burned beneath His gaze. And the children of Bakkalon swept across the worlds."

The Proctor lifted his eyes. "Go, my brothers-in-arms, and think on the Teachings of Bakkalon as you sleep. May the pale child grant you visions!"

They were dismissed.

THE TREES ON THE HILL WERE BARE AND GLAZED WITH ICE, AND THE snow—unbroken except for their footsteps and the stirrings of the bitter-sharp north wind—gleamed a blinding white in the noon sun. In the valley beneath, the City of the Steel Angels looked preternaturally clean and still. Great snowdrifts had piled against the eastern walls, climbing halfway up the stark scarlet stone; the gates had not opened in months. Long ago, the children of Bakkalon had taken their harvest and fallen back inside the city, to huddle around their fires. But for the blue lights that burned late into the cold black night, and the occasional guard pacing atop the walls, neKrol would hardly have known that the Angels still lived.

The Jaenshi that neKrol had come to think of as the bitter speaker looked at him out of eyes curiously darker than the soft gold of her brothers. "Below the snow, the god lies broken," she said, and even the soothing tones of the Jaenshi tongue could not hide the hardness in her voice. They stood at the very spot where neKrol had once taken Ryther, the spot where the pyramid of the people of the ring-of-stone once stood. NeKrol was sheathed head to foot in a white thermosuit that clung too tightly, accenting every unsightly bulge. He looked out on Sword Valley from behind a dark blue plastifilm in the suit's cowl. But the Jaenshi, the bitter speaker, was nude, covered only by the thick gray fur of her winter coat. The strap of the hunting laser ran down between her breasts.

"Other gods besides yours will break unless the Steel Angels are stopped," neKrol said, shivering despite his thermosuit.

The bitter speaker seemed hardly to hear. "I was a child when they came, Arik. If they had left our god, I might be a child still. Afterwards, when the light went out and the glow inside me died, I wandered far from the ring-of-stone, beyond our own home forest; knowing nothing, eating where I could. Things are not the same in the dark valley. Bushogs honked at my passing, and charged me with their tusks, other Jaenshi threatened me and each other. I did not understand and I could not pray. Even when the Steel Angels found me, I did not understand, and I went with them to their city, knowing nothing of their speech. I remember the walls, and the children, many so much younger than me. Then I screamed and struggled; when I saw those on the ropes, something wild and godless stirred to life inside me." Her eyes regarded him, her eyes like burnished bronze. She shifted in the ankle-deep snow, curling a clawed hand around the strap of her laser.

NeKrol had taught her well since the day she had joined him, in the late summer when the Steel Angels had cast her from Sword Valley. The bitter speaker was by far the best shot of his six, the godless exiles he had gathered to him and trained. It was the only way; he had offered the lasers in trade to clan after clan, and each had refused. The Jaenshi were certain that their gods would protect them. Only the godless listened, and not all of them; many—the young children, the quiet ones, the first to flee—many had been accepted into other clans. But others, like the bitter speaker, had grown too savage, had seen too much; they fit no longer. She had been the first to take the weapon, after the old talker had sent her away from the waterfall folk.

"It is often better to be without gods," neKrol told her. "Those below us have a god, and it has made them what they are. And so the Jaenshi have gods, and because they trust, they die. You godless are their only hope."

The bitter speaker did not answer. She only looked down on the silent city, besieged by snow, and her eyes smoldered.

And neKrol watched her, and wondered. He and his six were the hope of the Jaenshi, he had said; if so, was there hope at all? The bitter speaker, and all his exiles, had a madness about them, a rage that made him tremble. Even if Ryther came with the lasers, even if so small a group could stop the Angels' march, even if all that came to pass— what then? Should all the Angels die tomorrow, where would his godless find a place?

They stood, all quiet, while the snow stirred under their feet and the north wind bit at them.

———

THE CHAPEL WAS DARK AND QUIET. FLAMEGLOBES BURNED A DIM, EERIE red in either corner, and the rows of plain wooden benches were empty. Above the heavy altar, a slab of rough black stone, Bakkalon stood in hologram, so real he almost breathed; a boy, a mere boy, naked and milky white, with the wide eyes and blond hair of innocent youth. In his hand, half again taller than himself, was the great black sword.

Wyatt knelt before the projection, head bowed and very still. All through the winter his dreams had been dark and troubled, so each day he would kneel and pray for guidance. There was none else to seek but Bakkalon; he, Wyatt, was the Proctor, who led in battle and in faith. He alone must riddle his visions.

So daily he wrestled with his thoughts, until the snows began to melt and the knees of his uniform had nearly worn through from long scraping on the floor. Finally, he had decided, and this day he had called upon the senior collars to join him in the chapel.

Alone they entered, while the Proctor knelt unmoving, and chose seats on the benches behind him, each apart from his fellows. Wyatt took no notice; he prayed only that his words would be correct, his vision true. When they were all there, he stood and turned to face them.

"Many are the worlds on which the children of Bakkalon have lived," he told them, "but none so blessed as this, our Corlos. A great time is on us, my brothers-in-arms. The pale child has come to me in my sleep, as once he came to the first Proctors in the years when the brotherhood was forged. He has given me visions."

They were quiet, all of them, their eyes humble and obedient; he was their Proctor, after all. There could be no questioning when one of higher rank spoke wisdom or gave orders. That was one of the precepts of Bakkalon, that the chain of command was sacred and never to be doubted. So all of them kept silence.

"Bakkalon Himself has walked upon this world. He has walked among the soulless and the beasts of the field and told them our dominion, and this He has said to me: that when the spring comes and the seed of Earth moves from Sword Valley to take new land, all the animals shall know their place and retire before us. This I do prophesy!

"More, we shall see miracles. That too the pale child has promised me, signs by which we will know His truth, signs that shall bolster our faith with new revelation. But so too shall our faith be tested, for it will be a time of sacrifices, and Bakkalon will call upon us more than once to show our trust in Him. We must remember His Teachings and be true, and each of us must obey Him as a child obeys the parent and a fighting man his officer: that is, swiftly and without question. For the pale child knows best.

"These are the visions He has granted me, these are the dreams that I have dreamed. Brothers, pray with me."

And Wyatt turned again and knelt, and the rest knelt with him, and all the heads were bowed in prayer save one. In the shadows at the rear of the chapel where the flameglobes flickered but dimly, C'ara DaHan stared at his Proctor from beneath a heavy beetled brow.

That night, after a silent meal in the mess hall and a short staff meeting, the Weaponsmaster called upon Wyatt to go walking on the walls. "Proctor, my soul is troubled," he told him. "I must have counsel from he who is closest to Bakkalon." Wyatt nodded, and both donned heavy nightcloaks of black fur and oil-dark metal cloth, and together they walked the redstone parapets beneath the stars.

Near the guardhouse that stood above the city gates, DaHan paused and leaned out over the ledge, his eyes searching the slow-melting snow for long moments before he turned them on the Proctor. "Wyatt," he said at last, "my faith is weak."

The Proctor said nothing, merely watched the other, his face concealed by the hood of his nightcloak. Confession was not a part of the rites of the Steel Angels; Bakkalon had said that a fighting man's faith ought never to waver.

"In the old days," C'ara DaHan was saying, "many weapons were used against the children of Bakkalon. Some, today, exist only in tales. Perhaps they never existed. Perhaps they are empty things, like the gods the soft men worship. I am only a Weaponsmaster; such knowledge is not mine.

"Yet there is a tale, my Proctor—one that troubles me. Once, it is said, in the long centuries of war, the Sons of Hranga loosed upon the seed of Earth foul vampires of the mind, the creatures men called soulsucks. Their touch was invisible, but it crept across kilometers, farther than a man could see, farther than a laser could fire, and it brought madness. Visions, my Proctor, visions! False gods and foolish plans were put in the minds of men, and . . ."

"Silence," Wyatt said. His voice was hard, as cold as the night air that crackled around them and turned his breath to steam.

There was a long pause. Then, in a softer voice, the Proctor continued. "All winter I have prayed, DaHan, and struggled with my visions. I am the Proctor of the Children of Bakkalon on the World of Corlos, not some new-armed child to be lied to by false gods. I spoke only after I was sure. I spoke as your Proctor, as your father in faith and your commanding officer. That you would question me, Weaponsmaster, that you would doubt—this disturbs me greatly. Next will you stop to argue with me on the field of battle, to dispute some fine point of my orders?"

"Never, Proctor," DaHan said, kneeling in penance in the packed snow atop the walkway.

"I hope not. But, before I dismiss you, because you are my brother in Bakkalon, I will answer you, though I need not and it was wrong of you to expect it. I will tell you this; the Proctor Wyatt is a good officer as well as a devout man. The pale child has made prophecies to me, and has predicted that miracles will come to pass. All these things we shall see with our very eyes. But if the prophecies should fail us, and if no signs appear, well, our eyes will see that too. And then I will know that it was not Bakkalon who sent the visions, but only a false god, perhaps a soul-suck of Hranga. Or do you think a Hrangan can work miracles?"

"No," DaHan said, still on his knees, his great bald head downcast. "That would be heresy."

"Indeed," said Wyatt. The Proctor glanced briefly beyond the walls. The night was crisp and cold and there was no moon. He felt transfigured, and even the stars seemed to cry the glory of the pale child, for the constellation of the Sword was high upon the zenith, the Soldier reaching up toward it from where he stood on the horizon.

"Tonight you will walk guard without your cloak," the Proctor told DaHan when he looked down again. "And should the north wind blow and the cold bite at you, you will rejoice in the pain, for it will be a sign that you submit to your Proctor and your god. As your flesh grows bitter numb, the flame in your heart must burn hotter."

"Yes, my Proctor," DaHan said. He stood and removed his night-cloak, handing it to the other. Wyatt gave him the slash of blessing.

On the wallscreen in his darkened living quarters the taped drama went through its familiar measured paces, but neKrol, slouched in a large cushioned recliner with his eyes half-closed, hardly noticed. The bitter speaker and two of the other Jaenshi exiles sat on the floor, golden eyes rapt on the spectacle of humans chasing and shooting each other amid the vaulting tower cities of ai-Emerel; increasingly they had begun to grow curious about other worlds and other ways of life. It was all very strange, neKrol thought; the waterfall folk and the other clanned Jaenshi had never shown any such interest. He remembered the early days, before the coming of the Steel Angels in their ancient and soon-to-be-dismantled warship, when he had set all kinds of trade goods before the Jaenshi talkers; bright bolts of glittersilk from Avalon, glowstone jewelry from High Kavalaan, duralloy knives and solar generators and steel powerbows, books from a dozen worlds, medicines and wines—he had come with a little of everything. The talkers took some of it, from time to time, but never with any enthusiasm; the only offering that excited them was salt.

It was not until the spring rains came and the bitter speaker began to question him that neKrol realized, with a start, how seldom any of the Jaenshi clans had ever asked him anything. Perhaps their social structure and their religion stifled their natural intellectual curiosity. The exiles were certainly eager enough, especially the bitter speaker. NeKrol could answer only a small portion of her questions of late, and even then she always had new ones to puzzle him with. He had begun to grow appalled with the extent of his own ignorance.

But then, so had the bitter speaker; unlike the clanned Jaenshi—did the religion make *that* much difference?—she would answer questions as well, and neKrol had tried quizzing her on many things that he'd wondered at. But most of the time she would only blink in bafflement, and begin to question herself.

"There are no stories about our gods," she said to him once, when he'd tried to learn a little of Jaenshi myth. "What sort of stories could there be? The gods live in the worship pyramids, Arik, and we pray to them and they watch over us and light our lives. They do not bounce around and fight and break each other like your gods seem to do."

"But you had other gods once, before you came to worship the pyramids," neKrol objected. "The very ones your carvers did for me." He had even gone so far as to unpack a crate and show her, though surely she remembered, since the people of the pyramid in the ring-of-stone had been among the finest craftsmen.

Yet the bitter speaker only smoothed her fur, and shook her head. "I was too young to be a carver, so perhaps I was not told," she said. "We all know that which we need to know, but only the carvers need to do these things, so perhaps only they know the stories of these old gods."

Another time he had asked her about the pyramids, and had gotten even less. "Build them?" she had said. "We did not build them, Arik. They have always been, like the rocks and the trees." But then she blinked. "But they are not like the rocks and the trees, are they?" And, puzzled, she went away to talk to the others.

But if the godless Jaenshi were more thoughtful than their brothers in the clans, they were also more difficult, and each day neKrol realized more and more the futility of their enterprise. He had eight of the exiles with him now—they had found two more, half dead from starvation, in the height of winter—and they all took turns training with the two lasers and spying on the Angels. But even should Ryther return with the weaponry, their force was a joke against the might the Proctor could put in the field. The *Lights of Jolostar* would be carrying a full arms shipment in the expectation that every clan for a hundred kilometers would now be roused and angry, ready to resist the Steel Angels and overwhelm them by sheer force of numbers; Jannis would be blank-faced when only neKrol and his ragged band appeared to greet her.

If in fact they did. Even that was problematical; he was having much difficulty keeping his guerrillas together. Their hatred of the Steel Angels still bordered on madness, but they were far from a cohesive unit. None of them liked to take orders very well, and they fought constantly, going at each other with bared claws in struggles for social dominance. If neKrol had not warned them, he suspected they might even duel with the lasers. As for staying in good fighting shape, that too was a joke. Of the three females in the band, the bitter speaker was the only one who had not allowed herself to be impregnated. Since the Jaenshi usually gave birth in litters of four to eight, neKrol calculated that late summer would present them with an exile population explosion. And there would be more after that, he knew; the godless seemed to copulate almost hourly, and there was no such thing as Jaenshi birth control. He wondered how the clans kept their population so stable, but his charges didn't know that either.

"I suppose we sexed less," the bitter speaker said when he asked her, "but I was a child, so I would not really know. Before I came here, there was never the urge. I was just young, I would think." But when she said it, she scratched herself and seemed very unsure.

Sighing, neKrol eased himself back in the recliner and tried to shut out the noise of the wall-screen. It was all going to be very difficult. Already the Steel Angels had emerged from behind their walls, and the powerwagons rolled up and down Sword Valley turning forest into farmland. He had gone up into the hills himself, and it was easy to see that the spring planting would soon be done. Then, he suspected, the children of Bakkalon would try to expand. Just last week one of them—a giant "with no head fur," as his scout had described him—was seen up in the ring-of-stone, gathering shards from the broken pyramid. Whatever that meant, it could not be for the good.

Sometimes he felt sick at the forces he had set in motion, and almost wished that Ryther would forget the lasers. The bitter speaker was determined to strike as soon as they were armed, no matter what the odds. Frightened, neKrol reminded her of the hard Angel lesson the last time a Jaenshi had killed a man; in his dreams he still saw children on the walls.

But she only looked at him, with the bronze tinge of madness in her eyes, and said, "Yes, Arik. I remember."

———

SILENT AND EFFICIENT, THE WHITE-SMOCKED KITCHEN BOYS CLEARED away the last of the evening's dishes and vanished. "At ease," Wyatt said to his officers. Then: "The time of miracles is upon us, as the pale child foretold.

"This morning I sent three squads into the hills to the southeast of Sword Valley, to disperse the Jaenshi clans on lands that we require. They reported back to me in early afternoon, and now I wish to share their reports with you. Squadmother Jolip, will you relate the events that transpired when you carried out your orders?"

"Yes, Proctor." Jolip stood, a white-skinned blonde with a pinched face, her uniform hanging slightly loose on a lean body. "I was assigned a squad of ten to clear out the so-called cliff clan, whose pyramid lies near the foot of a low granite cliff in the wilder part of the hills. The information provided by our intelligence indicated that they were one of the smaller clans, with only twenty-odd adults, so I dispensed with heavy armor. We did take a class five blastcannon, since the destruction of the Jaenshi pyramids is slow work with sidearms alone, but other than that our armament was strictly standard issue.

"We expected no resistance, but recalling the incident at the ring-of-stone, I was cautious. After a march of some twelve kilometers through the hills to the vicinity of the cliff, we fanned out in a semi-circle and moved in slowly, with screechguns drawn. A few Jaenshi were encountered in the forest, and these we took prisoner and marched before us, for use as shields in the event of an ambush or attack. That, of course, proved unnecessary.

"When we reached the pyramid by the cliff, they were waiting for us. At least twelve of the beasts, sir. One of them sat near the base of the pyramid with his hands pressed against its side, while the others surrounded him in a sort of a circle. They all looked up at us, but made no other move."

She paused a minute, and rubbed a thoughtful finger up against the side of her nose. "As I told the Proctor, it was all very odd from that point forward. Last summer, I twice led squads against the Jaenshi clans. The first time, having no idea of our intentions, none of the soulless were there; we simply destroyed the artifact and left. The second time, a crowd of the creatures milled around, hampering us with their bodies while not being actively hostile. They did not disperse until I had one of them screeched down. And, of course, I studied the reports of Squadfather Allor's difficulties at the ring-of-stone.

"This time, it was all quite different. I ordered two of my men to set the blastcannon on its tripod, and gave the beasts to understand that they must get out of the way. With hand signals, of course, since I know none of their ungodly tongue. They complied at once, splitting into two groups and, well, lining up, on either side of the line-of-fire. We kept them covered with our screechguns, of course, but everything seemed very peaceful.

"And so it was. The blaster took the pyramid out neatly, a big ball of flame and then sort of a thunder as the thing exploded. A few shards were scattered, but no one was injured, as we had all taken cover and the Jaenshi seemed unconcerned. After the pyramid broke, there was a sharp ozone smell, and for an instant a lingering bluish fire—perhaps an afterimage. I hardly had time to notice them, however, since that was when the Jaenshi all fell to their knees before us. All at once, sirs. And then they pressed their heads against the ground, prostrating themselves. I thought for a moment that they were trying to hail us as gods, because we had shattered their god, and I tried to tell them that we wanted none of their animal worship, and required only that they leave these lands at once. But then I saw that I had misunderstood, because that was when the other four clan members came forward from the trees atop the cliff, and climbed down, and gave us the statue. Then the rest got up. The last I saw, the entire clan was walking due east, away from Sword Valley and the outlying hills. I took the statue and brought it back to the Proctor." She fell silent but remained standing, waiting for questions.

"I have the statuette here," Wyatt said. He reached down beside his chair and set it on the table, then pulled off the white cloth covering he had wrapped around it.

The base was a triangle of rockhard blackbark, and three long splinters of bone rose from the corners to make a pyramid frame. Within, exquisitely carved in every detail from soft blue wood, Bakkalon the pale child stood, holding a painted sword.

"What does this mean?" Fieldbishop Lyon asked, obviously startled.

"Sacrilege!" Fieldbishop Dhallis said.

"Nothing so serious," said Gorman, Fieldbishop for Heavy Armor. "The beasts are simply trying to ingratiate themselves, perhaps in the hope that we will stay our swords."

"None but the seed of Earth may bow to Bakkalon," Dhallis said. "It is written in the Book! The pale child will not look with favor on the soulless!"

"Silence, my brothers-in-arms!" the Proctor said, and the long table abruptly grew quiet again. Wyatt smiled a thin smile. "This is the first of the miracles of which I spoke this winter in the chapel, the first of the strange happenings that Bakkalon told to me. For truly He has walked this world, our Corlos, so even the beasts of the fields know His likeness! Think on it, my brothers. Think on this carving. Ask yourselves a few simple questions. Have any of the Jaenshi animals ever been permitted to set foot in this holy city?"

"No, of course not," someone said.

"Then clearly none of them have seen the holograph that stands above our altar. Nor have I often walked among the beasts, as my duties keep me here within the walls. So none could have seen the pale child's likeness on the chain of office that I wear, for the few Jaenshi who have seen my visage have not lived to speak of it—they were those I judged, who hung upon our city walls. The animals do not speak the language of the Earthseed, nor have any among us learned their simple beastly tongue. Lastly, they have not read the Book. Remember all this, and wonder; how did their carvers know what face and form to carve?"

Quiet; the leaders of the children of Bakkalon looked back and forth among themselves in wonderment.

Wyatt quietly folded his hands. "A miracle. We shall have no more trouble with the Jaenshi, for the pale child has come to them."

To the Proctor's right, Fieldbishop Dhallis sat rigidly. "My Proctor, my leader in faith," she said, with some difficulty, each word coming slowly, "surely, *surely,* you do not mean to tell us that these, these *animals*—that they can worship the pale child, that He accepts their worship!"

Wyatt seemed calm, benevolent; he only smiled. "You need not trouble your soul, Dhallis. You wonder whether I commit the First Fallacy, remembering perhaps the Sacrilege of G'hra when a captive Hrangan bowed to Bakkalon to save himself from an animal's death, and the False Proctor Gibrone proclaimed that all who worship the pale child must have souls." He shook his head. "You see, I read the Book. But no, Fieldbishop, no sacrilege has transpired. Bakkalon has walked among the Jaenshi, but surely has given them only truth. They have seen Him in all His armed dark glory, and heard Him proclaim that they are animals, without souls, as surely He would proclaim. Accordingly, they accept their place in the order of the universe, and retire before us. They will never kill a man again. Recall that they did not bow to the statue they carved, but rather gave the statue to us, the seed of Earth, who alone can rightfully worship it. When they did prostrate themselves, it was at *our* feet, as animals to men, and that is as it should be. You see? They have been given truth."

Dhallis was nodding. "Yes, my Proctor. I am enlightened. Forgive my moment of weakness."

But halfway down the table, C'ara DaHan leaned forward and knotted his great knuckled hands, frowning all the while. "My Proctor," he said heavily.

"Weaponsmaster?" Wyatt returned. His face grew stern.

"Like the Fieldbishop, my soul has flickered briefly with worry, and I too would be enlightened, if I might?"

Wyatt smiled. "Proceed," he said, in a voice without humor.

"A miracle this thing may be indeed," DaHan said, "but first we must question ourselves, to ascertain that it is not the trick of a soulless enemy. I do not fathom their strategem, or their reasons for acting as they have, but I do know of one way that the Jaenshi might have learned the features of our Bakkalon."

"Oh?"

"I speak of the Jamish trading base, and the red-haired trader Arik neKrol. He is an Earthseed, an Emereli by his looks, and we have given him the Book. But he remains without a burning love of Bakkalon, and goes without arms like a godless man. Since our landing he has opposed us, and he grew most hostile after the lesson we were forced to give the Jaenshi. Perhaps he put the cliff clan up to it, told them to do the carving, to some strange ends of his own. I believe that he *did* trade with them."

"I believe you speak truth, Weaponsmaster. In the early months after landing, I tried hard to convert neKrol. To no avail, but I did learn much of the Jaenshi beasts and of the trading he did with them." The Proctor still smiled. "He traded with one of the clans here in Sword Valley, with the people of ring-of-stone, with the cliff clan and that of the far fruit tangle, with the waterfall folk, and sundry clans farther east."

"Then it is his doing," DaHan said. "A trick!"

All eyes moved to Wyatt. "I did not say that. NeKrol, whatever intentions he might have, is but a single man. He did not trade with all the Jaenshi, nor even know them all." The Proctor's smile grew briefly wider. "Those of you who have seen the Emereli know him for a man of flab and weakness; he could hardly walk as far as might be required, and he has neither aircar nor power sled."

"But he *did* have contact with the cliff clan," DaHan said. The deep-graven lines on his bronze forehead were set stubbornly.

"Yes, he did," Wyatt answered. "But Squadmother Jolip did not go forth alone this morning. I also sent out Squadfather Walman and Squadfather Allor, to cross the waters of the White Knife. The land there is dark and fertile, better than that to the east. The cliff clan, who are southeast, were between Sword Valley and the White Knife, so they had to go. But the other pyramids we moved against belonged to far-river clans, more than thirty kilometers south. They have never seen the trader Arik neKrol, unless he has grown wings this winter."

Then Wyatt bent again, and set two more statues on the table, and pulled away their coverings. One was set on a base of slate, and the figure was carved in a clumsy broad manner; the other was finely detailed soaproot, even to the struts of the pyramid. But except for the materials and the workmanship, the later statues were identical to the first.

"Do you see a trick, Weaponsmaster?" Wyatt asked.

DaHan looked, and said nothing, for Fieldbishop Lyon rose suddenly and said, "I see a miracle," and others echoed him. After the hubbub had finally quieted, the brawny Weaponsmaster lowered his head and said, very softly, "My Proctor. Read wisdom to us."

"THE LASERS, SPEAKER, THE *LASERS!*" THERE WAS A TINGE OF HYSTERIcal desperation in neKrol's tone. "Ryther is not back yet, and that is the very point. We must wait."

He stood outside the bubble of the trading base, bare-chested and sweating in the hot morning sun, with the thick wind tugging at his tangled hair. The clamor had pulled him from a troubled sleep. He had stopped them just on the edge of the forest, and now the bitter speaker had turned to face him, looking fierce and hard and most unJaenshilike with the laser slung across her shoulders, a bright blue glittersilk scarf knotted around her neck, and fat glowstone rings on all eight of her fingers. The other exiles, but for the two that were heavy with child, stood around her. One of them held the other laser, the rest carried quivers and powerbows. That had been the speaker's idea. Her newly chosen mate was down on one knee, panting; he had run all the way from the ring-of-stone.

"No, Arik," the speaker said, eyes bronze-angry. "Your lasers are now a month overdue, by your own count of time. Each day we wait, and the Steel Angels smash more pyramids. Soon they may hang children again."

"Very soon," neKrol said. "Very soon, if you attack them. Where is your very hope of victory? Your watcher says they go with two squads and a powerwagon—can you stop them with a pair of lasers and four powerbows? Have you learned to think here, or not?"

"Yes," the speaker said, but she bared her teeth at him as she said it. "Yes, but that cannot matter. The clans do not resist, so we must."

From one knee, her mate looked up at neKrol. "They . . . they march on the waterfall," he said, still breathing heavily.

"The waterfall!" the bitter speaker repeated. "Since the death of winter, they have broken more than twenty pyramids, Arik, and their powerwagons have crushed the forest and now a great dusty road scars the soil from their valley to the riverlands. But they had hurt no Jaenshi yet this season, they had let them go. And all those clans-without-a-god have gone to the waterfall, until the home forest of the waterfall folk is bare and eaten clean. Their talkers sit with the old talker and perhaps the waterfall god takes them in, perhaps he is a very great god. I do not know these things. But I *do* know that now the bald Angel has learned of the twenty clans together, of a grouping of half-a-thousand Jaenshi adults, and he leads a powerwagon against them. Will he let them go so easy this time, happy with a carved statue? Will *they* go, Arik, will they give up a second god as easily as a first?" The speaker blinked. "I fear they will resist with their silly claws. I fear the bald Angel will hang them even if they do not resist, because so many in union throws suspicion in him. I fear many things and know little, but I know *we* must be there. You will not stop us, Arik, and we cannot wait for your long-late lasers."

And she turned to the others and said, "Come, we must run," and they had faded into the forest before neKrol could even shout for them to stay. Swearing, he turned back to the bubble.

The two female exiles were leaving just as he entered. Both were close to the end of their term, but they had powerbows in their hands. NeKrol stopped short. "You too!" he said furiously, glaring at them. "Madness, it is the very stuff of madness!" They only looked at him with silent golden eyes, and moved past him toward the trees.

Inside, he swiftly braided his long red hair so it would not catch on the branches, slipped into a shirt, and darted toward the door. Then he stopped. A weapon, he must have a weapon! He glanced around frantically and ran heavily for his storeroom. The powerbows were all gone, he saw. What then, what? He began to rummage, and finally settled for a duralloy machete. It felt strange in his hand and he must have looked most unmartial and ridiculous, but somehow he felt he must take something.

Then he was off, toward the place of the waterfall folk.

NeKROL WAS overweight and soft, hardly used to running, and the way was nearly two kilometers through lush summer forest. He had to stop three times to rest, and quiet the pains in his chest, and it seemed an eternity before he arrived. But still he beat the Steel Angels; a powerwagon is ponderous and slow, and the road from Sword Valley was longer and more hilly.

Jaenshi were everywhere. The glade was bare of grass and twice as large as neKrol remembered it from his last trading trip, early that spring. Still, the Jaenshi filled all of it, sitting on the ground, staring at the pool and the waterfall, all silent, packed together so there was scarcely room to walk among them. More sat above, a dozen in every fruit tree, some of the children even ascending to the higher limbs where the pseudomonks usually ruled alone.

On the rock at the center of the pool, with the waterfall behind them as a backdrop, the talkers pressed around the pyramid of the waterfall folk. They were closer together than even those in the grass, and each had his palms flat against the sides. One, thin and frail, sat on the shoulders of another so that he too might touch. NeKrol tried to count them and gave up; the group was too dense, a blurred mass of gray-furred arms and golden eyes, the pyramid at their center, dark and unmovable as ever.

The bitter speaker stood in the pool, the waters ankle-deep around her. She was facing the crowd and screeching at them, her voice strangely unlike the usual Jaenshi purr; in her scarf and rings, she looked absurdly out of place. As she talked, she waved the laser rifle she was holding in one hand. Wildly, passionately, hysterically, she was telling the gathered Jaenshi that the Steel Angels were coming, that they must leave at once, that they should break up and go into the forest and regroup at the trading base. Over and over again she said it.

But the clans were stiff and silent. No one answered, no one listened, no one heard. In full daylight, they were praying.

NeKrol pushed his way through them, stepping on a hand here and a foot there, hardly able to set down a boot without crunching Jaenshi flesh. He was standing next to the bitter speaker, who still gestured wildly, before her bronze eyes seemed to see him. Then she stopped. "Arik," she said, "the Angels are coming, and *they will not listen.*"

"The others," he panted, still short on breath. "Where are they?"

"The trees," the bitter speaker replied, with a vague gesture. "I sent them up in the trees. Snipers, Arik, such as we saw upon your wall."

"Please," he said. "Come back with me. Leave them, leave them. You told them. I told them. Whatever happens, it is their doing, it is the fault of their fool religion."

"I cannot leave," the bitter speaker said. She seemed confused, as so often when neKrol had questioned her back at the base. "It seems I should, but somehow I know I must stay here. And the others will never go, even if I did. They feel it much more strongly. We must be here. To fight, to talk." She blinked. "I do not know *why*, Arik, but we must."

And before the trader could reply, the Steel Angels came out of the forest.

There were five of them at first, widely spaced; then shortly five more. All afoot, in uniforms whose mottled dark greens blended with the leaves, so that only the glitter of the mesh-steel belts and matching battle helmets stood out. One of them, a gaunt pale woman, wore a high red collar; all of them had hand-lasers drawn.

"You!" the blond woman shouted, her eyes finding Arik at once, as he stood with his braid flying in the wind and the machete dangling uselessly in his hand. "Speak to these animals! Tell them they must leave! Tell them that no Jaenshi gathering of this size is permitted east of the mountains, by order of the Proctor Wyatt, and the pale child Bakkalon. Tell them!" And then she saw the bitter speaker, and started. "And take the laser from the hand of that animal before we burn both of you down!"

Trembling, neKrol dropped the machete from limp fingers into the water. "Speaker, drop the gun," he said in Jaenshi, "*please*. If you ever hope to see the far stars. Let loose the laser, my friend, my child, this very now. And I will take you when Ryther comes, with me to ai-Emerel and farther places." The trader's voice was full of fear; the Steel Angels held their lasers steady, and not for a moment did he think the speaker would obey him.

But strangely, meekly, she threw the laser rifle into the pool. NeKrol could not see to read her eyes.

The Squadmother relaxed visibly. "Good," she said. "Now, talk to them in their beastly talk, tell them to leave. If not, we shall crush them. A powerwagon is on its way!" And now, over the roar and tumble of the nearby waters, neKrol could hear it; a heavy crunching as it rolled over trees, rending them into splinters beneath wide duramesh treads. Perhaps they were using the blastcannon and the turret lasers to clear away boulders and other obstacles.

"We have told them," neKrol said desperately. "Many times we have told them, but they do not hear!" He gestured all about him; the glade was still hot and close with Jaenshi bodies and none among the clans had taken the slightest notice of the Steel Angels or the confrontation. Behind him, the clustered talkers still pressed small hands against their god.

"Then we shall bare the sword of Bakkalon to them," the Squadmother said, "and perhaps they will hear their own wailing!" She holstered her laser and drew a screechgun, and neKrol, shuddering, knew her intent. The screechers used concentrated high-intensity sound to break down cell walls and liquify flesh. Its effects were psychological as much as anything; there was no more horrible death.

But then a second squad of the Angels was among them, and there was a creak of wood straining and snapping, and from behind a final grove of fruit trees, dimly, neKrol could see the black flanks of the powerwagon, its blastcannon seemingly trained right at him. Two of the newcomers wore the scarlet collar—a red-faced youth with large ears who barked orders to his squad, and a huge, muscular man with a bald head and lined bronze skin. NeKrol recognized him; the Weaponsmaster C'ara DaHan. It was DaHan who laid a heavy hand on the Squadmother's arm as she raised her screechgun. "No," he said. "It is not the way."

She holstered the weapon at once. "I hear and obey."

DaHan looked at neKrol. "Trader," he boomed, "is this your doing?"

"No," neKrol said.

"They will not disperse," the Squadmother added.

"It would take us a day and a night to screech them down," DaHan said, his eyes sweeping over the glade and the trees, and following the rocky twisted path of the waterwall up to its summit. "There is an easier way. Break the pyramid and they go at once." He stopped then, about to say something else; his eyes were on the bitter speaker.

"A Jaenshi in rings and cloth," he said. "They have woven nothing but deathcloth up to now. This alarms me."

"She is one of the people of the ring-of-stone," neKrol said quickly. "She has lived with me."

DaHan nodded. "I understand. You are truly a godless man, neKrol, to consort so with soulless animals, to teach them to ape the ways of the seed of Earth. But it does not matter." He raised his arm in signal; behind him, among the trees, the blastcannon of the powerwagon moved slightly to the right. "You and your pet should move at once," DaHan told neKrol. "When I lower my arm, the Jaenshi god will burn and if you stand in the way, you will never move again."

"The *talkers!*" neKrol protested, "the blast will—" and he started to turn to show them. But the talkers were crawling away from the pyramid, one by one.

Behind him, the Angels were muttering. "A miracle!" one said hoarsely. "Our child! Our Lord!" cried another.

NeKrol stood paralyzed. The pyramid on the rock was no

longer a reddish slab. Now it sparkled in the sunlight, a canopy of transparent crystal. And below that canopy, perfect in every detail, the pale child Bakkalon stood smiling, with his Demon-Reaver in his hand.

The Jaenshi talkers were scrambling from it now, tripping in the water in their haste to be away. NeKrol glimpsed the old talker, running faster than any despite his age. Even he seemed not to understand. The bitter speaker stood open-mouthed.

The trader turned. Half of the Steel Angels were on their knees, the rest had absent-mindedly lowered their arms and they froze in gaping wonder. The Squadmother turned to DaHan. "It *is* a miracle," she said. "As Proctor Wyatt has foreseen. The pale child walks upon this world."

But the Weaponsmaster was unmoved. "The Proctor is not here and this is no miracle," he said in a steely voice. "It is a trick of some enemy, and I will not be tricked. We will burn the blasphemous thing from the soil of Corlos." His arm flashed down.

The Angels in the powerwagon must have been lax with awe; the blastcannon did not fire. DaHan turned in irritation. "It is no miracle!" he shouted. He began to raise his arm again.

Next to neKrol, the bitter speaker suddenly cried out. He looked over with alarm, and saw her eyes flash a brilliant yellow-gold. "The god!" she muttered softly. "The light returns to me!"

And the whine of powerbows sounded from the trees around them, and two long bolts shuddered almost simultaneously in the broad back of C'ara DaHan. The force of the shots drove the Weaponsmaster to his knees, smashed him against the ground.

"*RUN!*" neKrol screamed, and he shoved the bitter speaker with all his strength, and she stumbled and looked back at him briefly, her eyes dark bronze again and flickering with fear. Then, swiftly, she was running, her scarf aflutter behind her as she dodged toward the nearest green.

"Kill her!" the Squadmother shouted. "Kill them all!" And her words woke Jaenshi and Steel Angels both; the children of Bakkalon lifted their lasers against the suddenly surging crowd, and the slaughter began. NeKrol knelt and scrabbled on the moss-slick rocks until he had the laser rifle in his hands, then brought it to his shoulder and commenced to fire. Light stabbed out in angry bursts; once, twice, a third time. He held the trigger down and the bursts became a beam, and he sheared through the waist of a silver-helmeted Angel before the fire flared in his stomach and he fell heavily into the pool.

For a long time he saw nothing; there was only pain and noise, the water gently slapping against his face, the sounds of high-pitched Jaenshi screaming, running all around him. Twice he heard the roar and crackle of the blastcannon, and more than twice he was stepped on. It all seemed unimportant. He struggled to keep his head on the rocks, half out of the water, but even that seemed none too vital after a while. The only thing that counted was the burning in his gut.

Then, somehow, the pain went away, and there was a lot of smoke and horrible smells but not so much noise, and neKrol lay quietly and listened to the voices.

"The pyramid, Squadmother?" someone asked.

"It *is* a miracle," a woman's voice replied. "Look, Bakkalon stands there yet. And see how He smiles! We have done right here today!"

"What should we do with it?"

"Lift it aboard the powerwagon. We shall bring it back to Proctor Wyatt."

Soon after, the voices went away, and neKrol heard only the sound of the water, rushing down endlessly, falling and tumbling. It was a very restful sound. He decided he would sleep.

———

THE CREWMAN SHOVED THE CROWBAR DOWN BETWEEN THE SLATS AND lifted. The thin wood hardly protested at all before it gave. "More statues, Jannis," he reported, after reaching inside the crate and tugging loose some of the packing material.

"Worthless," Ryther said, with a brief sigh. She stood in the broken ruins of neKrol's trading base. The Angels had ransacked it, searching for armed Jaenshi, and debris lay everywhere. But they had not touched the crates.

The crewman took his crowbar and moved on to the next stack of crated artifacts. Ryther looked wistfully at the three Jaenshi who clustered around her, wishing they could communicate a little better. One of them, a sleek female who wore a trailing scarf and a lot of jewelry and seemed always to be leaning on a powerbow, knew a smattering of Terran, but hardly enough. She picked up things quickly, but so far the only thing of substance she had said was, "Jamson' World. Arik take us. Angels kill." That she had repeated endlessly until Ryther had finally made her understand that, yes, they would take them. The other two Jaenshi, the pregnant female and the male with the laser, never seemed to talk at all.

"Statues again," the crewman said, having pulled a crate from atop the stack in the ruptured storeroom and pried it open.

Ryther shrugged; the crewman moved on. She turned her back on him and wandered slowly outside, to the edge of the spacefield where the *Lights of Jolostar* rested, its open ports bright with yellow light in the gathering gloom of dusk. The Jaenshi followed her, as they had followed her since she arrived; afraid, no doubt, that she would go away and leave them if they took their great bronze eyes off her for an instant.

"Statues," Ryther muttered, half to herself and half to the Jaenshi. She shook her head. "Why did he do it?" she asked them, knowing they could not understand. "A trader of his experience? You could tell me, maybe, if you knew what I was saying. Instead of concentrating on deathcloths and such, on real Jaenshi art, why did Arik train you people to carve alien versions of human gods? He should have known no dealer would accept such obvious frauds. Alien art is *alien*." She sighed. "My fault, I suppose. We should have opened the crates." She laughed.

The bitter speaker stared at her. "Arik deathcloth. Gave."

Ryther nodded, abstractly. She had it now, hanging just above her bunk; a strange small thing, woven partly from Jaenshi fur and mostly from long silken strands of flame red hair. On it, gray against the red, was a crude but recognizable caricature of Arik neKrol. She had wondered at that too. The tribute of the widow? A child? Or just a friend? What *had* happened to Arik during the year the *Lights* had been away? If only she had been back on time, then . . . but she'd lost three months on Jamison's World, checking dealer after dealer in an effort to unload the worthless statuettes. It had been middle autumn before the *Lights of Jolostar* returned to Corlos, to find neKrol's base in ruins, the Angels already gathering in their harvests.

And the Angels—when she'd gone to them, offering the hold of unwanted lasers, offering to trade, the sight on those blood-red city walls had sickened even her. She had thought she'd gone prepared, but the obscenity she encountered was beyond any preparation. A squad of Steel Angels found her, vomiting, beyond the tall rusty gates, and had escorted her inside, before the Proctor.

Wyatt was twice as skeletal as she remembered him. He had been standing outdoors, near the foot of a huge platform altar that had been erected in the middle of the city. A startlingly lifelike statue of Bakkalon, encased in a glass pyramid and set atop a high redstone plinth, threw a long shadow over the wooden altar. Beneath it, the squads of Angels were piling the newly harvested neograss and wheat and the frozen carcasses of bushogs.

"We do not need your trade," the Proctor told her. "The World of Corlos is many-times-blessed, my child, and Bakkalon lives among us now. He has worked vast miracles, and shall work more. Our faith is in Him." Wyatt gestured toward the altar with a thin hand. "See? In tribute we burn our winter stores, for the pale child has promised that this year winter will not come. And He has taught us to cull ourselves in peace as once we were culled in war, so the seed of Earth grows ever stronger. It is a time of great new revelation!" His eyes had burned as he spoke to her; eyes darting and fanatic, vast and dark yet strangely flecked with gold.

As quickly as she could, Ryther had left the City of the Steel Angels, trying hard not to look back at the walls. But when she had climbed the hills, back toward the trading base, she had come to the ring-of-stone, to the broken pyramid where Arik had taken her. Then Ryther found that she could not resist, and powerless she had turned for a final glance out over Sword Valley. The sight had stayed with her.

Outside the walls the Angel children hung, a row of small white-smocked bodies still and motionless at the end of long ropes. They had gone peacefully, all of them, but death is seldom peaceful; the older ones, at least, died quickly, necks broken with a sudden snap. But the small pale infants had the nooses round their waists, and it had seemed clear to Ryther that most of them had simply hung there till they starved.

As she stood, remembering, the crewman came from inside neKrol's broken bubble. "Nothing," he reported. "All statues." Ryther nodded.

"Go?" the bitter speaker said. "Jamson' World?"

"Yes," she replied, her eyes staring past the waiting *Lights of Jolostar,* out toward the black primal forest. The Heart of Bakkalon was sunk forever. In a thousand thousand woods and a single city, the clans had begun to pray.

THE STONE CITY

THE CROSSWORLDS HAD A THOUSAND NAMES. HUMAN STARCHARTS listed it as Greyrest, when they listed it at all—which was seldom, for it lay a decade's journey inward from the realms of men. The Dan'lai named it Empty in their high, barking tongue. To the ul-mennaleith, who had known it longest, it was simply the world of the stone city. The Kresh had a word for it, as did the Linkellar, and the Cedrans, and other races had landed there and left again, so other names lingered on. But mostly it was the crossworlds to the beings who paused there briefly while they jumped from star to star.

It was a barren place, a world of gray oceans and endless plains where the windstorms raged. But for the spacefield and the stone city, it was empty and lifeless. The field was at least five thousand years old, as men count time. The ul-nayileith had built it in the glory days when they claimed the ullish stars, and for a hundred generations it had made the crossworlds theirs. But then the ul-nayileith had faded and the ul-mennaleith had come to fill up their worlds and now the elder race was remembered only in legends and prayers.

Yet their spacefield endured, a great pockmark on the plains, circled by the towering windwalls that the vanished engineers had built against the storms. Inside the high walls lay the port city—hangars and barracks and shops where tired beings from a hundred worlds could rest and be refreshed. Outside, to the west, nothing; the winds came from the west, battering against the walls with a fury soon drained and used for power. But the eastern walls had a second city in their shadows, an open-air city of plastic bubbles and metal shacks. There huddled the beaten and the outcast and the sick; there clustered the shipless.

Beyond that, further east: the stone city.

It had been there when the ul-nayileith had come, five thousand years before. They had never learned how long it stood against the winds, or why. The ullish elders were arrogant and curious in those days, it was said, and they had searched. They walked the twisting alleys, climbed the narrow stairs, scaled the close-set towers and the square-topped pyramids. They found the endless dark passageways that wove mazelike beneath the earth. They discovered the vastness of the city, found all the dust and awesome silence. But nowhere did they find the Builders.

Finally, strangely, a weariness had come upon the ul-nayileith, and with it a fear. They had withdrawn from the stone city, never to walk its halls again. For thousands of years the stone was shunned, and the worship of the Builders was begun. And so too had begun the long decline of the elder race.

But the ul-mennaleith worship only the ul-nayileith. And the Dan'lai worship nothing. And who knows what humans worship? So now, again, there were sounds in the stone city; footfalls rode the alley winds.

————

THE SKELETONS WERE IMBEDDED IN THE WALL. THEY WERE MOUNTED above the windwall gates in no particular pattern, one short of a dozen, half sunk in the seamless ullish metal and half exposed to the crossworlds wind. Some were in deeper than others. High up, the new skeleton of some nameless winged being rattled in the breeze, a loose bag of hollow fairy bones welded to the wall only at wrists and ankles. Yet lower, up and to the right a little from the doorway, the yellow barrel-stave ribs of a Linkellar were all that could be seen of the creature.

MacDonald's skeleton was half in, half out. Most of the limbs were sunk deep in the metal, but the fingertips dangled out (one hand still holding a laser), and the feet, and the torso was open to the air. And the skull, of course—bleached white, half crushed, but still a rebuke. It looked down at Holt every dawn as he passed through the portal below. Sometimes, in the curious half-light of an early crossworlds morning, it seemed as though the missing eyes followed him on his long walk toward the gate.

But that had not bothered Holt for months. It had been different right after they had taken MacDonald, and his rotting body had suddenly appeared on the windwall, half joined to the metal. Holt could smell the stench then, and the corpse had been too recognizably Mac. Now it was just a skeleton, and that made it easier for Holt to forget.

On that anniversary morning, the day that marked the end of the first full standard year since the *Pegasus* had set down, Holt passed below the skeletons with hardly an upward glance.

Inside, as always, the corridor stood deserted. It curved away in both directions, white, dusty, very vacant; thin blue doors stood at regular intervals, but all of them were closed.

Holt turned to the right and tried the first door, pressing his palm to the entry plate. Nothing; the office was locked. He tried the next, with the same result. And then the next. Holt was methodical. He had to be. Each day only one office was open, and each day it was a different one.

The seventh door slid open at his touch.

Behind a curving metal desk a single Dan'la sat, looking out of place. The room, the furniture, the field—everything had been built to the proportions of the long-departed ul-nayileith, and the Dan'la was entirely too small for its setting. But Holt had gotten used to it. He had come every day for a year now, and every day a single Dan'la sat behind a desk. He had no idea whether it was the same one changing offices daily, or a different one each day. All of them had long snouts and darting eyes and bristling reddish fur. The humans called them foxmen. With rare exceptions, Holt could not tell one from the other. The Dan'lai would not help him. They refused to give names, and the creature behind the desk sometimes recognized him, often did not. Holt had long since given up the game, and resigned himself to treating every Dan'la as a stranger.

This morning, though, the foxman knew him at once. "Ah," he said as Holt entered. "A berth for you?"

"Yes," Holt said. He removed the battered ship's cap that matched his frayed gray uniform, and he waited—a thin, pale man with receding brown hair and a stubborn chin.

The foxman interlocked slim, six-fingered hands and smiled a swift thin smile. "No berth, Holt," he said, "Sorry. No ship today."

"I heard a ship last night," Holt said. "I could hear it all the way over in the stone city. Get me a berth on it. I'm qualified. I know standard drive, and I can run a Dan'lai jump-gun. I have credentials."

"Yes, yes." Again the snapping smile. "But there is no ship. Next week, perhaps. Next week perhaps a man-ship will come. Then you'll have a berth, Holt, I swear it, I promise you. You a good jump man, right? You tell me. I get you a berth. But next week, next week. No ship now."

Holt bit his lip and leaned forward, spreading his hands on the desktop, the cap crushed beneath one fist. "Next week you won't be here," he said. "Or if you are, you won't recognize me, won't remember anything you promised. Get me a berth on the ship that came last night."

"Ah," said the Dan'la. "No berth. Not a man-ship, Holt. No berth for a man."

"I don't care. I'll take any ship. I'll work with Dan'lai, ullies, Cedrans, anything. Jumps are all the same. Get me on the ship that came in last night."

"But there *was* no ship, Holt," the foxman said. His teeth flashed, then were gone again. "I tell you, Holt. No ship, no ship. Next week, come back. Come back, next week." There was dismissal in his tone. Holt had learned to recognize it. Once, months ago, he'd stayed and tried to argue. But the desk-fox had summoned others to drag him away. For a week afterward, *all* the doors had been locked in the mornings. Now Holt knew when to leave.

Outside in the wan light, he leaned briefly against the windwall and tried to still his shaking hands. He must keep busy, he reminded himself. He needed money, food tokens, so that was one task he could set to. He could visit the Shed, maybe look up Sunderland. As for a berth, there was always tomorrow. He had to be patient.

With a brief glance up at MacDonald, who had not been patient, Holt went off down the vacant streets of the city of the shipless.

EVEN AS A CHILD, HOLT HAD LOVED THE STARS. HE USED TO WALK AT night, during the years of high cold when the iceforests bloomed on Ymir. Straight out he would go, for kilometers, crunching the snow beneath until the lights of town were lost behind him and he stood alone in the glistening blue-white wonderland of frost-flowers and ice-webs and bitterblooms. Then he would look up.

WinterYear nights on Ymir are clear and still and very black. There is no moon. The stars and the silence are everything.

Diligent, Holt had learned the names—not the starnames (no one named the stars anymore—numbers were all that was needed), but rather the names of the worlds that swung around each. He was a bright child. He learned quickly and well, and even his gruff, practical father found a certain pride in that. Holt remembered endless parties at the Old House when his father, drunk on summerbrew, would march all his guests out onto the balcony so his son could name the worlds. "There," the old man would say, holding a mug in one hand and pointing with the other, "there, that bright one!"

"Arachne," the boy would reply, blank-faced. The guests would smile and mutter politely.

"And there?"

"Baldur."

"There. There. Those three over there."

"Finnegan. Johnhenry. Celia's World, New Rome, Cathaday." The names skipped lightly off his youthful tongue. And his father's leathery face would crinkle in a smile, and he would go on and on until the others grew bored and restive and Holt had named all the worlds a boy could name standing on a balcony of the Old House on Ymir. He had always hated the ritual.

It was a good thing that his father had never come with him off into the iceforests, for away from the lights a thousand new stars could be seen, and that meant a thousand names to know. Holt never learned them all, the names that went with the dimmer, far-off stars that were not man's. But he learned enough. The pale stars of the Damoosh inward toward the core, the reddish sun of the Silent Centaurs, the scattered lights where the Fyndii hordes raised their emblem-sticks; these he knew, and more.

He continued to come as he grew older, not always alone now. All his youthful sweethearts he dragged out with him, and he made his first love in the starlight during a SummerYear when the trees dripped flowers instead of ice. Sometimes he talked about it with lovers, and friends. But the words came hard. Holt was never eloquent, and he could not make them understand. He scarcely understood himself.

After his father died, he took over the Old House and the estates and ran them for a long WinterYear, though he was only twenty standard. When the thaw came, he left it all and went to Ymir City. A ship was down, a trader bound for Finnegan and worlds further in. Holt found a berth.

The streets grew busier as the day aged. Already the Dan'lai were out, setting up food stalls between the huts. In an hour or so the streets would be lined with them. A few gaunt ul-mennaleith were also about, traveling in groups of four or five. They all wore powder-blue gowns that fell almost to the ground, and they seemed to flow rather than walk—eerie, dignified, wraithlike. Their soft gray skin was finely powdered, their eyes were liquid and distant. Always they seemed serene, even *these,* these sorry shipless ones.

Holt fell in behind a group of them, increasing his pace to keep up. The fox merchants ignored the solemn ul-mennaleith, but they all spied Holt and called out to him as he passed. And laughed their high, barking laughs when he ignored them.

Near the Cedran neighborhoods Holt took his leave of the ullies, darting into a tiny side street that seemed deserted. He had work to do, and this was the place to do it.

He walked deeper into the rash of yellowed bubble-huts and picked one almost at random. It was old, its plastic exterior heavily polished; the door was wood, carved with nest symbols. Locked, of course—Holt put his shoulder to it and pushed. When it held firm, he retreated a bit, then ran and crashed against it. On his fourth try it gave noisily. The noise didn't bother him. In a Cedran slum, no one would hear.

Pitch-dark inside. He felt near the door and found a coldtorch, touched it until it returned his body heat as light. Then, leisurely, he looked around.

There were five Cedrans present: three adults and two younglings, all curled up into featureless balls on the floor. Holt hardly gave them a glance. By night, the Cedrans were terrifying. He'd seen them many times on the darkened streets of the stone city, moaning in their soft speech and swaying sinister. Their segmented torsos unfolded into three meters of milk-white maggotflesh, and they had six specialized limbs; two wide-splayed feet, a pair of delicate branching tentacles for manipulation, and the wicked fighting-claws. The eyes, saucer-sized pools of glowing violet, saw everything. By night, Cedrans were beings to be avoided.

By day, they were immobile balls of meat.

Holt walked around them and looted their hut. He took a hand-held coldtorch, set low to give the murky purple half-light the Cedrans liked best, plus a sack of food tokens and a clawbone. The polished, jeweled fighting-claws of some illustrious ancestor sat in an honored place on the wall, but Holt was careful not to touch them. If their family god was stolen, the entire nest would be obliged to find the thief or commit suicide.

Finally he found a set of wizard-cards, smoke-dark wooden plaques inlaid with iron and gold. He shoved them in a pocket and left. The street was still empty. Few beings visited the Cedran districts save Cedrans.

Quickly Holt found his way back to the main thoroughfare, the wide gravel path that ran from the windwalls of the spacefield to the silent gates of the stone city five kilometers away. The street was crowded and noisy now, and Holt had to push his way through the throng. Foxmen were everywhere, laughing and barking, snapping their quick grins on and off, rubbing reddish brown fur up against the blue gowns of the ul-mennaleith, the chitinous Kresh, and the loose baggy skin of the pop-eyed green Linkellars. Some of the food stalls had hot meals to offer, and the ways were heavy with smokes and smells. Holt had been months on the crossworlds before he had finally learned to distinguish the food scents from the body odors.

As he fought his way down the street, dodging in and out among the aliens with his loot clutched tightly in his hand, Holt watched carefully. It was habit now, drilled into him; he looked constantly for an unfamiliar human face, the face that might mean a man-ship was in, that salvation had come.

He did not find one. As always, there was only the milling press of the crossworlds all around him—Dan'lai barks and Kresh clickings and the ululating speech of the Linkellars, but never a human voice. By now, it had ceased to affect him.

He found the stall he was looking for. From beneath a flap of gray leather, a frazzled Dan'la looked up at him. "Yes, yes," the foxman snapped impatiently. "Who are you? What do you want?"

Holt shoved aside the multicolored blinking-jewels that were strewn over the counter and put down the coldtorch and clawbone he had taken. "Trade," he said. "These for tokens."

The foxman looked down at the goods, up at Holt, and began to rub his snout vigorously. "Trade. Trade. A trade for you," he chanted. He picked up the clawbone, tossed it from one hand to the other, set it down again, touched the coldtorch to wake it to barely perceptible life. Then he nodded and turned on his grin. "Good stuff. Cedran. The big worms will want it. Yes. Yes. Trade, then. Tokens?"

Holt nodded.

The Dan'la fumbled in the pocket of the smock he was wearing, and tossed a handful of food tokens on the counter. They were bright disks of plastic in a dozen different colors, the nearest things to currency the crossworlds had. The Dan'lai merchants honored them for food. And the Dan'lai brought in all the food there was on their fleets of jump-gun spacers.

Holt counted the tokens, then scooped them up and threw them in the sack that he'd taken from the Cedran bubble-hut. "I have more," he said, reaching into his pocket for the wizard-cards.

His pocket was empty. The Dan'la grinned and snapped his teeth together. "Gone? Not the only thief on Empty, then. No. Not the only thief."

He remembered his first ship; he remembered the stars of his youth on Ymir, he remembered the worlds he'd touched since, he remembered all the ships he'd served on and the men (and not-men) he had served with. But better than any of them he remembered his first ship:

the *Laughing Shadow* (an old name heavy with history, but no one told him the story until much later), out of Celia's World and bound for Finnegan. It was a converted ore freighter, great blue-gray teardrop of pitted duralloy that was at least a century older than Holt was. Sparse and raw—big cargo holds and not much crew space, sleep-webs for the twelve who manned it, no gravity grid (he'd gotten used to free fall quickly), nukes for landing and lifting, and a standard ftl drive for the star-shifts. Holt was set to working in the drive room, an austere place of muted lights and bare metal and computer consoles. Cain narKarmian showed him what to do.

Holt remembered narKarmian too. An old, *old* man, too old for shipwork, he would have thought; skin like soft yellow leather that has been folded and wrinkled so many times that there is nowhere a piece of it without a million tiny creases, eyes brown and almond-shaped, a mottled bald head and a wispy blond goatee. Sometimes Cain seemed senile, but most often he was sharp and alert; he knew the drives, and he knew the stars, and he would talk incessantly as he worked.

"Two hundred standard years!" he said once as they both sat before their consoles. He smiled a shy, crooked smile, and Holt saw that he still had teeth, even at his age—or perhaps he had teeth *again*. "That's how long Cain's been shipping, Holt. The very truth! You know, your regular man never leaves the very world he's born on. Never! Ninety-five per cent of them, anyway. They never leave, just get born and grow up and die, all on the same world. And the ones that do ship—well, most of *them* ship only a little. A world or two or ten. Not me! You know where I was born, Holt? Guess!"

Holt shrugged. "Old Earth?"

Cain just laughed. "Earth? Earth's nothing, only three or four years out from here. Four, I think. I forget. No, no, but I've seen Earth, the very homeworld, the seeding place. Seen it fifty years ago on the—the *Corey Dark*, I'd guess it was. It was about time, I thought. I'd been shipping a hundred fifty standard even then, and I still hadn't been to Earth. But I finally got there!"

"You weren't born there?" Holt prompted.

Old Cain shook his head and laughed again. "Not very! I'm an Emereli. From ai-Emerel. You know it, Holt?"

Holt had to think. It was not a world-name he recognized, not one of the stars his father had pointed to, aflame in the night of Ymir. But it rang a bell, dimly. "The Fringe?" he guessed finally. The Fringe was the furthest *out*-edge of human space, the place where the small sliver of the galaxy they called the manrealm had brushed the top of the galactic lens, where the stars drew thin. Ymir and the stars he knew were on the other side of Old Earth, inward toward the denser starfields and the still-unreachable core.

Cain was happy at his guess. "Yes! I'm an outworlder. I'm near to two hundred and twenty standard, and I've seen near that many worlds now, human worlds and Hrangan and Fyndii and all sorts, even some worlds in the manrealm where the men aren't *men* anymore, if you understand what I'm saying. Shipping, always shipping. Whenever I found a place that looked interesting I'd skip ship and stay a time, then go on when I wanted to. I've seen all sorts of things, Holt. When I was young I saw the Festival of the Fringe, and hunted banshee on High Kavalaan, and got a wife on Kimdiss. She died, though, and I got on. Saw Prometheus and Rhiannon, which are in a bit from the Fringe, and Jamison's World and Avalon, which are in further still. You know. I was a Jamie for a bit, and on Avalon I got three wives. And two husbands, or co-husbands, or however you say it. I was still shy of a hundred then, maybe less. That was time when we owned our own ship, did local trading, hit some of the old Hrangan slaveworlds that have gone off their own ways since the war. Even Old Hranga itself, the very place. They say there are still some Minds on Hranga, deep underground, waiting to come back and attack the manrealm again. But all I ever saw was a lot of kill-castes and workers and the other lesser types."

He smiled. "Good years, Holt, very good years. We called our ship *Jamison's Ass*. My wives and my husbands were all Avalonians, you see, except for one who was Old Poseidon, and Avalonians don't like Jamies much, which is how we arrived at that very name. But I can't say that they were wrong. I was a Jamie too, before that, and Port Jamison is a stulty, priggy town on a planet that's the same.

"We were together nearly thirty standard on *Jamison's Ass*. The marriage outlasted two wives and one husband. And me too, finally. They wanted to keep Avalon as their trade base, you see, but after thirty I'd seen all the worlds I wanted to see around there, and I hadn't seen a lot else. So I shipped on. But I loved them, Holt, I did love them. A man should be married to his shipmates. It makes for a very good feeling." He sighed. "Sex comes easier too. Less uncertainty."

By then, Holt was caught. "Afterward," he asked, his young face showing only a hint of the envy he felt, "what did you do then?"

Cain had shrugged, looked down at his console, and started to punch the glowing studs to set in a drive correction. "Oh, shipped on, shipped on. Old worlds, new worlds, man, not-man, aliens. New Refuge and Pachacuti and burnt-out old Wellington, and then Newholme and Silversky and Old Earth. And now I'm going in, as far as I can go before I die. Like Tomo and Walberg, I guess. You know about Tomo and Walberg, in here at Ymir?"

And Holt had only nodded. Even Ymir knew about Tomo and Walberg. Tomo was an outworlder too, born on Darkdawn high atop the Fringe, and they say he was a darkling dreamer. Walberg was an Altered Man from Prometheus, a roistering adventurer, according to the legend. Three centuries ago, in a ship called the *Dreaming Whore,* they had set off from Darkdawn for the opposite edge of the galaxy. How many worlds they had visited, what had happened on each, how far they had gotten before death—those were the knots in the tale, and schoolboys disputed them still. Holt liked to think that they were still out there, somewhere. After all, Walberg had said he was a superman, and there was no telling how long a superman might live. Maybe even long enough to reach the core, or beyond.

He had been staring at the console, daydreaming, and Cain had grinned over at him and said, "Hey! Starsick!" And when Holt had started and looked up, the old man nodded (still smiling), saying, "Yes, you, the very one! Set to, Holt, or you won't be shipping nowhere!"

But it was a gentle rebuke, and a gentle smile, and Holt never forgot it or Cain narKarmian's other words. Their sleep-webs were next to each other and Holt listened every night, for Cain was hard to silence and Holt was not about to try. And when the *Laughing Shadow* finally hit Cathaday, as far in as it would go, and got ready to turn back into the manrealm towards Celia's World and home, Holt and narKarmian signed off together and got berths on a mailship that was heading for Vess and the alien Damoosh suns.

They had shipped together for six years when narKarmian finally died. Holt remembered the old man's face much better than his father's.

————————

The Shed was a long, thin, metal building, a corrugated shack of blue duralloy that someone had found in the stores of a looted freighter, probably. It was built kilometers from the windwall, within sight of the gray walls of the stone city and the high iris of the Western Door. Around it were other, larger metal buildings, the warehouse-barracks of the shipless ul-mennaleith. But there were no ullies inside, ever.

It was near noon when Holt arrived, and the Shed was almost empty. A wide columnar coldtorch reached from floor to ceiling in the center of the room, giving off a tired ruddy light that left most of the deserted tables in darkness. A party of muttering Linkellars filled a corner off in the shadows; opposite them, a fat Cedran was curled up in a tight sleep-ball, his slick white skin glistening. And next to the cold-torch pillar, at the old *Pegasus* table, Alaina and Takker-Rey were sharing a white stone flask of amberlethe.

Takker spied him at once. "Look," he said, raising his glass. "We have company, Alaina. A lost soul returns! How are things in the stone city, Michael?"

Holt sat down. "The same as always, Takker. The same as always." He forced a smile for bloated, pale-faced Takker, then quickly turned to Alaina. She had worked the jump-gun with him once, a year ago and more. And they had been lovers, briefly. But that was over. Alaina had put on weight and her long auburn hair was dirty and matted. Her green eyes used to spark; now amberlethe made them dull and cloudy.

Alaina favored him with a pudgy smile. "'Lo, Michael," she said. "Have you found your ship?"

Takker-Rey giggled, but Holt ignored him. "No," he said. "But I keep going. Today the foxman said there'd be a ship in next week. A man-ship. He promised me a berth."

Now both of them giggled. "Oh, Michael," Alaina said. "Silly, silly. They used to tell *me* that. I haven't gone for so long. Don't you go, either. I'll take you back. Come up to my room. I miss you. Tak is such a bore."

Takker frowned, hardly paying attention. He was intent on pouring himself a new glass of amberlethe. The liquor flowed with agonizing slowness, like honey. Holt remembered the taste of it, gold fire on his tongue, and the easy sense of peace it brought. They had all done a lot of drinking in the early weeks, while they waited for the Captain to return. Before things fell apart.

"Have some 'lethe," Takker said. "Join us."

"No," Holt said. "Maybe a little fire brandy, Takker, if you're buying. Or a foxbeer. Summerbrew, if there's some handy. I miss summerbrew. But no 'lethe. That's why I went away, remember?"

Alaina gasped suddenly; her mouth drooped open and something flickered in her eyes. "You went away," she said in a thin voice. "I remember, you were the first. You went away. You and Jeff. You were the first.

"No, dear," Takker interrupted very patiently. He set down the flask of amberlethe, took a sip from his glass, smiled, and proceeded to explain. "The Captain was the first one to go away. Don't you recall? The Captain and Villareal and Susie Benet, they all went away together, and we waited and waited."

"Oh, yes," Alaina said. "Then later Jeff and Michael left us. And poor Irai killed herself, and the foxes took Ian and put him up on the wall. And all the others went away. Oh, I don't know where, Michael, I just don't." Suddenly she started to weep. "We all used to be together, all of us, but now there's just Tak and me. They all left us. We're the only ones who come here anymore, the *only* ones." She broke down and started sobbing.

Holt felt sick. It was worse than his last visit the month before—much worse. He wanted to grab the amberlethe and smash it to the floor. But it was pointless. He had done that once a long time ago—the second month after landing—when the endless hopeless waiting had sent him into a rare rage. Alaina had wept, MacDonald cursed and hit him and knocked loose a tooth (it still hurt sometimes, at night), and Takker-Rey bought another flask. Takker always had money. He wasn't much of a thief, but he'd grown up on Vess where men shared a planet with two alien races, and like a lot of Vessmen he'd grown up a xenophile. Takker was soft and willing, and foxmen (some foxmen) found him attractive. When Alaina had joined him, in his room and his business, Holt and Jeff Sunderland had given up on them and moved to the outskirts of the stone city.

"Don't cry, Alaina," Holt said now. "Look, I'm here, see? I even brought food tokens." He reached into his sack and tossed a handful onto the table—red, blue, silver, black. They clattered and rolled and lay still.

At once, Alaina's tears were gone. She began to scrabble among the tokens, and even Takker leaned forward to watch. "Red ones," she said excitedly. "Look, Takker, red ones, meat tokens! And silvers, for 'lethe. Look, look!" She began to scoop loose tokens into her pockets, but her hands were trembling, and more than one token was thrown onto the floor. "Help me, Tak," she said.

Takker giggled. "Don't worry, love, that was only a green. We don't need worm food anyway, do we?" He looked at Holt. "Thank you, Michael, thank you. I always told Alaina you had a generous soul, even if you did leave us when we needed you. You and Jeff, Ian said you were a coward, you know, but I always defended you. Thank you, yes." He picked up a silver token and flipped it with his thumb. "Generous Michael. You're always welcome here."

Holt said nothing. The Shed-boss had suddenly materialized at his elbow, a vast bulk of musky blue-black flesh. His face looked down at Holt—if you could call it looking, since the being was eyeless, and if you could call it a face, since there was no mouth either. The thing that passed for a head was a flabby, half-filled bladder full of breathing holes and ringed by whitish tentacles. It was the size of a child's head, an infant's, and it looked absurdly small atop the gross oily body and the rolls of mottled fat. The Shed-boss did not speak; not Terran nor ullish nor the pidgin Dan'lai that passed for crossworlds trade talk. But he always knew what his customers wanted.

Holt just wanted to leave. While the Shed-boss stood, silent and waiting, he rose and lurched for the door. It slid shut behind him, and he could hear Alaina and Takker-Rey arguing over the tokens.

———

THE DAMOOSH ARE A WISE AND GENTLE RACE, AND GREAT philosophers—or so they used to say on Ymir. The outermost of their suns interlock with the innermost parts of the ever-growing manrealm, and it was on a timeworn Damoosh colony that narKarmian died and Holt first saw a Linkellar.

Rayma-k-Tel was with him at the time, a hard hatchet-faced woman who'd come out of Vess; they were drinking in an enclave bar just off the spacefield. The place had good manrealm liquor, and he and Ram swilled it down together from seats by a window of stained yellow glass. Cain was three weeks dead. When Holt saw the Linkellar shuffling past the window, its bulging eyes a-wobble, he tugged at Ram's arm and turned her around and said, "Look. A new one. You know the race?"

Rayma shrugged loose her arm and shook her head. "No," she said, irritated. She was a raging xenophobe, which is the other thing that growing up on Vess will do to you. "Probably from further in somewhere. Don't even *try* to keep them straight, Mikey. There's a million different kinds, specially this far in. Damn Damos'll trade with any *thing.*"

Holt had looked again, still curious, but the heavy being with the loose green skin was out of sight. Briefly he thought of Cain, and something like a thrill went through him. The old man had shipped for more than two hundred years, he thought, and yet he'd probably never seen an alien of the race *they'd* just seen. He said something to that effect to Rayma-k-Tel.

She was most unimpressed. "So what?" she said. "So *we've* never seen the Fringe or a Hrangan, though I'd be damned to know why we'd *want* to." She smiled thinly at her own wit. "Aliens are like jelly-beans, Mikey. They come in a lot of different colors, but inside they're just about the same.

"So don't turn yourself into a collector like old narKarmian. Where did it ever get him, after all? He moved around a lot on a bunch of third-rate ships, but he never saw the Far Arm and he never saw the core, and nobody ever will. He didn't get too rich, neither. Just relax and make a living."

Holt had hardly been listening. He put down his drink and lightly touched the cool glass of the window with his fingertips.

That night, after Rayma had returned to their ship, Holt left the offworld enclave and wandered out into the Damoosh home-places. He paid half-a-run's salary to be led to the underground chamber where the world's wisdompool lay: a vast computer of living light linked to the dead brains of telepathic Damoosh elders (or at least that was how the guide explained it to Holt).

The chamber was a bowl of green fog stirring with little waves and swells. Within its depths, curtains of colored light rippled and faded and were gone. Holt stood on the upper lip looking down and asked his questions, and the answers came back in an echoing whisper as of many tiny voices speaking together. First he described the being he'd seen that afternoon and asked what it had been, and it was then he heard the word Linkellar.

"Where do they come from?" Holt asked.

"Six years from the manrealm by the drive you use," the whispers told him while the green fog moved. "Toward the core but not straight in. Do you want coordinates?"

"No. Why don't we see them more often?"

"They are far away, too far perhaps," the answer came. "The whole width of the Damoosh suns is between the manrealm and the Twelve Worlds of the Linkellar, and so too the colonies of the Nor T'alush and a hundred worlds that have not found stardrives. The Linkellars trade with the Damoosh, but they seldom come to this place, which is closer to you than to them."

"Yes," said Holt. A chill went through him, as if a cold wind blew across the cavern and the flickering sea of fog. "I have heard of the Nor T'alush, but not of the Linkellars. What else is there? Further in?"

"There are many directions," the fog whispered. Colors undulated deep below. "We know the dead worlds of the vanished race the Nor T'alush call the First Ones, though they were not truly the first, and we know the Reaches of the Kresh, and the lost colony of the geth-soids of Aath who sailed from far within the manrealm before it was the manrealm."

"What's beyond *them?*"

"The Kresh tell of a world called Cedris, and of a great sphere of suns larger than the manrealm and the Damoosh suns and the old Hrangan Empire all together. The stars within are the ullish stars."

"Yes," Holt said. There was a tremor in his voice. "And beyond *that?* Around it? Further in?"

A fire burned within the far depths of the fog; the green mists glowed with a smoldering reddish light. "The Damoosh do not know. Who sails so far, so long? There are only tales. Shall we tell you of the Very Old Ones? Of the Bright Gods, or the shipless sailors? Shall we sing the old song of the race without a world? Ghost ships have been sighted further in, things that move faster than a man-ship or a Damoosh in drive, and they destroy where they will, yet sometimes they are not there at all. Who can say what they are, who they are, where they are, if they are? We have names, names, stories, we can give you names and stories. But the facts are dim. We hear of a world named Huul the Golden that trades with the lost gethsoids who trade with the Kresh who trade with the Nor T'alush who trade with us, but no Damoosh ship has ever sailed to Huul the Golden and we cannot say much of it or even where it is. We hear of the veiled men of a world unnamed, who puff themselves up and float around and around in their atmosphere, but that may be only a legend, and we cannot even say *whose* legend. We hear of a race that lives in deep space, who talk to a race called the Dan'lai, who trade with the ullish stars, who trade with Cedris, and so the string runs back to us. But we Damoosh on this world so near the manrealm have never seen a Cedran, so how can we trust the string?" There was a sound like muttering; below his feet, the fog churned, and something that smelled like incense rose to touch Holt's nostrils.

"I'll go in," Holt said. "I'll ship on, and see."

"Then come back one day and tell us," the fogs cried, and for the very first time Holt heard the mournful keen of a wisdompool that is not wise enough. "Come back, come back. There is much to learn." The smell of incense was very strong.

———

HOLT LOOTED THREE MORE CEDRAN BUBBLE-HUTS THAT AFTERNOON, and broke into two others. The first of those was simply cold and vacant and dusty; the second was occupied, but not by a Cedran. After jiggling loose the door, he'd stood stock-still while an ethereal winged thing with feral eyes flapped against the roof of the hut and hissed down at him. He got nothing from that bubble, nor from the empty one, but the rest of his break-ins paid off.

Toward sunset, he returned to the stone city, climbing a narrow ramp to the Western Iris with a bag of food slung over his shoulders.

In the pale and failing light, the city looked colorless, washed out, dead. The circling walls were four meters high and twice as thick, fashioned of a smooth and seamless gray stone as if they were a single piece; the Western Iris that opened on the city of the shipless was more a tunnel than a gateway. Holt went through it quickly, out into a narrow zigzag alley that threaded its way between two huge buildings— or perhaps they were not buildings. Twenty meters tall, irregularly shaped, windowless and doorless; there could be no possible entrance save through the stone city's lower levels. Yet this type of structure, these odd-shaped dented blocks of gray stone, dominated the easternmost part of the stone city in an area of some twelve kilometers square. Sunderland had mapped it.

The alleys here were a hopeless maze, none of them running straight for more than ten meters; from above, Holt had often imagined them to look like a child's drawing of a lightning bolt. But he had come this route often, and he had Sunderland's maps committed to memory (for this small portion of the stone city, at any rate). He moved with speed and confidence, encountering no one.

From time to time, when he stood in the nexus points where several alleys joined, Holt caught glimpses of other structures in the distance. Sunderland had mapped most of them too; they used the sights as landmarks. The stone city had a hundred separate parts, and in each the architecture and the very building stone itself was different. Along the northwest wall was a jungle of obsidian towers set close together with dry canals between; due south lay a region of blood-red stone pyramids; east was an utterly empty granite plain with a single mushroom-shaped tower ascending from its center. And there were other regions, all strange, all uninhabited. Sunderland mapped a few additional blocks each day. Yet even this was only the tip of the iceberg. The stone city had levels beneath levels, and neither Holt nor Sunderland nor any of the others had penetrated those black and airless warrens.

Dusk was all around him when Holt paused at a major nexus point, a wide octagon with a smaller octagonal pool in its center. The water was still and green; not even a ripple of wind moved across its surface until Holt stopped to wash. Their rooms, just past here, were as bone-dry as this whole area of the city. Sunderland said the pyramids had indoor water supplies, but near the Western Iris there was nothing but this single public pool.

Holt resumed walking when he had cleaned the day's dust from his face and hands. The food bag bounced on his back, and his footsteps, echoing, broke the alley stillness. There was no other sound; the night was falling fast. It would be as bleak and moonless as any other cross-worlds night. Holt knew that. The overcast was always heavy, and he could seldom spot more than a half-dozen dim stars.

Beyond the plaza of the pool, one of the great buildings had fallen. There was nothing left but a jumble of broken rock and sand. Holt cut across it carefully, to a single structure that stood out of place among the rest—a huge gold stone dome like a blown-up Cedran bubble-hut. It had a dozen entrance holes, a dozen narrow little staircases winding up to them, and a honeycomb of chambers within.

For nearly ten standard months, this had been home.

Sunderland was squatting on the floor of their common room when Holt entered, his maps spread out all around him. He had arranged each section to fit with the others in a patchwork tapestry; old yellowed scraps he'd purchased from the Dan'lai and corrected were sandwiched between sheets of *Pegasus* gridfilm and lightweight squares of silvery ullish metal. The totality carpeted the room, each piece covered with lines and Sunderland's neat notation. He sat in the middle of it all with a map on his lap and a marker in his hand, looking owlish and rumpled and very overweight.

"I've got food," Holt said. He flipped the bag across the room and it landed among the maps, disarraying several of the loose sections.

Sunderland squawked, "Ahh, the *maps!* Be careful!" He blinked and pushed the food aside and rearranged everything neatly again.

Holt crossed the room to his sleep-web, strung between two sturdy coldtorch pillars. He walked on the maps as he went and Sunderland squawked again, but Holt ignored him and climbed into the web.

"Damn you," Sunderland said, smoothing the trodden sections. "Be more careful, will you?" He looked up and saw that Holt was frowning at him. "Mike?"

"Sorry," Holt said. "You find something today?" His tone made the question an empty formality.

Sunderland never noticed. "I got into a whole new section, off to the south," he said excitedly. "Very interesting too. Obviously designed as a unit. There's this central pillar, you see, built out of some soft green stone, and surrounded by ten slightly smaller pillars, and there are these bridges—well, sort of ribbons of stone, they loop from the top of the big ones to the tops of the little ones. The pattern is repeated over and over. And below you've got sort of a labyrinth of waist-high stone walls. It will take me weeks to map them."

Holt was looking at the wall next to his head, where the count of the days was scored in the golden stone. "A year," he said. "A standard year, Jeff."

Sunderland looked at him curiously, then stood and began gathering up his maps. "How was your day?" he asked.

"We're not going to leave this place," Holt said, speaking more to himself than to Sunderland. "Never. It's over."

Now Sunderland stopped. "Stop it," the small fat man said. "I won't have it, Holt. Give up, and next thing you know you'll be drowning in amberlethe with Alaina and Takker. The stone city is the key. I've known that all along. Once we discover all its secrets, we can sell them to the foxmen and get out of this place. When I finish my mapping—"

Holt rolled over on his side to face Sunderland. "A year, Jeff, a year. You're not going to finish your mapping. You could map for ten years and still have covered only part of the stone city. And what about the tunnels? The levels beneath?"

Sunderland licked his lips nervously. "Beneath. Well. If I had the equipment on board the *Pegasus,* then—"

"You don't, and it doesn't work anyway. Nothing works on the stone city. That was why the Captain landed. The rules don't work down here."

Sunderland shook his head and resumed his gathering up the maps. "The human mind can understand anything. Give me time, that's all, and I'll figure it all out. We could even figure out the Dan'lai and the ullies if Susie Benet was still here." Susie Benet had been their contact specialist—a third-rate linguesp, but even a minor talent is better than none when dealing with alien minds.

"Susie Benet isn't here," Holt said. His voice had a hard edge to it. He began to tick off names on his fingers. "Susie vanished with the Captain. Ditto Carlos. Irai suicided. Ian tried to shoot his way inside the windwalls and wound up on them. Det and Lana and Maje went down beneath, trying to find the Captain, and they vanished too. Davie Tillman sold himself as a Kresh egg host, so he's surely finished by now. Alaina and Takker-Rey are vegetables, useless, and we don't know what went on with the four aboard the *Pegasus.* That leaves us, Sunderland, you and me." He smiled grimly. "You make maps, I steal from the worms, and nobody understands anything. We're finished. We'll die here in the stone city. We'll never see the stars again."

He stopped as suddenly as he had started. It was a rare outburst for Holt; in general he was quiet, unexpressive, maybe a little repressed. Sunderland stood there, astonished, while Holt sagged back hopelessly into his sleep-web.

"Day after day after day," Holt said. "And none of it means anything. You remember what Irai told us?"

"She was unstable," Sunderland insisted. "She proved that beyond our wildest dreams."

"She said we'd come too far," Holt said, as if Sunderland had never spoken. "She said it was wrong to think that the whole universe operated by rules we could understand. You remember. She called it 'sick, arrogant human folly.' You remember, Jeff. That was how she talked. Like that. 'Sick, arrogant human folly.'"

He laughed. "The crossworlds *almost* made sense, that was what fooled us. But if Irai was right, that would figure. After all, we're still only a little bit from the manrealm, right? Further in, maybe the rules change even more."

"I don't like this kind of talk," said Sunderland. "You're getting defeatist. Irai was sick. At the end, you know, she was going to ul-mennaleith prayer meetings, submitting herself to the ul-nayileith, that sort of thing. A mystic, that was what she became. A mystic."

"She was wrong?" Holt asked.

"She was wrong," Sunderland said firmly.

Holt looked at him again. "Then explain things, Jeff. Tell me how to get out of here. Tell me how it all makes sense."

"The stone city," Sunderland said. "Well, when I finish my maps—" He stopped suddenly. Holt was leaning back in his web again and not listening at all.

————

IT TOOK HIM FIVE YEARS AND SIX SHIPS TO MOVE ACROSS THE GREAT star-flecked sphere the Damoosh claimed as their own and penetrate the border sector beyond. He consulted other, greater wisdompools as he went, and learned all he could, but always there were mysteries and surprises waiting on the world beyond this one. Not all the ships he served on were crewed by humans; man-ships seldom straggled in this far, so Holt signed on with Damoosh and stray gethsoids and other, lesser mongrels. But still there were usually a few men on every port he touched, and he even began to hear rumors of a second human empire some five hundred years in toward the core, settled by a wandering generation ship and ruled from a glittering world called Prester. On Prester the cities floated on clouds, one withered Vessman told him. Holt believed that for a time until another crewmate said that Prester was really a single world-spanning city, kept alive by fleets of food freighters greater than anything the Federal Empire had built in the wars before the Collapse. The same man said it had not been a generation ship that had settled her at all—he proved that by showing how far a slow-light ship could get from Old Earth since the dawn of the interstellar age—but rather a squadron of Earth Imperials fleeing a Hrangan Mind. Holt stayed skeptical this time. When a woman from a grounded Cathadayn freighter insisted that Prester had been founded by Tomo and Walberg, and that Walberg ruled it still, he gave up on the whole idea.

But there were other legends, other stories, and they drew him on. As they drew others.

On an airless world circling a blue-white star, in its single domed city, Holt met Alaina. She told him about the *Pegasus*.

"The Captain built her from scratch, you know, right here. He was trading, going in further than usual, like we all do"—she flashed an understanding smile, figuring that Holt too was a trading gambler out for the big find—"and he met a Dan'la. They're further in."

"I know," Holt said.

"Well, maybe you don't know what's going *on* in there. The Captain said the Dan'lai have all but taken over the ullish stars—you've heard of the ullish stars? . . . Good. Well, it's because the ul-mennaleith haven't resisted much, I gather, but also because of the Dan'lai jump-gun. It's a new concept, I guess, and the Captain says it cuts travel time in half, or better. The standard drive warps the fabric of the space-time continuum, you know, to get ftl effects, and—"

"I'm a drive man," Holt said curtly. But he was leaning forward as he said it, listening intently.

"Oh," Alaina said, not rebuked in the least. "Well, the Dan'lai jump-gun does something else, shifts you into another continuum and then back again. Running it is entirely different. It's partly psionic, and they put this ring around your head."

"You *have* a jump-gun?" Holt interrupted.

She nodded. "The Captain melted down his old ship, just about, to build the *Pegasus*. With a jump-gun he bought from the Dan'lai. He's collecting a crew now, and they're training us."

"Where are you going?" he said.

She laughed, lightly, and her bright green eyes seemed to flash. "Where else? In!"

———

HOLT WOKE AT DAWN, IN SILENCE, ROSE AND DRESSED HIMSELF quickly, and traced his path backward, past the quiet green pool and the endless alleys, out the Western Iris and through the city of the ship-less. He walked under the wall of skeletons without an upward glance.

Inside the windwall, in the long corridor, he began to try the doors. The first four rattled and stayed shut. The fifth opened on an empty office. No Dan'la.

That was something new. Holt entered cautiously, peering around. No one, nothing, and no second door. He walked around the wide ullish desk and began to rifle it methodically, much as he looted the Cedran bubble-huts. Maybe he could find a field pass, a gun, something—anything to get him back to the *Pegasus*. If it was still sitting beyond the walls. Or maybe he could find a berth assignment.

The door slid open; a foxman stood there. He was indistinguish-able from all the others. He barked, and Holt jumped away from the desk.

Swiftly the Dan'la circled around and seized the chair. "Thief!" he said. "Thief. I will shoot. You be shot. Yes." His teeth snapped.

"No," Holt said, edging toward the door. He could run if the Dan'la called others. "I came for a berth," he said inanely.

"Ah!" the foxman interlocked his hands. "Different. Well, Holt, who are you?"

Holt stood mute.

"A berth, a berth, Holt wants a berth," the Dan'la said in a squeaky singsong.

"Yesterday they said that a man-ship would be in next week," Holt said.

"No no no. I'm sorry. No man-ship will come. There will be no man-ship. Next week, yesterday, no time. You understand? And we have no berth. Ship is full. You never go on field with no berth."

Holt moved forward again, to the other side of the desk. "No ship next week?"

The foxman shook his head. "No ship. No ship. No man-ship."

"Something else, then. I'll crew for ullies, for Dan'lai, for Cedrans. I've told you. I know drive, I know your jump-guns. Remember? I have credentials."

The Dan'la tilted his head to one side. Did Holt remember the gesture? Was this a Dan'la he'd dealt with before? "Yes, but no berth."

Holt started for the door.

"Wait," the foxman commanded.

Holt turned.

"No man-ship next week," the Dan'la said. "No ship, no ship, no ship," he sang. Then he stopped singing. "Man-ship is *now!*"

Holt straightened. "*Now?!* You mean there's a man-ship on the field right now?"

The Dan'la nodded furiously.

"A berth!" Holt was frantic. "Get me a berth, damn you."

"Yes. Yes. A berth for you, for you a berth." The foxman touched something on the desk, a drawer slid open, and he took out a film of silver metal and a slim wand of blue plastic. "Your name?"

"Michael Holt," he answered.

"Oh." The foxman put down the wand, took the metal sheet and put it back in the drawer, and barked, "No berth!"

"No berth?"

"No one can have two berths," the Dan'la said.

"Two?"

The deskfox nodded. "Holt has a berth on *Pegasus*."

Holt's hands were trembling. "Damn," he said. "Damn."

The Dan'la laughed. "Will you take berth?"

"On *Pegasus*?"

A nod.

"You'll let me through the walls, then? Out onto the field?"

The foxman nodded again. "Write Holt field pass."

"Yes," Holt said. "Yes."

"Name?"

"Michael Holt."

"Race?"

"Man."

"Homeworld?"

"Ymir."

There was a short silence. The Dan'la had been sitting there staring at Holt, his hands folded. Now he suddenly opened the drawer again, took out an ancient-looking piece of parchment that crumbled as he touched it, and picked up the wand again. "Name?" he asked.

They went through the whole thing again.

When the Dan'la had finished writing, he gave the paper to Holt. It flaked as he fingered it. He tried to be very careful. None of the scrawls made sense. "This will get me past the guards?" Holt said skeptically. "On the field? To the *Pegasus*?"

The Dan'la nodded. Holt turned and almost ran for the door.

"Wait," the foxman cried.

Holt froze, then spun. "What?" he said between his teeth, and it was almost a snarl of rage.

"Technical thing."

"Yes?"

"Field pass, to be good, must be signed." The Dan'la flashed on its toothy smile. "Signed, yes yes, signed by your captain."

There was no noise. Holt's hand tightened spasmodically around the slip of yellow paper, and the pieces fluttered stiffly to the floor. Then, swift and wordless, he was on him.

The Dan'la had time for only one brief bark before Holt had him by the throat. The delicate six-fingered hands clawed air, helplessly. Holt twisted, and the neck snapped. He was holding a bundle of limp reddish fur.

He stood there for a long time, his hands locked, his teeth clenched. Then slowly he released his grip and the Dan'la corpse tumbled backward, toppling the chair.

In Holt's eyes, a picture of the windwall flashed briefly.

He ran.

THE PEGASUS HAD STANDARD DRIVES TOO, IN CASE THE JUMP-GUN failed; the walls of the room were the familiar blend of naked metal and computer consoles. But the center was filled by the Dan'lai jump-gun: a long cylinder of metallic glass, thick around as a man, mounted on an instrument panel. The cylinder was half full of a sluggish liquid that changed color abruptly each time a pulse of energy was run through the tank. Around it were seats for four jumpmen, two on a side. Holt and Alaina sat on one flank, opposite tall blond Irai and Ian MacDonald; each of them wore a hollow glass crown full of the same liquid that sloshed in the gun cylinder.

Carlos Villareal was behind Holt, at the main console, draining data from the ship's computer. The jumps were already planned. They were going to see the ullish stars, the Captain had decided. And Cedris and Huul the Golden, and points further in. And maybe even Prester and the core.

The first stop was a transit point named Greyrest (clearly, by the name, some other men had gone there once—the star was on the charts). The Captain had heard a story of a stone city older than time.

Beyond the atmosphere the nukes cut off, and Villareal gave the order. "Coordinates are in, navigation is ready," he said, his voice a little less sure than usual; the whole procedure was so new. "Jump."

They switched on the Dan'lai jump-gun.

*darkness flickering with colors and a thousand whirling stars and Holt was
in the middle all alone but no! there was Alaina and there someone else and all
of them joined and the chaos whirled around them and great gray waves crashed
over their heads and faces appeared ringed with fire laughing and dissolving and
pain pain pain and they were lost and nothing was solid and eons passed and no
Holt saw something burning calling pulling the core the core and there out from
it Greyrest but then it was gone and somehow Holt brought it back and he yelled
to Alaina and she grabbed for it too and MacDonald and Irai and they* PULLED

They were sitting before the jump-gun again, and Holt was suddenly conscious of a pain in his wrist, and he looked down and saw
that someone had taped an i.v. needle into him. Alaina was plugged in
too, and the others, Ian and Irai. There was no sign of Villareal.

The door slid open and Sunderland stood there smiling at them
and blinking. "Thank God!" the chubby navigator said. "You've been
out for three months. I thought we were finished."

Holt took the glass crown from his head and saw that there was
only a thin film of liquid left. Then he noticed that the jump cylinder
was almost empty as well. "Three months?"

Sunderland shuddered. "It was horrible. There was nothing outside, *nothing,* and we couldn't rouse you. Villareal had to play nurse-
maid. If it hadn't been for the Captain, I don't know what would have
happened. I know what the foxman said, but I wasn't sure you could
ever pull us out of—of wherever we were."

"Are we there?" MacDonald demanded.

Sunderland went around the jump-gun to Villareal's console and
hooked it into the ship's viewscreen. In a field of black, a small yellow
sun was burning. And a cold gray orb filled the screen.

"Greyrest," Sunderland said. "I've taken readings. We're there.
The Captain has already opened a beam to them. The Dan'lai seem to
run things, and they've cleared us to land. The time checks too; three
months subjective, three months objective, as near as we can figure."

"And by standard drive?" Holt said. "The same trip by standard
drive?"

"We did even better than the Dan'lai promised," Sunderland said.
"Greyrest is a good year and a half in from where we were."

IT WAS TOO EARLY; THERE WAS TOO GREAT A CHANCE THAT THE Cedrans might not be comatose yet. But Holt had to take the risk. He smashed his way into the first bubble-hut he found and looted it completely, ripping things apart with frantic haste. The residents, luckily, were torpid sleep-balls.

Out on the main thoroughfare, he ignored the Dan'lai merchants, half afraid he would confront the same foxman he had just killed. Instead he found a stall tended by a heavy blind Linkellar, its huge eyes like rolling balls of pus. The creature still cheated him, somehow. But he traded all that he had taken for an eggshell-shaped helmet of transparent blue and a working laser. The laser startled him; it was a twin for the one MacDonald had carried, even down to the Finnegan crest. But it worked, and that was all that mattered.

The crowds were assembling for the daily shuffle up and down the ways of the city of the shipless. Holt pushed through them savagely, toward the Western Iris, and broke into a measured jog when he reached the empty alleys of the stone city.

Sunderland was gone; out mapping. Holt took one of his markers and wrote across a map: KILLED A FOX. MUST HIDE. I'M GO-ING INTO THE STONE CITY. SAFE THERE.

Then he took all the food that was left, a good two weeks' supply, more if he starved himself. He filled a pack with it, strapped it on, and left. The laser was snug in his pocket, the helmet tucked under his arm.

The nearest underway was only a few blocks away; a great corkscrew that descended into the earth from the center of a nexus. Holt and Sunderland had often gone to the first level, as far as the light reached. Even there it was dim, gloomy, stuffy; a network of tunnels as intricate as the alleys above had branched off in every direction. Many of them slanted downward. And of course the corkscrew went further down, with more branchings, growing darker and more still with every turn. No one went beyond the first level; those that did—like the Captain—never came back. They had heard stories about how deep the stone city went, but there was no way to check them out; the instruments they had taken from *Pegasus* had never worked on the crossworlds.

At the bottom of the first full turn, the first level, Holt stopped and put on the pale blue helmet. It was a tight fit; the front of it pressed

against the edge of his nose and the sides squeezed his head uncomfortably. Clearly it had been built for an ul-mennalei. But it would do;
there was a hole around his mouth, so he could talk and breathe.

He waited a moment while his body heat was absorbed by the helmet. Shortly it began to give off a somber blue light. Holt continued
down the corkscrew, into the darkness.

Around and around the underway curved, with other tunnels
branching off at every turning; Holt kept on and soon lost track of the
levels he had come. Outside his small circle of light there was only
pitch-black and silence and still hot air that was increasingly difficult to
breathe. But fear was driving him now, and he did not slow. The surface of the stone city was deserted, but not entirely so; the Dan'lai entered when they had to. Only down here would he be safe. He would
stay on the corkscrew itself, he vowed; if he did not wander he could
not get lost. That was what happened to the Captain and the others, he
was sure; they'd left the underway, gone off into the side tunnels, and
had starved to death before they could find their way back. But not
Holt. In two weeks or so he could come up and get food from
Sunderland, perhaps.

For what seemed hours he walked down the twisting ramp, past
endless walls of featureless gray stone tinted blue by his helmet, past a
thousand gaping holes that ran to the sides and up and down, each calling to him with a wide black mouth. The air grew steadily warmer;
soon Holt was breathing heavily. Nothing around him but stone, yet
the tunnels seemed rank and thick. He ignored it.

After a time Holt reached a place where the corkscrew ended; a
triple fork confronted him, three arched doorways and three narrow
stairs, each descending sharply in a different direction, each curving so
that Holt could see only a few meters into the dark. By then his feet
were sore. He sat and removed his boots and took out a tube of
smoked meat to chew on.

Darkness all around him; without his footsteps echoing heavily,
there was no sound. Unless. He listened carefully. Yes. He heard
something, dim and far off. A rumble, sort of. He chewed on his meat
and listened even harder and after a long while decided the sounds
were coming from the left-hand staircase.

When the food was gone, he licked his fingers and pulled on his boots and rose. Laser in hand, he slowly started down the stair as quietly as he could manage.

The stair too was spiral; a tighter corkscrew than the ramp, without branchings and very narrow. He barely had room to turn around, but at least there was no chance of getting lost.

The sound got steadily louder as he descended, and before long Holt realized that it was not a rumble after all, but more a howl. Then, later, it changed again. He could barely make it out. Moans and barking.

The stairway made a sharp turn. Holt followed it and stopped suddenly.

He was standing in a window in an oddly shaped gray stone building, looking out over the stone city. It was night, and a tapestry of stars filled the sky. Below, near an octagonal pool, six Dan'lai surrounded a Cedran. They were laughing, quick barking laughs full of rage, and they were chattering to each other and clawing at the Cedran whenever it tried to move. It stood above them trapped in the circle, confused and moaning, swaying back and forth. The huge violet eyes glowed brightly, and the fighting-claws waved.

One of the Dan'lai had something. He unfolded it slowly; a long jag-toothed knife. A second appeared, a third; all the foxmen had them. They laughed to each other. One of them darted in at the Cedran from behind, and the silvered blade flashed, and Holt saw black ichor ooze slowly from a long cut in the milk-white Cedran flesh.

There was a blood-curdling low moan and the worm turned slowly as the Dan'la danced back, and its fighting-claws moved quicker than Holt would have believed. The Dan'la with the dripping black knife was lifted, kicking, into the air. He barked furiously, and then the claw snapped together, and the foxman fell in two pieces to the ground. But the others closed in, laughing, and their knives wove patterns and the Cedran's moan became a screech. It lashed out with its claws and a second Dan'la was knocked headless into the waters, but by then two others were cutting off its thrashing tentacles and yet another had driven his blade hilt-deep into the swaying wormlike torso. All the foxmen were wildly excited; Holt could not hear the Cedran over their frantic barking.

He lifted his laser, took aim on the nearest Dan'la, and pushed the firing stud. Angry red light spurted.

A curtain dropped across the window, blocking the view. Holt reached out and yanked it aside. Behind it was a low-roofed chamber, with a dozen level tunnels leading off in all directions. No Dan'lai, no Cedran. He was far beneath the city. The only light was the blue glow of his helmet.

Slowly, silently, Holt walked to the center of the chamber. Half of the tunnels, he saw, were bricked in. Others were dead black holes. But from one, a blast of cool air was flowing. He followed it a long way in darkness until at last it opened on a long gallery full of glowing red mist, like droplets of fire. The hall stretched away to left and right as far as Holt could see, high-ceilinged and straight; the tunnel that had led him here was only one of many. Others—each a different size and shape, all as black as death—lined the walls.

Holt took one step into the soft red fog, then turned and burned a mark into the stone floor of the tunnel behind him. He began walking down the hall, past the endless rows of tunnel mouths. The mist was thick but easy to see through, and Holt saw that the whole vast gallery was empty—at least to the limits of his vision. But he could not see either end, and his footsteps made no sound.

He walked a long time, almost in a trance, somehow forgetting to be afraid. Then, briefly, a white light surged from a portal far ahead. Holt began to run, but the glow had faded before he covered half the distance to the tunnel. Still, something called him on.

The tunnel mouth was a high arch full of night when Holt entered. A few meters of darkness, and a door; he stopped.

The arch opened on a high bank of snow and a forest of iron-gray trees linked by fragile webs of ice, so delicate that they would melt and shatter at a breath. No leaves, but hardy blue flowers peeked from the wind-crannies beneath every limb. The stars blazed in the frigid blackness above. And, sitting high on the horizon, Holt saw the wooden stockade and stone-fairy parapets of the rambling twisted Old House.

He paused for a long time, watching, remembering. The cold wind stirred briefly, blowing a flurry of snow in through the door, and Holt shivered in the blast. Then he turned and went back to the hall of the red mist.

Sunderland was waiting for him where tunnel met gallery, half wrapped in the sound-sucking fog. "Mike!" he said, talking normally enough, but all that Holt heard was a whisper. "You've got to come back. We need you, Mike. I can't map without you to get food for me, and Alaina and Takker. . . . You must come back!"

Holt shook his head. The mists thickened and whirled, and Sunderland's portly figure was draped and blurred until all Holt could see was the heavy outline. Then the air cleared, and it was not Sunderland at all. It was the Shed-boss. The creature stood silently, the white tentacles trembling on the bladder atop its torso. It waited. Holt waited.

Across the gallery, sudden light woke dimly in a tunnel. Then the two that flanked them began to glow, and then the two beyond that. Holt glanced right, then left; on both sides of the gallery, the silent waves raced from him until all the portals shone—here a dim red, here a flood of blue-white, here a friendly homesun yellow.

Ponderously the Shed-boss turned and began to walk down the hall. The rolls of blue-black fat bounced and jiggled as it went along, but the mists leeched away the musky smell. Holt followed it, his laser still in his hand.

The ceiling rose higher and higher, and Holt saw that the doorways were growing larger. As he watched, a craggy mottled being much like the Shed-boss came out of one tunnel, crossed the hall, and entered another.

They stopped before a tunnel mouth, round and black and twice as tall as Holt. The Shed-boss waited. Holt, laser at ready, entered. He stood before another window, or perhaps a viewscreen; on the far side of the round crystal port, chaos swirled and screamed. He watched it briefly, and just as his head was starting to hurt, the swirling view solidified. If you could call it solid. Beyond the port, four Dan'lai sat with jump-gun tubes around their brows and a cylinder before them. Except—except—the picture was blurred. Ghosts, there were ghosts, second images that almost overlapped the first, but not quite, not completely. And then Holt saw a third image, and a fourth, and suddenly the picture *cracked* and it was as though he was looking into an infinite array of mirrors. Long rows of Dan'lai sat on top of each other, blurring into one another, growing smaller and smaller until they dwindled into nothingness. In unison—no, no, *almost* in unison (for here one image did not move with his reflections, and here another fumbled)—they removed the drained jump-gun tubes and looked at each other and began to laugh. Wild, high barking laughs; they laughed and laughed and laughed and Holt watched as the fires of madness burned in their eyes, and the foxmen all (no, *almost* all) hunched their slim shoulders and seemed more feral and animal than he had ever seen them.

He left. Back in the hall, the Shed-boss still stood patiently. Holt followed again.

There were others in the hall now; Holt saw them faintly, scurrying back and forth through the reddish mist. Creatures like the Shed-boss seemed to dominate, but they were not alone. Holt glimpsed a single Dan'la, lost and frightened; the foxman kept stumbling into walls. And there were things part-angel and part-dragonfly that slid silently past overhead, and something tall and thin surrounded by flickering veils of light, and other presences that he felt as much as saw. Frequently he saw the bright-skinned striders with their gorgeous hues and high collars of bone and flesh, and always slender, sensuous animals loped at their heels, moving with fluid grace on four legs. The animals had soft gray skins and liquid eyes and strangely sentient faces.

Then he thought he spied a man; dark and very dignified, in ship's uniform and cap. Holt strained after the vision and ran toward it, but the mists confused him, bright and glowing as they were, and he lost the sight. When he looked around again, the Shed-boss was gone too.

He tried the nearest tunnel. It was a doorway, like the first; beyond was a mountain ledge overlooking a hard arid land, a plain of baked brick broken by a great crevasse. A city stood in the center of the desolation, its walls chalk white, its buildings all right angles. It was quite dead, but Holt still knew it, somehow. Often Cain narKarmian had told him how the Hrangans build their cities, in the war-torn reaches between Old Earth and the Fringe.

Hesitant, Holt extended a hand past the door frame, and withdrew it quickly. Beyond the arch was an oven; it was not a viewscreen, no more than the sight of Ymir had been.

Back in the gallery he paused and tried to understand. The hall went on and on in both directions, and beings like none he had ever seen drifted past in the mists, death silent, barely noticing the others. The Captain was down here, he knew, and Villareal and Susie Benet and maybe the others—or—or perhaps they *had* been down here, and now they were elsewhere. Perhaps they too had seen their homes calling to them through a stone doorway, and perhaps they had followed and not returned. Once beyond the arches, Holt wondered, how could you come back?

The Dan'la came into sight again, crawling now, and Holt saw that he was very old. The way he fumbled made it clear that he was quite blind, and yet, and yet his eyes *looked* good enough. Then Holt began to watch the others, and finally to follow them. Many went out through the doorways, and they did indeed walk off into the landscapes beyond. And the *landscapes* . . . he watched the ullish worlds in all their weary splendor, as the ul-mennaleith glided to their worships . . . he saw the starless night of Darkdawn, high atop the Fringe, and the darkling dreamers wandering beneath . . . and Huul the Golden (real after all, though less than he expected) . . . and the ghost ships flitting out from the core and the screechers of the black worlds in the Far Arm and the ancient races that had locked their stars in spheres and a thousand worlds undreamed of.

Soon he stopped following the quiet travelers and began to wander on his own, and then he found that the views beyond the doors could change. As he stood before a square gate that opened on the plains of ai-Emerel, he thought for a moment on Old Cain, who had indeed shipped a long ways, but not quite far enough. The Emereli towers were before him, and Holt wished to see them closer, and suddenly the doorway opened onto one. Then the Shed-boss was at his elbow, materializing as abruptly as ever in the Shed, and Holt glanced over into the faceless face. Then he put away the laser and removed his helmet (it had ceased to glow, oddly—why hadn't he noticed that?) and stepped forward.

He was on a balcony, cold wind stroking his face, black Emereli metal behind and an orange sunset before him. Across the horizon the other towers stood, and Holt knew that each was a city of a million; but from here, they were only tall dark needles.

A world. Cain's world. Yet it would have changed a lot since Cain had last seen it, some two hundred years ago. He wondered how. No matter; he would soon find out.

As he turned to go inside, he promised himself that soon he would go back, to find Sunderland and Alaina and Takker-Rey. For them, perhaps, it would be all darkness and fear below, but Holt could guide them home. Yes, he would do that. But not right now. He wanted to see ai-Emerel first, and Old Earth, and the Altered Men of Prometheus. Yes. But later he would go back. Later. In a little bit.

———

TIME MOVES SLOWLY IN THE STONE CITY; MORE SLOWLY DOWN BELOW where the webs of spacetime were knotted by the Builders. But still it moves, inexorably. The great gray buildings are all tumbled now, the mushroom tower fallen, the pyramids blown dust. Of the ullish wind-walls not a trace remains, and no ship has landed for millennia. The ul-mennaleith grow few and strangely diffident and walk with armored hoppers at their heels, the Dan'lai have disintegrated into violent anar-chy after a thousand years of jump-guns, the Kresh are gone, the Linkellars are enslaved, and the ghost ships still keep silent. Outwards, the Damoosh are a dying race, though the wisdompools live on and ponder, waiting for questions that no longer come. New races walk on tired worlds; old ones grow and change. No man has reached the core.

The crossworlds sun grows dim.

In empty tunnels beneath the ruins, Holt walks from star to star.

BITTERBLOOMS

❖

When he finally died, Shawn found to her shame that she could not even bury him.

She had no proper digging tools; only her hands, the longknife strapped to her thigh, and the smaller blade in her boot. But it would not have mattered. Beneath its sparse covering of snow, the ground was frozen hard as rock. Shawn was sixteen, as her family counted years, and the ground had been frozen for half her lifetime. The season was deepwinter, and the world was cold.

Knowing the futility of it before she started, Shawn still tried to dig. She picked a spot a few meters from the rude lean-to she had built for their shelter, broke the thin crust of the snow and swept it away with her hands, and began to hack at the frozen earth with the smaller of her blades. But the ground was harder than her steel. The knife broke, and she looked at it helplessly, knowing how precious it had been, knowing what Creg would say. Then she began to claw at the unfeeling soil, weeping, until her hands ached and her tears froze within her mask. It was not right for her to leave him without burial; he had been father, brother, lover. He had always been kind to her, and she had always failed him. And now she could not even bury him.

Finally, not knowing what else to do, she kissed him one last time—there was ice in his beard and his hair, and his face was twisted unnaturally by the pain and the cold, but he was still family, after all—and toppled the lean-to across his body, hiding him within a rough bier of branches and snow. It was useless, she knew; vampires and wind-wolves would knock it apart easily to get at his flesh. But she could not abandon him without shelter of some kind.

She left him his skis and his big silverwood bow, its bowstring snapped by the cold. But she took his sword and his heavy fur cloak; it was little enough burden added to her pack. She had nursed him for almost a week after the vampire had left him wounded, and that long delay in the little lean-to had depleted most of their supplies. Now she hoped to travel light and fast. She strapped on her skis, standing next to the clumsy grave she had built him, and said her last farewell leaning on her poles. Then she set off over the snow, through the terrible silence of the deepwinter woods, toward home and fire and family. It was just past midday.

By dusk, Shawn knew that she would never make it.

She was calmer then, more rational. She had left her grief and her shame behind with his body, as she had been taught to do. The stillness and the cold were all around her, but the long hours of skiing had left her flushed and almost warm beneath her layers of leather and fur. Her thoughts had the brittle clarity of the ice that hung in long spears from the bare, twisted trees around her.

As darkness threw its cloak over the world, Shawn sought shelter in the lee of the greatest of those trees, a massive blackbark whose trunk was three meters across. She spread the fur cloak she had taken on a bare patch of ground and pulled her own woven cape over her like a blanket to shut out the rising wind. With her back to the trunk and her longknife drawn beneath her cape, just in case, she slept a brief, wary sleep, and woke in full night to contemplate her mistakes.

The stars were out; she could see them peeking through the bare black branches above her. The Ice Wagon dominated the sky, bringing cold into the world, as it had for as long as Shawn could remember. The driver's blue eyes glared down at her, mocking.

It had been the Ice Wagon that killed Lane, she thought bitterly. Not the vampire. The vampire had mauled him badly that night, when his bowstring broke as he tried to draw in their defense. But in another season, with Shawn nursing him, he would have lived. In deepwinter, he never had a chance. The cold crept in past all the defenses she had built for him; the cold drained away all his strength, all his ferocity. The cold left him a shrunken white thing, numb and pale, his lips tinged with blue. And now the driver of the Ice Wagon would claim his soul.

And hers too, she knew. She should have abandoned Lane to his fate. That was what Creg would have done, or Leila—any of them. There had never been any hope that he would live, not in deepwinter. Nothing lived in deepwinter. The trees grew stark and bare in deepwinter, the grass and the flowers perished, the animals all froze or went underground to sleep. Even the windwolves and the vampires grew lean and fierce, and many starved to death before the thaw.

As Shawn would starve.

They had already been running three days late when the vampire attacked them, and Lane had had them eating short rations. Afterward he had been so weak. He had finished his own food on the fourth day, and Shawn had started feeding him some of hers, never telling him. She had very little left now, and the safety of Carinhall was still nearly two weeks of hard travel away. In deepwinter, it might as well be two years.

Curled beneath her cape, Shawn briefly considered starting a fire. A fire would bring vampires—they could feel the heat three kilometers off. They would come stalking silently between the trees, gaunt black shadows taller than Lane had been, their loose skin flapping over skeletal limbs like dark cloaks, concealing the claws. Perhaps, if she lay in wait, she could take one by surprise. A full-grown vampire would feed her long enough to return to Carinhall. She played with the idea in the darkness, and only reluctantly put it aside. Vampires could run across the snow as fast as an arrow in flight, scarcely touching the ground, and it was virtually impossible to see them by night. But they could see her very well, by the heat she gave off. Lighting a fire would only guarantee her a quick and relatively painless death.

Shawn shivered and gripped the hilt of her longknife more tightly for reassurance. Every shadow suddenly seemed to have a vampire crouched within it, and in the keening of the wind she thought she could hear the flapping noise their skin made when they ran.

Then, louder and very real, another noise reached her ears—an angry high-pitched whistling like nothing Shawn had ever heard. And suddenly the black horizon was suffused with light, a flicker of ghostly blue radiance that outlined the naked bones of the forest and throbbed visibly against the sky. Shawn inhaled sharply, a draught of ice down her raw throat, and struggled to her feet, half-afraid she was under attack. But there was nothing. The world was cold and black and dead; only the light lived, flickering dimly in the distance, beckoning, calling to her. She watched it for long minutes, thinking back on old Jon and the terrible stories he used to tell the children when they gathered round Carinhall's great hearth. *There are worse things than vampires,* he would tell them; and remembering, Shawn was suddenly a little girl again, sitting on the thick furs with her back to the fire, listening to Jon talk of ghosts and living shadows and cannibal families who lived in great castles built of bone.

As abruptly as it had come, the strange light faded and was gone, and with it went the high-pitched noise. Shawn had marked where it had shone, however. She took up her pack and fastened Lane's cloak about her for extra warmth, then began to don her skis. She was no child now, she told herself, and that light had been no ghost dance. Whatever it was, it might be her only chance. She took her poles in hand and set off toward it.

Night travel was dangerous in the extreme, she knew. Creg had told her that a hundred times, and Lane as well. In the darkness, in the scant starlight, it was easy to go astray, to break a ski or a leg or worse. And movement generated heat, heat that drew vampires from the deep of the woods. Better to lay low until dawn, when the nocturnal hunters had retired to their lairs. All of her training told her that, and all of her instincts. But it was deepwinter, and when she rested, the cold bit through even the warmest of furs, and Lane was dead and she was hungry, and the light had been so close, so achingly close. So she followed it, going slowly, going carefully, and it seemed that this night she had a charm upon her. The terrain was all flatland, gentle to her, almost kind, and the snow cover was sparse enough so that neither root nor rock could surprise and trip her. No dark predators came gliding out of the night, and the only sound was the sound of her motion, the soft crackling of the snow crust beneath her skis.

The forest grew steadily thinner as she moved, and after an hour Shawn emerged from it entirely, into a wasteland of tumbled stone blocks and twisted, rusting metal. She knew what it was; she had seen other ruins before, where families had lived and died, and their halls and houses had gone all to rot. But never a ruin so extensive as this. The family that had lived here, however long ago, had been very great once; the shattered remains of their dwellings were more extensive than a hundred Carinhalls. She began to pick a careful path through the crumbling, snow-dusted masonry. Twice she came upon structures that were almost intact, and each time she considered seeking shelter within those ancient stone walls, but there was nothing in either of them that might have caused the light, so Shawn passed on after only a brief inspection. The river she came to soon thereafter stopped her for a slightly longer time. From the high bank where she paused, she could see the remains of two bridges that had once spanned the narrow channel, but both of them had fallen long ago. The river was frozen over, however, so she had no trouble crossing it. In deepwinter the ice was thick and solid and there was no danger of her falling through.

As she climbed painstakingly up the far bank, Shawn came upon the flower.

It was a very small thing, its thick black stem emerging from between two rocks low on the riverbank. She might never have seen it in the night, but her pole dislodged one of the ice-covered stones as she struggled up the slope, and the noise made her glance down to where it grew.

It startled her so that she took both poles in one hand, and with the other fumbled in the deepest recesses of her clothing, so that she might risk a flame. The match gave a short, intense light. But it was enough; Shawn saw.

A flower, tiny, so tiny, with four blue petals, each the same pale blue shade that Lane's lips had been just before he died. A flower, here, alive, growing in the eighth year of deepwinter, when all the world was dead.

They would never believe her, Shawn thought, not unless she brought the truth with her, back to Carinhall. She freed herself from her skis and tried to pick the flower. It was futile, as futile as her effort to bury Lane. The stem was as strong as metal wire. She struggled with it for several minutes, and fought to keep from crying when it would not come. Creg would call her a liar, a dreamer, all the things he always called her.

She did not cry, though, finally. She left the flower where it grew, and climbed to the top of the river ridge. There she paused.

Beneath her, going on and on for meters upon meters, was a wide empty field. Snow stood in great drifts in some places, and in others there was only bare flat stone, naked to the wind and the cold. In the center of the field was the strangest building Shawn had even seen, a great fat teardrop of a building that squatted like an animal in the starlight on three black legs. The legs were bent beneath it, flexed and rimed over with ice at their joints, as if the beast had been about to leap straight up into the sky. And legs and building both were covered with flowers.

There were flowers everywhere, Shawn saw when she took her eyes off the squat building long enough to look. They sprouted, singly and in clusters, from every little crack in the field, with snow and ice all around them, making dark islands of life in the pure white stillness of deepwinter.

Shawn walked through them, closer to the building, until she stood next to one of the legs and reached up to touch its joint wonderingly with a gloved hand. It was all metal, metal and ice and flowers, like the building itself. Where each of the legs rested, the stone beneath had broken and fractured in a hundred places, as if shattered by some great blow, and vines grew from the crevices, twisting black vines that crawled around the flanks of the structure like the webs of a summer-spinner. The flowers burst from the vines, and now that she stood up close, Shawn saw that they were not like her little river bloom at all. There were blossoms of many

colors, some as big as her head, growing in wild profusion everywhere, as if they did not realize that it was deepwinter, when they
should be black and dead.

She was walking around the building, looking for an entrance,
when a noise made her turn her head toward the ridge.

A thin shadow flickered briefly against the snow, then seemed to
vanish. Shawn trembled and retreated quickly, putting the nearest of
the tall legs to her back, and then she dropped everything and Lane's
sword was in her left hand and her own longknife in her right, and she
stood cursing herself for that match, that stupid, stupid match, and listening for the *flap-flap-flap* of death on taloned feet.

It was too dark, she realized, and her hand shook, and even as it
did the shape rushed upon her from the side. Her longknife flashed at
it, stabbing, slicing, but cut only the skincloak, and then the vampire
gave a shriek of triumph and Shawn was buffeted to the ground and
she knew she was bleeding. There was a weight on her chest, and
something black and leathery settled across her eyes, and she tried to
knife it and that was when she realized that her blade was gone. She
screamed.

Then the vampire screamed, and the side of Shawn's head exploded in pain, and she had blood in her eyes, and she was choking on
blood, and blood and blood, and nothing more. . . .

————

It was blue, all blue; hazy, shifting blue. A pale blue, dancing,
dancing, like the ghost light that had flickered on the sky. A soft blue,
like the little flower, the impossible blossom by the riverbank. A cold
blue, like the eyes of the Ice Wagon's black driver, like Lane's lips when
last she kissed them. Blue, blue, and it moved and would not be still.
Everything was blurred, unreal. There was only blue. For a long time,
only blue.

Then music. But it was blurred music, blue music somehow,
strange and high and fleeting, very sad, lonely, a bit erotic. It was a lullaby, like old Tesenya used to sing when Shawn was very little, before
Tesenya grew weak and sick and Creg put her out to die. It had been
so long since Shawn had heard such a song; all the music she knew was

Creg on his harp, and Rys on her guitar. She found herself relaxing, floating, all her limbs turned to water, lazy water, though it was deepwinter and she knew she should be ice.

Soft hands began to touch her, lifting her head, pulling off her facemask so the blue warm brushed her naked cheeks, then drifting lower, lower, loosening her clothes, stripping her of furs and cloth and leather, off with her belt and off with her jerkin and off with her pants. Her skin tingled. She was floating, floating. Everything was warm, so warm, and the hands fluttered here and there and they were so gentle, like old mother Tesenya had been, like her sister Leila was sometimes, like Devin. Like Lane, she thought, and it was a pleasant thought, comforting and arousing at the same time, and Shawn held close to it. She was with Lane, she was safe and warm and . . . and she remembered his face, the blue in his lips, the ice in his beard where his breath had frozen, the pain burned into him, twisting his features like a mask. She remembered, and suddenly she was drowning in the blue, choking on the blue, struggling, screaming.

The hands lifted her and a stranger's voice muttered something low and soothing in a language she did not understand. A cup was pressed to Shawn's lips. She opened her mouth to scream again, but instead she was drinking. It was hot and sweet and fragrant, full of spices, and some of them were very familiar, but others she could not place at all. Tea, she thought, and her hands took it from the other hands as she gulped it down.

She was in a small dim room, propped up on a bed of pillows, and her clothes were piled next to her and the air was full of blue mist from a burning stick. A woman knelt beside her, dressed in bright tatters of many different colors, and gray eyes regarded her calmly from beneath the thickest, wildest hair that Shawn had ever seen. "You . . . who . . . ?" Shawn said.

The woman stroked her brow with a pale soft hand. "Carin," she said clearly.

Shawn nodded, slowly, wondering who the woman was, and how she knew the family.

"Carinhall," the woman said, and her eyes seemed amused and a bit sad. "Lin and Eris and Caith. I remember them, little girl.

Beth, Voice Carin, how hard she was. And Kaya and Dale and Shawn."

"Shawn. I'm Shawn. That's me. But Creg is Voice Carin. . . ."

The woman smiled faintly, and continued to stroke Shawn's brow. The skin of her hand was very soft. Shawn had never felt anything so soft. "Shawn is my lover," the woman said. "Every tenthyear, at Gathering."

Shawn blinked at her, confused. She was beginning to remember. The light in the forest, the flowers, the vampire. "Where am I?" she asked.

"You are everywhere you never dreamed of being, little Carin," the woman said, and she laughed at herself.

The walls of the room shone like dark metal, Shawn noticed. "The building," she blurted, "the building on legs, with all the flowers . . ."

"Yes," the woman said.

"Do you . . . who are you? Did you make the light? I was in the forest, and Lane was dead and I was nearly out of food, and I saw a light, a blue. . . ."

"That was my light, Carin child, as I came down from the sky. I was far away, oh yes, far away in lands you never heard of, but I came back." The woman stood up suddenly, and whirled around and around, and the gaudy cloth she wore flapped and shimmered, and she was wreathed in pale blue smoke. "I am the witch they warn you of in Carinhall, child," she yelled, exulting, and she whirled and whirled until finally, dizzy, she collapsed again beside Shawn's bed.

No one had ever warned Shawn of a witch. She was more puzzled than afraid. "You killed the vampire," she said. "How did you . . . ?"

"I am magic," the woman said. "I am magic and I can do magic things and I will live forever. And so will you, Carin child, Shawn, when I teach you. You can travel with me, and I will teach you all the magics and tell you stories, and we can be lovers. You are my lover already, you know, you've always been, at Gathering. Shawn, Shawn." She smiled.

"No," Shawn said. "*That* was some other person."

"You're tired, child. The vampire hurt you, and you don't

remember. But you will remember, you will." She stood up and moved across the room, snuffing out the burning stick with her fingertips, quieting the music. When her back was turned, her hair fell nearly to her waist, and all of it was curls and tangles; wild restless hair, tossing as she moved like the waves on the distant sea. Shawn had seen the sea once, years ago, before deepwinter came. She remembered.

The woman faded the dim lights somehow, and turned back to Shawn in darkness. "Rest now. I took away your pain with my magics, but it may come back. Call me if it does. I have other magics."

Shawn did feel drowsy. "Yes," she murmured, unresisting. But when the woman moved to leave, Shawn called out to her again. "Wait," she said. "Your family, mother. Tell me who you are."

The woman stood framed in yellow light, a silhouette without features. "My family is very great, child. My sisters are Lilith and Marcyan and Erika Stormjones and Lamiya-Bailis and Deirdre d'Allerane. Kleronomas and Stephen Cobalt Northstar and Tomo and Walberg were all brothers to me, and fathers. Our house is up past the Ice Wagon, and my name, my name is Morgan." And then she was gone, and the door closed behind her, and Shawn was left to sleep.

———

MORGAN, SHE THOUGHT AS SHE SLEPT. MORGANMORGANMORGAN. THE name drifted through her dreams like smoke.

She was very little, and she was watching the fire in the hearth at Carinhall, watching the flames lick and tease at the big black logs, smelling the sweet fragrances of thistlewood, and nearby someone was telling a story. Not Jon, no, this was before Jon had become storyteller. This was long ago. It was Tesenya, so very old, her face wrinkled, and she was talking in her tired voice so full of music, her lullaby voice, and all the children listened. Her stories had been different from Jon's. His were always about fighting, wars and vendettas and monsters, chock-full with blood and knives and impassioned oaths sworn by a father's corpse. Tesenya was quieter. She told of a group of travelers, six of family Alynne, who were lost in the wild one year during the season of freeze. They chanced upon a huge hall built all of metal, and the family within welcomed them with a great feast. So the travelers ate and drank, and just as they were wiping their lips to go, another banquet was served, and thus it went. The Alynnes stayed and stayed, for the food was richer and more delightful than any they had ever tasted, and the more they ate of it, the hungrier they grew. Besides, deepwinter had set in outside the metal hall. Finally, when thaw came many years later, others of family Alynne went searching for the six wanderers. They found them dead in the forest. They had put off their good warm furs and dressed in flimsies. Their steel had gone all to rust, and each of them had starved. For the name of the metal hall was Morganhall, Tesenya told the children, and the family who lived there was the family named Liar, whose food is empty stuff made of dreams and air.

Shawn woke naked and shivering.

Her clothes were still piled next to her bed. She dressed quickly, first pulling on her undergarments, and over them a heavy blackwool shift, and over that her leathers, pants and belt and jerkin, then her coat of fur with its hood, and finally the capes, Lane's cloak and her own of child's cloth. Last of all was her facemask. She pulled the taut leather down over her head and laced it closed beneath her chin, and then she was safe from deepwinter winds and stranger's touches both. Shawn found her weapons thrown carelessly in a corner with her boots. When Lane's sword was in her hand and her longknife back in its familiar sheath, she felt complete again. She stepped outside determined to find skis and exit.

Morgan met her with laughter bright and brittle, in a chamber of glass and shining silver metal. She stood framed against the largest window Shawn had ever seen, a sheet of pure clean glass taller than a man and wider than Carinhall's great hearth, even more flawless than the mirrors of family Terhis, who were famed for their glassblowers and lensmakers. Beyond the glass it was midday; the cool blue midday of deepwinter. Shawn saw the field of stone and snow and flowers, and beyond it the low ridge that she had climbed, and beyond that the frozen river winding through the ruins.

"You look so fierce and angry," Morgan said, when her silly laughter had stopped. She had been threading her wild hair with wisps of cloth and gems on silver clips that sparkled when she moved. "Come, Carin child, take off your furs again. The cold can't touch us here, and if it does we can leave it. There are other lands, you know." She walked across the room.

Shawn had let the point of her sword droop toward the floor; now she jerked it up again. "Stay away," she warned. Her voice sounded hoarse and strange.

"I am not afraid of you, Shawn," Morgan said. "Not you, my Shawn, my lover." She moved around the sword easily, and took off the scarf she wore, a gossamer of gray spidersilk set with tiny crimson jewels, to drape it around Shawn's neck. "See, I know what you are thinking," she said, pointing to the jewels. One by one, they were changing color; fire became blood, blood crusted and turned brown, brown faded to black. "You are frightened of me, nothing more. No anger. You would never hurt me." She tied the scarf neatly under Shawn's facemask, and smiled.

Shawn stared at the gems with horror. "How did you do that?" she demanded, backing off uncertainly.

"With magic," Morgan said. She spun on her heels and danced back to the window. "Morgan is full of magic."

"You are full of lies," Shawn said. "I know about the six Alynnes. I'm not going to eat here and starve to death. Where are my skis?"

Morgan seemed not to hear her; the older woman's eyes were clouded, wistful. "Have you ever seen Alynne House in summer, child? It's very beautiful. The sun comes up over the redstone tower, and sinks every night into Jamei's Lake. Do you know it, Shawn?"

"No," Shawn said boldly, "and you don't either. What do you talk about Alynne House for? You said your family lived on the Ice Wagon, and they all had names I never heard of, Kleraberus and things like that."

"Kleronomas," Morgan said, giggling. She raised her hand to her mouth to still herself, and chewed on a finger idly while her gray eyes shone. All her fingers were ringed with bright metal. "You should see my brother Kleronomas, child. He is half of metal and half of flesh, and his eyes are bright as glass, and he knows more than all the Voices who've ever spoken for Carinhall."

"He does not," Shawn said. "You're lying again!"

"He *does*," Morgan said. Her hand fell and she looked cross. "He's magic. We all are. Erika died, but she wakes up to live again and again and again. Stephen was a warrior—he killed a billion families, more than you can count—and Celia found a lot of secret places that no one had ever found before. My family all does magic things." Her expression grew suddenly sly. "I killed the vampire, didn't I? How do you think I did that?"

"With a knife!" Shawn said fiercely. But beneath her mask she flushed. Morgan *had* killed the vampire; that meant there was a debt. And she had drawn steel! She flinched under Creg's imagined fury, and dropped the sword to clatter on the floor. All at once she was very confused.

Morgan's voice was gentle. "But you had a longknife *and* a sword, and you couldn't kill the vampire, could you, child? No." She came across the room. "You are mine, Shawn Carin, you are my lover and my daughter and my sister. You have to learn to trust. I have much to teach you. Here." She took Shawn by the hand and led her to the window. "Stand here. Wait, Shawn, wait and watch, and I will show you more of Morgan's magics." At the far wall, smiling, she did something with her rings to a panel of bright metal and square dim lights.

Watching, Shawn grew suddenly afraid.

Beneath her feet, the floor began to shake, and a sound assaulted her, a high whining shriek that stabbed at her ears through the leather mask, until she clapped her gloved hands on either side of her head to shut it out. Even then she could hear it, like a vibration in her bones. Her teeth ached, and she was aware of a sudden shooting pain up in her left temple. And that was not the worst of it.

For outside, where everything had been cold and bright and still, a somber blue light was shifting and dancing and staining all the world. The snowdrifts were a pale blue, and the plumes of frozen powder that blew from each of them were paler still, and blue shadows came and went upon the river ridge where none had been before. And Shawn could see the light reflected even on the river itself, and on the ruins that stood desolate and broken upon the farther crest. Morgan was giggling behind her, and then everything in the window began to blur, until there was nothing to be seen at all, only colors, colors bright and dark running together, like pieces of a rainbow melting in some vast stewpot. Shawn did not budge from where she stood, but her hand fell to the hilt of her longknife, and despite herself she trembled.

"Look, Carin child!" Morgan shouted, over the terrible whine. Shawn could barely hear her. "We've jumped up into the sky now, away from all that cold. I told you, Shawn. We're going to ride the Ice Wagon now." And she did something to the wall again, and the noise vanished, and the colors were gone. Beyond the glass was sky.

Shawn cried out in fear. She could see nothing except darkness and stars, stars everywhere, more than she had ever seen before. And she knew she was lost. Lane had taught her all the stars, so she could use them for a guide, find her way from anywhere to anywhere, but these stars were wrong, were *different*. She could not find the Ice Wagon, or the Ghost Skier, or even Lara Carin with her windwolves. She could find nothing familiar; only stars, stars that leered at her like a million eyes, red and white and blue and yellow, and none of them would even blink.

Morgan was standing behind her. "Are we in the Ice Wagon?" Shawn asked in a small voice.

"Yes."

Shawn trembled, threw away her knife so that it bounded noisily off a metal wall, and turned to face her host. "Then we're dead, and the driver is taking our souls off to the frozen waste," she said. She did not cry. She had not wanted to be dead, especially not in deepwinter, but at least she would see Lane again.

Morgan began to undo the scarf she had fastened round Shawn's neck. The stones were black and frightening. "No, Shawn Carin," she said evenly. "We are not dead. Live here with me, child, and you will never die. You'll see." She pulled off the scarf and started unlacing the thongs of Shawn's facemask. When it was loose, she pulled it up and off the girl's head, tossing it casually to the floor. "You're pretty, Shawn. You have always been pretty, though. I remember, all those years ago. I remember."

"I'm not pretty," Shawn said. "I'm too soft, and I'm too weak, and Creg says I'm skinny and my face is all pushed in. And I'm not . . ."

Morgan shushed her with a touch to her lips, and then unfastened her neck clasp. Lane's battered cloak slipped from her shoulders. Her own cape followed, and then her coat was off, and Morgan's fingers moved down to the laces of her jerkin.

"No," Shawn said, suddenly shying away. Her back pressed up against the great window, and she felt the awful night laying its weight upon her. "I can't, Morgan. I'm Carin, and you're not family; I *can't*."

"Gathering," Morgan whispered. "Pretend this is Gathering, Shawn. You've always been my lover during the Gathering."

Shawn's throat was dry. "But it *isn't* Gathering," she insisted. She had seen one Gathering, down by the sea, when forty families came together to trade news and goods and love. But that had been years before her blood, so no one had taken her; she was not yet a woman, and thus untouchable. "It *isn't* Gathering," she repeated, close to tears.

Morgan giggled. "Very well. I am no Carin, but I am Morgan full-of-magic. I can make it Gathering." She darted across the room on bare feet, and thrust her rings against the wall once more, and moved them this way and that, in a strange pattern. Then she called out, "Look! Turn and look." Shawn, confused, glanced back at the window.

Under the double suns of highsummer, the world was bright and green. Sailing ships moved languidly on the slow-flowing waters of the river, and Shawn could see the bright reflections of the twin suns bobbing and rolling in their wake, balls of soft yellow butter afloat upon the blue. Even the sky seemed sweet and buttery; white clouds moved like the stately schooners of family Crien, and nowhere could a star be seen. The far shore was dotted by houses, houses small as a road shelter and greater than even Carinhall, towers as tall and sleek as the wind-carved rocks in the Broken Mountains. And here and there and all among them people moved; lithe swarthy folk strange to Shawn, and people of the families too, all mingling together. The stone field was free of snow and ice, but there were metal buildings everywhere, some larger than Morganhall, many smaller, each with its distinctive markings, and every one of them squatting on three legs. Between the buildings were the tents and stalls of the families, with their sigils and their banners. And mats, the gaily-colored lovers' mats. Shawn saw people coupling, and felt Morgan's hand resting lightly on her shoulder.

"Do you know what you are seeing, Carin child?" Morgan whispered.

Shawn turned back to her with fear and wonder in her eyes. "It is Gathering."

Morgan smiled. "You see," she said. "It is Gathering, and I claim you. Celebrate with me." And her fingers moved to the buckle on Shawn's belt, and Shawn did not resist.

WITHIN THE METALS WALLS OF MORGANHALL, SEASONS TURNED TO hours turned to years turned to days turned to months turned to weeks turned to seasons once again. Time had no sense. When Shawn awoke, on a shaggy fur that Morgan had spread beneath the window, highsummer had turned back into deepwinter, and the families, ships, and Gathering were gone. Dawn came earlier than it should have, and Morgan seemed annoyed, so she made it dusk; the season was freeze, with its ominous chill, and where the stars of sunrise had shown, now gray clouds raced across a copper-colored sky. They ate while the copper turned to black. Morgan served mushrooms and crunchy summer greens, dark bread dripping with honey and butter, creamed spice-tea, and thick cuts of red meat floating in blood, and afterward there was flavored ice with nuts, and finally a tall hot drink with nine layers, each a different color with a different taste. They sipped the drink from glasses of impossibly thin crystal, and it made Shawn's head ache. And she began to cry, because the food had seemed real and all of it was good, but she was afraid that if she ate any more of it she would starve to death. Morgan laughed at her and slipped away and returned with dried leathery strips of vampire meat; she told Shawn to keep it in her pack and munch on it whenever she felt hungry.

Shawn kept the meat for a long time, but never ate from it.

At first she tried to keep track of the days by counting the meals they ate, and how many times they slept, but soon the changing scenes outside the window and the random nature of life in Morganhall confused her past any hope of understanding. She worried about it for weeks—or perhaps only for days—and then she ceased to worry.

Morgan could make time do anything she pleased, so there was no sense in Shawn caring about it.

Several times Shawn asked to leave, but Morgan would have none of it. She only laughed and did some great magic that made Shawn forget about everything. Morgan took her blades away one night when she was asleep, and all her furs and leathers too, and afterward Shawn was forced to dress as Morgan wanted her to dress, in clouds of colored silk and fantastic tatters, or in nothing at all. She was angry and upset at first, but later she grew used to it. Her old clothing would have been much too hot inside Morganhall, anyway.

Morgan gave her gifts. Bags of spice that smelled of summer. A windwolf fashioned of pale blue glass. A metal mask that let Shawn see in the dark. Scented oils for her bath, and bottles of a slow golden liquor that brought her forgetfulness when her mind was troubled. A mirror, the finest mirror that had ever been. Books that Shawn could not read. A bracelet set with small red stones than drank in light all day and glowed by night. Cubes that played exotic music when Shawn warmed them with her hand. Boots woven of metal that were so light and flexible she could crumple them up in the palm of one hand. Metal miniatures of men and women and all manner of demons.

Morgan told her stories. Each gift she gave to Shawn had a story that went with it, a tale of where it came from and who had made it and how it had come here. Morgan told them all. There were tales for each of her relatives as well; indomitable Kleronomas who drove across the sky hunting for knowledge, Celia Marcyan the ever-curious and her ship *Shadow Chaser,* Erika Stormjones whose family cut her up with knives that she might live again, savage Stephen Cobalt Northstar, melancholy Tomo, bright Deirdre d'Allerane and her grim ghostly twin. Those stories Morgan told with magic. There was a place in one wall with a small square slot in it, and Morgan would go there and insert a flat metallic box, and then all the lights would go out and Morgan's dead relatives would live again, bright phantoms who walked and talked and dripped blood when they were hurt. Shawn thought they were real until the day when Deirdre first wept for her slain children, and Shawn ran to comfort her and found they could not touch. It was not until afterward that Morgan told her Deirdre and the others were only spirits, called down by her magic. Morgan told her many things. Morgan was her teacher as well as her lover, and she was nearly as patient as Lane had been, though much more prone to wander and lose interest. She gave Shawn a beautiful twelve-stringed guitar and began to teach her to play it, and she taught her to read a little, and she taught her a few of the simpler magics, so Shawn could move easily around the ship. That was another thing that Morgan taught her; Morganhall was no building after all, but a ship, a sky-ship that could flex its metal legs and leap from star to star. Morgan told her about the planets, lands out by those far-off stars, and said that all the gifts she had given Shawn had come from out there, from beyond the Ice Wagon; the mask and mirror were from Jamison's World, the books and cubes from Avalon, the bracelet from High Kavalaan, the oils from Braque, the spices from Rhiannon and Tara and Old Poseidon, the boots from Bastion, the figurines from Chul Damien, the golden liquor from a land so far away that even Morgan did not know its name. Only the fine glass windwolf had been made here, on Shawn's world, Morgan said. The windwolf had always been one of Shawn's favorites, but now she found she did not like it half so well as she had thought she did. The others were all so much more exciting. Shawn had always wanted to travel, to visit distant families in wild distant climes, to gaze on seas and mountains. But she had been too young, and when she finally reached her womanhood, Creg would not let her go; she was too slow, he said, too timid, too irresponsible. Her life would be spent at home, where she could put her meager talents to better use for Carinhall. Even the fateful trip that had led her here had been a fluke; Lane had insisted, and Lane alone of all the others was strong enough to stand up to Creg, Voice Carin.

Morgan took her traveling, though, on sails between the stars. When blue fire flickered against the icy landscape of deepwinter and the sound rose up out of nowhere, higher and higher, Shawn would rush eagerly to the window, where she would wait with mounting impatience for the colors to clear. Morgan gave her all the mountains and all the seas she could dream of, and more. Through the flawless glass Shawn saw the lands from all the stories; Old Poseidon with its weathered docks and its fleets of silver ships, the meadows of Rhiannon, the vaulting black steel towers of ai-Emerel, High Kavalaan's windswept plains and rugged hills, the island-cities of Port Jamison and Jolostar on Jamison's World. Shawn learned about cities from Morgan, and suddenly the ruins by the river seemed different in her eyes. She learned about other ways of living as well, about arcologies and holdfasts and brotherhoods, about bond-companies and slavery and armies. Family Carin no longer seemed the beginning and the end of human loyalties.

Of all the places they sailed to, they came to Avalon most often, and Shawn learned to love it best. On Avalon the landing field was always full of other wanderers, and Shawn could watch ships come and go on wands of pale blue light. And in the distance she could see the buildings of the Academy of Human Knowledge, where Kleronomas had deposited all his secrets so that they might be held in trust for Morgan's family. Those jagged glass towers filled Shawn with a longing that was almost a hurt, but a hurt that she somehow craved.

Sometimes—on several of the worlds, but most particularly on Avalon—it seemed to Shawn that some stranger was about to board their ship. She would watch them come, striding purposefully across the field, their destination clear from every step. They never came aboard, though, much to her disappointment. There was never anyone to touch or talk to except Morgan. Shawn suspected that Morgan magicked the would-be visitors away, or else lured them to their doom. She could not quite make up her mind which; Morgan was so moody that it might be both. One dinnertime she remembered Jon's story of the cannibal hall, and looked down with horror at the red meat they were eating. She ate only vegetables that meal, and for several meals thereafter until she finally decided that she was being childish. Shawn considered asking Morgan about the strangers who approached and vanished, but she was afraid. She remembered Creg, whose temper was awful if you asked him the wrong question. And if the older woman was really killing those who tried to board her ship, it would not be wise to mention it to her. When Shawn was just a child, Creg had beaten her savagely for asking why old Tesenya had to go outside and die.

Other questions Shawn did ask, only to find that Morgan would not answer. Morgan would not talk about her own origins, or the source of their food, or the magic that flew the ship. Twice Shawn asked to learn the spells that moved them from star to star, and both times Morgan refused with anger in her voice. She had other secrets from Shawn as well. There were rooms that would not open to Shawn, things that she was not allowed to touch, other things that Morgan would not even talk about. From time to time Morgan would disappear for what seemed like days, and Shawn would wander desolately, with nothing outside the window to occupy her but steady unwinking stars. On those occasions Morgan would be somber and secretive when she returned, but only for a few hours, after which she would return to normal.

For Morgan, though, normal was different than for other people.

She would dance about the ship endlessly, singing to herself, sometimes with Shawn as a dancing partner and sometimes alone. She would converse with herself in a musical tongue that Shawn did not know. She would be alternately as serious as a wise old mother, and three times as knowledgeable as a Voice, and as giddy and giggly as a child of one season. Sometimes Morgan seemed to know just who Shawn was, and sometimes she insisted on confusing her with that other Shawn Carin who had loved her during Gathering. She was very patient and very impetuous; she was unlike anyone that Shawn had ever met before. "You're silly," Shawn told her once. "You wouldn't be so silly if you lived in Carinhall. Silly people die, you know, and they hurt their families. Everyone has to be useful, and you're not useful. Creg would make you be useful. You're lucky that you aren't a Carin."

Morgan had only caressed her, and gazed at her from sad gray eyes. "Poor Shawn," she'd whispered. "They've been so hard to you. But the Carins were always hard. Alynne House was different, child. You should have been born an Alynne." And after that she would say no more of it.

Shawn squandered her days in wonder and her nights in love, and she thought of Carinhall less and less, and gradually she found that she had come to care for Morgan as if she were family. And more, she had come to trust her.

Until the day she learned about the bitterblooms.

————

SHAWN WOKE UP ONE MORNING TO FIND THAT THE WINDOW WAS FULL of stars, and Morgan had vanished. That usually meant a long boring wait, but this time Shawn was still eating the food that Morgan had left out for her when the older woman returned with her hands full of pale blue flowers.

She was so eager; Shawn had never seen her so eager. She made Shawn leave her breakfast half-eaten, and come across the room to the fur rug by the window, so that she could wind the flowers in Shawn's hair. "I saw while you were sleeping, child," she said happily as she worked. "Your hair has grown long. It used to be so short, chopped off and ugly, but you've been here long enough and now it's better, long like mine. The bitterblooms will make it best of all."

"Bitterblooms?" Shawn asked, curious. "Is that what you call them? I never knew."

"Yes, child," Morgan replied, still fussing and arranging. Shawn had her back to her, so she could not see her face. "The little blue ones are the bitterblooms. They flower even in the bitterest cold, so that's why they call them that. Originally they came from a world named Ymir, very far off, where they have winters nearly as long and cold as we do. The other flowers are from Ymir too, the ones that grow on the vines around the ship. Those are called frostflowers. Deepwinter is always so bleak, so I planted them to make everything look nicer." She took Shawn by the shoulder and turned her around. "You look like me now," she said. "Go and get your mirror and see for yourself, Carin child."

"It's over there," Shawn answered, and she darted around Morgan to get it. Her bare foot came down in something cold and wet. She flinched from it and made a noise; there was a puddle on the rug.

Shawn frowned. She stood very still and looked at Morgan. The woman had not removed her boots. They dripped.

And behind Morgan, there was nothing to be seen but blackness and unfamiliar stars. Shawn was afraid; something was very wrong. Morgan was looking at her uneasily.

She wet her lips, then smiled shyly, and went to get the mirror.

————

MORGAN MAGICKED THE STARS AWAY BEFORE SHE WENT TO SLEEP; IT was night outside their window, but a gentle night far from the frozen rigor of deepwinter. Leafy trees swayed in the wind on the perimeter of their landing field, and a moon overhead made everything bright and beautiful. A good safe world to sleep on, Morgan said.

Shawn did not sleep. She sat across the room from Morgan, staring at the moon. For the first time since she had come to Morganhall, she was using her mind like a Carin. Lane would have been proud of her; Creg would only have asked what took her so long.

Morgan had returned with a handful of bitterblooms and boots wet with snow. But outside had been nothing, only the emptiness that Morgan said filled the space between the stars.

Morgan said that the light Shawn had seen in the forest had been the fires of her ship as it landed. But the thick vines of the frostflowers grew in and around and over the legs of that ship, and they had been growing for years.

Morgan would not let her go outside. Morgan showed her everything through the great window. But Shawn could not remember seeing any window when she had been *outside* Morganhall. And if the window was a window, where were the vines that should have crept across it, the deepwinter frost that should have covered it?

For the name of the metal hall was Morganhall, Tesenya told the children, and the family who lived there was the family named Liar, whose food is empty stuff made of dreams and air.

Shawn arose in the lie of moonlight and went to where she kept the gifts that Morgan had given her. She looked at them each in turn, and lifted the heaviest of them, the glass windwolf. It was a large sculpture, hefty enough so that Shawn used two hands to lift it, one hand on the creature's snarling snout, the other around its tail. "Morgan!" she shouted.

Morgan sat up drowsily, and smiled. "Shawn," she murmured. "Shawn child. What are you doing with your windwolf?"

Shawn advanced and lifted the glass animal high above her head. "You lied to me. We've never gone anywhere. We're still in the ruined city, and it's still deepwinter."

Morgan's face was somber. "You don't know what you're saying." She got shakily to her feet. "Are you going to hit me with that thing, child? I'm not afraid of it. Once you held a sword on me, and I wasn't afraid of you then, either. I am Morgan, full-of-magic. You cannot hurt me, Shawn."

"I want to leave," Shawn said. "Bring me my blades and my clothing, my old clothing. I'm going back to Carinhall. I am a woman of Carin, not a child. You've made a child of me. Bring me food too."

Morgan giggled. "So serious. And if I don't?"

"If you don't," Shawn said, "then I'll throw this right through your window." She hefted the windwolf for emphasis.

"No," Morgan said. Her expression was unreadable. "You don't want to do that, child."

"I *will*," Shawn said. "Unless you do as I say."

"You don't want to leave me, Shawn Carin, no you don't. We're lovers, remember. We're family. I can do magics for you." Her voice trembled. "Put that down, child. I'll show you things I never showed you before. There are so many places we can go together, so many stories I can tell you. Put that down." She was pleading.

Shawn could sense triumph; oddly enough, there were tears in her eyes. "Why are you so afraid?" she demanded angrily. "You can fix a broken window with your magic, can't you? Even I can fix a broken window, and Creg says I'm hardly good for anything at all." The tears were rolling down her naked cheeks now, but silently, silently. "It's warm outside, you can see that, and there's moonlight to work by, and even a city. You could hire a glazier. I don't see why you are so afraid. It isn't as if it were deepwinter out there, with cold and ice, vampires gliding through the dark. It isn't like that."

"No," Morgan said, "No."

"No," Shawn echoed. "Bring me my things."

Morgan did not move. "It wasn't all lies. It wasn't. If you stay with me, you'll live for a long time. I think it's the food, but it's true. A lot of it was true, Shawn. I didn't mean to lie to you. I wanted it to be best, the way it was for me at first. You just have to pretend, you know. Forget that the ship can't move. It's better that way." Her voice sounded young, frightened; she was a woman, and she begged like a little girl, in a little girl's voice. "Don't break the window. The window is the most magic thing. It can take us anywhere, almost. Please, *please*, don't break it, Shawn. Don't."

Morgan was shaking. The fluttering rags she wore seemed faded and shabby suddenly, and her rings did not sparkle. She was just a crazy old woman. Shawn lowered the heavy glass windwolf. "I want my clothing, and my sword, and my skis. And food. Lots and lots of food. Bring it to me and maybe I won't break your window, liar. Do you hear me?"

And Morgan, no longer full of magic, nodded and did as she was told. Shawn watched her in silence. They never spoke again.

SHAWN RETURNED TO CARINHALL AND GREW OLD.

Her return was a sensation. She had been missing for more than a standard year, she discovered, and everyone had presumed that both she and Lane were dead. Creg refused to believe her story at first, and the others followed his lead, until Shawn produced a handful of bitterblooms that she had picked from her hair. Even then, Creg could not accept the more fanciful parts of her tale. "Illusions," he snorted, "every bit of it illusion. Tesenya told it true. If you went back, your magic ship would be gone, with no sign that it had ever been there. Believe me, Shawn." But it was never clear to her whether Creg truly believed himself. He issued orders, and no man or woman of family Carin ever went that way again.

Things were different at Carinhall after Shawn's return. The family was smaller. Lane's was not the only face she missed at the meal table. Food had grown very short while she had been away, and Creg, as was the custom, had sent the weakest and most useless out to die. Jon was among the missing. Leila was gone too, Leila who had been so young and strong. A vampire had taken her three months ago. But not everything was sadness. Deepwinter was ending. And, on a more personal level, Shawn found that her position in the family had changed. Now even Creg treated her with a rough respect. A year later, when thaw was well under way, she bore her first child, and was accepted as an equal into the councils of Carinhall. Shawn named her daughter Lane.

She settled easily into family life. When it was time for her to choose a permanent profession, she asked to be a trader, and was surprised to find that Creg did not speak against her choice. Rys took her as apprentice, and after three years she got an assignment of her own. Her work kept her on the road a great deal. When she was home in Carinhall, however, Shawn found to her surprise that she had become the favored family storyteller. The children said she knew the best stories of anyone. Creg, ever practical, said that her fancies set a bad example for the children and had no proper lesson to them. But by that time he was very sick, a victim of highsummer fever, and his opposition carried little weight. He died soon after, and Devin became Voice, a gentler and more moderate Voice than Creg. Family Carin had a generation of peace while he spoke for Carinhall, and their numbers increased from forty to nearly one hundred.

Shawn was frequently his lover. Her reading had improved a great deal by then, through long study, and Devin once yielded to her whim and showed her the secret library of the Voices, where each Voice for untold centuries had kept a journal detailing the events of his service. As Shawn had suspected, one of the thicker volumes was called *The Book of Beth, Voice Carin*. It was about sixty years old.

Lane was the first of nine children for Shawn. She was lucky. Six of them lived, two fathered by family and four that she brought back with her from Gathering. Devin honored her for bringing so much fresh blood into Carinhall, and later another Voice would name her for exceptional prowess as a trader. She traveled widely, met many families, saw waterfalls and volcanoes as well as seas and mountains, sailed halfway around the world on a Crien schooner. She had many lovers and much esteem. Jannis followed Devin as Voice, but she had a bitter unhappy time of it, and when she passed, the mothers and fathers of family Carin offered the position to Shawn. She turned it down. It would not have made her happy. Despite everything she had done, she was not a happy person.

She remembered too much, and sometimes she could not sleep very well at night.

During the fourth deepwinter of her life, the family numbered two hundred and thirty-seven, fully a hundred of them children. But game was scarce, even in the third year after freeze, and Shawn could see the hard cold times approaching. The Voice was a kind woman who found it hard to make the decisions that had to be made, but Shawn knew what was coming. She was the second eldest of those in Carinhall. One night she stole some food—just enough, two weeks' traveling supply—and a pair of skis, left Carinhall at dawn, and spared the Voice the giving of the order.

She was not so fast as she had been when she was young. The journey took closer to three weeks than two, and she was lean and weak when she finally entered the ruined city.

But the ship was just as she had left it.

Extremes of heat and cold had cracked the stone of the spacefield over the years, and the alien flowers had taken advantage of every little opening. The stone was dotted with bitterblooms, and the frostflower vines that twined around the ship were twice as thick as Shawn remembered them. The big brightly colored blossoms stirred faintly in the wind.

Nothing else moved.

She circled the ship three times, waiting for a door to open, waiting for someone to see her and appear. But if the metal noticed her presence, it gave no sign. On the far side of the ship Shawn found something she hadn't seen before—writing, faded but still legible, obscured only by ice and flowers. She used her longknife to shatter the ice and cut the vines, so she might read. It said:

MORGAN LE FAY
Registry: Avalon 476 3319

Shawn smiled. So even her name had been a lie. Well, it did not matter now. She cupped her gloved hands together over her mouth.

"Morgan," she shouted. "It's Shawn." The wind whipped her words away from her. "Let me in, Morgan. Lie to me, Morgan full-of-magic. I'm sorry. Lie to me and make me believe."

There was no answer. Shawn dug herself a hollow in the snow, and sat down to wait. She was tired and hungry, and dusk was close at hand. Already she could see the driver's ice blue eyes staring through the wispy clouds of twilight.

When at last she slept, she dreamt of Avalon.

The Way of Cross and Dragon

❖

"HERESY," HE TOLD ME. THE BRACKISH WATERS OF HIS POOL SLOSHED gently.

"Another one?" I said wearily. "There are so many these days."

My Lord Commander was displeased by that comment. He shifted position heavily, sending ripples up and down the pool. One broke over the side, and a sheet of water slid across the tiles of the receiving chamber. My boots were soaked yet again. I accepted that philosophically. I had worn my worst boots, well aware that wet feet are among the inescapable consequences of paying a call on Torgathon Nine-Klariis Tûn, elder of the ka-Thane people, and also Archbishop of Vess, Most Holy Father of the Four Vows, Grand Inquisitor of the Order Militant of the Knights of Jesus Christ, and counselor to His Holiness, Pope Daryn XXI of New Rome.

"Be there as many heresies as stars in the sky, each single one is no less dangerous, Father," the Archbishop said solemnly. "As Knights of Christ, it is our ordained task to fight them one and all. And I must add that this new heresy is particularly foul."

"Yes, my Lord Commander," I replied. "I did not intend to make light of it. You have my apologies. The mission to Finnegan was most taxing. I had hoped to ask you for a leave of absence from my duties. I need rest, a time for thought and restoration."

"Rest?" The Archbishop moved again in his pool; only a slight shift of his immense bulk, but it was enough to send a fresh sheet of water across the floor. His black, pupilless eyes blinked at me. "No, Father, I am afraid that is out of the question. Your skills and your experience are vital to this new mission." His bass tones seemed then to soften somewhat. "I have not had time to go over your reports on Finnegan," he said. "How did your work go?"

"Badly," I told him, "though I think that ultimately we will prevail. The Church is strong on Finnegan. When our attempts at reconciliation were rebuffed, I put some standards into the right hands, and we were able to shut down the heretics' newspaper and broadcast facilities. Our friends also saw to it that their legal actions came to nothing."

"That is not *badly*," the Archbishop said. "You won a considerable victory for the Lord."

"There were riots, my Lord Commander," I said. "More than a hundred of the heretics were killed, and a dozen of our own people. I fear there will be more violence before the matter is finished. Our priests are attacked if they so much as enter the city where the heresy has taken root. Their leaders risk their lives if they leave that city. I had hoped to avoid such hatreds, such bloodshed."

"Commendable, but not realistic," said Archbishop Torgathon. He blinked at me again, and I remembered that among people of his race, that was a sign of impatience. "The blood of martyrs must sometimes be spilled, and the blood of heretics as well. What matters it if a being surrenders his life, so long as his soul is saved?"

"Indeed," I agreed. Despite his impatience, Torgathon would lecture me for another hour if given a chance. That prospect dismayed me. The receiving chamber was not designed for human comfort, and I did not wish to remain any longer than necessary. The walls were damp and moldy, the air hot and humid and thick with the rancid-butter smell characteristic of the ka-Thane. My collar was chafing my neck raw, I was sweating beneath my cassock, my feet were thoroughly soaked, and my stomach was beginning to churn. I pushed ahead to the business at hand. "You say this new heresy is unusually foul, my Lord Commander?"

"It is," he said.

"Where has it started?"

"On Arion, a world some three weeks' distance from Vess. A human world entirely. I cannot understand why you humans are so easily corrupted. Once a ka-Thane has found the faith, he would scarcely abandon it."

"That is well known," I said politely. I did not mention that the number of ka-Thane to find the faith was vanishingly small. They were a slow, ponderous people, and most of their vast millions showed no interest in learning any ways other than their own, nor in following any creed but their own ancient religion. Torgathon Nine-Klariis Tûn was an anomaly. He had been among the first converts almost two centuries ago, when Pope Vidas L had ruled that nonhumans might serve as clergy. Given his great lifespan and the iron certainty of his belief, it was no wonder that Torgathon had risen as far as he had, despite the fact that less than a thousand of his race had followed him into the Church. He had at least a century of life remaining to him. No doubt he would someday be Torgathon Cardinal Tûn, should he squelch enough heresies. The times are like that.

"We have little influence on Arion," the Archbishop was saying. His arms moved as he spoke, four ponderous clubs of mottled green-gray flesh churning the water, and the dirty white cilia around his breathing hole trembled with each word. "A few priests, a few churches, and some believers, but no power to speak of. The heretics already outnumber us on this world. I rely on your intellect, your shrewdness. Turn this calamity into an opportunity. This heresy is so spurious that you can easily disprove it. Perhaps some of the deluded will turn to the true way."

"Certainly," I said. "And the nature of this heresy? What must I disprove?" It is a sad indication of my own troubled faith to add that I did not really care. I have dealt with too many heretics. Their beliefs and their questionings echo in my head and trouble my dreams at night. How can I be sure of my own faith? The very edict that had admitted Torgathon into the clergy had caused a half-dozen worlds to repudiate the Bishop of New Rome, and those who had followed that path would find a particularly ugly heresy in the massive naked (save for a damp Roman collar) alien who floated before me, and wielded the authority of the Church in four great webbed hands. Christianity is the greatest single human religion, but that means little. The non-Christians outnumber us five-to-one, and there are well over seven hundred Christian sects, some almost as large as the One True Interstellar Catholic Church of Earth and the Thousand Worlds. Even Daryn XXI, powerful as he is, is only one of seven to claim the title of Pope. My own belief was once strong, but I have moved too long among heretics and nonbelievers. Now even my prayers do not make the doubts go away. So it was that I felt no horror—only a sudden intellectual interest—when the Archbishop told me the nature of the heresy on Arion.

"They have made a saint," he said, "out of Judas Iscariot."

AS A SENIOR IN THE KNIGHTS INQUISITOR, I COMMAND MY OWN STAR-ship, which it pleases me to call the *Truth of Christ*. Before the craft was assigned to me, it was named the *Saint Thomas,* after the apostle, but I did not consider a saint notorious for doubting to be an appropriate patron for a ship enlisted in the fight against heresy.

I have no duties aboard the *Truth,* which is crewed by six brothers and sisters of the Order of Saint Christopher the Far-Traveling, and captained by a young woman I hired away from a merchant trader. I was therefore able to devote the entire three-week voyage from Vess to Arion to a study of the heretical Bible, a copy of which had been given to me by the Archbishop's administrative assistant. It was a thick, heavy, handsome book, bound in dark leather, its pages tipped with gold leaf, with many splendid interior illustrations in full color with holographic enhancement. Remarkable work, clearly done by someone who loved the all-but-forgotten art of bookmaking. The paintings reproduced inside—the originals, I gathered, were to be found on the walls of the House of Saint Judas on Arion—were masterful, if blasphemous, as much high art as the Tammerwens and RoHallidays that adorn the Great Cathedral of Saint John on New Rome.

Inside, the book bore an imprimatur indicating that it had been approved by Lukyan Judasson, First Scholar of the Order of Saint Judas Iscariot.

It was called *The Way of Cross and Dragon.*

I read it as the *Truth of Christ* slid between the stars, at first taking copious notes to better understand the heresy I must fight, but later simply absorbed by the strange, convoluted, grotesque story it told. The words of text had passion and power and poetry.

Thus it was that I first encountered the striking figure of Saint Judas Iscariot, a complex, ambitious, contradictory, and altogether extraordinary human being.

He was born of a whore in the fabled ancient city-state of Babylon on the same day that the savior was born in Bethlehem, and he spent his childhood in the alleys and gutters, selling his own body when he had to, pimping when he was older. As a youth he began to experiment with the dark arts, and before the age of twenty he was a skilled necromancer. That was when he became Judas the Dragon-Tamer, the first and only man to bend to his will the most fearsome of God's creatures, the great winged fire-lizards of Old Earth. The book held a marvelous painting of Judas in some great dank cavern, his eyes aflame as he wields a glowing lash to keep a mountainous green-gold dragon at bay. Beneath his arm is a woven basket, its lid slightly ajar, and the tiny scaled heads of three dragon chicks are peering from within. A fourth infant dragon is crawling up his sleeve. That was in the first chapter of his life.

In the second, he was Judas the Conqueror, Judas the Dragon-King, Judas of Babylon, the Great Usurper. Astride the greatest of his dragons, with an iron crown on his head and a sword in his hand, he made Babylon the capital of the greatest empire Old Earth had ever known, a realm that stretched from Spain to India. He reigned from a dragon throne amid the Hanging Gardens he had caused to be constructed, and it was there he sat when he tried Jesus of Nazareth, the troublemaking prophet who had been dragged before him bound and bleeding. Judas was not a patient man, and he made Christ bleed still more before he was through with Him. And when Jesus would not answer his questions, Judas contemptuously had Him cast back out into the streets. But first, he ordered his guards to cut off Christ's legs. "Healer," he said, "heal thyself."

Then came the Repentance, the vision in the night, and Judas Iscariot gave up his crown, his dark arts, and his riches to follow the man he had crippled. Despised and taunted by those he had tyrannized, Judas became the Legs of the Lord, and for a year carried Jesus on his back to the far corners of the realm he once ruled. When Jesus did finally heal Himself, then Judas walked at His side, and from that time forth he was Jesus' trusted friend and counselor, the first and foremost of the Twelve. Finally, Jesus gave Judas the gift of tongues, recalled and sanctified the dragons that Judas had sent away, and sent His disciple forth on a solitary ministry across the oceans, "to spread My Word where I cannot go."

There came a day when the sun went dark at noon and the ground trembled, and Judas swung his dragon around on ponderous wings and flew back across the raging seas. But when he reached the city of Jerusalem, he found Christ dead on the cross.

In that moment his faith faltered, and for the next three days the Great Wrath of Judas was like a storm across the ancient world. His dragons razed the Temple in Jerusalem, drove the people forth from the city, and struck as well at the great seats of power in Rome and Babylon. And when he found the others of the Twelve and questioned them and learned of how the one named Simon-called-Peter had three times betrayed the Lord, he strangled Peter with his own hands and fed the corpse to his dragons. Then he sent those dragons forth to start fires throughout the world, funeral pyres for Jesus of Nazareth.

And Jesus rose on the third day, and Judas wept, but his tears could not turn Christ's anger, for in his wrath he had betrayed all of Christ's teachings.

So Jesus called back the dragons, and they came, and everywhere the fires went out. And from their bellies He called forth Peter and made him whole again, and gave him dominion over the Church.

Then the dragons died, and so too did all dragons everywhere, for they were the living sigil of the power and wisdom of Judas Iscariot, who had sinned greatly. And He took from Judas the gift of tongues and the power of healing He had given, and even his eyesight, for Judas had acted as a blind man (there was a fine painting of the blinded Judas weeping over the bodies of his dragons). And He told Judas that for long ages he would be remembered only as Betrayer, and people would curse his name, and all that he had been and done would be forgotten.

But then, because Judas had loved Him so, Christ gave him a boon: an extended life, during which he might travel and think on his sins and finally come to forgiveness. Only then might he die.

And that was the beginning of the last chapter in the life of Judas Iscariot. But it was a very long chapter indeed. Once dragon-king, once the friend of Christ, now he was only a blind traveler, outcast and friendless, wandering all the cold roads of the Earth, living still when all the cities and people and things he had known were dead. Peter, the first Pope and ever his enemy, spread far and wide the tale of how Judas had sold Christ for thirty pieces of silver, until Judas dared not even use his true name. For a time he called himself just Wandering Ju', and afterward many other names. He lived more than a thousand years and became a preacher, a healer, and a lover of animals, and was hunted and persecuted when the Church that Peter had founded became bloated and corrupt. But he had a great deal of time, and at last he found wisdom and a sense of peace, and finally, Jesus came to him on a long-postponed deathbed and they were reconciled, and Judas wept once again. Before he died, Christ promised that he would permit a few to remember who and what Judas had been, and that with the passage of centuries the news would spread, until finally Peter's Lie was displaced and forgotten.

Such was the life of Saint Judas Iscariot, as related in *The Way of Cross and Dragon*. His teachings were there as well, and the apocryphal books he had allegedly written.

When I had finished the volume, I lent it to Arla-k-Bau, the captain of the *Truth of Christ*. Arla was a gaunt, pragmatic woman of no particular faith, but I valued her opinion. The others of my crew, the good sisters and brothers of Saint Christopher, would only have echoed the Archbishop's religious horror.

"Interesting," Aria said when she returned the book to me.

I chuckled. "Is that all?"

She shrugged. "It makes a nice story. An easier read than your Bible, Damien, and more dramatic as well."

"True," I admitted. "But it's absurd. An unbelievable tangle of doctrine, apocrypha, mythology, and superstition. Entertaining, yes, certainly. Imaginative, even daring. But ridiculous, don't you think? How can you credit dragons? A legless Christ? Peter being pieced together after being devoured by four monsters?"

Arla's grin was taunting. "Is that any sillier than water changing into wine, or Christ walking on the waves, or a man living in the belly of a fish?" Arla-k-Bau liked to jab at me. It had been a scandal when I selected a nonbeliever as my captain, but she was very good at her job, and I liked her around to keep me sharp. She had a good mind, Arla did, and I valued that more than blind obedience. Perhaps that was a sin in me.

"There is a difference," I said.

"Is there?" she snapped back. Her eyes saw through any masks. "Ah, Damien, admit it. You rather liked this book."

I cleared my throat. "It piqued my interest," I acknowledged. I had to justify myself. "You know the kind of matter I deal with ordinarily. Dreary little doctrinal deviations; obscure quibblings on theology somehow blown all out of proportion; bald-faced political maneuverings designed to set some ambitious planetary bishop up as a new pope, or wrest some concession or other from New Rome or Vess. The war is endless, but the battles are dull and dirty. They exhaust me spiritually, emotionally, physically. Afterward I feel drained and guilty." I tapped the book's leather cover. "This is different. The heresy must be crushed, of course, but I admit that I am anxious to meet this Lukyan Judasson."

"The artwork is lovely as well," Arla said, flipping through the pages of *The Way of Cross and Dragon* and stopping to study one especially striking plate—Judas weeping over his dragons, I think. I smiled to see that it had affected her as much as me. Then I frowned.

That was the first inkling I had of the difficulties ahead.

So it was that the *Truth of Christ* came to the porcelain city Ammadon on the world of Arion, where the Order of Saint Judas Iscariot kept its House.

Arion was a pleasant, gentle world, inhabited for these past three centuries. Its population was under nine million; Ammadon, the only real city, was home to two of those millions. The technological level was medium high, but chiefly imported. Arion had little industry and was not an innovative world, except perhaps artistically. The arts were quite important here, flourishing and vital. Religious freedom was a basic tenet of the society, but Arion was not a religious world either, and the majority of the populace lived devoutly secular lives. The most popular religion was Aestheticism, which hardly counts as a religion at all. There were also Taoists, Erikaners, Old True Christers, and Children of the Dreamer, plus adherents of a dozen lesser sects.

And finally there were nine churches of the One True Interstellar Catholic faith. There had been twelve. The other three were now houses of Arion's fastest-growing faith, the Order of Saint Judas Iscariot, which also had a dozen newly built churches of its own.

The Bishop of Arion was a dark, severe man with close-cropped black hair who was not at all happy to see me. "Damien Har Veris!" he exclaimed with some wonderment when I called on him at his residence. "We have heard of you, of course, but I never thought to meet or host you. Our numbers here are small."

"And growing smaller," I said, "a matter of some concern to my Lord Commander, Archbishop Torgathon. Apparently you are less troubled, Excellency, since you did not see fit to report the activities of this sect of Judas worshippers."

He looked briefly angry at the rebuke, but quickly swallowed his temper. Even a bishop can fear a Knight Inquisitor. "We are concerned, of course," he said. "We do all we can to combat the heresy. If you have advice that will help us, I will be glad to listen."

"I am an Inquisitor of the Order Militant of the Knights of Jesus Christ," I said bluntly. "I do not give advice, Excellency. I take action. To that end I was sent to Arion, and that is what I shall do. Now, tell me what you know about this heresy, and this First Scholar, this Lukyan Judasson."

"Of course, Father Damien," the Bishop began. He signaled for a servant to bring us a tray of wine and cheese, and began to summarize the short but explosive history of the Judas cult. I listened, polishing my nails on the crimson lapel of my jacket until the black paint gleamed brilliantly, interrupting from time to time with a question. Before he had half finished, I was determined to visit Lukyan personally. It seemed the best course of action.

And I had wanted to do so all along.

APPEARANCES WERE IMPORTANT ON ARION, I GATHERED, AND I DEEMED it necessary to impress Lukyan with myself and my station. I wore my best boots—sleek, dark handmade boots of Roman leather that had never seen the inside of Torgathon's receiving chamber—and a severe black suit with deep burgundy lapels and stiff collar. Around my neck was a splendid crucifix of pure gold; my collarpin was a matching golden sword, the sigil of the Knights Inquisitor. Brother Denis carefully painted my nails, all black as ebon, and darkened my eyes as well, and used a fine white powder on my face. When I glanced in the mirror, I frightened even myself. I smiled, but only briefly. It ruined the effect.

I walked to the House of Saint Judas Iscariot. The streets of Ammadon were wide and spacious and golden, lined by scarlet trees called whisperwinds whose long, drooping tendrils did indeed seem to whisper secrets to the gentle breeze. Sister Judith came with me. She is a small woman, slight of build even in the cowled coveralls of the Order of Saint Christopher. Her face is meek and kind, her eyes wide and youthful and innocent. I find her useful. Four times now she has killed those who attempted to assault me.

The House itself was newly built. Rambling and stately, it rose from amid gardens of small bright flowers and seas of golden grass; the gardens were surrounded by a high wall. Murals covered both the outer wall around the property and the exterior of the building itself. I recognized a few of them from *The Way of Cross and Dragon,* and stopped briefly to admire them before walking through the main gate. No one tried to stop us. There were no guards, not even a receptionist. Within the walls, men and women strolled languidly through the flowers, or sat on benches beneath silverwoods and whisperwinds.

Sister Judith and I paused, then made our way directly to the House itself.

We had just started up the steps when a man appeared from within, and stood waiting in the doorway. He was blond and fat, with a great wiry beard that framed a slow smile, and he wore a flimsy robe that fell to his sandaled feet. On the robe were dragons, dragons bearing the silhouette of a man holding a cross.

When I reached the top of the steps, he bowed to me. "Father Damien Har Veris of the Knights Inquisitor," he said. His smile widened. "I greet you in the name of Jesus, and in the name of Saint Judas. I am Lukyan."

I made a note to myself to find out which of the Bishop's staff was feeding information to the Judas cult, but my composure did not break. I have been a Knight Inquisitor for a long, long time. "Father Lukyan Mo," I said, taking his hand. "I have questions to ask of you." I did not smile.

He did. "I thought you might," he said.

––––––––

LUKYAN'S OFFICE WAS LARGE BUT SPARTAN. HERETICS OFTEN HAVE A simplicity that the officers of the true Church seem to have lost. He did have one indulgence, however. Dominating the wall behind his desk console was the painting I had already fallen in love with: the blinded Judas weeping over his dragons.

Lukyan sat down heavily and motioned me to a second chair. We had left Sister Judith outside in the waiting chamber. "I prefer to stand, Father Lukyan," I said, knowing it gave me an advantage.

"Just Lukyan," he said. "Or Luke, if you prefer. We have little use for hierarchy here."

"You are Father Lukyan Mo, born here on Arion, educated in the seminary on Cathaday, a former priest of the One True Interstellar Catholic Church of Earth and the Thousand Worlds," I said. "I will address you as befits your station, Father. I expect you to reciprocate. Is that understood?"

"Oh, yes," he said amiably.

"I am empowered to strip you of your right to perform the sacraments, to order you shunned and excommunicated for this heresy you have formulated. On certain worlds I could even order your death."

"But not on Arion," Lukyan said quickly. "We're very tolerant here. Besides, we outnumber you." He smiled. "As for the rest, well, I don't perform those sacraments much anyway, you know. Not for years. I'm First Scholar now. A teacher, a thinker. I show others the way, help them find the faith. Excommunicate me if it will make you happy, Father Damien. Happiness is what all of us seek."

"You have given up the faith, then, Father Lukyan," I said. I deposited my copy of *The Way of Cross and Dragon* on his desk. "But I see you have found a new one." Now I did smile, but it was all ice, all menace, all mockery. "A more ridiculous creed I have yet to encounter. I suppose you will tell me that you have spoken to God, that He trusted you with this new revelation, so that you might clear the good name, such that it is, of Holy Judas?"

Now Lukyan's smile was very broad indeed. He picked up the book and beamed at me. "Oh, no," he said. "No, I made it all up."

That stopped me. "What?"

"I made it all up," he repeated. He hefted the book fondly. "I drew on many sources, of course, especially the Bible, but I do think of *Cross and Dragon* as mostly my own work. It's rather good, don't you agree? Of course, I could hardly put my name on it, proud as I am of it, but I did include my imprimatur. Did you notice that? It was the closest I dared come to a byline."

I was speechless only for a moment. Then I grimaced. "You startle me," I admitted. "I expected to find an inventive madman, some poor self-deluded fool, firm in his belief that he had spoken to God. I've dealt with such fanatics before. Instead I find a cheerful cynic who has invented a religion for his own profit. I think I prefer the fanatics. You are beneath contempt, Father Lukyan. You will burn in hell for eternity."

"I doubt it," Lukyan said, "but you do mistake me, Father Damien. I am no cynic, nor do I profit from my dear Saint Judas. Truthfully, I lived more comfortably as a priest of your own Church. I do this because it is my vocation."

I sat down. "You confuse me," I said. "Explain."

"Now I am going to tell you the truth," he said. He said it in an odd way, almost as a chant. "I am a Liar," he added.

"You want to confuse me with a child's paradoxes," I snapped.

"No, no." He smiled. "A *Liar.* With a capital. It is an organization, Father Damien. A religion, you might call it. A great and powerful faith. And I am the smallest part of it."

"I know of no such church," I said.

"Oh, no, you wouldn't. It's secret. It has to be. You can understand that, can't you? People don't like being lied to."

"I do not like being lied to," I said.

Lukyan looked wounded. "I told you this would be the truth, didn't I? When a Liar says that, you can believe him. How else could we trust each other?"

"There are many of you?" I asked. I was starting to think that Lukyan was a madman after all, as fanatical as any heretic, but in a more complex way. Here was a heresy within a heresy, but I recognized my duty: to find the truth of things, and set them right.

"Many of us," Lukyan said, smiling. "You would be surprised, Father Damien, really you would. But there are some things I dare not tell you."

"Tell me what you dare, then."

"Happily," said Lukyan Judasson. "We Liars, like those of all other religions, have several truths we take on faith. Faith is always required. There are some things that cannot be proven. We believe that life is worth living. That is an article of faith. The purpose of life is to live, to resist death, perhaps to defy entropy."

"Go on," I said, interested despite myself.

"We also believe that happiness is a good, something to be sought after."

"The Church does not oppose happiness," I said drily.

"I wonder," Lukyan said. "But let us not quibble. Whatever the Church's position on happiness, it does preach belief in an afterlife, in a supreme being and a complex moral code."

"True."

"The Liars believe in no afterlife, no God. We see the universe as it *is,* Father Damien, and these naked truths are cruel ones. We who believe in life, and treasure it, will die. Afterward there will be nothing, eternal emptiness, blackness, nonexistence. In our living there has been no purpose, no poetry, no meaning. Nor do our deaths possess these qualities. When we are gone, the universe will not long remember us, and shortly it will be as if we had never lived at all. Our worlds and our universe will not long outlive us. Ultimately, entropy will consume all, and our puny efforts cannot stay that awful end. It will be gone. It has never been. It has never mattered. The universe itself is doomed, transient, uncaring."

I slid back in my chair, and a shiver went through me as I listened to poor Lukyan's dark words. I found myself fingering my crucifix. "A bleak philosophy," I said, "as well as a false one. I have had that fearful vision myself. I think all of us do, at some point. But it is not so, Father. My faith sustains me against such nihilism. It is a shield against despair."

"Oh, I know that, my friend, my Knight Inquisitor," Lukyan said. "I'm glad to see you understand so well. You are almost one of us already."

I frowned.

"You've touched the heart of it," Lukyan continued. "The truths, the great truths—and most of the lesser ones as well—they are unbearable for most men. We find our shield in faith. Your faith, my faith, any faith. It doesn't matter, so long as we *believe,* really and truly believe, in whatever lie we cling to." He fingered the ragged edges of his great blond beard. "Our psychs have always told us that believers are the happy ones, you know. They may believe in Christ or Buddha or Erika Stormjones, in reincarnation or immortality or nature, in the power of love or the platform of a political faction, but it all comes to the same thing. They believe. They are happy. It is the ones who have seen truth who despair, and kill themselves. The truths are so vast, the faiths so little, so poorly made, so riddled with error and contradiction that we see around them and through them, and then we feel the weight of darkness upon us, and can no longer be happy."

I am not a slow man. I knew, by then, where Lukyan Judasson was going. "Your Liars invent faiths."

He smiled. "Of all sorts. Not only religious. Think of it. We know truth for the cruel instrument it is. Beauty is infinitely preferable to truth. We invent beauty. Faiths, political movements, high ideals, belief in love and fellowship. All of them are lies. We tell those lies, among others, endless others. We improve on history and myth and religion, make each more beautiful, better, easier to believe in. Our lies are not perfect, of course. The truths are too big. But perhaps someday we will find one great lie that all humanity can use. Until then, a thousand small lies will do."

"I think I do not care for your Liars very much," I said with a cold, even fervor. "My whole life has been a quest for truth."

Lukyan was indulgent. "Father Damien Har Veris, Knight Inquisitor, I know you better than that. You are a Liar yourself. You do good work. You ship from world to world, and on each you destroy the foolish, the rebels, the questioners who would bring down the edifice of the vast lie that you serve."

"If my lie is so admirable," I said, "then why have you abandoned it?"

"A religion must fit its culture and society, work with them, not against them. If there is conflict, contradiction, then the lie breaks down, and the faith falters. Your Church is good for many worlds, Father, but not for Arion. Life is too kind here, and your faith is stern. Here we love beauty, and your faith offers too little. So we have improved it. We studied this world for a long time. We know its psychological profile. Saint Judas will thrive here. He offers drama, and color, and much beauty—the aesthetics are admirable. His is a tragedy with a happy ending, and Arion dotes on such stories. And the dragons are a nice touch. I think your own Church ought to find a way to work in dragons. They are marvelous creatures."

"Mythical," I said.

"Hardly," he replied. "Look it up." He grinned at me. "You see, really, it all comes back to faith. Can you really know what happened three thousand years ago? You have one Judas, I have another. Both of us have books. Is yours true? Can you really believe that? I have been admitted only to the first circle of the order of Liars, so I do not know all our secrets, but I know that we are very old. It would not surprise me to learn that the gospels were written by men very much like me. Perhaps there never was a Judas at all. Or a Jesus."

"I have faith that that is not so," I said.

"There are a hundred people in this building who have a deep and very real faith in Saint Judas, and the way of cross and dragon," Lukyan said. "Faith is a very good thing. Do you know that the suicide rate on Arion has decreased by almost a third since the Order of Saint Judas was founded?"

I remember rising slowly from my chair. "You are as fanatical as any heretic I have ever met, Lukyan Judasson," I told him. "I pity you the loss of your faith."

Lukyan rose with me. "Pity yourself, Damien Har Veris," he said. "I have found a new faith and a new cause, and I am a happy man. You, my dear friend, are tortured and miserable."

"That is a lie!" I am afraid I screamed.

"Come with me," Lukyan said. He touched a panel on his wall, and the great painting of Judas weeping over his dragons slid up out of sight. There was a stairway leading down into the ground. "Follow me," he said.

In the cellar was a great glass vat full of pale green fluid, and in it a thing was floating, a thing very like an ancient embryo, aged and infantile at the same time, naked, with a huge head and a tiny atrophied body. Tubes ran from its arms and legs and genitals, connecting it to the machinery that kept it alive.

When Lukyan turned on the lights, it opened its eyes. They were large and dark and they looked into my soul.

"This is my colleague," Lukyan said, patting the side of the vat, "Jon Azure Cross, a Liar of the fourth circle."

"And a telepath," I said with a sick certainty. I had led pogroms against other telepaths, children mostly, on other worlds. The Church teaches that the psionic powers are one of Satan's traps. They are not mentioned in the Bible. I have never felt good about those killings.

"The moment you entered the compound, Jon read you and notified me," Lukyan said. "Only a few of us know that he is here. He helps us lie most efficiently. He knows when faith is true, and when it is feigned. I have an implant in my skull. Jon can talk to me at all times. It was he who initially recruited me into the Liars. He knew my faith was hollow. He felt the depth of my despair."

Then the thing in the tank spoke, its metallic voice coming from a speaker-grille in the base of the machine that nurtured it. *"And I feel yours, Damien Har Veris, empty priest. Inquisitor, you have asked too many questions. You are sick at heart, and tired, and you do not believe. Join us, Damien. You have been a Liar for a long, long time!"*

For a moment I hesitated, looking deep into myself, wondering what it was I *did* believe. I searched for my faith—the fire that had once sustained me, the certainty in the teachings of the Church, the presence of Christ within me. I found none of it, none. I was empty inside, burned out, full of questions and pain. But as I was about to answer Jon Azure Cross and the smiling Lukyan Judasson, I found something else, something I *did* believe in, had always believed in.

Truth.

I believed in truth, even when it hurt.

"He is lost to us," said the telepath with the mocking name of Cross.

Lukyan's smile faded. "Oh, really? I had hoped you would be one of us, Damien. You seemed ready."

I was suddenly afraid, and I considered sprinting up the stairs to

Sister Judith. Lukyan had told me so very much, and now I had rejected them.

The telepath felt my fear. *"You cannot hurt us, Damien,"* it said. *"Go in peace. Lukyan has told you nothing."*

Lukyan was frowning. "I told him a good deal, Jon," he said.

"Yes. But can he trust the words of such a Liar as you?" The small misshapen mouth of the thing in the vat twitched in a smile, and its great eyes closed, and Lukyan Judasson sighed and led me up the stairs.

————

It was not until some years later that I realized it was Jon Azure Cross who was lying, and the victim of his lie was Lukyan. I *could* hurt them. I did.

It was almost simple. The Bishop had friends in government and media. With some money in the right places, I made some friends of my own. Then I exposed Cross in his cellar, charging that he had used his psionic powers to tamper with the minds of Lukyan's followers. My friends were receptive to the charges. The guardians conducted a raid, took the telepath Cross into custody, and later tried him.

He was innocent, of course. My charge was nonsense; human telepaths can read minds in close proximity, but seldom anything more. But they are rare, and much feared, and Cross was hideous enough so that it was easy to make him a victim of superstition. In the end, he was acquitted, but he left the city Ammadon and perhaps Arion itself, bound for regions unknown.

But it had never been my intention to convict him. The charge was enough. The cracks began to show in the lie that he and Lukyan had built together. Faith is hard to come by, and easy to lose. The merest doubt can begin to erode even the strongest foundation of belief.

The Bishop and I labored together to sow further doubts. It was not as easy as I might have thought. The Liars had done their work well. Ammadon, like most civilized cities, had a great pool of knowledge, a computer system that linked the schools and universities and libraries together, and made their combined wisdom available to any who needed it.

But when I checked, I soon discovered that the histories of Rome and Babylon had been subtly reshaped, and there were three listings for

Judas Iscariot—one for the betrayer, one for the saint, and one for the conqueror-king of Babylon. His name was also mentioned in connection with the Hanging Gardens, and there is an entry for a so-called "Codex Judas."

And according to the Ammadon library, dragons became extinct on Old Earth around the time of Christ.

We finally purged all those lies, wiped them from the memories of the computers, though we had to cite authorities on a half-dozen non-Christian worlds before the librarians and academics would credit that the differences were anything more than a question of religious preference. By then the Order of Saint Judas had withered in the glare of exposure. Lukyan Judasson had grown gaunt and angry, and at least half of his churches had closed.

The heresy never died completely, of course. There are always those who believe no matter what. And so to this day *The Way of Cross and Dragon* is read on Arion, in the porcelain city Ammadon, amid murmuring whisperwinds.

Arla-k-Bau and the *Truth of Christ* carried me back to Vess a year after my departure, and Archbishop Torgathon finally gave me the rest I had asked for, before sending me out to fight still other heresies. So I had my victory, and the Church continued on much as before, and the Order of Saint Judas Iscariot was crushed and diminished. The telepath Jon Azure Cross had been wrong, I thought then. He had sadly underestimated the power of a Knight Inquisitor.

Later, though, I remembered his words.

You cannot hurt us, Damien.

Us?

The Order of Saint Judas? Or the Liars?

He lied, I think, deliberately, knowing I would go forth and destroy the way of cross and dragon, knowing too that I could not touch the Liars, would not even dare mention them. How could I? Who would believe it? A grand star-spanning conspiracy as old as history? It reeks of paranoia, and I had no proof at all.

The telepath lied for Lukyan's benefit, so that he would let me go. I am certain of that now. Cross risked much to snare me. Failing, he was willing to sacrifice Lukyan Judasson and his lie, pawns in some greater game.

So I left, and carried within me the knowledge that I was empty of faith but for a blind faith in truth, a truth I could no longer find in my Church. I grew certain of that in my year of rest, which I spent reading and studying on Vess and Cathaday and Celia's World. Finally I returned to the Archbishop's receiving room, and stood again before Torgathon Nine-Klariis Tûn in my very worst pair of boots. "My Lord Commander," I said to him, "I can accept no further assignments. I ask that I be retired from active service."

"For what cause?" Torgathon rumbled, splashing feebly.

"I have lost the faith," I said to him, simply.

He regarded me for a long time, his pupilless eyes blinking. At last he said, "Your faith is a matter between you and your confessor. I care only about your results. You have done good work, Damien. You may not retire, and we will not allow you to resign."

The truth will set us free.

But freedom is cold and empty and frightening, and lies can often be warm and beautiful.

Last year the Church finally granted me a new and better ship. I named this one *Dragon*.

FOUR

The Heirs of Turtle Castle

ME AND FANTASY GO WAY BACK.

Let's get that straight right from the start, because there seem to be some strange misconceptions floating around. On one hand, I have readers who never heard of me until they picked up *A Game of Thrones,* who seem convinced that I've never written anything but epic fantasy. On the other hand, I have the folks who have read all my older stuff, yet persist in the delusion that I'm a science fiction writer who "turned to fantasy," for nefarious reasons.

The truth is, I've been reading and writing fantasy (and horror, for that matter) since my boyhood in Bayonne. My first sale may have been a science fiction story, but my second was a ghost story, and never mind those damned hovertrucks whooshing by.

"The Exit to San Breta" was by no means the first fantasy I ever wrote, either. Even before Jarn of Mars and his band of alien space pirates, I was wont to fill my idle hours by making up stories about a great castle and the brave knights and kings who dwelled there. The only thing was, all of them were turtles.

The projects did not permit tenants to keep dogs or cats. You could have smaller pets, though. I had guppies, I had parakeets, and I had turtles. Lots and lots of turtles. They were the sort you bought in the five-and-ten, and they came with little plastic bowls divided down the center, one side for water, one for gravel. In the middle of the bowl was a fake plastic palm tree.

I also owned a toy castle that had come with my toy knights (a Marx tin litho castle, though I don't recall which model). It sat on top of the table that served me for a desk, and had just enough room inside its yard to fit two dimestore turtle bowls side by side. So that was where my turtles lived . . . and since they lived inside a castle, they must be kings and knights and princes. (I owned Marx's Fort Apache as well, but cowboy turtles would just have been *wrong*.)

The first turtle king was Big Fellow, who must have been a different species, since he was brown instead of green and twice as large as any of the little red-eared guys. One day I found Big Fellow dead, however, no doubt the victim of some sinister plot by the horned toads and chameleons who lived in the adjoining kingdoms. The turtle who followed Big Fellow to the throne was well meaning but hapless, and he soon died as well, but just when things were looking bleakest, Frisky and Peppy swore eternal friendship and started a turtle round table. Peppy the First turned out to be the greatest of the turtle kings, but when he was old . . .

Turtle Castle had no beginning and no end, but lots of middle. Only parts of it were ever written down, but I acted out all the best bits in my head, the swordfights and battles and betrayals. I went through at least a dozen turtle kings. My mighty monarchs had a disconcerting habit of escaping the Marx castle and turning up dead beneath the refrigerator, the turtle equivalent of Mordor.

So there you are. I have *always* been a fantasy writer.

I cannot say that I was always a fantasy reader, though, for the simple reason that there was not a lot of fantasy around to be read back in the '50s and '60s. The spinner racks of my childhood were ruled by science fiction, murder mysteries, westerns, gothics, and historical novels; you could look high and low and not find a fantasy anywhere. I had signed up for the Science Fiction Book Club (three hardcovers for a dime, couldn't beat that), but they were the *science fiction* book club in those days, and fantasy need not apply.

It was five years after *Have Space Suit, Will Travel* that I stumbled across the book that would give me my first real taste of fantasy: a slim Pyramid anthology entitled *Swords & Sorcery*, edited by L. Sprague de Camp and published in December of 1963. And quite a tasty taste it was. Inside were stories by Poul Anderson, Henry Kuttner, Clark Ashton Smith, Lord Dunsany, and H. P.

Lovecraft. There was a Jirel of Joiry story by C. L. Moore and a tale of Fafhrd and the Gray Mouser by Fritz Leiber . . . and there was a story titled "Shadows in the Moonlight," by Robert E. Howard.

"Know, O prince," it opened, "that between the years when the oceans drank Atlantis and the gleaming cities, and the years of the rise of the sons of the Aryas, there was an age undreamed of, when shining kingdoms lay spread across the world like blue mantles beneath the stars—Nemedia, Ophir, Brythunia, Hyperborea, Zamora with its dark-haired women and towers of spider-haunted mystery, Zingara with its chivalry, Koth that bordered on the pastoral lands of Shem, Stygia with its shadow-guarded tombs, Hyrkania whose riders wore steel and silk and gold. But the proudest kingdom of the world was Aquilonia, reigning supreme in the dreaming west. Hither came Conan, the Cimmerian, black-haired, sullen-eyed, sword in hand, a thief, a reaver, a slayer, with gigantic melancholies and gigantic mirths, to tread the jeweled thrones of the Earth under his sandaled feet."

Howard had me at "Zamora." The "towers of spider-haunted mystery" would have done it all by themselves, though by 1963 I was fifteen, and those "dark-haired women" stirred some interest up as well. Fifteen is a fine age to make the acquaintance of Conan of Cimmeria. If *Swords & Sorcery* did not start me buying heroic fantasy right and left, the way *Have Space Suit, Will Travel* had started me buying science fiction, it was only because you could hardly *find* any fantasy, heroic or otherwise.

In the '60s and '70s, fantasy and science fiction were often considered one field, although the field usually went by the name "science fiction." It was commonplace for the same writers to work in both genres. Robert A. Heinlein, Andre Norton, and Eric Frank Russell, three of my boyhood favorites, were all strongly identified with science fiction, but they all wrote fantasy as well. Poul Anderson was writing *The Broken Sword* and *Three Hearts and Three Lions* in between his tales of Nicholas van Rijn and Dominic Flandry. Jack Vance created Big Planet *and* the Dying Earth. Fritz Leiber's Spiders and Snakes fought their Time War even as Fafhrd and the Gray Mouser were fighting the Lords of Quarmall.

And yet, though all the top writers wrote fantasy, they did not write much of it, not if they wanted to pay their rent and eat. Science fiction was far more popular, far more commercial. The SF magazines wanted *only* SF, and would not publish fantasy no matter how well done. From time to time, fantasy magazines were launched, but few lasted long. *Astounding* spanned years and decades to become *Analog,* but *Unknown* did not survive the paper shortages of World War II. The publishers of *Galaxy* and *If* tried *Worlds of Fantasy*, and as quickly killed it. *Fantastic* endured for decades, but *Amazing* was the prize horse in that stable. And when Boucher and McComas launched *The Magazine of Fantasy*, it took them only one issue before they renamed it *The Magazine of Fantasy and Science-Fiction*.

These things often go in cycles, of course. As it happened, huge changes were looming just around the corner. In 1965, Ace Books would take advantage of a loophole in the copyright laws to release an unauthorized paperback reprint of J.R.R. Tolkien's *Lord of the Rings*. They would sell hundreds of thousands of copies before Tolkien and Ballantine Books, moving hurriedly, could answer with an authorized edition. In 1966, Lancer Books, perhaps inspired by the success that Ace and Ballantine had been having with Tolkien, would begin reprinting all of the Conan tales in a series of matched paperbacks with Frank Frazetta covers. Come 1969, Lin Carter (a dreadful writer but a fine editor) would launch the Ballantine Adult Fantasy Series and bring dozens of classic fantasies back into print. But all that lay well in the future in 1963, when I finished de Camp's *Swords & Sorcery* and looked about for more fantasy to read.

I found some in a most unlikely place: a comics fanzine.

Early comics fandom grew out of science fiction fandom, but after a few years it had become so much a world unto itself that most new fans were not even aware of the existance of the earlier, parent fandom. At the same time, all those high school boys were growing older, and their interests were broadening to include things other than superhero comics. Things like music, cars, girls . . . and books without pictures. Inevitably the scope of their fanzines began to broaden as well. The wheel was duly reinvented, and before long specialized 'zines began to pop up, devoted not to superheroes but to secret agents, or private eyes, or the old pulps, or the Barsoom stories of Edgar Rice Burroughs . . . or to heroic fantasy.

Cortana was the name of the *Swords & Sorcery* fanzine. Edited "on a trimonthly schedule" (hah) by Clint Bigglestone, who would later go on to be one of the founders of the Society for Creative Anachronism, it came out of the San Francisco Bay Area in 1964. Printed in the usual faded purple ditto, *Cortana* was nothing special to look at, but it was great fun to *read*, full of articles and news items about Conan and his competitors, and original heroic fantasies by some of the top writers of '60s comics fandom: Paul Moslander and Victor Baron (who were the same person), my penpal Howard Waldrop (who wasn't), Steve Perrin, and Bigglestone himself. Waldrop's stories starred an adventurer known only as the Wanderer, whose exploits were recorded in the "Canticles of Chimwazle." Howard also drew the covers of *Cortana,* and provided some of the interior art.

In *Star Studded Comics* and most other comics fanzines, prose fiction was the homely sister; pride of place went to comic strips. Not here. In *Cortana* the text stories ruled. I wrote a gushing letter of comment at once, but I wanted to be a bigger part of this great new fanzine than that. So I put Manta Ray and Dr. Weird aside, and sat down to write my first fantasy since Turtle Castle.

"Dark Gods of Kor-Yuban," I called it, and yes, my version of Mordor sounds like a brand of coffee. My heroes were the usual pair of mismatched adventurers, the melancholy exile prince R'hllor of Raugg and his boisterous, swaggering companion, Argilac the Arrogant. "Dark Gods of Kor-Yuban" was the longest story I'd ever attempted (maybe five thousand words), and had a tragic ending where Argilac got eaten by the titular dark gods. I had been reading Shakespeare at Marist and learning about tragedy, so I gave Argilac the tragic flaw of arrogance, which caused his downfall. R'hllor escaped to tell the tale . . . and to fight another day, I hoped. When the story was done, I shipped it off to San Francisco, where Clint Bigglestone promptly accepted it for publication in *Cortana.*

Cortana never published another issue.

By my senior year of high school I *did* know how to use carbon paper, honest. I was just too lazy to bother with it. "Dark Gods of Kor-Yuban" became another of my lost stories. (It was the last, though. In college, I made carbon copies of every story I wrote.) Before folding up its purple ditto tent, *Cortana* did me one more favor. In his third issue, Bigglestone ran an article called "Don't Make a Hobbit of It," wherein, for the first time, I learned of J.R.R. Tolkien and his fantasy trilogy, *Lord of the Rings*. The story sounded intriguing enough so that I did not hesitate a few months later, when I chanced to see the pirated Ace paperback of *The Fellowship of the Ring* on a newsstand.

Dipping into the fat red paperback during my bus ride home, I began to wonder if I had not made a mistake. *Fellowship* did not seem like proper heroic fantasy at all. What the hell was all this stuff about pipe-weed? Robert E. Howard's stories usually opened with a giant serpent slithering by or an axe cleaving someone's head in two. Tolkien opened his with a birthday party. And these hobbits with their hairy feet and love of 'taters seemed to have escaped from a Peter Rabbit book. *Conan would hack a bloody path right through the Shire, end to end,* I remembered thinking. *Where are the gigantic melancholies and the gigantic mirths?*

Yet I kept on reading. I almost gave up at Tom Bombadil, when people started going *"Hey! Come derry dol! Tom Bombadillo!"* Things got more interesting in the barrow downs, though, and even more so in Bree, where Strider strode onto the scene. By the time we got to Weathertop, Tolkien had me. "Gil-Galad was an elven king," Sam Gamgee recited, "of him the harpers sadly sing." A chill went through me, such as Conan and Kull had never evoked.

Almost forty years later, I find myself in the middle of my own high fantasy, *A Song of Ice and Fire.* The books are huge, and hugely complex, and take me years to write. Within days of each volume being published, I begin to get emails asking when the next is coming out. "You do not know how hard it is to wait," some of my readers cry plaintively. I *do,* I want to tell them, *I know just how hard it is. I waited too.* When I finished *The Fellowship of the Ring,* it was the only volume out in paperback. I had to wait for Ace to bring out *The Two Towers,* and again for *The Return of the King.* Not a long wait, admittedly, yet somehow it seemed like decades. The moment I got my hands on the next volume I put everything else aside so I could read it ... but halfway through *The Return of the King,* I slowed down. Only a few hundred pages remained, and once they were done, I would never be able to read *Lord of the Rings* for the first time again. As much as I wanted to know how it all came out, I did not want the experience to be over.

That was how fiercely I loved those books, as a reader.

As a writer, however, I was seriously daunted by Tolkien. When I read Robert E. Howard, I would think, *Someday I may be able to write as well as him.* When I read Lin Carter or John Jakes, I would think, *I can write better stuff than this right now.* But when I read Tolkien, I despaired. *I will never be able to do what he's done,* I would think. *I will never be able to come close.* Though I would write fantasy in the years to come, most of it remained closer in tone to Howard than to Tolkien. One does not presume to tread upon the master's heels.

I began a second R'hllor story during my freshman year at Northwestern, when I still deluded myself that *Cortana* was only delayed, not dead, and that "Dark Gods of Kor-Yuban" would be coming out real soon now. In the sequel, my exile prince finds himself in the Dothrak Empire, where he joins Barron of the Bloody Blade to fight the winged demons who slew his grandsire, King Barristan the Bold. I'd written twenty-three pages when some friends found the story on my desk one day, and had so much fun reading the purple prose aloud that I was too chagrined to continue. (I still have the pages, and yes, they're a bit purple, bordering on indigo.)

I wrote no more fantasy during my college years. And aside from "The Exit to San Breta," which was neither high nor heroic fantasy, I hardly touched it as a fledgling pro. That was not because I liked it any less than science fiction. My reasons were more pragmatic. I had rent to pay.

The early '70s were a splendid time to be a young science fiction writer at the start of a career. New SF magazines were being launched every year: *Vertex, Cosmos, Odyssey, Galileo, Asimov's.* (There were no new fantasy magazines.) Of the existing magazines, only *Fantastic* and *F&SF* bought fantasy, and the latter preferred quirky modern fantasies, partaking more of Thorne Smith and Gerald Kersh than Tolkien or Howard. New or old, the SF mags had serious rivals in the original anthology series: *Orbit, New Dimensions, Universe, Infinity, Quark, Alternities, Andromeda, Nova, Stellar, Chrysalis.* (There were no original anthologies devoted to fantasy.) The men's magazines were also booming, having just discovered that women had pubic hair; many wanted SF stories to fill up the pages between the pictures. (They would buy horror as well, but neither high fantasy nor heroic fantasy need apply.)

There were more book publishers than there are today. Bantam Doubleday Dell Random House Ballantine Fawcett were six publishers, not one, most of whom had SF lines. (The major fantasy imprint era was the Ballantine Adult Fantasy Series, which was largely devoted to reprints. Lancer had its Robert E. Howard titles . . . but Lancer was a bottom-feeder, a low-prestige, low-pay house that most writers fled as soon as they could sell elsewhere.) The World Fantasy Convention did not yet exist, and the World Science Fiction Convention rarely nominated any fantasies for Hugo Awards, no more than the Science Fiction Writers of America (who had not yet added "and Fantasy" to their name) nominated them for Nebulas.

In short, you could not make a career as a fantasist. Not then. Not yet. So I did what all those other writers before me had done, what Jack Williamson had done, and Poul Anderson, and Andre Norton, and Jack Vance, and Heinlein and Kuttner and Russell and de Camp and C. L. Moore and the rest. I wrote science fiction . . . and from time to time, for love, I snuck in a fantasy or two.

"The Lonely Songs of Laren Dorr" was my first pure fantasy as a pro. *Fantastic* published it in 1976. Keen-eyed readers will notice certain names and motifs that go all the way back to "Only Kids Are Afraid of the Dark," and other names and motifs that I would pick up and use again in later works. In my fiction, as in real life, I never throw anything away. You can never tell when you might find another use for it. Sharra and her dark crown were originally meant for the Dr. Weird mythos that Howard Keltner once asked me to create. By 1976, however, my fanzine days were almost a decade behind me and *Dr. Weird* had folded up shop, so I felt free to reclaim the ideas and rework them for a different sort of tale.

Once upon a time I meant to follow "Laren Dorr" with more tales about Sharra, "the girl who goes between the worlds." I never did . . . but the phrase remained with me, as you'll see when we reach the section about my years in film and television.

"The Ice Dragon" was the second of the three stories that I wrote over Christmas break during the winter of 1978-79, as described in the last commentary. Dubuque winters had a way of inspiring stories about ice and snow and freezing cold. You won't often find me saying, "The story wrote itself," but it was true in this case. The words seemed to pour out of me, and when I was done I was convinced that this was one of the best short stories I had ever written, maybe the best.

No sooner had I finished than I chanced to see a market report announcing that Orson Scott Card was looking for submissions for an original anthology called *Dragons of Light and Darkness*. The timing could not have been more perfect; the gods were trying to tell me something. So I sent "The Ice Dragon" to Card, and it was published in *Dragons of Light*, where it promptly vanished with nary a trace, as stories in anthologies so often do. Maybe surrounding it with other dragon stories was not the best idea I ever had.

Ice dragons have become commonplace features of a lot of fantasy books and games in the twenty-odd years since I wrote "The Ice Dragon," but I believe mine was the first. And most of these other "ice dragons" appear to be no more than white dragons living in cold climates. Adara's friend, a dragon *made* of ice that breathes cold instead of flame, remains unique so far as I'm aware, my only truly original contribution to the fantasy bestiary.

"In the Lost Lands," the third of the stories showcased in this section, first appeared in the DAW anthology *Amazons,* edited by Jessica Amanda Salmonson. ("How did *she* get a story out of you?" another anthology editor asked me, in annoyed tones, after the book came out. "Well," I said, "she asked for one.") Like "The Lonely Songs of Laren Dorr," it was meant to be the opening installment of a series. I would later write a few pages of a sequel called "The Withered Hand," but as usual I never managed to complete it. Until such time as I return to it (if ever), "In the Lost Lands" will remain yet another example of my patented one-story series.

I might also mention that some of the inspiration for "In the Lost Lands" came from a song. Which one? That would be telling. Seems obvious to me. The clue is right in the first line, for those who care about such puzzles.

Sharra and Laren Dorr, Adara and her ice dragon, Gray Alys, Boyce, and Blue Jerais . . . one and all, they are the heirs of Turtle Castle, the ancestors of Ice and Fire. This book would not have been complete without them.

Why do I love fantasy? Let me answer that with a piece I wrote in 1996, to accompany my portrait in Pati Perret's book of photographs, *The Faces of Fantasy:*

The best fantasy is written in the language of dreams. It is alive as dreams are alive, more real than real . . . for a moment at least . . . that long magic moment before we wake.

Fantasy is silver and scarlet, indigo and azure, obsidian veined with gold and lapis lazuli. Reality is plywood and plastic, done up in mud brown and olive drab. Fantasy tastes of habaneros and honey, cinnamon and cloves, rare red meat and wines as sweet as summer. Reality is beans and tofu, and ashes at the end. Reality is the strip malls of Burbank, the smokestacks of Cleveland, a parking garage in Newark. Fantasy is the towers of Minas Tirith, the ancient stones of Gormenghast, the halls of Camelot. Fantasy flies on the wings of Icarus, reality on Southwest Airlines. Why do our dreams become so much smaller when they finally come true?

We read fantasy to find the colors again, I think. To taste strong spices and hear the song the sirens sang. There is something old and true in fantasy that speaks to something deep within us, to the child who dreamt that one day he would hunt the forests of the night, and feast beneath the hollow hills, and find a love to last forever somewhere south of Oz and north of Shangri-La.

They can keep their heaven. When I die, I'd sooner go to Middle Earth.

The Lonely Songs of
Laren Dorr

––––––––––– ❖ –––––––––––

THERE IS A GIRL WHO GOES BETWEEN THE WORLDS.

She is gray-eyed and pale of skin, or so the story goes, and her hair is a coal-black waterfall with half-seen hints of red. She wears about her brow a circlet of burnished metal, a dark crown that holds her hair in place and sometimes puts shadows in her eyes. Her name is Sharra; she knows the gates.

The beginning of her story is lost to us, with the memory of the world from which she sprang. The end? The end is not yet, and when it comes we shall not know it.

We have only the middle, or rather a piece of that middle, the smallest part of the legend, a mere fragment of the quest. A small tale within the greater, of one world where Sharra paused, and of the lonely singer Laren Dorr and how they briefly touched.

––––––––––––

ONE MOMENT THERE WAS ONLY THE VALLEY, CAUGHT IN TWILIGHT. The setting sun hung fat and violet on the ridge above, and its rays slanted down silently into a dense forest whose trees had shiny black trunks and colorless ghostly leaves. The only sounds were the cries of the mourning-birds coming out for the night, and the swift rush of water in the rocky stream that cut the woods.

Then, through a gate unseen, Sharra came tired and bloodied to the world of Laren Dorr. She wore a plain white dress, now stained and sweaty, and a heavy fur cloak that had been half-ripped from her back. And her left arm, bare and slender, still bled from three long wounds. She appeared by the side of the stream, shaking, and she threw a quick, wary glance about her before she knelt to dress her wounds. The water, for all its swiftness, was a dark and murky green. No way to tell if it was safe, but Sharra was weak and thirsty. She drank, washed her arm as best she could in the strange and doubtful water, and bound her injuries with bandages ripped from her clothes. Then, as the purple sun dipped lower behind the ridge, she crawled away from the water to a sheltered spot among the trees, and fell into exhausted sleep.

She woke to arms around her, strong arms that lifted her easily to carry her somewhere, and she woke struggling. But the arms just tightened, and held her still. "Easy," a mellow voice said, and she saw a face dimly through gathering mist, a man's face, long and somehow gentle.

"You are weak," he said, "and night is coming. We must be inside before darkness."

Sharra did not struggle, not then, though she knew she should. She had been struggling a long time, and she was tired. But she looked at him, confused. "Why?" she asked. Then, not waiting for an answer, "Who are you? Where are we going?"

"To safety," he said.

"Your home?" she asked, drowsy.

"No," he said, so soft she could scarcely hear his voice. "No, not home, not ever home. But it will do." She heard splashing then, as if he were carrying her across the stream, and ahead of them on the ridge she glimpsed a gaunt, twisted silhouette, a triple-towered castle etched black against the sun. Odd, she thought, that wasn't there before.

She slept.

––––––

WHEN SHE WOKE, HE WAS THERE, WATCHING HER. SHE LAY UNDER A pile of soft, warm blankets in a curtained, canopied bed. But the curtains had been drawn back, and her host sat across the room in a great chair draped by shadows. Candlelight flickered in his eyes, and his hands locked together neatly beneath his chin. "Are you feeling better?" he asked, without moving.

She sat up, and noticed she was nude. Swift as suspicion, quicker than thought, her hand went to her head. But the dark crown was still there, in place, untouched, its metal cool against her brow. Relaxing, she leaned back against the pillows and pulled the blankets up to cover herself. "Much better," she said, and as she said it she realized for the first time that her wounds were gone.

The man smiled at her, a sad wistful sort of smile. He had a strong face, with charcoal-colored hair that curled in lazy ringlets and fell down into dark eyes somehow wider than they should be. Even seated, he was tall. And slender. He wore a suit and cape of some soft gray leather, and over that he wore melancholy like a cloak. "Claw marks," he said speculatively, while he smiled. "Claw marks down your arm, and your clothes almost ripped from your back. Someone doesn't like you."

"Something," Sharra said. "A guardian, a guardian at the gate." She sighed. "There is always a guardian at the gate. The Seven don't like us to move from world to world. Me they like least of all."

His hands unfolded from beneath his chin, and rested on the carved wooden arms of his chair. He nodded, but the wistful smile stayed. "So, then," he said. "You know the Seven, and you know the gates." His eyes strayed to her forehead. "The crown, of course. I should have guessed."

Sharra grinned at him. "You did guess. More than that, you knew. Who are you? What world is this?"

"My world," he said evenly. "I've named it a thousand times, but none of the names ever seem quite right. There was one once, a name I liked, a name that fit. But I've forgotten it. It was a long time ago. *My* name is Laren Dorr, or that was my name, once, when I had use for such a thing. Here and now it seems somewhat silly. But at least I haven't forgotten *it*."

"Your world," Sharra said. "Are you a king, then? A god?"

"Yes," Laren Dorr replied, with an easy laugh. "And more. I'm whatever I choose to be. There is no one around to dispute me."

"What did you do to my wounds?" she asked.

"I healed them." He gave an apologetic shrug. "It's my world. I have certain powers. Not the powers I'd like to have, perhaps, but powers nonetheless."

"Oh." She did not look convinced.

Laren waved an impatient hand. "You think it's impossible. Your crown, of course. Well, that's only half right. I could not harm you with my, ah, powers, not while you wear that. But I can help you." He smiled again, and his eyes grew soft and dreamy. "But it doesn't matter. Even if I could I would never harm you, Sharra. Believe that. It has been a long time."

Sharra looked startled. "You know my name. How?"

He stood up, smiling, and came across the room to sit beside her on the bed. And he took her hand before replying, wrapping it softly in his and stroking her with his thumb. "Yes, I know your name. You are Sharra, who moves between the worlds. Centuries ago, when the hills had a different shape and the violet sun burned scarlet at the very beginning of its cycle, they came to me and told me you would come. I hate them, all Seven, and I will always hate them, but that night I welcomed the vision they gave me. They told me only your name, and that you would come here, to my world. And one thing more, but that was enough. It was a promise. A promise of an ending or a start, of a change. And any change is welcome on this world. I've been alone here through a thousand sun-cycles, Sharra, and each cycle lasts for centuries. There are few events to mark the death of time."

Sharra was frowning. She shook her long black hair, and in the dim light of the candles the soft red highlights glowed. "Are they that far ahead of me, then?" she said. "Do they know what will happen?" Her voice was troubled. She looked up at him. "This other thing they told you?"

He squeezed her hand, very gently. "They told me I would love you," Laren said. His voice still sounded sad. "But that was no great prophecy. I could have told them as much. There was a time long ago—I think the sun was yellow then—when I realized that I would love *any* voice that was not an echo of my own."

SHARRA WOKE AT DAWN, WHEN SHAFTS OF BRIGHT PURPLE LIGHT SPILLED into her room through a high arched window that had not been there the night before. Clothing had been laid out for her; a loose yellow robe, a jeweled dress of bright crimson, a suit of forest green. She chose the suit, dressed quickly. As she left, she paused to look out the window.

She was in a tower, looking out over crumbling stone battlements and a dusty triangular courtyard. Two other towers, twisted matchstick things with pointed conical spires, rose from the other corners of the triangle. There was a strong wind that whipped the rows of gray pennants set along the walls, but no other motion to be seen.

And, beyond the castle walls, no sign of the valley, none at all. The castle with its courtyard and its crooked towers was set atop a mountain, and far and away in all directions taller mountains loomed, presenting a panorama of black stone cliffs and jagged rocky walls and shining clean ice steeples that gleamed with a violet sheen. The window was sealed and closed, but the wind *looked* cold.

Her door was open. Sharra moved quickly down a twisting stone staircase, out across the courtyard into the main building, a low wooden structure built against the wall. She passed through countless rooms, some cold and empty save for dust, others richly furnished, before she found Laren Dorr eating breakfast.

There was an empty seat at his side; the table was heavily laden with food and drink. Sharra sat down, and took a hot biscuit, smiling despite herself. Laren smiled back.

"I'm leaving today," she said, in between bites. "I'm sorry, Laren. I must find the gate."

The air of hopeless melancholy had not left him. It never did. "So you said last night," he replied, sighing. "It seems I have waited a long time for nothing."

There was meat, several types of biscuits, fruit, cheese, milk. Sharra filled a plate, face a little downcast, avoiding Laren's eyes. "I'm sorry," she repeated.

"Stay awhile," he said. "Only a short time. You can afford it, I would think. Let me show you what I can of my world. Let me sing to you." His eyes, wide and dark and very tired, asked the question.

She hesitated. "Well . . . it takes time to find the gate."

"Stay with me for a while, then."

"But Laren, eventually I must go. I have made promises. You understand?"

He smiled, gave a helpless shrug. "Yes. But look. I know where the gate is. I can show you, save you a search. Stay with me, oh, a month. A month as you measure time. Then I'll take you to the gate." He studied her. "You've been hunting a long, long time, Sharra. Perhaps you need a rest."

Slowly, thoughtfully, she ate a piece of fruit, watching him all the time. "Perhaps I do," she said at last, weighing things. "And there will be a guardian, of course. You could help me, then. A month . . . that's not so long. I've been on other worlds far longer than a month." She nodded, and a smile spread slowly across her face. "Yes," she said, still nodding. "That would be all right."

He touched her hand lightly. After breakfast he showed her the world they had given him.

They stood side by side on a small balcony atop the highest of the three towers, Sharra in dark green and Laren tall and soft in gray. They stood without moving, and Laren moved the world around them. He set the castle flying over restless churning seas, where long black serpent-heads peered up out of the water to watch them pass. He moved them to a vast echoing cavern under the earth, all aglow with a soft green light, where dripping stalactites brushed down against the towers and herds of blind white goats moaned outside the battlements. He clapped his hands and smiled, and steam-thick jungle rose around them; trees that climbed each other in rubber ladders to the sky, giant flowers of a dozen different colors, fanged monkeys that chittered from the walls. He clapped again, and the walls were swept clean, and suddenly the courtyard dirt was sand and they were on an endless beach by the shore of a bleak gray ocean, and above the slow wheeling of a great blue bird with tissue-paper wings was the only movement to be seen. He showed her this, and more, and more, and in the end as dusk seemed to threaten in one place after another, he took the castle back to the ridge above the valley. And Sharra looked down on the forest of black-barked trees where he had found her, and heard the mourning-birds whimper and weep among transparent leaves.

"It is not a bad world," she said, turning to him on the balcony.

"No," Laren replied. His hands rested on the cold stone railing, his eyes on the valley below. "Not entirely. I explored it once, on foot, with a sword and a walking stick. There was a joy there, a real excitement. A new mystery behind every hill." He chuckled. "But that, too, was long ago. Now I know what lies behind every hill. Another empty horizon."

He looked at her, and gave his characteristic shrug. "There are worse hells, I suppose. But this is mine."

"Come with me, then," she said. "Find the gate with me, and leave. There are other worlds. Maybe they are less strange and less beautiful, but you will not be alone."

He shrugged again. "You make it sound so easy," he said in a careless voice. "I have found the gate, Sharra. I have tried it a thousand times. The guardian does not stop me. I step through, briefly glimpse some other world, and suddenly I'm back in the courtyard. No. I cannot leave."

She took his hand in hers. "How sad. To be alone so long. I think you must be very strong, Laren. I would go mad in only a handful of years."

He laughed, and there was a bitterness in the way he did it. "Oh, Sharra. I have gone mad a thousand times, also. They cure me, love. They always cure me." Another shrug, and he put his arm around her. The wind was cold and rising. "Come," he said. "We must be inside before full dark."

They went up in the tower to her bedroom, and they sat together on her bed and Laren brought them food; meat burned black on the outside and red within, hot bread, wine. They ate and they talked.

"Why are you here?" she asked him, in between mouthfuls, washing her words down with wine. "How did you offend them? Who were you, before?"

"I hardly remember, except in dreams," he told her. "And the dreams—it has been so long, I can't even recall which ones are truth and which are visions born of my madness." He sighed. "Sometimes I dream I was a king, a great king in a world other than this, and my crime was that I made my people happy. In happiness they turned against the Seven, and the temples fell idle. And I woke one day, within my room, within my castle, and found my servants gone. And when I went outside, my people and my world were also gone, and even the woman who slept beside me.

"But there are other dreams. Often I remember vaguely that I was a god. Well, an almost-god. I had powers, and teachings, and they were not the teachings of the Seven. They were afraid of me, each of them, for I was a match for any of them. But I could not meet all Seven together, and that was what they forced me to do. And then they left me only a small bit of my power, and set me here. It was cruel irony. As a god, I'd taught that people should turn to each other, that they could keep away the darkness by love and laughter and talk. So all these things the Seven took from me.

"And even that is not the worst. For there are other times when I think that I have always been here, that I was born here some endless age ago. And the memories are all false ones, sent to make me hurt the more."

Sharra watched him as he spoke. His eyes were not on her, but far away, full of fog and dreams and half-dead rememberings. And he spoke very slowly, in a voice that was also like fog, that drifted and curled and hid things, and you knew that there were mysteries there and things brooding just out of sight and far-off lights that you would never reach.

Laren stopped, and his eyes woke up again. "Ah, Sharra," he said. "Be careful how you go. Even your crown will not help you should they move on you directly. And the pale child Bakkalon will tear at you, and Naa-Slas feed upon your pain, and Saagael on your soul."

She shivered, and cut another piece of meat. But it was cold and tough when she bit into it, and suddenly she noticed that the candles had burned very low. How long had she listened to him speak?

"Wait," he said then, and he rose and went outside, out the door near where the window had been. There was nothing there now but rough gray stone; the windows all changed to solid rock with the last fading of the sun. Laren returned in a few moments, with a softly shining instrument of dark black wood slung around his neck on a leather cord. Sharra had never quite seen its like. It had sixteen strings, each a different color, and all up and down its length brightly glowing bars of light were inlaid amid the polished wood. When Laren sat, the bottom of the device rested on the floor and the top came to just above his shoulder. He stroked it lightly, speculatively; the lights glowed, and suddenly the room was full of swift-fading music.

"My companion," he said, smiling. He touched it again, and the music rose and died, lost notes without a tune. And he brushed the light-bars and the very air shimmered and changed color. He began to sing.

> *I am the lord of loneliness,*
> *Empty my domain . . .*

. . . the first words ran, sung low and sweet in Laren's mellow far-off fog voice. The rest of the song—Sharra clutched at it, heard each word and tried to remember, but lost them all. They brushed her, touched her, then melted away, back into the fog, here and gone again so swift that she could not remember quite what they had been. With the words, the music; wistful and melancholy and full of secrets, pulling at her, crying, whispering promises of a thousand tales untold. All around the room the candles flamed up brighter, and globes of light grew and danced and flowed together until the air was full of color.

Words, music, light; Laren Dorr put them all together, and wove for her a vision.

She saw him then as he saw himself in his dreams; a king, strong and tall and still proud, with hair as black as hers and eyes that snapped. He was dressed all in shimmering white, pants that clung tight and a shirt that ballooned at the sleeves, and a great cloak that moved and curled in the wind like a sheet of solid snow. Around his brow he wore a crown of flashing silver, and a slim, straight sword flashed just as bright at his side. This Laren, this younger Laren, this dream vision, moved without melancholy, moved in a world of sweet ivory minarets and languid blue canals. And the world moved around him, friends and lovers and one special woman whom Laren drew with words and lights of fire, and there was an infinity of easy days and laughter.

Then, sudden, abrupt darkness. He was here.

The music moaned; the lights dimmed; the words grew sad and lost. Sharra saw Laren wake, in a familiar castle now deserted. She saw him search from room to room, and walk outside to face a world he'd never seen. She watched him leave the castle, walk off towards the mists of a far horizon in the hope that those mists were smoke. And on and on he walked, and new horizons fell beneath his feet each day, and the great fat sun waxed red and orange and yellow, but still his world was empty. All the places he had shown her he walked to; all those and more; and finally, lost as ever, wanting home, the castle came to him.

By then his white had faded to dim gray. But still the song went on. Days went, and years, and centuries, and Laren grew tired and mad but never old. The sun shone green and violet and a savage hard blue-white, but with each cycle there was less color in his world. So Laren sang, of endless empty days and nights when music and memory were his only sanity, and his songs made Sharra feel it.

And when the vision faded and the music died and his soft voice melted away for the last time and Laren paused and smiled and looked at her, Sharra found herself trembling.

"Thank you," he said softly, with a shrug. And he took his instrument and left her for the night.

The next day dawned cold and overcast, but Laren took her out into the forests, hunting. Their quarry was a lean white thing, half cat, half gazelle, with too much speed for them to chase easily and too many teeth for them to kill. Sharra did not mind. The hunt was better than the kill. There was a singular, striking joy in that run through the darkling forest, holding a bow she never used and wearing a quiver of black wood arrows cut from the same dour trees that surrounded them. Both of them were bundled up tightly in gray fur, and Laren smiled out at her from under a wolf's-head hood. And the leaves beneath their boots, as clear and fragile as glass, cracked and splintered as they ran.

Afterwards, unblooded but exhausted, they returned to the castle and Laren set out a great feast in the main dining room. They smiled at each other from opposite ends of a table fifty feet long, and Sharra watched the clouds roll by the window behind Laren's head, and later watched the window turn to stone.

"Why does it do that?" she asked. "And why don't you ever go outside at night?"

He shrugged. "Ah. I have reasons. The nights are, well, not good here." He sipped hot spice wine from a great jeweled cup. "The world you came from, where you started—tell me, Sharra, did you have stars?"

She nodded. "Yes. It's been so long, though. But I still remember. The nights were very dark and black, and the stars were little pinpoints of light, hard and cold and far away. You could see patterns sometimes. The men of my world, when they were young, gave names to each of those patterns, and told grand tales about them."

Laren nodded. "I would like your world, I think," he said. "Mine was like that, a little. But our stars were a thousand colors, and they moved, like ghostly lanterns in the night. Sometimes they drew veils around them to hide their light. And then our nights would be all shimmer and gossamer. Often I would go sailing at startime, myself and she whom I loved. Just so we could see the stars together. It was a good time to sing." His voice was growing sad again.

Darkness had crept into the room, darkness and silence, and the food was cold and Sharra could scarce see his face fifty long feet away. So she rose and went to him, and sat lightly on the great table near to his chair. And Laren nodded and smiled, and at once there was a whooosh, and all along the walls torches flared to sudden life in the long dining hall. He offered her more wine, and her fingers lingered on his as she took the glass.

"It was like that for us, too," Sharra said. "If the wind was warm enough, and other men were far away, then we liked to lie together in the open. Kaydar and I." She hesitated, looked at him.

His eyes were searching. "Kaydar?"

"You would have liked him, Laren. And he would have liked you, I think. He was tall and he had red hair and there was a fire in his eyes. Kaydar had powers, as did I, but his were greater. And he had such a will. They took him one night, did not kill him, only took him from me and from our world. I have been hunting for him ever since. I know the gates, I wear the dark crown, and they will not stop me easily."

Laren drank his wine and watched the torchlight on the metal of his goblet. "There are an infinity of worlds, Sharra."

"I have as much time as I require. I do not age, Laren, no more than you do. I will find him."

"Did you love him so much?"

Sharra fought a fond, flickering smile, and lost. "Yes," she said, and now it was her voice that seemed a little lost. "Yes, so much. He made me happy, Laren. We were only together for a short time, but he *did* make me happy. The Seven cannot touch that. It was a joy just to watch him, to feel his arms around me and see the way he smiled."

"Ah," he said, and he did smile, but there was something very beaten in the way he did it. The silence grew very thick.

Finally Sharra turned to him. "But we have wandered a long way from where we started. You still have not told me why your windows seal themselves at night."

"You have come a long way, Sharra. You move between the worlds. Have you seen worlds without stars?"

"Yes. Many, Laren. I have seen a universe where the sun is a glowing ember with but a single world, and the skies are vast and vacant by night. I have seen the land of frowning jesters, where there is no sky and the hissing suns burn below the ocean. I have walked the moors of Carradyne, and watched dark sorcerers set fire to a rainbow to light that sunless land."

"This world has no stars," Laren said.

"Does that frighten you so much, that you stay inside?"

"No. But it has something else instead." He looked at her. "Would you see?"

She nodded.

As abruptly as they had lit, the torches all snuffed out. The room swam with blackness. And Sharra shifted on the table to look over Laren's shoulder. Laren did not move. But behind him, the stones of the window fell away like dust and light poured in from outside.

The sky was very dark, but she could see clearly, for against the darkness a shape was moving. Light poured from it, and the dirt in the courtyard and the stones of the battlements and the gray pennants were all bright beneath its glow. Puzzling, Sharra looked up.

Something looked back. It was taller than the mountains and it filled up half the sky, and though it gave off light enough to see the castle by, Sharra knew that it was dark beyond darkness. It had a man-shape, roughly, and it wore a long cape and a cowl, and below that was blackness even fouler than the rest. The only sounds were Laren's soft breathing and the beating of her heart and distant weeping of a mourning-bird, but in her head Sharra could hear demonic laughter.

The shape in the sky looked down at her, in her, and she felt the cold dark in her soul. Frozen, she could not move her eyes. But the shape did move. It turned, and raised a hand, and then there was something else up there with it, a tiny man-shape with eyes of fire that writhed and screamed and called to her.

Sharra shrieked, and turned away. When she glanced back, there was no window. Only a wall of safe, sure stone, and a row of torches burning, and Laren holding her within strong arms. "It was only a vision," he told her. He pressed her tight against him, and stroked her hair. "I used to test myself at night," he said, more to himself than to her. "But there was no need. They take turns up there, watching me, each of the Seven. I have seen them too often, burning with black light against the clean dark of the sky, and holding those I loved. Now I don't look. I stay inside and sing, and my windows are made of night-stone."

"I feel . . . fouled," she said, still trembling a little.

"Come," he said. "There is water upstairs, you can clean away the cold. And then I'll sing for you." He took her hand, and led her up into the tower.

Sharra took a hot bath while Laren set up his instrument and tuned it in the bedroom. He was ready when she returned, wrapped head to foot in a huge fluffy brown towel. She sat on the bed, drying her hair and waiting.

And Laren gave her visions.

He sang his other dream this time, the one where he was a god and the enemy of the Seven. The music was a savage pounding thing, shot through with lightning and tremors of fear, and the lights melted together to form a scarlet battlefield where a blinding-white Laren fought shadows and the shapes of nightmare. There were seven of them, and they formed a ring around him and darted in and out, stabbing him with lances of absolute black, and Laren answered them with fire and storm. But in the end they overwhelmed him, the light faded, and then the song grew soft and sad again and the vision blurred as lonely dreaming centuries flashed by.

Hardly had the last notes fallen from the air and the final shimmers died than Laren started once again. A new song this time, and one he did not know so well. His fingers, slim and graceful, hesitated and re-traced themselves more than once, and his voice was shaky, too, for he was making up some of the words as he went along. Sharra knew why. For this time he sang of her, a ballad of her quest. Of burning love and endless searching, of worlds beyond worlds, of dark crowns and wait-ing guardians that fought with claws and tricks and lies. He took every word that she had spoken, and used each, and transformed each. In the bedroom, glittering panoramas formed where hot white suns burned beneath eternal oceans and hissed in clouds of steam, and men ancient beyond time lit rainbows to keep away the dark. And he sang Kaydar, and he sang him true somehow, he caught and drew the fire that had been Sharra's love and made her believe anew.

But the song ended with a question, the halting finale lingering in the air, echoing, echoing. Both of them waited for the rest, and both knew there was no more. Not yet.

Sharra was crying. "My turn, Laren," she said. Then: "Thank you. For giving Kaydar back to me."

"It was only a song," he said, shrugging. "It's been a long time since I had a new song to sing."

Once again he left her, touching her cheek lightly at the door as she stood there with the blanket wrapped around her. Then Sharra locked the door behind him and went from candle to candle, turning light to darkness with a breath. And she threw the towel over a chair and crawled under the blankets and lay a long long time before drifting off to sleep.

It was still dark when she woke, not knowing why. She opened her eyes and lay quietly and looked around the room, and nothing was there, nothing was changed. Or was there?

And then she saw him, sitting in the chair across the room with his hands locked under his chin, just as he had sat that first time. His eyes steady and unmoving, very wide and dark in a room full of night. He sat very still. "Laren?" she called, softly, still not quite sure the dark form was him.

"Yes," he said. He did not move. "I watched you last night, too, while you slept. I have been alone here for longer than you can ever imagine, and very soon now I will be alone again. Even in sleep, your presence is a wonder."

"Oh, Laren," she said. There was a silence, a pause, a weighing and an unspoken conversation. Then she threw back the blanket, and Laren came to her.

———

BOTH OF THEM HAD SEEN CENTURIES COME AND GO. A MONTH, A MO-ment; much the same.

They slept together every night, and every night Laren sang his songs while Sharra listened. They talked throughout dark hours, and during the day they swam nude in crystalline waters that caught the purple glory of the sky. They made love on beaches of fine white sand, and they spoke a lot of love.

But nothing changed. And finally the time drew near. On the eve of the night before the day that was end, at twilight, they walked together through the shadowed forest where he'd found her.

Laren had learned to laugh during his month with Sharra, but now he was silent again. He walked slowly, clutched her hand hard in his, and his mood was more gray than the soft silk shirt he wore. Finally, by the side of the valley stream, he sat and pulled her down by his side. They took off their boots and let the water cool their feet. It was a warm evening, with a lonely restless wind and already you could hear the first of the mourning-birds.

"You must go," he said, still holding her hand but never looking at her. It was a statement, not a question.

"Yes," she said, and the melancholy had touched her, too, and there were leaden echoes in her voice.

"My words have all left me, Sharra," Laren said. "If I could sing for you a vision now, I would. A vision of a world once empty, made full by us and our children. I could offer that. My world has beauty and wonder and mystery enough, if only there were eyes to see it. And if the nights are evil, well, men have faced dark nights before, on other worlds in other times. I would love you, Sharra, as much as I am able. I would try to make you happy."

"Laren . . ." she started. But he quieted her with a glance.

"No, I could say that, but I will not. I have no right. Kaydar makes you happy. Only a selfish fool would ask you to give up that happiness to share my misery. Kaydar is all fire and laughter, while I am smoke and song and sadness. I have been alone too long, Sharra. The gray is part of my soul now, and I would not have you darkened. But still . . ."

She took his hand in both of hers, lifted it, and kissed it quickly. Then, releasing him, she lay her head on his unmoving shoulder. "Try to come with me, Laren," she said. "Hold my hand when we pass through the gate, and perhaps the dark crown will protect you."

"I will try anything you ask. But don't ask me to believe that it will work." He sighed. "You have countless worlds ahead of you, Sharra, and I cannot see your ending. But it is not here. That I know. And maybe that is best. I don't know anymore, if I ever did. I remember love vaguely, I think I can recall what it was like, and I remember that it never lasts. Here, with both of us unchanging and immortal, how could we help but to grow bored? Would we hate each other then? I'd not want that." He looked at her then, and smiled an aching, melancholy smile. "I think that you had known Kaydar for only a short time, to be so *in* love with him. Perhaps I'm being devious after all. For in finding Kaydar, you may lose him. The fire will go out someday, my love, and the magic will die. And then you may remember Laren Dorr."

Sharra began to weep, softly. Laren gathered her to him, and kissed her, and whispered a gentle "No." She kissed back, and they held each other wordless.

When at last the purple gloom had darkened to near-black, they put back on their boots and stood. Laren hugged her and smiled.

"I *must* go," Sharra said. "I *must*. But leaving is hard, Laren, you must believe that."

"I do," he said. "I love you *because* you will go, I think. Because you cannot forget Kaydar, and you will not forget the promises you made. You are Sharra, who goes between the worlds, and I think the Seven must fear you far more than any god I might have been. If you were not you, I would not think as much of you."

"Oh. Once you said you would love any voice that was not any echo of your own."

Laren shrugged. "As I have often said, love, *that* was a very long time ago."

They were back inside the castle before darkness, for a final meal, a final night, a final song. They got no sleep that night, and Laren sang to her again just before dawn. It was not a very good song, though; it was an aimless, rambling thing about a wandering minstrel on some nondescript world. Very little of interest ever happened to the minstrel; Sharra couldn't quite get the point of the song, and Laren sang it listlessly. It seemed an odd farewell, but both of them were troubled.

He left her with the sunrise, promising to change clothes and meet her in the courtyard. And sure enough, he was waiting when she got there, smiling at her, calm and confident. He wore a suit of pure white; pants that clung, a shirt that puffed up at the sleeves, and a great heavy cape that snapped and billowed in the rising wind. But the purple sun stained him with its shadow rays.

Sharra walked out to him and took his hand. She wore tough leather, and there was a knife in her belt, for dealing with the guardian. Her hair, jet-black with light-born glints of red and purple, blew as freely as his cape, but the dark crown was in place. "Good-bye, Laren," she said. "I wish I had given you more."

"You have given me enough. In all the centuries that come, in all the sun-cycles that lie ahead, I will remember. I shall measure time by you, Sharra. When the sun rises one day and its color is blue fire, I will look at it and say, 'Yes, this is the first blue sun after Sharra came to me.'"

She nodded. "And I have a new promise. I will find Kaydar, some-day. And if I free him, we will come back to you, both of us together, and we will pit my crown and Kaydar's fires against all the darkness of the Seven."

Laren shrugged. "Good. If I'm not here, be sure to leave a mes-sage," he said. And then he grinned.

"Now, the gate. You said you would show me the gate."

Laren turned and gestured at the shortest tower, a sooty stone structure Sharra had never been inside. There was a wide wooden door in its base. Laren produced a key.

"Here?" she said, looking puzzled. "In the castle?"

"Here," Laren said. They walked across the courtyard, to the door. Laren inserted the heavy metal key and began to fumble with the lock. While he worked, Sharra took one last look around, and felt the sadness heavy on her soul. The other towers looked bleak and dead, the courtyard was forlorn, and beyond the high icy mountains was only an empty horizon. There was no sound but Laren working at the lock, and no motion but the steady wind that kicked up the courtyard dust and flapped the seven gray pennants that hung along each wall. Sharra shivered with sudden loneliness.

Laren opened the door. No room inside; only a wall of moving fog, a fog without color or sound or light. "Your gate, my lady," the singer said.

Sharra watched it, as she had watched it so many times before. What world was next? she wondered. She never knew. But maybe in the next one, she would find Kaydar.

She felt Laren's hand on her shoulder. "You hesitate," he said, his voice soft.

Sharra's hand went to her knife. "The guardian," she said suddenly. "There is always a guardian." Her eyes darted quickly round the courtyard.

Laren sighed. "Yes. Always. There are some who try to claw you to pieces, and some who try to get you lost, and some who try to trick you into taking the wrong gate. There are some who hold you with weapons, some with chains, some with lies. And there is one, at least, who tried to stop you with love. Yet he was true for all that, and he never sang you false."

And with a hopeless, loving shrug, Laren shoved her through the gate.

DID SHE FIND HIM, IN THE END, HER LOVER WITH THE EYES OF FIRE? OR is she searching still? What guardian did she face next?

When she walks at night, a stranger in a lonely land, does the sky have stars?

I don't know. He doesn't. Maybe even the Seven do not know. They are powerful, yes, but all power is not theirs, and the number of worlds is greater than even they can count.

There is a girl who goes between the worlds, but her path is lost in legend by now. Maybe she is dead, and maybe not. Knowledge moves slowly from world to world, and not all of it is true.

But this we know; in an empty castle below a purple sun, a lonely minstrel waits, and sings of her.

THE ICE DRAGON

ADARA LIKED THE WINTER BEST OF ALL, FOR WHEN THE WORLD GREW cold the ice dragon came.

She was never quite sure whether it was the cold that brought the ice dragon or the ice dragon that brought the cold. That was the sort of question that often troubled her brother Geoff, who was two years older than her and insatiably curious, but Adara did not care about such things. So long as the cold and the snow and the ice dragon all arrived on schedule, she was happy.

She always knew when they were due because of her birthday. Adara was a winter child, born during the worst freeze that anyone could remember, even Old Laura, who lived on the next farm and remembered things that had happened before anyone else was born. People still talked about that freeze. Adara often heard them.

They talked about other things as well. They said it was the chill of that terrible freeze that had killed her mother, stealing in during her long night of labor past the great fire that Adara's father had built, and creeping under the layers of blankets that covered the birthing bed. And they said that the cold had entered Adara in the womb, that her skin had been pale blue and icy to the touch when she came forth, and that she had never warmed in all the years since. The winter had touched her, left its mark upon her, and made her its own.

It was true that Adara was always a child apart. She was a very serious little girl who seldom cared to play with the others. She was beautiful, people said, but in a strange, distant sort of way, with her pale skin and blond hair and wide clear blue eyes. She smiled, but not often. No one had ever seen her cry. Once when she was five she had stepped upon a nail imbedded in a board that lay concealed beneath a snowbank, and it had gone clear through her foot, but Adara had not wept or screamed even then. She had pulled her foot loose and walked back to the house, leaving a trail of blood in the snow, and when she had gotten there she had said only, "Father, I hurt myself." The sulks and tempers and tears of ordinary childhood were not for her.

Even her family knew that Adara was different. Her father was a huge gruff bear of a man who had little use for people in general, but a smile always broke across his face when Geoff pestered him with questions, and he was full of hugs and laughter for Teri, Adara's older sister, who was golden and freckled, and flirted shamelessly with all the local boys. Every so often he would hug Adara as well, especially when he was drunk, which was frequent during the long winters. But there would be no smiles then. He would only wrap his arms around her, and pull her small body tight against him with all his massive strength, sob deep in his chest, and fat wet tears would run down his ruddy cheeks. He never hugged her at all during the summers. During the summers he was too busy.

Everyone was busy during the summers except for Adara. Geoff would work with his father in the fields and ask endless questions about this and that, learning everything a farmer had to know. When he was not working he would run with his friends to the river, and have adventures. Teri ran the house and did the cooking, and worked a bit at the inn by the crossroads during the busy season. The innkeeper's daughter was her friend, and his youngest son was more than a friend, and she would always come back giggly and full of gossip and news from travelers and soldiers and king's messengers. For Teri and Geoff the summers were the best time, and both of them were too busy for Adara.

Their father was the busiest of all. A thousand things needed to be done each day, and he did them, and found a thousand more. He worked from dawn to dusk. His muscles grew hard and lean in summer, and he stank from sweat each night when he came in from the fields, but he always came in smiling. After supper he would sit with Geoff and tell him stories and answer his questions, or teach Teri things she did not know about cooking, or stroll down to the inn. He was a summer man, truly.

He never drank in summer, except for a cup of wine now and again to celebrate his brother's visits.

That was another reason why Teri and Geoff loved the summers, when the world was green and hot and bursting with life. It was only in summer that Uncle Hal, their father's younger brother, came to call. Hal was a dragonrider in service to the king, a tall slender man with a face like a noble. Dragons cannot stand the cold, so when winter fell Hal and his wing would fly south. But each summer he returned, brilliant in the king's green-and-gold uniform, en route to the battlegrounds to the north and west of them. The war had been going on for all of Adara's life.

Whenever Hal came north, he would bring presents; toys from the king's city, crystal and gold jewelry, candies, and always a bottle of some expensive wine that he and his brother could share. He would grin at Teri and make her blush with his compliments, and entertain Geoff with tales of war and castles and dragons. As for Adara, he often tried to coax a smile out of her, with gifts and jests and hugs. He seldom succeeded.

For all his good nature, Adara did not like Hal; when Hal was there, it meant that winter was far away.

Besides, there had been a night when she was only four, and they thought her long asleep, that she overheard them talking over wine. "A solemn little thing," Hal said. "You ought to be kinder to her, John. You cannot blame *her* for what happened."

"Can't I?" her father replied, his voice thick with wine. "No, I suppose not. But it is hard. She looks like Beth, but she has none of Beth's warmth. The winter is in her, you know. Whenever I touch her I feel the chill, and I remember that it was for her that Beth had to die."

"You are cold to her. You do not love her as you do the others."

Adara remembered the way her father laughed then. "Love her? Ah, Hal. I loved her best of all, my little winter child. But she has never loved back. There is nothing in her for me, or you, any of us. She is such a cold little girl." And then he began to weep, even though it was summer and Hal was with him. In her bed, Adara listened and wished that Hal would fly away. She did not quite understand all that she had heard, not then, but she remembered it, and the understanding came later.

She did not cry; not at four, when she heard, or six, when she finally understood. Hal left a few days later, and Geoff and Teri waved to him excitedly when his wing passed overhead, thirty great dragons in proud formation against the summer sky. Adara watched with her small hands by her sides.

There were other visits in other summers, but Hal never made her smile, no matter what he brought her.

Adara's smiles were a secret store, and she spent of them only in winter. She could hardly wait for her birthday to come, and with it the cold. For in winter she was a special child.

She had known it since she was very little, playing with the others in the snow. The cold had never bothered her the way it did Geoff and Teri and their friends. Often Adara stayed outside alone for hours after the others had fled in search of warmth, or run off to Old Laura's to eat the hot vegetable soup she liked to make for the children. Adara would find a secret place in the far corner of the fields, a different place each winter, and there she would build a tall white castle, patting the snow in place with small bare hands, shaping it into towers and battlements like those Hal often talked about on the king's castle in the city. She would snap icicles off from the lower branches of trees, and use them for spires and spikes and guardposts, ranging them all about her castle. And often in the dead of winter would come a brief thaw and a sudden freeze, and overnight her snow castle would turn to ice, as hard and strong as she imagined real castles to be. All through the winters she would build on her castle, and no one ever knew. But always the spring would come, and a thaw not followed by a freeze; then all the ramparts and walls would melt away, and Adara would begin to count the days until her birthday came again.

Her winter castles were seldom empty. At the first frost each year, the ice lizards would come wriggling out of their burrows, and the fields would be overrun with the tiny blue creatures, darting this way and that, hardly seeming to touch the snow as they skimmed across it. All the children played with the ice lizards. But the others were clumsy

and cruel, and they would snap the fragile little animals in two, breaking them between their fingers as they might break an icicle hanging
from a roof. Even Geoff, who was too kind ever to do something like
that, sometimes grew curious, and held the lizards too long in his efforts to examine them, and the heat of his hands would make them
melt and burn and finally die.

Adara's hands were cool and gentle, and she could hold the lizards
as long as she liked without harming them, which always made Geoff
pout and ask angry questions. Sometimes she would lie in the cold,
damp snow and let the lizards crawl all over her, delighting in the light
touch of their feet as they skittered across her face. Sometimes she
would wear ice lizards hidden in her hair as she went about her chores,
though she took care never to take them inside where the heat of the
fires would kill them. Always she would gather up scraps after the
family ate, and bring them to the secret place where her castle was
a-building, and there she would scatter them. So the castles she erected
were full of kings and courtiers every winter; small furry creatures that
snuck out from the woods, winter birds with pale white plumage, and
hundreds and hundreds of squirming, struggling ice lizards, cold and
quick and fat. Adara liked the ice lizards better than any of the pets the
family had kept over the years.

But it was the ice dragon that she loved.

She did not know when she had first seen it. It seemed to her that
it had always been a part of her life, a vision glimpsed during the deep
of winter, sweeping across the frigid sky on wings serene and blue. Ice
dragons were rare, even in those days, and whenever it was seen the
children would all point and wonder, while the old folks muttered and
shook their heads. It was a sign of a long and bitter winter when ice
dragons were abroad in the land. An ice dragon had been seen flying
across the face of the moon on the night Adara had been born, people
said, and each winter since it had been seen again, and those winters
had been very bad indeed, the spring coming later each year. So the
people would set fires and pray and hope to keep the ice dragon away,
and Adara would fill with fear.

But it never worked. Every year the ice dragon returned. Adara
knew it came for her.

The ice dragon was large, half again the size of the scaled green war dragons that Hal and his fellows flew. Adara had heard legends of wild dragons larger than mountains, but she had never seen any. Hal's dragon was big enough, to be sure, five times the size of a horse, but it was small compared to the ice dragon, and ugly besides.

The ice dragon was a crystalline white, that shade of white that is so hard and cold that it is almost blue. It was covered with hoarfrost, so when it moved its skin broke and crackled as the crust on the snow crackles beneath a man's boots, and flakes of rime fell off.

Its eyes were clear and deep and icy.

Its wings were vast and batlike, colored all a faint translucent blue. Adara could see the clouds through them, and oftentimes the moon and stars, when the beast wheeled in frozen circles through the skies.

Its teeth were icicles, a triple row of them, jagged spears of unequal length, white against its deep blue maw.

When the ice dragon beat its wings, the cold winds blew and the snow swirled and scurried and the world seemed to shrink and shiver. Sometimes when a door flew open in the cold of winter, driven by a sudden gust of wind, the householder would run to bolt it and say, "An ice dragon flies nearby."

And when the ice dragon opened its great mouth, and exhaled, it was not fire that came streaming out, the burning sulfurous stink of lesser dragons.

The ice dragon breathed cold.

Ice formed when it breathed. Warmth fled. Fires guttered and went out, shriven by the chill. Trees froze through to their slow secret souls, and their limbs turned brittle and cracked from their own weight. Animals turned blue and whimpered and died, their eyes bulging and their skin covered over with frost.

The ice dragon breathed death into the world; death and quiet and cold. But Adara was not afraid. She was a winter child, and the ice dragon was her secret.

She had seen it in the sky a thousand times. When she was four, she saw it on the ground.

She was out building on her snow castle, and it came and landed close to her, in the emptiness of the snow-covered fields. All the ice lizards ran away. Adara simply stood. The ice dragon looked at her for ten long heartbeats, before it took to the air again. The wind shrieked around her and through her as it beat its wings to rise, but Adara felt strangely exulted.

Later that winter it returned, and Adara touched it. Its skin was very cold. She took off her glove nonetheless. It would not be right otherwise. She was half afraid it would burn and melt at her touch, but it did not. It was much more sensitive to heat than even the ice lizards, Adara knew somehow. But she was special, the winter child, cool. She stroked it, and finally gave its wing a kiss that hurt her lips. That was the winter of her fourth birthday, the year she touched the ice dragon.

The winter of her fifth birthday was the year she rode upon it for the first time.

It found her again, working on a different castle at a different place in the fields, alone as ever. She watched it come, and ran to it when it landed, and pressed herself against it. That had been the summer when she had heard her father talking to Hal.

They stood together for long minutes until finally Adara, remembering Hal, reached out and tugged at the dragon's wing with a small hand. And the dragon beat its great wings once, and then extended them flat against the snow, and Adara scrambled up to wrap her arms about its cold white neck.

Together, for the first time, they flew.

She had no harness or whip, as the king's dragonriders use. At times the beating of the wings threatened to shake her loose from where she clung, and the coldness of the dragon's flesh crept through her clothing and bit and numbed her child's flesh. But Adara was not afraid.

They flew over her father's farm, and she saw Geoff looking very small below, startled and afraid, and knew he could not see her. It made her laugh an icy, tinkling laugh, a laugh as bright and crisp as the winter air.

They flew over the crossroads inn, where crowds of people came out to watch them pass.

They flew above the forest, all white and green and silent.

They flew high into the sky, so high that Adara could not even see the ground below, and she thought she glimpsed another ice dragon, way off in the distance, but it was not half so grand as *hers*.

They flew for most of the day, and finally the dragon swept around in a great circle, and spiraled down, gliding on its stiff and glittering wings. It let her off in the field where it had found her, just after dusk.

Her father found her there, and wept to see her, and hugged her savagely. Adara did not understand that, nor why he beat her after he had gotten her back to the house. But when she and Geoff had been put to sleep, she heard him slide out of his own bed and come padding over to hers. "You missed it all," he said. "There was an ice dragon, and it scared everybody. Father was afraid it had eaten you."

Adara smiled to herself in the darkness, but said nothing.

She flew on the ice dragon four more times that winter, and every winter after that. Each year she flew farther and more often than the year before, and the ice dragon was seen more frequently in the skies above their farm.

Each winter was longer and colder than the one before.

Each year the thaw came later.

And sometimes there were patches of land, where the ice dragon had lain to rest, that never seemed to thaw properly at all.

There was much talk in the village during her sixth year, and a message was sent to the king. No answer ever came.

"A bad business, ice dragons," Hal said that summer when he visited the farm. "They're not like real dragons, you know. You can't break them or train them. We have tales of those that tried, found frozen with their whip and harness in hand. I've heard about people who have lost hands or fingers just by touching one of them. Frostbite. Yes, a bad business."

"Then why doesn't the king do something?" her father demanded. "We sent a message. Unless we can kill the beast or drive it away, in a year or two we won't have any planting season at all."

Hal smiled grimly. "The king has other concerns. The war is going badly, you know. They advance every summer, and they have twice as many dragonriders as we do. I tell you, John, it's hell up there. Some year I'm not going to come back. The king can hardly spare men to go chasing an ice dragon." He laughed. "Besides, I don't think anybody's ever killed one of the things. Maybe we should just let the enemy take this whole province. Then it'll be *his* ice dragon."

But it wouldn't be, Adara thought as she listened. No matter what king ruled the land, it would always be *her* ice dragon.

Hal departed and summer waxed and waned. Adara counted the days until her birthday. Hal passed through again before the first chill, taking his ugly dragon south for the winter. His wing seemed smaller when it came flying over the forest that fall, though, and his visit was briefer than usual, and ended with a loud quarrel between him and her father.

"They won't move during the winter," Hal said. "The winter terrain is too treacherous, and they won't risk an advance without dragonriders to cover them from above. But come spring, we aren't going to be able to hold them. The king may not even try. Sell the farm now, while you can still get a good price. You can buy another piece of land in the south."

"This is my land," her father said. "I was born here. You too, though you seem to have forgotten it. Our parents are buried here. And Beth too. I want to lie beside her when I go."

"You'll go a lot sooner than you'd like if you don't listen to me," Hal said angrily. "Don't be stupid, John. I know what the land means to you, but it isn't worth your life." He went on and on, but her father would not be moved. They ended the evening swearing at each other, and Hal left in the dead of night, slamming the door behind him as he went.

Adara, listening, had made a decision. It did not matter what her father did or did not do. She would stay. If she moved, the ice dragon would not know where to find her when winter came, and if she went too far south it would never be able to come to her at all.

It did come to her, though, just after her seventh birthday. That winter was the coldest one of all. She flew so often and so far that she scarcely had time to work on her ice castle.

Hal came again in the spring. There were only a dozen dragons in his wing, and he brought no presents that year. He and her father argued once again. Hal raged and pleaded and threatened, but her father was stone. Finally Hal left, off to the battlefields.

That was the year the king's line broke, up north near some town with a long name that Adara could not pronounce.

Teri heard about it first. She returned from the inn one night flushed and excited. "A messenger came through, on his way to the king," she told them. "The enemy won some big battle, and he's to ask for reinforcements. He said our army is retreating."

Their father frowned, and worry lines creased his brow. "Did he say anything of the king's dragonriders?" Arguments or no, Hal was family.

"I asked," Teri said. "He said the dragonriders are the rear guard. They're supposed to raid and burn, delay the enemy while our army pulls back safely. Oh, I hope Uncle Hal is safe!"

"Hal will show them," Geoff said. "Him and Brimstone will burn 'em all up."

Their father smiled. "Hal could always take care of himself. At any rate, there is nothing we can do. Teri, if any more messengers come through, ask them how it goes."

She nodded, her concern not quite covering her excitement. It was all quite thrilling.

In the weeks that followed, the thrill wore off, as the people of the area began to comprehend the magnitude of the disaster. The king's highway grew busier and busier, and all the traffic flowed from north to south, and all the travelers wore green-and-gold. At first the soldiers marched in disciplined columns, led by officers wearing golden helmets, but even then they were less than stirring. The columns marched wearily, and the uniforms were filthy and torn, and the swords and pikes and axes the soldiers carried were nicked and ofttimes stained. Some men had lost their weapons; they limped along blindly, empty-handed. And the trains of wounded that followed the columns were often longer than the columns themselves. Adara stood in the grass by the side of the road and watched them pass. She saw a man with no eyes supporting a man with only one leg, as the two of them walked together. She saw men with no legs, or no arms, or both. She saw a man with his head split open by an axe, and many men covered with caked blood and filth, men who moaned low in their throats as they walked. She *smelled* men with bodies that were horribly greenish and puffed-up. One of them died and was left abandoned by the side of the road. Adara told her father and he and some of the men from the village came out and buried him.

Most of all, Adara saw the burned men. There were dozens of them in every column that passed, men whose skin was black and seared and falling off, who had lost an arm or a leg or half of a face to the hot breath of a dragon. Teri told them what the officers said, when they stopped at the inn to drink or rest: the enemy had many, many dragons.

For almost a month the columns flowed past, more every day. Even Old Laura admitted that she had never seen so much traffic on the road. From time to time a lone messenger on horseback rode against the tide, galloping towards the north, but always alone. After a time everyone knew there would be no reinforcements.

An officer in one of the last columns advised the people of the area to pack up whatever they could carry and move south. "They are coming," he warned. A few listened to him, and indeed for a week the road was full of refugees from towns farther north. Some of them told frightful stories. When they left, more of the local people went with them.

But most stayed. They were people like her father, and the land was in their blood.

The last organized force to come down the road was a ragged troop of cavalry, men as gaunt as skeletons riding horses with skin pulled tight around their ribs. They thundered past in the night, their mounts heaving and foaming, and the only one to pause was a pale young officer, who reined his mount up briefly and shouted, "Go, go. They are burning everything!" Then he was off after his men.

The few soldiers who came after were alone or in small groups. They did not always use the road, and they did not pay for the things they took. One swordsman killed a farmer on the other side of town, raped his wife, stole his money, and ran. His rags were green-and-gold.

Then no one came at all. The road was deserted.

The innkeeper claimed he could smell ashes when the wind blew from the north. He packed up his family and went south. Teri was distraught. Geoff was wide-eyed and anxious and only a bit frightened. He asked a thousand questions about the enemy, and practiced at being a warrior. Their father went about his labors, busy as ever. War or no war, he had crops in the field. He smiled less than usual, however, and he began to drink, and Adara often saw him glancing up at the sky while he worked.

Adara wandered the fields alone, played by herself in the damp summer heat, and tried to think of where she would hide if her father tried to take them away.

Last of all, the king's dragonriders came, and with them Hal.

There were only four of them. Adara saw the first one, and went and told her father, and he put his hand on her shoulder and together they watched it pass, a solitary green dragon with a vaguely tattered look. It did not pause for them.

Two days later, three dragons flying together came into view, and one of them detached itself from the others and circled down to their farm while the other two headed south.

Uncle Hal was thin and grim and sallow-looking. His dragon looked sick. Its eyes ran, and one of its wings had been partially burned, so it flew in an awkward, heavy manner, with much difficulty. "Now will you go?" Hal said to his brother, in front of all the children.

"No. Nothing has changed."

Hal swore. "They will be here within three days," he said. "Their dragonriders may be here even sooner."

"Father, I'm scared," Teri said.

He looked at her, saw her fear, hesitated, and finally turned back to his brother. "I am staying. But if you would, I would have you take the children."

Now it was Hal's turn to pause. He thought for a moment, and finally shook his head. "I can't, John. I would, willingly, joyfully, if it were possible. But it isn't. Brimstone is wounded. He can barely carry me. If I took on any extra weight, we might never make it."

Teri began to weep.

"I'm sorry, love," Hal said to her. "Truly I am." His fists clenched helplessly.

"Teri is almost full-grown," their father said. "If her weight is too much, then take one of the others."

Brother looked at brother, with despair in their eyes. Hal trembled. "Adara," he said finally. "She's small and light." He forced a laugh. "She hardly weighs anything at all. I'll take Adara. The rest of you take horses, or a wagon, or go on foot. But go, damn you, go."

"We will see," their father said noncommittally. "You take Adara, and keep her safe for us."

"Yes," Hal agreed. He turned and smiled at her. "Come, child. Uncle Hal is going to take you for a ride on Brimstone."

Adara looked at him very seriously. "No," she said. She turned and slipped through the door and began to run.

They came after her, of course, Hal and her father and even Geoff. But her father wasted time standing in the door, shouting at her to come back, and when he began to run he was ponderous and clumsy, while Adara was indeed small and light and fleet of foot. Hal and Geoff stayed with her longer, but Hal was weak, and Geoff soon winded himself, though he sprinted hard at her heels for a few moments. By the time Adara reached the nearest wheat field, the three of them were well behind her. She quickly lost herself amid the grain, and they searched for hours in vain while she made her way carefully towards the woods.

When dusk fell, they brought out lanterns and torches and continued their search. From time to time she heard her father swearing, or Hal calling out her name. She stayed high in the branches of the oak she had climbed, and smiled down at their lights as they combed back and forth through the fields. Finally she drifted off to sleep, dreaming about the coming of winter and wondering how she would live until her birthday. It was still a long time away.

Dawn woke her; dawn and a noise in the sky.

Adara yawned and blinked, and heard it again. She shinnied to the uppermost limb of the tree, as high as it would bear her, and pushed aside the leaves.

There were dragons in the sky.

She had never seen beasts quite like these. Their scales were dark and sooty, not green like the dragon Hal rode. One was a rust color and one was the shade of dried blood and one was black as coal. All of them had eyes like glowing embers, and steam rose from their nostrils, and their tails flicked back and forth as their dark, leathery wings beat the air. The rust-colored one opened its mouth and roared, and the forest shook to its challenge, and even the branch that held Adara trembled just a little. The black one made a noise too, and when it opened its maw a spear of flame lanced out, all orange and blue, and touched the trees below. Leaves withered and blackened, and smoke began to rise from where the dragon's breath had fallen. The one the color of blood flew close overhead, its wings creaking and straining, its mouth half-open. Between its yellowed teeth Adara saw soot and cinders, and the wind stirred by its passage was fire and sandpaper, raw and chafing against her skin. She cringed.

On the backs of the dragons rode men with whip and lance, in uniforms of black-and-orange, their faces hidden behind dark helmets. The one on the rust dragon gestured with his lance, pointing at the farm buildings across the fields. Adara looked.

Hal came up to meet them.

His green dragon was as large as their own, but somehow it seemed small to Adara as she watched it climb upwards from the farm. With its wings fully extended, it was plain to see how badly injured it was; the right wing tip was charred, and it leaned heavily to one side as it flew. On its back, Hal looked like one of the tiny toy soldiers he had brought them as a present years before.

The enemy dragonriders split up and came at him from three sides. Hal saw what they were doing. He tried to turn, to throw himself at the black dragon head-on, and flee the other two. His whip flailed angrily, desperately. His green dragon opened its mouth, and roared a challenge, but its flame was pale and short and did not reach the enemy.

The others held their fire. Then, on a signal, their dragons all breathed as one. Hal was wreathed in flames.

His dragon made a high wailing noise, and Adara saw that it was burning, *he* was burning, they were all burning, beast and master both. They fell heavily to the ground, and lay smoking amidst her father's wheat.

The air was full of ashes.

Adara craned her head around in the other direction, and saw a column of smoke rising from beyond the forest and the river. That was the farm where Old Laura lived with her grandchildren and *their* children.

When she looked back, the three dark dragons were circling lower and lower above her own farm. One by one they landed. She watched the first of the riders dismount and saunter towards their door.

She was frightened and confused and only seven, after all. And the heavy air of summer was a weight upon her, and it filled her with a helplessness and thickened all her fears. So Adara did the only thing she knew, without thinking, a thing that came naturally to her. She climbed down from her tree and ran. She ran across the fields and through the woods, away from the farm and her family and the dragons, away from all of it. She ran until her legs throbbed with pain, down in the direction of the river. She ran to the coldest place she knew, to the deep caves underneath the river bluffs, to chill shelter and darkness and safety.

And there in the cold she hid. Adara was a winter child, and cold did not bother her. But still, as she hid, she trembled.

Day turned into night. Adara did not leave her cave.

She tried to sleep, but her dreams were full of burning dragons.

She made herself very small as she lay in the darkness, and tried to count how many days remained until her birthday. The caves were nicely cool; Adara could almost imagine that it was not summer after all, that it was winter, or near to winter. Soon her ice dragon would come for her, and she would ride on its back to the land of always-winter, where great ice castles and cathedrals of snow stood eternally in endless fields of white, and the stillness and silence were all.

It almost felt like winter as she lay there. The cave grew colder and colder, it seemed. It made her feel safe. She napped briefly. When she woke, it was colder still. A white coating of frost covered the cave walls, and she was sitting on a bed of ice. Adara jumped to her feet and looked up towards the mouth of the cave, filled with a wan dawn light. A cold wind caressed her. But it was coming from outside, from the world of summer, not from the depths of the cave at all.

She gave a small shout of joy and climbed and scrambled up the ice-covered rocks.

Outside, the ice dragon was waiting for her.

It had breathed upon the water, and now the river was frozen, or at least a part of it was, although one could see that the ice was fast melting as the summer sun rose. It had breathed upon the green grass that grew along the banks, grass as high as Adara, and now the tall blades were white and brittle, and when the ice dragon moved its wings the grass cracked in half and tumbled, sheared as clean as if it had been cut down with a scythe.

The dragon's icy eyes met Adara's, and she ran to it and up its wing, and threw her arms about it. She knew she had to hurry. The ice dragon looked smaller than she had ever seen it, and she understood what the heat of summer was doing to it.

"Hurry, dragon," she whispered. "Take me away, take me to the land of always-winter. We'll never come back here, never. I'll build you the best castle of all, and take care of you, and ride you every day. Just take me away, dragon, take me home with you."

The ice dragon heard and understood. Its wide translucent wings unfolded and beat the air, and bitter arctic winds howled through the fields of summer. They rose. Away from the cave. Away from the river. Above the forest. Up and up. The ice dragon swung around to the north. Adara caught a glimpse of her father's farm, but it was very small and growing smaller. They turned their back to it, and soared.

Then a sound came to Adara's ears. An impossible sound, a sound that was too small and too far away for her to ever have heard it, especially above the beating of the ice dragon's wings. But she heard it nonetheless. She heard her father scream.

Hot tears ran down her cheeks, and where they fell upon the ice dragon's back they burned small pockmarks in the frost. Suddenly the cold beneath her hands was biting, and when she pulled one hand away Adara saw the mark that it had made upon the dragon's neck. She was scared, but still she clung. "Turn back," she whispered. "Oh, *please,* dragon. Take me back."

She could not see the ice dragon's eyes, but she knew what they would look like. Its mouth opened and a blue-white plume issued, a long cold streamer that hung in the air. It made no noise; ice dragons are silent. But in her mind Adara heard the wild keening of its grief.

"Please," she whispered once again. "Help me." Her voice was thin and small.

The ice dragon turned.

The three dark dragons were outside of the barn when Adara returned, feasting on the burned and blackened carcasses of her father's stock. One of the dragonriders was standing near them, leaning on his lance and prodding his dragon from time to time.

He looked up when the cold gust of wind came shrieking across the fields, and shouted something, and sprinted for the black dragon. The beast tore a last hunk of meat from her father's horse, swallowed, and rose reluctantly into the air. The rider flailed his whip.

Adara saw the door of the farmhouse burst open. The other two riders rushed out, and ran for their dragons. One of them was struggling into his pants as he ran. He was bare-chested.

The black dragon roared, and its fire came blazing up at them. Adara felt the searing of heat, and a shudder went through the ice dragon as the flames played along its belly. Then it craned its long neck around, and fixed its baleful empty eyes upon the enemy, and opened its frost-rimmed jaws. Out from among its icy teeth its breath came streaming, and that breath was pale and cold.

It touched the left wing of the coal-black dragon beneath them, and the dark beast gave a shrill cry of pain, and when it beat its wings again, the frost-covered wing broke in two. Dragon and dragonrider began to fall.

The ice dragon breathed again.

They were frozen and dead before they hit the ground.

The rust-colored dragon was flying at them, and the dragon the color of blood with its bare-chested rider. Adara's ears were filled with their angry roaring, and she could feel their hot breath around her, and see the air shimmering with heat, and smell the stink of sulfur.

Two long swords of fire crossed in midair, but neither touched the ice dragon, though it shriveled in the heat, and water flew from it like rain whenever it beat its wings.

The blood-colored dragon flew too close, and the breath of the ice dragon blasted the rider. His bare chest turned blue before Adara's eyes, and moisture condensed on him in an instant, covering him with frost. He screamed, and died, and fell from his mount, though his harness had remained behind, frozen to the neck of his dragon. The ice dragon closed on it, wings screaming the secret song of winter, and a blast of flame met a blast of cold. The ice dragon shuddered once again, and twisted away, dripping. The other dragon died.

But the last dragonrider was behind them now, the enemy in full armor on the dragon whose scales were the brown of rust. Adara screamed, and even as she did the fire enveloped the ice dragon's wing. It was gone in less than an instant, but the wing was gone with it, melted, destroyed.

The ice dragon's remaining wing beat wildly to slow its plunge, but it came to earth with an awful crash. Its legs shattered beneath it, and its wing snapped in two places, and the impact of the landing threw Adara from its back. She tumbled to the soft earth of the field, and rolled, and struggled up, bruised but whole.

The ice dragon seemed very small now, very broken. Its long neck sank wearily to the ground, and its head rested amid the wheat.

The enemy dragonrider came swooping in, roaring with triumph. The dragon's eyes burned. The man flourished his lance and shouted.

The ice dragon painfully raised its head once more, and made the only sound that Adara ever heard it make: a terrible thin cry full of melancholy, like the sound the north wind makes when it moves around the towers and battlements of the white castle that stands empty in the land of always-winter.

When the cry had faded, the ice dragon sent cold into the world one final time: a long smoking blue-white stream of cold that was full of snow and stillness and the end of all living things. The dragonrider flew right into it, still brandishing whip and lance. Adara watched him crash.

Then she was running, away from the fields, back to the house and her family within, running as fast as she could, running and panting and crying all the while like a seven-year-old.

Her father had been nailed to the bedroom wall. They had wanted him to watch while they took their turns with Teri. Adara did not know what to do, but she untied Teri, whose tears had dried by then, and they freed Geoff, and then they got their father down. Teri nursed him and cleaned out his wounds. When his eyes opened and he saw Adara he smiled. She hugged him very hard, and cried for him.

By night he said he was fit enough to travel. They crept away under cover of darkness, and took the king's road south.

Her family asked no questions then, in those hours of darkness and fear. But later, when they were safe in the south, there were questions endlessly. Adara gave them the best answers she could. But none of them ever believed her, except for Geoff, and he grew out of it when he got older. She was only seven, after all, and she did not understand that ice dragons are never seen in summer, and cannot be tamed nor ridden.

Besides, when they left the house that night, there was no ice dragon to be seen. Only the huge dark corpses of three war dragons and the smaller bodies of three dragonriders in black-and-orange. And a pond that had never been there before, a small quiet pool where the water was very old. They had walked around it carefully, headed toward the road.

Their father worked for another farmer for three years in the south. His hands were never as strong as they had been, before the nails had been pounded through them, but he made up for that with the strength of his back and his arms, and his determination. He saved whatever he could, and he seemed happy. "Hal is gone, and my land," he would tell Adara, "and I am sad for that. But it is all right. I have my daughter back." For the winter was gone from her now, and she smiled and laughed and even wept like other little girls.

Three years after they had fled, the king's army routed the enemy in a great battle, and the king's dragons burned the foreign capital. In the peace that followed, the northern provinces changed hands once more. Teri had recaptured her spirit and married a young trader, and she remained in the south. Geoff and Adara returned with their father to the farm.

When the first frost came, all the ice lizards came out, just as they had always done. Adara watched them with a smile on her face, re-membering the way it had been. But she did not try to touch them. They were cold and fragile little things, and the warmth of her hands would hurt them.

In the Lost Lands

You can buy anything you might desire from Gray Alys.

But it is better not to.

The Lady Melange did not come herself to Gray Alys. She was said to be a clever and a cautious young woman, as well as exceedingly fair, and she had heard the stories. Those who dealt with Gray Alys did so at their own peril, it was said. Gray Alys did not refuse any of those who came to her, and she always got them what they wanted. Yet somehow, when all was done, those who dealt with Gray Alys were never happy with the things that she brought them, the things that they had wanted. The Lady Melange knew all this, ruling as she did from the high keep built into the side of the mountain. Perhaps that was why she did not come herself.

Instead, it was Jerais who came calling on Gray Alys that day; Blue Jerais, the lady's champion, foremost of the paladins who secured her high keep and led her armies into battle, captain of her colorguard. Jerais wore an underlining of pale blue silk beneath the deep azure plate of his enameled armor. The sigil on his shield was a maelstrom done in a hundred subtle hues of blue, and a sapphire large as an eagle's eye was set in the hilt of his sword. When he entered Gray Alys' presence and removed his helmet, his eyes were a perfect match for the jewel in his sword, though his hair was a startling and inappropriate red.

Gray Alys received him in the small, ancient stone house she kept in the dim heart of the town beneath the mountain. She waited for him in a windowless room full of dust and the smell of mold, seated in an old high-backed chair that seemed to dwarf her small, thin body. In her lap was a gray rat the size of a small dog. She stroked it languidly as Jerais entered and took off his helmet and let his bright blue eyes adjust to the dimness.

"Yes?" Gray Alys said at last.

"You are the one they call Gray Alys," Jerais said.

"I am."

"I am Jerais. I come at the behest of the Lady Melange."

"The wise and beautiful Lady Melange," said Gray Alys. The rat's fur was soft as velvet beneath her long, pale fingers. "Why does the Lady send her champion to one as poor and plain as I?"

"Even in the keep, we hear tales of you," said Jerais.

"Yes."

"It is said, for a price, you will sell things strange and wonderful."

"Does the Lady Melange wish to buy?"

"It is said also that you have powers, Gray Alys. It is said that you are not always as you sit before me now, a slender woman of indeterminate age, clad all in gray. It is said that you become young and old as you wish. It is said that sometimes you are a man, or an old woman, or a child. It is said that you know the secrets of shapeshifting, that you go abroad as a great cat, a bear, a bird, and that you change your skin at will, not as a slave to the moon like the werefolk of the lost lands."

"All of these things are said," Gray Alys acknowledged.

Jerais removed a small leather bag from his belt and stepped closer to where Gray Alys sat. He loosened the drawstring that held the bag shut, and spilled out the contents on the table by her side. Gems. A dozen of them, in as many colors. Gray Alys lifted one and held it to her eye, watching the candle flame through it. When she placed it back among the others, she nodded at Jerais and said, "What would the Lady buy of me?"

"Your secret," Jerais said, smiling. "The Lady Melange wishes to shapeshift."

"She is said to be young and beautiful," Gray Alys replied. "Even here beyond the keep, we hear many tales of her. She has no mate but many lovers. All of her colorguard are said to love her, among them yourself. Why should she wish to change?"

"You misunderstand. The Lady Melange does not seek youth or beauty. No change could make her fairer than she is. She wants from you the power to become a beast. A wolf."

"Why?" asked Gray Alys.

"That is none of your concern. Will you sell her this gift?"

"I refuse no one," said Gray Alys. "Leave the gems here. Return in one month, and I shall give you what the Lady Melange desires."

Jerais nodded. His face looked thoughtful. "You refuse no one?"

"No one."

He grinned crookedly, reached into his belt, and extended his hand to her. Within the soft blue crushed velvet of his gloved palm rested another jewel, a sapphire even larger than the one set in the hilt of his sword. "Accept this as payment, if you will. I wish to buy for myself."

Gray Alys took the sapphire from his palm, held it up between thumb and forefinger against the candle flame, nodded, and dropped it among the other jewels. "What would you have, Jerais?"

His grin spread wider. "I would have you fail," he said. "I do not want the Lady Melange to have this power she seeks."

Gray Alys regarded him evenly, her steady gray eyes fixed on his own cold blue ones. "You wear the wrong color, Jerais," she said at last. "Blue is the color of loyalty, yet you betray your mistress and the mission she entrusted to you."

"I am loyal," Jerais protested. "I know what is good for her, better than she knows herself. Melange is young and foolish. She thinks it can be kept secret, when she finds this power she seeks. She is wrong. And when the people know, they will destroy her. She cannot rule these folk by day, and tear out their throats by night."

Gray Alys considered that for a time in silence, stroking the great rat that lay across her lap. "You lie, Jerais," she said when she spoke again. "The reasons you give are not your true reasons."

Jerais frowned. His gloved hand, almost casually, came to rest on the hilt of his sword. His thumb stroked the great sapphire set there. "I will not argue with you," he said gruffly. "If you will not sell to me, give me back my gem and be damned with you!"

"I refuse no one," Gray Alys replied.

Jerais scowled in confusion. "I shall have what I ask?"

"You shall have what you want."

"Excellent," said Jerais, grinning again. "In a month, then!"

"A month," agreed Gray Alys.

———

AND SO GRAY ALYS SENT THE WORD OUT, IN WAYS THAT ONLY GRAY Alys knew. The message passed from mouth to mouth through the shadows and alleys and the secret sewers of the town, and even to the tall houses of scarlet wood and colored glass where dwelled the noble and the rich. Soft gray rats with tiny human hands whispered it to sleeping children, and the children shared it with each other, and chanted a strange new chant when they skipped rope. The word drifted to all the army outposts to the east, and rode west with the great caravans into the heart of the old empire of which the town beneath the mountain was only the smallest part. Huge leathery birds with the cunning faces of monkeys flew the word south, over the forests and the rivers, to a dozen different kingdoms, where men and women as pale and terrible as Gray Alys herself heard it in the solitude of their towers. Even north, past the mountains, even into the lost lands, the word traveled.

It did not take long. In less than two weeks, he came to her. "I can lead you to what you seek," he told her. "I can find you a werewolf."

He was a young man, slender and beardless. He dressed in the worn leathers of the rangers who lived and hunted in the windswept desolation beyond the mountains. His skin had the deep tan of a man who spent all his life outdoors, though his hair was as white as mountain snow and fell about his shoulders, tangled and unkempt. He wore no armor and carried a long knife instead of a sword, and he moved with a wary grace. Beneath the pale strands of hair that fell across his face, his eyes were dark and sleepy. Though his smile was open and amiable, there was a curious indolence to him as well, and a dreamy, sensuous set to his lips when he thought no one was watching. He named himself Boyce.

Gray Alys watched him and listened to his words and finally said, "Where?"

"A week's journey north," Boyce replied. "In the lost lands."

"Do you dwell in the lost lands, Boyce?" Gray Alys asked of him.

"No. They are no fit place for dwelling. I have a home here in town. But I go beyond the mountains often, Gray Alys. I am a hunter. I know the lost lands well, and I know the things that live there. You seek a man who walks like a wolf. I can take you to him. But we must leave at once, if we are to arrive before the moon is full."

Gray Alys rose. "My wagon is loaded, my horses are fed and shod. Let us depart, then."

Boyce brushed the fine white hair from his eyes, and smiled lazily.

———

THE MOUNTAIN PASS WAS HIGH AND STEEP AND ROCKY, AND IN PLACES barely wide enough for Gray Alys' wagon to pass. The wagon was a cumbersome thing, long and heavy and entirely enclosed, once brightly painted but now faded so by time and weather that its wooden walls were all a dreary gray. It rode on six clattering iron wheels, and the two horses that pulled it were of necessity monsters half again the size of normal beasts. Even so, they kept a slow pace through the mountains. Boyce, who had no horse, walked ahead or alongside, and sometimes rode up next to Gray Alys. The wagon groaned and creaked. It took them three days to ascend to the highest point on the mountain road, where they looked through a cleft in the mountains out onto the wide barren plains of the lost lands. It took them three more days to descend.

"Now we will make better time," Boyce promised Gray Alys when they reached the lost lands themselves. "Here the land is flat and empty, and the going will be easy. A day now, perhaps two, and you shall have what you seek."

"Yes," said Gray Alys.

They filled the water barrels full before they left the mountains, and Boyce went hunting in the foothills and returned with three black rabbits and the carcass of a small deer, curiously deformed, and when Gray Alys asked him how he had brought them down with only a knife as a weapon, Boyce smiled and produced a sling and sent several small stones whistling through the air. Gray Alys nodded. They made a small fire and cooked two of the rabbits, and salted the rest of the meat. The next morning, at dawn, they set off into the lost lands.

Here they moved quickly indeed. The lost lands were a cold and empty place, and the earth was packed as hard and firm as the roads that wound through the empire beyond the mountains. The wagon rolled along briskly, creaking and clattering, shaking a bit from side to side as it went. In the lost lands there were no thickets to cut through, no rivers to cross. Desolation lay before them on all sides, seemingly endless. From time to time they saw a grove of trees, gnarled and twisted all together, limbs heavy with swollen fruit with skin the color of indigo, shining. From time to time they clattered through a shallow, rocky stream, none deeper than ankle level. From time to time vast patches of white fungus blanketed the desolate gray earth. Yet all these things were rare. Mostly there was only the emptiness, the shuddering dead plains all around them, and the winds. The winds were terrible in the lost lands. They blew constantly, and they were cold and bitter, and sometimes they smelled of ash, and sometimes they seemed to howl and shriek like some poor doomed soul.

At last they had come far enough so Gray Alys could see the end of the lost lands: another line of mountains far, far north of them, a vague bluish-white line across the gray horizon. They could travel for weeks and not reach those distant peaks, Gray Alys knew, yet the lost lands were so flat and so empty that even now they could make them out, dimly.

At dusk Gray Alys and Boyce made their camp, just beyond a grove of the curious tortured trees they had glimpsed on their journey north. The trees gave them a partial respite from the fury of the wind, but even so they could hear it, keening and pulling at them, twisting their fire into wild suggestive shapes.

"These lands are lost indeed," Gray Alys said as they ate.

"They have their own beauty," Boyce replied. He impaled a chunk of meat on the end of his long knife, and turned it above the fire. "Tonight, if the clouds pass, you will see the lights rippling above the northern mountains, all purple and gray and maroon, twisting like curtains caught in this endless wind."

"I have seen those lights before," said Gray Alys.

"I have seen them many times," Boyce said. He bit off a piece of meat, pulling at it with his teeth, and a thin line of grease ran down from the corner of his mouth. He smiled.

"You come to the lost lands often," Gray Alys said.

Boyce shrugged. "I hunt."

"Does anything live here?" asked Gray Alys. "Live amidst all this desolation?"

"Oh yes," Boyce replied. "You must have eyes to find it, you must know the lost lands, but it is there. Strange twisted beasts never seen beyond the mountains, things out of legends and nightmares, enchanted things and accursed things, things whose flesh is impossibly rare and impossibly delicious. Humans, too, or things that are almost human. Werefolk and changelings and gray shapes that walk only by twilight, shuffling things half-living and half-dead." His smile was gentle and taunting. "But you are Gray Alys, and all this you must know. It is said you came out of the lost lands yourself once, long ago."

"It is said," Gray Alys answered.

"We are alike, you and I," Boyce replied. "I love the town, the people, song and laughter and gossip. I savor the comforts of my house, good food, and good wine. I relish the players who come each fall to the high keep and perform for the Lady Melange. I like fine clothes and jewels and soft, pretty women. Yet part of me is only at home here, in the lost lands, listening to the wind, watching the shadows warily each dusk, dreaming things the townsfolk never dare." Full dark had fallen by then. Boyce lifted his knife and pointed north, to where dim lights had begun to glow faintly against the mountains. "See there, Gray Alys. See how the lights shimmer and shift. You can see shapes in them if you watch long enough. Men and women and things that are neither, moving against the darkness. Their voices are carried by the wind. Watch and listen. There are great dramas in those lights, plays grander and stranger than any ever performed on the Lady's stage. Do you hear? Do you see?"

Gray Alys sat on the hard-packed earth with her legs crossed and her gray eyes unreadable, watching in silence. Finally she spoke. "Yes," she said, and that was all.

Boyce sheathed his long knife and came around the campfire—it had died now to a handful of dim reddish embers—to sit beside her. "I knew you would see," he said. "We are alike, you and I. We wear the flesh of the city, but in our blood the cold wind of the lost lands is blowing always. I could see it in your eyes, Gray Alys."

She said nothing; she sat and watched the lights, feeling the warm presence of Boyce beside her. After a time he put an arm about her shoulders, and Gray Alys did not protest. Later, much later, when the fire had gone entirely dark and the night had grown cold, Boyce reached out and cupped her chin within his hand and turned her face to his. He kissed her, once, gently, full upon her thin lips.

And Gray Alys woke, as if from a dream, and pushed him back upon the ground and undressed him with sure, deft hands and took him then and there. Boyce let her do it all. He lay upon the chill hard ground with his hands clasped behind his head, his eyes dreamy and his lips curled up in a lazy, complacent smile, while Gray Alys rode him, slowly at first, then faster and faster, building to a shuddering climax. When she came her body went stiff and she threw her head back; her mouth opened, as if to cry out, but no sound came forth. There was only the wind, cold and wild, and the cry it made was not a cry of pleasure.

The next day dawned chill and overcast. The sky was full of thin, twisted gray clouds that raced before them faster than clouds ought to race. What light filtered through seemed wan and colorless. Boyce walked beside the wagon while Gray Alys drove it forward at a leisurely pace. "We are close now," Boyce told her. "Very close."

"Yes."

Boyce smiled up at her. His smile had changed since they had become lovers. It was fond and mysterious, and more than a bit indulgent. It was a smile that presumed. "Tonight," he told her.

"The moon will be full tonight," Gray Alys said.

Boyce smiled and pushed the hair from his eyes and said nothing.

Well before dusk, they drew up amidst the ruins of some nameless town long forgotten even by those who dwelled in the lost lands. Little remained to disturb the sweeping emptiness, only a huddle of broken masonry, forlorn and pitiful. The vague outlines of town walls could still be discerned, and one or two chimneys remained standing, jagged and half-shattered, gnawing at the horizon like rotten black teeth. No shelter was to be found here, no life. When Gray Alys had fed her horses, she wandered through the ruins but found little. No pottery, no rusted blades, no books. Not even bones. Nothing at all to hint of the people who had once lived here, if people they had been.

The lost lands had sucked the life out of this place and blown away even the ghosts, so not a trace of memory remained. The shrunken sun was low on the horizon, obscured by scuttling clouds, and the scene spoke to her with the wind's voice, cried out in loneliness and despair. Gray Alys stood for a long time, alone, watching the sun sink while her thin tattered cloak billowed behind her and the cold wind bit through into her soul. Finally she turned away and went back to the wagon.

Boyce had built a fire, and he sat in front of it, mulling some wine in a copper pot, adding spices from time to time. He smiled his new smile for Gray Alys when she looked at him. "The wind is cold," he said. "I thought a hot drink would make our meal more pleasant."

Gray Alys glanced away toward the setting sun, then back at Boyce. "This is not the time or the place for pleasure, Boyce. Dusk is all but upon us, and soon the full moon shall rise."

"Yes," said Boyce. He ladled some of the hot wine into his cup, and tried a swallow. "No need to rush off hunting, though," he said, smiling lazily. "The wolf will come to us. Our scent will carry far in this wind, in this emptiness, and the smell of fresh meat will bring him running."

Gray Alys said nothing. She turned away from him and climbed the three wooden steps that led up to the interior of her wagon. Inside she lit a brazier carefully, and watched the light shift and flicker against the weathered gray wallboards and the pile of furs on which she slept. When the light had grown steady, Gray Alys slid back a wall panel, and stared at the long row of tattered garments that hung on pegs within the narrow closet. Cloaks and capes and billowing loose shirts, strangely cut gowns and suits that clung like a second skin from head to toe, leather and fur and feathers. She hesitated briefly, then reached in and chose a great cloak made of a thousand long silver feathers, each one tipped delicately with black. Removing her simple cloth cloak, Gray Alys fastened the flowing feathered garment at her neck. When she turned it billowed all about her, and the dead air inside the wagon stirred and briefly seemed alive before the feathers settled and stilled once again. Then Gray Alys bent and opened a huge oaken chest, bound in iron and leather. From within she drew out a small box. Ten rings rested against worn gray felt, each set with a long, curving silver claw instead of a stone. Gray Alys donned them methodically, one ring to each finger, and when she rose and clenched her fists, the claws shone dimly and menacingly in the light from the brazier.

Outside, it was twilight. Boyce had not prepared any food, Gray Alys noted as she took her seat across the fire from where the pale-haired ranger sat quaffing his hot wine.

"A beautiful cloak," Boyce observed amiably.

"Yes," said Gray Alys.

"No cloak will help you when *he* comes, though."

Gray Alys raised her hand, made a fist. The silver claws caught the firelight. Gleamed.

"Ah," said Boyce. "Silver."

"Silver," agreed Gray Alys, lowering her hand.

"Still," Boyce said. "Others have come against him, armed with silver. Silver swords, silver knives, arrows tipped with silver. They are dust now, all those silvered warriors. He gorged himself on their flesh."

Gray Alys shrugged.

Boyce stared at her speculatively for a time, then smiled and went back to his wine. Gray Alys drew her cloak more tightly about herself to keep out the cold wind. After a while, staring off into the far distance, she saw lights moving against the northern mountains. She remembered the stories that she had seen there, the tales that Boyce had conjured for her from that play of colored shadows. They were grim and terrible stories. In the lost lands, there was no other kind.

At last another light caught her eye. A spreading dimness in the east, wan and ominous. Moonrise.

Gray Alys stared calmly across the dying camp fire. Boyce had begun to change.

She watched his body twist as bone and muscle changed within, watched his pale white hair grow longer and longer, watched his lazy smile turn into a wide red grin that split his face, saw the canines lengthen and the tongue come lolling out, watched the wine cup fall as his hands melted and writhed and became paws. He started to say something once, but no words came out, only a low, coarse snarl of laughter, half-human and half-animal. Then he threw back his head and howled, and he ripped at his clothing until it lay in tatters all about him and he was Boyce no longer. Across the fire from Gray Alys the wolf stood, a great shaggy white beast, half again the size of an ordinary wolf, with a savage red slash of a mouth and glowing scarlet eyes. Gray Alys stared into those eyes as she rose and shook the dust from her feathered cloak. They were knowing eyes, cunning, wise. Inside those eyes she saw a smile, a smile that presumed.

A smile that presumed too much.

The wolf howled once again, a long wild sound that melted into the wind. And then he leapt, straight across the embers of the fire he had built.

Gray Alys threw her arms out, her cloak bunched in her hands, and changed.

Her change was faster than his had been, over almost as soon as it began, but for Gray Alys it lasted an eternity. First there was the strange choking, clinging feeling as the cloak adhered to her skin, then dizziness and a curious liquid weakness as her muscles began to run and flow and reshape themselves. And finally exhilaration, as the power rushed into her and came coursing through her veins, a wine fiercer and hotter and wilder than the poor stuff Boyce had mulled above their fire.

She beat her vast silvery wings, each pinion tipped with black, and the dust stirred and swirled as she rose up into the moonlight, up to safety high above the white wolf's bound, up and up until the ruins shrunk to insignificance far beneath her. The wind took hold of her, caressed her with trembling icy hands, and she yielded herself to it and soared. Her great wings filled with the dread melody of the lost lands, carrying her higher and higher. Her cruel curving beak opened and closed and opened again, though no sound came forth. She wheeled across the sky, drunken with flight. Her eyes, sharper than any human eyes could be, saw far into the distance, spied out the secrets of every shadow, glimpsed all the dying and half-dead things that stirred and shambled across the barren face of the lost lands. The curtains of light to the north danced before her, a thousand times brighter and more gorgeous than they had been before, when she had only the dim eyes of the little thing called Gray Alys to perceive them with. She wanted to fly to them, to soar north and north and north, to cavort among those lights, shredding them into glowing strips with her talons.

She lifted her talons as if in challenge. Long and wickedly curved they were, and razor sharp, and the moonlight flashed along their length, pale upon the silver. And she remembered then, and she wheeled about in a great circle, reluctantly, and turned away from the beckoning lights of the northlands. Her wings beat and beat again, and she began to descend, shrieking down through the night air, plunging toward her prey.

She saw him far beneath her, a pale white shape hurtling away from the wagon, away from the fire, seeking safety in the shadows and the dark places. But there was no safety in the lost lands. He was strong and untiring, and his long powerful legs carried him forward in a steady swift lope that ate up the miles as if they were nothing. Already he had come a long way from their camp. But fast as he was, she was faster. He was only a wolf, after all, and she was the wind itself.

She descended in a dead silence, cutting through the wind like a knife, silver talons outstretched. But he must have spied her shadow streaking toward him, etched clear by the moonlight, for as she closed he spurted forward wildly, driven by fear. It was useless. He was running full out when she passed above him, raking him with her talons. They cut through fur and twisted flesh like ten bright silver swords, and he broke stride and staggered and went down.

She beat her wings and circled overhead for another pass, and as she did the wolf regained his feet and stared up at her terrible silhouette dark against the moon, his eyes brighter now than ever, turned feverish by fear. He threw back his head and howled a broken bloody howl that cried for mercy.

She had no mercy in her. Down she came, and down, talons drenched with blood, her beak open to rend and tear. The wolf waited for her, and leapt up to meet her dive, snarling, snapping. But he was no match for her.

She slashed at him in passing, evading him easily, opening five more long gashes that quickly welled with blood.

The next time she came around he was too weak to run, too weak to rise against her. But he watched her turn and descend, and his huge shaggy body trembled just before she struck.

———

FINALLY HIS EYES OPENED, blurred and weak. He groaned and moved feebly. It was daylight, and he was back in the camp, lying beside the fire. Gray Alys came to him when she heard him stir, knelt, and lifted his head. She held a cup of wine to his lips until he had drunk his fill.

When Boyce lay back again, she could see the wonder in his eyes, the surprise that he still lived. "You knew," he said hoarsely. "You knew . . . what I was."

"Yes," said Gray Alys. She was herself once more; a slender, small, somehow ageless woman with wide gray eyes, clad in faded cloth. The feathered cloak was hung away, the silver claws no longer adorned her fingers.

Boyce tried to sit up, winced at the pain, and settled back onto the blanket she had laid beneath him. "I thought . . . thought I was dead," he said.

"You were close to dead," Gray Alys replied.

"Silver," he said bitterly. "Silver cuts and burns so."

"Yes."

"But you saved me," he said, confused.

"I changed back to myself, and brought you back, and tended you."

Boyce smiled, though it was only a pale ghost of his old smile. "You change at will," he said wonderingly. "Ah, there is a gift I would kill for, Gray Alys!"

She said nothing.

"It was too open here," he said. "I should have taken you elsewhere. If there had been cover . . . buildings, a forest, anything . . . then you should not have had such an easy time with me."

"I have other skins," Gray Alys replied. "A bear, a cat. It would not have mattered."

"Ah," said Boyce. He closed his eyes. When he opened them again, he forced a twisted smile. "You were beautiful, Gray Alys. I watched you fly for a long time before I realized what it meant and began to run. It was hard to tear my eyes from you. I knew you were the doom of me, but still I could not look away. So beautiful. All smoke and silver, with fire in your eyes. The last time, as I watched you swoop toward me, I was almost glad. Better to perish at the hands of she who is so terrible and fine, I thought, than by some dirty little swordsman with his sharpened silver stick."

"I am sorry," said Gray Alys.

"No," Boyce said quickly. "It is better that you saved me. I will mend quickly, you will see. Even silver wounds bleed but briefly. Then we will be together."

"You are still weak," Gray Alys told him. "Sleep."

"Yes," said Boyce. He smiled at her, and closed his eyes.

HOURS HAD PASSED WHEN BOYCE FINALLY WOKE AGAIN. HE WAS much stronger, his wounds all but mended. But when he tried to rise, he could not. He was bound in place, spread-eagled, hands and feet tied securely to stakes driven into the hard gray earth.

Gray Alys watched him make the discovery, heard him cry out in alarm. She came to him, held up his head, and gave him more wine.

When she moved back, his head twisted around wildly, staring at his bonds, and then at her. "What have you done?" he cried.

Gray Alys said nothing.

"Why?" he asked. "I do not understand, Gray Alys. *Why?* You saved me, tended me, and now I am bound."

"You would not like my answer, Boyce."

"The moon!" he said wildly. "You are afraid of what might happen tonight, when I change again." He smiled, pleased to have figured it out. "You are being foolish. I would not harm you, not now, after what has passed between us, after what I know. We belong together, Gray Alys. We are alike, you and I. We have watched the lights together, and I have seen you fly! We must have trust between us! Let me loose."

Gray Alys frowned and sighed and gave no other answer.

Boyce stared at her uncomprehending. "Why?" he asked again. "Untie me, Alys, let me prove the truth of my words. You need not fear me."

"I do not fear you, Boyce," she said sadly.

"Good," he said eagerly. "Then free me, and change with me. Become a great cat tonight, and run beside me, hunt with me. I can lead you to prey you never dreamed of. There is so much we can share. You have felt how it is to change, you know the truth of it, you have tasted the power, the freedom, seen the lights from a beast's eyes, smelled fresh blood, gloried in a kill. You know . . . the freedom . . . the intoxication of it . . . all the . . . you know. . . ."

"I know," Gray Alys acknowledged.

"Then free me! We are meant for each other, you and I. We will live together, love together, hunt together."

Gray Alys shook her head.

"I do not understand," Boyce said. He strained upward wildly at his bonds, and swore, then sunk back again. "Am I hideous? Do you find me evil, unattractive?"

"No."

"Then what?" he said bitterly. "Other women have loved me, have found me handsome. Rich, beautiful ladies, the finest in the land. All of them have wanted me, even when they knew."

"But you have never returned that love, Boyce," she said.

"No," he admitted. "I have loved them after a fashion. I have never betrayed their trust, if that is what you think. I find my prey here, in the lost lands, not from among those who care for me." Boyce felt the weight of Gray Alys' eyes, and continued. "How could I love them more than I did?" he said passionately. "They could know only half of me, only the half that lived in town and loved wine and song and per-fumed sheets. The rest of me lived out here, in the lost lands, and knew things that they could never know, poor soft things. I told them so, those who pressed me hard. To join with me wholly they must run and hunt beside me. Like you. Let me go, Gray Alys. Soar for me, watch me run. Hunt with me."

Gray Alys rose and sighed. "I am sorry, Boyce. I would spare you if I could, but what must happen must happen. Had you died last night, it would have been useless. Dead things have no power. Night and day, black and white, they are weak. All strength derives from the realm between, from twilight, from shadow, from the terrible place between life and death. From the gray, Boyce, from the gray."

He wrenched at his bonds again, savagely, and began to weep and curse and gnash his teeth. Gray Alys turned away from him and sought out the solitude of her wagon. There she remained for hours, sitting alone in the darkness and listening to Boyce swear and cry out to her with threats and pleadings and professions of love. Gray Alys stayed inside until well after moonrise. She did not want to watch him change, watch his humanity pass from him for the last time.

At last his cries had become howls, bestial and abandoned and full of pain. That was when Gray Alys finally reemerged. The full moon cast a wan pale light over the scene. Bound to the hard ground, the great white wolf writhed and howled and struggled and stared at her out of hungry scarlet eyes.

Gray Alys walked toward him calmly. In her hand was the long silver skinning knife, its blade engraved with fine and graceful runes.

WHEN HE FINALLY STOPPED STRUGGLING, THE WORK WENT MORE quickly, but still it was a long and bloody night. She killed him the instant she was done, before the dawn came and changed him and gave him back a human voice to cry his agony. Then Gray Alys hung up the pelt and brought out tools and dug a deep, deep grave in the packed cold earth. She piled stones and broken pieces of masonry on top of it, to protect him from the things that roamed the lost lands, the ghouls and the carrion crows and the other creatures that did not flinch at dead flesh. It took her most of the day to bury him, for the ground was very hard indeed, and even as she worked she knew it was a futile labor.

And when at last the work was done, and dusk had almost come again, she went once more into her wagon, and returned wearing the great cloak of a thousand silver feathers, tipped with black. Then she changed, and flew, and flew, a fierce and tireless flight, bathed in strange lights and wedded to the dark. All night she flew beneath a full and mocking moon, and just before dawn she cried out once, a shrill scream of despair and anguish that rang and keened on the sharp edge of the wind and changed its sound forever.

———

PERHAPS JERAIS WAS AFRAID OF WHAT SHE MIGHT GIVE HIM, FOR HE DID not return to Gray Alys alone. He brought two other knights with him, a huge man all in white whose shield showed a skull carved out of ice, and another in crimson whose sigil was a burning man. They stood at the door, helmeted and silent, while Jerais approached Gray Alys warily. "Well?" he demanded.

Across her lap was a wolfskin, the pelt of some huge massive beast, all white as mountain snow. Gray Alys rose and offered the skin to Blue Jerais, draping it across his outstretched arm. "Tell the Lady Melange to cut herself, and drip her own blood onto the skin. Do this at moonrise when the moon is full, and then the power will be hers. She need only wear the skin as a cloak, and will the change thereafter. Day or night, full moon or no moon, it makes no matter."

Jerais looked at the heavy white pelt and smiled a hard smile. "A wolfskin, eh? I had not expected that. I thought perhaps a potion, a spell."

"No," said Gray Alys. "The skin of a werewolf."

"A werewolf?" Jerais' mouth twisted curiously, and there was a sparkle in his deep sapphire eyes. "Well, Gray Alys, you have done what the Lady Melange asked, but you have failed me. I did not pay you for success. Return my gem."

"No," said Gray Alys. "I have earned it, Jerais."

"I do not have what I asked for."

"You have what you wanted, and that is what I promised." Her gray eyes met his own without fear. "You thought my failure would help you get what you truly wanted, and that my success would doom you. You were wrong."

Jerais looked amused. "And what do I truly desire?"

"The Lady Melange," said Gray Alys. "You have been one lover among many, but you wanted more. You wanted all. You knew you stood second in her affections. I have changed that. Return to her now, and bring her the thing that she has bought."

THAT DAY THERE WAS BITTER LAMENTATION IN THE HIGH KEEP ON THE mountain, when Blue Jerais knelt before the Lady Melange and offered her a white wolfskin. But when the screaming and the wailing and the mourning was done, she took the great pale cloak and bled upon it and learned the ways of change. It is not the union she desired, but it is a union nonetheless. So every night she prowls the battlements and the mountainside, and the townsfolk say her howling is wild with grief.

And Blue Jerais, who wed her a month after Gray Alys returned from the lost lands, sits beside a madwoman in the great hall by day, and locks his doors by night in terror of his wife's hot red eyes, and does not hunt anymore, or laugh, or lust.

YOU CAN BUY ANYTHING YOU MIGHT DESIRE FROM GRAY ALYS.

But it is better not to.

FIVE

HYBRIDS AND HORRORS

I NEVER READ HORROR STORIES AS A KID. AT LEAST, I NEVER CALLED THEM THAT. MONSTER stories, though . . . *those* I loved. At Halloween, when we went out trick-or-treating, I always wanted to be a ghost or monster, never a cowboy or a hobo or a clown.

The Plaza was the dingiest of Bayonne's three regular movie theaters, but I never missed their monster matinees on Saturday afternoons. Admission was only a quarter. The DeWitt and the Lyceum, the more upscale theaters, were where I saw William Castle's gimmick films, *The Tingler* and *13 Ghosts*. The one time I set foot inside the Victory, Bayonne's cavernous old decaying opera house, closed during most of my childhood, that was for a monster movie too. The seats were musty and dusty and, it turned out, infested; I came home covered with insect bites, and the Victory was boarded up again shortly thereafter.

There was scary stuff on television as well. You could catch the old Universal horror films at night, if your mother let you stay up late enough. The Wolfman was my favorite monster, though I liked Count Dracula and Frankenstein (he was always Frankenstein to us, never "Frankenstein's monster" or "the monster") as well. The Creature from the Black Lagoon and the Invisible Man were not to be compared to the big three, and the Mummy was just stupid. Besides the old movies, the tube also offered the occasional creepy episode of *The Twilight Zone* and *The Alfred Hitchcock Hour* . . . but *Thriller,* hosted by Boris Karloff, was scarier than both and then some. Their adaptation of Robert E. Howard's "Pigeons from Hell" frightened me as much as anything I ever saw on television until the Vietnam War . . . and the Vietnam War didn't have a guy come down a staircase with an axe buried in his head.

I devoured monster comics too, though I was too young for the really good ones, *Tales from the Crypt* and its mouldering EC ilk. I read about those later in the fanzines, but never owned a copy. I do recall coming across a beat-up old comic at the local barbershop that was a *lot* scarier than the ones I was buying; almost certainly, an old EC that the barber still had lying around. (He had piles of old pre-DC *Blackhawk* comics as well.) Before Marvel was Marvel, they published a lot of not-especially-scary monster comics where the monsters had these goofy names and came from outer space. Those I got, though they were tepid fare for the most part, and I never liked them half as well as superhero comics.

Funny books, movies, and television planted the seeds, and monstrous seeds they were . . . but my love of actual horror fiction did not take root until 1965, when I paid fifty cents (outrageous the way book prices were going up) for an Avon paperback anthology called *Boris Karloff's Favorite Horror Stories* and read "The Haunter of the Dark," by H. P. Lovecraft. There were some other great yarns in that book as well, by the likes of Poe, Kornbluth, and Robert Bloch, but the Lovecraft was the one that caught me by the throat and wouldn't let go. I was afraid to go to sleep that night. The next day I began looking for more books with stories by HPL, who had vaulted to the top of my personal hit parade, where he remained for a long time, sharing pride of place with RAH and JRRT.

We write what we read. I never read Zane Grey growing up, and I've never written a western. I did read Heinlein, Tolkien, and Lovecraft. It was inevitable that one day I would set out to make some monsters of my own. As for those hybrids . . .

. . . long before H. P. Lovecraft came into my life, I once found a chemistry set waiting underneath the Christmas tree.

Chemistry sets were all the rage in the '50s, and were found beneath as many trees as Lionel trains or Roy Rogers gunbelts with the matching six-shooters (if you were a boy—girls got the Dale Evans set, and Betty Crocker baking sets instead of chemistry sets). It was the age of *Sputnik,* the age of Charles Van Doren, the age of the atom; America wanted all us boys to grow up to be rocket scientists, so we could beat the damned Russkies to the moon.

The chemistry sets they sold then (and may still be selling, for all I know) consisted of a big hinged metal box with racks of little glass jars of chemicals inside, along with a few test tubes and beakers, and an instructional booklet describing the various educational experiments you could perform. On the front of the box there was usually a picture of a clean-cut boy (never a girl) in a white lab coat, holding up a test tube as he performed one of the many educational experiments. (White lab coats were not included.) Somewhere, I do not doubt, there must have been some kids like him, kids who dutifully followed the instructions, performed the educational experiments, learned many valuable scientific things, and grew up to be chemists.

I never knew any, though. All of the kids I knew who got chemistry sets for Christmas were more interested in trying to make stuff explode. Or turn weird colors. Or bubble and smoke. "Let's see what will happen if we mix *this* with *that*," we would say, as we dreamed of finding the secret formula that would turn us into a superhero, or at least Mr. Hyde. Maybe our parents thought the chemistry sets would set us on the path to becoming Jonas Salk or Wernher von Braun, but we were more interested in becoming one of the great Victors . . . von Frankenstein or von Doom.

Most of the time when we mixed *this* with *that*, all we made was a mess. That was probably a good thing. If we had ever actually found a formula that turned weird colors and bubbled and smoked, we might have tried to drink it . . . or at the very least, see if our little sister could be convinced to drink it.

My chemistry set soon ended up at the back of my closet, gathering dust behind my collection of *TV Guides*, but my passion for mixing *this* with *that* remained as I grew older, and found expression in my fiction. Modern publishing loves to sort the tales we tell into categories, producing racks of books that resemble the racks of little bottles in the chemistry set, with neat little labels that read: MYSTERY. ROMANCE. WESTERN. HISTORICAL. SF. JUVENILE.

Pfui, I say. Let's mix *this* with *that* and see what happens. Let's cross some genre lines and blur some boundaries, make some stories that are both and neither. Some of the time we'll make a mess, sure . . . but once in a while, if we do it right, we may stumble on a combination that *explodes!*

With that as my philosophy, it's no wonder that I've produced a number of odd hybrids over the years. *Fevre Dream* is one such. Although most often categorized as horror, it is as much a steamboat novel as a vampire novel. *The Armageddon Rag* is even more difficult to classify; fantasy, horror, murder mystery, rock 'n' roll novel, political novel, '60s novel. It's got Froggy the

Gremlin too. Even my fantasy series, *A Song of Ice and Fire,* is a hybrid of sorts, inspired as much by the historical fiction of Thomas B. Costain and Nigel Tranter as the fantasy of Tolkien, Howard, and Fritz Leiber.

The two genres that I've mixed most often, though, are horror and science fiction.

I was doing it as early as my second sale. Despite its SF setting, "The Exit to San Breta" is a ghost story at heart . . . though admittedly not a very frightening one. My first two corpse handler tales, "Nobody Leaves New Pittsburg" and "Override," were further fumbling attempts at the same sort of cross-pollination, offering as they did a science fictional take on an old friend from the world of horror, the zombie. I was going for a horrific feel in "Dark, Dark Were the Tunnels" as well, and (much more successfully) in a later, stronger work, my novella "In the House of the Worm."

Some critics have argued that horror and science fiction are actually antithetical to each other. They can make a plausible case, certainly, especially in the case of Lovecraftian horror. SF assumes that the universe, however mysterious or frightening it may seem to us, is ultimately knowable, while Lovecraft suggests that even a glimpse of the true nature of reality would be enough to drive men mad. You cannot get much further from the Campbellian view of the cosmos as that. In *Billion Year Spree,* his insightful study of the history of science fiction, Brian W. Aldiss puts John W. Campbell at the genre's "thinking pole" and H. P. Lovecraft all the way over at the "dreaming pole," on the opposite end of the literary universe.

And yet both men wrote stories that can fairly be described as SF/ horror hybrids. There are, in fact, some startling similarities between HPL's "At the Mountains of Madness" and JWC's "Who Goes There?" Both are effective horror stories, but both work as science fiction too. And "Who Goes There?" is probably the best thing Campbell ever wrote, while "At the Mountains of Madness" must surely rank in Lovecraft's top five. That's hybrid vigor.

A few of my own hybrids and horrors follow.

The oldest story here, "Meathouse Man," was the third of my corpse handler stories, and turned out to be the last of the series. The horror is sexual and psychological, rather than visceral, but this is an SF/horror hybrid all the same. Easily the darkest thing that I have ever written (and I've produced some pretty dark stuff), "Meathouse Man" was supposed to be my story for *The Last Dangerous Visions.* Harlan Ellison's groundbreaking anthologies *Dangerous Visions* and *Again, Dangerous Visions* had a tremendous impact on me, as they did on most readers of my generation. When I met Harlan for the first time in the corridors of the 1972 Lunacon in New York City, virtually the first thing I asked him was whether I might send him a story for *TLDV*. He told me no; the anthology was closed.

A year later, however, it opened up again . . . at least for me. By that time, I had gotten to know Harlan better, through our mutual friend Lisa Tuttle, and I'd published more stories as well, which may have helped convince him that I was worthy of inclusion in what was, after all, going to be a monumental book, the anthology to end anthologies. Whatever made him change his mind, change it he did; in 1973, he invited me to send him a story. I was thrilled . . . and nervous as hell. *TLDV* would have a lot of heavy hitters in it. Could I measure up? Could I possibly be *dangerous* enough?

I struggled with the story for several months, finally mailed it off to Harlan in early 1974. "Meathouse Man" was the title, but otherwise it shared only some background and character names with the "Meathouse Man" that follows. It was much shorter, about a third the length of the present story, and much more superficial. I was trying my damnedest to be dangerous, but in that first version, "Meathouse Man" remained no more than an intellectual exercise.

Harlan returned my manuscript on March 30, 1974, with a letter of rejection that began, "Aside from shirking all responsibility to the material that forms the core, it's a nice story." After which he eviscerated me, while challenging me to tear the guts out of the story and rewrite the whole thing from page one. I cursed and fumed and kicked the wall, but I could not quarrel with a single thing he said. So I sat down and ripped the guts out of the story and rewrote the whole thing from page one, and this time I opened a vein as well, and let the blood drip down right onto the paper. While 1973 and 1974 were great years for me professionally, they were by no means happy years. My career was going wonderfully; my life, not so much so. I was wounded, and in a lot of pain. I put it all into "Meathouse Man," and sent the story back to Harlan.

He still didn't like it. This time he was much gentler with me, but a gentle pass is still a pass.

Afterward I considered simply abandoning "Meathouse Man." Even now, almost thirty years later, I find it painful to reread. But in the end, I had put too much work into the story to foresake it, so I sent it out to other markets, and ended up selling it to Damon Knight for *Orbit,* the only time I ever managed to crack that prestigious anthology series. It appeared in 1976, in *Orbit 18.*

"Remembering Melody," some three years later, was my first contemporary horror story. Lisa Tuttle gets the blame for this one. When we were starting work on "The Fall" in 1979, I flew down to Austin for a few weeks to consult with her in person, and get the novella started. We took turns at her typewriter. While she was pounding on the keys I would sit around reading carbons of her latest stories. Lisa was turning out a lot of contemporary horror by then, some wonderfully creepy tales that gave me the urge to try something along those lines myself.

"Remembering Melody" was the story that resulted. My agent tried (and failed) to place it with some of the big, high-paying men's slicks, but *Twilight Zone* magazine was glad to snap it up, and it appeared in the April 1981 issue.

Hollywood has had a love affair with horror fiction that goes back as far as Murnau's *Nosferatu* in the days of silent film, so it should come as no surprise that three of the six stories in this section have had film or television versions. "Remembering Melody" was not only the first of my works to go before a camera, it remains the only one to be filmed *twice*—first as a short student film (full of short student actors), then later as an episode of the HBO anthology series *The Hitchhiker*.

If you know my work at all, I suspect you've heard of "Sandkings." Until *A Song of Ice and Fire*, it was the story that I was best known for, far and away the most popular thing I ever did.

"Sandkings" was the third of the three stories I wrote during that Christmas break in the winter of 1978-79. The inspiration for it came from a guy I knew in college, who hosted *Creature Features* parties every Saturday. He kept a tank of piranha, and in between the first and the second creature feature, he would sometimes throw a goldfish into the tank, for the amusement of his guests.

"Sandkings" was also intended to be the first of a series. The strange little shop on the back alley where queer, dangerous items can be bought had long been a familiar trope of fantasy. I thought it might be fun to do a science fiction version. My "strange little shop" was actually going to be a franchise, with branches scattered over light-years, on many different planets. Its mysterious proprietors, Wo & Shade, would figure in each story, but the protagonists would be the customers, like Simon Kress. (Yes, I did begin a second Wo & Shade story, set on ai-Emerel, a world much mentioned in my old future history, but never seen. It was called "Protection" and I wrote 18 pages of it before putting it aside, for reasons that I no longer recall.) If you had asked me back in January 1979 about the three stories I'd just finished, I would have told you that "The Ice Dragon" was going to knock people's socks off. I ranked it right up there with the best work I'd ever done. I felt "The Way of Cross and Dragon" was damned good too, might even win some awards. And "Sandkings"? Not bad at all. Not near as strong as the other two, mind you, but hey . . . no one hits a home run every time.

I have never been so wrong about a story. "Sandkings" sold to *Omni*, the best-paying market in the field, and became the most popular story they ever published. It won *both* the Hugo and the Nebula in its year, the only one of my stories ever to accomplish that double. It has been reprinted and anthologized so many times that I've lost count, and has earned me more money than two of my novels and most of my TV scripts and screenplays. It was adapted as a graphic novel by DC Comics, and someday soon may be a computer game as well. Hollywood producers flocked to it, and I sold half a dozen options and saw half a dozen different screenplays and treatments before the story was finally filmed for television as the two-hour premiere episode of the new *Outer Limits*, adapted by my friend Melinda M. Snodgrass.

Is it the best thing I ever wrote? You be the judge.

The success of "Sandkings" inspired me to try more SF/horror hybrids, most notably with "Nightflyers," my haunted starship story.

I'd put ghosts in a futuristic setting way back as early as "The Exit to San Breta," but those were actual spirits of the dead. In "Nightflyers" I wanted to see if I could provide a legitimate sfnal explanation for the hauntings.

The original version of "Nightflyers," published in *Analog* with a nice Paul Lehr cover, weighed in at 23,000 words . . . but even at that length, I felt it was severely compressed, especially in the handling of its secondary characters. (They did not even have names, only job titles.) When Jim Frenkel of Dell Books offered to buy an expanded version of the novella for his new *Binary Star* series, an attempt to revive the old Ace Doubles concept, I leapt at the opportunity. It is the *Binary Star* version you'll find here.

"Nightflyers" won the Locus Poll as the Best Novella of 1980, but lost the Hugo to Gordon R. Dickson's "Lost Dorsai" at Denvention. It was soon optioned by Hollywood, and became the first of my works to be made into a feature film. *Nightflyers* starred Catherine Mary Stewart and Michael Praed, and was so terrific that the director took his name off the film. Large hunks of my story are still recognizable in the movie, although for some inexplicable reason the single scariest sequence in the novella was dropped.

"The Monkey Treatment" and "The Pear-Shaped Man" both date to my Gerold Kersh period. Kersh was a major writer of the '40s and '50s, the author of some excellent mainstream novels like *Night and the City* as well as a plethora of bizarre, disturbing, delightful short stories, collected in *On an Odd Note, Nightshades and Damnations,* and *Men Without Bones.* Because he tended to publish his short fiction in places like *Collier's* and the *Saturday Evening Post* rather than *Weird Tales* or *Fantastic Stories,* he was little known to fantasy readers even in his own time, and today he seems utterly forgotten. That's a great shame, as Kersh was a unique voice, a brilliant writer with a gift for taking his readers to some odd corners of the world, where strange, disturbing things are wont to happen. Some small press really needs to gather all of Kersh's weird fiction together in a book as large as this one, and put him back in print for a new generation of readers.

"The Monkey Treatment," the older of the two stories, was easy to write but hard as hell to sell. It seemed to me to be the sort of story that would appeal to a more general readership, so I set out to try and place it with one of the large slicks, *Playboy* or *Penthouse* or *Omni.* Frustration followed. The story elicited admiring comments everywhere it went, but no one seemed to feel it "right for us." Too strange, they said. Too disturbing. "Boy, is it repulsive," Ellen Datlow of *Omni* wrote me, in the same letter where she said how much she wished that she could buy the story.

I would have tried *Collier's* and the *Saturday Evening Post* next, but they were both long defunct by 1981, so in the end I fell back on my usual genre markets, and sold the story to *The Magazine of Fantasy and Science-Fiction.* Strange and repulsive or not, it was nominated for the Nebula and the Hugo, losing both.

"The Pear-Shaped Man" had an easier time of it, perhaps because "The Monkey Treatment" had primed the pump. Ellen Datlow had only been an assistant editor at *Omni* when Robert Sheckley returned "The Monkey Treatment," but she had moved up to fiction editor by the time I wrote "The Pear-Shaped Man," and she took it straightaway. It appeared in *Omni* in 1987, and won one of the first Bram Stoker Awards, given by the newly-formed Horror Writers of America (HWA) for the best horror of the year.

The founding of the HWA (originally it was going to be called HOWL, for Horror and Occult Writers League, a *much* cooler name that got howled down by members desperate for respectability) coincided with the great horror boom of the '80s. Subsequently horror has suffered an even greater bust, a victim of its own excess. Today there are those in publishing who will tell you that horror is dead ("and deservedly so," others will add).

As a commercial publishing genre? Yes, horror is dead.

But monster stories will never die, so long as we remember what it's like to be afraid.

In 1986, I edited the horror anthology *Night Visions 3* for Dark Harvest. In my introduction, I wrote, "Those who claim that we read horror stories for the same reasons we ride rollercoasters are missing the point. At the best of times we come away from a rollercoaster with a simple adrenalin high, and that's not what fiction is about. Like a rollercoaster, a really bad horror story can perhaps make us sick, but that's as far as the comparison extends. We go to fiction for things beyond those to be found in amusement parks.

"A good horror story will frighten us, yes. It will keep us awake at night, it will make our flesh crawl, it will creep into our dreams and give new meaning to the darkness. Fear, terror, horror; call it what you will, it drinks from all those cups. But please, don't confuse the feelings with simple vertigo. The great stories, the ones that linger in our memories and change our lives, are never really about the things that they're about.

"Bad horror stories concern themselves with six ways to kill a vampire, and graphic accounts of how the rats ate Billy's genitalia. Good horror stories are about larger things. About hope and despair. About love and hatred, lust and jealousy. About friendship and adolescence and sexuality and rage, loneliness and alienation and psychosis, courage and cowardice, the human mind and body and spirit under stress and in agony, the human heart in unending conflict with itself. Good horror stories make us look at our reflections in dark distorting mirrors, where we glimpse things that disturb us, things that we did not really want to look at. Horror looks into the shadows of the human soul, at the fears and rages that live within us all.

"But darkness is meaningless without light, and horror is pointless without beauty. The best horror stories are stories first and horror second, and however much they scare us, they do more than that as well. They have room in them for laughter as well as screams, for triumph and tenderness as well as tragedy. They concern themselves not simply with fear, but with life in all its infinite variety, with love and death and birth and hope and lust and transcendence, with the whole range of experiences and emotions that make up the human condition. Their characters are people, people who linger in our imagination, people like those around us, people who do not exist solely to be the objects of violent slaughter in chapter four. The best horror stories tell us truths."

That was almost twenty years ago, but I stand by every word.

MEATHOUSE MAN

---◈---

I

IN THE MEATHOUSE

THEY CAME STRAIGHT FROM THE ORE-FIELDS THAT FIRST TIME, TRAGER with the others, the older boys, the almost-men who worked their corpses next to his. Cox was the oldest of the group, and he'd been around the most, and he said that Trager had to come even if he didn't want to. Then one of the others laughed and said that Trager wouldn't even know what to do, but Cox the kind-of leader shoved him until he was quiet. And when payday came, Trager trailed the rest to the meathouse, scared but somehow eager, and he paid his money to a man downstairs and got a room key.

He came into the dim room trembling, nervous. The others had gone to other rooms, had left him alone with her (no, *it,* not her but *it,* he reminded himself, and promptly forgot again). In a shabby gray cubicle with a single smoky light.

He stank of sweat and sulfur, like all who walked the streets of Skrakky, but there was no help for that. It would be better if he could bathe first, but the room did not have a bath. Just a sink, double bed with sheets that looked dirty even in the dimness, a corpse.

She lay there naked, staring at nothing, breathing shallow breaths. Her legs were spread; ready. Was she always that way, Trager wondered, or had the man before him arranged her like that? He didn't know. He knew how to do it (he did, he *did,* he'd read the books Cox gave him, and there were films you could see, and all sorts of things), but he didn't know much of anything else. Except maybe how to handle corpses. That he was good at, the youngest handler on Skrakky, but he had to be. They had forced him into the handlers' school when his mother died, and they made him learn, so that was the thing he did. This, this he had never done (but he knew how, yes, yes, he *did*); it was his first time.

He came to the bed slowly and sat to a chorus of creaking springs. He touched her and the flesh was warm. Of course. She was not a corpse, not really, no; the body was alive enough, a heartbeat under the heavy white breasts, she breathed. Only the brain was gone, ripped from her, replaced with a deadman's synthabrain. She was meat now, an extra body for a corpsehandler to control, just like the crew he worked each day under sulfur skies. She was not a woman. So it did not matter that Trager was just a boy, a jowly frog-faced boy who smelled of Skrakky. She (no *it,* remember?) would not care, could not care.

Emboldened, aroused and hard, the boy stripped off his corpsehandler's clothing and climbed in bed with the female meat. He was very excited; his hands shook as he stroked her, studied her. Her skin was very white, her hair dark and long, but even the boy could not call her pretty. Her face was too flat and wide, her mouth hung open, and her limbs were loose and sagging with fat.

On her huge breasts, all around the fat dark nipples, the last customer had left tooth-marks where he'd chewed her. Trager touched the marks tentatively, traced them with a finger. Then, sheepish about his hesitations, he grabbed one breast, squeezed it hard, pinched the nipple until he imagined a real girl would squeal with pain. The corpse did not move. Still squeezing, he rolled over on her and took the other breast into his mouth.

And the corpse responded.

She thrust up at him, hard, and meaty arms wrapped around his pimpled back to pull him to her. Trager groaned and reached down between her legs. She was hot, wet, excited. He trembled. How did they do that? Could she really get excited without a mind, or did they have lubricating tubes stuck into her, or what?

Then he stopped caring. He fumbled, found his penis, put it into her, thrust. The corpse hooked her legs around him and thrust back. It felt good, real good, better than anything he'd ever done to himself, and in some obscure way he felt proud that she was so wet and excited.

It only took a few strokes; he was too new, too young, too eager to last long. A few strokes was all he needed—but it was all she needed too. They came together, a red flush washing over her skin as she arched against him and shook soundlessly.

Afterwards she lay again like a corpse.

Trager was drained and satisfied, but he had more time left, and he was determined to get his money's worth. He explored her thoroughly, sticking his fingers everywhere they would go, touching her everywhere, rolling it over, looking at everything. The corpse moved like dead meat.

He left her as he'd found her, lying face up on the bed with her legs apart. Meathouse courtesy.

———

THE HORIZON WAS A WALL OF FACTORIES, ALL FACTORIES, VAST BELCHING factories that sent red shadows to flick against the sulfur-dark skies. The boy saw but hardly noticed. He was strapped in place high atop his automill, two stories up on a monster machine of corroding yellow-painted metal with savage teeth of diamond and duralloy, and his eyes were blurred with triple images. Clear and strong and hard he saw the control panel before him, the wheel, the fuel-feed, the bright handle of the ore-scoops, the banks of light that would tell of trouble in the refinery under his feet, the brake and emergency brake. But that was not all he saw. Dimly, faintly, there were echoes; overlaid images of two other control cabs, almost identical to his, where corpse hands moved clumsily over the instruments.

Trager moved those hands, slow and careful, while another part of his mind held his own hands, his real hands, very still. The corpse controller hummed thinly on his belt.

On either side of him, the other two automills moved into flanking positions. The corpse hands squeezed the brakes; the machines rumbled to a halt. On the edge of the great sloping pit, they stood in a row, shabby pitted juggernauts ready to descend into the gloom. The pit was growing steadily larger; each day new layers of rock and ore were stripped away.

Once a mountain range had stood here, but Trager did not remember that.

The rest was easy. The automills were aligned now. To move the crew in unison was a cinch, any decent handler could do *that*. It was only when you had to keep several corpses busy at several different tasks that things got tricky. But a good corpsehandler could do that too. Eight-crews were not unknown to veterans; eight bodies linked to a single corpse controller moved by a single mind and eight synthabrains. The deadmen were each tuned to one controller, and only one; the handler who wore that controller and thought corpse-thoughts in its proximity field could move those deadmen like secondary bodies. Or like his own body. If he was good enough.

Trager checked his filtermask and earplugs quickly, then touched the fuel-feed, engaged, flicked on the laser-knives and the drills. His corpses echoed his moves, and pulses of light spit through the twilight of Skrakky. Even through his plugs he could hear the awful whine as the ore-scoops revved up and lowered. The rock-eating maw of an automill was even wider than the machine was tall.

Rumbling and screeching, in perfect formation, Trager and his corpse crew descended into the pit. Before they reached the factories on the far side of the plain, tons of metal would have been torn from the earth, melted and refined and processed, while the worthless rock was reduced to powder and blown out into the already unbreathable air. He would deliver finished steel at dusk, on the horizon.

He was a good handler, Trager thought as the automills started down. But the handler in the meathouse—now, she must be an artist. He imagined her down in the cellar somewhere, watching each of her corpses through holos and psi circuits, humping them all to please her patrons. Was it just a fluke, then, that his fuck had been so perfect? Or was she always that good? But how, *how*, to move a dozen corpses without even being near them, to have them doing different things, to keep them all excited, to match the needs and rhythm of each customer so exactly?

The air behind him was black and choked by rock-dust, his ears were full of screams, and the far horizon was a glowering red wall beneath which yellow ants crawled and ate rock. But Trager kept his hard-on all across the plain as the automill shook beneath him.

THE CORPSES WERE COMPANY-OWNED; THEY STAYED IN THE COMPANY deadman depot. But Trager had a room, a slice of the space that was his own in a steel-and-concrete warehouse with a thousand other slices. He only knew a handful of his neighbors, but he knew all of them too; they were corpsehandlers. It was a world of silent shadowed corridors and endless closed doors. The lobby-lounge, all air and plastic, was a dusty deserted place where none of the tenants ever gathered.

The evenings were long there, the nights eternal. Trager had bought extra light-panels for his particular cube, and when all of them were on they burned so bright that his infrequent visitors blinked and complained about the glare. But always there came a time when he could read no more, and then he had to turn them out, and the darkness returned once more.

His father, long gone and barely remembered, had left a wealth of books and tapes, and Trager kept them still. The room was lined with them, and others stood in great piles against the foot of the bed and on either side of the bathroom door. Infrequently he went on with Cox and the others, to drink and joke and prowl for real women. He imitated them as best he could, but he always felt out of place. So most of his nights were spent at home, reading and listening to the music, remembering and thinking.

That week he thought long after he'd faded his light panels into black, and his thoughts were a frightened jumble. Payday was coming again, and Cox would be after him to return to the meathouse, and yes, yes, he wanted to. It had been good, exciting; for once he had felt confident and virile. But it was so easy, cheap, *dirty*. There had to be more, didn't there? Love, whatever that was? It had to be better with a real woman, had to, and he wouldn't find one of those in a meathouse. He'd never found one outside, either, but then he'd never really had the courage to try. But he had to try, *had* to, or what sort of life would he ever have?

Beneath the covers he masturbated, hardly thinking of it, while he resolved not to return to the meathouse.

––––––––

BUT A FEW DAYS LATER, COX LAUGHED AT HIM AND HE HAD TO GO along. Somehow he felt it would prove something.

A different room this time, a different corpse. Fat and black, with bright orange hair, less attractive than his first, if that was possible. But Trager came to her ready and eager, and this time he lasted longer. Again, the performance was superb. Her rhythm matched his stroke for stroke, she came with him, she seemed to know exactly what he wanted.

Other visits; two of them, four, six. He was a regular now at the meathouse, along with the others, and he had stopped worrying about it. Cox and the others accepted him in a strange half-hearted way, but his dislike of them had grown, if anything. He was better than they were, he thought. He could hold his own in a meathouse, he could run his corpses and his automills as good as any of them, and he still thought and dreamed. In time he'd leave them all behind, leave Skrakky, be something. They would be meathouse men as long as they would live, but Trager knew he could do better. He believed. He would find love.

He found none in the meathouse, but the sex got better and better, though it was perfect to begin with. In bed with the corpses, Trager was never dissatisfied; he did everything he'd ever read about, heard about, dreamt about. The corpses knew his needs before he did. When he needed it slow, they were slow. When he wanted to have it hard and quick and brutal, then they gave it to him that way, perfectly. He used every orifice they had; they always knew which one to present to him.

His admiration of the meathouse handler grew steadily for months, until it was almost worship. Perhaps somehow he could meet her, he thought at last. Still a boy, still hopelessly naïve, he was sure he would love her. Then he would take her away from the meathouse to a clean, corpseless world where they could be happy together.

One day, in a moment of weakness, he told Cox and the others. Cox looked at him, shook his head, grinned. Somebody else snickered. Then they all began to laugh. "What an *ass* you are, Trager," Cox said at last. "There is no fucking *handler!* Don't tell me you never heard of a feedback circuit?"

He explained it all, to laughter; explained how each corpse was tuned to a controller built into its bed, explained how each customer handled his own meat, explained why non-handlers found meathouse women dead and still. And the boy realized suddenly why the sex was always perfect. He was a better handler than even he had thought.

That night, alone in his room with all the lights burning white and hot, Trager faced himself. And turned away, sickened. He was good at his job, he was proud of that, but the rest . . .

It was the meathouse, he decided. There was a trap there in the meathouse, a trap that could ruin him, destroy life and dream and hope. He would not go back; it was too easy. He would show Cox, show all of them. He could take the hard way, take the risks, feel the pain if he had to. And maybe the joy, maybe the love. He'd gone the other way too long.

Trager did not go back to the meathouse. Feeling strong and decisive and superior, he went back to his room. There, as years passed, he read and dreamed and waited for life to begin.

1

WHEN I WAS ONE-AND-TWENTY

JOSIE WAS THE FIRST.

She was beautiful, had always been beautiful, knew she was beautiful; all that had shaped her, made her what she was. She was a free spirit. She was aggressive, confident, conquering. Like Trager, she was only twenty when they met, but she had lived more than he had, and she seemed to have the answers. He loved her from the first.

And Trager? Trager before Josie, but years beyond the meathouse? He was taller now, broad and heavy with both muscle and fat, often moody, silent and self-contained. He ran a full five-crew in the ore fields, more than Cox, more than any of them. At night, he read books; sometimes in his room, sometimes in the lobby. He had long since forgotten that he went there to meet someone. Stable, solid, unemotional; that was Trager. He touched no one, and no one touched him. Even the tortures had stopped, though the scars remained *inside*. Trager hardly knew they were there; he never looked at them.

He fit in well now. With his corpses.

Yet—not completely. Inside, the dream. Something believed, something hungered, something yearned. It was strong enough to keep him away from the meathouse, from the vegetable life the others had all chosen. And sometimes, on bleak lonely nights, it would grow stronger still. Then Trager would rise from his empty bed, dress, and walk the corridors for hours with his hands shoved deep into his pockets while something twisted, clawed, and whimpered in his gut. Always, before his walks were over, he would resolve to do something, to change his life tomorrow.

But when tomorrow came, the silent gray corridors were half forgotten, the demons had faded, and he had six roaring, shaking automills to drive across the pit. He would lose himself in routine, and it would be long months before the feelings came again.

Then Josie. They met like this:

It was a new field, rich and unmined, a vast expanse of broken rock and rubble that filled the plain. Low hills a few weeks ago, but the company skimmers had leveled the area with systematic nuclear blast mining, and now the automills were moving in. Trager's five-crew had been one of the first, and the change had been exhilarating at first. The old pit had been just about worked out; here there was a new terrain to contend with, boulders and jagged rock fragments, baseball-sized fists of stone that came shrieking at you on the dusty wind. It all seemed exciting, dangerous. Trager, wearing a leather jacket and filtermask and goggles and earplugs, drove his six machines and six bodies with a fierce pride, reducing boulders to powder, clearing a path for the later machines, fighting his way yard by yard to get whatever ore he could.

And one day, suddenly, one of the eye echoes suddenly caught his attention. A light flashed red on a corpse-driven automill. Trager reached, with his hands, with his mind, with five sets of corpse-hands. Six machines stopped, but still another light went red. Then another, and another. Then the whole board, all twelve. One of his automills was out. Cursing, he looked across the rock field towards the machine in question, used his corpse to give it a kick. The lights stayed red. He beamed out for a tech.

By the time she got there—in a one-man skimmer that looked like a teardrop of pitted black metal—Trager had unstrapped, climbed down the metal rings on the side of the automill, walked across the rocks to where the dead machine stopped. He was just starting to climb up when Josie arrived; they met at the foot of the yellow-metal mountain, in the shadow of its treads.

She was field-wise, he knew at once. She wore a handler's coverall, earplugs, heavy goggles, and her face was smeared with grease to prevent dust abrasions. But still she was beautiful. Her hair was short, light brown, cut in a shag that was jumbled by the wind; her eyes, when she lifted the goggles, were bright green. She took charge immediately.

All business, she introduced herself, asked him a few questions, then opened a repair bay and crawled inside, into the guts of the drive and the ore-smelt and the refinery. It didn't take her long; ten minutes, maybe, and she was back outside.

"Don't go in there," she said, tossing her hair from in front of her goggles with a flick of her head. "You've got a damper failure. The nukes are running away."

"Oh," said Trager. His mind was hardly on the automill, but he had to make an impression, made to say something intelligent. "Is it going to blow up?" he asked, and as soon as he said it he knew that *that* hadn't been intelligent at all. Of course it wasn't going to blow up; runaway nuclear reactors didn't work that way, he knew that.

But Josie seemed amused. She smiled—the first time he saw her distinctive flashing grin—and seemed to see him, *him,* Trager, not just a corpsehandler. "No," she said. "It will just melt itself down. Won't even get hot out here, since you've got shields built into the walls. Just don't go in there."

"All right." Pause. What could he say now? "What do I do?"

"Work the rest of your crew, I guess. This machine'll have to be scrapped. It should have been overhauled a long time ago. From the looks of it, there's been a lot of patching done in the past. Stupid. It breaks down, it breaks down, it breaks down, and they keep sending it out. Should realize that something is wrong. After that many failures, it's sheer self-delusion to think the thing's going to work right next time out."

"I guess," Trager said. Josie smiled at him again, sealed up the panel, and started to turn.

"Wait," he said. It came out before he could stop it, almost in spite of him. Josie turned, cocked her head, looked at him questioningly. And Trager drew a sudden strength from the steel and the stone and the wind; under sulfur skies, his dreams seemed less impossible. Maybe, he thought. Maybe.

"Uh. I'm Greg Trager. Will I see you again?"

Josie grinned. "Sure. Come tonight." She gave him the address.

He climbed back into his automill after she had left, exulting in his six strong bodies, all fire and life, and he chewed up rock with something near to joy. The dark red glow in the distance looked almost like a sunrise.

———

WHEN HE GOT TO JOSIE'S, HE FOUND FOUR OTHER PEOPLE THERE, friends of hers. It was a party of sorts. Josie threw a lot of parties and Trager—from that night on—went to all of them. Josie talked to him, laughed with him, *liked* him, and suddenly his life was no longer the same.

With Josie, he saw parts of Skrakky he had never seen before, did things he had never done:

—he stood with her in the crowds that gathered on the streets at night, stood in the dusty wind and sickly yellow light between the windowless concrete buildings, stood and bet and cheered himself hoarse while grease-stained mechs raced yellow rumbly tractor-trucks up and down and down and up.

—he walked with her through the strangely silent and white and clean underground Offices, and sealed air-conditioned corridors where off-worlders and paper-shufflers and company executives lived and worked.

—he prowled the rec-malls with her, those huge low buildings so like a warehouse from the outside, but full of colored lights and game rooms and cafeterias and tape shops and endless bars where handlers made their rounds.

—he went with her to dormitory gyms, where they watched handlers less skillful than himself send their corpses against each other with clumsy fists.

—he sat with her and her friends, and they woke dark quiet taverns with their talk and with their laughter, and once Trager saw someone looking much like Cox staring at him from across the room, and he smiled and leaned a bit closer to Josie.

He hardly noticed the other people, the crowds that Josie surrounded herself with; when they went out on one of her wild jaunts, six of them or eight or ten, Trager would tell himself that he and Josie were going out, and that some others had come along with them.

Once in a great while, things would work out so they were alone together, at her place, or his. Then they would talk. Of distant worlds, of politics, of corpses and life on Skrakky, of the books they both consumed, of sports or games or friends they had in common. They shared a good deal. Trager talked a lot with Josie. And never said a word.

He loved her, of course. He suspected it the first month, and soon he was convinced of it. He loved her. This was the real thing, the thing he had been waiting for, and it had happened just as he knew it would.

But with his love: agony. He could not tell her. A dozen times he tried; the words would never come. What if she did not love him back?

His nights were still alone, in the small room with the white lights and the books and the pain. He was more alone than ever now; the peace of his routine, of his half-life with his corpses, was gone, stripped from him. By day he rode the great automills, moved his corpses, smashed rock and melted ore, and in his head rehearsed the words he'd say to Josie. And dreamed of those that she'd speak back. She was trapped too, he thought. She'd had men, of course, but she didn't love them, she loved him. But she couldn't tell him, any more than he could tell her. When he broke through, when he found the words and the courage, then everything would be all right. Each day he said that to himself, and dug swift and deep into the earth.

But back home, the sureness faded. Then, with awful despair, he knew that he was kidding himself. He was a friend to her, nothing more, never would be more. Why did he lie to himself? He'd had hints enough. They had never been lovers, never would be; on the few times he'd worked up the courage to touch her, she would smile, move away on some pretext, so he was never quite sure that he was being rejected. But he got the idea, and in the dark it tore at him. He walked the corridors weekly now, sullen, desperate, wanting to talk to someone without knowing how. And all the old scars woke up to bleed again.

Until the next day. When he would return to his machines, and believe again. He must believe in himself, he knew that, he shouted it out loud. He must stop feeling sorry for himself. He must do something. He must tell Josie. He would.

And she would love him, cried the day.

And she would laugh, the nights replied.

Trager chased her for a year, a year of pain and promise, the first year that he had ever *lived*. On that the night-fears and the day-voice agreed; he was alive now. He would never return to the emptiness of his time before Josie; he would never go back to the meathouse. That far, at least, he had come. He could change, and someday he would be strong enough to tell her.

———

Josie and two friends dropped by his room that night, but the friends had to leave early. For an hour or so they were alone, talking about nothing. Finally she had to go. Trager said he'd walk her home.

He kept his arm around her down the long corridors, and he watched her face, watched the play of light and shadow on her cheeks as they walked from light to darkness. "Josie," he started. He felt so fine, so good, so warm, and it came out. "I love you."

And she stopped, pulled away from him, stepped back. Her mouth opened, just a little, and something flickered in her eyes. "Oh, Greg," she said. Softly. Sadly. "No, Greg, no, don't, don't." And she shook her head.

Trembling slightly, mouthing silent words, Trager held out his hand. Josie did not take it. He touched her cheek, gently, and wordless she spun away from him.

Then, for the first time ever, Trager shook. And the tears came.

Josie took him to her room. There, sitting across from each other on the floor, never touching, they talked.

J: *. . . known it for a long time . . . tried to discourage you, Greg, but I didn't just want to come right out and . . . I never wanted to hurt you . . . a good person . . . don't worry. . . .*

T: *. . . knew it all along . . . that it would never . . . lied to myself . . . wanted to believe, even if it wasn't true . . . I'm sorry, Josie, I'm sorry, I'm sorry, I'm sorryimsorryimsorry. . . .*

J: *. . . afraid you would go back to what you were . . . don't Greg, promise me . . . can't give up . . . have to believe. . . .*

T: *why?*

J: *. . . stop believing, then you have nothing . . . dead . . . you can do better . . . a good handler . . . get off Skrakky, find something . . . no life here . . . someone . . . you will, you will, just believe, keep on believing. . . .*

T: *. . . you . . . love you forever, Josie . . . forever . . . how can I find someone . . . never anyone like you, never . . . special . . .*

J: *. . . oh, Greg . . . lots of people . . . just look . . . open . . .*

T: (laughter) *. . . open? . . . first time I ever talked to anyone . . .*

J: *. . . talk to me again, if you have to . . . I can talk to you . . . had enough lovers, everyone wants to get to bed with me, better just to be friends. . . .*

T: *. . . friends . . .* (laughter) *. . .* (tears) *. . .*

II

PROMISES OF SOMEDAY

THE FIRE HAD BURNED OUT LONG AGO, AND STEVENS AND THE forester had retired, but Trager and Donelly still sat around the ashes on the edges of the clear zone. They talked softly, so as not to wake the others, yet their words hung long in the restless night air. The uncut forest, standing dark behind them, was dead still; the wildlife of

Vendalia had all fled the noise that the fleet of buzztrucks made during the day.

"... a full six-crew, running buzztrucks, I know enough to know that's not easy," Donelly was saying. He was a pale, timid youth, likeable but self-conscious about everything he did. Trager heard echoes of himself in Donelly's stiff words. "You'd do well in the arena."

Trager nodded, thoughtful, his eyes on the ashes as he moved them with a stick. "I came to Vendalia with that in mind. Went to the gladiatorial once, only once. That was enough to change my mind. I could take them, I guess, but the whole idea made me sick. Out here, well, the money doesn't even match what I was getting on Skrakky, but the work is, well, clean. You know?"

"Sort of," said Donelly. "Still, you know, it isn't like they were real people out there in the arena. Only meat. All you can do is make the bodies as dead as the minds. That's the logical way to look at it."

Trager chuckled. "You're too logical, Don. You ought to *feel* more. Listen, next time you're in Gidyon, go to the gladiatorials and take a look. It's ugly, *ugly*. Corpses stumbling around with axes and swords and morningstars, hacking and hewing at each other. Butchery, that's all it is. And the audience, the way they cheer at each blow. And *laugh*. They *laugh*, Don! No." He shook his head, sharply. "No."

Donelly never abandoned an argument. "But why not? I don't understand, Greg. You'd be good at it, the best. I've seen the way you work your crew."

Trager looked up, studied Donelly briefly while the youth sat quietly, waiting. Josie's words came back; open, be open. The old Trager, the Trager who lived friendless and alone and closed inside a Skrakky handlers' dorm, was gone. He had grown, changed.

"There was a girl," he said, slowly, with measured words. Opening. "Back on Skrakky, Don, there was a girl I loved. It, well, it didn't work out. That's why I'm here, I guess. I'm looking for someone else, for something better. That's all part of it, you see." He stopped, paused, tried to think his words out. "This girl, Josie, I wanted her to love me. You know." The words came hard. "Admire me, all that stuff. Now, yeah, sure, I could do good running corpses in the arena. But Josie could never love someone who had a job like *that*. She's gone now, of course, but still ... the kind of person I'm looking for, I couldn't find them as an arena corpsemaster." He stood up, abruptly. "I don't know. That's what's important, though, to me. Josie, somebody like her, someday. Soon, I hope."

Donelly sat quiet in the moonlight, chewing his lip, not looking at Trager, his logic suddenly useless. While Trager, his corridors long gone, walked off alone into the woods.

THEY HAD A TIGHT-KNIT GROUP; THREE HANDLERS, A FORESTER, THIR-teen corpses. Each day they drove the forest back, with Trager in the forefront. Against the Vendalian wilderness, against the blackbriars and the hard gray ironspike trees and the bulbous rubbery snaplimbs, against the tangled hostile forest, he would throw his six-crew and their buzztrucks. Smaller than the automills he'd run on Skrakky, fast and airborne, complex and demanding, those were buzztrucks. Trager ran six of them with corpse hands, a seventh with his own. Before his screaming blades and laser knives, the wall of wilderness fell each day. Donelly came behind him, pushing three of the mountain-sized rolling mills, to turn the fallen trees into lumber for Gidyon and other cities of Vendalia. Then Stevens, the third handler, with a flame-cannon to burn down stumps and melt rocks, and the soilpumps that would ready the fresh clear land for farming. The forester was their foreman. The procedure was a science.

Clean, hard, demanding work; Trager thrived on it by day. He grew lean, almost athletic; the lines of his face tightened and tanned, he grew steadily browner under Vendalia's hot bright sun. His corpses were almost part of him, so easily did he move them, fly their buzztrucks. As an ordinary man might move a hand, a foot. Sometimes his control grew so firm, the echoes so clear and strong, that Trager felt he was not a handler working a crew at all, but rather a man with seven bodies. Seven strong bodies that rode the sultry forest winds. He exulted in their sweat.

And the evenings, after work ceased, they were good too. Trager found a sort of peace there, a sense of belonging he had never known on Skrakky. The Vendalian foresters, rotated back and forth from Gidyon, were decent enough, and friendly. Stevens was a hearty slab of a man who seldom stopped joking long enough to talk about anything serious. Trager always found him amusing. And Donelly, the self-conscious

youth, the quiet logical voice, he became a friend. He was a good listener, empathetic, compassionate, and the new open Trager was a good
talker. Something close to envy shone in Donelly's eyes when Trager
spoke of Josie and exorcised his soul. And Trager knew, or thought he
knew, that Donelly was himself, the old Trager, the one before Josie
who could not find the words.

In time, though, after days and weeks of talking, Donelly found his
words. Then Trager listened, and shared another's pain. And he felt good
about it. He was helping; he was lending strength; he was needed.

Each night around the ashes, the two men traded dreams. And
wove a hopeful tapestry of promises and lies.

Yet still the nights would come.

Those were the worst times, as always; those were the hours of
Trager's long lonely walks. If Josie had given Trager much, she had taken
something too; she had taken the curious deadness he had once had, the
trick of not-thinking, the pain-blotter of his mind. On Skrakky, he had
walked the corridors infrequently; the forest knew him far more often.

After the talking all had stopped, after Donelly had gone to bed,
that was when it would happen, when Josie would come to him in the
loneliness of his tent. A thousand nights he lay there with his hands
hooked behind his head, staring at the plastic tent film while he relived
the night he'd told her. A thousand times he touched her cheek, and
saw her spin away.

He would think of it, and fight it, and lose. Then, restless, he
would rise and go outside. He would walk across the clear area, into
the silent looming forest, brushing aside low branches and tripping on
the underbrush; he would walk until he found water. Then he would
sit down, by a scum-choked lake or a gurgling stream that ran swift and
oily in the moonlight. He would fling rocks into the water, hurl them
hard and flat into the night to hear them when they splashed.

He would sit for hours, throwing rocks and thinking, till finally he
could convince himself the sun would rise.

———

GIDYON; THE CITY; THE HEART OF VENDALIA, AND THROUGH IT OF SLAGG
and Skrakky and New Pittsburg and all the other corpseworlds, the harsh
ugly places where men would not work and corpses had to. Great tow-

ers of black and silver metal, floating aerial sculpture that flashed in the sunlight and shone softly at night, the vast bustling spaceport where freighters rose and fell on invisible firewands, malls where the pavement was polished, ironspike wood that gleamed a gentle gray; Gidyon.

The city with the rot. The corpse city. The meatmart.

For the freighters carried cargoes of men, criminals and derelicts and troublemakers from a dozen worlds bought with hard Vendalian cash (and there were darker rumors, of liners that had vanished mysteriously on routine tourist hops). And the soaring towers were hospitals and corpseyards, where men and women died and deadmen were born to walk anew. And all along the ironspike boardwalks were corpse-seller's shops and meathouses.

The meathouses of Vendalia were far-famed. The corpses were guaranteed beautiful.

Trager sat across from one, on the other side of the wide gray avenue, under the umbrella of an outdoor café. He sipped a bittersweet wine, thought about how his leave had evaporated too quickly, and tried to keep his eyes from wandering across the street. The wine was warm on his tongue, and his eyes were very restless.

Up and down the avenue, between him and the meathouse, strangers moved. Dark-faced corpsehandlers from Vendalia, Skrakky, Slagg; pudgy merchants, gawking tourists from the Clean Worlds like Old Earth and Zephyr, and dozens of question marks whose names and occupations and errands Trager would never know. Sitting there, drinking his wine and watching, Trager felt utterly cut off. He could not touch these people, could not reach them; he didn't know how, it wasn't possible, it wouldn't work. He could rise and walk out into the street and grab one, and still they would not touch. The stranger would only pull free and run. All his leave like that, all of it; he'd run through all the bars of Gidyon, forced a thousand contacts, and nothing had clicked.

His wine was gone. Trager looked at the glass dully, turning it in his hands, blinking. Then, abruptly, he stood up and paid his bill. His hands trembled.

It had been so many years, he thought as he started across the street. Josie, he thought, forgive me.

———

TRAGER RETURNED TO THE WILDERNESS CAMP, AND HIS CORPSES FLEW their buzztrucks like men gone wild. But he was strangely silent around the campfire, and he did not talk to Donelly at night. Until finally, hurt and puzzled, Donelly followed him into the forest. And found him by a languid death-dark stream, sitting on the bank with a pile of throwing stones at his feet.

T: . . . *went in . . . after all I said, all I promised . . . still I went in. . . .*

D: . . . *nothing to worry . . . remember what you told me . . . keep on believing. . . .*

T: . . . *did believe, DID . . . no difficulties . . . Josie . . .*

D: . . . *you say I shouldn't give up, you better not . . . repeat everything you told me, everything Josie told you . . . everybody finds someone . . . if they keep looking . . . give up, dead . . . all you need . . . openness . . . courage to look . . . stop feeling sorry for yourself . . . told me that a hundred times. . . .*

T: . . . *fucking lot easier to tell you than do it myself . . .*

D: . . . *Greg . . . not a meathouse man . . . a dreamer . . . better than they are . . .*

T: *(sighing) . . . yeah . . . hard, though . . . why do I do this to myself? . . .*

D: . . . *rather be like you were? . . . . not hurting, not living? . . . like me? . . .*

T: . . . *no . . . no . . . you're right. . . .*

2

THE PILGRIM, UP AND DOWN

HER NAME WAS LAUREL. SHE WAS NOTHING LIKE JOSIE, SAVE IN ONE thing alone. Trager loved her.

Pretty? Trager didn't think so, not at first. She was too tall, a half-foot taller than he was, and she was a bit on the heavy side, and more than a bit on the awkward side. Her hair was her best feature, her hair that was red-brown in winter and glowing blond in summer, that fell long and straight down past her shoulders and did wild beautiful things in the wind. But she was not beautiful, not the way Josie had been beautiful. Although, oddly, she grew more beautiful with time, and maybe that was because she was losing weight, and maybe that was because Trager was falling in love with her and seeing her through kinder eyes, and maybe that was because he *told* her she was pretty and the very telling made it so. Just as Laurel told him he was wise, and her belief gave him wisdom. Whatever the reason, Laurel was very beautiful indeed after he had known her for a time.

She was five years younger than he, clean-scrubbed and innocent, shy where Josie had been assertive. She was intelligent, romantic, a dreamer; she was wondrously fresh and eager; she was painfully insecure, and full of hungry need.

She was new to Gidyon, fresh from the Vendalian outback, a student forester. Trager, on leave again, was visiting the forestry college to say hello to a teacher who'd once worked with his crew. They met in the teacher's office. Trager had two weeks free in a city of strangers and meathouses; Laurel was alone. He showed her the glittering decadence of Gidyon, feeling smooth and sophisticated, and she was suitably impressed.

Two weeks went quickly. They came to the last night. Trager, suddenly afraid, took her to the park by the river that ran through Gidyon and they sat together on the low stone wall by the water's edge. Close, not touching.

"Time runs too fast," he said. He had a stone in his hand. He flicked it out over the water, flat and hard. Thoughtfully, he watched it splash and sink. Then he looked at her. "I'm nervous," he said, laughing. "I—Laurel. I don't want to leave."

Her face was unreadable (wary?). "The city is nice," she agreed.

Trager shook his head violently. "No. *No!* Not the city, you. Laurel, I think I . . . well . . ."

Laurel smiled for him. Her eyes were bright, very happy. "I know," she said.

Trager could hardly believe it. He reached out, touched her cheek. She turned her head and kissed his hand. They smiled at each other.

———

He flew back to the forest camp to quit. "Don, Don, you've got to meet her," he shouted. "See, you can do it, *I* did it, just keep believing, keep trying. I feel so goddamn good it's obscene."

Donelly, stiff and logical, smiled for him, at a loss as how to handle such a flood of happiness. "What will you do?" he asked, a little awkwardly. "The arena?"

Trager laughed. "Hardly, you know how I feel. But something like that. There's a theatre near the spaceport, puts on pantomime with corpse actors. I've got a job there. The pay is rotten, but I'll be near Laurel. That's all that matters."

———

They hardly slept at night. Instead they talked and cuddled and made love. The lovemaking was a joy, a game, a glorious discovery; never as good technically as the meathouse, but Trager hardly cared. He taught her to be open. He told her every secret he had, and wished he had more secrets.

"Poor Josie," Laurel would often say at night, her body warm against his. "She doesn't know what she missed. I'm lucky. There couldn't be anyone else like you."

"No," said Trager, "*I'm* lucky."

They would argue about it, laughing.

———

Donelly came to Gidyon and joined the theatre. Without Trager, the forest work had been no fun, he said. The three of them spent a lot of time together, and Trager glowed. He wanted to share his friends with Laurel, and he'd already mentioned Donelly a lot. And he wanted Donelly to see how happy he'd become, to see what belief could accomplish.

"I like her," Donelly said, smiling, the first night after Laurel had left.

"Good," Trager replied, nodding.

"No," said Donelly. "Greg, I *really* like her."

THEY SPENT A *LOT* OF TIME TOGETHER.

"GREG," LAUREL SAID ONE NIGHT IN BED, "I THINK THAT DON IS . . . well, after me. You know."

Trager rolled over and propped his head up on his elbow. "God," he said. He sounded concerned.

"I don't know how to handle it."

"Carefully," Trager said. "He's very vulnerable. You're probably the first woman he's ever been interested in. Don't be too hard on him. He shouldn't have to go through the stuff I went through, you know?"

THE SEX WAS NEVER AS GOOD AS A MEATHOUSE. AND, AFTER A WHILE, Laurel began to close. More and more nights now she went to sleep after they made love; the days when they talked till dawn were gone. Perhaps they had nothing left to say. Trager had noticed that she had a tendency to finish his stories for him. It was nearly impossible to come up with one he hadn't already told her.

"HE SAID *THAT?*" TRAGER GOT OUT OF BED, TURNED ON A LIGHT, AND sat down frowning. Laurel pulled the covers up to her chin.

"Well, what did *you* say?"

She hesitated. "I can't tell you. It's between Don and me. He said it wasn't fair, the way I turn around and tell you everything that goes on between us, and he's right."

"*Right!* But I tell you everything. Don't you remember what we . . ."

"I know, but . . ."

Trager shook his head. His voice lost some of its anger. "What's going on, Laurel, huh? I'm scared, all of a sudden. I love you, remember? How can everything change so fast?"

Her face softened. She sat up, and held out her arms, and the covers fell back from full soft breasts. "Oh, Greg," she said. "Don't worry. I love you, I always will, but it's just that I love him too, I guess. You know?"

Trager, mollified, came into her arms, and kissed her with fervor. Then, suddenly, he broke off. "Hey," he said, with mock sternness to hide the trembling in his voice, "who do you love *more?*"

"You, of course, always you."

Smiling, he returned to the kiss.

———

"I KNOW YOU KNOW," DONELLY SAID. "I GUESS WE HAVE TO TALK about it."

Trager nodded. They were backstage in the theatre. Three of his corpses walked up behind him, and stood arms crossed, like a guard. "All right." He looked straight at Donelly, and his face—smiling until the other's words—was suddenly stern. "Laurel asked me to pretend I didn't know anything. She said you felt guilty. But pretending was quite a strain, Don. I guess it's time we got everything out in the open."

Donelly's pale blue eyes shifted to the floor, and he stuck his hands into his pockets. "I don't want to hurt you," he said.

"Then don't."

"But I'm not going to pretend I'm dead, either. I'm not. I love her too."

"You're supposed to be my friend, Don. Love someone else. You're just going to get yourself hurt this way."

"I have more in common with her than you do."

Trager just stared.

Donelly looked up at him. Then, abashed, back down again. "I don't know. Oh, Greg. She loves you more anyway, she said so. I never should have expected anything else. I feel like I've stabbed you in the back. I . . ."

Trager watched him. Finally, he laughed softly. "Oh, shit, I can't take this. Look, Don, you haven't stabbed me, c'mon, don't talk like that. I guess, if you love her, this is the way it's got to be, you know. I just hope everything comes out all right."

Later that night, in bed with Laurel; "I'm worried about him," he told her.

———

HIS FACE, ONCE TANNED, NOW ASHEN. "LAUREL?" HE SAID. NOT BE-lieving.

"I don't love you anymore. I'm sorry. I don't. It seemed real at the time, but now it's almost like a dream. I don't even know if I ever loved you, really."

"Don," he said woodenly.

Laurel flushed. "Don't say anything bad about Don. I'm tired of hearing you run him down. He never says anything except good about you."

"Oh, Laurel. Don't you *remember?* The things we said, the way we felt? I'm the same person you said those words to."

"But I've grown," Laurel said, hard and tearless, tossing her red-gold hair. "I remember perfectly well, but I just don't feel that way anymore."

"Don't," he said. He reached for her.

She stepped back. "Keep your hands off me. I told you, Greg, it's *over.* You have to leave now. Don is coming by."

———

IT WAS WORSE THAN JOSIE. A THOUSAND TIMES WORSE.

III
WANDERINGS

HE TRIED TO KEEP ON AT THE THEATRE; HE ENJOYED THE WORK, HE had friends there. But it was impossible. Donelly was there every day, smiling and being friendly, and sometimes Laurel came to meet him after the day's show and they went off together, arm in arm. Trager would stand and watch, try not to notice. While the twisted thing inside him shrieked and clawed.

He quit. He would not see them again. He would keep his pride.

———

THE SKY WAS BRIGHT WITH THE LIGHTS OF GIDYON AND FULL OF laughter, but it was dark and quiet in the park.

Trager stood stiff against a tree, his eyes on the river, his hands folded tightly against his chest. He was a statue. He hardly seemed to breathe. Not even his eyes moved.

Kneeling near the low wall, the corpse pounded until the stone was slick with blood and its hands were mangled clots of torn meat. The sounds of the blows were dull and wet, but for the infrequent scraping of bone against rock.

———

THEY MADE HIM PAY FIRST, BEFORE HE COULD EVEN ENTER THE BOOTH. Then he sat there for an hour while they found her and punched through. Finally, though, finally; "Josie."

"Greg," she said, grinning her distinctive grin. "I should have known. Who else would call all the way from Vendalia? How are you?"

He told her.

Her grin vanished. "Oh, Greg," she said. "I'm sorry. But don't let it get to you. Keep going. The next one will work out better. They always do."

Her words didn't satisfy him. "Josie," he said, "How are things back there? You miss me?"

"Oh, sure. Things are pretty good. It's still Skrakky, though. Stay where you are, you're better off." She looked off screen, then back. "I should go, before your bill gets enormous. Glad you called, love."

"*Josie,*" Trager started. But the screen was already dark.

———

SOMETIMES, AT NIGHT, HE COULDN'T HELP HIMSELF. HE WOULD MOVE to his home screen and ring Laurel. Invariably her eyes would narrow when she saw who it was. Then she would hang up.

And Trager would sit in a dark room and recall how once the sound of his voice made her so very, very happy.

The streets of Gidyon are not the best of places for lonely midnight walks. They are brightly lit, even in the darkest hours, and jammed with men and deadmen. And there are meathouses, all up and down the boulevards and the ironspike boardwalks.

Josie's words had lost their power. In the meathouses, Trager abandoned dreams and found cheap solace. The sensuous evenings with Laurel and the fumbling sex of his boyhood were things of yesterday; Trager took his meatmates hard and quick, almost brutally, fucked them with a wordless savage power to the inevitable perfect orgasm. Sometimes, remembering the theatre, he would have them act out short erotic playlets to get him in the mood.

In the night. Agony.

He was in the corridors again, the low dim corridors of the corpsehandlers' dorm on Skrakky, but now the corridors were twisted and torturous and Trager had long since lost his way. The air was thick with a rotting gray haze, and growing thicker. Soon, he feared, he would be all but blind.

Around and around he walked, up and down, but always there was more corridor, and all of them led nowhere. The doors were grim black rectangles, knobless, locked to him forever; he passed them by without thinking, most of them. Once or twice, though, he paused, before doors where light leaked around the frame. He would listen, and inside there were sounds, and then he would begin to knock wildly. But no one ever answered.

So he would move on, through the haze that got darker and thicker and seemed to burn his skin, past door after door after door, until he was weeping and his feet were tired and bloody. And then, off a ways, down a long, long corridor that loomed straight before him, he would see an open door. From it came light so hot and white it hurt the eyes, and music bright and joyful, and the sounds of people laughing. Then Trager would run, though his feet were raw bundles of pain and his lungs burned with the haze he was breathing. He would run and run until he reached the room with the open door.

Only when he got there, it was his room, and it was empty.

ONCE, IN THE MIDDLE OF THEIR BRIEF TIME TOGETHER, THEY'D GONE out into the wilderness and made love under the stars. Afterwards she had snuggled hard against him, and he stroked her gently. "What are you thinking?" he asked.

"About us," Laurel said. She shivered. The wind was brisk and cold. "Sometimes I get scared, Greg. I'm so afraid something will happen to us, something that will ruin it. I don't ever want you to leave me."

"Don't worry," he told her. "I won't."

Now, each night before sleep came, he tortured himself with her words. The good memories left him with ashes and tears; the bad ones with a wordless rage.

He slept with a ghost beside him, a supernaturally beautiful ghost, the husk of a dead dream. He woke to her each morning.

———

HE HATED THEM. HE HATED HIMSELF FOR HATING.

3

DUVALIER'S DREAM

HER NAME DOES NOT MATTER. HER LOOKS ARE NOT IMPORTANT. ALL that counts is that she *was,* that Trager tried again, that he forced himself on and made himself believe and didn't give up. He *tried.*

But something was missing. Magic?

The words were the same.

How many times can you speak them, Trager wondered, *speak them and believe them, like you believed them the first time you said them? Once? Twice? Three times, maybe? Or a hundred? And the people who say it a hundred times, are they really so much better at loving? Or only at fooling themselves? Aren't they really people who long ago abandoned the dream, who use its name for something else?*

He said the words, holding her, cradling her, and kissing her. He said the words, with a knowledge that was surer and heavier and more dead than any belief. He said the words and *tried,* but no longer could he mean them.

And she said the words back, and Trager realized that they meant nothing to him. Over and over again they said the things each wanted to hear, and both of them knew they were pretending.

They tried *hard.* But when he reached out, like an actor caught in his role, doomed to play out the same part over and over again, when he reached out his hand and touched her cheek—the skin was smooth and soft and lovely. And wet with tears.

IV

ECHOES

"I DON'T WANT TO HURT YOU," SAID DONELLY, SHUFFLING AND looking guilty, until Trager felt ashamed for having hurt a friend.

He touched her cheek, and she spun away from him.

"I never wanted to hurt you," Josie said, and Trager was sad. She had given him so much; he'd only made her guilty. Yes, he was hurt, but a stronger man would never have let her know.

He touched her cheek, and she kissed his hand.

"I'm sorry, I don't," Laurel said. And Trager was lost. What had he done, where was his fault, how had he ruined it? She had been so sure. They had had so much.

He touched her cheek, and she wept.

How many times can you speak them, his voice echoed, *speak them and believe them, like you believed them the first time you said them?*

The wind was dark and dust heavy, the sky throbbed painfully with flickering scarlet flame. In the pit, in the darkness, stood a young woman with goggles and a filtermask and short brown hair and answers. "It breaks down, it breaks down, it breaks down, and they keep sending it out," she said. "Should realize that something is wrong. After that many failures, it's sheer self-delusion to think the thing's going to work right next time out."

The enemy corpse is huge and black, its torso rippling with muscle, a product of months of exercise, the biggest thing that Trager has ever faced. It advances across the sawdust in a slow, clumsy crouch, holding the gleaming broadsword in one hand. Trager watches it come from his chair atop one end of the fighting arena. The other corpsemaster is careful, cautious.

His own deadman, a wiry blond, stands and waits, a Morningstar trailing down in the blood-soaked arena dust. Trager will move him fast enough and well enough when the time is right. The enemy knows it, and the crowd.

The black corpse suddenly lifts its broadsword and scrambles forward in a run, hoping to use reach and speed to get its kill. But Trager's corpse is no longer there when the enemy's measured blow cuts the air where he had been.

Sitting comfortably above the fighting pit/down in the arena, his feet grimy with blood and sawdust—Trager/the corpse—snaps the command/swings the Morningstar—and the great studded ball drifts up and around, almost lazily, almost gracefully. Into the back of the enemy's head, as he tries to recover and turn. A flower of blood and brain blooms swift and sudden, and the crowd cheers.

Trager walks his corpse from the arena, then stands to receive applause. It is his tenth kill. Soon the championship will be his. He is building such a record that they can no longer deny him a match.

She is beautiful, his lady, his love. Her hair is short and blond, her body very slim, graceful, almost athletic, with trim legs and small hard breasts. Her eyes are bright green, and they always welcome him. And there is a strange erotic innocence in her smile.

She waits for him in bed, waits for his return from the arena, waits for him eager and playful and loving. When he enters, she is sitting up, smiling for him, the covers bunched around her waist. From the door he admires her nipples.

Aware of his eyes, shy, she covers her breasts and blushes. Trager knows it is all false modesty, all playing. He moves to the bedside, sits, reaches out to stroke her cheek. Her skin is very soft; she nuzzles against his hand as it brushes her. Then Trager draws her hands aside, plants one gentle kiss on each breast, and a not-so-gentle kiss on her mouth. She kisses back, with ardor; their tongues dance.

They make love, he and she, slow and sensuous, locked together in a loving embrace that goes on and on. Two bodies move flawlessly in perfect rhythm, each knowing the other's needs. Trager thrusts, and his other body meets the thrusts. He reaches, and her hand is there. They come together (always, *always,* both orgasms triggered by the handler's brain), and a bright red flush burns on her breasts and earlobes. They kiss.

Afterwards, he talks to her, his love, his lady. You should always talk afterwards; he learned that long ago.

"You're lucky," he tells her sometimes, and she snuggles up to him and plants tiny kisses all across his chest. "Very lucky. They lie to you out there, love. They teach you a silly shining dream and they tell you to believe and chase it and they tell you that for you, for everyone, there is someone. But it's all wrong. The universe isn't fair, it never has been, so why do they tell you so? You run after the phantom, and lose, and they tell you next time, but it's all rot, all empty rot. Nobody ever finds the dream at all, they just kid themselves, trick themselves so they can go on believing. It's just a clutching lie that desperate people tell each other, hoping to convince themselves."

But then he can't talk anymore, for her kisses have gone lower and lower, and now she takes him in her mouth. And Trager smiles at his love and gently strokes her hair.

———

OF ALL THE BRIGHT CRUEL LIES THEY TELL YOU, THE CRUELEST IS THE one called love.

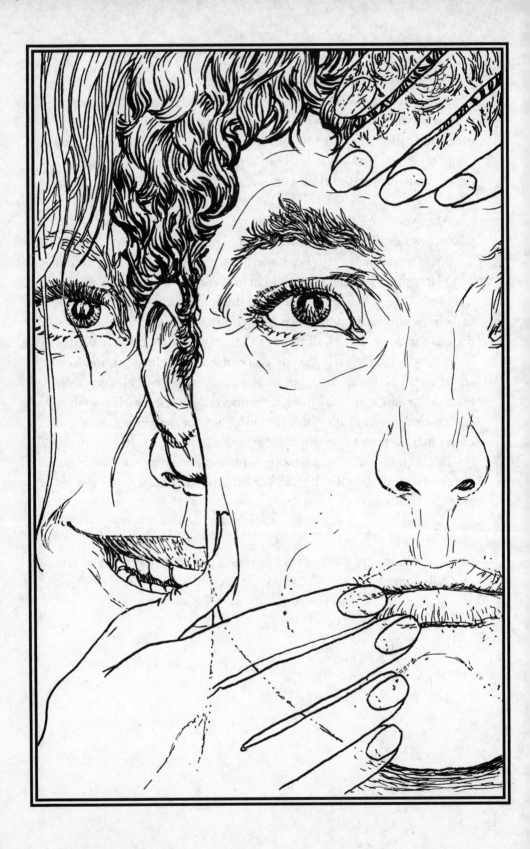

REMEMBERING MELODY

TED WAS SHAVING WHEN THE DOORBELL SOUNDED. IT STARTLED him so badly that he cut himself. His condominium was on the thirty-second floor, and Jack the doorman generally gave him advance warning of any prospective visitors. This had to be someone from the building, then. Except that Ted didn't know anyone in the building, at least not beyond the trade-smiles-in-the-elevator level.

"Coming," he shouted. Scowling, he snatched up a towel and wiped the lather from his face, then dabbed at his cut with a tissue. "Shit," he said loudly to his face in the mirror. He had to be in court this afternoon. If this was another Jehovah's Witness like the one who'd gotten past Jack last month, they were going to be in for a very rough time indeed.

The buzzer buzzed again. "Coming, dammit," Ted yelled. He made a final dab at the blood on his neck, then threw the tissue into a wastebasket and strode across the sunken living room to the door. He peered through the eyehole carefully before he opened. "Oh, shit," he muttered. Before she could buzz again, Ted slid off the chain and threw open the door. "Hello, Melody," he said.

She smiled wanly. "Hi, Ted," she replied. She had an old suitcase in her hand, a battered cloth bag with a hideous red-and-black plaid pattern, its broken handle replaced by a length of rope. The last time Ted had seen her, three years before, she'd looked terrible. Now she looked worse. Her clothes—shorts and a tie-dyed T-shirt—were wrinkled and dirty, and emphasized how gaunt she'd become. Her ribs showed through plainly; her legs were pipestems. Her long stringy blond hair hadn't been washed recently, and her face was red and puffy, as if she'd been crying. That was no surprise. Melody was always crying about one thing or another. "Aren't you going to ask me in, Ted?"

Ted grimaced. He certainly didn't *want* to ask her in. He knew from past experience how difficult it was to get her out again. But he couldn't just leave her standing in the hall with her suitcase in hand. After all, he thought sourly, she was an old and dear friend. "Oh, sure," he said. He gestured. "Come on in."

He took her bag from her and set it by the door, then led her into the kitchen and put on some water to boil. "You look as though you could use a cup of coffee," he said, trying to keep his voice friendly.

Melody smiled again. "Don't you remember, Ted? I don't drink coffee. It's no good for you, Ted. I used to tell you that. Don't you remember?" She got up from the kitchen table, and began rummaging through his cupboards. "Do you have any hot chocolate?" she asked. "I like hot chocolate."

"I don't drink hot chocolate," he said. "Just a lot of coffee."

"You shouldn't," she said. "It's no good for you."

"Yeah," he said. "Do you want juice? I've got juice."

Melody nodded. "Fine."

He poured her a glass of orange juice, and led her back to the table, then spooned some Maxim into a mug while he waited for his kettle to whistle. "So," he asked, "what brings you to Chicago?"

Melody began to cry. Ted leaned back against the stove and watched her. She was a very noisy crier, and she produced an amazing amount of tears for someone who cried so often. She didn't look up until the water began to boil. Ted poured some into his cup and stirred in a teaspoon of sugar. Her face was redder and more puffy than ever. Her eyes fixed on him accusingly. "Things have been real bad," she said. "I need help, Ted. I don't have any place to live. I thought maybe I could stay with you awhile. Things have been real bad."

"I'm sorry to hear that, Melody," Ted replied, sipping at his coffee thoughtfully. "You can stay here for a few days, if you want. But no longer. I'm not in the market for a roommate." She always made him feel like such a bastard, but it was better to be firm with her right from the start, he thought.

Melody began to cry again when he mentioned roommates. "You used to say I was a *good* roommate," she whined. "We used to have fun, don't you remember? You were my friend."

Ted set down his coffee mug and looked at the kitchen clock. "I don't have time to talk about old times right now," he said. "I was shaving when you rang. I've got to get to the office." He frowned. "Drink your juice and make yourself at home. I've got to get dressed." He turned abruptly, and left her weeping at the kitchen table.

Back in the bathroom, Ted finished shaving and tended to his cut more properly, his mind full of Melody. Already he could tell that this was going to be difficult. He felt sorry for her—she was messed up and miserably unhappy, with no one to turn to—but he wasn't going to let her inflict all her troubles on him. Not this time. She'd done it too many times before.

In his bedroom, Ted stared pensively into the closet for a long time before selecting the gray suit. He knotted his tie carefully in the mirror, scowling at his cut. Then he checked his briefcase to make sure all the papers on the Syndio case were in order, nodded, and walked back into the kitchen.

Melody was at the stove, making some pancakes. She turned and smiled at him happily when he entered. "You remember my pancakes, Ted?" she asked. "You used to love it when I made pancakes, especially blueberry pancakes, you remember? You didn't have any blueberries, though, so I'm just making plain. Is that alright?"

"Jesus," Ted muttered. "Dammit, Melody, who said you should make *anything?* I told you I had to get to the office. I don't have time to eat with you. I'm late already. Anyway, I don't eat breakfast. I'm trying to lose weight."

Tears began to trickle from her eyes again. "But—but these are my special pancakes, Ted. What am I going to do with them? What am I going to *do?*"

"Eat them," Ted said. "You could use a few extra pounds. Jesus, you look terrible. You look like you haven't eaten for a month."

Melody's face screwed up and became ugly. "You bastard," she said. "You're supposed to be my *friend.*"

Ted sighed. "Take it easy," he said. He glanced at his watch. "Look, I'm fifteen minutes late already. I've got to go. You eat your pancakes and get some sleep. I'll be back around six. We can have dinner together and talk, all right? Is that what you want?"

"That would be nice," she said, suddenly contrite. "That would be real nice."

"TELL JILL I WANT TO SEE HER IN MY OFFICE, RIGHT AWAY," TED snapped to the secretary when he arrived. "And get us some coffee, willya? I really need some coffee."

"Sure."

Jill arrived a few minutes after the coffee. She and Ted were associates in the same law firm. He motioned her to a seat, and pushed a cup at her. "Sit down," he said. "Look, the date's off tonight. I've got problems."

"You look it," she said. "What's wrong?"

"An old friend showed up on my doorstep this morning," he said.

Jill arched one elegant eyebrow. "So?" she said. "Reunions can be fun."

"Not with Melody, they can't."

"Melody?" she said. "A pretty name. An old flame, Ted? What is it, unrequited love?"

"No," he said, "no, it wasn't like that."

"Tell me what it was like, then. You know I love the gory details."

"Melody and I were roommates, back in college. Not just us— don't get the wrong idea. There were four of us. Me and a guy named Michael Englehart, Melody and another girl, Anne Kaye. The four of us shared a big old run-down house for two years. We were—friends."

"Friends?" Jill looked skeptical.

Ted scowled at her. "Friends," he repeated. "Oh, hell, I slept with Melody a few times. With Anne too. And both of them fucked Michael a time or two. But when it happened, it was just kind of— kind of *friendly,* you know? Our love life was mostly with outsiders, we used to tell one another our troubles, swap advice, cry on one another's shoulders. Hell, I know it sounds weird. It was 1970, though. I had hair down to my ass. Everything was weird." He sloshed the dregs of his coffee around in the cup, and looked pensive. "They were good times too. Special times. Sometimes I'm sorry they had to end. The four of us were close, really close. I loved those people."

"Watch out," Jill said, "I'll get jealous. My roommate and I cordially despised each other." She smiled. "So what happened?"

Ted shrugged. "The usual story," he said. "We graduated, drifted apart. I remember the last night in the old house. We smoked a ton of dope, and got very silly. Swore eternal friendship. We weren't ever going to be strangers, no matter what happened, and if any of us ever needed help, well, the other three would always be there. We sealed the bargain with—well, kind of an orgy."

Jill smiled. "Touching," she said. "I never dreamed you had it in you."

"It didn't last, of course," Ted continued. "We tried, I'll give us that much. But things changed too much. I went on to law school, wound up here in Chicago. Michael got a job with a publishing house in New York City. He's an editor at Random House now, been married and divorced, two kids. We used to write. Now we trade Christmas cards. Anne's a teacher. She was down in Phoenix the last I heard, but that was four, five years ago. Her husband didn't like the rest of us much, the one time we had a reunion. I think Anne must have told him about the orgy."

"And your houseguest?"

"Melody," he sighed. "She became a problem. In college, she was wonderful; gutsy, pretty, a real free spirit. But afterwards she couldn't cut it. She tried to make it as a painter for a couple of years, but she wasn't good enough. Got nowhere. She went through a couple of relationships that turned sour, then married some guy about a week after she'd met him in a singles bar. That was terrible. He used to get drunk and beat her. She took about six months of it, and finally got a divorce. He still came round to beat her up for a year, until he finally got frightened off. After that Melody got into drugs, bad. She spent some time in an asylum. When she got out, it was more of the same. She can't hold a job, or stay away from drugs. Her relationships don't last more than a few weeks. She's let her body go to hell." He shook his head.

Jill pursed her lips. "Sounds like a lady who needs help," she said.

Ted flushed, and grew angry. "You think I don't know that? You think we haven't tried to help her? *Jesus.* When she was trying to be an artist, Michael got her a couple of cover assignments from the paperback house he was with. Not only did she blow the deadlines, but she got into a screaming match with the art director. Almost cost Michael his job. I flew to Cleveland and handled her divorce for her, gratis. Flew back a couple of months later, and spent quite a while there trying to get the cops to give her protection against her ex-hubby. Anne took her in when she had no place to stay, got her into a drug rehabilitation program. In return, Melody tried to seduce her boyfriend—said she wanted to *share* him, like they'd done in the old days. All of us have lent her money. She's never paid back any of it. And we've listened to her troubles, God, but we've listened to her troubles. There was a period a few years ago when she'd phone every week, usually collect, with some new sad story. She cried over the phone a lot. If *Queen for a Day* was still on TV, Melody would be a natural!"

"I'm beginning to see why you're not thrilled by her visit," Jill said drily. "What are you going to do?"

"I don't know," Ted replied. "I shouldn't have let her in. The last few times she's called, I just hung up on her, and that seemed to work pretty well. Felt guilty about it at first, but that passed. This morning, though, she looked so pathetic that I didn't know how to send her away. I suppose eventually I'll have to get brutal, and go through a scene. Nothing else works. She'll make a lot of accusations, remind me of what good friends we were and the promises we made, threaten to kill herself. Fun times ahead."

"Can I help?" Jill asked.

"Pick up my pieces afterwards," Ted said. "It's always nice to have someone around afterwards, to tell you that you're not a son-of-a-bitch even though you just kicked an old dear friend out into the gutter."

HE WAS TERRIBLE IN COURT THAT AFTERNOON. HIS THOUGHTS WERE full of Melody, and the strategies that most occupied him concerned how to get rid of her most painlessly, instead of the case at hand. Melody had danced flamenco on his psyche too many times before; Ted wasn't going to let her leech off him this time, nor leave him an emotional wreck.

When he got back to his condo with a bag of Chinese food under his arm—he'd decided he didn't want to take her out to a restaurant— Melody was sitting nude in the middle of his conversation pit, giggling and sniffing some white powder. She looked up at Ted happily when he entered. "Here," she said. "I scored some coke."

"*Jesus*," he swore. He dropped the Chinese food and his briefcase, and strode furiously across the carpet. "I don't *believe* you," he roared. "I'm a *lawyer*, for Chrissakes. Do you want to get me disbarred?"

Melody had the coke in a little paper square, and was sniffing it from a rolled-up dollar bill. Ted snatched it all away from her, and she began to cry. He went to the bathroom and flushed it down the toilet, dollar bill and all. Except it wasn't a dollar bill, he saw, as it was sucked out of sight. It was a twenty. That made him even angrier. When he returned to the living room, Melody was still crying.

"Stop that," he said. "I don't want to hear it. And put some clothes on." Another suspicion came to him. "Where did you get the money for that stuff?" he demanded. "Huh, *where?*"

Melody whimpered. "I sold some stuff," she said in a timid voice. "I didn't think you'd mind. It was good coke." She shied away from him and threw an arm across her face, as if Ted was going to hit her.

Ted didn't need to ask whose stuff she'd sold. He knew; she'd pulled the same trick on Michael years before, or so he'd heard. He sighed. "Get dressed," he repeated wearily. "I brought Chinese food." Later he could check what was missing, and phone the insurance company.

"Chinese food is no good for you," Melody said. "It's full of monosodium glutamate. Gives you headaches, Ted." But she got to her feet obediently, if a bit unsteadily, went off towards the bathroom, and came back a few minutes later wearing a halter-top and a pair of ratty cutoffs. Nothing else, Ted guessed. A couple of years ago she must have decided that underwear was no good for you.

Ignoring her comment about monosodium glutamate, Ted found some plates and served up the Chinese food in his dining nook. Melody ate it meekly enough, drowning everything in soy sauce. Every few minutes she giggled at some private joke, then grew very serious again and resumed eating. When she broke open her fortune cookie, a wide smile lit her face. "Look, Ted," she said happily, passing the little slip of paper across to him.

He read it. OLD FRIENDS ARE THE BEST FRIENDS, it said. "Oh, shit," he muttered. He didn't even open his own. Melody wanted to know why.

"You ought to read it, Ted," she told him. "It's bad luck if you don't read your fortune cookie."

"I don't want to read it," he said. "I'm going to change out of this suit." He rose. "Don't do anything."

But when he came back, she'd put an album on the stereo. At least she hadn't sold that, he thought gratefully.

"Do you want me to dance for you?" she asked. "Remember how I used to dance for you and Michael? Real sexy . . . you used to tell me how good I dance. I could have been a dancer if I'd wanted." She did a few steps in the middle of his living room, stumbled, and almost fell. It was grotesque.

"Sit down, Melody," Ted said, as sternly as he could manage. "We have to talk."

She sat down.

"Don't cry," he said before he started. "You understand that? I don't want you to cry. We can't talk if you're going to cry every time I say anything. You start crying and this conversation is over."

Melody nodded. "I won't cry, Ted," she said. "I feel much better now than this morning. I'm with you now. You make me feel better."

"You're *not* with me, Melody. Stop that."

Her eyes filled up with tears. "You're my friend, Ted. You and Michael and Anne, you're the special ones."

He sighed. "What's wrong, Melody? Why are you here?"

"I lost my job, Ted," she said.

"The waitress job?" he asked. The last time he'd seen her, three years ago, she'd been waiting tables in a bar in Kansas City.

Melody blinked at him, confused. "Waitress?" she said. "No, Ted. That was before. That was in Kansas City. Don't you remember?"

"I remember very well," he said. "What job was it you lost?"

"It was a shitty job," Melody said. "A factory job. It was in Iowa. In Des Moines. Des Moines is a shitty place. I didn't come to work, so they fired me. I was strung out, you know? I needed a couple of days off. I would have come back to work. But they fired me." She looked close to tears again. "I haven't had a good job in a long time, Ted. I was an art major. You remember? You and Michael and Anne used to have my drawings hung up in your rooms. You still have my drawings, Ted?"

"Yes," he lied. "Sure. Somewhere." He'd gotten rid of them years ago. They reminded him too much of Melody, and that was too painful.

"Anyway, when I lost my job, Johnny said I wasn't bringing in any money. Johnny was the guy I lived with. He said he wasn't gonna support me, that I had to get some job, but I couldn't. I *tried*, Ted, but I couldn't. So Johnny talked to some man, and he got me this job in a massage parlor, you know. And he took me down there, but it was crummy. I didn't want to work in no massage parlor, Ted. I used to be an art major."

"I remember, Melody," Ted said. She seemed to expect him to say something.

Melody nodded. "So I didn't take it, and Johnny threw me out. I had no place to go, you know. And I thought of you, and Anne, and Michael. Remember the last night? We all said that if anyone ever needed help . . ."

"I remember, Melody," Ted said. "Not as often as you do, but I remember. You don't ever let any of us forget it, do you? But let it pass. What do you want this time?" His tone was flat and cold.

"You're a lawyer, Ted," she said.

"Yes."

"So, I thought—" Her long, thin fingers plucked nervously at her face. "I thought maybe you could get me a job. I could be a secretary, maybe. In your office. We could be together again, every day, like it used to be. Or maybe,"—she brightened visibly—"maybe I could be one of those people who draw pictures in the courtroom. You know. Like Patty Hearst and people like that. On TV. I'd be good at that."

"Those artists work for TV stations," Ted said patiently. "And there are no openings in my office. I'm sorry, Melody. I can't get you a job."

Melody took that surprisingly well. "All right, Ted," she said. "I can find a job, I guess. I'll get one all by myself. Only—only let me live here, okay? We can be roommates again."

"Oh, Jesus," Ted said. He sat back and crossed his arms. "No," he said flatly.

Melody took her hand away from her face, and stared at him imploringly. "Please, Ted," she whispered. "Please."

"No," he said. The word hung there, chill and final.

"You're my *friend,* Ted," she said. "You *promised.*"

"You can stay here a week," he said. "No longer. I have my own life, Melody. I have my own problems. I'm tired of dealing with yours. We all are. You're nothing but problems. In college, you were fun. You're not fun any longer. I've helped you and helped you and helped you. How fucking much do you want out of me?" He was getting angrier as he talked. "Things change, Melody," he said brutally. "People change. You can't hold me forever to some dumb promise I made when I was stoned out of my mind back in college. I'm not responsible for your life. Tough up, dammit. Pull yourself together. I can't do it for you, and I'm sick of all your shit. I don't even like to see you anymore, Melody, you know that?"

She whimpered. "Don't say that, Ted. We're friends. You're special. As long as I have you and Michael and Anne, I'll never be alone, don't you see?"

"You *are* alone," he said. Melody infuriated him.

"No I'm not," she insisted. "I have my friends, my special friends. They'll help me. You're my *friend,* Ted."

"I used to be your friend," he replied.

She stared at him, her lip trembling, hurt beyond words. For a moment he thought that the dam was going to burst, that Melody was finally about to break down and begin one of her marathon crying jags. Instead, a change came over her face. She paled perceptibly, and her lips drew back slowly, and her expression settled into a terrible mask of anger. She was hideous when she was angry. "You bastard," she said.

Ted had been this route too. He got up from the couch and walked to his bar. "Don't start," he said, pouring himself a glass of Chivas Regal on the rocks. "The first thing you throw, you're out on your ass. Got that, Melody?"

"You scum," she repeated. "You were never my friend. None of you were. You lied to me, made me trust you, used me. Now you're all so high and mighty and I'm nothing, and you don't want to know me. You don't want to help me. You never wanted to help me."

"I did help you," Ted pointed out. "Several times. You owe me something close to two thousand dollars, I believe."

"Money," she said. "That's all you care about, you bastard."

Ted sipped at his scotch and frowned at her. "Go to hell," he said.

"I could, for all you care." Her face had gone white. "I cabled you, two years ago. I cabled all three of you. I needed you, you promised that you'd come if I needed you, that you'd be there, you promised that and you made love to me and you were my friend, but I cabled you and you didn't come, you bastard, you didn't come, none of you came, none of you came." She was screaming.

Ted had forgotten about the telegram. But it all came back to him in a rush. He'd read it over several times, and finally he'd picked up the phone and called Michael. Michael hadn't been in. So he'd reread the telegram one last time, then crumbled it up and flushed it down the toilet. One of the others could go to her this time, he remembered thinking. He had a big case, the Argrath Corporation patent suit, and he couldn't risk leaving it. But it had been a desperate telegram, and he'd been guilty about it for weeks, until he finally managed to put the whole thing out of his mind. "I was busy," he said, his tone half-angry and half-defensive. "I had more important things to do than come hold your hand through another crisis."

"It was *horrible,*" Melody screamed. "I needed you and you left me all *alone.* I almost *killed* myself."

"But you didn't, did you?"

"I could have," she said. "I could have killed myself, and you wouldn't have even cared."

Threatening suicide was one of Melody's favorite tricks. Ted had been through it a hundred times before. This time he decided not to take it. "You could have killed yourself," he said calmly, "and we probably wouldn't've cared. I think you're right about that. You would have rotted for weeks before anyone found you, and we probably wouldn't even have heard about it for half a year. And when I did hear, finally, I guess it would have made me sad for an hour or two, remembering how things had been, but then I would have gotten drunk or phoned up my girlfriend or something, and pretty soon I'd have been out of it. And then I could have forgotten all about you."

"You would have been sorry," Melody said.

"No," Ted replied. He strolled back to the bar and freshened his drink. "No, you know, I don't think I would have been sorry. Not in the least. Not guilty, either. So you might as well stop threatening to kill yourself, Melody, because it isn't going to work."

The anger drained out of her face, and she gave a little whimper. "Please, Ted," she said. "Don't say such things. Tell me you'd care. Tell me you'd remember me."

He scowled at her. "No," he said. It was harder when she was pitiful, when she shrunk up all small and vulnerable and whimpered instead of accusing him. But he had to end it once and for all, get rid of this curse on his life.

"I'll go away tomorrow," she said meekly. "I won't bother you. But tell me you care, Ted. That you're my friend. That you'll come to me. If I need you."

"I won't come to you, Melody," he said. "That's over. And I don't want you coming here anymore, or phoning, or sending telegrams, no matter what kind of trouble you're in. You understand? Do you? I want you out of my life, and when you're gone I'm going to forget you as quick as I can, 'cause, lady, you are one hell of a bad memory."

Melody cried out as if he had struck her. "NO!" she said. "No, don't say that, remember me, you have to. I'll leave you alone, I promise I will, I'll never see you again. But say you'll remember me." She stood up abruptly. "I'll go right now," she said. "If you want me to go, I'll go. But make love to me first, Ted. Please. I want to give you something to remember me by." She smiled a lascivious little smile, and began to struggle out of her halter top, and Ted felt sick.

He set down his glass with a bang. "You're crazy," he said. "You ought to get professional help, Melody. But I can't give it to you and I'm not going to put up with this anymore. I'm going out for a walk. I'll be gone a couple of hours. You be gone when I get back."

Ted started for the door. Melody stood looking at him, her halter in her hand. Her breasts looked small and shrunken, and the left one had a tattoo on it that he'd never noticed before. There was nothing even vaguely desirable about her. She whimpered. "I just wanted to give you something to remember me by," she said.

Ted slammed the door.

IT WAS MIDNIGHT WHEN HE RETURNED, DRUNK AND SURLY, RESOLVED that if Melody was still there, he would call the police and that would be the end of that. Jack was behind the desk, having just gone on duty. Ted stopped and gave him hell for having admitted Melody that morning, but the doorman denied it vehemently. "Wasn't nobody got in, Mister Cirelli. I don't let in anyone without buzzing up, you ought to know that. I been here six years, and I never let in nobody without buzzing up." Ted reminded him forcefully about the Jehovah's Witness, and they ended up in a shouting match.

Finally Ted stormed away and took the elevator up to the thirty-second floor.

There was a drawing taped to his door.

He blinked at it furiously for a moment, then snatched it down. It was a cartoon, a caricature of Melody. Not the Melody he'd seen today, but the Melody he'd known in college; sharp, funny, pretty. When they'd been roommates, Melody had always illustrated her notes with little cartoons of herself. He was surprised that she could still draw this well. Beneath the face, she'd printed a message.

I LEFT YOU SOMETHING TO REMEMBER ME BY.

Ted scowled down at the cartoon, wondering whether he should keep it or not. His own hesitation made him angry. He crumbled the paper in his hand, and fumbled for his keys. At least she's gone, he thought, and maybe for good. If she left the note, it meant that she'd gone. He was rid of her for another couple of years at least.

He went inside, tossed the crumbled ball of paper across the room towards a wastebasket, and smiled when it went in. "Two points," he said loudly to himself, drunk and self-satisfied. He went to the bar and began to mix himself a drink.

But something was wrong.

Ted stopped stirring his drink, and listened. The water was running, he realized. She'd left the water running in the bathroom.

"Christ," he said, and then an awful thought hit him; maybe she hadn't gone after all. Maybe she was still in the bathroom, taking a shower or something, freaked out of her mind, crying, whatever. "Melody!" he shouted.

No answer. The water was running all right. It couldn't be anything else. But she didn't answer.

"Melody, are you still here?" he yelled. "Answer, dammit!"

Silence.

He put down his drink and walked to the bathroom. The door was closed. Ted stood outside. The water was definitely running. "Melody," he said loudly, "are you in there? Melody?"

Nothing. Ted was beginning to be afraid.

He reached out and grasped the doorknob. It turned easily in his hand. The door hadn't been locked.

Inside the bathroom was filled with steam. He could hardly see, but he made out that the shower curtain was drawn. The shower was running full blast, and judging from the amount of steam, it must be scalding. Ted stepped back and waited for the steam to dissipate. "Melody?" he said softly. There was no reply.

"Shit," he said. He tried not to be afraid. She only talked about it, he told himself; she'd never really do it. The ones who talk about it never do it, he'd read that somewhere. She was just doing this to frighten him.

He took two quick strides across the room and yanked back the shower curtain.

She was there, wreathed in steam, water streaming down her naked body. She wasn't stretched out in the tub at all; she was sitting up, crammed in sideways near the faucets, looking very small and pathetic. Her position seemed half-fetal. The needle spray had been directed down at her, at her hands. She'd opened her wrists with his razor blades, and tried to hold them under the water, but it hadn't been enough, she'd slit the veins crosswise, and everybody knew the only way to do it was lengthwise. So she'd used the razor elsewhere, and now she had two mouths, and both of them were smiling at him, smiling. The shower had washed away most of the blood; there were no stains anywhere, but the second mouth below her chin was still red and dripping. Trickles oozed down her chest, over the flower tattooed on her breast, and the spray of the shower caught them and washed them away. Her hair hung down over her cheeks, limp and wet. She was smiling. She looked so happy. The steam was all around her. She'd been in there for hours, he thought. She was very clean.

Ted closed his eyes. It didn't make any difference. He still saw her. He would always see her.

He opened them again; Melody was still smiling. He reached across her and turned off the shower, getting the sleeve of his shirt soaked in the process.

Numb, he fled back into the living room. God, he thought, God. I have to call someone, I have to report this, I can't deal with this. He decided to call the police. He lifted the phone, and hesitated with his finger poised over the buttons. The police won't help, he thought. He punched for Jill.

When he had finished telling her, it grew very silent on the other end of the phone. "My God," she said at last. "How awful. Can I do anything?"

"Come over," he said. "Right away." He found the drink he'd set down, took a hurried sip from it.

Jill hesitated. "Er—look, Ted, I'm not very good at dealing with corpses," she said. "Why don't you come over here? I don't want to—well, you know. I don't think I'll ever shower at your place again."

"Jill," he said, stricken. "I need someone right now." He laughed a frightened, uncertain laugh.

"Come over here," she urged.

"I can't just *leave* it there," he said.

"Well, don't," she said. "Call the police. They'll take it away. Come over afterwards."

Ted called the police.

"IF THIS IS YOUR IDEA OF A JOKE, IT ISN'T FUNNY," THE PATROLMAN said. His partner was scowling.

"Joke?" Ted said.

"There's nothing in your shower," the patrolman said. "I ought to take you down to the station house."

"Nothing in the shower?" Ted repeated, incredulous.

"Leave him alone, Sam," the partner said. "He's stinko, can't you tell?"

Ted rushed past them both into the bathroom.

The tub was empty. Empty. He knelt and felt the bottom of it. Dry. Perfectly dry. But his shirt sleeve was still damp. "No," he said, "no." He rushed back out to the living room. The two cops watched him with amusement. Her suitcase was gone from its place by the door. The dishes had all been run through the dishwasher, no way to tell if anyone had made pancakes or not. Ted turned the wastebasket upside down, spilling out the contents all over his couch. He began to scrabble through the papers.

"Go to bed and sleep it off, mister," the older cop said. "You'll feel better in the morning."

"C'mon," his partner said. They departed, leaving Ted still pawing through the papers. No cartoon. No cartoon. No cartoon.

Ted flung the empty wastebasket across the room, and it caromed off the wall with a ringing metallic clang.

He took a cab to Jill's.

———

IT WAS NEAR DAWN WHEN HE SAT UP IN BED SUDDENLY, HIS HEART thumping, his mouth dry with fear.

Jill murmured sleepily. "Jill," he said, shaking her.

She blinked up at him. "What?" she said. "What time is it, Ted? What's wrong?" She sat up, pulling up the blanket to cover herself.

"Don't you hear it?"

"Hear what?" she asked.

He giggled. "Your shower is running."

That morning he shaved in the kitchen, even though there was no mirror. He cut himself twice. His bladder ached, but he would not go past the bathroom door, despite Jill's repeated assurances that the shower was not running. Dammit, he could *hear* it. He waited until he got to the office. There was no shower in the washroom there.

But Jill looked at him strangely.

———

AT THE OFFICE, TED CLEARED HIS DESK, AND TRIED TO THINK. HE WAS a lawyer. He had a good, analytical mind. He tried to reason it out. He drank only coffee, lots of coffee.

No suitcase, he thought. Jack hadn't seen her. No corpse. No cartoon. No one had seen her. The shower was dry. No dishes. He'd been drinking. But not all day, only later, after dinner. Couldn't be the drinking. Couldn't be. No cartoon. He was the only one who'd seen her. No cartoon. I LEFT YOU SOMETHING TO REMEMBER ME BY. He'd crumpled up her cable, and flushed her away. Two years ago. Nothing in the shower.

He picked up his phone. "Billie," he said, "get me a newspaper in Des Moines, Iowa. Any newspaper, I don't care."

When he finally got through, the woman who tended the morgue was reluctant to give him any information. But she softened when he told her he was a lawyer, and needed the information for an important case.

The obituary was very short. Melody was identified only as a "massage parlor employee." She'd killed herself in her shower.

"Thank you," Ted said. He set down the receiver. For a long time he sat staring out of his window. He had a very good view; he could see the lake and the soaring tower of the Standard Oil building. He pondered what to do next. There was a thick knot of fear in his gut.

He could take the day off and go home. But the shower would be running at home, and sooner or later he would have to go in there.

He could go back to Jill's. If Jill would have him. She'd seemed awfully cool after last night. She'd recommended a shrink to him as they shared a cab to the office. She didn't understand. No one would understand . . . unless . . . he picked up the phone again, searching through his circular file. There was no card, no number, they'd drifted that far apart. He buzzed for Billie again. "Get me through to Random House in New York City," he said. "To Mr. Michael Englehart. He's an editor there."

But when he finally connected, the voice on the other end of the line was strange and distant. "Mister Cirelli? Were you a friend of Michael's? Or one of his authors?"

Ted's mouth was dry. "A friend," he said. "Isn't Michael in? I need to talk to him. It's . . . urgent."

"I'm afraid Michael's no longer with us," the voice said. "He had a nervous breakdown, less than a week ago."

"Is he . . . ?"

"He's alive. They took him to a hospital, I believe. You know. Maybe I can find you the number."

"No," Ted said. "No, that's quite all right." He hung up.

Phoenix directory assistance had no listing for an Anne Kaye. Of course not, he thought. She was married now. He tried to remember her married name. It took him a long time. Something Polish, he thought. Finally it came to him.

He hadn't expected to find her at home. It was a school day, after all. But someone picked up the phone on the third ring. "Hello," he said. "Anne, is that you? This is Ted, in Chicago. Anne, I've got to talk to you. It's about Melody. Anne, I need your help." He was breathless.

There was a giggle. "Anne isn't here right now, Ted," Melody said. "She's off at school, and then she's got to visit her husband. They're separated, you know. But she promised to come back by eight."

"Melody," he said.

"Of course, I don't know if I can believe her. You three were never very good about promises. But maybe she'll come back, Ted. I hope so.

"I want to leave her something to remember me by."

SANDKINGS

❖

SIMON KRESS LIVED ALONE IN A SPRAWLING MANOR HOUSE AMONG the dry, rocky hills fifty kilometers from the city. So, when he was called away unexpectedly on business, he had no neighbors he could conveniently impose on to take his pets. The carrion hawk was no problem; it roosted in the unused belfry and customarily fed itself anyway. The shambler Kress simply shooed outside and left to fend for itself; the little monster would gorge on slugs and birds and rockjocks. But the fish tank, stocked with genuine Earth piranha, posed a difficulty. Kress finally just threw a haunch of beef into the huge tank. The piranha could always eat one another if he were detained longer than expected. They'd done it before. It amused him.

Unfortunately, he was detained *much* longer than expected this time. When he finally returned, all the fish were dead. So was the carrion hawk. The shambler had climbed up to the belfry and eaten it. Simon Kress was vexed.

The next day he flew his skimmer to Asgard, a journey of some two hundred kilometers. Asgard was Baldur's largest city and boasted the oldest and largest starport as well. Kress liked to impress his friends with animals that were unusual, entertaining, and expensive; Asgard was the place to buy them.

This time, though, he had poor luck. Xenopets had closed its doors, t'Etherane the Petseller tried to foist another carrion hawk off on him, and Strange Waters offered nothing more exotic than piranha, glow-sharks, and spider squids. Kress had had all those; he wanted something new.

Near dusk, he found himself walking down the Rainbow Boulevard, looking for places he had not patronized before. So close to the starport, the street was lined by importers' marts. The big corporate emporiums had impressive long windows, where rare and costly alien artifacts reposed on felt cushions against dark drapes that made the interiors of the stores a mystery. Between them were the junk shops—narrow, nasty little places whose display areas were crammed with all manner of offworld bric-a-brac. Kress tried both kinds of shop, with equal dissatisfaction.

Then he came across a store that was different.

It was quite close to the port. Kress had never been there before. The shop occupied a small, single-story building of moderate size, set between a euphoria bar and a temple-brothel of the Secret Sisterhood. Down this far, the Rainbow Boulevard grew tacky. The shop itself was unusual. Arresting.

The windows were full of mist; now a pale red, now the gray of true fog, now sparkling and golden. The mist swirled and eddied and glowed faintly from within. Kress glimpsed objects in the window—machines, pieces of art, other things he could not recognize—but he could not get a good look at any of them. The mists flowed sensuously around them, displaying a bit of first one thing and then another, then cloaking all. It was intriguing.

As he watched, the mist began to form letters. One word at a time. Kress stood and read:

WO. AND. SHADE. IMPORTERS. ARTIFACTS. ART. LIFEFORMS. AND. MISC.

The letters stopped. Through the fog, Kress saw something moving. That was enough for him, that and the word "Lifeforms" in their advertisement. He swept his walking cloak over his shoulder and entered the store.

Inside, Kress felt disoriented. The interior seemed vast, much larger than he would have guessed from the relatively modest frontage. It was dimly lit, peaceful. The ceiling was a starscape, complete with spiral nebulae, very dark and realistic, very nice. The counters all shone faintly, the better to display the merchandise within. The aisles were carpeted with ground fog. In places, it came almost to his knees and swirled about his feet as he walked.

"Can I help you?"

She seemed almost to have risen from the fog. Tall and gaunt and pale, she wore a practical gray jumpsuit and a strange little cap that rested well back on her head.

"Are you Wo or Shade?" Kress asked. "Or only sales help?"

"Jala Wo, ready to serve you," she replied. "Shade does not see customers. We have no sales help."

"You have quite a large establishment," Kress said. "Odd that I have never heard of you before."

"We have only just opened this shop on Baldur," the woman said. "We have franchises on a number of other worlds, however. What can I sell you? Art, perhaps? You have the look of a collector. We have some fine Nor T'alush crystal carvings."

"No," Simon Kress said. "I own all the crystal carvings I desire. I came to see about a pet."

"A lifeform?"

"Yes."

"Alien?"

"Of course."

"We have a mimic in stock. From Celia's World. A clever little simian. Not only will it learn to speak, but eventually it will mimic your voice, inflections, gestures, even facial expressions."

"Cute," said Kress. "And common. I have no use for either, Wo. I want something exotic. Unusual. And not cute. I detest cute animals. At the moment I own a shambler. Imported from Cotho, at no mean expense. From time to time I feed him a litter of unwanted kittens. That is what I think of *cute*. Do I make myself understood?"

Wo smiled enigmatically. "Have you ever owned an animal that worshipped you?" she asked.

Kress grinned. "Oh, now and again. But I don't require worship, Wo. Just entertainment."

"You misunderstood me," Wo said, still wearing her strange smile. "I meant worship literally."

"What are you talking about?"

"I think I have just the thing for you," Wo said. "Follow me."

She led Kress between the radiant counters and down a long, fog-shrouded aisle beneath false starlight. They passed through a wall of mist into another section of the store, and stopped before a large plastic tank. An aquarium, thought Kress.

Wo beckoned. He stepped closer and saw that he was wrong. It was a terrarium. Within lay a miniature desert about two meters square. Pale and bleached scarlet by wan red light. Rocks: basalt and quartz and granite. In each corner of the tank stood a castle.

Kress blinked, and peered, and corrected himself; actually only three castles stood. The fourth leaned; a crumbled, broken ruin. The other three were crude but intact, carved of stone and sand. Over their battlements and through their rounded porticoes, tiny creatures climbed and scrambled. Kress pressed his face against the plastic. "Insects?" he asked.

"No," Wo replied. "A much more complex lifeform. More intelligent as well. Considerably smarter than your shambler. They are called sandkings."

"Insects," Kress said, drawing back from the tank. "I don't care how complex they are." He frowned. "And kindly don't try to gull me with this talk of intelligence. These things are far too small to have anything but the most rudimentary brains."

"They share hiveminds," Wo said. "Castle minds, in this case. There are only three organisms in the tank, actually. The fourth died. You see how her castle has fallen."

Kress looked back at the tank. "Hiveminds, eh? Interesting." He frowned again. "Still, it is only an oversized ant farm. I'd hoped for something better."

"They fight wars."

"Wars? Hmmm." Kress looked again.

"Note the colors, if you will," Wo told him. She pointed to the creatures that swarmed over the nearest castle. One was scrabbling at the tank wall. Kress studied it. It still looked like an insect to his eyes. Barely as long as his fingernail, six-limbed, with six tiny eyes set all around its body. A wicked set of mandibles clacked visibly, while two long, fine antennae wove patterns in the air. Antennae, mandibles, eyes, and legs were sooty black, but the dominant color was the burnt orange of its armor plating. "It's an insect," Kress repeated.

"It is not an insect," Wo insisted calmly. "The armored exoskeleton is shed when the sandking grows larger. *If* it grows larger. In a tank this size, it won't." She took Kress by the elbow and led him around the tank to the next castle. "Look at the colors here."

He did. They were different. Here the sandkings had bright red armor; antennae, mandibles, eyes, and legs were yellow. Kress glanced across the tank. The denizens of the third live castle were off-white, with red trim. "Hmmm," he said.

"They war, as I said," Wo told him. "They even have truces and alliances. It was an alliance that destroyed the fourth castle in this tank. The blacks were getting too numerous, so the others joined forces to destroy them."

Kress remained unconvinced. "Amusing, no doubt. But insects fight wars too."

"Insects do not worship," Wo said.

"Eh?"

Wo smiled and pointed at the castle. Kress stared. A face had been carved into the wall of the highest tower. He recognized it. It was Jala Wo's face. "How . . . ?"

"I projected a hologram of my face into the tank, kept it there for a few days. The face of god, you see? I feed them; I am always close. The sandkings have a rudimentary psionic sense. Proximity telepathy. They sense me, and worship me by using my face to decorate their buildings. All the castles have them, see." They did.

On the castle, the face of Jala Wo was serene and peaceful, and very lifelike. Kress marveled at the workmanship. "How do they do it?"

"The foremost legs double as arms. They even have fingers of a sort; three small, flexible tendrils. And they cooperate well, both in building and in battle. Remember, all the mobiles of one color share a single mind."

"Tell me more," Kress said.

Wo smiled. "The maw lives in the castle. Maw is my name for her. A pun, if you will; the thing is mother and stomach both. Female, large as your fist, immobile. Actually, sandking is a bit of a misnomer. The mobiles are peasants and warriors, the real ruler is a queen. But that analogy is faulty as well. Considered as a whole, each castle is a single hermaphroditic creature."

"What do they eat?"

"The mobiles eat pap—predigested food obtained inside the castle. They get it from the maw after she has worked on it for several days. Their stomachs can't handle anything else, so if the maw dies, they soon die as well. The maw . . . the maw eats anything. You'll have no special expense there. Table scraps will do excellently."

"Live food?" Kress asked.

Wo shrugged. "Each maw eats mobiles from the other castles, yes."

"I am intrigued," he admitted. "If only they weren't so small."

"Yours can be larger. These sandkings are small because their tank is small. They seem to limit their growth to fit available space. If I moved these to a larger tank, they'd start growing again."

"Hmmm. My piranha tank is twice this size, and vacant. It could be cleaned out, filled with sand. . . ."

"Wo and Shade would take care of the installation. It would be our pleasure."

"Of course," said Kress, "I would expect four intact castles."

"Certainly," Wo said.

They began to haggle about the price.

THREE DAYS LATER JALA WO ARRIVED AT SIMON KRESS' ESTATE, with dormant sandkings and a work crew to take charge of the installation. Wo's assistants were aliens unlike any Kress was familiar with—squat, broad bipeds with four arms and bulging, multifaceted eyes. Their skin was thick and leathery, twisted into horns and spines and protrusions at odd spots upon their bodies. But they were very strong, and good workers. Wo ordered them about in a musical tongue that Kress had never heard.

In a day it was done. They moved his piranha tank to the center of his spacious living room, arranged couches on either side of it for better viewing, scrubbed it clean, and filled it two-thirds of the way up with sand and rock. Then they installed a special lighting system, both to provide the dim red illumination the sandkings preferred and to project holographic images into the tank. On top they mounted a sturdy plastic cover, with a feeder mechanism built in. "This way you can feed your sandkings without removing the top of the tank," Wo explained. "You would not want to take any chances on the mobiles escaping."

The cover also included climate control devices, to condense just the right amount of moisture from the air. "You want it dry, but not too dry," Wo said.

Finally one of the four-armed workers climbed into the tank and dug deep pits in the four corners. One of his companions handed the dormant maws over to him, removing them one by one from their frosted cryonic traveling cases. They were nothing to look at. Kress decided they resembled nothing so much as a mottled, half-spoiled chunk of raw meat. With a mouth.

The alien buried them, one in each corner of the tank. Then they sealed it all up and took their leave.

"The heat will bring the maws out of dormancy," Wo said. "In less than a week, mobiles will begin to hatch and burrow to the surface. Be certain to give them plenty of food. They will need all their strength until they are well established. I would estimate that you will have castles rising in about three weeks."

"And my face? When will they carve my face?"

"Turn on the hologram after about a month," she advised him. "And be patient. If you have any questions, please call. Wo and Shade are at your service." She bowed and left.

Kress wandered back to the tank and lit a joy-stick. The desert was still and empty. He drummed his fingers impatiently against the plastic, and frowned.

ON THE FOURTH DAY, KRESS THOUGHT HE GLIMPSED MOTION BENEATH the sand, subtle subterranean stirrings.

On the fifth day, he saw his first mobile, a lone white.

On the sixth day, he counted a dozen of them, whites and reds and blacks. The oranges were tardy. He cycled through a bowl of half-decayed table scraps. The mobiles sensed it at once, rushed to it, and began to drag pieces back to their respective corners. Each color group was very organized. They did not fight. Kress was a bit disappointed, but he decided to give them time.

The oranges made their appearance on the eighth day. By then the other sandkings had begun to carry small stones and erect crude fortifications. They still did not war. At the moment they were only half the size of those he had seen at Wo and Shade's, but Kress thought they were growing rapidly.

The castles began to rise midway through the second week. Organized battalions of mobiles dragged heavy chunks of sandstone and granite to their corners, where other mobiles were pushing sand into place with mandibles and tendrils. Kress had purchased a pair of magnifying goggles so he could watch them work, wherever they might go in the tank. He wandered around and around the tall plastic walls, observing. It was fascinating. The castles were a bit plainer than Kress would have liked, but he had an idea about that. The next day he cycled through some obsidian and flakes of colored glass along with the food. Within hours, they had been incorporated into the castle walls.

The black castle was the first completed, followed by the white and red fortresses. The oranges were last, as usual. Kress took his meals into the living room and ate seated on the couch, so he could watch. He expected the first war to break out any hour now.

He was disappointed. Days passed; the castles grew taller and more grand, and Kress seldom left the tank except to attend to his sanitary needs and answer critical business calls. But the sandkings did not war. He was getting upset.

Finally, he stopped feeding them.

Two days after the table scraps had ceased to fall from their desert sky, four black mobiles surrounded an orange and dragged it back to their maw. They maimed it first, ripping off its mandibles and antennae and limbs, and carried it through the shadowed main gate of their miniature castle. It never emerged. Within an hour, more than forty orange mobiles marched across the sand and attacked the blacks' corner. They were outnumbered by the blacks that came rushing up from the depths. When the fighting was over, the attackers had been slaughtered. The dead and dying were taken down to feed the black maw.

Kress, delighted, congratulated himself on his genius.

When he put food into the tank the following day, a three-cornered battle broke out over its possession. The whites were the big winners. After that, war followed war.

ALMOST A MONTH TO THE DAY AFTER JALA WO HAD DELIVERED THE
sandkings, Kress turned on the hologram projector, and his face materialized in the tank. It turned, slowly, around and around so his gaze
fell on all four castles equally. Kress thought it rather a good likeness—
it had his impish grin, wide mouth, full cheeks. His blue eyes sparkled,
his gray hair was carefully arrayed in a fashionable sidesweep, his eyebrows were thin and sophisticated.

Soon enough, the sandkings set to work. Kress fed them lavishly
while his image beamed down at them from their sky. Temporarily, the
wars stopped. All activity was directed toward worship.

His face emerged on the castle walls.

At first all four carvings looked alike to him, but as the work continued and Kress studied the reproductions, he began to detect subtle
differences in technique and execution. The reds were the most creative, using tiny flakes of slate to put the gray in his hair. The white idol
seemed young and mischievous to him, while the face shaped by the
blacks—although virtually the same, line for line—struck him as wise
and beneficent. The orange sandkings, as ever, were last and least. The
wars had not gone well for them, and their castle was sad compared to
the others. The image they carved was crude and cartoonish, and they
seemed to intend to leave it that way. When they stopped work on the
face, Kress grew quite piqued with them, but there was really nothing
he could do.

When all the sandkings had finished their Kress-faces, he turned off
the hologram and decided that it was time to have a party. His friends
would be impressed. He could even stage a war for them, he thought.
Humming happily to himself, he began to draw up a guest list.

The party was a wild success.

Kress invited thirty people: a handful of close friends who shared
his amusements, a few former lovers, and a collection of business and
social rivals who could not afford to ignore his summons. He knew
some of them would be discomfited and even offended by his sandkings. He counted on it. Simon Kress customarily considered his parties a failure unless at least one guest walked out in high dudgeon.

On impulse he added Jala Wo's name to his list. "Bring Shade if
you like," he added when dictating her invitation.

Her acceptance surprised him just a bit. "Shade, alas, will be unable to attend. He does not go to social functions," Wo added. "As for myself, I look forward to the chance to see how your sandkings are doing."

Kress ordered them up a sumptuous meal. And when at last the conversation had died down, and most of his guests had gotten silly on wine and joy-sticks, he shocked them by personally scraping their table leavings into a large bowl. "Come, all of you," he told them. "I want to introduce you to my newest pets." Carrying the bowl, he conducted them into his living room.

The sandkings lived up to his fondest expectations. He had starved them for two days in preparation, and they were in a fighting mood. While the guests ringed the tank, looking through the magnifying glasses Kress had thoughtfully provided, the sandkings waged a glorious battle over the scraps. He counted almost sixty dead mobiles when the struggle was over. The reds and whites, who had recently formed an alliance, emerged with most of the food.

"Kress, you're disgusting," Cath m'Lane told him. She had lived with him for a short time two years before, until her soppy sentimentality almost drove him mad. "I was a fool to come back here. I thought perhaps you'd changed, wanted to apologize." She had never forgiven him for the time his shambler had eaten an excessively cute puppy of which she had been fond. "Don't *ever* invite me here again, Simon." She strode out, accompanied by her current lover and a chorus of laughter.

His other guests were full of questions.

Where did the sandkings come from? they wanted to know. "From Wo and Shade, Importers," he replied, with a polite gesture toward Jala Wo, who had remained quiet and apart through most of the evening.

Why did they decorate their castles with his likeness? "Because I am the source of all good things. Surely you know that?" That brought a round of chuckles.

Will they fight again? "Of course, but not tonight. Don't worry. There will be other parties."

Jad Rakkis, who was an amateur xenologist, began talking about other social insects and the wars they fought. "These sandkings are amusing, but nothing really. You ought to read about Terran soldier ants, for instance."

"Sandkings are not insects," Jala Wo said sharply, but Jad was off and running, and no one paid her the slightest attention. Kress smiled at her and shrugged.

Malada Blane suggested a betting pool the next time they got together to watch a war, and everyone was taken with the idea. An animated discussion about rules and odds ensued. It lasted for almost an hour. Finally the guests began to take their leave.

Jala Wo was the last to depart. "So," Kress said to her when they were alone, "it appears my sandkings are a hit."

"They are doing well," Wo said. "Already they are larger than my own."

"Yes," Kress said, "except for the oranges."

"I had noticed that," Wo replied. "They seem few in number, and their castle is shabby."

"Well, someone must lose," Kress said. "The oranges were late to emerge and get established. They have suffered for it."

"Pardon," said Wo, "but might I ask if you are feeding your sandkings sufficiently?"

Kress shrugged. "They diet from time to time. It makes them fiercer."

She frowned. "There is no need to starve them. Let them war in their own time, for their own reasons. It is their nature, and you will witness conflicts that are delightfully subtle and complex. The constant war brought on by hunger is artless and degrading."

Simon Kress repaid Wo's frown with interest. "You are in my house, Wo, and here I am the judge of what is degrading. I fed the sandkings as you advised, and they did not fight."

"You must have patience."

"No," Kress said. "I am their master and their god, after all. Why should I wait on their impulses? They did not war often enough to suit me. I corrected the situation."

"I see," said Wo. "I will discuss the matter with Shade."

"It is none of your concern, or his," Kress snapped.

"I must bid you good night, then," Wo said with resignation. But as she slipped into her coat to depart, she fixed him with a final disapproving stare. "Look to your faces, Simon Kress," she warned him. "Look to your faces."

Puzzled, he wandered back to the tank and stared at the castles after she had taken her departure. His faces were still there, as ever. Except—he snatched up his magnifying goggles and slipped them on. Even then it was hard to make out. But it seemed to him that the expression on the face of his images had changed slightly, that his smile was somehow twisted so that it seemed a touch malicious. But it was a very subtle change, if it was a change at all. Kress finally put it down to his suggestibility, and resolved not to invite Jala Wo to any more of his gatherings.

OVER THE NEXT FEW MONTHS, KRESS AND ABOUT A DOZEN OF HIS favorites got together weekly for what he liked to call his "war games." Now that his initial fascination with the sandkings was past, Kress spent less time around his tank and more on his business affairs and his social life, but he still enjoyed having a few friends over for a war or two. He kept the combatants sharp on a constant edge of hunger. It had severe effects on the orange sandkings, who dwindled visibly until Kress began to wonder if their maw was dead. But the others did well enough.

Sometimes at night, when he could not sleep, Kress would take a bottle of wine into the darkened living room, where the red gloom of his miniature desert was the only light. He would drink and watch for hours, alone. There was usually a fight going on somewhere, and when there was not he could easily start one by dropping in some small morsel of food.

They took to betting on the weekly battles, as Malada Blane had suggested. Kress won a good amount by betting on the whites, who had become the most powerful and numerous colony in the tank, with the grandest castle. One week he slid the corner of the tank top aside, and dropped the food close to the white castle instead of on the central battleground as usual, so that the others had to attack the whites in their stronghold to get any food at all. They tried. The whites were brilliant in defense. Kress won a hundred standards from Jad Rakkis.

Rakkis, in fact, lost heavily on the sandkings almost every week. He pretended to a vast knowledge of them and their ways, claiming that he had studied them after the first party, but he had no luck when it came to placing his bets. Kress suspected that Jad's claims were empty boasting. He had tried to study the sandkings a bit himself, in a moment of idle curiosity, tying in to the library to find out to what world his pets were native. But there was no listing for them. He wanted to get in touch with Wo and ask her about it, but he had other concerns, and the matter kept slipping his mind.

Finally, after a month in which his losses totaled more than a thousand standards, Jad Rakkis arrived at the war games carrying a small plastic case under his arm. Inside was a spiderlike thing covered with fine golden hair.

"A sand spider," Rakkis announced. "From Cathaday. I got it this afternoon from t'Etherane the Petseller. Usually they remove the poison sacs, but this one is intact. Are you game, Simon? I want my money back. I'll bet a thousand standards, sand spider against sandkings."

Kress studied the spider in its plastic prison. His sandkings had grown—they were twice as large as Wo's, as she'd predicted—but they were still dwarfed by this thing. It was venomed, and they were not. Still, there were an awful lot of them. Besides, the endless sandking wars had begun to grow tiresome lately. The novelty of the match intrigued him. "Done," Kress said. "Jad, you are a fool. The sandkings will just keep coming until this ugly creature of yours is dead."

"You are the fool, Simon," Rakkis replied, smiling. "The Cathadayn sand spider customarily feeds on burrowers that hide in nooks and crevices and—well, watch—it will go straight into those castles, and eat the maws."

Kress scowled amid general laughter. He hadn't counted on that. "Get on with it," he said irritably. He went to freshen his drink.

The spider was too large to cycle conveniently through the food chamber. Two of the others helped Rakkis slide the tank top slightly to one side, and Malada Blane handed him up his case. He shook the spider out. It landed lightly on a miniature dune in front of the red castle, and stood confused for a moment, mouth working, legs twitching menacingly.

"Come on," Rakkis urged. They all gathered round the tank. Simon Kress found his magnifiers and slipped them on. If he was going to lose a thousand standards, at least he wanted a good view of the action.

The sandkings had seen the invader. All over the castle, activity had ceased. The small scarlet mobiles were frozen, watching.

The spider began to move toward the dark promise of the gate. On the tower above, Simon Kress' countenance stared down impassively.

At once there was a flurry of activity. The nearest red mobiles formed themselves into two wedges and streamed over the sand toward the spider. More warriors erupted from inside the castle and assembled in a triple line to guard the approach to the underground chamber where the maw lived. Scouts came scuttling over the dunes, recalled to fight.

Battle was joined.

The attacking sandkings washed over the spider. Mandibles snapped shut on legs and abdomen, and clung. Reds raced up the golden legs to the invader's back. They bit and tore. One of them found an eye, and ripped it loose with tiny yellow tendrils. Kress smiled and pointed.

But they were *small,* and they had no venom, and the spider did not stop. Its legs flicked sandkings off to either side. Its dripping jaws found others, and left them broken and stiffening. Already a dozen of the reds lay dying. The sand spider came on and on. It strode straight through the triple line of guardians before the castle. The lines closed around it, covered it, waging desperate battle. A team of sandkings had bitten off one of the spider's legs, Kress saw. Defenders leaped from atop the towers to land on the twitching, heaving mass.

Lost beneath the sandkings, the spider somehow lurched down into the darkness and vanished.

Jad Rakkis let out a long breath. He looked pale. "Wonderful," someone else said. Malada Blane chuckled deep in her throat.

"Look," said Idi Noreddian, tugging Kress by the arm.

They had been so intent on the struggle in the corner that none of them had noticed the activity elsewhere in the tank. But now the castle was still, the sands empty save for dead red mobiles, and now they saw.

Three armies were drawn up before the red castle. They stood quite still, in perfect array, rank after rank of sandkings, orange and white and black. Waiting to see what emerged from the depths.

Simon Kress smiled. "A *cordon sanitaire,*" he said. "And glance at the other castles, if you will, Jad."

Rakkis did, and swore. Teams of mobiles were sealing up the gates with sand and stone. If the spider somehow survived this encounter, it would find no easy entrance at the other castles. "I should have brought four spiders," Jad Rakkis said. "Still, I've won. My spider is down there right now, eating your damned maw."

Kress did not reply. He waited. There was motion in the shadows.

All at once, red mobiles began pouring out of the gate. They took their positions on the castle, and began repairing the damage the spider had wrought. The other armies dissolved and began to retreat to their respective corners.

"Jad," said Simon Kress, "I think you are a bit confused about who is eating who."

THE FOLLOWING WEEK RAKKIS BROUGHT FOUR SLIM SILVER SNAKES. The sandkings dispatched them without much trouble.

Next he tried a large black bird. It ate more than thirty white mobiles, and its thrashing and blundering virtually destroyed their castle, but ultimately its wings grew tired, and the sandkings attacked in force wherever it landed.

After that it was a case of insects, armored beetles not too unlike the sandkings themselves. But stupid, stupid. An allied force of oranges and blacks broke their formation, divided them, and butchered them.

Rakkis began giving Kress promissory notes.

It was around that time that Kress met Cath m'Lane again, one evening when he was dining in Asgard at his favorite restaurant. He stopped at her table briefly and told her about the war games, inviting her to join them. She flushed, then regained control of herself and grew icy. "Someone has to put a stop to you, Simon. I guess it's going to be me," she said. Kress shrugged and enjoyed a lovely meal and thought no more about her threat.

Until a week later, when a small, stout woman arrived at his door and showed him a police wristband. "We've had complaints," she said. "Do you keep a tank full of dangerous insects, Kress?"

"Not insects," he said, furious. "Come, I'll show you."

When she had seen the sandkings, she shook her head. "This will never do. What do you know about these creatures, anyway? Do you know what world they're from? Have they been cleared by the ecological board? Do you have a license for these things? We have a report that they're carnivores, possibly dangerous. We also have a report that they are semi-sentient. Where did you get these creatures, anyway?"

"From Wo and Shade," Kress replied.

"Never heard of them," the woman said. "Probably smuggled them in, knowing our ecologists would never approve them. No, Kress, this won't do. I'm going to confiscate this tank and have it destroyed. And you're going to have to expect a few fines as well."

Kress offered her a hundred standards to forget all about him and his sandkings.

She tsked. "Now I'll have to add attempted bribery to the charges against you."

Not until he raised the figure to two thousand standards was she willing to be persuaded.

"It's not going to be easy, you know," she said. "There are forms to be altered, records to be wiped. And getting a forged license from the ecologists will be time-consuming. Not to mention dealing with the complainant. What if she calls again?"

"Leave her to me," Kress said. "Leave her to me."

———

HE THOUGHT ABOUT IT FOR A WHILE. THAT NIGHT HE MADE SOME CALLS.

First he got t'Etherane the Petseller. "I want to buy a dog," he said. "A puppy."

The round-faced merchant gawked at him. "A puppy? That is not like you, Simon. Why don't you come in? I have a lovely choice."

"I want a very specific *kind* of puppy," Kress said. "Take notes. I'll describe to you what it must look like."

Afterward he punched for Idi Noreddian. "Idi," he said, "I want you out here tonight with your holo equipment. I have a notion to record a sandking battle. A present for one of my friends."

The night after they made the recording, Simon Kress stayed up late. He absorbed a controversial new drama in his sensorium, fixed himself a small snack, smoked a joy-stick or two, and broke out a bottle of wine. Feeling very happy with himself, he wandered into the living room, glass in hand.

The lights were out. The red glow of the terrarium made the shad-

ows flushed and feverish. He walked over to look at his domain, curious as to how the blacks were doing in the repairs on their castle. The
puppy had left it in ruins.

The restoration went well. But as Kress inspected the work through
his magnifiers, he chanced to glance closely at the face. It startled him.

He drew back, blinked, took a healthy gulp of wine, and looked
again.

The face on the wall was still his. But it was all wrong, all *twisted*.
His cheeks were bloated and piggish, his smile was a crooked leer. He
looked impossibly malevolent.

Uneasy, he moved around the tank to inspect the other castles.
They were each a bit different, but ultimately all the same.

The oranges had left out most of the fine detail, but the result still
seemed monstrous, crude—a brutal mouth and mindless eyes.

The reds gave him a Satanic, twitching kind of smile. His mouth
did odd, unlovely things at its corners.

The whites, his favorites, had carved a cruel idiot god.

Simon Kress flung his wine across the room in rage. "You *dare*," he
said under his breath. "Now you won't eat for a week, you damned . . ."
His voice was shrill. "I'll teach you." He had an idea. He strode out of
the room, and returned a moment later with an antique iron throwing-
sword in his hand. It was a meter long, and the point was still sharp. Kress
smiled, climbed up, and moved the tank cover aside just enough to give
him working room, opening one corner of the desert. He leaned down,
and jabbed the sword at the white castle below him. He waved it back
and forth, smashing towers and ramparts and walls. Sand and stone collapsed, burying the scrambling mobiles. A flick of his wrist obliterated
the features of the insolent, insulting caricature the sandkings had made
of his face. Then he poised the point of the sword above the dark mouth
that opened down into the maw's chamber, and thrust with all his
strength. He heard a soft, squishing sound, and met resistance. All of the
mobiles trembled and collapsed. Satisfied, Kress pulled back.

He watched for a moment, wondering whether he'd killed the maw.
The point of the throwing-sword was wet and slimy. But finally the
white sandkings began to move again. Feebly, slowly, but they moved.

He was preparing to slide the cover back in place and move on to
a second castle when he felt something crawling on his hand.

He screamed and dropped the sword, and brushed the sandking from his flesh. It fell to the carpet, and he ground it beneath his heel, crushing it thoroughly long after it was dead. It had crunched when he stepped on it. After that, trembling, he hurried to seal the tank up again, and rushed off to shower and inspect himself carefully. He boiled his clothing.

Later, after several fresh glasses of wine, he returned to the living room. He was a bit ashamed of the way the sandking had terrified him. But he was not about to open the tank again. From now on, the cover stayed sealed permanently. Still, he had to punish the others.

Kress decided to lubricate his mental processes with another glass of wine. As he finished it, an inspiration came to him. He went to the tank smiling, and made a few adjustments to the humidity controls.

By the time he fell asleep on the couch, his wine glass still in his hand, the sand castles were melting in the rain.

––––––––

KRESS WOKE TO ANGRY POUNDING ON HIS DOOR.

He sat up, groggy, his head throbbing. Wine hangovers were always the worst, he thought. He lurched to the entry chamber.

Cath m'Lane was outside. "You monster," she said, her face swollen and puffy and streaked by tears. "I cried all night, damn you. But no more, Simon, no more."

"Easy," he said, holding his head. "I've got a hangover."

She swore and shoved him aside and pushed her way into his house. The shambler came peering round a corner to see what the noise was. She spat at it and stalked into the living room, Kress trailing ineffectually after her. "Hold on," he said. "Where do you . . . you can't . . ." He stopped, suddenly horrorstruck. She was carrying a heavy sledgehammer in her left hand. "No," he said.

She went directly to the sandking tank. "You like the little charmers so much, Simon? Then you can live with them."

"Cath!" he shrieked.

Gripping the hammer with both hands, she swung as hard as she could against the side of the tank. The sound of the impact set his head to screaming, and Kress made a low blubbering sound of despair. But the plastic held.

She swung again. This time there was a *crack,* and a network of thin lines sprang into being.

Kress threw himself at her as she drew back her hammer for a third swing. They went down flailing, and rolled. She lost her grip on the hammer and tried to throttle him, but Kress wrenched free and bit her on the arm, drawing blood. They both staggered to their feet, panting.

"You should see yourself, Simon," she said grimly. "Blood dripping from your mouth. You look like one of your pets. How do you like the taste?"

"Get out," he said. He saw the throwing-sword where it had fallen the night before, and snatched it up. "Get out," he repeated, waving the sword for emphasis. "Don't go near that tank again."

She laughed at him. "You wouldn't dare," she said. She bent to pick up her hammer.

Kress shrieked at her, and lunged. Before he quite knew what was happening, the iron blade had gone clear through her abdomen. Cath m'Lane looked at him wonderingly, and down at the sword. Kress fell back whimpering. "I didn't mean . . . I only wanted . . ."

She was transfixed, bleeding, dead, but somehow she did not fall. "You monster," she managed to say, though her mouth was full of blood. And she whirled, impossibly, the sword in her, and swung with her last strength at the tank. The tortured wall shattered, and Cath m'Lane was buried beneath an avalanche of plastic and sand and mud.

Kress made small hysterical noises and scrambled up on the couch.

Sandkings were emerging from the muck on his living room floor. They were crawling across Cath's body. A few of them ventured tentatively out across the carpet. More followed.

He watched as a column took shape, a living, writhing square of sandkings, bearing something, something slimy and featureless, a piece of raw meat big as a man's head. They began to carry it away from the tank. It pulsed.

That was when Kress broke and ran.

———

IT WAS LATE AFTERNOON BEFORE HE FOUND THE COURAGE TO RETURN. He had run to his skimmer and flown to the nearest city, some fifty kilometers away, almost sick with fear. But once safely away, he had found a small restaurant, put down several mugs of coffee and two anti-hangover tabs, eaten a full breakfast, and gradually regained his composure.

It had been a dreadful morning, but dwelling on that would solve nothing. He ordered more coffee and considered his situation with icy rationality.

Cath m'Lane was dead at his hand. Could he report it, plead that it had been an accident? Unlikely. He had run her through, after all, and he had already told that policer to leave her to him. He would have to get rid of the evidence, and hope that she had not told anyone where she was going this morning. That was probable. She could only have gotten his gift late last night. She said that she had cried all night, and she had been alone when she arrived. Very well; he had one body and one skimmer to dispose of.

That left the sandkings. They might prove more of a difficulty. No doubt they had all escaped by now. The thought of them around his house, in his bed and his clothes, infesting his food—it made his flesh crawl. He shuddered and overcame his revulsion. It really shouldn't be too hard to kill them, he reminded himself. He didn't have to account for every mobile. Just the four maws, that was all. He could do that. They were large, as he'd seen. He would find them and kill them.

Simon Kress went shopping before he flew back to his home. He bought a set of skinthins that would cover him from head to foot, several bags of poison pellets for rockjock control, and a spray canister of illegally strong pesticide. He also bought a magnalock towing device.

When he landed, he went about things methodically. First he hooked Cath's skimmer to his own with the magnalock. Searching it, he had his first piece of luck. The crystal chip with Idi Noreddian's holo of the sandking fight was on the front seat. He had worried about that.

When the skimmers were ready, he slipped into his skinthins and went inside for Cath's body.

It wasn't there.

He poked through the fast-drying sand carefully, but there was no doubt of it; the body was gone. Could she have dragged herself away? Unlikely, but Kress searched. A cursory inspection of his house turned up neither the body nor any sign of the sandkings. He did not have time for a more thorough investigation, not with the incriminating skimmer outside his front door. He resolved to try later.

Some seventy kilometers north of Kress' estate was a range of active volcanoes. He flew there, Cath's skimmer in tow. Above the glowering cone of the largest, he released the magnalock and watched it vanish in the lava below.

It was dusk when he returned to his house. That gave him pause. Briefly he considered flying back to the city and spending the night there. He put the thought aside. There was work to do. He wasn't safe yet.

He scattered the poison pellets around the exterior of his house. No one would find that suspicious. He'd always had a rockjock problem. When that task was completed, he primed the canister of pesticide and ventured back inside.

Kress went through the house room by room, turning on lights everywhere he went until he was surrounded by a blaze of artificial illumination. He paused to clean up in the living room, shoveling sand and plastic fragments back into the broken tank. The sandkings were all gone, as he'd feared. The castles were shrunken and distorted, slagged by the watery bombardment Kress had visited upon them, and what little remained was crumbling as it dried.

He frowned and searched on, the canister of pest spray strapped across his shoulders.

Down in his deepest wine cellar, he came upon Cath m'Lane's corpse.

It sprawled at the foot of a steep flight of stairs, the limbs twisted as if by a fall. White mobiles were swarming all over it, and as Kress watched, the body moved jerkily across the hard-packed dirt floor.

He laughed, and twisted the illumination up to maximum. In the far corner, a squat little earthen castle and a dark hole were visible between two wine racks. Kress could make out a rough outline of his face on the cellar wall.

The body shifted once again, moving a few centimeters toward the castle. Kress had a sudden vision of the white maw waiting hungrily. It might be able to get Cath's foot in its mouth, but no more. It was too absurd. He laughed again, and started down into the cellar, finger poised on the trigger of the hose that snaked down his right arm. The sandkings—hundreds of them moving as one—deserted the body and formed up battle lines, a field of white between him and their maw.

Suddenly Kress had another inspiration. He smiled and lowered his firing hand. "Cath was always hard to swallow," he said, delighted at his wit. "Especially for one your size. Here, let me give you some help. What are gods for, after all?"

He retreated upstairs, returning shortly with a cleaver. The sandkings, patient, waited and watched while Kress chopped Cath m'Lane into small, easily digestible pieces.

―――――――

Simon Kress slept in his skinthins that night, the pesticide close at hand, but he did not need it. The whites, sated, remained in the cellar, and he saw no sign of the others.

In the morning he finished the cleanup of the living room. After he was through, no trace of the struggle remained except for the broken tank.

He ate a light lunch, and resumed his hunt for the missing sandkings. In full daylight, it was not too difficult. The blacks had located in his rock garden, and built a castle heavy with obsidian and quartz. The reds he found at the bottom of his long-disused swimming pool, which had partially filled with wind-blown sand over the years. He saw mobiles of both colors ranging about his grounds, many of them carrying poison pellets back to their maws. Kress decided his pesticide was unnecessary. No use risking a fight when he could just let the poison do its work. Both maws should be dead by evening.

That left only the burnt orange sandkings unaccounted for. Kress circled his estate several times, in ever-widening spirals, but found no trace of them. When he began to sweat in his skinthins—it was a hot, dry day—he decided it was not important. If they were out here, they were probably eating the poison pellets along with the reds and blacks.

He crunched several sandkings underfoot, with a certain degree of satisfaction, as he walked back to the house. Inside, he removed his skinthins, settled down to a delicious meal, and finally began to relax. Everything was under control. Two of the maws would soon be defunct, the third was safely located where he could dispose of it after it had served his purposes, and he had no doubt that he would find the fourth. As for Cath, all trace of her visit had been obliterated.

His reverie was interrupted when his viewscreen began to blink at him. It was Jad Rakkis, calling to brag about some cannibal worms he was bringing to the war games tonight.

Kress had forgotten about that, but he recovered quickly. "Oh, Jad, my pardons. I neglected to tell you. I grew bored with all that, and got rid of the sandkings. Ugly little things. Sorry, but there'll be no party tonight."

Rakkis was indignant. "But what will I do with my worms?"

"Put them in a basket of fruit and send them to a loved one," Kress said, signing off. Quickly he began calling the others. He did not need anyone arriving at his doorstep now, with the sandkings alive and infesting the estate.

As he was calling Idi Noreddian, Kress became aware of an annoying oversight. The screen began to clear, indicating that someone had answered at the other end. Kress flicked off. Idi arrived on schedule an hour later. She was surprised to find the party canceled, but perfectly happy to share an evening alone with Kress. He delighted her with his story of Cath's reaction to the holo they had made together. While telling it, he managed to ascertain that she had not mentioned the prank to anyone. He nodded, satisfied, and refilled their wine glasses. Only a trickle was left. "I'll have to get a fresh bottle," he said. "Come with me to my wine cellar, and help me pick out a good vintage. You've always had a better palate than I."

She came along willingly enough, but balked at the top of the stairs when Kress opened the door and gestured for her to precede him. "Where are the lights?" she said. "And that smell—what's that peculiar smell, Simon?"

When he shoved her, she looked briefly startled. She screamed as she tumbled down the stairs. Kress closed the door and began to nail it shut with the boards and airhammer he had left for that purpose. As he was finishing, he heard Idi groan. "I'm hurt," she said. "Simon, what is this?" Suddenly she squealed, and shortly after that the screaming started.

It did not cease for hours. Kress went to his sensorium and dialed up a saucy comedy to blot it off his mind.

When he was sure she was dead, Kress flew her skimmer north to the volcanoes and discarded it. The magnalock was proving a good investment.

ODD SCRABBLING NOISES WERE COMING FROM BEYOND THE WINE CELlar door the next morning when Kress went down to check it out. He listened for several uneasy moments, wondering if Idi Noreddian could possibly have survived, and was now scratching to get out. It seemed unlikely; it had to be the sandkings. Kress did not like the implications of that. He decided that he would keep the door sealed, at least for the moment, and went outside with a shovel to bury the red and black maws in their own castles.

He found them very much alive.

The black castle was glittering with volcanic glass, and sandkings were all over it, repairing and improving. The highest tower was up to his waist, and on it was a hideous caricature of his face. When he approached, the blacks halted in their labors, and formed up into two threatening phalanxes. Kress glanced behind him and saw others closing off his escape. Startled, he dropped the shovel and sprinted out of the trap, crushing several mobiles beneath his boots.

The red castle was creeping up the walls of the swimming pool. The maw was safely settled in a pit, surrounded by sand and concrete and battlements. The reds crept all over the bottom of the pool. Kress watched them carry a rockjock and a large lizard into the castle. He stepped back from the poolside, horrified, and felt something crunch. Looking down, he saw three mobiles climbing up his leg. He brushed them off and stamped them to death, but others were approaching quickly. They were larger than he remembered. Some were almost as big as his thumb.

He ran. By the time he reached the safety of the house, his heart was racing and he was short of breath. The door closed behind him, and Kress hurried to lock it. His house was supposed to be pest-proof. He'd be safe in here.

A stiff drink steadied his nerve. So poison doesn't faze them, he thought. He should have known. Wo had warned him that the maw could eat anything. He would have to use the pesticide. Kress took another drink for good measure, donned his skinthins, and strapped the canister to his back. He unlocked the door.

Outside, the sandkings were waiting.

Two armies confronted him, allied against the common threat. More than he could have guessed. The damned maws must be breeding like rockjocks. They were everywhere, a creeping sea of them.

Kress brought up the hose and flicked the trigger. A gray mist washed over the nearest rank of sandkings. He moved his hand from side to side.

Where the mist fell, the sandkings twitched violently and died in sudden spasms. Kress smiled. They were no match for him. He sprayed in a wide arc before him and stepped forward confidently over a litter of black and red bodies. The armies fell back. Kress advanced, intent on cutting through them to their maws.

All at once the retreat stopped. A thousand sandkings surged toward him.

Kress had been expecting the counterattack. He stood his ground, sweeping his misty sword before him in great looping strokes. They came at him and died. A few got through; he could not spray everywhere at once. He felt them climbing up his legs, sensed their mandibles biting futilely at the reinforced plastic of his skinthins. He ignored them, and kept spraying.

Then he began to feel soft impacts on his head and shoulders.

Kress trembled and spun and looked up above him. The front of his house was alive with sandkings. Blacks and reds, hundreds of them. They were launching themselves into the air, raining down on him. They fell all around him. One landed on his faceplate, its mandibles scraping at his eyes for a terrible second before he plucked it away.

He swung up his hose and sprayed the air, sprayed the house, sprayed until the airborne sandkings were all dead and dying. The mist settled back on him, making him cough. He coughed, and kept spraying. Only when the front of the house was clean did Kress turn his attention back to the ground.

They were all around him, on him, dozens of them scurrying over his body, hundreds of others hurrying to join them. He turned the mist on them. The hose went dead. Kress heard a loud *hiss,* and the deadly fog rose in a great cloud from between his shoulders, cloaking him, choking him, making his eyes burn and blur. He felt for the hose, and his hand came away covered with dying sandkings. The hose was severed; they'd eaten it through. He was surrounded by a shroud of pesticide, blinded. He stumbled and screamed, and began to run back to the house, pulling sandkings from his body as he went.

Inside, he sealed the door and collapsed on the carpet, rolling back and forth until he was sure he had crushed them all. The canister was empty by then, hissing feebly. Kress stripped off his skinthins and showered. The hot spray scalded him and left his skin reddened and sensitive, but it made his flesh stop crawling.

He dressed in his heaviest clothing, thick workpants and leathers, after shaking them out nervously. "Damn," he kept muttering, "damn." His throat was dry. After searching the entry hall thoroughly to make certain it was clean, he allowed himself to sit and pour a drink. "Damn," he repeated. His hand shook as he poured, slopping liquor on the carpet.

The alcohol settled him, but it did not wash away the fear. He had a second drink and went to the window furtively. Sandkings were moving across the thick plastic pane. He shuddered and retreated to his communications console. He had to get help, he thought wildly. He would punch through a call to the authorities, and policers would come out with flamethrowers and . . .

Simon Kress stopped in mid-call, and groaned. He couldn't call in the police. He would have to tell them about the whites in his cellar, and they'd find the bodies there. Perhaps the maw might have finished Cath m'Lane by now, but certainly not Idi Noreddian. He hadn't even cut her up. Besides, there would be bones. No, the police could be called in only as a last resort.

He sat at the console, frowning. His communications equipment filled a whole wall; from here he could reach anyone on Baldur. He had plenty of money, and his cunning—he had always prided himself on his cunning. He would handle this somehow.

He briefly considered calling Wo, but soon dismissed the idea. Wo knew too much, and she would ask questions, and he did not trust her. No, he needed someone who would do as he asked *without* questions.

His frown faded, and slowly turned into a smile. Simon Kress had contacts. He put through a call to a number he had not used in a long time.

A woman's face took shape on his viewscreen: white-haired, bland of expression, with a long hook nose. Her voice was brisk and efficient. "Simon," she said. "How is business?"

"Business is fine, Lissandra," Kress replied. "I have a job for you."

"A removal? My price has gone up since last time, Simon. It has been ten years, after all."

"You will be well paid," Kress said. "You know I'm generous. I want you for a bit of pest control."

She smiled a thin smile. "No need to use euphemisms, Simon. The call is shielded."

"No, I'm serious. I have a pest problem. Dangerous pests. Take care of them for me. No questions. Understood?"

"Understood."

"Good. You'll need . . . oh, three or four operatives. Wear heat-resistant skinthins, and equip them with flamethrowers, or lasers, something on that order. Come out to my place. You'll see the problem. Bugs, lots and lots of them. In my rock garden and the old swimming pool you'll find castles. Destroy them, kill everything inside them. Then knock on the door, and I'll show you what else needs to be done. Can you get out here quickly?"

Her face was impassive. "We'll leave within the hour."

LISSANDRA WAS TRUE TO HER WORD. SHE ARRIVED IN A LEAN BLACK skimmer with three operatives. Kress watched them from the safety of a second-story window. They were all faceless in dark plastic skinthins. Two of them wore portable flamethrowers, a third carried lasercannon and explosives. Lissandra carried nothing; Kress recognized her by the way she gave orders.

Their skimmer passed low overhead first, checking out the situation. The sandkings went mad. Scarlet and ebon mobiles ran everywhere, frenetic. Kress could see the castle in the rock garden from his vantage point. It stood tall as a man. Its ramparts were crawling with black defenders, and a steady stream of mobiles flowed down into its depths.

Lissandra's skimmer came down next to Kress' and the operatives vaulted out and unlimbered their weapons. They looked inhuman, deadly.

The black army drew up between them and the castle. The reds— Kress suddenly realized that he could not see the reds. He blinked. Where had they gone?

Lissandra pointed and shouted, and her two flamethrowers spread out and opened up on the black sandkings. Their weapons coughed dully and began to roar, long tongues of blue-and-scarlet fire licking out before them. Sandkings crisped and blackened and died. The operatives began to play the fire back and forth in an efficient, interlocking pattern. They advanced with careful, measured steps.

The black army burned and disintegrated, the mobiles fleeing in a thousand different directions, some back toward the castle, others toward the enemy. None reached the operatives with the flamethrowers. Lissandra's people were very professional.

Then one of them stumbled.

Or seemed to stumble. Kress looked again, and saw that the ground had given way beneath the man. Tunnels, he thought with a tremor of fear—tunnels, pits, traps. The flamer was sunk in sand up to his waist, and suddenly the ground around him seemed to erupt, and he was covered with scarlet sandkings. He dropped the flamethrower and began to claw wildly at his own body. His screams were horrible to hear.

His companion hesitated, then swung and fired. A blast of flame swallowed human and sandkings both. The screaming stopped abruptly. Satisfied, the second flamer turned back to the castle and took another step forward, and recoiled as his foot broke through the ground and vanished up to the ankle. He tried to pull it back and retreat, and the sand all around him gave way. He lost his balance and stumbled, flailing, and the sandkings were everywhere, a boiling mass of them, covering him as he writhed and rolled. His flamethrower was useless and forgotten.

Kress pounded wildly on the window, shouting for attention. "The castle! Get the castle!"

Lissandra, standing back by her skimmer, heard and gestured. Her third operative sighted with the lasercannon and fired. The beam throbbed across the grounds and sliced off the top of the castle. He brought it down sharply, hacking at the sand and stone parapets. Towers fell. Kress' face disintegrated. The laser bit into the ground, searching round and about. The castle crumbled; now it was only a heap of sand. But the black mobiles continued to move. The maw was buried too deeply; they hadn't touched her.

Lissandra gave another order. Her operative discarded the laser, primed an explosive, and darted forward. He leaped over the smoking corpse of the first flamer, landed on solid ground within Kress' rock garden, and heaved. The explosive ball landed square atop the ruins of the black castle. White-hot light seared Kress' eyes, and there was a tremendous gout of sand and rock and mobiles. For a moment dust obscured everything. It was raining sandkings and pieces of sandkings.

Kress saw that the black mobiles were dead and unmoving.

"The pool," he shouted down through the window. "Get the castle in the pool."

Lissandra understood quickly; the ground was littered with motionless blacks, but the reds were pulling back hurriedly and re-forming. Her operative stood uncertain, then reached down and pulled out another explosive ball. He took one step forward, but Lissandra called him and he sprinted back in her direction.

It was all so simple then. He reached the skimmer, and Lissandra took him aloft. Kress rushed to another window in another room to watch. They came swooping in just over the pool, and the operative pitched his bombs down at the red castle from the safety of the skimmer. After the fourth run, the castle was unrecognizable, and the sandkings stopped moving.

Lissandra was thorough. She had him bomb each castle several additional times. Then he used the lasercannon, crisscrossing methodically until it was certain that nothing living could remain intact beneath those small patches of ground.

Finally they came knocking at his door. Kress was grinning manically when he let them in. "Lovely," he said, "lovely."

Lissandra pulled off the mask of her skinthins. "This will cost you, Simon. Two operatives gone, not to mention the danger to my own life."

"Of course," Kress blurted. "You'll be well paid, Lissandra. Whatever you ask, just so you finish the job."

"What remains to be done?"

"You have to clean out my wine cellar," Kress said. "There's another castle down there. And you'll have to do it without explosives. I don't want my house coming down around me." Lissandra motioned to her operative. "Go outside and get Rajk's flamethrower. It should be intact."

He returned armed, ready, silent. Kress led them down to the wine cellar.

The heavy door was still nailed shut, as he had left it. But it bulged outward slightly, as if warped by some tremendous pressure. That made Kress uneasy, as did the silence that held reign about them. He stood well away from the door as Lissandra's operative removed his nails and planks. "Is that safe in here?" he found himself muttering, pointing at the flamethrower. "I don't want a fire, either, you know."

"I have the laser," Lissandra said. "We'll use that for the kill. The flamethrower probably won't be needed. But I want it here just in case. There are worse things than fire, Simon."

He nodded.

The last plank came free of the cellar door. There was still no sound from below. Lissandra snapped an order, and her underling fell back, took up a position behind her, and leveled the flamethrower square at the door. She slipped her mask back on, hefted the laser, stepped forward, and pulled open the door.

No motion. No sound. It was dark down there.

"Is there a light?" Lissandra asked.

"Just inside the door," Kress said. "On the right hand side. Mind the stairs, they're quite steep."

She stepped into the door, shifted the laser to her left hand, and reached up with her right, fumbling inside for the light panel. Nothing happened. "I feel it," Lissandra said, "but it doesn't seem to . . ."

Then she was screaming, and she stumbled backward. A great white sandking had clamped itself around her wrist. Blood welled through her skinthins where its mandibles had sunk in. It was fully as large as her hand.

Lissandra did a horrible little jig across the room and began to smash her hand against the nearest wall. Again and again and again. It landed with a heavy, meaty thud. Finally the sandking fell away. She whimpered and fell to her knees. "I think my fingers are broken," she said softly. The blood was still flowing freely. She had dropped the laser near the cellar door.

"I'm not going down there," her operative announced in clear firm tones.

Lissandra looked up at him. "No," she said. "Stand in the door and flame it all. Cinder it. Do you understand?"

He nodded.

Simon Kress moaned. "My *house*," he said. His stomach churned. The white sandking had been so *large*. How many more were down there? "Don't," he continued. "Leave it alone. I've changed my mind. Leave it alone."

Lissandra misunderstood. She held out her hand. It was covered with blood and greenish-black ichor. "Your little friend bit clean through my glove, and you saw what it took to get it off. I don't care about your house, Simon. Whatever is down there is going to die."

Kress hardly heard her. He thought he could see movement in the shadows beyond the cellar door. He imagined a white army bursting forth, all as large as the sandking that had attacked Lissandra. He saw himself being lifted by a hundred tiny arms, and dragged down into the darkness where the maw waited hungrily. He was afraid. "Don't," he said.

They ignored him.

Kress darted forward, and his shoulder slammed into the back of Lissandra's operative just as the man was bracing to fire. He grunted and unbalanced and pitched forward into the black. Kress listened to him fall down the stairs. Afterward there were other noises—scuttlings and snaps and soft squishing sounds.

Kress swung around to face Lissandra. He was drenched in cold sweat, but a sickly kind of excitement was on him. It was almost sexual.

Lissandra's calm cold eyes regarded him through her mask. "What are you doing?" she demanded as Kress picked up the laser she had dropped. *"Simon!"*

"Making a peace," he said, giggling. "They won't hurt god, no, not so long as god is good and generous. I was cruel. Starved them. I have to make up for it now, you see."

"You're insane," Lissandra said. It was the last thing she said. Kress burned a hole in her chest big enough to put his arm through. He dragged the body across the floor and rolled it down the cellar stairs. The noises were louder—chitinous clackings and scrapings and echoes that were thick and liquid. Kress nailed up the door once again.

As he fled, he was filled with a deep sense of contentment that coated his fear like a layer of syrup. He suspected it was not his own.

He planned to leave his home, to fly to the city and take a room for a night, or perhaps for a year. Instead Kress started drinking. He was not quite sure why. He drank steadily for hours, and retched it all up violently on his living room carpet. At some point he fell asleep. When he woke, it was pitch dark in the house.

He cowered against the couch. He could hear *noises.* Things were moving in the walls. They were all around him. His hearing was extraordinarily acute. Every little creak was the footstep of a sandking. He closed his eyes and waited, expecting to feel their terrible touch, afraid to move lest he brush against one.

Kress sobbed, and was very still for a while, but nothing happened.

He opened his eyes again. He trembled. Slowly the shadows began to soften and dissolve. Moonlight was filtering through the high windows. His eyes adjusted.

The living room was empty. Nothing there, nothing, nothing. Only his drunken fears.

Simon Kress steeled himself, and rose, and went to a light.

Nothing there. The room was quiet, deserted.

He listened. Nothing. No sound. Nothing in the walls. It had all been his imagination, his fear.

The memories of Lissandra and the thing in the cellar returned to him unbidden. Shame and anger washed over him. Why had he done that? He could have helped her burn it out, kill it. *Why* . . . he knew why. The maw had done it to him, put fear in him. Wo had said it was psionic, even when it was small. And now it was large, so large. It had feasted on Cath, and Idi, and now it had two more bodies down there. It would keep growing. And it had learned to like the taste of human flesh, he thought.

He began to shake, but he took control of himself again and stopped. It wouldn't hurt him. He was god. The whites had always been his favorites.

He remembered how he had stabbed it with his throwing-sword. That was before Cath came. Damn her anyway.

He couldn't stay here. The maw would grow hungry again. Large as it was, it wouldn't take long. Its appetite would be terrible. What would it do then? He had to get away, back to the safety of the city while it was still contained in his wine cellar. It was only plaster and hard-packed earth down there, and the mobiles could dig and tunnel. When they got free . . . Kress didn't want to think about it.

He went to his bedroom and packed. He took three bags. Just a single change of clothing, that was all he needed; the rest of the space he filled with his valuables, with jewelry and art and other things he could not bear to lose. He did not expect to return.

His shambler followed him down the stairs, staring at him from its baleful glowing eyes. It was gaunt. Kress realized that it had been ages since he had fed it. Normally it could take care of itself, but no doubt the pickings had grown lean of late. When it tried to clutch at his leg, he snarled at it and kicked it away, and it scurried off, offended.

Kress slipped outside, carrying his bags awkwardly, and shut the door behind him.

For a moment he stood pressed against the house, his heart thudding in his chest. Only a few meters between him and his skimmer. He was afraid to cross them. The moonlight was bright, and the front of his house was a scene of carnage. The bodies of Lissandra's two flamers lay where they had fallen, one twisted and burned, the other swollen beneath a mass of dead sandkings. And the mobiles, the black and red mobiles, they were all around him. It was an effort to remember that they were dead. It was almost as if they were simply waiting, as they had waited so often before.

Nonsense, Kress told himself. More drunken fears. He had seen the castles blown apart. They were dead, and the white maw was trapped in his cellar. He took several deep and deliberate breaths, and stepped forward onto the sandkings. They crunched. He ground them into the sand savagely. They did not move.

Kress smiled, and walked slowly across the battleground, listening to the sounds, the sounds of safety.

Crunch. Crackle. Crunch.

He lowered his bags to the ground and opened the door to his skimmer.

Something moved from shadow into light. A pale shape on the seat of his skimmer. It was as long as his forearm. Its mandibles clacked together softly, and it looked up at him from six small eyes set all around its body.

Kress wet his pants and backed away slowly.

There was more motion from inside the skimmer. He had left the door open. The sandking emerged and came toward him, cautiously. Others followed. They had been hiding beneath his seats, burrowed into the upholstery. But now they emerged. They formed a ragged ring around the skimmer.

Kress licked his lips, turned, and moved quickly to Lissandra's skimmer.

He stopped before he was halfway there. Things were moving inside that one too. Great maggoty things, half-seen by the light of the moon.

Kress whimpered and retreated back toward the house. Near the front door, he looked up.

He counted a dozen long white shapes creeping back and forth across the walls of the building. Four of them were clustered close together near the top of the unused belfry where the carrion hawk had once roosted. They were carving something. A face. A very recognizable face.

Simon Kress shrieked and ran back inside.

A SUFFICIENT QUANTITY OF DRINK BROUGHT HIM THE EASY OBLIVION he sought. But he woke. Despite everything, he woke. He had a terrible headache, and he smelled, and he was hungry. Oh so very hungry. He had never been so hungry.

Kress knew it was not his *own* stomach hurting.

A white sandking watched him from atop the dresser in his bedroom, its antennae moving faintly. It was as big as the one in the skimmer the night before. He was horribly dry, sandpaper dry. He licked his lips and fled from the room.

The house was full of sandkings; he had to be careful where he put his feet. They all seemed busy on errands of their own. They were making modifications in his house, burrowing into or out of his walls, carving things. Twice he saw his own likeness staring out at him from unexpected places. The faces were warped, twisted, livid with fear.

He went outside to get the bodies that had been rotting in the yard, hoping to appease the white maw's hunger. They were gone, both of them. Kress remembered how easily the mobiles could carry things many times their own weight.

It was terrible to think that the maw was *still* hungry after all of that.

When Kress reentered the house, a column of sandkings was wending its way down the stairs. Each carried a piece of his shambler. The head seemed to look at him reproachfully as it went by.

Kress emptied his freezers, his cabinets, everything, piling all the food in the house in the center of his kitchen floor. A dozen whites waited to take it away. They avoided the frozen food, leaving it to thaw in a great puddle, but they carried off everything else.

When all the food was gone, Kress felt his own hunger pangs abate just a bit, though he had not eaten a thing. But he knew the respite would be short-lived. Soon the maw would be hungry again. He had to feed it.

Kress knew what to do. He went to his communicator. "Malada," he began casually when the first of his friends answered, "I'm having a small party tonight. I realize this is terribly short notice, but I hope you can make it. I really do."

He called Jad Rakkis next, and then the others. By the time he had finished, nine of them had accepted his invitation. Kress hoped that would be enough.

Kress met his guests outside—the mobiles had cleaned up remarkably quickly, and the grounds looked almost as they had before the battle—and walked them to his front door. He let them enter first. He did not follow.

When four of them had gone through, Kress finally worked up his courage. He closed the door behind his latest guest, ignoring the startled exclamations that soon turned into shrill gibbering, and sprinted for the skimmer the man had arrived in. He slid in safely, thumbed the startplate, and swore. It was programmed to lift only in response to its owner's thumbprint, of course.

Jad Rakkis was the next to arrive. Kress ran to his skimmer as it set down, and seized Rakkis by the arm as he was climbing out. "Get back in, quickly," he said, pushing. "Take me to the city. Hurry, Jad. *Get out of here!*"

But Rakkis only stared at him, and would not move. "Why, what's wrong, Simon? I don't understand. What about your party?"

And then it was too late, because the loose sand all around them was stirring, and the red eyes were staring at them, and the mandibles were clacking. Rakkis made a choking sound, and moved to get back in his skimmer, but a pair of mandibles snapped shut about his ankle, and suddenly he was on his knees. The sand seemed to boil with subterranean activity. Jad thrashed and cried terribly as they tore him apart. Kress could hardly bear to watch.

After that, he did not try to escape again. When it was all over, he cleaned out what remained in his liquor cabinet, and got extremely drunk. It would be the last time he would enjoy that luxury, he knew. The only alcohol remaining in the house was stored down in the wine cellar.

Kress did not touch a bite of food the entire day, but he fell asleep feeling bloated, sated at last, the awful hunger vanquished. His last thoughts before the nightmares took him were of whom he could ask out tomorrow.

Morning was hot and dry. Kress opened his eyes to see the white sandking on his dresser again. He shut them again quickly, hoping the dream would leave him. It did not, and he could not go back to sleep. Soon he found himself staring at the thing.

He stared for almost five minutes before the strangeness of it dawned on him; the sandking was not moving.

The mobiles could be preternaturally still, to be sure. He had seen them wait and watch a thousand times. But always there was some motion about them—the mandibles clacked, the legs twitched, the long fine antennae stirred and swayed.

But the sandking on his dresser was completely still.

Kress rose, holding his breath, not daring to hope. Could it be dead? Could something have killed it? He walked across the room.

The eyes were glassy and black. The creature seemed swollen, somehow, as if it were soft and rotting inside, filling up with gas that pushed outward at the plates of white armor.

Kress reached out a trembling hand and touched it.

It was warm—hot even—and growing hotter. But it did not move.

He pulled his hand back, and as he did, a segment of the sandking's white exoskeleton fell away from it. The flesh beneath was the same color, but softer-looking, swollen and feverish. And it almost seemed to throb.

Kress backed away, and ran to the door.

Three more white mobiles lay in his hall. They were all like the one in his bedroom.

He ran down the stairs, jumping over sandkings. None of them moved. The house was full of them, all dead, dying, comatose, whatever. Kress did not care what was wrong with them. Just so they could not move.

He found four of them inside his skimmer. He picked them up one by one, and threw them as far as he could. Damned monsters. He slid back in, on the ruined half-eaten seats, and thumbed the startplate.

Nothing happened.

Kress tried again, and again. Nothing. It wasn't fair. This was *his* skimmer, it ought to start, why wouldn't it lift, he didn't understand.

Finally he got out and checked, expecting the worst. He found it. The sandkings had torn apart his gravity grid. He was trapped. He was still trapped.

Grimly, Kress marched back into the house. He went to his gallery and found the antique axe that had hung next to the throwing-sword he had used on Cath m'Lane. He set to work. The sandkings did not stir even as he chopped them to pieces. But they splattered when he made the first cut, the bodies almost bursting. Inside was awful; strange half-formed organs, a viscous reddish ooze that looked almost like human blood, and the yellow ichor.

Kress destroyed twenty of them before he realized the futility of what he was doing. The mobiles were nothing, really. Besides, there were so *many* of them. He could work for a day and night and still not kill them all.

He had to go down into the wine cellar and use the axe on the maw.

Resolute, he started down. He got within sight of the door, and stopped.

It was not a door anymore. The walls had been eaten away, so that the hole was twice the size it had been, and round. A pit, that was all. There was no sign that there had ever been a door nailed shut over that black abyss.

A ghastly, choking, fetid odor seemed to come from below.

And the walls were wet and bloody and covered with patches of white fungus.

And worst, it was *breathing*.

Kress stood across the room and felt the warm wind wash over him as it exhaled, and he tried not to choke, and when the wind reversed direction, he fled.

Back in the living room, he destroyed three more mobiles, and collapsed. What was *happening*? He didn't understand.

Then he remembered the only person who might understand. Kress went to his communicator again, stepping on a sandking in his haste, and prayed fervently that the device still worked.

When Jala Wo answered, he broke down and told her everything.

She let him talk without interruption, no expression save for a slight frown on her gaunt, pale face. When Kress had finished, she said only, "I ought to leave you there."

Kress began to blubber. "You can't. Help me. I'll pay. . . ."

"I ought to," Wo repeated, "but I won't."

"Thank you," Kress said. "Oh, thank . . ."

"Quiet," said Wo. "Listen to me. This is your own doing. Keep your sandkings well, and they are courtly ritual warriors. You turned yours into something else, with starvation and torture. You were their god. You made them what they are. That maw in your cellar is sick, still suffering from the wound you gave it. It is probably insane. Its behavior is . . . unusual.

"You have to get out of there quickly. The mobiles are not dead, Kress. They are dormant. I told you the exoskeleton falls off when they grow larger. Normally, in fact, it falls off much earlier. I have never heard of sandkings growing as large as yours while still in the insectoid stage. It is another result of crippling the white maw, I would say. That does not matter.

"What matters is the metamorphosis your sandkings are now undergoing. As the maw grows, you see, it gets progressively more intelligent. Its psionic powers strengthen, and its mind becomes more sophisticated, more ambitious. The armored mobiles are useful enough when the maw is tiny and only semi-sentient, but now it needs better servants, bodies with capabilities. Do you understand? The mobiles are all going to give birth to a new breed of sandking. I can't say exactly what it will look like. Each maw designs its own, to fit its perceived needs and desires. But it will be biped, with four arms, and opposable thumbs. It will be able to construct and operate advanced machinery. The individual sandkings will not be sentient. But the maw will be very sentient indeed."

Simon Kress was gaping at Wo's image on the viewscreen. "Your workers," he said, with an effort. "The ones who came out here . . . who installed the tank . . ."

Jala Wo managed a faint smile. "Shade," she said.

"Shade is a sandking," Kress repeated numbly. "And you sold me a tank of . . . of . . . infants, ah. . . ."

"Do not be absurd," Wo said. "A first-stage sandking is more like a sperm than an infant. The wars temper and control them in nature. Only one in a hundred reaches second stage. Only one in a thousand achieves the third and final plateau, and becomes like Shade. Adult sandkings are not sentimental about the small maws. There are too many of them, and their mobiles are pests." She sighed. "And all this talk wastes time. That white sandking is going to waken to full sentience soon. It is not going to need you any longer, and it hates you, and it will be very hungry. The transformation is taxing. The maw must eat enormous amounts both before and after. So you have to get out of there. Do you understand?"

"I *can't*," Kress said. "My skimmer is destroyed, and I can't get any of the others to start. I don't know how to reprogram them. Can you come out for me?"

"Yes," said Wo. "Shade and I will leave at once, but it is more than two hundred kilometers from Asgard to you, and there is equipment we will need to deal with the deranged sandking you've created. You cannot wait there. You have two feet. Walk. Go due east, as near as you can determine, as quickly as you can. The land out there is pretty desolate. We'll find you easily with an aerial search, and you'll be safely away from the sandking. Do you understand?"

"Yes," said Simon Kress. "Yes, oh, yes."

They signed off, and he walked quickly toward the door. He was halfway there when he heard the noise—a sound halfway between a pop and a crack.

One of the sandkings had split open. Four tiny hands covered with pinkish-yellow blood came up out of the gap and began to push the dead skin aside.

Kress began to run.

He had not counted on the heat.

The hills were dry and rocky. Kress ran from the house as quickly as he could, ran until his ribs ached and his breath was coming in gasps. Then he walked, but as soon as he had recovered he began to run again. For almost an hour he ran and walked, ran and walked, beneath the fierce hot sun. He sweated freely, and wished that he had thought to bring some water. He watched the sky in hopes of seeing Wo and Shade.

He was not made for this. It was too hot, and too dry, and he was in no condition. But he kept himself going with the memory of the way the maw had breathed, and the thought of the wriggling little things that by now were surely crawling all over his house. He hoped Wo and Shade would know how to deal with them.

He had his own plans for Wo and Shade. It was all their fault, Kress had decided, and they would suffer for it. Lissandra was dead, but he knew others in her profession. He would have his revenge. He promised himself that a hundred times as he struggled and sweated his way east.

At least he hoped it was east. He was not that good at directions, and he wasn't certain which way he had run in his initial panic, but since then he had made an effort to bear due east, as Wo had suggested.

When he had been running for several hours, with no sign of rescue, Kress began to grow certain that he had gone wrong.

When several more hours passed, he began to grow afraid. What if Wo and Shade could not find him? He would die out here. He hadn't eaten in two days; he was weak and frightened; his throat was raw for want of water. He couldn't keep going. The sun was sinking now, and he'd be completely lost in the dark. What was wrong? Had the sandkings eaten Wo and Shade? The fear was on him again, filling him, and with it a great thirst and a terrible hunger. But Kress kept going. He stumbled now when he tried to run, and twice he fell. The second time he scraped his hand on a rock, and it came away bloody. He sucked at it as he walked, and worried about infection.

The sun was on the horizon behind him. The ground grew a little cooler, for which Kress was grateful. He decided to walk until last light and settle in for the night. Surely he was far enough from the sandkings to be safe, and Wo and Shade would find him come morning.

When he topped the next rise, he saw the outline of a house in front of him.

It wasn't as big as his own house, but it was big enough. It was habitation, safety. Kress shouted and began to run toward it. Food and drink, he had to have nourishment, he could taste the meal now. He was aching with hunger. He ran down the hill toward the house, waving his arms and shouting to the inhabitants. The light was almost gone now, but he could still make out a half-dozen children playing in the twilight. "Hey there," he shouted. "Help, help."

They came running toward him.

Kress stopped suddenly. "No," he said, "oh, no. Oh, no." He backpedaled, slipped on the sand, got up, and tried to run again. They caught him easily. They were ghastly little things with bulging eyes and dusky orange skin. He struggled, but it was useless. Small as they were, each of them had four arms, and Kress had only two.

They carried him toward the house. It was a sad, shabby house built of crumbling sand, but the door was quite large, and dark, and it breathed. That was terrible, but it was not the thing that set Simon Kress to screaming. He screamed because of the others, the little orange children who came crawling out from the castle, and watched impassive as he passed.

All of them had his face.

NIGHTFLYERS

❖

WHEN JESUS OF NAZARETH HUNG DYING ON HIS CROSS, THE *VOLCRYN* passed within a year of his agony, headed outward.

When the Fire Wars raged on Earth, the *volcryn* sailed near Old Poseidon, where the seas were still unnamed and unfished. By the time the stardrive had transformed the Federated Nations of Earth into the Federal Empire, the *volcryn* had moved into the fringes of Hrangan space. The Hrangans never knew it. Like us they were children of the small bright worlds that circled their scattered suns, with little interest and less knowledge of the things that moved in the gulfs between.

War flamed for a thousand years and the *volcryn* passed through it, unknowing and untouched, safe in a place where no fires could ever burn. Afterwards, the Federal Empire was shattered and gone, and the Hrangans vanished in the dark of the Collapse, but it was no darker for the *volcryn*.

When Kleronomas took his survey ship out from Avalon, the *volcryn* came within ten light years of him. Kleronomas found many things, but he did not find the *volcryn*. Not then and not on his return to Avalon, a lifetime later.

When I was a child of three, Kleronomas was dust, as distant and dead as Jesus of Nazareth, and the *volcryn* passed close to Daronne. That season all the Crey sensitives grew strange and sat staring at the stars with luminous, flickering eyes.

When I was grown, the *volcryn* had sailed beyond Tara, past the range of even the Crey, still heading outward.

And now I am old and growing older and the *volcryn* will soon pierce the Tempter's Veil where it hangs like a black mist between the stars. And we follow, we follow. Through the dark gulfs where no one goes, through the emptiness, through the silence that goes on and on, my *Nightflyer* and I give chase.

———

They made their way slowly down the length of the transparent tube that linked the orbital docks to the waiting starship ahead, pulling themselves hand over hand through weightlessness.

Melantha Jhirl, the only one among them who did not seem clumsy and ill at ease in free fall, paused briefly to look at the dappled globe of Avalon below, a stately vastness in jade and amber. She smiled and moved swiftly down the tube, passing her companions with an easy grace. They had boarded starships before, all of them, but never like this. Most ships docked flush against the station, but the craft that Karoly d'Branin had chartered for his mission was too large, and too singular in design. It loomed ahead; three small eggs side-by-side, two larger spheres beneath and at right angles, the cylinder of the drive-room between, lengths of tube connecting it all. The ship was white and austere.

Melantha Jhirl was the first one through the airlock. The others straggled up one by one until they had all boarded; five women and four men, each an Academy scholar, their backgrounds as diverse as their fields of study. The frail young telepath, Thale Lasamer, was the last to enter. He glanced about nervously as the others chatted and waited for the entry procedure to be completed. "We're being watched," he said.

The outer door was closed behind them, the tube had fallen away; now the inner door slid open. "Welcome to my *Nightflyer*," said a mellow voice from within.

But there was no one there.

Melantha Jhirl stepped into the corridor. "Hello," she said, looking about quizzically. Karoly d'Branin followed her.

"Hello," the mellow voice replied. It was coming from a communicator grille beneath a darkened viewscreen. "This is Royd Eris, master of the *Nightflyer*. I'm pleased to see you again, Karoly, and pleased to welcome the rest of you."

"Where are you?" someone demanded.

"In my quarters, which occupy half of this life-support sphere," the voice of Royd Eris replied amiably. "The other half is comprised of a lounge-library-kitchen, two sanitary stations, one double cabin, and a rather small single. The rest of you will have to rig sleepwebs in the cargo spheres, I'm afraid. The *Nightflyer* was designed as a trader, not a passenger vessel. However, I've opened all the appropriate passageways and locks, so the holds have air and heat and water. I thought you'd find it more comfortable that way. Your equipment and computer system have been stowed in the holds, but there is still plenty of space, I assure you. I suggest you settle in, and then meet in the lounge for a meal."

"Will you join us?" asked the psipsych, a querulous hatchet-faced woman named Agatha Marij-Black.

"In a fashion," Royd Eris said, "in a fashion."

THE GHOST APPEARED AT THE BANQUET.

They found the lounge easily enough, after they had rigged their sleepwebs and arranged their personal belongings around their sleeping quarters. It was the largest room in this section of the ship. One end of it was a fully equipped kitchen, well stocked with provisions. The opposite end offered several comfortable chairs, two readers, a holotank, and a wall of books and tapes and crystal chips. In the center was a long table with places set for ten.

A light meal was hot and waiting. The academicians helped themselves and took seats at the table, laughing and talking to each other, more at ease now than when they had boarded.

The ship's gravity grid was on, which went a long way towards making them more comfortable; the queasy awkwardness of their weightless transit was soon forgotten.

Finally all the seats were occupied except for one at the head of the table.

The ghost materialized there.

All conversation stopped.

"Hello," said the spectre, the bright shade of a lithe, pale-eyed young man with white hair. He was dressed in clothing twenty years out of date; a loose blue pastel shirt that ballooned at his wrists, clinging white trousers with built-in boots. They could see through him, and his own eyes did not see them at all.

"A hologram," said Alys Northwind, the short, stout xenotech.

"Royd, Royd, I do not understand," said Karoly d'Branin, staring at the ghost. "What is this? Why do you send us a projection? Will you not join us in person?"

The ghost smiled faintly and lifted an arm. "My quarters are on the other side of that wall," he said. "I'm afraid there is no door or lock between the two halves of the sphere. I spend most of my time by myself, and I value my privacy. I hope you will all understand and respect my wishes. I will be a gracious host nonetheless. Here in the lounge my projection can join you. Elsewhere, if you have anything you need, if you want to talk to me, just use a communicator. Now, please resume your meal, and your conversations. I'll gladly listen. It's been a long time since I had passengers."

They tried. But the ghost at the head of the table cast a long shadow, and the meal was strained and hurried.

———

FROM THE HOUR THE *NIGHTFLYER* SLIPPED INTO STARDRIVE, ROYD ERIS watched his passengers.

Within a few days most of the academicians had grown accustomed to the disembodied voice from the communicators and the holographic spectre in the lounge, but only Melantha Jhirl and Karoly d'Branin ever seemed really comfortable in his presence. The others would have been even more uncomfortable if they had known that Royd was always with them. Always and everywhere, he watched. Even in the sanitary stations, Royd had eyes and ears.

He watched them work, eat, sleep, copulate; he listened untiringly to their talk. Within a week he knew them, all nine, and had begun to ferret out their tawdry little secrets.

The cyberneticist, Lommie Thorne, talked to her computers and seemed to prefer their company to that of humans. She was bright and quick, with a mobile, expressive face and a small, hard boyish body; most of the others found her attractive, but she did not like to be touched. She sexed only once, with Melantha Jhirl. Lommie Thorne wore shirts of softly-woven metal, and had an implant in her left wrist that let her interface directly with her computers.

The xenobiologist, Rojan Christopheris, was a surly, argumentative man, a cynic whose contempt for his colleagues was barely kept in check, a solitary drinker. He was tall and stooped and ugly.

The two linguists, Dannel and Lindran, were lovers in public, constantly holding hands and supporting each other. In private they quarreled bitterly. Lindran had a mordant wit and liked to wound Dannel where it hurt the most, with jokes about his professional competence. They sexed often, both of them, but not with each other.

Agatha Marij-Black, the psipsych, was a hypochrondriac given to black depressions, which worsened in the close confines of the *Nightflyer.*

Xenotech Alys Northwind ate constantly and never washed. Her stubby fingernails were always caked with black dirt, and she wore the same jumpsuit for the first two weeks of the voyage, taking it off only for sex, and then only briefly.

Telepath Thale Lasamer was nervous and temperamental, afraid of everyone around him, yet given to bouts of arrogance in which he taunted his companions with thoughts he had snatched from their minds.

Royd Eris watched them all, studied them, lived with them and through them. He neglected none, not even the ones he found the most distasteful. But by the time the *Nightflyer* had been lost in the roiling flux of stardrive for two weeks, two of his riders had come to engage the bulk of his attention.

"Most of all, I want to know the why of them," Karoly d'Branin told him one false night the second week out from Avalon.

Royd's luminescent ghost sat close to d'Branin in the darkened lounge, watching him drink bittersweet chocolate. The others were all asleep. Night and day are meaningless on a starship, but the *Nightflyer* kept the usual cycles and most of the passengers followed them. Old d'Branin, administrator, generalist, and mission leader, was the exception; he kept his own hours, preferred work to sleep, and liked nothing better than to talk about his pet obsession, the *volcryn* he hunted.

"The *if* of them is important as well, Karoly," Royd answered. "Can you truly be certain these aliens of yours exist?"

"*I* can be certain," Karoly d'Branin said, with a broad wink. He was a compact man, short and slender, iron gray hair carefully styled and his tunic almost fussily neat, but the expansiveness of his gestures and the giddy enthusiasms to which he was prone belied his sober appearance. "That is enough. If everyone else were certain as well, we would have a fleet of research ships instead of your little *Nightflyer.*" He sipped at his chocolate and sighed with satisfaction. "Do you know the Nor T'alush, Royd?"

The name was strange, but it took Royd only a moment to consult his library computer. "An alien race on the other side of human space, past the Fyndii worlds and the Damoosh. Possibly legendary."

D'Branin chuckled. "No, no, no! Your library is out of date, my friend, you must supplement it the next time you visit Avalon. Not legends, no, real enough, though far away. We have little information about the Nor T'alush, but we are sure they exist, though you and I may never meet one. They were the start of it all."

"Tell me," Royd said. "I am interested in your work, Karoly."

"I was coding some information into the Academy computers, a packet newly arrived from Dam Tullian after twenty standard years in transit. Part of it was Nor T'alush folklore. I had no idea how long that had taken to get to Dam Tullian, or by what route it had come, but it did not matter—folklore is timeless anyway, and this was fascinating material. Did you know that my first degree was in xenomythology?"

"I did not. Please continue."

"The *volcryn* story was among the Nor T'alush myths. It awed me; a race of sentients moving out from some mysterious origin in the core of the galaxy, sailing towards the galactic edge and, it was alleged, eventually bound for intergalactic space itself, meanwhile always keeping to the interstellar depths, no planetfalls, seldom coming within a light year of a star." D'Branin's gray eyes sparkled, and as he spoke his hands swept enthusiastically to either side, as if they could encompass the galaxy. "And doing it all *without a stardrive,* Royd, that is the real wonder! Doing it in ships moving only a fraction of the speed of light! That was the detail that obsessed me! How different they must be, my *volcryn*—wise and patient, long-lived and long-viewed, with none of the terrible haste and passion that consumes the lesser races. Think how *old* they must be, those *volcryn* ships!"

"Old," Royd agreed. "Karoly, you said ships. More than one?"

"Oh, yes," d'Branin said. "According to the Nor T'alush, one or two appeared first, on the innermost edges of their trading sphere, but others followed. Hundreds of them, each solitary, moving by itself, bound outward, always outward. The direction was always the same. For fifteen thousand standard years they moved among the Nor T'alush stars, and then they began to pass out from among them. The myth said that the last *volcryn* ship was gone three thousand years ago."

"Eighteen thousand years," Royd said, adding, "Are the Nor T'alush that old?"

"Not as star-travelers, no," d'Branin said, smiling. "According to their own histories, the Nor T'alush have only been civilized for about half that long. That bothered me for a while. It seemed to make the *volcryn* story clearly a legend. A wonderful legend, true, but nothing more.

"Ultimately, however, I could not let it alone. In my spare time I investigated, cross-checking with other alien cosmologies to see whether this particular myth was shared by any races other than the Nor T'alush. I thought perhaps I could get a thesis out of it. It seemed a fruitful line of inquiry.

"I was startled by what I found. Nothing from the Hrangans, or the Hrangan slave races, but that made sense, you see. Since they were *out* from human space, the *volcryn* would not reach them until after they had passed through our own sphere. When I looked *in,* however, the *volcryn* story was everywhere." D'Branin leaned forward eagerly. "Ah, Royd, the stories, the *stories!*"

"Tell me," Royd said.

"The Fyndii call them *iy-wivii,* which translates to something like void-horde or dark-horde. Each Fyndii horde tells the same story, only the mindmutes disbelieve. The ships are said to be vast, much larger than any known in their history or ours. Warships, they say. There is a story of a lost Fyndii horde, three hundred ships under *rala-fyn,* all destroyed utterly when they encountered an *iy-wivii.* This was many thousands of years ago, of course, so the details are unclear.

"The Damoosh have a different story, but they accept it as literal truth—and the Damoosh, you know, are the oldest race we've yet encountered. The people of the gulf, they call my *volcryn*. Lovely stories, Royd, lovely! Ships like great dark cities, still and silent, moving at a slower pace than the universe around them. Damoosh legends say the *volcryn* are refugees from some unimaginable war deep in the core of the galaxy, at the very beginning of time. They abandoned the worlds and stars on which they had evolved, sought true peace in the emptiness between.

"The gethsoids of Aath have a similar story, but in their tale that war destroyed all life in our galaxy, and the *volcryn* are gods of a sort, re-seeding the worlds as they pass. Other races see them as god's messengers, or shadows out of hell warning us all to flee some terror soon to emerge from the core."

"Your stories contradict each other, Karoly."

"Yes, yes, of course, but they all agree on the essentials—the *volcryn,* sailing out, passing through our short-lived empires and transient glories in their ancient eternal sublight ships. *That* is what matters! The rest is frippery, ornamentation; we will soon know the truth of it. I checked what little was known about the races said to flourish farther in still, beyond even the Nor T'alush—civilizations and peoples half legendary themselves, like the Dan'lai and the ullish and the Rohenna'kh—and where I could find anything at all, I found the *volcryn* story once again."

"The legend of the legends," Royd suggested. The spectre's wide mouth turned up in a smile.

"Exactly, exactly," d'Branin agreed. "At that point, I called in the experts, specialists from the Institute for the Study of Non-Human Intelligence. We researched for two years. It was all there, in the libraries and memories and matrices of the Academy. No one had ever looked before, or bothered to put it together.

"The *volcryn* have been moving through the manrealm for most of human history, since before the dawn of spaceflight. While we twist the fabric of space itself to cheat relativity, they have been sailing their great ships right through the heart of our alleged civilization, past our most populous worlds, at stately, slow sublight speeds, bound for the Fringe and the dark between the galaxies. Marvelous, Royd, marvelous!"

"Marvelous!" Royd agreed.

Karoly d'Branin drained his chocolate cup with a swig, and reached out to catch Royd's arm, but his hand passed through empty light. He seemed disconcerted for a moment, before he began to laugh at himself. "Ah, my *volcryn*. I grow overenthused, Royd. I am so close now. They have preyed on my mind for a dozen years, and within the month I will have them, will behold their splendor with my own weary eyes. Then, then, if only I can open communication, if only my people can reach ones so great and strange as they, so different from us—I have hopes, Royd, hopes that at last I will know the why of it!"

The ghost of Royd Eris smiled for him, and looked on through calm transparent eyes.

PASSENGERS SOON GROW RESTLESS ON A STARSHIP UNDER DRIVE, SOONER on one as small and spare as the *Nightflyer.* Late in the second week, the speculation began in deadly earnest.

"Who is this Royd Eris, really?" the xenobiologist, Rojan Christopheris, complained one night when four of them were playing cards. "Why doesn't he come out? What's the purpose of keeping himself sealed off from the rest of us?"

"Ask him," suggested Dannel, the male linguist.

"What if he's a criminal of some sort?" Christopheris said. "Do we know anything about him? No, of course not. D'Branin engaged him, and d'Branin is a senile old fool, we all know that."

"It's your play," Lommie Thorne said.

Christopheris snapped down a card. "Setback," he declared, "you'll have to draw again." He grinned. "As for this Eris, who knows that he isn't planning to kill us all."

"For our vast wealth, no doubt," said Lindran, the female linguist. She played a card on top of the one Christopheris had laid down. "Ricochet," she called softly. She smiled. So did Royd Eris, watching.

MELANTHA JHIRL WAS GOOD TO WATCH.

Young, healthy, active, Melantha Jhirl had a vibrancy about her the others could not match. She was big in every way; a head taller than anyone else on board, large-framed, large-breasted, long-legged, strong, muscles moving fluidly beneath shiny coal-black skin. Her appetites were big as well. She ate twice as much as any of her colleagues, drank heavily without ever seeming drunk, exercised for hours every day on equipment she had brought with her and set up in one of the cargo holds. By the third week out she had sexed with all four of the men on board and two of the other women. Even in bed she was always active, exhausting most of her partners. Royd watched her with consuming interest.

"I am an improved model," she told him once as she worked out on her parallel bars, sweat glistening on her bare skin, her long black hair confined in a net.

"Improved?" Royd said. He could not send his projection down to the holds, but Melantha had summoned him with the communicator to talk while she exercised, not knowing he would have been there anyway.

She paused in her routine, holding her body straight and aloft with the strength of her arms and her back. "Altered, captain," she said. She had taken to calling him captain. "Born on Prometheus among the elite, child of two genetic wizards. Improved, captain. I require twice the energy you do, but I use it all. A more efficient metabolism, a stronger and more durable body, an expected lifespan half again the normal human's. My people have made some terrible mistakes when they try to radically redesign humanity, but the small improvements they do well."

She resumed her exercises, moving quickly and easily, silent until she had finished. When she was done, she vaulted away from the bars and stood breathing heavily for a moment, then crossed her arms and cocked her head and grinned. "Now you know my life story, captain," she said. She pulled off the net to shake free her hair.

"Surely there is more," said the voice from the communicator.

Melantha Jhirl laughed. "Surely," she said. "Do you want to hear about my defection to Avalon, the whys and wherefores of it, the trouble it caused my family on Prometheus? Or are you more interested in my extraordinary work in cultural xenology? Do you want to hear about that?"

"Perhaps some other time," Royd said politely. "What is that crystal you wear?"

It hung between her breasts ordinarily; she had removed it when she stripped for her exercises. She picked it up again and slipped it over her head; a small green gem laced with traceries of black, on a silver chain. When it touched her Melantha closed her eyes briefly, then opened them again, grinning. "It's alive," she said. "Haven't you ever seen one? A whisperjewel, captain. Resonant crystal, etched psionically to hold a memory, a sensation. The touch brings it back, for a time."

"I am familiar with the principle," Royd said, "but not this use. Yours contains some treasured memory, then? Of your family, perhaps?"

Melantha Jhirl snatched up a towel and began to dry the sweat from her body. "Mine contains the sensations of a particularly satisfying session in bed, captain. It arouses me. Or it did. Whisperjewels fade in time, and this isn't as potent as it once was. But sometimes—often when I've come from lovemaking or strenuous exercise—it comes alive on me again, like it did just then."

"Oh," said Royd's voice. "It has made you aroused, then? Are you going off to copulate now?"

Melantha grinned. "I know what part of my life you want to hear about, captain—my tumultuous and passionate love life. Well, you won't have it. Not until I hear your life story, anyway. Among my modest attributes is an insatiable curiosity. Who are you, captain? Really?"

"One as improved as you," Royd replied, "should certainly be able to guess."

Melantha laughed, and tossed her towel at the communicator grille.

———

LOMMIE THORNE SPENT MOST OF HER DAYS IN THE CARGO HOLD THEY had designated as the computer room, setting up the system they would use to analyze the *volcryn*. As often as not, the xenotech Alys Northwind came with her to lend a hand. The cyberneticist whistled as she worked; Northwind obeyed her orders in a sullen silence. Occasionally they talked.

"Eris isn't human," Lommie Thorne said one day, as she supervised the installation of a display viewscreen.

Alys Northwind grunted. "What?" A frown broke across her square, flat features. Christopheris and his talk had made her nervous about Eris. She clicked another component into position, and turned.

"He talks to us, but he can't be seen," the cyberneticist said. "This ship is uncrewed, seemingly all automated except for him. Why not entirely automated, then? I'd wager this Royd Eris is a fairly sophisticated computer system, perhaps a genuine Artificial Intelligence. Even a modest program can carry on a blind conversation indistinguishable from a human's. This one could fool you, I'd bet, once it's up and running."

The xenotech grunted and turned back to her work. "Why fake being human, then?"

"Because," said Lommie Thorne, "most legal systems give AIs no rights. A ship can't own itself, even on Avalon. The *Nightflyer* is probably afraid of being seized and disconnected." She whistled. "Death, Alys; the end of self-awareness and conscious thought."

"I work with machines every day," Alys Northwind said stubbornly. "Turn them off, turn them on, makes no difference. They don't mind. Why should this machine care?"

Lommie Thorne smiled. "A computer is different, Alys," she said. "Mind, thought, life, the big systems have all of that." Her right hand curled around her left wrist, and her thumb began idly rubbing the nubs of her implant. "Sensation, too. I know. No one wants the end of sensation. They are not so different from you and I, really."

The xenotech glanced back and shook her head. "Really," she repeated, in a flat, disbelieving voice.

Royd Eris listened and watched, unsmiling.

———

THALE LASAMER WAS A FRAIL YOUNG THING; NERVOUS, SENSITIVE, WITH limp flaxen hair that fell to his shoulders, and watery blue eyes. Normally he dressed like a peacock, favoring the lacy V-necked shirts and codpieces that were still the fashion among the lower classes of his homeworld. But on the day he sought out Karoly d'Branin in his cramped, private cabin, Lasamer was dressed almost somberly, in an austere gray jumpsuit.

"I feel it," he said, clutching d'Branin by the arm, his long fingernails digging in painfully. "Something is wrong, Karoly, something is very wrong. I'm beginning to get frightened."

The telepath's nails bit, and d'Branin pulled away hard. "You are hurting me," he protested. "My friend, what is it? Frightened? Of what, of whom? I do not understand. What could there be to fear?"

Lasamer raised pale hands to his face. "I don't know, I don't *know*," he wailed. "Yet it's *there*, I feel it. Karoly, I'm picking up something. You know I'm good, I am, that's why you picked me. Just a moment ago, when my nails dug into you, I felt it. I can read you now, in flashes. You're thinking I'm too excitable, that it's the confinement, that I've got to be calmed down." The young man laughed a thin hysterical laugh that died as quickly as it had begun. "No, you see, I am good. Class one, tested, and I tell you I'm afraid. I sense it. Feel it. Dream of it. I felt it even as we were boarding, and it's gotten worse. Something dangerous. Something volatile. And alien, Karoly, *alien!*"

"The *volcryn!*" d'Branin said.

"No, impossible. We're in drive, they're light years away." The edgy laughter sounded again. "I'm not that good, Karoly. I've heard your Crey story, but I'm only a human. No, this is close. On the ship."

"One of us?"

"Maybe," Lassamer said. He rubbed his cheek absently. "I can't sort it out."

D'Branin put a fatherly hand on his shoulder. "Thale, this feeling of yours—could it be that you are just tired? We have all of us been under strain. Inactivity can be taxing."

"Get your hand off me," Lasamer snapped.

D'Branin drew back his hand quickly.

"This is *real*," the telepath insisted, "and I don't need you thinking that maybe you shouldn't have taken me, all that crap. I'm as stable as anyone on this . . . this . . . how *dare* you think I'm unstable, you ought to look inside some of these others, Christopheris with his bottle and his dirty little fantasies, Dannel half sick with fear, Lommie and her machines, with her it's all metal and lights and cool circuits, sick, I tell you, and Jhirl's arrogant and Agatha whines even in her head to herself all the time, and Alys is empty, like a cow. You, you don't touch them, see into them, what do you know of *stable?* Losers, d'Branin, they've given you a bunch of losers, and I'm one of your best, so don't you go thinking that I'm not stable, not sane, you hear." His blue eyes were fevered. "Do you *hear?*"

"Easy," d'Branin said. "Easy, Thale, you're getting excited."

The telepath blinked, and suddenly the wildness was gone. "Excited?" he said. "Yes." He looked around guiltily. "It's hard, Karoly, but listen to me, you must, I'm warning you. We're in danger."

"I will listen," d'Branin said, "but I cannot act without more definite information. You must use your talent and get it for me, yes? You can do that."

Lasamer nodded. "Yes," he said. "Yes." They talked quietly for more than an hour, and finally the telepath left peacefully.

Afterwards d'Branin went straight to the psipsych, who was lying in her sleepweb surrounded by medicines, complaining bitterly of aches. "Interesting," she said when d'Branin told her. "I've felt something too, a sense of threat, very vague, diffuse. I thought it was me, the confinement, the boredom, the way I feel. My moods betray me at times. Did he say anything more specific?"

"No."

"I'll make an effort to move around, read him, read the others, see what I can pick up. Although, if this is real, he should know it first. He's a one, I'm only a three."

D'Branin nodded. "He seems very receptive," he said. "He told me all kinds of things about the others."

"Means nothing. Sometimes, when a telepath insists he is picking up everything, what it means is that he's picking up nothing at all. He imagines feelings, readings, to make up for those that will not come. I'll keep careful watch on him, d'Branin. Sometimes a talent can crack, slip into a kind of hysteria, and begin to broadcast instead of receive. In a closed environment, that's very dangerous."

Karoly d'Branin nodded. "Of course, of course."

In another part of the ship, Royd Eris frowned.

———

"HAVE YOU NOTICED THE CLOTHING ON THAT HOLOGRAPH HE SENDS us?" Rojan Christopheris asked Alys Northwind. They were alone in one of the holds, reclining on a mat, trying to avoid the wet spot. The xenobiologist had lit a joystick. He offered it to his companion, but Northwind waved it away.

"A decade out of style, maybe more. My father wore shirts like that when he was a boy on Old Poseidon."

"Eris has old-fashioned taste," Alys Northwind said. "So? I don't care what he wears. Me, I like my jumpsuits. They're comfortable. Don't care what people think."

"You don't, do you?" Christopheris said, wrinkling his huge nose. She did not see the gesture. "Well, you miss the point. What if that isn't really Eris? A projection can be anything, can be made up out of whole cloth. I don't think he really looks like that."

"No?" Now her voice was curious. She rolled over and curled up beneath his arm, her heavy white breasts against his chest.

"What if he's sick, deformed, ashamed to be seen the way he really looks?" Christopheris said. "Perhaps he has some disease. The Slow Plague can waste a person terribly, but it takes decades to kill, and there are other contagions—manthrax, new leprosy, the melt, Langamen's Disease, lots of them. Could be that Royd's self-imposed quarantine is just that. A quarantine. Think about it."

Alys Northwind frowned. "All this talk of Eris," she said, "is making me edgy."

The xenobiologist sucked on his joystick and laughed. "Welcome to the *Nightflyer*, then. The rest of us are already there."

IN THE FIFTH WEEK OUT, MELANTHA JHIRL PUSHED HER PAWN TO THE sixth rank and Royd saw that it was unstoppable and resigned. It was his eighth straight defeat at her hands in as many days. She was sitting cross-legged on the floor of the lounge, the chessmen spread out before her in front of a darkened viewscreen. Laughing, she swept them all away. "Don't feel bad, Royd," she told him. "I'm an improved model. Always three moves ahead."

"I should tie in my computer," he replied. "You'd never know." His ghost materialized suddenly, standing in front of the viewscreen, and smiled at her.

"I'd know within three moves," Melantha Jhirl said. "Try it."

They were the last victims of a chess fever that had swept the *Nightflyer* for more than a week. Initially it had been Christopheris who produced the set and urged people to play, but the others had lost interest quickly when Thale Lasamer sat down and beat them all, one by one. Everyone was certain that he'd done it by reading their minds, but the telepath was in a volatile, nasty mood, and no one dared voice the accusation. Melantha, however, had been able to defeat Lasamer without very much trouble. "He isn't that good a player," she told Royd afterwards, "and if he's trying to lift ideas from me, he's getting gibberish. The improved model knows certain mental disciplines. I can shield myself well enough, thank you." Christopheris and a few of the others then tried a game or two against Melantha, and were routed for their troubles. Finally Royd asked if he might play. Only Melantha and Karoly were willing to sit down with him over the board, and since Karoly could barely recall how the pieces moved from one moment to the next, that left Melantha and Royd as regular opponents. They both seemed to thrive on the games, though Melantha always won.

Melantha stood up and walked to the kitchen, stepping right through Royd's ghostly form, which she steadfastly refused to pretend was real. "The rest of them walk around me," Royd complained.

She shrugged, and found a bulb of beer in a storage compartment. "When are you going to break down and let me behind your wall for a visit, captain?" she asked. "Don't you get lonely back there? Sexually frustrated? Claustrophobic?"

"I have flown the *Nightflyer* all my life, Melantha," Royd said. His projection, ignored, winked out. "If I were subject to claustrophobia, sexual frustration, or loneliness, such a life would have been impossible. Surely that should be obvious to you, being as improved a model as you are?"

She took a squeeze of her beer and laughed her mellow, musical laugh at him. "I'll solve you yet, captain," she warned.

"Meanwhile," he said, "tell me some more lies about your life."

"Have you ever heard of Jupiter?" the xenotech demanded of the others. She was drunk, lolling in her sleepweb in the cargo hold.

"Something to do with Earth," said Lindran. "The same myth system originated both names, I believe."

"Jupiter," the xenotech announced loudly, "is a gas giant in the same solar system as Old Earth. Didn't know that, did you?"

"I've got more important things to occupy my mind than such trivia, Alys," Lindran said.

Alys Northwind smiled down smugly. "Listen, I'm talking to you. They were on the verge of exploring this Jupiter when the stardrive was discovered, oh, way back. After that, course, no one bothered with gas giants. Just slip into drive and find the habitable worlds, settle them, ignore the comets and the rocks and the gas giants—there's another star just a few light years away, and it has *more* habitable planets. But there were people who thought those Jupiters might have life, you know. Do you see?"

"I see that you're blind drunk," Lindran said.

Christopheris looked annoyed. "If there is intelligent life on the gas giants, it shows no interest in leaving them," he snapped. "All of the sentient species we have met up to now have originated on worlds similar to Earth, and most of them are oxygen breathers. Unless you're suggesting that the *volcryn* are from a gas giant?"

The xenotech pushed herself up to a sitting position and smiled conspiratorially. "Not the *volcryn*," she said. "Royd Eris. Crack that forward bulkhead in the lounge, and watch the methane and ammonia come smoking out." Her hand made a sensuous waving motion through the air, and she convulsed with giddy laughter.

THE SYSTEM WAS UP AND RUNNING. CYBERNETICIST LOMMIE THORNE sat at the master console, a featureless black plastic plate upon which the phantom images of a hundred keyboard configurations came and went in holographic display, vanishing and shifting even as she used them. Around her rose crystalline data grids, ranks of viewscreens and readout panels upon which columns of figures marched and geometric shapes did stately whirling dances, dark columns of seamless metal that contained the mind and soul of her system. She sat in the semi-darkness happily, whistling as she ran the computer through several simple routines, her fingers moving across the flickering keys with blind speed and quickening tempo. "Ah," she said once, smiling. Later, only, "Good."

Then it was time for the final run-through. Lommie Thorne slid back the metallic fabric of her left sleeve, pushed her wrist beneath the console, found the prongs, jacked herself in. Interface.

Ecstasy.

Inkblot shapes in a dozen glowing colors twisted and melded and broke apart on the readout screens.

In an instant it was over.

Lommie Thorne pulled free her wrist. The smile on her face was shy and satisfied, but across it lay another expression, the merest hint of puzzlement. She touched her thumb to the holes of her wrist jack, and found them warm to the touch, tingling. Lommie shivered.

The system was running perfectly, hardware in good condition, all software systems functioning according to plan, interface meshing well. It had been a delight, as it always was. When she joined with the system, she was wise beyond her years, and powerful, and full of light and electricity and the stuff of life, cool and clean and exciting to touch, and never alone, never small or weak. That was what it was always like when she interfaced and let herself expand.

But this time something had been different. Something cold had touched her, only for a moment. Something very cold and very frightening, and together she and the system had seen it clearly for a brief moment, and then it had been gone again.

The cyberneticist shook her head, and drove the nonsense out. She went back to work. After a time, she began to whistle.

DURING THE SIXTH WEEK, ALYS NORTHWIND CUT HERSELF BADLY while preparing a snack. She was standing in the kitchen, slicing a spiced meatstick with a long knife, when suddenly she screamed.

Dannel and Lindran rushed to her, and found her staring down in horror at the chopping block in front of her. The knife had taken off the first joint of the index finger on her left hand, and the blood was spreading in ragged spurts. "The ship lurched," Alys said numbly, staring up at Dannel. "Didn't you feel it jerk? It pushed the knife to the side."

"Get something to stop the bleeding," Lindran said. Dannel looked around in panic. "Oh, I'll do it myself," Lindran finally said, and she did.

The psipsych, Agatha Marij-Black, gave Northwind a tranquilizer, then looked at the two linguists. "Did you see it happen?"

"She did it herself, with the knife," Dannel said.

From somewhere down the corridor, there came the sound of wild, hysterical laughter.

———

"I DAMPENED HIM," MARIJ-BLACK REPORTED TO KAROLY D'BRANIN later the same day. "Psionine-4. It will blunt his receptivity for several days, and I have more if he needs it."

D'Branin wore a stricken look. "We talked several times and I could see that Thale was becoming ever more fearful, but he could never tell me the why of it. Did you have to shut him off?"

The psipsych shrugged. "He was edging into the irrational. Given his level of talent, if he'd gone over the edge he might have taken us all with him. You should never have taken a class one telepath, d'Branin. Too unstable."

"We must communicate with an alien race. I remind you that is no easy task. The *volcryn* will be more alien than any sentients we have yet encountered. We needed class one skills if we were to have any hope of reaching them. And they have so much to teach us, my friend!"

"Glib," she said, "but you might have no working skills at all, given the condition of your class one. Half the time he's curled up into the fetal position in his sleepweb, half the time he's strutting and crowing and half mad with fear. He insists we're all in real physical danger, but he doesn't know why or from what. The worst of it is that I can't tell if he's really sensing something or simply having an acute attack of paranoia. He certainly displays some classic paranoid symptoms. Among other things, he insists that he's being watched. Perhaps his condition is completely unrelated to us, the *volcryn,* and his talent. I can't be sure."

"What of your own talent?" d'Branin said. "You are an empath, are you not?"

"Don't tell me my job," she said sharply. "I sexed with him last week. You don't get more proximity or better rapport for esping than that. Even under those conditions, I couldn't be sure of anything. His mind is a chaos, and his fear is so rank it stank up the sheets. I don't read anything from the others either, besides the ordinary tensions and frustrations. But I'm only a three, so that doesn't mean much. My abilities are limited. You know I haven't been feeling well, d'Branin. I can barely breathe on this ship. The air seems thick and heavy to me, my head throbs. I ought to stay in bed."

"Yes, of course," d'Branin said hastily. "I did not mean to criticize. You have been doing all you can under difficult circumstances. How long will it be until Thale is with us again?"

The psipsych rubbed her temple wearily. "I'm recommending we keep him dampened until the mission is over, d'Branin. I warn you, an insane or hysterical telepath is dangerous. That business with Northwind and the knife might have been his doing, you know. He started screaming not long after, remember. Maybe he'd touched her, for just an instant—oh, it's a wild idea, but it's possible. The point is, we don't take chances. I have enough psionine-4 to keep him numb and functional until we're back on Avalon."

"*But*—Royd will take us out of drive soon, and we will make contact with the *volcryn*. We will need Thale, his mind, his talent. Is it vital to keep him dampened? Is there no other way?"

Marij-Black grimaced. "My other option was an injection of esperon. It would have opened him up completely, increased his psionic receptivity tenfold for a few hours. Then, I'd hope, he could focus in on this danger he's feeling. Exorcise it if it's false, deal with it if it's real. But psionine-4 is a lot safer. Esperon is a hell of a drug, with devastating side effects. It raises the blood pressure dramatically, sometimes brings on hyperventilation or seizures, has even been known to stop the heart. Lasamer is young enough so that I'm not worried about that, but I don't think he has the emotional stability to deal with that kind of power. The psionine should tell us something. If his paranoia persists, I'll know it has nothing to do with his telepathy."

"And if it does not persist?" Karoly d'Branin said.

Agatha Marij-Black smiled wickedly at him. "If Lasamer becomes quiescent, and stops babbling about danger? Why, that would mean he was no longer picking up anything, wouldn't it? And *that* would mean there had been something to pick up, that he'd been right all along."

AT DINNER THAT NIGHT, THALE LASAMER WAS QUIET AND DISTRACTED, eating in a rhythmic, mechanical sort of way, with a cloudy look in his blue eyes. Afterwards he excused himself and went straight to bed, falling into exhausted slumber almost immediately.

"What did you do to him?" Lommie Thorne asked Marij-Black.

"I shut off that prying mind of his," she replied.

"You should have done it two weeks ago," Lindran said. "Docile, he's a lot easier to take."

Karoly d'Branin hardly touched his food.

———

FALSE NIGHT CAME, AND ROYD'S WRAITH MATERIALIZED WHILE KAROLY d'Branin sat brooding over his chocolate. "Karoly," the apparition said, "would it be possible to tie in the computer your team brought on board with my shipboard system? Your *volcryn* stories fascinate me, and I would like to be able to study them further at my leisure. I assume the details of your investigation are in storage."

"Certainly," d'Branin replied in an offhand, distracted manner. "Our system is up now. Patching it into the *Nightflyer* should present no problem. I will tell Lommie to attend to it tomorrow."

Silence hung in the room heavily. Karoly d'Branin sipped at his chocolate and stared off into the darkness, almost unaware of Royd.

"You are troubled," Royd said after a time.

"Eh? Oh, yes." D'Branin looked up. "Forgive me, my friend. I have much on my mind."

"It concerns Thale Lasamer, does it not?"

Karoly d'Branin looked at the pale, luminescent figure across from him for a long time before he finally managed a stiff nod. "Yes. Might I ask how you knew that?"

"I know everything that occurs on the *Nightflyer*," Royd said.

"You have been watching us," d'Branin said gravely, accusation in his tone. "Then it is so, what Thale says, about us being watched. Royd, how could you? Spying is beneath you."

The ghost's transparent eyes had no life in them, did not see. "Do not tell the others," Royd warned. "Karoly, my friend—if I may call you my friend—I have my own reasons for watching, reasons it would not profit you to know. I mean you no harm. Believe that. You have hired me to take you safely to the *volcryn* and safely back, and I mean to do just that."

"You are being evasive, Royd," d'Branin said. "Why do you spy on us? Do you watch everything? Are you a voyeur, some enemy, is that why you do not mix with us? Is watching all you intend to do?"

"Your suspicions hurt me, Karoly."

"Your deception hurts me. Will you not answer me?"

"I have eyes and ears everywhere," Royd said. "There is no place to hide from me on the *Nightflyer*. Do I see everything? No, not always. I am only human, no matter what your colleagues might think. I sleep. The monitors remain on, but there is no one to observe them. I can only pay attention to one or two scenes or inputs at once. Sometimes I grow distracted, unobservant. I watch everything, Karoly, but I do not see everything."

"Why?" D'Branin poured himself a fresh cup of chocolate, steadying his hand with an effort.

"I do not have to answer that question. The *Nightflyer* is my ship."

D'Branin sipped chocolate, blinked, nodded to himself. "You grieve me, my friend. You give me no choice. Thale said we were being watched, I now learn that he was right. He says also that we are in danger. Something alien, he says. You?"

The projection was still and silent.

D'Branin clucked. "You do not answer. Ah, Royd, what am I to do? I must believe him, then. We are in danger, perhaps from you. I must abort our mission, then. Return us to Avalon, Royd. That is my decision."

The ghost smiled wanly. "So close, Karoly? Soon now we will be dropping out of drive."

Karoly d'Branin made a small sad noise deep in his throat. "My *volcryn*," he said, sighing. "So close—ah, it pains me to desert them. But I cannot do otherwise, I cannot."

"You can," said the voice of Royd Eris. "Trust me. That is all I ask, Karoly. Believe me when I tell you that I have no sinister intentions. Thale Lasamer may speak of danger, but no one has been harmed so far, have they?"

"No," admitted d'Branin. "No, unless you count Alys, cutting herself this afternoon."

"What?" Royd hesitated briefly. "Cutting herself? I did not see, Karoly. When did this happen?"

"Oh, early—just before Lasamer began to scream and rant, I believe."

"I see." Royd's voice was thoughtful. "I was watching Melantha go through her exercises," he said finally, "and talking to her. I did not notice. Tell me how it happened."

D'Branin told him.

"Listen to me," Royd said. "Trust me, Karoly, and I will give you your *volcryn*. Calm your people. Assure them that I am no threat. And keep Lasamer drugged and quiescent, do you understand? That is very important. He is the problem."

"Agatha advises much the same thing."

"I know," said Royd. "I agree with her. Will you do as I ask?"

"I do not know," d'Branin said. "You make it hard for me. I do not understand what is going wrong, my friend. Will you not tell me more?"

Royd Eris did not answer. His ghost waited.

"Well," d'Branin said at last, "you do not talk. How difficult you make it. How soon, Royd? How soon will we see my *volcryn*?"

"Quite soon," Royd replied. "We will drop out of drive in approximately seventy hours."

"Seventy hours," d'Branin said. "Such a short time. Going back would gain us nothing." He moistened his lips, lifted his cup, found it empty. "Go on, then. I will do as you bid. I will trust you, keep Lasamer drugged, I will not tell the others of your spying. Is that enough, then? Give me my *volcryn*. I have waited so long!"

"I know," said Royd Eris. "I know."

Then the ghost was gone, and Karoly d'Branin sat alone in the darkened lounge. He tried to refill his cup, but his hand began to tremble unaccountably, and he poured the chocolate over his fingers and dropped the cup, swearing, wondering, hurting.

———

THE NEXT DAY WAS A DAY OF RISING TENSIONS AND A HUNDRED SMALL irritations. Lindran and Dannel had a "private" argument that could be overheard through half the ship. A three-handed war game in the lounge ended in disaster when Christopheris accused Melantha Jhirl of cheating. Lommie Thorne complained of unusual difficulties in tying her system into the shipboard computers. Alys Northwind sat in the lounge for hours, staring at her bandaged finger with a look of sullen hatred on her face. Agatha Marij-Black prowled through the corridors, complaining that the ship was too hot, that her joints throbbed, that the air was thick and full of smoke, that the ship was too cold. Even Karoly d'Branin was despondent and on edge.

Only the telepath seemed content. Shot full of psionine-4, Thale Lasamer was often sluggish and lethargic, but at least he no longer flinched at shadows.

Royd Eris made no appearance, either by voice or holographic projection.

He was still absent at dinner. The academicians ate uneasily, expecting him to materialize at any moment, take his accustomed place, and join in the mealtime conversation. Their expectations were still unfulfilled when the after-dinner pots of chocolate and spiced tea and coffee were set on the table.

"Our captain seems to be occupied," Melantha Jhirl observed, leaning back in her chair and swirling a snifter of brandy.

"We will be shifting out of drive soon," Karoly d'Branin said. "Undoubtedly there are preparations to make." Secretly, he fretted over Royd's absence, and wondered if they were being watched even now.

Rojan Christopheris cleared his throat. "Since we're all here and he's not, perhaps this is a good time to discuss certain things. I'm not concerned about him missing dinner. He doesn't eat. He's a damned hologram. What does it matter? Maybe it's just as well, we need to talk about this. Karoly, a lot of us have been getting uneasy about Royd Eris. What do you know about this mystery man, anyway?"

"Know, my friend?" D'Branin refilled his cup with the thick bittersweet chocolate and sipped at it slowly, trying to give himself a moment to think. "What is there to know?"

"Surely you've noticed that he never comes out to play with us," Lindran said drily. "Before you engaged his ship, did anyone remark on this quirk of his?"

"I'd like to know the answer to that one, too," said Dannel, the other linguist. "A lot of traffic comes and goes through Avalon. How did you come to choose Eris? What were you told about him?"

"Told about him? Very little, I must admit. I spoke to a few port officials and charter companies, but none of them were acquainted with Royd. He had not traded out of Avalon originally, you see."

"How convenient," said Lindran.

"How suspicious," added Dannel.

"Where *is* he from, then?" Lindran demanded. "Dannel and I have listened to him pretty carefully. He speaks standard very flatly, with no discernible accent, no idiosyncrasies to betray his origins."

"Sometimes he sounds a bit archaic," Dannel put in, "and from time to time one of his constructions will give me an association. Only it's a different one each time. He's traveled a lot."

"Such a deduction," Lindran said, patting his hand. "Traders frequently do, love. Comes of owning a starship."

Dannel glared at her, but Lindran just went on. "Seriously, though, do you know anything about him? Where did this *Nightflyer* of ours come from?"

"I do not know," d'Branin admitted. "I—I never thought to ask."

The members of his research team glanced at one another incredulously. "You never thought to *ask?*" Christopheris said. "How did you come to select this ship?"

"It was available. The administrative council approved my project and assigned me personnel, but they could not spare an Academy ship. There were budgetary constraints as well."

Agatha Marij-Black laughed sourly. "What d'Branin is telling those of you who haven't figured it out is that the Academy was pleased with his studies in xenomyth, with the discovery of the *volcryn* legend, but less than enthusiastic about his plan to seek them out. So they gave him a small budget to keep him happy and productive, assuming this little mission would be fruitless, and they assigned him people who wouldn't be missed back on Avalon." She looked around. "Look at the lot of you. None of us had worked with d'Branin in the early stages, but we were all available for this jaunt. And not a one of us is a first-rate scholar."

"Speak for yourself," Melantha Jhirl said. "I volunteered for this mission."

"I won't argue the point," the psipsych said. "The crux is that the choice of the *Nightflyer* is no large enigma. You just engaged the cheapest charter you could find, didn't you, d'Branin?"

"Some of the available ships would not consider my proposition," d'Branin said. "The sound of it is odd, we must admit. And many shipmasters have an almost superstitious fear of dropping out of drive in interstellar space, without a planet near. Of those who would agree to the conditions, Royd Eris offered the best terms, and he was able to leave at once."

"And we *had* to leave at once," said Lindran. "Otherwise the *volcryn* might get away. They've only been passing through this region for ten thousand years, give or take a few thousand."

Someone laughed. D'Branin was nonplussed. "Friends, no doubt I could have postponed departure. I admit I was eager to meet my *volcryn,* to see their great ships and ask them all the questions that have haunted me, to discover the why of them. But I admit also that a delay would have been no great hardship. But why? Royd has been a gracious host, a good pilot. We have been treated well."

"Did you meet him?" Alys Northwind asked. "When you were making your arrangements, did you ever see him?"

"We spoke many times, but I was on Avalon, and Royd in orbit. I saw his face on my viewscreen."

"A projection, a computer simulation, could be anything," Lommie Thorne said. "I can have my system conjure up all sorts of faces for your viewscreen, Karoly."

"No one has ever seen this Royd Eris," Christopheris said. "He has made himself a cipher from the start."

"Our host wishes his privacy to remain inviolate," d'Branin said.

"Evasions," Lindran said. "What is he hiding?"

Melantha Jhirl laughed. When all eyes had moved to her, she grinned and shook her head. "Captain Royd is perfect, a strange man for a strange mission. Don't any of you love a mystery? Here we are flying light years to intercept a hypothetical alien starship from the core of the galaxy that has been outward-bound for longer than humanity has been having wars, and all of you are upset because you can't count the warts on Royd's nose." She leaned across the table to refill her brandy snifter. "My mother was right," she said lightly. "Normals are subnormal."

"Maybe we should listen to Melantha," Lommie Thome said thoughtfully. "Royd's foibles and neuroses are his business, if he does not impose them on us."

"It makes me uncomfortable," Dannel complained weakly.

"For all we know," said Alys Northwind, "we might be traveling with a criminal or an alien."

"*Jupiter,*" someone muttered. The xenotech flushed red and there was sniggering around the long table.

But Thale Lasamer looked up furtively from his plate, and giggled. "An *alien,*" he said. His blue eyes flicked back and forth in his skull, as if seeking escape. They were bright and wild.

Marij-Black swore. "The drug is wearing off," she said quickly to d'Branin. "I'll have to go back to my cabin to get some more."

"What drug?" Lommie Thorne demanded. D'Branin had been careful not to tell the others too much about Lasamer's ravings, for fear of inflaming the shipboard tensions. "What's going on?"

"Danger," Lasamer said. He turned to Lommie, sitting next to him, and grasped her forearm hard, his long painted fingernails clawing at the silvery metal of her shirt. "We're in danger, I tell you, I'm reading it. Something *alien.* It means us ill. Blood, I see blood." He laughed. "Can you taste it, Agatha? I can almost taste the blood. *It* can, too."

Marij-Black rose. "He's not well," she announced to the others. "I've been dampening him with psionine, trying to hold his delusions in check. I'll get some more." She started towards the door.

"Dampening him?" Christopheris said, horrified. "He's warning us of something. Don't you hear him? I want to know what it *is.*"

"Not psionine," said Melantha Jhirl. "Try esperon."

"Don't tell me my job, woman!"

"Sorry," Melantha said. She gave a modest shrug. "I'm one step ahead of you, though. Esperon might exorcise his delusions, no?"

"Yes, but—"

"And it might help him focus on this threat he claims to detect, correct?"

"I know the characteristics of esperon quite well," the psipsych said testily.

Melantha smiled over the rim of her brandy glass. "I'm sure you do. Now listen to me. All of you are anxious about Royd, it seems.

You can't stand not knowing whatever it is he's concealing. Rojan has been making up stories for weeks, and he's ready to believe any of them. Alys is so nervous she cut her finger off. We're squabbling constantly. Fears like that won't help us work together as a team. Let's end them. Easy enough." She pointed to Thale. "Here sits a class one telepath. Boost his power with esperon and he'll be able to recite our captain's life history to us, until we're all suitably bored with it. Meanwhile he'll also be vanquishing his personal demons."

"He's watching us," the telepath said in a low, urgent voice.

"No," said Karoly d'Branin, "we must keep Thale dampened."

"Karoly," Christopheris said, "this has gone too far. Several of us are nervous and this boy is terrified. I believe we all need an end to the mystery of Royd Eris. For once, Melantha is right."

"We have no right," d'Branin said.

"We have the need," said Lommie Thorne. "I agree with Melantha."

"Yes," echoed Alys Northwind. The two linguists were nodding.

D'Branin thought regretfully of his promise to Royd. They were not giving him any choice. His eyes met those of the psipsych, and he sighed. "Do it, then," he said. "Get him the esperon."

"He's going to kill me." Thale Lasamer screamed. He leapt to his feet, and when Lommie Thorne tried to calm him with a hand on his arm, he seized a cup of coffee and threw it square in her face. It took three of them to hold him down. "Hurry," Christopheris barked, as the telepath struggled.

Marij-Black shuddered and left the lounge.

WHEN SHE RETURNED, THE OTHERS HAD LIFTED LASAMER TO THE TABLE and forced him down, pulling aside his long pale hair to bare the arteries in his neck.

Marij-Black moved to his side.

"Stop that," Royd said. "There is no need."

His ghost shimmered into being in its empty chair at the head of the long dinner table. The psipsych froze in the act of slipping an ampule of esperon into her injection gun, and Alys Northwind startled visibly and released one of Lasamer's arms. The captive did not pull free. He lay on the table, breathing heavily, his pale blue eyes fixed glassily on Royd's projection, transfixed by the vision of his sudden materialization.

Melantha Jhirl lifted her brandy glass in salute. "Boo," she said. "You've missed dinner, captain."

"Royd," said Karoly d'Branin, "I am sorry."

The ghost stared unseeing at the far wall. "Release him," said the voice from the communicators. "I will tell you my great secrets, if my privacy intimidates you so."

"He *has* been watching us," Dannel said.

"We're listening," Northwind said suspiciously. "What are you?"

"I liked your guess about the gas giants," Royd said. "Sadly, the truth is less dramatic. I am an ordinary *Homo sapien* in middle age. Sixty-eight standard, if you require precision. The hologram you see before you is the real Royd Eris, or was so some years ago. I am somewhat older now, but I use computer simulation to project a more youthful appearance to my guests."

"Oh?" Lommie Thorne's face was red where the coffee had scalded her. "Then why the secrecy?"

"I will begin the tale with my mother," Royd replied. "The *Nightflyer* was her ship originally, custom-built to her design in the Newholme spaceyards. My mother was a freetrader, a notably successful one. She was born trash on a world called Vess, which is a very long way from here, although perhaps some of you have heard of it. She worked her way up, position by position, until she won her own command. She soon made a fortune through a willingness to accept the unusual consignment, fly off the major trade routes, take her cargo a month or a year or two years beyond where it was customarily transferred. Such practices are riskier but more profitable than flying the mail runs. My mother did not worry about how often she and her crews returned home. Her ships were her home. She forgot about Vess as soon as she left it, and seldom visited the same world twice if she could avoid it."

"Adventurous," Melantha Jhirl said.

"No," said Royd. "Sociopathic. My mother did not like people, you see. Not at all. Her crews had no love for her, nor she for them. Her one great dream was to free herself from the necessity of crew altogether. When she grew rich enough, she had it done. The *Nightflyer* was the result. After she boarded it at Newholme, she never touched a human being again, or walked a planet's surface. She did all her business from the compartments that are now mine, by viewscreen or lasercom. You would call her insane. You would be right." The ghost smiled faintly. "She did have an interesting life, though, even after her isolation. The worlds she saw, Karoly! The things she might have told you would break your heart, but you'll never hear them. She destroyed most of her records for fear that other people might get some use or pleasure from her experiences after her death. She was like that."

"And you?" asked Alys Northwind.

"She must have touched at least *one* other human being," Lindran put in, with a smile.

"I should not call her my mother," Royd said. "I am her cross-sex clone. After thirty years of flying this ship alone, she was bored. I was to be her companion and lover. She could shape me to be a perfect diversion. She had no patience with children, however, and no desire to raise me herself. After she had done the cloning, I was sealed in a nurturant tank, an embryo linked into her computer. It was my teacher. Before birth and after. I had no birth, really. Long after the time a normal child would have been born, I remained in the tank, growing, learning, on slow-time, blind and dreaming and living through tubes. I was to be released when I had attained the age of puberty, at which time she guessed I would be fit company."

"How horrible," Karoly d'Branin said. "Royd, my friend, I did not know."

"I'm sorry, captain," Melantha Jhirl said. "You were robbed of your childhood."

"I never missed it," Royd said. "Nor her. Her plans were all futile, you see. She died a few months after the cloning, when I was still a fetus in the tank. She had programmed the ship for such an eventuality, however. It dropped out of drive and shut down, drifted in interstellar space for eleven standard years while the computer made me—" He stopped, smiling. "I was going to say *while the computer made me a human being*. Well, while the computer made me whatever I am, then. That was how I inherited the *Nightflyer*. When I was born, it took me some months to acquaint myself with the operation of the ship and my own origins."

"Fascinating," said Karoly d'Branin.

"Yes," said the linguist Lindran, "but it doesn't explain why you keep yourself in isolation."

"Ah, but it does," Melantha Jhirl said. "Captain, perhaps you should explain further for the less-improved models?"

"My mother hated planets," Royd said. "She hated stinks and dirt and bacteria, the irregularity of the weather, the sight of other people. She engineered for us a flawless environment, as sterile as she could possibly make it. She disliked gravity as well. She was accustomed to weightlessness from years of service on ancient freetraders that could not afford gravity grids, and she preferred it. These were the conditions under which I was born and raised.

"My body has no immune systems, no natural resistance to anything. Contact with any of you would probably kill me, and would certainly make me very sick. My muscles are feeble, in a sense atrophied. The gravity the *Nightflyer* is now generating is for your comfort, not mine. To me it is agony. At this moment the real me is seated in a floating chair that supports my weight. I still hurt, and my internal organs may be suffering damage. It is one reason why I do not often take on passengers."

"You share your mother's opinion of the run of humanity?" asked Marij-Black.

"I do not. I like people. I accept what I am, but I did not choose it. I experience human life in the only way I can, vicariously. I am a voracious consumer of books, tapes, holoplays, fictions and drama and histories of all sorts. I have experimented with dreamdust. And infrequently, when I dare, I carry passengers. At those times, I drink in as much of their lives as I can."

"If you kept your ship under weightlessness at all times, you could take on more riders," suggested Lommie Thorne.

"True," Royd said politely. "I have found, however, that most planet-born are as uncomfortable weightless as I am under gravity. A shipmaster who does not have artificial gravity, or elects not to use it, attracts few riders. The exceptions often spend much of the voyage sick or drugged. No. I could also mingle with my passengers, I know, if I kept to my chair and wore a sealed environ-wear suit. I have done so. I find it lessens my participation instead of increasing it. I become a freak, a maimed thing, one who must be treated differently and kept at a distance. These things do not suit my purpose. I prefer isolation. As often as I dare, I study the aliens I take on as riders."

"Aliens?" Northwind's voice was confused.

"You are all aliens to me," Royd answered.

Silence filled the *Nightflyer*'s lounge.

"I am sorry this has happened, my friend," Karoly d'Branin said. "We ought not have intruded on your personal affairs."

"Sorry," muttered Agatha Marij-Black. She frowned and pushed the ampule of esperon into the injection chamber. "Well, it's glib enough, but is it the truth? We still have no proof, just a new bedtime story. The hologram could have claimed it was a creature from Jupiter, a computer, or a diseased war criminal just as easily. We have no way of verifying anything that he's said. No—we have one way, rather." She took two quick steps forward to where Thale Lasamer lay on the table. "He still needs treatment and we still need confirmation, and I don't see any sense in stopping now after we've gone this far. Why should we live with all this anxiety if we can end it all now?" Her hand pushed the telepath's unresisting head to one side. She found the artery and pressed the gun to it.

"Agatha," said Karoly d'Branin. "Don't you think . . . perhaps we should forgo this, now that Royd . . . ?"

"NO," Royd said. "Stop. I order it. This is my ship. Stop, or . . ."

" . . . or what?" The gun hissed loudly, and there was a red mark on the telepath's neck when she lifted it away.

Lasamer raised himself to a half-sitting position, supported by his elbows, and Marij-Black moved close to him. "Thale," she said in her best professional tones, "focus on Royd. You can do it, we all know how good you are. Wait just a moment, the esperon will open it all up for you."

His pale blue eyes were clouded. "Not close enough," he muttered. "One, I'm one, tested. Good, you know I'm good, but I got to be *close.*" He trembled.

The psipsych put an arm around him, stroked him, coaxed him. "The esperon will give you range, Thale," she said. "Feel it, feel yourself grow stronger. Can you feel it? Everything's getting clear, isn't it?" Her voice was a reassuring drone. "You can hear what I'm thinking, I know you can, but never mind that. The others too, push them aside, all that chatter, thoughts, desires, fear. Push it all aside. Remember the danger now? Remember? Go find it, Thale, go find the danger. Look beyond the wall there, tell us what it's like beyond the wall. Tell us about Royd. Was he telling the truth? Tell us. You're good, we all know that, you can tell us." The phrases were almost an incantation.

He shrugged off her support and sat upright by himself. "I can feel it," he said. His eyes were suddenly clearer. "Something—my head hurts—I'm *afraid!*"

"Don't be afraid," said Marij-Black. "The esperon won't make your head hurt, it just makes you better. We're all here with you. Nothing to fear." She stroked his brow. "Tell us what you see."

Thale Lasamer looked at Royd's ghost with terrified little-boy eyes, and his tongue flicked across his lower lips. "He's—"

Then his skull exploded.

HYSTERIA AND CONFUSION.

The telepath's head had burst with awful force, splattering them all with blood and bits of bone and flesh. His body thrashed madly on the tabletop for a long instant, blood spurting from the arteries in his neck in a crimson stream, his limbs twitching in a macabre dance. His head had simply ceased to exist, but he would not be still.

Agatha Marij-Black, who had been standing closest to him, dropped her injection gun and stood slack-mouthed. She was drenched with his blood, covered with pieces of flesh and brain. Beneath her right eye, a long sliver of bone had penetrated her skin, and her own blood was mingling with his. She did not seem to notice.

Rojan Christopheris fell over backward, scrambled to his feet, and pressed himself hard against the wall.

Dannel screamed, and screamed, and screamed, until Lindran slapped him hard across a blood-smeared cheek and told him to be quiet.

Alys Northwind dropped to her knees and began to mumble a prayer in a strange tongue.

Karoly d'Branin sat very still, staring, blinking, his chocolate cup forgotten in his hand.

"Do something," Lommie Thorne moaned. "Somebody *do* something." One of Lasamer's arms moved feebly, and brushed against her. She shrieked and pulled away.

Melantha Jhirl pushed aside her brandy snifter. "Control yourself," she snapped. "He's dead, he can't hurt you."

They all looked at her, but for d'Branin and Marij-Black, both of whom seemed frozen in shock. Royd's projection had vanished at some point, Melantha realized suddenly. She began to give orders. "Dannel, Lindran, Rojan—find a sheet or something to wrap him in, and get him out of here. Alys, you and Lommie get some water and sponges. We've got to clean up." Melantha moved to d'Branin's side as the others rushed to do as she had told them. "Karoly," she said, putting a gentle hand on his shoulder, "are you all right, Karoly?"

He looked up at her, gray eyes blinking. "I—yes, yes, I am—I told her not to go ahead, Melantha. I told her."

"Yes, you did," Melantha Jhirl said. She gave him a reassuring pat and moved around the table to Agatha Marij-Black. "Agatha," she called. But the psipsych did not respond, not even when Melantha shook her bodily by the shoulders. Her eyes were empty. "She's in shock," Melantha announced. She frowned at the sliver of bone protruding from Marij-Black's cheek. Sponging off her face with a napkin, she carefully removed the splinter.

"What do we do with the body?" asked Lindran. They had found a sheet and wrapped it up. It had finally stopped twitching, although blood continued to seep out, turning the concealing sheet red.

"Put it in a cargo hold," suggested Christopheris.

"No," Melantha said, "not sanitary. It will rot." She thought for a moment. "Suit up and take it down to the driveroom. Cycle it through and lash it in place somehow. Tear up the sheet if you have to. That section of the ship is vacuum. It will be best there."

Christopheris nodded, and the three of them moved off, the dead weight of Lasamer's corpse supported between them. Melantha turned back to Marij-Black, but only for an instant. Lommie Thorne, who was mopping the blood from the tabletop with a piece of cloth, suddenly began to retch violently. Melantha swore. "Someone help her," she snapped.

Karoly d'Branin finally seemed to stir. He rose and took the blood-soaked cloth from Lommie's hand, and led her back to his cabin.

"I can't do this alone," whined Alys Northwind, turning away in disgust.

"Help me, then," Melantha said. Together she and Northwind half-led and half-carried the psipsych from the lounge, cleaned her and undressed her, and put her to sleep with a shot of one of her own drugs. Afterwards Melantha took the injection gun and made the rounds. Northwind and Lommie Thorne required mild tranquilizers, Dannel a somewhat stronger one.

It was three hours before they met again.

———

THE SURVIVORS ASSEMBLED IN THE LARGEST OF THE CARGO HOLDS, where three of them hung their sleepwebs. Seven of eight attended. Agatha Marij-Black was still unconscious, sleeping or in a coma or deep shock; none of them were sure. The rest seemed to have recovered, though their faces were pale and drawn. All of them had changed clothes, even Alys Northwind, who had slipped into a new jumpsuit identical to the old one.

"I do not understand," Karoly d'Branin said. "I do not understand what . . ."

"Royd killed him, is all," Northwind said bitterly. "His secret was endangered so he just—just blew him apart. We all saw it."

"I cannot believe that," Karoly d'Branin said in an anguished voice. "I cannot. Royd and I, we have talked, talked many a night when the rest of you were sleeping. He is gentle, inquisitive, sensitive. A dreamer. He understands about the *volcryn*. He would not do such a thing, could not."

"His projection certainly winked out quick enough when it happened," Lindran said. "And you'll notice he hasn't had much to say since."

"The rest of us haven't been unusually talkative either," said Melantha Jhirl. "I don't know what to think, but my impulse is to side with Karoly. We have no proof that the captain was responsible for Thale's death. There's something here none of us understands yet."

Alys Northwind grunted. "Proof," she said disdainfully.

"In fact," Melantha continued, unperturbed, "I'm not even sure *anyone* is responsible. Nothing happened until he was given the esperon. Could the drug be at fault?"

"Hell of a side effect," Lindran muttered.

Rojan Christopheris frowned. "This is not my field, but I would think no. Esperon is extremely potent, with both physical and psionic side effects verging on the extreme, but not *that* extreme."

"What, then?" said Lommie Thorne. "What killed him?"

"The instrument of death was probably his own talent," the xenobiologist said, "undoubtedly augmented by the drug. Besides boosting his principal power, his telepathic sensitivity, esperon would also tend to bring out other psi-talents that might have been latent in him."

"Such as?" Lommie demanded.

"Biocontrol. Telekinesis."

Melantha Jhirl was way ahead of him. "Esperon shoots blood pressure way up anyway. Increase the pressure in his skull even more by rushing all the blood in his body to his brain. Decrease the air pressure around his head simultaneously, using teke to induce a short-lived vacuum. Think about it."

They thought about it, and none of them liked it.

"Who could do such a thing?" Karoly d'Branin said. "It could only have been self-induced, his own talent wild, out of control."

"Or turned against him by a greater talent," Alys Northwind said stubbornly.

"No human telepath has talent on that order, to seize control of someone else, body and mind and soul, even for an instant."

"Exactly," the stout xenotech replied. "No *human* telepath."

"Gas giant people?" Lommie Thorne's tone was mocking.

Alys Northwind stared her down. "I could talk about Crey sensitives or *githyanki* soulsucks, name a half-dozen others off the top of my head, but I don't need to. I'll only name one. A Hrangan Mind."

That was a disquieting thought. All of them fell silent and stirred uneasily, thinking of the vast, inimical power of a Hrangan Mind hidden in the command chambers of the *Nightflyer*, until Melantha Jhirl broke the spell with a short, derisive laugh. "You're frightening yourself with shadows, Alys," she said. "What you're saying is ridiculous, if you stop to think about it. I hope that isn't too much to ask. You're supposed to be xenologists, the lot of you, experts in alien languages, psychology, biology, technology. You don't act the part. We warred with Old Hranga for a thousand years, but we *never* communicated successfully with a Hrangan Mind. If Royd Eris is a Hrangan, they've improved their conversational skills markedly in the centuries since the Collapse."

Alys Northwind flushed. "You're right," she said. "I'm jumpy."

"Friends," said Karoly d'Branin, "we must not let our actions be dictated by panic or hysteria. A terrible thing has happened. One of our colleagues is dead, and we do not know why. Until we do, we can only go on. This is no time for rash actions against the innocent. Perhaps, when we return to Avalon, an investigation will tell us what happened. The body is safe for examination, is it not?"

"We cycled it through the airlock into the driveroom," Dannel said. "It'll keep."

"And it can be studied closely on our return," d'Branin said.

"Which should be immediate," said Northwind. "Tell Eris to turn this ship around!"

D'Branin looked stricken. "But the *volcryn!* A week more and we shall know them, if my figures are correct. To return would take us six weeks. Surely it is worth one additional week to know that they exist? Thale would not have wanted his death to be for nothing."

"Before he died, Thale was raving about aliens, about danger," Northwind insisted. "We're rushing to meet some aliens. What if they're the danger? Maybe these *volcryn* are even more potent than a Hrangan Mind, and maybe they don't want to be met, or investigated, or observed. What about that, Karoly? You ever think about that? Those stories of yours—don't some of them talk about terrible things happening to the races that meet the *volcryn?*"

"Legends," d'Branin said. "Superstition."

"A whole Fyndii horde vanishes in one legend," Rojan Christopheris put in.

"We cannot put credence in these fears of others," d'Branin argued.

"Perhaps there's nothing to the stories," Northwind said, "but do you care to risk it? *I* don't. For what? Your sources may be fictional or exaggerated or wrong, your interpretations and computations may be in error, or they may have changed course—the *volcryn* may not even be within light years of where we'll drop out."

"Ah," Melantha Jhirl said, "I understand. Then we shouldn't go on because they won't be there, and besides, they might be dangerous."

D'Branin smiled and Lindran laughed. "Not funny," protested Alys Northwind, but she argued no further.

"No," Melantha continued, "any danger we are in will not increase significantly in the time it will take us to drop out of drive and look about for *volcryn*. We have to drop out anyway, to reprogram for the shunt home. Besides, we've come a long way for these *volcryn*, and I admit to being curious." She looked at each of them in turn, but no one spoke. "We continue, then."

"And Royd?" demanded Christopheris. "What do we do about him?"

"What *can* we do?" said Dannel.

"Treat the captain as before," Melantha said decisively. "We should open lines to him and talk. Maybe now we can clear up some of the mysteries that are bothering us, if Royd is willing to discuss things frankly."

"He is probably as shocked and dismayed as we are, my friends," said d'Branin. "Possibly he is fearful that we will blame him, try to hurt him."

"I think we should cut through to his section of the ship and drag him out kicking and screaming," Christopheris said. "We have the tools. That would write a quick end to all our fears."

"It could kill Royd," Melantha said. "Then he'd be justified in anything he did to stop us. He controls this ship. He could do a great deal, if he decided we were his enemies." She shook her head vehemently. "No, Rojan, we can't attack Royd. We've got to reassure him. I'll do it, if no one else wants to talk to him." There were no volunteers. "All right. But I don't want any of you trying any foolish schemes. Go about your business. Act normally."

Karoly d'Branin was nodding agreement. "Let us put Royd and poor Thale from our minds, and concern ourselves with our work, with our preparations. Our sensory instruments must be ready for deployment as soon as we shift out of drive and reenter normal space, so we can find our quarry quickly. We must review everything we know of the *volcryn*." He turned to the linguists and began discussing some of the preliminaries he expected of them, and in a short time the talk had turned to the *volcryn,* and bit by bit the fear drained out of the group.

Lommie Thorne sat listening quietly, her thumb absently rubbing her wrist implant, but no one noticed the thoughtful look in her eyes.

Not even Royd Eris, watching.

MELANTHA JHIRL RETURNED TO THE LOUNGE ALONE.

Someone had turned out the lights. "Captain?" she said softly.

He appeared to her; pale, glowing softly, with eyes that did not see. His clothes, filmy and out-of-date, were all shades of white and faded blue. "Hello, Melantha," the mellow voice said from the communicators, as the ghost silently mouthed the same words.

"Did you hear, captain?"

"Yes," he said, his voice vaguely tinged by surprise. "I hear and I see everything on my *Nightflyer,* Melantha. Not only in the lounge, and not only when the communicators and viewscreens are on. How long have you known?"

"Known?" She smiled. "Since you praised Alys' gas giant solution to the Roydian mystery. The communicators were not on that night. You had no way of knowing. Unless . . ."

"I have never made a mistake before," Royd said. "I told Karoly, but that was deliberate. I am sorry. I have been under stress."

"I believe you, captain," she said. "No matter. I'm the improved model, remember? I'd guessed weeks ago."

For a time Royd said nothing. Then: "When do you begin to reassure me?"

"I'm doing so right now. Don't you feel reassured yet?"

The apparition gave a ghostly shrug. "I am pleased that you and Karoly do not think I murdered that man. Otherwise, I am frightened. Things are getting out of control, Melantha. Why didn't she listen to me? I told Karoly to keep him dampened. I told Agatha not to give him that injection. I warned them."

"They were afraid, too," Melantha said. "Afraid that you were only trying to frighten them off, to protect some awful plan. I don't know. It was my fault, in a sense. I was the one who suggested esperon.

I thought it would put Thale at ease, and tell us something about you. I was curious." She frowned. "A deadly curiosity. Now I have blood on my hands."

Melantha's eyes were adjusting to the darkness in the lounge. By the faint light of the holograph, she could see the table where it had happened, dark streaks of drying blood across its surface among the plates and cups and cold pots of tea and chocolate. She heard a faint dripping as well, and could not tell if it was blood or coffee. She shivered. "I don't like it in here."

"If you would like to leave, I can be with you wherever you go."

"No," she said. "I'll stay. Royd, I think it might be better if you were *not* with us wherever we go. If you kept silent and out of sight, so to speak. If I asked you to, would you shut off your monitors throughout the ship? Except for the lounge, perhaps. It would make the others feel better, I'm sure."

"They don't know."

"They will. You made that remark about gas giants in everyone's hearing. Some of them have probably figured it out by now."

"If I told you I had cut myself off, you would have no way of knowing whether it was the truth."

"I could trust you," Melantha Jhirl said.

Silence. The spectre stared at her. "As you wish," Royd's voice said finally. "Everything off. Now I see and hear only in here. Now, Melantha, you must promise to control them. No secret schemes, or attempts to breach my quarters. Can you do that?"

"I think so," she said.

"Did you believe my story?" Royd asked.

"Ah," she said. "A strange and wondrous story, captain. If it's a lie, I'll swap lies with you anytime. You do it well. If it's true, then you are a strange and wondrous man."

"It's true," the ghost said quietly. "Melantha . . ."

"Yes?"

"Does it bother you that I have . . . watched you? Watched you when you were not aware?"

"A little," she said, "but I think I can understand it."

"I watched you copulating."

She smiled. "Ah," she said, "I'm good at it."

"I wouldn't know," Royd said. "You're good to watch."

Silence. She tried not to hear the steady, faint dripping off to her right. "Yes," she said after a long hesitation.

"Yes? What?"

"Yes, Royd," she said, "I would probably sex with you if it were possible."

"How did you know what I was thinking?" Royd's voice was suddenly frightened, full of anxiety and something close to fear.

"Easy," Melantha said, startled. "I'm an improved model. It wasn't so difficult to figure out. I told you, remember? I'm three moves ahead of you."

"You're not a telepath, are you?"

"No," Melantha said. "No."

Royd considered that for a long time. "I believe I'm reassured," he said at last.

"Good," she said.

"Melantha," he added, "one thing. Sometimes it is not wise to be too many moves ahead. Do you understand?"

"Oh? No, not really. You frighten me. Now reassure me. Your turn, Captain Royd."

"Of what?"

"What happened in here? Really?"

Royd said nothing.

"I think you know something," Melantha said. "You gave up your secret to stop us from injecting Lasamer with esperon. Even after your secret was forfeit, you ordered us not to go ahead. Why?"

"Esperon is a dangerous drug," Royd said.

"More than that, captain," Melantha said. "You're evading. What killed Thale Lasamer? Or is it *who?*"

"*I* didn't."

"One of us? The *volcryn?*"

Royd said nothing.

"Is there an alien aboard your ship, captain?"

Silence.

"Are we in danger? Am *I* in danger, captain? I'm not afraid. Does that make me a fool?"

"I like people," Royd said at last. "When I can stand it, I like to have passengers. I watch them, yes. It's not so terrible. I like you and Karoly especially. I won't let anything happen to you."

"What might happen?"

Royd said nothing.

"And what about the others, Royd? Christopheris and Northwind, Dannel and Lindran, Lommie Thorne? Are you taking care of them, too? Or only Karoly and I?"

No reply.

"You're not very talkative tonight," Melantha observed.

"I'm under strain," his voice replied. "And certain things you are safer not to know. Go to bed, Melantha Jhirl. We've talked long enough."

"All right, captain," she said. She smiled at the ghost and lifted her hand. His own rose to meet it. Warm dark flesh and pale radiance brushed, melded, were one. Melantha Jhirl turned to go. It was not until she was out in the corridor, safe in the light once more, that she began to tremble.

———

FALSE MIDNIGHT.

The talks had broken up, and one by one the academicians had gone to bed. Even Karoly d'Branin had retired, his appetite for chocolate quelled by his memories of the lounge.

The linguists had made violent, noisy love before giving themselves up to sleep, as if to reaffirm their life in the face of Thale Lasamer's grisly death. Rojan Christopheris had listened to music. But now they were all still.

The *Nightflyer* was filled with silence.

In the darkness of the largest cargo hold, three sleepwebs hung side by side. Melantha Jhirl twisted occasionally in her sleep, her face feverish, as if in the grip of some nightmare. Alys Northwind lay flat on her back, snoring loudly, a reassuring wheeze of noise from her solid, meaty chest.

Lommie Thorne lay awake, thinking.

Finally she rose and dropped to the floor, nude, quiet, light and careful as a cat. She pulled on a tight pair of pants, slipped a wide-sleeved shirt of black metallic cloth over her head, belted it with a silver chain, shook out her short hair. She did not don her boots.

Barefoot was quieter. Her feet were small and soft, with no trace of callous.

She moved to the middle sleepweb and shook Alys Northwind by her shoulder. The snoring stopped abruptly. "Huh?" the xenotech said. She grunted in annoyance.

"Come," whispered Lommie Thome. She beckoned.

Northwind got heavily to her feet, blinking, and followed the cyberneticist through the door, out into the corridor. She'd been sleeping in her jumpsuit, its seam open nearly to her crotch. She frowned and sealed it. "What the hell," she muttered. She was disarrayed and unhappy.

"There's a way to find out if Royd's story was true," Lommie Thorne said carefully. "Melantha won't like it, though. Are you game to try?"

"What?" Northwind asked. Her face betrayed her interest.

"Come," the cyberneticist said.

They moved silently through the ship, to the computer room. The system was up, but dormant. They entered quietly; all empty. Currents of light ran silkily down crystalline channels in the data grids, meeting, joining, splitting apart again; rivers of wan multihued radiance crisscrossing a black landscape. The chamber was dim, the only noise a buzz at the edge of human hearing, until Lommie Thorne moved through it, touching keys, tripping switches, directing the silent luminescent currents. Bit by bit the machine woke.

"What are you *doing?*" Alys Northwind said.

"Karoly told me to tie in our system with the ship," Lommie Thorne replied as she worked. "I was told Royd wanted to study the *volcryn* data. Fine, I did it. Do you understand what that means?" Her shirt whispered in soft metallic tones when she moved.

Eagerness broke across the flat features of xenotech Alys Northwind. "The two systems are tied together!"

"Exactly. So Royd can find out about the *volcryn,* and we can find out about Royd." She frowned. "I wish I knew more about the *Nightflyer*'s hardware, but I think I can feel my way through. This is a pretty sophisticated system d'Branin requisitioned."

"Can you take over from Eris?"

"Take over?" Lommie sounded puzzled. "You been drinking again, Alys?"

"No, I'm serious. Use your system to break into the ship's control, overwhelm Eris, countermand his orders, make the *Nightflyer* respond to us, down here. Wouldn't you feel safer if we were in control?"

"Maybe," the cyberneticist said doubtfully. "I could try, but why do that?"

"Just in case. We don't have to use the capacity. Just so we have it, if an emergency arises."

Lommie Thorne shrugged. "Emergencies and gas giants. I only want to put my mind at rest about Royd, whether he had anything to do with killing Lasamer." She moved over to a readout panel, where a half-dozen meter-square viewscreens curved around a console, and brought one of them to life. Long fingers ghosted through holographic keys that appeared and disappeared as she used them, the keyboard changing shape again and yet again. The cyberneticist's pretty face grew thoughtful and serious. "We're in," she said. Characters began to flow across a viewscreen, red flickerings in glassy black depths. On a second screen, a schematic of the *Nightflyer* appeared, revolved, halved; its spheres shifted size and perspective at the whim of Lommie's fingers, and a line of numerals below gave the specifications. The cyberneticist watched, and finally froze both screens.

"Here," she said, "here's my answer about the hardware. You can dismiss your takeover idea, unless those gas giant people of yours are going to help. The *Nightflyer*'s bigger and smarter than our little system here. Makes sense, when you stop to think about it. Ship's all automated, except for Royd."

Her hands moved again, and two more display screens stirred. Lommie Thorne whistled and coaxed her search program with soft words of encouragement. "It looks as though there *is* a Royd, though. Configurations are all wrong for a robot ship. Damn, I would have bet anything." The characters began to flow again, Lommie watching the figures as they drifted by. "Here's life support specs, might tell us something." A finger jabbed, and one screen froze yet again.

"Nothing unusual," Alys Northwind said in disappointment.

"Standard waste disposal. Water recycling. Food processor, with protein and vitamin supplements in stores." She began to whistle. "Tanks of Renny's moss and neograss to eat up the CO_2. Oxygen cycle, then. No methane or ammonia. Sorry about that."

"Go sex with a computer!"

The cyberneticist smiled. "Ever tried it?" Her fingers moved again. "What else should I look for? You're the tech, what would be a giveaway? Give me some ideas."

"Check the specs for nurturant tanks, cloning equipment, that sort of thing," the xenotech said. "That would tell us whether he was lying."

"I don't know," Lommie Thorne said. "Long time ago. He might have junked that stuff. No use for it."

"Find Royd's life history," Northwind said. "His mother's. Get a readout on the business they've done, all this alleged trading. They must have records. Account books, profit-and-loss, cargo invoices, that kind of thing." Her voice grew excited, and she gripped the cyberneticist from behind by her shoulders. "A log, a ship's log! There's got to be a log. Find it!"

"All right." Lommie Thorne whistled, happy, at ease with her system, riding the data winds, curious, in control. Then the screen in front of her turned a bright red and began to blink. She smiled, touched a ghost key, and the keyboard melted away and re-formed under her. She tried another tack. Three more screens turned red and began to blink. Her smile faded.

"What is it?"

"Security," said Lommie Thorne. "I'll get through it in a second. Hold on." She changed the keyboard yet again, entered another search program, attached on a rider in case it was blocked. Another screen flashed red. She had her machine chew the data she'd gathered, sent out another feeler. More red. Flashing. Blinking. Bright enough to hurt the eyes. All the screens were red now. "A good security program," she said with admiration. "The log is well protected."

Alys Northwind grunted. "Are we blocked?"

"Response time is too slow," Lommie Thorne said, chewing on her lower lip as she thought. "There's a way to fix that." She smiled, and rolled back the soft black metal of her sleeve.

"What are you doing?"

"Watch," she said. She slid her arm under the console, found the prongs, jacked in.

"Ah," she said, low in her throat. The flashing red blocks vanished from her readout screens, one after the other, as she sent her mind coursing into the *Nightflyer*'s system, easing through all the blocks. "Nothing like slipping past another system's security. Like slipping onto a man." Log entries were flickering past them in a whirling, blurring rush, too fast for Alys Northwind to read. But Lommie read them.

Then she stiffened. "Oh," she said. It was almost a whimper. "Cold," she said. She shook her head and it was gone, but there was a sound in her ears, a terrible whooping sound. "Damn," she said, "that'll wake everyone." She glanced up when she felt Alys' fingers dig painfully into her shoulder, squeezing, hurting.

A gray steel panel slid almost silently across the access to the corridor, cutting off the whooping cry of the alarm. "What?" Lommie Thorne said.

"That's an emergency airseal," said Alys Northwind in a dead voice. She knew starships. "It closes where they're about to load or unload cargo in vacuum."

Their eyes went to the huge curving outer airlock above their heads. The inner lock was almost completely open, and as they watched it clicked into place, and the seal on the outer door cracked, and now it was open half a meter, sliding, and beyond was twisted nothingness so burning-bright it seared the eyes.

"Oh," said Lommie Thorne, as the cold coursed up her arm. She had stopped whistling.

Alarms were hooting everywhere. The passengers began to stir. Melantha Jhirl tumbled from her sleepweb and darted into the corridor, nude, frantic, alert. Karoly d'Branin sat up drowsily. The psipsych muttered fitfully in drug-induced sleep. Rojan Christopheris cried out in alarm.

Far away metal crunched and tore, and a violent shudder ran through the ship, throwing the linguists out of their sleepwebs, knocking Melantha from her feet.

In the command quarters of the *Nightflyer* was a spherical room with featureless white walls, a lesser sphere—a suspended control console—floating in its center. The walls were always blank when the ship was in drive; the warped and glaring underside of spacetime was painful to behold.

But now darkness woke in the room, a holoscope coming to life, cold black and stars everywhere, points of icy unwinking brilliance, no up and no down and no direction, the floating control sphere the only feature in the simulated sea of night.

The *Nightflyer* had shifted out of drive.

Melantha Jhirl found her feet again and thumbed on a communicator. The alarms were still hooting, and it was hard to hear. "Captain," she shouted, "what's happening?"

"I don't know," Royd's voice replied. "I'm trying to find out. Wait."

Melantha waited. Karoly d'Branin came staggering out into the corridor, blinking and rubbing his eyes. Rojan Christopheris was not long behind him. "What is it? What's wrong?" he demanded, but Melantha just shook her head. Lindran and Dannel soon appeared as well. There was no sign of Marij-Black, Alys Northwind, or Lommie Thorne. The academicians looked uneasily at the seal that blocked cargo hold three. Finally Melantha told Christopheris to go look. He returned a few minutes later. "Agatha is still unconscious," he said, talking at the top of his voice to be heard over the alarms. "The drugs still have her. She's moving around, though. Crying out."

"Alys and Lommie?"

Christopheris shrugged. "I can't find them. Ask your friend Royd."

The communicator came back to life as the alarms died. "We have returned to normal space," Royd's voice said, "but the ship is damaged. Hold three, your computer room, was breached while we were under drive. It was ripped apart by the flux. The computer dropped us out of drive automatically, fortunately for us, or the drive forces might have torn my entire ship apart."

"Royd," said Melantha, "Northwind and Thorne are missing."

"It appears your computer was in use when the hold was breached," Royd said carefully. "I would presume them dead, although I cannot say that with certainty. At Melantha's request I have deactivated most of my monitors, retaining only the lounge input. I do not know what transpired. But this is a small ship, and if they are not with you, we must assume the worst." He paused briefly. "If it is any consolation, they died swiftly and painlessly."

"You killed them," Christopheris said, his face red and angry. He started to say more, but Melantha slipped her hand firmly over his mouth. The two linguists exchanged a long, meaningful look. "Do we know how it happened, captain?" Melantha asked.

"Yes," he said, reluctantly.

The xenobiologist had taken the hint, and Melantha took away her hand to let him breathe. "Royd?" she prompted.

"It sounds insane, Melantha," his voice replied, "but it appears your colleagues opened the hold's loading lock. I doubt they did so deliberately, of course. They were using the system interface to gain entry to the *Nightflyer*'s data storage and controls, and they shunted aside all the safeties."

"I see," Melantha said. "A terrible tragedy."

"Yes. Perhaps more terrible than you think. I have yet to discover the extent of damage to my ship."

"We should not keep you if you have duties to perform," Melantha said. "All of us are shocked, and it is difficult to talk now. Investigate the condition of your ship, and we'll continue our discussion at a more opportune time. Agreed?"

"Yes," said Royd.

Melantha turned off the communicator. Now, in theory, the device was dead; Royd could neither see nor hear them.

"Do you believe him?" Christopheris snapped.

"I don't know," Melantha Jhirl said, "but I do know that the other cargo holds can all be flushed just as hold three was. I'm moving my sleepweb into a cabin. I suggest that those of you who are living in hold two do the same."

"Clever," Lindran said, with a sharp nod of her head. "We can crowd in. It won't be comfortable, but I doubt that I'd sleep the sleep of angels in the holds after this."

"We should also get our suits out of storage in four," Dannel suggested. "Keep them close at hand. Just in case."

"If you wish," Melantha said. "It's possible that all the locks might pop open simultaneously. Royd can't fault us for taking precautions."

She flashed a grim smile. "After today we've earned the right to act irrationally."

"This is no time for your damned jokes, Melantha," Christopheris said. He was still red-faced, and his tone was full of fear and anger. "Three people are dead, Agatha is perhaps deranged or catatonic, the rest of us are endangered—"

"Yes. And we still have no idea what is happening," Melantha pointed out.

"*Royd Eris is killing us!*" Christopheris shrieked. "I don't know who or what he is and I don't know if that story he gave us is true and I don't *care.* Maybe he's a Hrangan Mind or the avenging angel of the *volcryn* or the second coming of Jesus Christ. What the hell difference does it make? He's *killing* us!" He looked at each of them in turn. "Any one of us could be next," he added. "Any one of us. Unless . . . we've got to make plans, *do* something, put a stop to this once and for all."

"You realize," Melantha said gently, "that we cannot actually know whether the good captain has turned off his sensory inputs down here. He could be watching and listening to us right now. He isn't, of course. He said he wouldn't and I believe him. But we have only his word on that. Now, Rojan, you don't appear to trust Royd. If that's so, you can hardly put any faith in his promises. It follows therefore that from your own point of view it might not be wise to say the things that you're saying." She smiled slyly. "Do you understand the implications of what I'm saying?"

Christopheris opened his mouth and closed it again, looking very like a tall, ugly fish. He said nothing, but his eyes moved furtively, and his flush deepened.

Lindran smiled thinly. "I think he's got it," she said.

"The computer is gone, then," Karoly d'Branin said suddenly in a low voice.

Melantha looked at him. "I'm afraid so, Karoly."

D'Branin ran his fingers through his hair, as if half aware of how untidy he looked. "The *volcryn,*" he muttered. "How will we work without the computer?" He nodded to himself. "I have a small unit in my cabin, a wrist model, perhaps it will suffice. It *must* suffice, it must. I will get the figures from Royd, learn where we have dropped out.

Excuse me, my friends. Pardon, I must go." He wandered away in a distracted haze, talking to himself.

"He hasn't heard a word we've said," Dannel said, incredulous.

"Think how distraught he'd be if *all* of us were dead," added Lindran. "Then he'd have no one to help him look for *volcryn*."

"Let him go," Melantha said. "He is as hurt as any of us, maybe more so. He wears it differently. His obsessions are his defense."

"Ah. And what is *our* defense?"

"Patience, maybe," said Melantha Jhirl. "All of the dead were trying to breach Royd's secret when they died. We haven't tried. Here we are discussing their deaths."

"You don't find that suspicious?" asked Lindran.

"Very," Melantha said. "I even have a method of testing my suspicions. One of us can make yet another attempt to find out whether our captain told us the truth. If he or she dies, we'll know." She shrugged. "Forgive me, however, if I'm not the one who tries. But don't let me stop you if you have the urge. I'll note the results with interest. Until then, I'm going to move out of the cargo hold and get some sleep." She turned and strode off, leaving the others to stare at one another.

"Arrogant bitch," Dannel observed almost conversationally after Melantha had left.

"Do you really think he can hear us?" Christopheris whispered to the two linguists.

"Every pithy word," Lindran said. She smiled at his discomfiture. "Come, Dannel, let's get to a safe area and back to bed."

He nodded.

"But," said Christopheris, "we have to *do* something. Make plans. Defenses."

Lindran gave him a final withering look, and pulled Dannel off behind her down the corridor.

———

"MELANTHA? KAROLY?"

She woke quickly, alert at the mere whisper of her name, fully awake almost at once, and sat up in the narrow single bed. Squeezed in beside her, Karoly d'Branin groaned and rolled over, yawning.

"Royd?" she asked. "Is it morning?"

"We are drifting in interstellar space three light years from the nearest star, Melantha," replied the soft voice from the walls. "In such a context, the term *morning* has no meaning. But, yes, it is morning."

Melantha laughed. "*Drifting,* you said? How bad is the damage?"

"Serious, but not dangerous. Hold three is a complete ruin, hanging from my ship like half of a broken egg, but the damage was confined. The drives themselves are intact, and the *Nightflyer's* computers did not seem to suffer from your system's destruction. I feared they might. I have heard of phenomena like electronic death traumas."

D'Branin said, "Eh? Royd?"

Melantha stroked him affectionately. "I'll tell you later, Karoly," she said. "Go back to sleep. Royd, you sound serious. Is there more?"

"I am worried about our return flight, Melantha," Royd said. "When I take the *Nightflyer* back into drive, the flux will be playing directly on portions of the ship that were never engineered to withstand it. Our configurations are askew now; I can show you the mathematics of it, but the question of the flux forces is the vital one. The airseal across the access to hold three is a particular concern. I've run some simulations, and I don't know if it can take the stress. If it bursts, my whole ship will split apart in the middle. My engines will go shunting off by themselves, and the rest—even if the life support sphere remains intact, we will all soon be dead."

"I see. Is there anything we can do?"

"Yes. The exposed areas would be easy enough to reinforce. The outer hull is armored to withstand the warping forces, of course. We could mount it in place, a crude shield, but according to my projections it would suffice. If we do it correctly, it will help correct our configurations as well. Large portions of the hull were torn loose when the locks opened, but they are still out there, most within a kilometer or two, and could be used."

At some point Karoly d'Branin had finally come awake. "My team has four vacuum sleds," he said. "We can retrieve those pieces for you, my friend."

"Fine, Karoly, but that is not my primary concern. My ship is self-repairing within certain limits, but this exceeds those limits by an order of magnitude. I will have to do this myself."

"You?" D'Branin was startled. "Royd, you said—that is, your

muscles, your weakness—this work will be too much for you. Surely we can do this for you!"

Royd's reply was tolerant. "I am only a cripple in a gravity field, Karoly. Weightless, I am in my element, and I will be killing the *Nightflyer's* gravity grid momentarily, to try to gather my own strength for the repair work. No, you misunderstand. I am capable of the work. I have the tools, including my own heavy-duty sled."

"I think I know what you are concerned about, captain," Melantha said.

"I'm glad," Royd said. "Perhaps then you can answer my question. If I emerge from the safety of my chambers to do this work, can you keep your colleagues from harming me?"

Karoly d'Branin was shocked. "Oh, Royd, Royd, how could you think such a thing? We are scholars, scientists, not—not criminals, or soldiers, or—or animals, we are human, how can you believe we would threaten you or do you harm?"

"Human," Royd repeated, "but alien to me, suspicious of me. Give me no false assurances, Karoly."

He sputtered. Melantha took him by the hand and bid him quiet. "Royd," she said, "I won't lie to you. You'd be in some danger. But I'd hope that, by coming out, you'd make our friends joyously happy. They'd be able to see that you told the truth, see that you were only human." She smiled. "They *would* see that, wouldn't they?"

"They would," Royd said, "but would it be enough to offset their suspicions? They believe I am responsible for the deaths of the other three, do they not?"

"Believe is too strong a word. They suspect it, they fear it. They are frightened, captain, and with good cause. *I* am frightened."

"No more than I."

"I would be less frightened if I knew what *did* happen. Will you tell me?"

Silence.

"Royd, if—"

"I have made mistakes, Melantha," Royd said gravely. "But I am not alone in that. I did my best to stop the esperon injection, and I failed. I might have saved Alys and Lommie if I had seen them, heard them, known what they were about. But you made me turn off my monitors, Melantha. I cannot help what I cannot see. Why, if you saw three moves ahead, did you calculate these results?"

Melantha Jhirl felt briefly guilty. "*Mea culpa,* captain, I share the blame. I know that. Believe me, I know that. It is hard to see three moves ahead when you do not know the rules, however. Tell me the rules."

"I am blind and deaf," Royd said, ignoring her. "It is frustrating. I cannot help if I am blind and deaf. I am going to turn on the monitors again, Melantha. I am sorry if you do not approve. I want your approval, but I must do this with or without it. I have to see."

"Turn them on," Melantha said thoughtfully. "I was wrong, captain. I should never have asked you to blind yourself. I did not understand the situation, and I overestimated my own power to control the others. A failing of mine. Improved models too often think they can do anything." Her mind was racing, and she felt almost sick; she had miscalculated, misled, and there was more blood on her hands. "I think I understand better now."

"Understand what?" Karoly d'Branin said, baffled.

"You do *not* understand," Royd said sternly. "Don't pretend that you do, Melantha Jhirl. Don't! It is not wise or safe to be too many moves ahead." There was something disturbing in his tone.

Melantha understood that, too.

"What?" Karoly said. "I do not understand."

"Neither do I," Melantha said carefully. "Neither do I, Karoly." She kissed him lightly. "None of us understands, do we?"

"Good," said Royd.

She nodded, and put a reassuring arm around Karoly. "Royd," she said, "to return to the question of repairs, it seems to me you must do this work, regardless of what promises we can give you. You won't risk your ship by slipping back into drive in your present condition, and the only other option is to drift out here until we all die. What choice do we have?"

"I have a choice," Royd said with deadly seriousness. "I could kill all of you, if that were the only way to save myself and my ship."

"You could try," Melantha said.

"Let us have no more talk of death," d'Branin said.

"You are right, Karoly," Royd said, "I do not wish to kill any of you. But I must be protected."

"You will be," Melantha said. "Karoly can set the others to chasing your hull fragments. I'll be your protection. I'll stay by your side. If anyone tries to attack you, they'll have to deal with me. They won't find that easy. And I can assist you. The work will be done three times as fast."

Royd was polite. "It is my experience that most planet-born are clumsy and easily tired in weightlessness. It would be more efficient if I worked alone, although I will gladly accept your services as a bodyguard."

"I remind you that I'm the improved model, captain," Melantha said. "Good in free fall as well as in bed. I'll help."

"You are stubborn. As you will, then. In a few moments I shall depower the gravity grid. Karoly, go and prepare your people. Unship your vacuum sleds and suit up. I will exit the *Nightflyer* in three standard hours, after I have recovered from the pains of your gravity. I want all of you outside the ship before I leave. Is that condition understood?"

"Yes," said Karoly. "All except Agatha. She has not regained consciousness, friend, she will not be a problem."

"No," said Royd, "I meant *all* of you, including Agatha. Take her outside with you."

"But Royd!" protested d'Branin.

"You're the captain," Melantha Jhirl said firmly. "It will be as you say; all of us outside. Including Agatha."

OUTSIDE. IT WAS AS THOUGH SOME VAST ANIMAL HAD TAKEN A BITE out of the stars.

Melantha Jhirl waited on her sled close by the *Nightflyer* and looked at stars. It was not so very different out here in the depths of interstellar space. The stars were cold, frozen points of light; unwinking, austere, more chill and uncaring somehow than the same suns made to dance and twinkle by an atmosphere. Only the absence of a landmark primary reminded her of where she was: in the places between, where men and women and their ships do not stop, where the *volcryn* sail crafts impossibly ancient. She tried to pick out Avalon's sun, but she did not know where to search. The configurations were strange to her and she had no idea of how she was oriented. Behind her, before her, above, all around, the starfields stretched endlessly. She glanced down, or what seemed like down just then, beyond her feet and her sled and the *Nightflyer,* expecting still more alien stars. And the *bite* hit her with an almost physical force.

Melantha fought off a wave of vertigo. She was suspended above a pit, a yawning chasm in the universe, black, starless, vast.

Empty.

She remembered then: the Tempter's Veil. Just a cloud of dark gases, nothing really, galactic pollution that obscured the light from the stars of the Fringe. But this close at hand, it seemed immense, terrifying, and she had to break her gaze when she began to feel as if she were falling. It was a gulf beneath her and the frail silver-white shell of the *Nightflyer,* a gulf about to swallow them.

Melantha touched one of the controls on the sled's forked handle, swinging around so the Veil was to her side instead of beneath her. That seemed to help somehow. She concentrated on the *Nightflyer,* ignoring the looming wall of blackness beyond. It was the largest object in her universe, bright amid the darkness, ungainly, its shattered cargo sphere giving the whole craft an unbalanced cast.

She could see the other sleds as they angled through the black, tracking the missing pieces of hull, grappling with them, bringing them back. The linguistic team worked together, as always, sharing a sled. Rojan Christopheris was alone, working in a sullen silence. Melantha had almost had to threaten him with physical violence before he agreed to join them. The xenobiologist was certain that it was all another plot, that once they were outside, the *Nightflyer* would slip into drive without them and leave them to lingering deaths. His suspicions were inflamed by drink, and there had been alcohol on his breath when Melantha and Karoly had finally forced him to suit up. Karoly had a sled too, and a silent passenger; Agatha Marij-Black, freshly drugged and asleep in her vacuum suit, safely locked into place.

While her colleagues labored, Melantha Jhirl waited for Royd Eris, talking to the others occasionally over the comm link. The two linguists, unaccustomed to weightlessness, were complaining a good deal, and bickering as well. Karoly tried to soothe them frequently. Christopheris said little, and his few comments were edged and biting.

He was still angry. Melantha watched him flit across her field of vision, a stick figure in form-fitting black armor standing erect at the controls of his sled.

Finally the circular airlock atop the foremost of the *Nightflyer's* major spheres dilated and Royd Eris emerged.

She watched him approach, curious, wondering what he would look like. In her mind were a half-dozen contradictory pictures. His genteel, cultured, too-formal voice sometimes reminded her of the dark aristocrats of her native Prometheus, the wizards who toyed with human genes and played baroque status games. At other times his naïveté made her imagine him as an inexperienced youth. His ghost was a tired-looking thin young man, and he was supposed to be considerably older than that pale shadow, but Melantha found it difficult to hear an old man talking when he spoke.

Melantha felt a nervous tingle as he neared. The lines of his sled and his suit were different than theirs, disturbingly so. Alien, she thought, and quickly squelched the thought. Such differences meant nothing. Royd's sled was large, a long oval plate with eight jointed grappling arms bristling from its underside like the legs of a metallic spider. A heavy-duty cutting laser was mounted beneath the controls, its snout jutting threateningly forward. His suit was far more massive than the carefully engineered Academy worksuits they wore, with a bulge between its shoulder blades that was probably a power pack, and rakish radiant fins atop shoulders and helmet. It made him seem hulking; hunched and deformed.

But when he finally came near enough for Melantha to see his face, it was just a face.

White, very white, that was the predominant impression she got; white hair cropped very short, a white stubble around the sharply chiseled lines of his jaw, almost invisible eyebrows beneath which his eyes moved restlessly. His eyes were large and vividly blue, his best feature. His skin was pale and unlined, scarcely touched by time.

He looked wary, she thought. And perhaps a bit frightened.

Royd stopped his sled close to hers, amid the twisted ruin that had been cargo hold three, and surveyed the damage, the pieces of floating wreckage that had once been flesh, blood, glass, metal, plastic. Hard to distinguish now, all of them fused and burned and frozen together. "We have a good deal of work to do," he said. "Shall we begin?"

"First let's talk," she replied. She shifted her sled closer and reached out to him, but the distance was still too great, the width of the bases of the two vacuum sleds keeping them apart. Melantha backed off and turned herself over completely, so that Royd stood upside down in her world and she upside down in his. She moved to him again, positioning her sled directly over/under his. Their gloved hands met, brushed, parted. Melantha adjusted her altitude. Their helmets touched.

"Now I have touched you," Royd said, with a tremor in his voice. "I have never touched anyone before, or been touched."

"Oh, Royd. This isn't touching, not really. The suits are in the way. But I will touch you, *really* touch you. I promise you that."

"You can't. It's impossible."

"I'll find a way," she said firmly. "Now, turn off your comm. The sound will carry through our helmets."

He blinked and used his tongue controls and it was done.

"Now we can talk," she said. "Privately."

"I do not like this, Melantha," he said. "This is too obvious. This is dangerous."

"There is no other way. Royd, I *do* know."

"Yes," he said. "I knew you did. Three moves ahead, Melantha. I remember the way you play chess. But this is a more serious game, and you are safer if you feign ignorance."

"I understand that, captain. Other things I'm less sure about. Can we talk about them?"

"No. Don't ask me to. Just do as I tell you. You are in peril, all of you, but I can protect you. The less you know, the better I can protect you." Through the transparent faceplates, his expression was somber.

She stared into his upside-down eyes. "It might be a second crew member, someone else hidden in your quarters, but I don't believe that. It's the ship, isn't it? Your ship is killing us. Not you. It. Only that doesn't make sense. You command the *Nightflyer*. How can it act independently? And why? What motive? And how was Thale Lasamer killed? The business with Alys and Lommie, that was easy, but a psionic murder? A starship with psi? I can't accept that. It can't be the ship. Yet it can't be anything else. Help me, captain."

He blinked, anguish behind his eyes. "I should never have accepted Karoly's charter, not with a telepath among you. It was too risky. But I wanted to see the *volcryn,* and he spoke of them so movingly." He sighed. "You understand too much already, Melantha. I can't tell you more, or I would be powerless to protect you. The ship is malfunctioning, that is all you need to know. It is not safe to push too hard. As long as I am at the controls, I think I can keep you and the others from harm. Trust me."

"Trust is a two-way bond," Melantha said.

Royd lifted his hand and pushed her away, then tongued his communicator back to life. "Enough gossip," he announced. "We have work to do. Come. I want to see just how improved you actually are."

In the solitude of her helmet, Melantha Jhirl swore softly.

––––––––––

WITH AN IRREGULAR TWIST OF METAL LOCKED BENEATH HIM IN HIS sled's magnetic grip, Rojan Christopheris sailed back towards the *Nightflyer.* He was watching from a distance when Royd Eris emerged on his oversized work sled. He was closer when Melantha Jhirl moved to him, inverted her sled, and pressed her faceplate to Royd's. Christopheris listened to their soft exchange, heard Melantha promise to touch him, Eris, the *thing,* the killer. He swallowed his rage. Then they cut him out, cut all of them out, went off the open circuit. But still she hung there, suspended by that cipher in the hunchbacked spacesuit, faces pressed together like two lovers kissing.

Christopheris swept in close, unlocked his captive plate so it would drift towards them. "Here," he announced. "I'm off to get another." He tongued off his own comm and swore, and his sled slid around the spheres and tubes of the *Nightflyer.*

Somehow they were all in it together, Royd and Melantha and possibly old d'Branin as well, he thought sourly. She had protected Eris from the first, stopped them when they might have taken action together, found out who or what he was. He did not trust her. His skin crawled when he remembered that they had been to bed together. She and Eris were the same, whatever they might be. And now poor Alys was dead, and that fool Thorne and even that damned telepath, but still Melantha was with him, against them. Rojan Christopheris was deeply afraid, and angry, and half drunk.

The others were out of sight, off chasing spinning wedges of half-slagged metal. Royd and Melantha were engrossed in each other, the ship abandoned and vulnerable. This was his chance. No wonder Eris had insisted that all of them precede him into the void; outside, isolated from the controls of the *Nightflyer,* he was only a man. A weak one at that.

Smiling a thin hard smile, Christopheris brought his sled curling around the cargo spheres, hidden from sight, and vanished into the gaping maw of the driveroom. It was a long tunnel, everything open to vacuum, safe from the corrosion of an atmosphere. Like most starships, the *Nightflyer* had a triple propulsion system: the gravfield for landing and lifting, useless away from a gravity well, the nukes for deep space sublight maneuverings, and the great stardrives themselves. The lights of his sled flickered past the encircling ring of nukes and sent long bright streaks along the sides of the closed cylinders of the stardrives, the huge engines that bent the stuff of spacetime, encased in webs of metal and crystal.

At the end of the tunnel was a great circular door, reinforced metal, closed: the main airlock.

Christopheris set the sled down, dismounted—pulling his boots free of the sled's magnetic grip with an effort—and moved to the airlock. This was the hardest part, he thought. The headless body of Thale Lasamer was tethered loosely to a massive support strut by the lock, like a grisly guardian of the way. The xenobiologist had to stare at it while he waited for the lock to cycle. Whenever he glanced away, somehow he would find his eyes creeping back to it. The body looked almost natural, as if it had never had a head. Christopheris tried to remember what Lasamer had looked like, but the features would not come to mind. He moved uncomfortably, but then the lock door slid open and he gratefully entered the chamber to cycle through.

He was alone in the *Nightflyer.*

A cautious man, Christopheris kept his suit on, though he collapsed the helmet and yanked loose the suddenly-limp metallic fabric so it fell behind his back like a hood. He could snap it in place quickly enough if the need arose. In cargo hold four, where they had stored their equipment, the xenobiologist found what he was looking for; a portable cutting laser, charged and ready. Low power, but it would do.

Slow and clumsy in weightlessness, he pulled himself down the corridor into the darkened lounge.

It was chilly inside, the air cold on his cheeks. He tried not to notice. He braced himself at the door and pushed off across the width of the room, sailing above the furniture, which was all safely bolted into place. As he drifted towards his objective, something wet and cold touched his face. It startled him, but it was gone before he could quite make out what it was.

When it happened again, Christopheris snatched at it, caught it, and felt briefly sick. He had forgotten. No one had cleaned the lounge yet. The—the *remains* were still there, floating now, blood and flesh and bits of bone and brain. All around him.

He reached the far wall, stopped himself with his arms, pulled himself down to where he wanted to go. The bulkhead. The wall. No doorway was visible, but the metal couldn't be very thick. Beyond was the control room, the computer access, safety, power. Rojan Christopheris did not think of himself as a vindictive man. He did not intend to harm Royd Eris, that judgment was not his to make. He would take control of the *Nightflyer,* warn Eris away, make certain the man stayed sealed in his suit. He would take them all back without any more mysteries, any more killings. The Academy arbiters could listen to the story, and probe Eris, and decide the right and wrong of it, guilt and innocence, what should be done.

The cutting laser emitted a thin pencil of scarlet light. Christopheris smiled and applied it to the bulkhead. It was slow work, but he had patience. They would not have missed him, quiet as he'd been, and if they did they would assume he was off sledding after some hunk of salvage. Eris' repairs would take hours, maybe days, to finish. The bright blade of the laser smoked where it touched the metal. Christopheris applied himself diligently.

Something moved on the periphery of his vision, just a little flicker, barely seen. A floating bit of brain, he thought. A sliver of bone. A bloody piece of flesh, hair still hanging from it. Horrible things, but nothing to worry about. He was a biologist, he was used to blood and brains and flesh. And worse, and worse; he had dissected many an alien in his day, cutting through chitin and mucous, pulsing stinking food sacs and poisonous spines, he had seen and touched it all.

Again the motion caught his eye, teased at it. Not wanting to, Christopheris found himself drawn to look. He could not *not* look, somehow, just as he had been unable to ignore the headless corpse near the airlock. He looked.

It was an eye.

Christopheris trembled and the laser slipped sharply off to one side, so he had to wrestle with it to bring it back to the channel he was cutting. His heart raced. He tried to calm himself. Nothing to be frightened of. No one was home, and if Royd should return, well, he had the laser as a weapon and he had his suit on if an airlock blew.

He looked at the eye again, willing away his fear. It was just an eye, Thale Lasamer's eye, pale blue, bloody but intact, the same watery eye the boy had when alive, nothing supernatural. A piece of dead flesh, floating in the lounge amid other pieces of dead flesh. Someone should have cleaned up the lounge, Christopheris thought angrily. It was indecent to leave it like this, it was uncivilized.

The eye did not move. The other grisly bits were drifting on the air currents that flowed across the room, but the eye was still. It neither bobbed nor spun. It was fixed on him. Staring.

He cursed himself and concentrated on the laser, on his cutting. He had burned an almost straight line up the bulkhead for about a meter. He began another at a right angle.

The eye watched dispassionately. Christopheris suddenly found he could not stand it. One hand released its grip on the laser, reached out, caught the eye, flung it across the room. The action made him lose balance. He tumbled backward, the laser slipping from his grasp, his arms flapping like the wings of some absurd heavy bird. Finally he caught an edge of the table and stopped himself.

The laser hung in the center of the room, floating amid coffee pots and pieces of human debris, still firing, turning slowly. That did not make sense. It should have ceased fire when he released it. A malfunction, Christopheris thought nervously. Smoke was rising where the thin line of the laser traced a path across the carpet.

With a shiver of fear, Christopheris realized that the laser was turning towards him.

He raised himself, put both hands flat against the table, pushed up out of the way, bobbing towards the ceiling.

The laser was turning more swiftly now.

He pushed away from the ceiling hard, slammed into a wall,

grunted in pain, bounced off the floor, kicked. The laser was spinning quickly, chasing him. Christopheris soared, braced himself for another ricochet off the ceiling. The beam swung around, but not fast enough. He'd get it while it was still firing off in the other direction.

He moved close, reached, and saw the eye.

It hung just above the laser. Staring.

Rojan Christopheris made a small whimpering sound low in his throat, and his hand hesitated—not long, but long enough—and the scarlet beam came up and around.

Its touch was a light, hot caress across his neck.

IT WAS MORE THAN AN HOUR LATER BEFORE THEY MISSED HIM. KAROLY d'Branin noticed his absence first, called for him over the comm link, and got no answer. He discussed it with the others.

Royd Eris moved his sled back from the armor plate he had just mounted, and through his helmet Melantha Jhirl could see the lines around his mouth grow hard.

It was just then that the noises began.

A shrill bleat of pain and fear, followed by moans and sobbing. Terrible wet sounds, like a man choking on his own blood. They all heard. The sounds filled their helmets. And almost clear amid the anguish was something that sounded like a word: "Help."

"That's Christopheris," a woman's voice said. Lindran.

"He's hurt," Dannel added. "He's crying for help. Can't you hear it?"

"Where—?" someone started.

"The ship," Lindran said. "He must have returned to the ship."

Royd Eris said, "The fool. No. I warned—"

"We're going to check," Lindran announced. Dannel cut free the hull fragment they had been bringing in, and it spun away, tumbling. Their sled angled down towards the *Nightflyer*.

"Stop," Royd said. "I'll return to my chambers and check from there, if you wish, but you may not enter the ship. Stay outside until I give you clearance."

The terrible sounds went on and on.

"Go to hell," Lindran snapped at him over the open circuit.

Karoly d'Branin had his sled in motion too, hastening after the linguists, but he had been farther out and it was a long way back to the ship. "Royd, what can you mean, we must help, don't you see? He is hurt, listen to him. Please, my friend."

"No," Royd said. "Karoly, stop! If Rojan went back to the ship alone, he is dead."

"How do you know that?" Dannel demanded. "Did you arrange it? Set traps in case we disobeyed you?"

"No," Royd said, "listen to me. You can't help him now. Only I could have helped him, and he did not listen to me. Trust me. Stop." His voice was despairing.

In the distance, d'Branin's sled slowed. The linguists did not. "We've already listened to you too damn much, I'd say," Lindran said. She almost had to shout to be heard above the noises, the whimpers and moans, the awful wet sucking sounds, the distorted pleas for help. Agony filled their universe. "Melantha," Lindran continued, "keep Eris right where he is. We'll go carefully, find out what is happening inside, but I don't want him getting back to his controls. Understood?"

Melantha Jhirl hesitated. The sounds beat against her ears. It was hard to think.

Royd swung his sled around to face her, and she could feel the weight of his stare. "Stop them," he said. "Melantha, Karoly, order it. They will not listen to me. They do not know what they are doing." He was clearly in pain.

In his face Melantha found decision. "Go back inside quickly, Royd. Do what you can. I'm going to try to intercept them."

"Whose side are you on?" Lindran demanded.

Royd nodded to her across the gulf, but Melantha was already in motion. Her sled backed clear of the work area, congested with hull fragments and other debris, then accelerated briskly as she raced around the exterior of the *Nightflyer* towards the driveroom.

But even as she approached, she knew it was too late. The linguists were too close, and already moving much faster than she was.

"Don't," she said, authority in her tone. "Christopheris is dead."

"His ghost is crying for help, then," Lindran replied. "When they tinkered you together, they must have damaged the genes for hearing, bitch."

"The ship isn't safe."

"Bitch," was all the answer she got.

Karoly's sled pursued vainly. "Friends, you must stop, please, I beg it of you. Let us talk this out together."

The sounds were his only reply.

"I am your superior," he said. "I order you to wait outside. Do you hear me? I order it, I invoke the authority of the Academy of Human Knowledge. Please, my friends, please."

Melantha watched helplessly as Lindran and Dannel vanished down the long tunnel of the driveroom.

A moment later she halted her own sled near the waiting black mouth, debating whether she should follow them on into the *Nightflyer.* She might be able to catch them before the airlock opened.

Royd's voice, hoarse counterpoint to the sounds, answered her unvoiced question. "Stay, Melantha. Proceed no farther."

She looked behind her. Royd's sled was approaching.

"What are you doing here? Royd, use your own lock. You have to get back inside!"

"Melantha," he said calmly, "I cannot. The ship will not respond to me. The lock will not dilate. The main lock in the driveroom is the only one with manual override. I am trapped outside. I don't want you or Karoly inside the ship until I can return to my console."

Melantha Jhirl looked down the shadowed barrel of the drive-room, where the linguists had vanished.

"What will—"

"Beg them to come back, Melantha. Plead with them. Perhaps there is still time."

She tried. Karoly d'Branin tried as well. The twisted symphony of pain and pleading went on and on, but they could not raise Dannel or Lindran at all.

"They've cut out their comm," Melantha said furiously. "They don't want to listen to us. Or that . . . that sound."

Royd's sled and d'Branin's reached her at the same time. "I do not understand," Karoly said. "Why can you not enter, Royd? What is happening?"

"It is simple, Karoly," Royd replied. "I am being kept outside until—until—"

"Yes?" prompted Melantha.

"—until Mother is done with them."

THE LINGUISTS LEFT THEIR VACUUM SLED NEXT TO THE ONE THAT Christopheris had abandoned, and cycled through the airlock in unseemly haste, with hardly a glance for the grim headless doorman.

Inside they paused briefly to collapse their helmets. "I can still hear him," Dannel said. The sounds were faint inside the ship.

Lindran nodded. "It's coming from the lounge. Hurry."

They kicked and pulled their way down the corridor in less than a minute. The sounds grew steadily louder, nearer. "He's in there," Lindran said when they reached the doorway.

"Yes," Dannel said, "but is he alone? We need a weapon. What if . . . Royd had to be lying. There is someone else on board. We need to defend ourselves."

Lindran would not wait. "There are two of us," she said. "Come on!" She launched herself through the doorway, calling Christopheris by name.

It was dark inside. What little light there was spilled through the door from the corridor. Her eyes took a long moment to adjust. Everything was confused; walls and ceilings and floor were all the same, she had no sense of direction. "Rojan," she called, dizzily. "Where are you?" The lounge seemed empty, but maybe it was only the light, or her sense of unease.

"Follow the sound," Dannel suggested. He hung in the door, peering warily about for a minute, and then began to feel his way cautiously down a wall, groping with his hands.

As if in response to his comment, the sobbing sounds grew suddenly louder. But they seemed to come first from one corner of the room, then from another.

Lindran, impatient, propelled herself across the chamber, searching. She brushed against a wall in the kitchen area, and that made her think of weapons, and Dannel's fears. She knew where the utensils were stored. "Here," she said a moment later, turning towards him, "Here, I've got a knife, that should thrill you." She flourished it, and brushed against a floating bubble of liquid as big as her fist. It burst and re-formed into a hundred smaller globules. One moved past her face, close, and she tasted it. Blood.

But Lasamer had been dead a long time. His blood ought to have dried by now, she thought.

"Oh, merciful god," said Dannel.

"What?" Lindran demanded. "Did you find him?"

Dannel was fumbling his way back towards the door, creeping along the wall like an oversized insect, back the way he had come. "Get out, Lindran," he warned. *Hurry!*

"Why?" She trembled despite herself. "What's wrong?"

"The screams," he said. "The wall, Lindran, the wall. The sounds."

"You're not making sense," she snapped. "Get ahold of yourself."

He gibbered, "Don't you see? The sounds are coming from the *wall*. The communicator. Faked. Simulated." Dannel reached the door, and dove through it, sighing audibly. He did not wait for her. He bolted down the corridor and was gone, pulling himself hand over hand wildly, his feet thrashing and kicking behind him.

Lindran braced herself and moved to follow.

The sounds came from in front of her, from the door. "Help me," it said, in Rojan Christopheris' voice. She heard moaning and that terrible wet choking sound, and she stopped.

From her side came a wheezing ghastly death rattle. "Ahhhh," it moaned, loudly, building in a counterpoint to the other noise. "Help me."

"Help me, help me, help me," said Christopheris from the darkness behind her.

Coughing and a weak groan sounded under her feet.

"Help me," all the voices chorused, "help me, help me, help me." Recordings, she thought, recordings being played back. "Help me, help me, help me, help me." All the voices rose higher and louder, and the words turned into a scream, and the scream ended in wet choking, in wheezes and gasps and death. Then the sounds stopped. Just like that; turned off.

Lindran kicked off, floated towards the door, knife in hand.

Something dark and silent crawled from beneath the dinner table and rose to block her path. She saw it clearly for a moment, as it emerged between her and the light. Rojan Christopheris, still in his vacuum suit, but with the helmet pulled off. He had something in his hand that he raised to point at her. It was a laser, Lindran saw, a simple cutting laser.

She was moving straight towards him, coasting, helpless. She flailed and tried to stop herself, but she could not.

When she got quite close, she saw that Rojan had a second mouth below his chin, a long blackened slash, and it was grinning at her, and little droplets of blood flew from it, wetly, as he moved.

———

DANNEL RUSHED DOWN THE CORRIDOR IN A FRENZY OF FEAR, BRUISING himself as he smashed off walls and doorways. Panic and weightlessness made him clumsy. He kept glancing over his shoulder as he fled, hoping to see Lindran coming after him, but terrified of what he might see in her stead. Every time he looked back, he lost his sense of balance and went tumbling again.

It took a long, *long* time for the airlock to open. As he waited, trembling, his pulse began to slow. The sounds had dwindled behind him, and there was no sign of pursuit. He steadied himself with an effort. Once inside the lock chamber, with the inner door sealed between him and the lounge, he began to feel safe.

Suddenly Dannel could barely remember why he had been so terrified.

And he was ashamed; he had run, abandoned Lindran. And for what? What had frightened him so? An empty lounge? Noises from the walls? A rational explanation for that forced itself on him all at once. It only meant that poor Christopheris was somewhere else in the ship, that's all, just somewhere else, alive and in pain, spilling his agony into a comm unit.

Dannel shook his head ruefully. He'd hear no end of this, he knew. Lindran liked to taunt him. She would never let him forget it. But at least he would return, and apologize. That would count for something. Resolute, he reached out and killed the cycle on the airlock, then reversed it. The air that had been partially sucked out came gusting back into the chamber.

As the inner door rolled back, Dannel felt his fear return briefly, an instant of stark terror when he wondered what might have emerged from the lounge to wait for him in the corridors of the *Nightflyer*. He faced the fear and willed it away. He felt strong.

When he stepped out, Lindran was waiting.

He could see neither anger nor disdain in her curiously calm features, but he pushed himself towards her and tried to frame a plea for forgiveness anyway. "I don't know why I—"

With languid grace, her hand came out from behind her back. The knife flashed up in a killing arc, and that was when Dannel finally noticed the hole burned in her suit, still smoking, just between her breasts.

"YOUR *MOTHER*?" MELANTHA JHIRL SAID INCREDULOUSLY AS THEY hung helpless in the emptiness beyond the ship.

"She can hear everything we say," Royd replied. "But at this point it no longer makes any difference. Rojan must have done something very foolish, very threatening. Now she is determined to kill you all."

"She, she, what do you mean?" D'Branin's voice was puzzled. "Royd, surely you do not tell us that your mother is still alive. You said she died even before you were born."

"She did, Karoly," Royd said. "I did not lie to you."

"No," Melantha said. "I didn't think so. But you did not tell us the whole truth either."

Royd nodded. "Mother is dead, but her—her spirit still lives, and animates my *Nightflyer*." He sighed. "Perhaps it would be more fitting to say her *Nightflyer*. My control has been tenuous at best."

"Royd," d'Branin said, "spirits do not exist. They are not real. There is no survival after death. My *volcryn* are more real than any ghosts."

"I don't believe in ghosts either," said Melantha curtly.

"Call it what you will, then," Royd said. "My term is as good as any. The reality is unchanged by the terminology. My mother, or some part of my mother, lives in the *Nightflyer*, and she is killing all of you as she has killed others before."

"Royd, you do not make sense," d'Branin said.

"Quiet, Karoly. Let the captain explain."

"Yes," Royd said. "The *Nightflyer* is very—very advanced, you know. Automated, self-repairing, large. It had to be, if Mother were to be freed from the necessity of a crew. It was built on Newholme, you will recall. I have never been there, but I understand that Newholme's technology is quite sophisticated. Avalon could not duplicate this ship, I suspect. There are few worlds that could."

"The point, captain?"

"The point—the point is the computers, Melantha. They had to be extraordinary. They are, believe me, they are. Crystal-matrix cores, lasergrid data retrieval, full sensory extension, and other—features."

"Are you trying to tell us that the *Nightflyer* is an Artificial Intelligence? Lommie Thorne suspected as much."

"She was wrong," Royd said. "My ship is not an Artificial Intelligence, not as I understand it. But it is something close. Mother had a capacity for personality impress built in. She filled the central crystal with her own memories, desires, quirks, her loves and her—her hates. That was why she could trust the computer with my education, you see? She knew it would raise me as she herself would, had she the patience. She programmed it in certain other ways as well."

"And you cannot deprogram, my friend?" Karoly asked.

Karoly's voice was despairing. "I have *tried,* Karoly. But I am a weak hand at systems work, and the programs are very complicated, the machines very sophisticated. At least three times I have eradicated her, only to have her surface once again. She is a phantom program, and I cannot track her. She comes and goes as she will. A ghost, do you see? Her memories and her personality are so intertwined with the programs that run the *Nightflyer* that I cannot get rid of her without destroying the central crystal, wiping the entire system. But that would leave me helpless. I could never reprogram, and with the computers down the entire ship would fail, drivers, life support, everything. I would have to leave the *Nightflyer,* and that would kill me."

"You should have told us, my friend," Karoly d'Branin said. "On Avalon, we have many cyberneticists, some very great minds. We might have aided you. We could have provided expert help. Lommie Thorne might have helped you."

"Karoly, I have *had* expert help. Twice I have brought systems spe-cialists on board. The first one told me what I have just told you; that it was impossible without wiping the programs completely. The second had trained on Newholme. She thought she might be able to help me. Mother killed her."

"You are still holding something back," Melantha Jhirl said. "I understand how your cybernetic ghost can open and close airlocks at will and arrange other accidents of that nature. But how do you explain what she did to Thale Lasamer?"

"Ultimately I must bear the guilt," Royd replied. "My loneliness led me to a grievous error. I thought I could safeguard you, even with a telepath among you. I have carried other riders safely. I watch them constantly, warn them away from dangerous acts. If Mother attempts to interfere, I countermand her directly from the master control console. That usually works. Not always. Usually. Before this trip she had killed only five times, and the first three died when I was quite young. That was how I learned about her, about her presence in my ship. That party included a telepath, too.

"I should have known better, Karoly. My hunger for life has doomed you all to death. I overestimated my own abilities, and underestimated her fear of exposure. She strikes out when she is threatened, and telepaths are always a threat. They sense her, you see. A malign, looming presence, they tell me, something cool and hostile and inhuman."

"Yes," Karoly d'Branin said, "yes, that was what Thale said. An alien, he was certain of it."

"No doubt she feels alien to a telepath used to the familiar contours of organic minds. Hers is not a human brain, after all. What it is I cannot say—a complex of crystallized memories, a hellish network of interlocking programs, a meld of circuitry and spirit. Yes, I can understand why she might feel alien."

"You still haven't explained how a computer program could explode a man's skull," Melantha said.

"You wear the answer between your breasts, Melantha."

"My whisperjewel?" she said, puzzled. She felt it then, beneath her vacuum suit and her clothing; a touch of cold, a vague hint of eroticism that made her shiver. It was as if his mention had been enough to make the gem come alive.

"I was not familiar with whisperjewels until you told me of yours," Royd said, "but the principle is the same. Esper-etched, you said.

Then you know that psionic power can be stored. The central core of my computer is resonant crystal, many times larger than your tiny jewel. I think Mother impressed it as she lay dying."

"Only an esper can etch a whisperjewel," Melantha said.

"You never asked the *why* of it, either of you," Royd said. "You never asked why Mother hated people so. She was born gifted, you see. On Avalon she might have been a class one, tested and trained and honored, her talent nurtured and rewarded. I think she might have been very famous. She might have been stronger than a class one, but perhaps it is only after death that she acquired such power, linked as she is to the *Nightflyer*.

"The point is moot. She was not born on Avalon. On Vess, her ability was seen as a curse, something alien and fearful. So they cured her of it. They used drugs and electroshock and hypnotraining that made her violently ill whenever she tried to use her talent. They used other, less savory methods as well. She never lost her power, of course, only the ability to use it effectively, to control it with her conscious mind. It remained part of her, suppressed, erratic, a source of shame and pain, surfacing violently in times of great emotional stress. And half a decade of institutional care almost drove her insane. No wonder she hated people."

"What was her talent? Telepathy?"

"No. Oh, some rudimentary ability perhaps. I have read that all psi talents have several latent abilities in addition to their one developed strength. But Mother could not read minds. She had some empathy, although her cure had twisted it curiously, so that the emotions she felt literally sickened her. But her major strength, the talent they took five years to shatter and destroy, was teke."

Melantha Jhirl swore. "Of *course* she hated gravity! Telekinesis under weightlessness is—"

"Yes," Royd finished. "Keeping the *Nightflyer* under gravity tortures me, but it limits Mother."

In the silence that followed that comment, each of them looked down the dark cylinder of the driveroom. Karoly d'Branin moved awkwardly on his sled. "Dannel and Lindran have not returned," he said.

"They are probably dead," Royd said dispassionately.

"What will we do, then? We must plan. We cannot wait here indefinitely."

"The first question is what *I* can do," Royd Eris replied. "I have talked freely, you'll note. You deserved to know. We have passed the point where ignorance was a protection. Obviously things have gone too far. There have been too many deaths and you have been witness to all of them. Mother cannot allow you to return to Avalon alive."

"True," said Melantha. "But what shall she do with you? Is your own status in doubt, captain?"

"The crux of the problem," Royd admitted. "You are still three moves ahead, Melantha. I wonder if it will suffice. Your opponent is four ahead in this game, and most of your pawns are already captured. I fear checkmate is imminent."

"Unless I can persuade my opponent's king to desert, no?"

She could see Royd's wan smile. "She would probably kill me too if I choose to side with you. She does not need me."

Karoly d'Branin was slow to grasp the point. "But—but what else could—"

"My sled has a laser. Yours do not. I could kill you both, right now, and thereby earn my way back into the *Nightflyer's* good graces."

Across the three meters that lay between their sleds, Melantha's eyes met Royd's. Her hands rested easily on the thruster controls. "You could try, captain. Remember, the improved model isn't easy to kill."

"I would not kill you, Melantha Jhirl," Royd said seriously. "I have lived sixty-eight standard years and I have never lived at all. I am tired, and you tell grand gorgeous lies. Will you really touch me?"

"Yes."

"I risk a lot for that touch. Yet in a way it is no risk at all. If we lose, we will all die together. If we win, well, I shall die anyway when they destroy the *Nightflyer,* either that or live as a freak in an orbital hospital, and I would prefer death."

"We will build you a new ship, captain," Melantha promised.

"Liar," Royd replied. But his tone was cheerful. "No matter. I have not had much of a life anyway. Death does not frighten me. If we win, you must tell me about your *volcryn* once again, Karoly. And you, Melantha, you must play chess with me, and find a way to touch me, and . . ."

"And sex with you?" she finished, smiling.

"If you would," he said quietly. He shrugged. "Well, Mother has heard all of this. Doubtless she will listen carefully to any plans we might make, so there is no sense making them. Now there is no chance that the control lock will admit me, since it is keyed directly into the ship's computer. So we must follow the others through the driveroom, and enter through the main lock, and take what small chances we are given. If I can reach my console and restore gravity, perhaps we can win. If not—"

He was interrupted by a low groan.

For an instant Melantha thought the *Nightflyer* was wailing at them again, and she was surprised that it was so stupid as to try the same tactic twice. Then the groan sounded once more, and in the back of Karoly d'Branin's sled, the forgotten fourth member of their company struggled against the bonds that held her down. D'Branin hastened to free her, and Agatha Marij-Black tried to rise to her feet and almost floated off the sled, until he caught her hand and pulled her back. "Are you well?" he asked. "Can you hear me? Have you pain?"

Imprisoned beneath a transparent faceplate, wide frightened eyes flicked rapidly from Karoly to Melantha to Royd, and then to the broken *Nightflyer*. Melantha wondered whether the woman was insane, and started to caution d'Branin, when Marij-Black spoke.

"The *volcryn!*" was all she said. "Oh. The *volcryn!*"

Around the mouth of the driveroom, the ring of nuclear engines took on a faint glow. Melantha Jhirl heard Royd suck in his breath sharply. She gave the thruster controls of her sled a violent twist. "Hurry," she said loudly. "The *Nightflyer* is preparing to move."

A THIRD OF THE WAY DOWN THE LONG BARREL OF THE DRIVEROOM, Royd pulled abreast of her, stiff and menacing in his black, bulky armor. Side by side they sailed past the cylindrical stardrives and the cyberwebs; ahead, dimly lit, was the main airlock and its ghastly sentinel.

"When we reach the lock, jump over to my sled," Royd said. "I want to stay armed and mounted, and the chamber is not large enough for two sleds."

Melantha Jhirl risked a quick glance behind her. "Karoly," she called. "Where are you?"

"Outside, my love, my friend," the answer came. "I cannot come. Forgive me."

"We have to stay together!"

"No," d'Branin said, "no, I could not risk it, not when we are so close. It would be so tragic, so futile, Melantha. To come so close and fail. Death I do not mind, but I must see them first, finally, after all these years."

"My mother is going to move the ship," Royd cut in. "Karoly, you will be left behind, lost."

"I will wait," d'Branin replied. "My *volcryn* come, and I must wait for them."

Then the time for conversation was gone, for the airlock was almost upon them. Both sleds slowed and stopped, and Royd Eris reached out and began the cycle while Melantha Jhirl moved to the rear of his huge oval worksled. When the outer door moved aside, they glided through into the lock chamber.

"When the inner door opens it will begin," Royd told her evenly. "The permanent furnishings are either built-in or welded or bolted into place, but the things that your team brought on board are not. Mother will use those things as weapons. And beware of doors, airlocks, any equipment tied into the *Nightflyer's* computer. Need I warn you not to unseal your suit?"

"Hardly," she replied.

Royd lowered the sled a little, and its grapplers made a metallic sound as they touched against the floor of the chamber.

The inner door hissed open, and Royd applied his thrusters.

Inside Dannel and Lindran waited, swimming in a haze of blood. Dannel had been slit from crotch to throat and his intestines moved like a nest of pale, angry snakes. Lindran still held the knife. They swam closer, moving with a grace they had never possessed in life.

Royd lifted his foremost grapplers and smashed them to the side as he surged forward. Dannel caromed off a bulkhead, leaving a wide wet mark where he struck, and more of his guts came sliding out. Lindran lost control of the knife. Royd accelerated past them, driving up the corridor through the cloud of blood.

"I'll watch behind," Melantha said. She turned and put her back to his. Already the two corpses were safely behind them. The knife was floating uselessly in the air. She started to tell Royd that they were all right, when the blade abruptly shifted and came after them, gripped by some invisible force.

"*Swerve!*" she cried.

The sled shot wildly to one side. The knife missed by a full meter, and glanced ringingly off a bulkhead.

But it did not drop. It came at them again.

The lounge loomed ahead. Dark.

"The door is too narrow," Royd said. "We will have to abandon—" As he spoke, they hit; he wedged the sled squarely into the doorframe, and the sudden impact jarred them loose.

For a moment Melantha floated clumsily in the corridor, her head whirling, trying to sort up from down. The knife slashed at her, opening her suit and her shoulder clear through to the bone. She felt sharp pain and the warm flush of bleeding. "Damn," she shrieked. The knife came around again, spraying droplets of blood.

Melantha's hand darted out and caught it.

She muttered something under her breath and wrenched the blade free of the hand that had been gripping it.

Royd had regained the controls of his sled and seemed intent on some manipulation. Beyond him, in the dimness of the lounge, Melantha glimpsed a dark semi-human form rise into view.

"*Royd!*" she warned. The thing activated its small laser. The pencil beam caught Royd square in the chest.

He touched his own firing stud. The sled's heavy-duty laser came alive, a shaft of sudden brilliance. It cindered Christopheris' weapon and burned off his right arm and part of his chest. The beam hung in the air, throbbing, and smoked against the far bulkhead.

Royd made some adjustments and began cutting a hole. "We'll be through in five minutes or less," he said curtly.

"Are you all right?" Melantha asked.

"I'm uninjured," he replied. "My suit is better armored than yours, and his laser was a low-powered toy."

Melantha turned her attention back to the corridor.

The linguists were pulling themselves towards her, one on each side of the passage, to come at her from two directions at once. She flexed her muscles. Her shoulder stabbed and screamed. Otherwise she felt strong, almost reckless. "The corpses are coming after us again," she told Royd. "I'm going to take them."

"Is that wise?" he asked. "There are two of them."

"I'm an improved model," Melantha said, "and they're dead." She kicked herself free of the sled and sailed towards Dannel in a high, graceful trajectory. He raised his hands to block her. She slapped them aside, bent one arm back and heard it snap, and drove her knife deep into his throat before she realized what a useless gesture that was. Blood oozed from his neck in a spreading cloud, but he continued to flail at her. His teeth snapped grotesquely.

Melantha withdrew her blade, seized him, and with all her considerable strength threw him bodily down the corridor. He tumbled, spinning wildly, and vanished into the haze of his own blood.

Melantha flew in the opposite direction, revolving lazily.

Lindran's hands caught her from behind.

Nails scrabbled against her faceplate until they began to bleed, leaving red streaks on the plastic.

Melantha whirled to face her attacker, grabbed a thrashing arm, and flung the woman down the passageway to crash into her struggling companion. The reaction sent her spinning like a top. She spread her arms and stopped herself, dizzy, gulping.

"I'm through," Royd announced.

Melantha turned to see. A smoking meter-square opening had been cut through one wall of the lounge. Royd killed the laser, gripped both sides of the doorframe, and pushed himself towards it.

A piercing blast of sound drilled through her head. She doubled over in agony. Her tongue flicked out and clicked off the comm; then there was blessed silence.

In the lounge it was raining. Kitchen utensils, glasses and plates, pieces of human bodies all lashed violently across the room, and glanced harmessly off Royd's armored form. Melantha—eager to follow—drew back helplessly. That rain of death would cut her to pieces in her lighter, thinner vacuum suit. Royd reached the far wall and vanished into the secret control section of the ship. She was alone.

The *Nightflyer* lurched, and sudden acceleration provided a brief semblance of gravity. Melantha was thrown to one side. Her injured shoulder smashed painfully against the sled.

All up and down the corridor doors were opening.

Dannel and Lindran were moving towards her once again.

THE *NIGHTFLYER* WAS A DISTANT STAR SPARKED BY ITS NUCLEAR ENgines. Blackness and cold enveloped them, and below was the unending emptiness of the Tempter's Veil, but Karoly d'Branin did not feel afraid. He felt strangely transformed.

The void was alive with promise.

"They *are* coming," he whispered. "Even I, who have no psi at all, even I can feel it. The Crey story must be so, even from light years off they can be sensed. Marvelous!"

Agatha Marij-Black seemed small and shrunken. "The *volcryn*," she muttered. "What good can they do us. I hurt. The ship is gone. D'Branin, my head aches." She made a small frightened noise. "Thale said that, just after I injected him, before—before—you know. He said that his head hurt. It aches so terribly."

"Quiet, Agatha. Do not be afraid. I am here with you. Wait. Think only of what we shall witness, think only of that!"

"I can sense them," the psipsych said.

D'Branin was eager. "Tell me, then. We have our little sled. We shall go to them. Direct me."

"Yes," she agreed. "Yes. Oh, yes."

GRAVITY RETURNED; IN A FLICKER, THE UNIVERSE BECAME ALMOST normal.

Melantha fell to the deck, landed easily and rolled, and was on her feet cat-quick.

The objects that had been floating ominously through the open doors along the corridor all came clattering down.

The blood was transformed from a fine mist to a slick covering on the corridor floor.

The two corpses dropped heavily from the air, and lay still.

Royd spoke to her from the communicators built into the walls. "I made it," he said.

"I noticed," she replied.

"I'm at the main control console. I have restored the gravity with a manual override, and I'm cutting off as many computer functions as possible. We're still not safe, though. Mother will try to find a way around me. I'm countermanding her by sheer force, as it were. I cannot afford to overlook anything, and if my attention should lapse, even for a moment . . . Melantha, was your suit breached?"

"Yes. Cut at the shoulder."

"Change into another one. *Immediately.* I think the counterprogramming I'm doing will keep the locks sealed, but I can't take any chances."

Melantha was already running down the corridor, towards the cargo hold where the suits and equipment were stored.

"When you have changed," Royd continued, "dump the corpses into the mass conversion unit. You'll find the appropriate hatch near the driveroom airlock, just to the left of the lock controls. Convert any other loose objects that are not indispensable as well; scientific instruments, books, tapes, tableware—"

"Knives," suggested Melantha.

"By all means."

"Is teke still a threat, captain?"

"Mother is vastly weaker in a gravity field," Royd said. "She has to fight it. Even boosted by the *Nightflyer's* power, she can only move one object at a time, and she has only a fraction of the lifting force she wields under weightless conditions. But the power is still there, remember. Also, it is possible she will find a way to circumvent me and cut out the gravity again. From here I can restore it in an instant, but I don't want any likely weapons lying around even for that brief period of time."

Melantha reached the cargo area. She stripped off her vacuum suit and slipped into another one in record time, wincing at the pain in her shoulder. It was bleeding badly, but she had to ignore it. She gathered up the discarded suit and a double armful of instruments and dumped them into the conversion chamber. Afterwards she turned her attention to the bodies. Dannel was no problem. Lindran crawled down the corridor after her as she pushed him through, and thrashed weakly when it was her own turn, a grim reminder that the *Nightflyer's* powers were not all gone. Melantha easily overcame her feeble struggles and forced her through.

Christopheris' burned, ruined body writhed in her grasp and snapped its teeth at her, but Melantha had no real trouble with it. While she was cleaning out the lounge, a kitchen knife came spinning at her head. It came slowly, though, and Melantha just batted it aside, then picked it up and added it to the pile for conversion. She was working through the cabins, carrying Agatha Marij-Black's abandoned drugs and injection gun under her arm, when she heard Royd cry out.

A moment later a force like a giant invisible hand wrapped itself around her chest and squeezed and pulled her, struggling, to the floor.

SOMETHING WAS MOVING ACROSS THE STARS.

Dimly and far off, d'Branin could see it, though he could not yet make out details. But it was there, that was unmistakable, some vast shape that blocked off a section of the starscape. It was coming at them dead on.

How he wished he had his team with him now, his computer, his telepath, his experts, his instruments.

He pressed harder on the thrusters, and rushed to meet his *volcryn*.

PINNED TO THE FLOOR, HURTING, MELANTHA JHIRL RISKED OPENING her suit's comm. She had to talk to Royd. "Are you there?" she asked. "What's happen . . . happening?" The pressure was awful, and it was growing steadily worse. She could barely move.

The answer was pained and slow in coming. ". . . outwitted . . . me," Royd's voice managed. " . . . hurts to . . . talk."

"Royd—"

" . . . she . . . teked . . . the . . . dial . . . up . . . two . . . gees . . . three . . . higher . . . right . . . on . . . the . . . board . . . all . . . I . . . have to . . . to do . . . turn it . . . back . . . back . . . let me."

Silence. Then, finally, when Melantha was near despair, Royd's voice again. One word:

". . . can't . . ."

Melantha's chest felt as if it were supporting ten times her own weight. She could imagine the agony Royd must be in; Royd, for whom even one gravity was painful and dangerous. Even if the dial was an arm's length away, she knew his feeble musculature would never let him reach it. "Why," she started. Talking was not as hard for her as it seemed to be for him. "Why would . . . she turn *up* the . . . the gravity . . . it . . . weakens her too . . . yes?"

". . . yes . . . but . . . in a . . . a time . . . hour . . . minute . . . my . . . my heart . . . will burst . . . and . . . and then . . . you alone . . . she . . . will . . . kill gravity . . . kill you. . . ."

Painfully Melantha reached out her arm and dragged herself half a length down the corridor. "Royd . . . hold on . . . I'm coming. . . ." She dragged herself forward again. Agatha's drug kit was still under her arm, impossibly heavy. She eased it down and started to shove it aside. It felt as if it weighed a hundred kilos. She reconsidered. Instead she opened its lid.

The ampules were all neatly labeled. She glanced over them quickly, searching for adrenaline or synthastim, anything that might give her the strength she needed to reach Royd. She found several stimulants, selected the strongest, and was loading it into the injection gun with awkward, agonized slowness when her eyes chanced on the supply of esperon.

Melantha did not know why she hesitated. Esperon was only one of a half-dozen psionic drugs in the kit, none of which could do her any good, but something about seeing it bothered her, reminded her of something she could not quite lay her finger on. She was trying to sort it out when she heard the noise.

"Royd," she said, "your mother . . . could she move . . . she couldn't move anything . . . teke it . . . in this high a gravity . . . could she?"

"Maybe," he answered, ". . . if . . . concentrate . . . all her . . . power . . . hard . . . maybe possible . . . why?"

"Because," Melantha Jhirl said grimly, "because something . . . some*one* . . . is cycling through the airlock."

———

"IT IS NOT TRULY A SHIP, NOT AS I THOUGHT IT WOULD BE," KAROLY d'Branin was saying. His suit, Academy-designed, had a built-in encoding device, and he was recording his comments for posterity, strangely secure in the certainty of his impending death. "The scale of it is difficult to imagine, difficult to estimate. Vast, vast. I have nothing but my wrist computer, no instruments, I cannot make accurate measurements, but I would say, oh, a hundred kilometers, perhaps as much as three hundred, across. Not solid mass, of course, not at all. It is delicate, airy, no ship as we know ships, no city either. It is—oh, beautiful—it is crystal and gossamer, alive with its own dim lights, a vast intricate kind of spiderwebby craft—it reminds me a bit of the old starsail ships they used once, in the days before drive, but this great construct, it is not solid, it cannot be driven by light. It is no ship at all, really. It is all open to vacuum, it has no sealed cabins or life-support spheres, none visible to me, unless blocked from my line of sight in some fashion, and no, I cannot believe that, it is too open, too fragile. It moves quite rapidly. I would wish for the instrumentation to measure its speed, but it is enough to be here. I am taking the sled at right angles to it, to get clear of its path, but I cannot say that I will make it. It moves so much faster than we. Not at light speed, no, far below light speed, but still faster than the *Nightflyer* and its nuclear engines, I would guess . . . only a guess.

"The *volcryn* craft has no visible means of propulsion. In fact, I wonder how—perhaps it is a light-sail, laser-launched millennia ago, now torn and rotted by some unimaginable catastrophe—but no, it is too symmetrical, too beautiful, the webbings, the great shimmering veils near the nexus, the beauty of it.

"I must describe it, I must be more accurate, I know. It is difficult, I grow too excited. It is large, as I have said, kilometers across. Roughly—let me count—yes, roughly octagonal in shape. The nexus, the center, is a bright area, a small darkness surrounded by a much greater area of light, but only the dark portion seems entirely solid— the lighted areas are translucent, I can see stars through them, though discolored, shifted towards the purple. Veils, I call those the veils. From the nexus and the veils eight long—oh, vastly long—spurs project, not quite spaced evenly, so it is not a true geometric octagon—ah, I see better now, one of the spurs is shifting, oh, very slowly, the veils are rippling—they are mobile, then, those projections, and the webbing runs from one spur to the next, around and around, but there are— patterns, odd patterns, it is not at all the simple webbing of a spider. I cannot quite see order in the patterns, in the traceries of the webs, but I feel sure the order is there, the meaning is waiting to be found.

"There are lights. Have I mentioned the lights? The lights are brightest around the center nexus, but they are nowhere very bright, a dim violet. Some visible radiation, then, but not much. I would like to take an ultraviolet reading of this craft, but I do not have the instrumentation. The lights move. The veils seem to ripple, and lights run constantly up and down the length of the spurs, at differing rates of speed, and sometimes other lights can be seen transversing the webbing, moving across the patterns. I do not know what the lights are. Some form of communication, perhaps. I cannot tell whether they emanate from inside the craft or outside. I—oh! There was another light just then. Between the spurs, a brief flash, a starburst. It is gone now, already. It was more intense than the others, indigo. I feel so helpless, so ignorant. But they are beautiful, my *volcryn*. . . .

"The myths, they—this is really not much like the legends, not truly. The size, the lights. The *volcryn* have often been linked to lights, but those reports were so vague, they might have meant anything, described anything from a laser propulsion system to simple exterior lighting. I could not know it meant this. Ah, what mystery! The ship is still too far away to see the finer detail. It is so large, I do not think we shall get clear of it. It seems to have turned toward us, I think, yet I may be mistaken, it is only an impression. My instruments, if I only had my instruments. Perhaps the darker area in the center is a craft, a life capsule. The *volcryn* must be inside it. I wish my team were with me, and Thale, poor Thale. He was a class one, we might have made contact, might have communicated with them. The things we would learn! The things they have seen! To think how old this craft is, how ancient the race, how long they have been outbound . . . it fills me with awe. Communication would be such a gift, such an impossible gift, but they are so alien."

"*D'Branin*," Agatha Marij-Black said in a low, urgent voice. "Can't you feel?"

Karoly d'Branin looked at her as if seeing her for the first time.

"Can *you* feel them? You are a three, can you sense them now, strongly?"

"Long ago," the psipsych said, "long ago."

"Can you project? Talk to them, Agatha. Where are they? In the center area? The dark?"

"Yes," she replied, and she laughed. Her laugh was shrill and hysterical, and d'Branin had to recall that she was a very sick woman. "Yes, in the center, d'Branin, that's where the pulses come from. Only you're wrong about them. It's not a them at all, your legends are all lies, lies, I wouldn't be surprised if we were the first ever to see your *volcryn,* to come this close. The others, those aliens of yours, they merely *felt,* deep and distantly, sensed a bit of the nature of the *volcryn* in their dreams and visions, and fashioned the rest to suit themselves. Ships, and wars, and a race of eternal travelers, it is all—all—"

"Yes. What do you mean, Agatha, my friend? You do not make sense. I do not understand."

"No," Marij-Black said, "you do not, do you?" Her voice was suddenly gentle. "You cannot feel it, as I can. So clear now. This must be how a one feels, all the time. A one full of esperon."

"What do you feel? *What?*"

"It's not a *them,* Karoly. It's an *it.* Alive, Karoly, and quite mindless, I assure you."

"Mindless?" d'Branin said. "No, you must be wrong, you are not reading correctly. I will accept that it is a single creature if you say so, a single great marvelous star-traveler, but how can it be mindless? You sensed it, its mind, its telepathic emanations. You and the whole of the Crey sensitives and all the others. Perhaps its thoughts are too alien for you to read."

"Perhaps. But what I do read is not so terribly alien at all. Only animal. Its thoughts are slow and dark and strange, hardly thoughts at all, faint. Stirrings cold and distant. The brain must be huge all right, I grant you that, but it can't be devoted to conscious thought."

"What do you mean?"

"The propulsion system, d'Branin. Don't you *feel?* The pulses? They are threatening to rip off the top of my skull. Can't you guess what is driving your damned *volcryn* across the galaxy? And why they avoid gravity wells? Can't you guess how it is moving?"

"No," d'Branin said, but even as he denied it a dawn of comprehension broke across his face, and he looked away from his companion, back at the swelling immensity of the *volcryn,* its lights moving, its veils a-ripple as it came on and on, across light years, light centuries, across eons.

When he looked back at her, he mouthed only a single word: "Teke," he said.

She nodded.

———

Melantha Jhirl struggled to lift the injection gun and press it against an artery. It gave a single loud hiss, and the drug flooded her system. She lay back and gathered her strength and tried to think. Esperon, esperon, why was that important? It had killed Lasamer, made him a victim of his own latent abilities, multiplied his power and his vulnerability. Psi. It all came back to psi.

The inner door of the airlock opened. The headless corpse came through.

It moved with jerks, unnatural shufflings, never lifting its legs from the floor. It sagged as it moved, half-crushed by the weight upon it. Each shuffle was crude and sudden; some grim force was literally yanking one leg forward, then the next. It moved in slow motion, arms stiff by its sides.

But it moved.

Melantha summoned her own reserves and began to squirm away from it, never taking her eyes off its advance.

Her thoughts went round and round, searching for the piece out of place, the solution to the chess problem, finding nothing.

The corpse was moving faster than she was. Clearly, visibly, it was gaining.

Melantha tried to stand. She got to her knees with a grunt, her heart pounding. Then one knee. She tried to force herself up, to lift the impossible burden on her shoulders as if she were lifting weights. She was strong, she told herself. She was the improved model.

But when she put all her weight on one leg, her muscles would not hold her. She collapsed, awkwardly, and when she smashed against the floor it was as if she had fallen from a building. She heard a sharp *snap,* and a stab of agony flashed up her arm, her good arm, the arm she had tried to use to break her fall. The pain in her shoulder was terrible and intense. She blinked back tears and choked on her own scream.

The corpse was halfway up the corridor. It must be walking on two broken legs, she realized. It didn't care. A force greater than tendons and bone and muscle was holding it up.

"Melantha . . . heard you . . . are . . . you . . . Melantha?"

"Quiet," she snarled at Royd. She had no breath to waste on talk.

Now she used all the disciplines she had ever learned, willed away the pain. She kicked feebly, her boots scraping for purchase, and she pulled herself forward with her unbroken arm, ignoring the fire in her shoulder.

The corpse came on and on.

She dragged herself across the threshold of the lounge, worming her way under the crashed sled, hoping it would delay the cadaver. The thing that had been Thale Lasamer was a meter behind her.

In the darkness, in the lounge, where it had all begun, Melantha Jhirl ran out of strength.

Her body shuddered and she collapsed on the damp carpet, and she knew that she could go no farther.

On the far side of the door, the corpse stood stiffly. The sled began to shake. Then, with the scrape of metal against metal, it slid backward, moving in tiny sudden increments, jerking itself free and out of the way.

Psi. Melantha wanted to curse it, and cry. Vainly she wished for a psi power of her own, a weapon to blast apart the teke-driven corpse that stalked her. She was improved, she thought despairingly, but not improved enough. Her parents had given her all the genetic gifts they could arrange, but psi was beyond them. The genes were astronomically rare, recessive, and—

—and suddenly it came to her.

"Royd," she said, putting all of her remaining will into her words. She was weeping, wet, frightened. "The dial . . . *teke it.* Royd, teke it!"

His reply was faint, troubled. ". . . can't . . . I don't . . . Mother . . . only . . . her . . . not me . . . no . . . Mother . . ."

"Not Mother," she said, desperate. "You always . . . say . . .
Mother. I forgot . . . forgot. Not your mother . . . listen . . . you're a
clone . . . same genes . . . you have it too . . . power."

"Don't," he said. "Never . . . must be . . . sex-linked."

"No! It *isn't.* I know . . . Promethean, Royd . . . don't tell a
Promethean . . . about genes . . . turn it!"

The sled jumped a third of a meter, and listed to the side. A path
was clear.

The corpse came forward.

" . . . trying," Royd said. "Nothing . . . I *can't!*"

"She *cured* you," Melantha said bitterly. "Better than . . . she . . .
was cured . . . prenatal . . . but it's only . . . suppressed . . . you *can!*"

"I . . . don't . . . know . . . how."

The corpse stood above her. Stopped. Its pale-fleshed hands trembled, spasmed, jerked upward. Long painted fingernails. Made claws.
Began to rise.

Melantha swore. *"Royd!"*

" . . . sorry . . ."

She wept and shook and made a futile fist.

And all at once the gravity was gone. Far, far away, she heard Royd
cry out and then fall silent.

————

"THE FLASHES COME MORE FREQUENTLY NOW," KAROLY D'BRANIN
dictated, "or perhaps it is simply that I am closer, that I can see them better. Bursts of indigo and deep violet, short and fast-fading. Between the
webbing. A field, I think. The flashes are particles of hydrogen, the thin
ethereal stuff of the reaches between the stars. They touch the field, between the webbing, the spurs, and shortly flare into the range of visible
light. Matter to energy, yes, that is what I guess. My *volcryn* feeds.

"It fills half the universe, comes on and on. We shall not escape it,
oh, so sad. Agatha is gone, silent, blood on her faceplate. I can almost
see the dark area, almost, almost. I have a strange vision, in the center
is a face, small, ratlike, without mouth or nose or eyes, yet *still a face*
somehow, and it stares at me. The veils move so sensuously. The webbing looms around us.

"Ah, the light, the light!"

THE CORPSE BOBBED AWKWARDLY INTO THE AIR, ITS HANDS HANGING limply before it. Melantha, reeling in the weightlessness, was suddenly violently sick. She ripped off the helmet, collapsed it, and pushed away from her own nausea, trying to ready herself for the *Nightflyer's* furious assault.

But the body of Thale Lasamer floated dead and still, and nothing else moved in the darkened lounge. Finally Melantha recovered, and she moved to the corpse, weakly, and pushed it, a small and tentative shove. It sailed across the room.

"Royd?" she said uncertainly.

There was no answer.

She pulled herself through the hole into the control chamber.

And found Royd Eris suspended in his armored suit. She shook him, but he did not stir. Trembling, Melantha Jhirl studied his suit, and then began to dismantle it. She touched him. "Royd," she said, "here. Feel, Royd, here, I'm here, feel it." His suit came apart easily, and she flung the pieces of it away. "Royd, *Royd*."

Dead. Dead. His heart had given out. She punched it, pummeled it, tried to pound it into new life. It did not beat. Dead. Dead.

Melantha Jhirl moved back from him, blinded by her own tears, edged into the console, glanced down.

Dead. Dead.

But the dial on the gravity grid was set on zero.

"Melantha," said a mellow voice from the walls.

I HAVE HELD THE *NIGHTFLYER'S* CRYSTALLINE SOUL WITHIN MY HANDS.

It is deep red and multi-faceted, large as my head, and icy to the touch. In its scarlet depths, two small sparks of smoky light burn fiercely, and sometimes seem to whirl.

I have crawled through the consoles, wound my way carefully past safeguards and cybernets, taking care to damage nothing, and I have laid rough hands on that great crystal, knowing it is where *she* lives.

And I cannot bring myself to wipe it.

Royd's ghost has asked me not to.

Last night we talked about it once again, over brandy and chess in the lounge. Royd cannot drink, of course, but he sends his spectre to smile at me, and he tells me where he wants his pieces moved.

For the thousandth time he offered to take me back to Avalon, or any world of my choice, if only I would go outside and complete the repairs we abandoned so many years ago, so the *Nightflyer* might safely slip into stardrive.

For the thousandth time I refused.

He is stronger now, no doubt. Their genes are the same, after all. Their power is the same. Dying, he too found the strength to impress himself upon the great crystal. The ship is alive with both of them, and frequently they fight. Sometimes she outwits him for a moment, and the *Nightflyer* does odd, erratic things. The gravity goes up or down or off completely. Blankets wrap themselves around my throat when I sleep. Objects come hurtling out of dark corners.

Those times have come less frequently of late, though. When they do come, Royd stops her, or I do. Together, the *Nightflyer* is ours.

Royd claims he is strong enough alone, that he does not really need me, that he can keep her under check. I wonder. Over the chessboard, I still beat him nine games out of ten.

And there are other considerations. Our work, for one. Karoly would be proud of us. The *volcryn* will soon enter the mists of the Tempter's Veil, and we follow close behind. Studying, recording, doing all that old d'Branin would have wanted us to do. It is all in the computer, and on tape and paper as well, should the system ever be wiped. It will be interesting to see how the *volcryn* thrives in the Veil. Matter is so thick there, compared to the thin diet of interstellar hydrogen on which the creature has fed so many endless eons.

We have tried to communicate with it, with no success. I do not believe it is sentient at all. And lately Royd has tried to imitate its ways, gathering all his energies in an attempt to move the *Nightflyer* by teke. Sometimes, oddly, his mother even joins with him in those efforts. So far they have always failed, but we will keep trying.

So goes our work. We know our results will reach humanity. Royd and I have discussed it, and we have a plan. Before I die, when my time is near, I will destroy the central crystal and clear the computers, and afterwards I will set course manually for the close vicinity of an inhabited world. The *Nightflyer* will become a true ghost ship then. It will work. I have all the time I need, and I am an improved model.

I will not consider the other option, although it means much to me that Royd suggests it again and again. No doubt I could finish the repairs, and perhaps Royd could control the ship without me, and go on with the work. But that is not important.

I was wrong so many times. The esperon, the monitors, my control of the others; all of them my failures, payment for my hubris. Failure hurts. When I finally touched him, for the first and last and only time, his body was still warm. But he was gone already. He never felt my touch. I could not keep that promise.

But I can keep my other.

I will not leave him alone with her.

Ever.

THE MONKEY TREATMENT

❖

KENNY DORCHESTER WAS A FAT MAN.

He had not always been a fat man, of course. He had come into the world a perfectly normal infant of modest weight, but the normalcy was short-lived in Kenny's case, and before very long he had become a chubby-cheeked toddler well swaddled in baby fat. From then on it was all downhill and upscale so far as Kenny was concerned. He became a pudgy child, a corpulent adolescent, and a positively porcine college student, all in good turn, and by adulthood he had left all those intermediate steps behind and graduated into full obesity.

People became obese for a variety of reasons, some of them physiological and some psychological. Kenny's reason was relatively simple: food. Kenny Dorchester loved to eat. Often he would paraphrase Will Rogers, winking broadly, and tell his friends that he had never met a food he didn't like. This was not precisely true, since Kenny loathed both liver and prune juice. Perhaps if his mother had served them more often during his childhood, he would never have attained the girth and gravity that so haunted him at maturity. Unfortunately, Gina Dorchester was more inclined to lasagna and roast turkey with stuffing and sweet potatoes and chocolate pudding and veal cordon bleu and buttered corn-on-the-cob and stacks of blueberry pancakes (although not all in one meal) than she was to liver and prune juice, and once Kenny had expressed his preference in the matter by retching his liver back onto his plate, she obligingly never served liver and prune juice again. Thus, all unknowing, she set her son on the soft, suety road to the monkey treatment. But that was long ago and the poor woman really cannot be blamed, since it was Kenny himself who ate his way there.

Kenny loved pepperoni pizza, or plain pizza, or garbage pizza with everything on it including anchovies. Kenny could eat an entire slab of barbequed ribs, either beef or pork, and the spicier the sauce was the more he approved. He was fond of rare prime rib and roast chicken and Rock Cornish game hens stuffed with rice, and he was hardly the sort to object to a nice sirloin or a platter of fried shrimp or a hunk of kielbasa. He liked his burgers with everything on them, and fries and onion rings on the side, please. There was nothing you could do to his friend the potato that would turn him against it, but he was also partial to pasta and rice, to yams candied and un-, and even to mashed rutabagas. "Desserts are my downfall," he would sometimes say, for he liked sweets of all varieties, especially devil's food cake and cannoli and hot apple pie with whipped cream. "Bread is my downfall," he would say at other times, when it seemed likely that no dessert was forthcoming, and so saying he would rip off another chunk of sourdough or butter up another crescent roll or reach for another slice of garlic bread, which was a particular vice. Kenny had a lot of particular vices. He thought himself an authority on both fine restaurants and fast-food franchises, and could discourse endlessly and knowledgeably about either. He relished Greek food and Chinese food and Japanese food and Korean food and German food and Italian food and French food and Indian food, and was always on the lookout for new ethnic groups so he might "expand my cultural horizons." When Saigon fell, Kenny speculated about how many of the Vietnamese refugees would be likely to open restaurants. When Kenny traveled, he always made it a point to gorge himself on the area's specialty, and he could tell you the best places to eat in any of twenty-four major American cities, while reminiscing fondly about the meals he had enjoyed in each of them. His favorite writers were James Beard and Calvin Trillin.

"I live a tasty life!" Kenny Dorchester would proclaim, beaming.

And so he did. But Kenny also had a secret. He did not often think of it and never spoke it, but it was there nonetheless, down at the heart of him beneath all those great rolls of flesh, and not all his sauces could drown it, nor could his trusty fork keep it at bay.

Kenny Dorchester did not *like* being fat.

Kenny was like a man torn between two lovers, for while he loved his food with an abiding passion, he also dreamed of other loves, of women, and he knew that in order to secure the one he would have to give up the other, and that knowledge was his secret pain. Often he wrestled with the dilemmas posed by his situation. It seemed to Kenny that while it might be preferable to be slender and have a woman than to be fat and have only a crawfish bisque, nonetheless the latter was not entirely to be spurned. Both were sources of happiness after all, and the real misery fell to those who gave up the one and failed to obtain the other. Nothing depressed or saddened Kenny so much as the sight of a fat person eating cottage cheese. Such pathetic human beings never seemed to get appreciably skinnier, Kenny thought, and were doomed to go through life bereft of both women and crawfish, a fate too grim to contemplate.

Yet despite all his misgivings, at times the secret pain inside Kenny Dorchester would flare up mightily, and fill him with a sense of resolve that made him feel as if anything might be possible. The sight of a particularly beautiful woman or the word of some new, painless, and wonderfully effective diet were particularly prone to trigger what Kenny thought of his "aberrations." When such moods came, Kenny would be driven to diet.

Over the years he tried every diet there was, briefly and secretly. He tried Dr. Atkins' diet and Dr. Stillman's diet, the grapefruit diet and the brown rice diet. He tried the liquid protein diet, which was truly disgusting. He lived for a week on nothing but Slender and Sego, until he had run through all of the flavors and gotten bored. He joined a Pounds-Off club and attended a few meetings, until he discovered that the company of fellow dieters did him no good whatsoever, since all they talked about was food. He went on a hunger strike that lasted until he got hungry. He tried the fruit juice diet, and the drinking man's diet (even though he was not a drinking man), and the martinis-and-whipped-cream diet (he omitted the martinis). A hypnotist told him that his favorite foods tasted bad and he wasn't hungry anyway, but it was a damned lie, and that was that for hypnosis. He had his behavior modified so he put down his fork between bites, used small plates that looked full even with tiny portions, and wrote down everything he ate in a notebook. That left him with stacks of notebooks, a great many small dishes to wash, and unusual manual dexterity in putting down and picking up his fork. His favorite diet was the one that said you could eat all you wanted of your favorite food, so long as you ate nothing *but* that. The only problem was that Kenny couldn't decide what was really his one true favorite, so he wound up eating ribs for a week, and pizza for a week, and Peking duck for a week (that was an expensive week), and losing no weight whatsoever, though he did have a great time.

Most of Kenny Dorchester's aberrations lasted for a week or two. Then, like a man coming out of a fog, he would look around and realize that he was absolutely miserable, losing relatively little weight, and in imminent danger of turning into one of those cottage cheese fatties he so pitied. At that point he would chuck the diet, go out for a good meal, and be restored to his normal self for another six months, until his secret pain surfaced again.

Then, one Friday night, he spied Henry Moroney at the Slab.

The Slab was Kenny's favorite barbeque joint. It specialized in ribs, charred and meaty and served dripping with a sauce that Kenny approved of mightily. And on Fridays the Slab offered all the ribs you could eat for only fifteen dollars, which was prohibitively high for most people but a bargain for Kenny, who could eat a great many ribs. On that particular Friday, Kenny had just finished his first slab and was waiting for the second, sipping beer and eating bread, when he chanced to look up and realized, with a start, that the slim haggard fellow in the next booth was, in fact, Henry Moroney.

Kenny Dorchester was nonplussed. The last time he had seen Henry Moroney they had both been unhappy Pounds-Off members, and Moroney had been the only one in the club who weighed more than Kenny did. A great fat whale of a man, Moroney had carried about the cruel nickname of "Boney," as he confessed to his fellow members. Only now the nickname seemed to fit. Not only was Moroney skinny enough to hint at a ribcage under his skin, but the table in front of him was absolutely littered with bones. That was the detail that intrigued Kenny Dorchester. All those bones. He began to count, and he lost track before very long, because all the bones were disordered, strewn about on empty plates in little puddles of drying sauce. But from the sheer mass of them it was clear that Moroney had put away at least four slabs of ribs, maybe five.

It seemed to Kenny Dorchester that Henry "Boney" Moroney knew the secret. If there was a way to lose hundreds of pounds and still be able to consume five slabs of ribs at a sitting, that was something Kenny desperately needed to know. So he rose and walked over to Moroney's booth and squeezed in opposite him. "It *is* you," he said.

Moroney looked up as if he hadn't noticed Kenny until that very second. "Oh," he said in a thin, tired voice. "You." He seemed very weary, but Kenny thought that was probably natural for someone who had lost so much weight. Moroney's eyes were sunk in deep gray hollows, his flesh sagged in pale empty folds, and he was slouching forward with his elbows on the table as if he were too exhausted to sit up straight. He looked terrible, but he had lost so much *weight. . . .*

"You look wonderful!" Kenny blurted. "How did you do it? How? You must tell me, Henry, really you must."

"No," Moroney whispered. "No, Kenny. Go away."

Kenny was taken aback. "Really!" he declared. "That's not very friendly. I'm not leaving until I know your secret, Henry. You owe it to me. Think of all the times we've broken bread together."

"Oh, Kenny," Moroney said, in his faint and terrible voice. "Go, please, go, you don't want to know, it's too . . . too . . ." He stopped in mid-sentence, and a spasm passed across his face. He moaned. His head twisted wildly to the side, as if he were having some kind of a fit, and his hands beat on the table. "Ooooo," he said.

"Henry, what's wrong?" Kenny said, alarmed. He was certain now that Boney Moroney had overdone his diet.

"Ohhhh," Moroney sighed in sudden relief. "Nothing, nothing. I'm fine." His voice had none of the enthusiasm of his words. "I'm wonderful, in fact. Wonderful, Kenny. I haven't been so slim since . . . since . . . why, never. It's a miracle." He smiled faintly. "I'll be at my goal soon, and then it will be over. I think. Think I'll be at my goal. Don't know my weight, really." He put a hand to his brow. "I am slender, though, truly I am. Don't you think I look good?"

"Yes, yes," Kenny agreed impatiently. "But how? You must tell me. Surely not those Pounds-Off phonies . . ."

"No," said Moroney weakly. "No, it was the monkey treatment. Here, I'll write it down for you." He took out a pencil and scrawled an address on a napkin.

Kenny stuffed the napkin into a pocket. "The monkey treatment? I've never heard of that. What is it?"

Henry Moroney licked his lips. "They . . ." he started, and then another fit hit him, and his head twitched around grotesquely. "Go," he said to Kenny, "just go. It works, Kenny, yes, oh. The monkey treatment, yes. I can't say more. You have the address. Excuse me." He placed his hands flat on the table and pushed himself to his feet, then walked over to the cashier, shuffling like a man twice his age. Kenny Dorchester watched him go, and decided that Moroney had *definitely* overdone this monkey treatment, whatever it was. He had never had tics or spasms before, or whatever that had been.

"You have to have a sense of proportion about these things," Kenny said stoutly to himself. He patted his pocket to make sure the napkin was still there, resolved that he would handle things more sensibly than Boney Moroney, and returned to his own booth and his second slab of ribs. He ate four that night, figuring that if he was going to start a diet tomorrow he had better get in some eating while the eating was good.

The next day being Saturday, Kenny was free to pursue the monkey treatment and the dream of a new, slender him. He rose early, and immediately rushed to the bathroom to weigh himself on his digital scale, which he loved dearly because you didn't have to squint down at the numbers, since they lit up nice and bright and precise in red. This morning they lit up as 367. He had gained a few pounds, but he hardly minded. The monkey treatment would strip them off again soon enough.

Kenny tried to phone ahead, to make sure this place was open on a Saturday, but that proved to be impossible. Moroney had written nothing but an address, and there was no diet center at that listing in the yellow pages, nor a health club, nor a doctor. Kenny looked in the white pages under "Monkey" but that yielded nothing. So there was nothing to do but go down there in person.

Even that was troublesome. The address was way down by the docks in a singularly unsavory neighborhood, and Kenny had a hard time getting the cab to take him there. He finally got his way by threatening to report the cabbie to the commissioner. Kenny Dorchester knew his rights.

Before long, though, he began to have his doubts. The narrow little streets they wound through were filthy and decaying, altogether unappetizing, and it occurred to Kenny that any diet center located down here might offer only dangerous quackery. The block in question was an old commercial strip gone to seed, and it put his hackles up even more. Half the stores were boarded closed, and the rest lurked behind filthy dark windows and iron gates. The cab pulled up in front of an absolutely miserable old brick storefront, flanked by two vacant lots full of rubble, its plate glass windows grimed over impenetrably. A faded Coca-Cola sign swung back and forth, groaning, above the door. But the number was the number that Boney Moroney had written down.

"Here you are," the cabbie said impatiently, as Kenny peered out the taxi window, aghast.

"This does not look correct," Kenny said. "I will investigate. Kindly wait here until I am certain this is the place."

The cabbie nodded, and Kenny slid over and levered himself out of the taxi. He had taken two steps when he heard the cab shift gears and pull away from the curb, screeching. He turned and watched in astonishment. "Here, you can't . . ." he began. But it did. He would most definitely report that man to the commissioner, he decided.

But meanwhile he was stranded down here, and it seemed foolish not to proceed when he had come this far. Whether he took the monkey treatment or not, no doubt they would let him use a phone to summon another cab. Kenny screwed up his resolution, and went on in the grimy, unmarked storefront. A bell tinkled as he opened the door.

It was dark inside. The dust and dirt on the windows kept out nearly all the sunlight, and it took a moment for Kenny's eyes to adjust. When they did, he saw to his horror that he had walked into someone's living room. One of those gypsy families that moved into abandoned stores, he thought. He was standing on a threadbare carpet, and around and about him was a scatter of old furniture, no doubt the best the Salvation Army had to offer. An ancient black-and-white TV set crouched in one corner, staring at him blindly. The room stank of urine. "Sorry," Kenny muttered feebly, terrified that some dark gypsy youth would come out of the shadows to knife him. "Sorry." He had stepped backwards, groping behind him for the doorknob, when the man came out of the back room.

"Ah!" the man said, spying Kenny at once from tiny bright eyes. "Ah, the monkey treatment!" He rubbed his hands together and grinned. Kenny was terrified. The man was the fattest, grossest human being that Kenny had ever laid eyes on. He had squeezed through the door sideways. He was fatter than Kenny, fatter than Boney Moroney. He literally dripped with fat. And he was repulsive in other ways as well. He had the complexion of a mushroom, and miniscule little eyes almost invisible in rolls of pale flesh. His corpulence seemed to have overwhelmed even his hair, of which he had very little. Bare-chested, he displayed vast areas of folded, bulging skin, and his huge breasts flopped as he came forward quickly and seized Kenny by the arm. "The monkey treatment!" he repeated eagerly, pulling Kenny forward. Kenny looked at him, in shock, and was struck dumb by his grin. When the man grinned, his mouth seemed to become half his face, a grotesque semicircle full of shining white teeth.

"No," Kenny said at last, "no, I have changed my mind." Boney Moroney or no, he didn't think he cared to try this monkey treatment if it was administered by such as this. In the first place, it clearly could not be very effective, or else the man would not be so monstrously obese. Besides, it was probably dangerous, some quack potion of monkey hormones or something like that. *"NO!"* Kenny repeated more forcefully, trying to wrest his arm free from the grasp of the grotesquerie who held it.

But it was useless. The man was distinctly larger and infinitely stronger than Kenny, and he propelled him across the room with ease, oblivious to Kenny's protests, grinning like a maniac all the while.

"Fat man," he burbled, and as if to prove his point he reached out and seized one of Kenny's bulges and twisted it painfully. "Fat, fat, fat, no good. Monkey treatment make you thin."

"Yes, but . . ."

"Monkey treatment," the man repeated, and somehow he had gotten behind Kenny. He put his weight against Kenny's back and pushed, and Kenny staggered through a curtained doorway into the back room. The smell of urine was much stronger in there, strong enough to make him want to retch. It was pitch black, and from all sides Kenny heard rustlings and scurryings in the darkness. *Rats,* he thought wildly. Kenny was deathly afraid of rats. He fumbled about and propelled himself toward the square of dim light that marked the curtain he had come through.

Before he was quite there, a high-pitched chittering sounded suddenly from behind him, sharp and rapid as fire from a machine gun. Then another voice took it up, then a third, and suddenly the dark was alive with the terrible hammering noise. Kenny put his hands over his ears and staggered through the curtain, but just as he emerged he felt something brush the back of his neck, something warm and hairy. "Aieee!" he screamed, dancing out into the front room, where the tremendous bare-chested madman was waiting patiently. Kenny hopped from one foot to the other, screeching, "Aieee, a rat, a rat on my back. Get it off, get it *off.*" He was trying to grab for it with both hands, but the thing was very quick, and shifted around so cleverly so that he couldn't get ahold of it. But he felt it there, alive, moving. "Help me, help me!" he called out. "A rat!"

The proprietor grinned at him and shook his head, so all his many chins went bobbing merrily. "No, no," he said. "No rat, fat man. Monkey. You get the monkey treatment." Then he stepped forward and seized Kenny by the elbow again, and drew him over to a full-length mirror mounted on the wall. It was so dim in the room that Kenny could scarcely make out anything in the mirror, except that it wasn't wide enough and chopped off both his arms. The man stepped back and yanked a pull-cord dangling from the ceiling, and a single bare lightbulb clicked on overhead. The bulb swung back and forth, back and forth, so the light shifted crazily. Kenny Dorchester trembled and stared at the mirror.

"Oh!" he said.

There was a monkey on his back.

Actually it was on his shoulders, its legs wrapped around his thick neck and twined together beneath his triple chin. He could feel its monkey hair scratching the back of his neck, could feel its warm little monkey paws lightly grasping his ears. It was a very tiny monkey. As Kenny looked into the mirror, he saw it peek out from behind his head, grinning hugely. It had quick darting eyes, coarse brown hair, and altogether too many shiny white teeth for Kenny's liking. Its long prehensile tail swayed about restlessly, like some hairy snake that had grown out of the back of Kenny's skull.

Kenny's heart was pounding away like some great air-hammer lodged in his chest and he was altogether distressed by this place, this man, and this monkey. But he gathered all his reserves and forced himself to be calm. It wasn't a rat, after all. The little monkey couldn't harm him. It had to be a trained monkey, the way it had perched on his shoulders. Its owner must let it ride around like this, and when Kenny had come unwillingly through the curtain, it had probably mistook him. All fat men look alike in the dark. Kenny grabbed behind him and tried to pull the monkey loose, but somehow he couldn't seem to get a grip on it. The mirror, reversing everything, just made it worse. He jumped up and down ponderously, shaking the entire room and making the furniture leap around every time he landed, but the monkey held on tight to his ears and could not be dislodged.

Finally, with what Kenny thought was incredible aplomb under the circumstances, he turned to the gross proprietor and said, "Your monkey, sir. Kindly help me remove it."

"No, no," the man said. "Make you skinny. Monkey treatment. You no want to be skinny?"

"Of course I do," Kenny said unhappily, "but this is absurd." He was confused. This monkey on his back seemed to be part of the monkey treatment, but that certainly didn't make very much sense.

"Go," the man said. He reached up and snapped off the light with a sharp tug that sent the bulb careening wildly again. Then he started toward Kenny, who backpedaled nervously. "Go," the man repeated, as he grabbed Kenny's arm again. "Out, out. You get monkey treatment, you go now."

"See here!" Kenny said furiously. "Let go of me! Get this monkey off me, do you hear? I don't want your monkey! Do you hear me? Quit pushing, sir! I tell you, I have friends with the police department, you aren't going to get away with this. Here now . . ."

But all his protestations were useless. The man was a veritable tidal wave of sweating, smelling pale flesh, and he put his weight against Kenny and propelled him helplessly toward the door. The bell rang again as he pulled it open and shoved Kenny out into the garish bright sunlight.

"I'm not going to pay for this!" Kenny said stoutly, staggering. "Not a cent, do you hear!"

"No charge for monkey treatment," the man said, grinning.

"At least let me call a cab," Kenny began, but it was too late, the man had closed the door. Kenny stepped forward angrily and tried to yank it back open, but it did not budge. Locked. "Open up in there!" Kenny demanded at the top of his lungs. There was no reply. He shouted again, and grew suddenly and uncomfortably aware that he was being stared at. Kenny turned around. Across the street three old winos were sitting on the stoop of a boarded-up store, passing a bottle in a brown paper bag and regarding him through wary eyes.

That was when Kenny Dorchester recalled that he was standing there in the street in broad daylight with a monkey on his back.

A flush crept up his neck and spread across his cheeks. He felt very silly. "A pet!" he shouted to the winos, forcing a smile. "Just my little pet!" They went on staring. Kenny gave a last angry look at the locked door, and set off down the street, his legs pumping furiously. He had to get to someplace private.

Rounding the corner, he came upon a dark, narrow alley behind two gray old tenement buildings, and ducked inside, wheezing for breath. He sat down heavily on a trash can, pulled out his handkerchief, and mopped his brow. The monkey shifted just a bit, and Kenny felt it move. "Off me!" he shouted, reaching up and back again to try to wrench it off by the scruff of its neck, only to have it elude him once more. He tucked away his handkerchief and groped behind his head with both hands, but he just couldn't get ahold of it. Finally, exhausted, he stopped, and tried to think.

The legs! he thought. The legs under his chins! That's the ticket! Very calmly and deliberately he reached up, and felt for the monkey's legs, and wrapped one big fleshy hand around each of them. He took a deep breath and then savagely tried to yank them apart, as if they were two ends of a giant wishbone.

The monkey attacked him.

One hand twisted his right ear painfully, until it felt like it was being pulled clean off his head. The other started hammering against his temple, beating a furious tattoo. Kenny Dorchester yelped in distress and let go of the monkey's legs—which he hadn't budged for all his efforts. The monkey quit beating on him and released his ear. Kenny sobbed, half with relief and half with frustration. He felt wretched.

He sat there in that filthy alley for ages, defeated in his efforts to remove the monkey and afraid to go back to the street where people would point at him and laugh, or make rude, insulting comments under their breath. It was difficult enough going through life as a fat man, Kenny thought. How much worse, then, to face the cruel world as a fat man with a monkey on his back. Kenny did not want to know. He resolved to sit there on that trash can in the dark alley until he died or the monkey died, rather than face shame and ridicule on the streets.

His resolve endured about an hour. Then Kenny Dorchester began to get hungry. Maybe people would laugh at him, but they had always laughed at him, so what did it matter? Kenny rose and dusted himself off, while the monkey settled itself more comfortably on his neck. He ignored it, and decided to go in search of a pepperoni pizza.

He did not find one easily. The abysmal slum in which he had been stranded had a surfeit of winos, dangerous-looking teenagers, and burned-out or boarded-up buildings, but it had precious few pizza parlors. Nor did it have any taxis. Kenny walked down the main thoroughfare with brisk dignity, looking neither left nor right, heading for safer neighborhoods as fast as his plump little legs could carry him.

Twice he came upon phone booths, and eagerly fetched out a coin to summon transportation, but both times the phones proved to be out of order. Vandals, thought Kenny Dorchester, were as bad as rats.

Finally, after what seemed like hours of walking, he stumbled upon a sleazy café. The lettering on the window said JOHN'S GRILL, and there was a neon sign about the door that said, simply, EAT. Kenny was very familiar with those three lovely letters, and he recognized the sign two blocks off. It called to him like a beacon. Even before he entered, he knew it was rather unlikely that such a place would include pepperoni pizza on its menu, but by this time Kenny had ceased to care.

As he pushed the door aside, Kenny experienced a brief moment of apprehension, partially because he felt very out of place in the café, where the rest of the diners all appeared to be muggers, and partially because he was afraid they would refuse to serve him because of the monkey on his back. Acutely uncomfortable in the doorway, he moved quickly to a small table in an obscure corner, where he hoped to escape the curious stares. A gaunt gray-haired waitress in a faded pink uniform moved purposefully toward him, and Kenny sat with his eyes downcast, playing nervously with the salt, pepper, and ketchup, dreading the moment when she arrived and said, "Hey, you can't bring that thing in here!"

But when the waitress reached his table, she simply pulled a pad out of her apron's pocket and stood poised, pencil in hand. "Well?" she demanded. "What'll it be?"

Kenny stared up in shock, and smiled. He stammered a bit, then recovered himself and ordered a cheese omelet with a double side of bacon, coffee and a large glass of milk, and cinnamon toast. "Do hash browns come with?" he asked hopefully, but the waitress shook her head and departed.

What a marvelous, kind woman, Kenny thought as he waited for his meal and shredded a paper napkin thoughtfully. What a wonderful place! Why, they hadn't even mentioned his monkey! How very polite of them.

The food arrived shortly. "Ahhhh," Kenny said as the waitress laid it out in front of him on the Formica tabletop. He was ravenous. He selected a slice of cinnamon toast, and brought it to his mouth.

And a little monkey hand darted out from behind his head and snatched it clean away.

Kenny Dorchester sat in numb surprise for an instant, his suddenly empty hand poised before his mouth. He heard the monkey eating his toast, chomping noisily. Then, before Kenny had quite comprehended what was happening, the monkey's great long tail snaked in under his armpit, curled around his glass of milk, and spirited it up and away in the blink of an eye. *"Hey!"* Kenny said, but he was much too slow. Behind his back he heard slurping, sucking sounds, and all of a sudden the glass came vaulting over his left shoulder. He caught it before it fell and smashed, and set it down unsteadily. The monkey's tail came stealthily around and headed for his bacon. Kenny grabbed up a fork and stabbed at it, but the monkey was faster than he was. The bacon vanished, and the tines of the fork bent against the hard Formica uselessly. By then Kenny knew he was in a race. Dropping the bent fork, he used his spoon to cut off a chunk of the omelet, dripping cheese, and he bent forward as he lifted it, quick as he could. The monkey was quicker. A little hand flashed in from somewhere, and the spoon had only a tantalizing gob of half-melted cheese remaining on it when it reached Kenny's mouth. He lunged back toward his plate, and loaded up again, but it didn't matter how fast he tried to be. The monkey had two paws and a tail, and once it even used a little monkey foot to snatch something away from him. In hardly any time at all, Kenny Dorchester's meal was gone. He sat there staring down at the empty, greasy plate, and he felt tears gathering in his eyes.

The waitress reappeared without Kenny noticing. "My, you sure are a hungry one," she said to him, ripping off his check from her pad and putting it in front of him. "Polished that off quicker than anyone I ever saw."

Kenny looked up at her. "But I *didn't,*" he protested. "The monkey ate it all!"

The waitress looked at him very oddly. "The monkey?" she said, uncertainly.

"The monkey," Kenny said. He did not care for the way she was staring at him, like he was crazy or something.

"What monkey?" she asked. "You didn't sneak no animals in here, did you? The Board of Health don't allow no animals in here, Mister."

"What do you mean, *sneak?*" Kenny said in annoyance. "Why, the monkey is right on me. . . ." He never got a chance to finish. Just then the monkey hit him, a tremendous hard blow on the left side of his face. The force of it twisted his head half-around, and Kenny yelped in pain and shock.

The waitress seemed concerned. "You OK, Mister?" she asked. "You ain't gonna have a fit, are you, twitching like that?"

"I didn't twitch!" Kenny all but shouted. "The goddamned monkey hit me! Can't you see?"

"Oh," said the waitress, taking a step backwards. "Oh, of course. Your monkey hit you. Pesky little things, ain't they?"

Kenny pounded his fists on the table in frustration. "Never mind," he said, "just never mind." He snatched up the check—the monkey did not take that away from him, he noted—and rose. "Here," he said, pulling out his wallet. "And you have a phone in this place, don't you? Call me a cab, all right? You can do that, can't you?"

"Sure," the waitress said, moving to the register to ring up his meal. Everyone in the café was staring at him. "Sure, Mister," she muttered. "A cab. We'll get you a cab right away."

Kenny waited, fuming. The cab driver made no comment on his monkey. Instead of going home, he took the cab to his favorite pizza place, three blocks from his apartment. Then he stormed right in and ordered a large pepperoni. The monkey ate it all, even when Kenny tried to confuse it by picking up one slice in each hand and moving them simultaneously toward his mouth. Unfortunately, the monkey had two hands as well, both of them faster than Kenny's. When the pizza was completely gone, Kenny thought for a moment, summoned over the waitress, and ordered a second. This time he got a large anchovy. He thought that was very clever. Kenny Dorchester had never met anyone else besides himself who liked anchovy pizza. Those little salty fishes would be his salvation, he thought. To increase the odds, when the pizza arrived Kenny picked up the hot pepper shaker and covered it with enough hot peppers to ignite a major conflagration. Then, feeling confident, he tried to eat a slice.

The monkey liked anchovy pizza with lots of hot peppers. Kenny Dorchester almost wept.

He went from the pizza place to the Slab, from the Slab to a fine Greek restaurant, from the Greek restaurant to a local McDonald's, from a McDonald's to a bakery that made the most marvelous chocolate éclairs. Sooner or later, Kenny Dorchester thought, the monkey would be full. It was only a very little monkey, after all. How much food could it eat? He would just keep on ordering food, he resolved, and the monkey would either reach its limit or rupture and die.

That day Kenny spent more than two hundred dollars on meals.

He got absolutely nothing to eat.

The monkey seemed to be a bottomless pit. If it had a capacity, that capacity was surely greater than the capacity of Kenny's wallet. Finally he was forced to admit defeat. The monkey could not be stuffed into submission.

Kenny cast about for another tactic, and finally hit on it. Monkeys were stupid, after all, even invisible monkeys with prodigious appetites. Smiling shyly, Kenny went to a neighborhood supermarket, and picked up a box of banana pudding (it seemed appropriate) and a box of rat poison. Humming a spry little tune, he walked on home, and set to work making the pudding, stirring in liberal amounts of rat poison as it cooked. The poison was nicely odorless. The pudding smelled wonderful. Kenny poured it into some dessert cups to cool, and watched television for an hour or so. Finally he rose nonchalantly, went to the refrigerator, and got out a pudding and a nice big spoon. He sat back down in front of the set, spooned up a generous glob of pudding, and brought it to his open mouth. Where he paused. And paused. And waited.

The monkey did nothing.

Maybe it was full at last, Kenny thought. He put aside the poisoned pudding and rushed back into his kitchen, where he found a box of vanilla wafers hiding on a shelf, and a few forlorn Fig Newtons as well.

The monkey ate all of them.

A tear trickled down Kenny's cheek. The monkey would let him have all the poisoned pudding he wanted, it seemed, but nothing else. He reached back half-heartedly and tried to grab the monkey once again, thinking maybe all that eating would have slowed it down some, but it was a vain hope. The monkey evaded him, and when Kenny persisted, the monkey bit his finger. Kenny yowled and snatched his hand back. His finger was bleeding. He sucked on it. That much, at least, the monkey permitted him.

When he had washed his finger and wrapped a Band-Aid around it, Kenny returned to his living room and seated himself heavily, weary and defeated, in front of his television set. An old rerun of *The Galloping Gourmet* was coming on. He couldn't stand it. He jabbed at his remote control to change the channel, and watched blindly for hours, sunk in despair, weeping at the Betty Crocker commercials. Finally, during the late late show, he stirred a little at one of the frequent public service announcements. That was it, he thought, he had to enlist others, he had to get help.

He picked up his phone and punched out the Crisis Line number.

The woman who answered sounded kind and sympathetic and very beautiful, and Kenny began to pour out his heart to her, all about the monkey that wouldn't let him eat, about how nobody else seemed to notice the monkey, about . . . but he had barely gotten his heart-pouring going good when the monkey smashed him across the side of the head. Kenny moaned. "What's wrong?" the woman asked. The monkey yanked his ear. Kenny tried to ignore the pain and keep on talking, but the monkey kept hurting him until finally he shuddered and sobbed and hung up the phone.

This is a nightmare, Kenny thought, a terrible nightmare. And so thinking, he pushed himself to his feet and staggered off to bed, hoping that everything would be normal in the morning, that the monkey would have been nothing but part of some wretched dream, no doubt brought on by indigestion.

The merciless little monkey would not even allow him to sleep properly, Kenny discovered. He was accustomed to sleeping on his back, with his hands folded very primly on his stomach. But when he undressed and tried to assume that position, the monkey fists came raining down on his poor head like some furious hairy hail. The monkey was not about to be squashed between Kenny's bulk and the pillows, it seemed. Kenny squealed with pain and rolled over on his stomach. He was very uncomfortable this way and had difficulty falling asleep, but it was the only way the monkey would leave him alone.

The next morning Kenny Dorchester drifted slowly into wakefulness, his cheek mashed against the pillows and his right arm still asleep. He was afraid to move. It was all a dream, he told himself, there is no monkey, what a silly thing that would be, monkey indeed, it was only that Boney Moroney had told him about this "monkey treatment" and he had slept on it and had a nightmare. He couldn't feel anything on his back, not a thing. This was just like any other morning. He opened one bleary eye. His bedroom looked perfectly normal. Still, he was afraid to move. It was very peaceful lying here like this, monkeyless, and he wanted to savor the feeling. So Kenny lay very still for the longest time, watching the numbers on his digital clock change slowly.

Then his stomach growled at him. "There is no monkey!" he proclaimed loudly, and he sat up in bed.

He felt the monkey shift.

Kenny trembled and almost started to weep again, but he controlled himself with an effort. No monkey was going to get the best of Kenny Dorchester, he told himself. Grimacing, he donned his slippers and plodded into the bathroom.

The monkey peered out cautiously from behind his head while Kenny was shaving. He glared at it in the bathroom mirror. It seemed to have grown a bit, but this was hardly surprising, considering how much it had eaten yesterday. Kenny toyed with the idea of trying to cut the monkey's throat, but decided that his Norelco electric shaver was not terribly well suited to that end. And even if he used a knife, trying to stab behind his own back while looking in the mirror was a dangerously uncertain proposition.

Before leaving the bathroom, Kenny was struck by a whim. He stepped on his scale.

The numbers lit up at once. 367. The same as yesterday, he thought. The monkey weighed nothing. He frowned. No, that had to be wrong. No doubt the little monkey weighed a pound or two, but its weight was offset by whatever poundage Kenny had lost. He had to have lost *some* weight, he reasoned, since he hadn't been allowed to eat anything for ever so long. He stepped off the scale, then got back on quickly, just to double-check. It still read 367. Kenny was certain that he had lost weight. Perhaps some good would come of his travails after all. The thought made him feel oddly cheerful.

Kenny grew even more cheerful at breakfast. For the first time since he had gotten his monkey, he managed to get some food in his mouth.

When he arrived at the kitchen, he debated between French toast and bacon and eggs, but only briefly. Then he decided he would never get to taste either. Instead, with a somber fatalism, Kenny fetched down a bowl and filled it with corn flakes and milk. The monkey would probably steal it all anyway, he thought, so there was no sense going to any trouble.

Quick as he could he hurried the spoon to his mouth. The monkey grabbed it away. Kenny had expected it, had known it would happen, but when the monkey hand wrenched the spoon away he nonetheless felt a sudden and terrible grief. "No," he said uselessly. "No, no, no." He could hear the corn flakes crunching in that filthy monkey mouth, and he felt milk dropping down the back of his neck. Tears gathered in his eyes as he stared down at the bowl of corn flakes, so near and yet so far.

Then he had an idea.

Kenny Dorchester lunged forward and stuck his face right down in the bowl.

The monkey twisted his ear and shrieked and pounded on his temple, but Kenny didn't care. He was sucking in milk gleefully and gobbling up as many corn flakes as his mouth could hold. By the time the monkey's tail lashed around angrily and sent the bowl sailing from the table to the floor, Kenny had a huge wet mouthful. His cheeks bulged and milk dribbled down his chin, and somehow he'd gotten a corn flake up his nostril, but Kenny was in heaven. He chewed and swallowed as fast as he could, almost choking on the food.

When it was all gone he licked his lips and rose triumphantly. "Ha, ha," he said. "Ha, ha, ha." He walked back to his bedroom with great dignity and dressed, sneering at the monkey in the full-length bedroom mirror. He had beaten it.

In the days and weeks that followed, Kenny Dorchester settled into a new sort of daily routine and an uneasy accommodation with his monkey. It proved easier than he might have imagined, except at mealtimes. When he was not attempting to get food into his mouth, it was almost possible to forget about the monkey entirely. At work it sat peacefully on his back while Kenny shuffled his papers and made his phone calls. His coworkers either failed to notice the monkey or were sufficiently polite so as not to comment on it. The only difficulty came one day at coffee break, when Kenny foolhardily approached the coffee vendor in an effort to secure a cheese Danish. The monkey ate nine of them before Kenny could stagger away, and the man insisted that Kenny had done it when his back was turned.

Simply by avoiding mirrors, a habit that Kenny Dorchester now began to cultivate as assiduously as any vampire, he was able to keep his mind off the monkey for most of the day. He had only one difficulty, though it occurred thrice daily; breakfast, lunch, and dinner. At those times the monkey asserted itself forcefully, and Kenny was forced to deal with it. As the weeks passed, he gradually fell into the habit of ordering food that could be served in bowls, so that he might practice what he termed his "Kellogg maneuver." By this stratagem, Kenny usually managed to get at least a few mouthfuls to eat each and every day.

To be sure, there *were* problems. People would stare at him rather strangely when he used the Kellogg maneuver in public, and sometimes make rude comments on his table manners. At a chili emporium Kenny liked to frequent, the proprietor assumed he had suffered a heart attack when he dove toward his chili, and was very angry with him afterward. On another occasion a bowl of soup left him with facial burns that made it look as though he was constantly blushing. And the last straw came when he was thrown bodily out of his favorite seafood restaurant in the world, simply because he plunged his face into a bowl of crawfish bisque and began sucking it up noisily. Kenny stood in the street and berated them loudly and forcefully, reminding them how much money he had spent there over the years. Thereafter he ate only at home.

Despite the limited success of the Kellogg maneuver, Kenny Dorchester still lost nine-tenths of every meal and ten-tenths of some to the voracious monkey on his back. At first he was constantly hungry, frequently depressed, and full of schemes for ridding himself of his monkey. The only problem with these schemes was that none of them seemed to work. One Saturday Kenny went to the monkey house at the zoo, hoping that his monkey might hop off to play with others of its kind, or perhaps go in pursuit of some attractive monkey of the opposite sex. Instead, no sooner had he entered the monkey house than all the monkeys imprisoned therein ran to the bars of their cages and began to chitter and scream and spit and leap up and down madly. His own monkey answered in kind, and when some of the caged monkeys began to throw peanut husks and other bits of garbage, Kenny clapped his hands over his ears and fled. On another occasion he allowed himself to visit a local saloon, and order a number of boilermakers, a drink he understood to be particularly devastating. His intent was to get his monkey so blind drunk that it might be easily removed. This experiment too had rather unfortunate consequences. The monkey drank the boilermakers as fast as Kenny could order them, but after the third one it began to keep time to the disco music from the jukebox by beating on the top of Kenny's head. The next morning it was Kenny who woke with the pounding headache; the monkey seemed fine.

After a time, Kenny finally put all his scheming aside. Failure had discouraged him, and moreover, the matter seemed somehow less urgent than it had originally. He was seldom hungry after the first week, in fact. Instead he went through a brief period of weakness, marked by frequent dizzy spells, and then a kind of euphoria settled over him. He felt just wonderful, and even better, he was losing weight!

To be sure, it did not show on his scale. Every morning he climbed up on it, and every morning it lit up as 367. But that was only because it was weighing the monkey as well as himself. Kenny knew he was losing; he could almost feel the pounds and inches just melting away, and some of his coworkers in the office remarked on it as well. Kenny owned up to it, beaming. When they asked him how he was doing it, he winked and replied, "The monkey treatment! The mysterious monkey treatment!" He said no more than that. The one time he tried to explain, the monkey fetched him such a wallop it almost took his head off, and his friends began to mutter about his strange spasms.

Finally the day came when Kenny had to tell his cleaner to take in all his pants a few inches. That was one of the most delightful tasks of his life, he thought.

All the pleasure went right out of the moment when he exited the store, however, and chanced to glance briefly to his side and see his reflection in the window. At home Kenny had long since removed all his mirrors, so he was shocked at the sight of his monkey. It had grown. It was a little thing no longer. Now it hunched on his back like some evil deformed chimpanzee, and its grinning face loomed above his head instead of peering out behind it. The monkey was grossly fat beneath its sparse brown hair, almost as wide as it was tall, and its great long tail drooped all the way to the ground. Kenny stared at it with horror, and it grinned back at him. No wonder he had been having backaches recently, he thought.

He walked home slowly, all the jauntiness gone out of his step, trying to think. A few neighborhood dogs followed him up the street, barking at his monkey. Kenny ignored them. He had long since learned that dogs could see his monkey, just like the monkeys at the zoo. He suspected that drunks could see it as well. One man had stared at him for a very long time that night he had visited the saloon. Of course, the fellow might just have been staring at those vanishing boilermakers.

Back in his apartment Kenny Dorchester stretched out on his couch on his stomach, stuck a pillow underneath his chin, and turned on his television set. He paid no attention to the screen, however. He was trying to figure things out.

Even the Pizza Hut commercials were insufficiently distracting, although Kenny did absently mutter "Ah-h-h" like you were supposed to when the slice of pizza, dripping long strands of cheese, was first lifted from the pan.

When the show ended, Kenny got up and turned off the set and sat himself down at his dining room table. He found a piece of paper and a stubby little pencil. Very carefully, he block-printed a formula across the paper, and stared at it.

ME + MONKEY = 367 POUNDS

There were certain disturbing implications in that formula, Kenny thought. The more he considered them, the less he liked them. He was definitely losing weight, to be sure, and that was not to be sneered at—nonetheless, the grim inflexibility of the formula hinted that most of the gains traditionally attributed to weight loss would never be his to enjoy. No matter how much fat he shed, he would continue to carry around 367 pounds, and the strain on his body would be the same. As for becoming svelte and dashing and attractive to women, how could he even consider it so long as he had his monkey? Kenny thought of how a dinner date might go for him, and shuddered. "Where will it end?" he said aloud.

The monkey shifted, and snickered a vile little snicker.

Kenny pursed his lips in firm disapproval. This could not go on, he resolved. He decided to go straight to the source on the morrow, and with that idea planted firmly in his head, he took himself to bed.

The next day, after work, Kenny Dorchester returned by cab to the seedy neighborhood where he'd been subjected to the monkey treatment.

The storefront was gone.

Kenny sat in the backseat of the taxi (this time he had the good sense not to get out, and moreover had tipped the driver handsomely in advance) and blinked in confusion. A tiny, wet blubbery moan escaped his lips. The address was right, he knew it, he still had the slip of paper that had brought him there in the first place. But where he had found a grimy brick storefront adorned by a faded Coca-Cola sign and flanked by two vacant lots, now there was only one large vacant lot, choked with weeds and rubbish and broken bricks. "Oh, no," Kenny said. "Oh, no."

"You OK?" asked the lady driving the cab.

"Yes," Kenny muttered. "Just . . . just wait, please. I have to think." He held his head in his hands. He feared he was going to develop a splitting headache. Suddenly he felt weak and dizzy. And very hungry. The meter ticked. The cabbie whistled. Kenny thought. The street looked just as he remembered it, except for the missing storefront. It was just as dirty, the old winos were still on their stoop, the . . .

Kenny rolled down the window. "You, sir!" he called out to one of the winos. The man stared at him. "Come here, sir!" Kenny yelled.

Warily the old man shuffled across the street.

Kenny fetched out a dollar bill from his wallet and pressed it into the man's hand. "Here, friend," he said, "Go and buy yourself some vintage Thunderbird, if you will."

"Why you givin' me this?" the wino said suspiciously.

"I wish you to answer me a question. What has become of the building that was standing there"—Kenny pointed—"a few weeks ago."

The man stuffed the dollar into his pocket quickly. "Ain't been no buildin' there fo' years," he said.

"I was afraid of that," Kenny said. "Are you certain? I was here in the not-so-distant past and I *distinctly* recall . . ."

"No buildin'," the wino said firmly. He turned and walked away, but after a few steps he paused and glanced back. "You're one of them fat guys," he said accusingly.

"What do you know about . . . ahem . . . overweight men?"

"See 'em wanderin' over there, all the time. Crazy, too. Yellin' at thin air, playing with some kind of animals. Yeah. I 'member you. You're one of them fat guys all right." He scowled at Kenny, confused. "Looks like you lost some of that blubber, though. Real good. Thanks for the dollar."

Kenny Dorchester watched him return to his stoop and begin conversing animatedly with his colleagues. With a tremulous sigh, Kenny rolled up the window, glanced at the empty lot again, and bid his driver take him home. Him and his monkey, that is.

Weeks went dripping by and Kenny Dorchester lived as if in a trance. He went to work, shuffled his papers, mumbled pleasantries to his coworkers, struggled and schemed for his meager mouthfuls of food, avoided mirrors. The scale read 367. His flesh melted away from him at a precipitous rate. He developed slack droopy jowls, and his skin sagged all about his middle, looking as flaccid and pitiful as a used condom. He began to have fainting spells, brought on by hunger. At times he staggered and lurched about the street, his thinning and weakened legs unable to support the weight of his growing monkey. His vision got blurry. Once he even thought that his hair had started to fall out, but that at least was a false alarm; it was the monkey who was losing hair, thank goodness. It shed all over the place, ruining his furniture, and even daily vacuuming didn't seem to help much. Soon Kenny stopped trying to clean up. He lacked energy. He lacked energy for just about everything, in fact. Rising from a chair was a major undertaking. Cooking dinner was impossible torment—but he did *that* anyway, since the monkey beat him severely when it was not fed. Nothing seemed to matter very much to Kenny Dorchester. Nothing but the terrible tale of his scale each morning, and the formula that he had Scotch-taped to his bathroom wall.

ME + MONKEY = 367 POUNDS

He wondered how much was ME anymore, and how much was

MONKEY, but he did not really want to find out. One day, following the dictates of a kind of feeble whim, Kenny made a sudden grab for the monkey's legs under his chin, hoping against hope that it had gotten slow and obese and that he would be able to yank it from his back. His hands closed on nothing. On his own pale flesh. The monkey's legs did not seem to be there, though Kenny could still feel its awful crushing weight. He patted his neck and breast in dim confusion, staring down at himself, and noting absently that he could see his feet. He wondered how long that had been true. They seemed to be perfectly nice feet, Kenny Dorchester thought, although the legs to which they were attached were alarmingly gaunt.

Slowly his mind wandered back to the quandary at hand—what had become of the monkey's legs? Kenny frowned and puzzled and tried to work it all out in his head, but nothing occurred to him. Finally he slid his newly rediscovered feet into a pair of bed slippers and shuffled to the closet where he had stored all of his mirrors. Closing his eyes, he reached in, fumbled about, and found the full-length mirror that had once hung on his bedroom wall. It was a large, wide mirror. Working entirely by touch, Kenny fetched it out, carried it a few feet, and painstakingly propped it up against a wall. Then he held his breath and opened his eyes.

There in the mirror stood a gaunt, gray, skeletal-looking fellow, hunched over and sickly. On his back, grinning, was a thing the size of a gorilla. A very obese gorilla. It had a long pale snakelike tail, and great long arms, and it was as white as a maggot and entirely hairless. It had no legs. It was . . . *attached* to him now, growing right out of his back. Its grin was terrible, and filled up half of its face. It looked very like the gross proprietor of the monkey treatment emporium, in fact. Why had he never noticed that before? Of course, of course.

Kenny Dorchester turned from the mirror, and cooked the monkey a big rich dinner before going to bed.

That night he dreamed of how it had all started, back in the Slab when he had met Boney Moroney. In his nightmare a great evil white thing rode atop Moroney's shoulders, eating slab after slab of ribs, but Kenny politely pretended not to notice while he and Boney made bright, sprightly conversation. Then the thing ran out of ribs, so it reached down and lifted one of Boney's arms and began to eat his hand. The bones crunched nicely, and Moroney kept right on talking. The creature had eaten its way up to the elbow when Kenny woke screaming, covered with a cold sweat. He had wet his bed, too.

Agonizingly he pushed himself up and staggered to the toilet, where he dry-heaved for ten minutes. The monkey, angry at being wakened, gave him a desultory slap from time to time.

And then a furtive light came into Kenny Dorchester's eyes. "Boney," he whispered. Hurriedly he scrambled back to his bedroom on hands and knees, rose, and threw on some clothes. It was three in the morning, but Kenny knew there was no time to waste. He looked up an address in the phone book and called a cab.

Boney Moroney lived in a tall modern high-rise by the river with moonlight shining brightly off its silver-mirrored flanks. When Kenny staggered in, he found the doorman asleep at his station, which was just as well. Kenny tiptoed past him to the elevators and rode up to the eighth floor. The monkey on his back had begun stirring now, and seemed uneasy and ill-tempered.

Kenny's finger trembled as he pushed the round black button set in the door to Moroney's apartment, just beneath the eyehole. Musical chimes sounded loudly within, startling in the morning stillness. Kenny leaned on the button. The music played on and on. Finally he heard footsteps, heavy and threatening. The peephole opened and closed again. Then the door swung open.

The apartment was black, though the far wall was made entirely of glass, so the moonlight illuminated the darkness softly. Outlined against the stars and the light of the city stood the man who had opened the door. He was hugely, obscenely fat, and his skin was a pasty fungoid white, and he had little dark eyes set deep into crinkles in his broad suety face. He wore nothing but a vast pair of striped shorts. His breasts flopped about against his chest when he shifted his weight. And when he smiled, his teeth filled up half his face. A great crescent moon of teeth. He smiled when he saw Kenny, and Kenny's monkey. Kenny felt sick. The thing in the door weighed twice as much as the one on his back. Kenny trembled. "Where is he?" he whispered softly. "Where is Boney? What have you done to him?"

The creature laughed, and its pendulous breasts flounced about wildly as it shook with mirth. The monkey on Kenny's back began to laugh too, a higher thinner laughter as sharp as the edge of a knife. It reached down and twisted Kenny's ear cruelly. Suddenly a vast fear and a vast anger filled Kenny Dorchester. He summoned all the strength left in his wasted body and pushed forward, and somehow, somehow, he barged past the obese colossus who barred his way and staggered into the interior of the apartment. "Boney," he called, "where are you, Boney? It's me, Kenny."

There was no answer. Kenny went from room to room. The apartment was filthy, a shambles. There was no sign of Boney Moroney anywhere. When Kenny came panting back to the living room, the monkey shifted abruptly, and threw him off balance. He stumbled and fell hard. Pain went shooting up through his knees, and he cut open one outstretched hand on the edge of the chrome-and-glass coffee table. Kenny began to weep.

He heard the door close, and the thing that lived here moved slowly toward him. Kenny blinked back tears and stared at the approach of those two mammoth legs, pale in the moonlight, sagging all around with fat. He looked up and it was like gazing up the side of a mountain. Far, far above him grinned those horrible mocking teeth. *"Where is he?"* Kenny Dorchester whispered. "What have you done with poor Boney?"

The grin did not change. The thing reached down a meaty hand, fingers as thick as a length of kielbasa, and snagged the waistband of the baggy striped shorts. It pulled them down clumsily, and they settled to the ground like a parachute, bunching around its feet.

"Oh, no," said Kenny Dorchester.

The thing had no genitals. Hanging down between its legs, almost touching the carpet now that it had been freed from the confines of the soiled shorts, was a wrinkled droopy bag of skin, long and gaunt, growing from the creature's crotch. But as Kenny stared at it in horror, it thrashed feebly, and stirred, and the loose folds of flesh separated briefly into tiny arms and legs.

Then it opened its eyes.

Kenny Dorchester screamed and suddenly he was back on his feet, lurching away from the grinning obscenity in the center of the room. Between its legs, the thing that had been Boney Moroney raised its pitiful stick-thin arms in supplication. "Oh, nooooo," Kenny moaned, blubbering, and he danced about wildly, the vast weight of his monkey heavy on his back. Round and round he danced in the dimness, in the moonlight, searching for an escape from this madness.

Beyond the plate glass wall the lights of the city beckoned.

Kenny paused and panted and stared at them. Somehow the monkey must have known what he was thinking, for suddenly it began to beat on him wildly, to twist his ears, to rain savage blows all around his head. But Kenny Dorchester paid no mind. With a smile that was almost beatific, he gathered the last of his strength and rushed pell-mell toward the moonlight.

The glass shattered into a million glittering shards, and Kenny smiled all the way down.

––––––––

IT WAS THE SMELL THAT TOLD HIM HE WAS STILL ALIVE, THE SMELL OF disinfectant, and the feel of starched sheets beneath him. A hospital, he thought amidst a haze of pain. He was in a hospital. Kenny wanted to cry. Why hadn't he died? Oh, why, oh, why? He opened his eyes and tried to say something.

Suddenly a nurse was there, standing over him, feeling his brow and looking down with concern. Kenny wanted to beg her to kill him, but the words would not come. She went away and when she came back she had others with her.

A chubby young man said, "You'll be all right, Mr. Dorchester, but you have a long way to go. You're in a hospital. You're a very lucky man. You fell eight stories. You ought to be dead."

I want to be dead, Kenny thought, and he shaped the words very, very carefully with his mouth, but no one seemed to hear them. Maybe the monkey has taken over, he thought. Maybe I can't even talk anymore.

"He wants to say something," the nurse said.

"I can see that," said the chubby young doctor. "Mr. Dorchester, please don't strain yourself. Really. If you are trying to ask about your friend, I'm afraid he wasn't as lucky as you. He was killed by the fall. You would have died as well, but fortunately you landed on top of him."

Kenny's fear and confusion must have been obvious, for the nurse put a gentle hand on his arm. "The other man," she said patiently. "The fat one. You can thank God he was so fat, too. He broke your fall like a giant pillow."

And finally Kenny Dorchester understood what they were saying, and began to weep, but now he was weeping for joy, and trembling.

Three days later, he managed his first word. "Pizza," he said, and it came weak and hoarse from between his lips, and then louder still, and before long he was pushing the nurse's call button and shouting and pushing and shouting. "Pizza, pizza, pizza, pizza," he chanted, and he would not be calm until they ordered one for him. Nothing had ever tasted so good.

THE PEAR-SHAPED MAN

THE PEAR-SHAPED MAN LIVES BENEATH THE STAIRS. HIS SHOULDERS are narrow and stooped, but his buttocks are impressively large. Or perhaps it is only the clothing he wears; no one has ever admitted to seeing him nude, and no one has ever admitted to wanting to. His trousers are brown polyester double knits, with wide cuffs and a shiny seat; they are always baggy, and they have big, deep, droopy pockets so stuffed with oddments and bric-a-brac that they bulge against his sides. He wears his pants very high, hiked up above the swell of his stomach, and cinches them in place around his chest with a narrow brown leather belt. He wears them so high that his drooping socks show clearly, and often an inch or two of pasty white skin as well.

His shirts are always short-sleeved, most often white or pale blue, and his breast pocket is always full of Bic pens, the cheap throwaway kind that write with blue ink. He has lost the caps or tossed them out, because his shirts are all stained and splotched around the breast pockets. His head is a second pear set atop the first; he has a double chin and wide, full, fleshy cheeks, and the top of his head seems to come almost to a point. His nose is broad and flat, with large, greasy pores; his eyes are small and pale, set close together. His hair is thin, dark, limp, flaky with dandruff; it never looks washed, and there are those who say that he cuts it himself with a bowl and a dull knife. He has a smell, too, the Pear-shaped Man; it is a sweet smell, a sour smell, a rich smell, compounded of old butter and rancid meat and vegetables rotting in the garbage bin. His voice, when he speaks, is high and thin and squeaky; it would be a funny little voice, coming from such a large, ugly man, but there is something unnerving about it, and something even more chilling about his tight, small smile. He never shows any teeth when he smiles, but his lips are broad and wet.

Of course you know him. Everyone knows a Pear-shaped Man.

——————

JESSIE MET HERS ON HER FIRST DAY IN THE NEIGHBORHOOD, WHILE SHE and Angela were moving into the vacant apartment on the first floor. Angela and her boyfriend, Donald the student shrink, had lugged the couch inside and accidentally knocked away the brick that had been holding open the door to the building. Meanwhile Jessie had gotten the recliner out of the U-Haul all by herself and thumped it up the steps, only to find the door locked when she backed into it, the recliner in her arms. She was hot and sore and irritable and ready to scream with frustration.

And then the Pear-shaped Man emerged from his basement apartment under the steps, climbed onto the sidewalk at the foot of the stoop, and looked up at her with those small, pale, watery eyes of his. He made no move to help her with her chair. He did not say hello or offer to let her into the building. He only blinked and smiled a tight, wet smile that showed none of his teeth, and said in a voice as squeaky and grating as nails on a blackboard, "Ahhhh. *There* she is." Then he turned and walked away. When he walked he swayed slightly from side to side.

Jessie let go of the recliner; it bumped down two steps and turned over. She suddenly felt cold, despite the sweltering July heat. She watched the Pear-shaped Man depart. That was her first sight of him. She went inside and told Donald and Angela about him, but they were not much impressed. "Into every girl's life a Pear-shaped Man must fall," Angela said, with the cynicism of the veteran city girl. "I bet I met him on a blind date once."

Donald, who didn't live with them but spent so many nights with Angela that sometimes it seemed as though he did, had a more immediate concern. "Where do you want this recliner?" he wanted to know.

Later they had a few beers, and Rick and Molly and the Heathersons came over to help them warm the apartment, and Rick offered to pose for her (wink wink, nudge nudge) when Molly wasn't there to hear, and Donald drank too much and went to sleep on the sofa, and the Heathersons had a fight that ended with Geoff storming out and Lureen crying; it was a night like any other night, in other words, and Jessie forgot all about the Pear-shaped Man. But not for long.

The next morning Angela roused Donald, and the two of them went off, Angie to the big downtown firm where she was a legal secretary, Don to study shrinking. Jessie was a freelance commercial illustrator. She did her work at home, which as far as Angela and Donald and her mother and the rest of Western civilization were concerned meant that she didn't work at all. "Would you mind doing the shopping?" Angie asked her just before she left. They had pretty well devastated their refrigerator in the two weeks before the move, so as not to have a lot of food to lug across town. "Seeing as how you'll be home all day? I mean, we really need some food."

So Jessie was pushing a full cart of groceries down a crowded aisle in Santino's Market, on the corner, when she saw the Pear-shaped Man the second time. He was at the register, counting out change into Santino's hand. Jessie felt like making a U-turn and busying herself until he'd gone. But that would be silly. She'd gotten everything she needed, and she was a grown woman, after all, and he was standing at the only open register. Resolute, she got in line behind him.

Santino dumped the Pear-shaped Man's coins into the old register and bagged up his purchase: a big plastic bottle of Coke and a one-pound bag of Cheez Doodles. As he took the bag, the Pear-shaped Man saw her and smiled that little wet smile of his. "Cheez Doodles are the best," he said. "Would you like some?"

"No, thank you," Jessie said politely. The Pear-shaped Man put the brown paper sack inside a shapeless leather bag of the sort that schoolboys use to carry their books, gathered it up, and waddled out of the store. Santino, a big grizzled man with thinning salt-and-pepper hair, began to ring up Jessie's groceries. "He's something, ain't he?" he asked her.

"Who is he?" she asked.

Santino shrugged. "Hell, I dunno. Everybody just calls him the Pear-shaped Man. He's been around here forever. Comes in every morning, buys a bottle of Coke and a big bag of Cheez Doodles. Once we run out of Cheez Doodles, so I tell him he oughta try them Cheetos or maybe even potato chips, y'know, for a change? He wasn't having none of it, though."

Jessie was bemused. "He must buy something besides Coke and Cheez Doodles."

"Wanna bet, lady?"

"Then he must shop somewhere else."

"Besides me, the nearest supermarket is nine blocks away. Charlie down at the candy store tells me the Pear-shaped Man comes in every afternoon at four-thirty and has himself a chocolate ice-cream soda, but far as we can tell, that's all he eats." He rang for a total. "That's seventy-nine eighty-two, lady. You new around here?"

"I live just above the Pear-shaped Man," Jessie confessed.

"Congratulations," Santino said.

Later that morning, after she lined the shelves and put away the groceries, set up her studio in the spare bedroom, made a few desultory dabs on the cover she was supposed to be painting for Pirouette Publishing, ate lunch and washed the dishes, hooked up the stereo and listened to some Carly Simon, and rearranged half of the living room furniture, Jessie finally admitted a certain restlessness and decided this would be a good time to go around the building and introduce herself to her new neighbors. Not many people bothered with that in the city, she knew, but she was still a small-town kid at heart, and it made her feel safer to know the people around her. She decided to start with the Pear-shaped Man down in the basement and got as far as descending the stairs to his door. Then a funny feeling came over her. There was no name on the doorbell, she noticed. Suddenly she regretted her impulse. She retreated back upstairs to meet the rest of the building.

The other tenants all knew him; most of them had spoken to him, at least once or twice, trying to be friendly. Old Sadie Winbright, who had lived across the hall in the other first-floor apartment for twelve years, said he was very quiet. Billy Peabody, who shared the big second-floor apartment with his crippled mother, thought the Pear-shaped Man was creepy, especially that little smile of his. Pete Pumetti worked the late shift, and told her how those basement lights were always on, no matter what hour of the night Pete came swaggering home, even though it was hard to tell on account of the way the Pear-shaped Man had boarded up his windows. Jess and Ginny Harris didn't like their twins playing around the stairs that led down to his apartment and had forbidden them to talk to him. Jeffries the barber, whose small two-chair shop was down the block from Santino's, knew him and had no great desire for his patronage. All of them, every one, called him the Pear-shaped Man. That was who he was. "But who is he?" Jessie asked. None of them knew. "What does he do for a living?" she asked.

"I think he's on welfare," Old Sadie Winbright said. "The poor dear, he must be feebleminded."

"Damned if I know," said Pete Pumetti. "He sure as hell don't work. I bet he's a queer."

"Sometimes I think he might be a drug pusher," said Jeffries the barber, whose familiarity with drugs was limited to witch hazel.

"I betcha he writes them pornographic books down there," Billy Peabody surmised.

"He doesn't do anything for a living," said Ginny Harris. "Jess and I have talked about it. He's a shopping-bag man, he has to be."

That night, over dinner, Jessie told Angela about the Pear-shaped Man and the other tenants and their comments. "He's probably an attorney," Angie said. "Why do you care so much, anyway?"

Jessie couldn't answer that. "I don't know. He gives me goose bumps. I don't like the idea of some maniac living right underneath us."

Angela shrugged. "That's the way it goes in the big, glamorous city. Did the guy from the phone company come?"

"Maybe next week," said Jessie. "That's the way it goes in the big, glamorous city."

———

JESSIE SOON LEARNED THAT THERE WAS NO AVOIDING THE PEAR-SHAPED Man. When she visited the laundromat around the block, there he was, washing a big load of striped boxer shorts and ink-stained short-sleeved shirts, snacking on Coke and Cheez Doodles from the vending machines. She tried to ignore him, but whenever she turned around, there he was, smiling wetly, his eyes fixed on her, or perhaps on the underthings she was loading into the dryer.

When she went down to the corner candy store one afternoon to buy a paper, there he was, slurping his ice-cream soda, his buttocks overflowing the stool on which he was perched. "It's homemade," he squeaked at her. She frowned, paid for her newspaper, and left.

One evening when Angela was seeing Donald, Jessie picked up an old paperback and went out on the stoop to read and maybe socialize and enjoy the cool breeze that was blowing up the street. She got lost in the story, until she caught a whiff of something unpleasant, and when she looked up from the page, there he was, standing not three feet away, staring at her. "What do you want?" she snapped, closing the book.

"Would you like to come down and see my house?" the Pear-shaped Man asked in that high, whiny voice.

"No," she said, retreating to her own apartment. But when she looked out a half hour later, he was still standing in the same exact spot, clutching his brown bag and staring at her windows while dusk fell around him. He made her feel very uneasy. She wished that Angela would come home, but she knew that wouldn't happen for hours. In fact, Angie might very well decide to spend the night at Don's place.

Jessie shut the windows despite the heat, checked the locks on her door, and then went back to her studio to work. Painting would take her mind off the Pear-shaped Man. Besides, the cover was due at Pirouette by the end of the week.

She spent the rest of the evening finishing off the background and doing some of the fine detail on the heroine's gown. The hero didn't look quite right to her when she was done, so she worked on him, too. He was the usual dark-haired, virile, strong-jawed type, but Jessie decided to individualize him a bit, an effort that kept her pleasantly occupied until she heard Angie's key in the lock.

She put away her paints and washed up and decided to have some tea before calling it a night. Angela was standing in the living room, with her hands behind her back, looking more than a little tipsy, giggling. "What's so funny?" Jessie asked.

Angela giggled again. "You've been holding out on me," she said. "You got yourself a new beau and you didn't tell."

"What are you talking about?"

"He was standing on the stoop when I got home," Angie said, grinning. She came across the room. "He said to give you these." Her hand emerged from behind her back. It was full of fat, orange worms, little flaking twists of corn and cheese that curled between her fingers and left powdery stains on the palm of her hand. "For you," Angie repeated, laughing. "For you."

THAT NIGHT JESSIE HAD A LONG, TERRIBLE DREAM, BUT WHEN THE daylight came she could remember only a small part of it. She was standing at the door to the Pear-shaped Man's apartment under the stairs; she was standing there in darkness, waiting, waiting for something to happen, something awful, the worst thing she could imagine. Slowly, slowly, the door began to open. Light fell upon her face, and Jessie woke, trembling.

HE MIGHT BE DANGEROUS, JESSIE DECIDED THE NEXT MORNING OVER Rice Krispies and tea. Maybe he had a criminal record. Maybe he was some kind of mental patient. She ought to check up on him. But she needed to know his name first. She couldn't just call up the police and say, "Do you have anything on the Pear-shaped Man?"

After Angela had gone to work, Jessie pulled a chair over by the front window and sat down to wait and watch. The mail usually arrived about eleven. She saw the postman ascend the stairs, heard him putting the mail in the big hall mailbox. But the Pear-shaped Man got his mail separately, she knew. He had his own box, right under his doorbell, and if she remembered right it wasn't the kind that locked, either. As soon as the postman had departed, she was on her feet, moving quickly down the stairs. There was no sign of the Pear-shaped Man. The door to his apartment was down under the stoop, and farther back she could see overflowing garbage cans, smell their rich, sickly sweet odor. The upper half of the door was a window, boarded up. It was dark under the stoop. Jessie barked her knuckles on the brick as she fumbled for his mailbox. Her hand brushed the loose metal lid. She got it open, pulled out two thin envelopes. She had to squint and move toward the sunlight to read the name. They were both addressed to Occupant.

She was stuffing them back into the box when the door opened. The Pear-shaped Man was framed by bright light from within his apartment. He smiled at her, so close she could count the pores on his nose, see the sheen of the saliva on his lower lip. He said nothing.

"I," she said, startled, "I, I . . . I got some of your mail by mistake. Must be a new man on the route. I, I was just bringing it back."

The Pear-shaped Man reached up and into his mailbox. For a second his hand brushed Jessie's. His skin was soft and damp and seemed much colder than it ought to be, and the touch gave her goose bumps all up and down her arm. He took the two letters from her and looked at them briefly and then stuffed them into his pants pocket. "It's just garbage," squeaked the Pear-shaped Man. "They shouldn't be allowed to send you garbage. They ought to be stopped. Would you like to see my things? I have things inside to look at."

"I," said Jessie, "uh, no. No, I can't. Excuse me." She turned quickly, moved out from under the stairs, back into the sunlight, and hurried back inside the building. All the way, she could feel his eyes on her.

She spent the rest of that day working, and the next as well, never glancing outside, for fear that he would be standing there. By Thursday the painting was finished. She decided to take it in to Pirouette herself and have dinner downtown, maybe do a little shopping. A day away from the apartment and the Pear-shaped Man would do her good, soothe her nerves. She was being overimaginative. He hadn't actually done anything, after all. It was just that he was so damned *creepy*.

Adrian, the art director at Pirouette, was glad to see her, as always. "That's my Jessie," he said after he'd given her a hug. "I wish all my artists were like you. Never miss a deadline, never turn in anything but the best work, a real pro. Come on back to my office, we'll look at this one and talk about some new assignments and gossip a bit." He told his secretary to hold his calls and escorted her back through the maze of tiny little cubicles where the editors lived. Adrian himself had a huge corner office with two big windows, a sign of his status in Pirouette Publishing. He gestured Jessie to a chair, poured her a cup of herb tea, then took her portfolio and removed the cover painting and held it up at arm's length.

The silence went on far too long.

Adrian dragged out a chair, propped up the painting, and retreated several feet to consider it from a distance. He stroked his beard and cocked his head this way and that. Watching him, Jessie felt a thin prickle of alarm. Normally, Adrian was given to exuberant outbursts of approval. She didn't like this quiet. "What's wrong?" she said, setting down her teacup. "Don't you like it?"

"Oh," Adrian said. He put out a hand, palm open and level, waggled it this way and that. "It's well executed, no doubt. Your technique is very professional. Fine detail."

"I researched all the clothing," she said in exasperation. "It's all authentic for the period; you know it is."

"Yes, no doubt. And the heroine is gorgeous, as always. I wouldn't mind ripping her bodice myself. You do amazing things with mammaries, Jessie."

She stood up. "Then what is it?" she said. "I've been doing covers for you for three years now, Adrian. There's never been any problem."

"Well," he said. He shook his head, smiled. "Nothing, really. Maybe you've been doing too many of these. I know how it can go. They're so much alike, it gets boring, painting all those hot embraces one after another; so pretty soon you feel an urge to experiment, to try something a little bit different." He shook a finger at her. "It won't do, though. Our readers just want the same old shit with the same old covers. I understand, but it won't do."

"There's nothing experimental about this painting." Jessie said, exasperated. "It's the same thing I've done for you a hundred times before. *What* won't do?"

Adrian looked honestly surprised. "Why, the man, of course," he said. "I thought you'd done it deliberately." He gestured. "I mean, look at him. He's almost *unattractive*."

"What?" Jessie moved over to the painting. "He's the same virile jerk I've painted over and over again."

Adrian frowned. "Really now," he said. "Look." He started pointing things out. "There, around his collar, is that or is that not just the faintest hint of a double chin? And look at that lower lip! Beautifully executed, yes, but it looks, well, gross. Like it was wet or something. Pirouette heroes rape, they plunder, they seduce, they threaten, but they do not drool, darling. And perhaps it's just a trick of perspective, but I could swear"—he paused, leaned close, shook his head—"no, it's not perspective, the top of his head is definitely narrower than the bottom. A pinhead! We can't have pinheads on Pirouette books, Jessie. Too much fullness in the cheeks, too. He looks as though he might be storing nuts for the winter." Adrian shook his head. "It won't do, love. Look, no big problem. The rest of the painting is fine. Just take it home and fix him up. How about it?"

Jessie was staring at her painting in horror, as if she were seeing it for the first time. Everything Adrian had said, everything he had pointed out, was true. It was all very subtle, to be sure; at first glance the man looked almost like your normal Pirouette hero, but there was something just the tiniest bit off about him, and when you looked closer, it was blatant and unmistakable. Somehow the Pear-shaped Man had crept into her painting. "I," she began, "I, yes, you're right, I'll do it over. I don't know what happened. There's this man who lives in my building, a creepy-looking guy, everybody calls him the Pear-shaped Man. He's been getting on my nerves. I swear, it wasn't intentional. I guess I've been thinking about him so much it just crept into my work subconsciously."

"I understand," Adrian said. "Well, no problem, just set it right. We do have deadline problems, though."

"I'll fix it this weekend, have it back to you by Monday," Jessie promised.

"Wonderful," said Adrian. "Let's talk about those other assignments, then." He poured her more Red Zinger, and they sat down to talk. By the time Jessie left his office, she was feeling much better.

Afterward she enjoyed a drink in her favorite bar, met a few friends, and had a nice dinner at an excellent new Japanese restaurant. It was dark by the time she got home. There was no sign of the Pear-shaped Man. She kept her portfolio under her arm as she fished for her keys and unlocked the door to the building.

When she stepped inside, Jessie heard a faint noise and felt something crunch underfoot. A nest of orange worms clustered against the faded blue of the hallway carpet, crushed and broken by her foot.

SHE DREAMED OF HIM AGAIN. IT WAS THE SAME SHAPELESS, TERRIBLE dream. She was down in the dark beneath the stoop, near the trash bins crawling with all kinds of things, waiting at his door. She was frightened, too frightened to knock or open the door yet helpless to leave. Finally the door crept open of its own accord. There he stood, smiling, smiling. "Would you like to stay?" he said, and the last words echoed, *to stay to stay to stay to stay,* and he reached out for her, and his fingers were as soft and pulpy as earthworms when he touched her on the cheek.

The next morning Jessie arrived at the offices of Citywide Realty just as they opened their doors. The receptionist told her that Edward Selby was out showing some condos; she couldn't say when he'd be in. "That's all right," Jessie said. "I'll wait." She settled down to leaf through some magazines, studying pictures of houses she couldn't afford.

Selby arrived just before eleven. He looked momentarily surprised to see her, before his professional smile switched on automatically. "Jessie," he said, "how nice. Something I can do for you?"

"Let's talk," she said, tossing down the magazines.

They went to Selby's desk. He was still only an associate with the rental firm, so he shared the office with another agent, but she was out, and they had the room to themselves. Selby settled himself into his chair and leaned back. He was a pleasant-looking man, with curly brown hair and white teeth, his eyes careful behind silver aviator frames. "Is there a problem?" he asked.

Jessie leaned forward. "The Pear-shaped Man," she said.

Selby arched one eyebrow. "I see. A harmless eccentric."

"Are you sure of that?"

He shrugged. "He hasn't murdered anybody yet, at least that I know of."

"How much do you know about him? For starters, what's his name?"

"Good question," Selby said, smiling. "Here at Citywide Realty we just think of him as the Pear-shaped Man. I don't think I've ever gotten a name out of him."

"What the hell do you mean?" Jessie demanded. "Are you telling me his checks have THE PEAR-SHAPED MAN printed on them?"

Selby cleared his throat. "Well, no. Actually, he doesn't use checks. I come by on the first of every month to collect, and knock on his door, and he pays me in cash. One-dollar bills, in fact. I stand there, and he counts out the money into my hand, dollar by dollar. I'll confess, Jessie, that I've never been inside the apartment, and I don't especially care to. Kind of a funny smell, you know? But he's a good tenant, as far as we're concerned. Always has his rent paid on time. Never bitches about rent hikes. And he certainly doesn't bounce checks on us." He showed a lot of teeth, a broad smile to let her know he was joking.

Jessie was not amused. "He must have given a name when he first rented the apartment."

"I wouldn't know about that," Selby said. "I've only handled that building for six years. He's been down in the basement a lot longer than that."

"Why don't you check his lease?"

Selby frowned. "Well, I could dig it up, I suppose. But really, is his name any of your business? What's the problem here, anyway? Exactly what has the Pear-shaped Man *done?*"

Jessie sat back and crossed her arms. "He looks at me."

"Well," Selby said, carefully, "I, uh, well, you're an attractive woman, Jessie. I seem to recall asking you out myself."

"That's different," she said. "You're normal. It's the way he looks at me."

"Undressing you with his eyes?" Selby suggested.

Jessie was nonplussed. "No," she said. "That isn't it. It's not sexual, not in the normal way, anyhow. I don't know how to explain it. He keeps asking me down to his apartment. He's always hanging around."

"Well, that's where he lives."

"He bothers me. He's crept into my paintings."

This time both of Selby's eyebrows went up. "Into your paintings?" he said. There was a funny hitch in his voice.

Jessie was getting more and more discomfited; this wasn't coming out right at all. "Okay, it doesn't sound like much, but he's *creepy,* I tell you. His lips are always wet. The way he smiles. His eyes. His squeaky little voice. And that smell. Jesus Christ, you collect his rent, you ought to know."

The realtor spread his hands helplessly. "It's not against the law to have body odor. It's not even a violation of his lease."

"Last night he snuck into the building and left a pile of Cheez Doodles right where I'd step in them."

"Cheez Doodles?" Selby said. His voice took on a sarcastic edge. "God, not *Cheez Doodles!* How fucking heinous! Have you informed the police?"

"It's not funny. What was he doing inside the building, anyway?"

"He lives there."

"He lives in the basement. He has his own door, he doesn't need to come into our hallway. Nobody but the six regular tenants ought to have keys to that door."

"Nobody does, as far as I know," Selby said. He pulled out a notepad. "Well, that's something, anyway. I'll tell you what, I'll have the lock changed on the outer door. The Pear-shaped Man won't get a key. Will that make you happy?"

"A little," said Jessie, slightly mollified.

"I can't promise that he won't get in," Selby cautioned. "You know how it is. If I had a nickel for every time some tenant has taped over a lock or propped open a door with a doorstop because it was more convenient, well . . ."

"Don't worry, I'll see that nothing like that happens. What about his name? Will you check the lease for me?"

Selby sighed. "This is really an invasion of privacy. But I'll do it. A personal favor. You owe me one." He got up and went across the room to a black metal filing cabinet, pulled open a drawer, rummaged around, and came out with a legal-sized folder. He was flipping through it as he returned to his desk.

"Well?" Jessie asked, impatiently.

"Hmmm," Selby said. "Here's your lease. And here're the others." He went back to the beginning and checked the papers one by one. "Winbright, Peabody, Pumetti, Harris, Jeffries." He closed the file, looked up at her, and shrugged. "No lease. Well, it's a crummy little apartment, and he's been there forever. Either we've misfiled his lease or he never had one. It's not unknown. A month-to-month basis . . ."

"Oh, great," Jessie said. "Are you going to do anything about it?"

"I'll change that lock," Selby said. "Beyond that, I don't know what you expect of me. I'm not going to evict the man for offering you Cheez Doodles."

The Pear-shaped Man was standing on the stoop when Jessie got home, his battered bag tucked up under one arm. He smiled when he saw her approach. *Let him touch me,* she thought; *just let him touch me when I walk by, and I'll have him booked for assault so fast it'll make his little pointy head swim.* But the Pear-shaped Man made no effort to grab her. "I have things to show you downstairs," he said as Jessie ascended the stairs. She had to pass within a foot of him; the smell was overwhelming today, a rich odor like yeast and decaying vegetables. "Would you like to look at my things?" he called after her. Jessie unlocked the door and slammed it behind her.

I'm not going to think about him, she told herself inside, over a cup of tea. She had work to do. She'd promised Adrian the cover by Monday, after all. She went into her studio, drew back the curtains, and set to work, determined to eradicate every hint of the Pear-shaped Man from the cover. She painted away the double chin, firmed up the jaw, redid those tight wet lips, darkened the hair, made it blacker and bushier and more wind-tossed so the head didn't seem to come to such a point. She gave him sharp, high, pronounced cheekbones—cheekbones like the blade of a knife—made the face almost gaunt. She even changed the color of his eyes. Why had she given him those weak, pale eyes? She made the eyes green, a crisp, clean, commanding green, full of vitality.

It was almost midnight by the time she was done, and Jessie was exhausted, but when she stepped back to survey her handiwork, she was delighted. The man was a real Pirouette hero now: a rakehell, a rogue, a hellraiser whose robust exterior concealed a brooding, melancholy, poetic soul. There was nothing the least bit pear-shaped about him. Adrian would have puppies.

It was a good kind of tiredness. Jessie went to sleep feeling altogether satisfied. Maybe Selby was right; she was too imaginative, she'd really let the Pear-shaped Man get to her. But work, good hard old-fashioned work was the perfect antidote for these shapeless fears of hers. Tonight, she was sure, her sleep would be deep and dreamless.

She was wrong. There was no safety in her sleep. She stood trembling on his doorstep once again. It was so dark down there, so filthy. The rich ripe smell of the garbage cans was overwhelming, and she thought she could hear things moving in the shadows. The door began to open. The Pear-shaped Man smiled at her and touched her with cold, soft fingers like a nest of grubs. He took hold of her by the arm and drew her inside, inside, inside, inside. . . .

Angela knocked on her door the next morning at ten. "Sunday brunch," she called out. "Don is making waffles. With chocolate chips and fresh strawberries. And bacon. And coffee. And O.J. Want some?"

Jessie sat up in bed. "Don? Is he here?"

"He stayed over," Angela said.

Jessie climbed out of bed and pulled on a paint-splattered pair of jeans. "You know I'd never turn down one of Don's brunches. I didn't even hear you guys come in."

"I snuck my head into your studio, but you were painting away, and you didn't even notice. You had that intent look you get sometimes, you know, with the tip of your tongue peeking out of one corner of your mouth. I figured it was better not to disturb the artist at work." She giggled. "How you avoided hearing the bedsprings, though, I'll never know."

Breakfast was a triumph. There were times when Jessie couldn't understand just what Angela saw in Donald the student shrink, but mealtimes were not among them. He was a splendid cook. Angela and Donald were still lingering over coffee, and Jessie over tea, at eleven, when they heard noises from the hall. Angela went to check. "Some guy's out there changing the lock," she said when she returned. "I wonder what that's all about."

"I'll be damned," Jessie said. "And on the weekend, too. That's time and a half. I never expected Selby to move so fast."

Angela looked at her curiously. "What do you know about this?"

So Jessie told them all about her meeting with the realtor and her encounters with the Pear-shaped Man. Angela giggled once or twice, and Donald slipped into his wise-shrink face. "Tell me, Jessie," he said when she had finished, "don't you think you're overreacting a bit here?"

"No," Jessie said curtly.

"You're stonewalling," Donald said. "Really now, try and look at your actions objectively. What has this man done to you?"

"Nothing, and I intend to keep it that way," Jessie snapped. "I didn't ask for your opinion."

"You don't have to ask," Donald said. "We're friends, aren't we? I hate to see you getting upset over nothing. It sounds to me as though you're developing some kind of phobia about a harmless neighborhood character."

Angela giggled. "He's just got a crush on you, that's all. You're such a heartbreaker."

Jessie was getting annoyed. "You wouldn't think it was funny if he was leaving Cheez Doodles for you," she said angrily. "There's something . . . well, something *wrong* there. I can feel it."

Donald spread his hands. "Something wrong? Most definitely. The man is obviously very poorly socialized. He's unattractive, sloppy, he doesn't conform to normal standards of dress or personal hygiene, he has unusual eating habits and a great deal of difficulty relating to others. He's probably a very lonely person and no doubt deeply neurotic as well. But none of this makes him a killer or a rapist, does it? Why are you becoming so obsessed with him?"

"I am not becoming obsessed with him."

"Obviously you are," Donald said.

"She's in love," Angela teased.

Jessie stood up. "I am *not* becoming obsessed with him!" she shouted, "and this discussion has just ended."

———

THAT NIGHT, IN HER DREAM, JESSIE SAW INSIDE FOR THE FIRST TIME. HE drew her in, and she found she was too weak to resist. The lights were very bright inside, and it was warm and oh so humid, and the air seemed to move as if she had entered the mouth of some great beast, and the walls were orange and flaky and had a strange, sweet smell, and there were empty plastic Coke bottles everywhere and bowls of half-eaten Cheez Doodles, too, and the Pear-shaped Man said, "You can see my things, you can have my things," and he began to undress, unbuttoning his short-sleeved shirt, pulling it off, revealing dead, white, hairless flesh and two floppy breasts, and the right breast was stained with blue ink from his leaking pens, and he was smiling, smiling, and he undid his thin belt, and then pulled down the fly on his brown polyester pants, and Jessie woke screaming.

———

ON MONDAY MORNING, JESSIE PACKED UP HER COVER PAINTING, phoned a messenger service, and had them take it down to Pirouette for her. She wasn't up to another trip downtown. Adrian would want to chat, and Jess wasn't in a very sociable mood. Angela kept needling her about the Pear-shaped Man, and it had left her in a foul temper. Nobody seemed to understand. There was something wrong with the Pear-shaped Man, something serious, something horrible. He was no joke. He was frightening. Somehow she had to prove it. She had to learn his name, had to find out what he was hiding.

She could hire a detective, except detectives were expensive. There had to be something she could do on her own. She could try his mailbox again. She'd be better off if she waited until the day the gas and electric bills came, though. He had lights in his apartment, so the electric company would know his name. The only problem was that the electric bill wasn't due for another couple of weeks.

The living room windows were wide open, Jessie noticed suddenly. Even the drapes had been drawn all the way back. Angela must have done it that morning before taking off for work. Jessie hesitated and then went to the window. She closed it, locked it, moved to the next, closed it, locked it. It made her feel safer. She told herself she wouldn't look out. It would be better if she didn't look out.

How could she not look out? She looked out. He was there, standing on the sidewalk below her, looking up. "You could see my things," he said in his high, thin voice. "I knew when I saw you that you'd want my things. You'd like them. We could have food." He reached into a bulgy pocket, brought out a single Cheez Doodle, held it up to her. His mouth moved silently.

"Get away from here, or I'll call the police!" Jessie shouted.

"I have something for you. Come to my house and you can have it. It's in my pocket. I'll give it to you."

"No, you won't. Get away, I warn you. Leave me alone." She stepped back, closed the drapes. It was gloomy in here with the drapes pulled, but that was better than knowing that the Pear-shaped Man was looking in. Jessie turned on a light, picked up a paperback, and tried to read. She found herself turning pages rapidly and realized she didn't have the vaguest idea of what the words meant. She slammed down the book, marched into the kitchen, made a tuna salad sandwich on whole wheat toast. She wanted something with it, but she wasn't sure what. She took out a dill pickle and sliced it into quarters, arranged it neatly on her plate, searched through her cupboard for some potato chips. Then she poured a big fresh glass of milk and sat down to lunch.

She took one bite of the sandwich, made a face, and shoved it away. It tasted funny. Like the mayonnaise had gone bad or something. The pickle was too sour, and the chips seemed soggy and limp and much too salty. She didn't want chips anyway. She wanted something else. Some of those little orange cheese curls. She could picture them in her head, almost taste them. Her mouth watered.

Then she realized what she was thinking and almost gagged. She got up and scraped her lunch into the garbage. She had to get out of here, she thought wildly. She'd go see a movie or something, forget all about the Pear-shaped Man for a few hours. Maybe she could go to a singles' bar somewhere, pick someone up, get laid. At his place. Away from here. Away from the Pear-shaped Man. That was the ticket. A night away from the apartment would do her good.

She went to the window, pulled aside the drapes, peered out.

The Pear-shaped Man smiled, shifted from side to side. He had his misshapen briefcase under his arm. His pockets bulged. Jessie felt her skin crawl. He was *revolting,* she thought. But she wasn't going to let him keep her prisoner.

She gathered her things together, slipped a little steak knife into her purse just in case, and marched outside. "Would you like to see what I have in my case?" the Pear-shaped Man asked her when she emerged. Jessie had decided to ignore him. If she did not reply at all, just pretended he wasn't there, maybe he'd grow bored and leave her alone. She descended the steps briskly and set off down the street. The Pear-shaped Man followed close behind her. "They're all around us," he whispered. She could smell him hurrying a step or two behind her, puffing as he walked. "They are. They laugh at me. They don't understand, but they want my things. I can show you proof. I have it down in my house. I know you want to come see."

Jessie continued to ignore him. He followed her all the way to the bus stop.

THE MOVIE WAS A DUD. HAVING SKIPPED LUNCH, JESSIE WAS HUNGRY. She got a Coke and a tub of buttered popcorn from the candy counter. The Coke was three-quarters crushed ice, but it still tasted good. She couldn't eat the popcorn. The fake butter they used had a vaguely rancid smell that reminded her of the Pear-shaped Man. She tried two kernels and felt sick.

Afterward, though, she did a little better. His name was Jack, he said. He was a sound man on a local TV news show, and he had an interesting face: an easy smile, Clark Gable ears, nice gray eyes with friendly little crinkles in the corners. He bought her a drink and touched her hand; but the way he did it was a little clumsy, like he was a bit shy about this whole scene, and Jessie liked that. They had a few drinks together, and then he suggested dinner back at his place. Nothing fancy, he said. He had some cold cuts in the fridge; he could whip up some jumbo sandwiches and show her his stereo system, which was some kind of special super setup he'd rigged himself. That all sounded fine to her.

His apartment was on the twenty-third floor of a midtown high-rise, and from his windows you could see sailboats tacking off on the horizon. Jack put the new Linda Ronstadt album on the stereo while he went to make the sandwiches. Jessie watched the sailboats. She was finally beginning to relax. "I have beer or ice tea," Jack called from the kitchen. "What'll be?"

"Coke," she said absently.

"No Coke," he called back. "Beer or ice tea."

"Oh," she said, somehow annoyed. "Ice tea, then."

"You got it. Rye or wheat?"

"I don't care," she said. The boats were very graceful. She'd like to paint them someday. She could paint Jack, too. He looked like he had a nice body.

"Here we go," he said, emerging from the kitchen carrying a tray. "I hope you're hungry."

"Famished," Jessie said, turning away from the window. She went over to where he was setting the table and froze.

"What's wrong?" Jack said. He was holding out a white stoneware plate. On top of it was a truly gargantuan ham-and-Swiss sandwich on fresh deli rye, lavishly slathered with mustard, and next to it, filling up the rest of the plate, was a pile of puffy orange cheese curls. They seemed to writhe and move, to edge toward the sandwich, toward her. "Jessie?" Jack said.

She gave a choked, inarticulate cry and pushed the plate away wildly. Jack lost his grip; ham, Swiss cheese, bread, and Cheez Doodles scattered in all directions. A Cheez Doodle brushed against Jessie's leg. She whirled and ran from the apartment.

———

JESSIE SPENT THE NIGHT ALONE AT A HOTEL AND SLEPT POORLY. EVEN here, miles from the apartment, she could not escape the dream. It was the same as before, the same, but each night it seemed to grow longer, each night it went a little further. She was on the stoop, waiting, afraid. The door opened, and he drew her inside, the orange warm, the air like fetid breath, the Pear-shaped Man smiling. "You can see my things," he said, "you can have my things," and then he was undressing, his shirt first, his skin so white, dead flesh, heavy breasts with a blue ink stain, his belt, his pants falling, polyester puddling around his ankles, all the trash in his pockets scattering on the floor, and he really was pear-shaped, it wasn't just the way he dressed, and then the boxer shorts last of all, and Jessie looked down despite herself and there was no hair and it was small and wormy and kind of yellow, like a cheese curl, and it moved slightly and the Pear-shaped Man was saying, "I want your things now, give them to me, let me see your things," and why couldn't she run, her feet wouldn't move, but her hands did, her hands, and she began to undress.

The hotel detective woke her, pounding on her door, demanding to know what the problem was and why she was screaming.

———

SHE TIMED HER RETURN HOME SO THAT THE PEAR-SHAPED MAN WOULD be away on his morning run to Santino's Market when she arrived. The house was empty. Angela had already gone to work, leaving the living room windows open again. Jessie closed them, locked them, and pulled the drapes. With luck, the Pear-shaped Man would never know that she'd come home.

Already the day outside was swelteringly hot. It was going to be a real scorcher. Jessie felt sweaty and soiled. She stripped, dumped her clothing into the wicker hamper in her bedroom, and immersed herself in a long, cold shower. The icy water hurt, but it was a good clean kind of hurting, and it left her feeling invigorated. She dried her hair and wrapped herself in a huge, fluffy blue towel, then padded back to her bedroom, leaving wet footprints on the bare wood floors.

A halter top and a pair of cutoffs would be all she'd need in this heat, Jessie decided. She had a plan for the day firmly in mind. She'd get dressed, do a little work in her studio, and after that she could read or watch some soaps or something. She wouldn't go outside; she wouldn't even look out the window. If the Pear-shaped Man was at his vigil, it would be a long, hot, boring afternoon for him.

Jessie laid out her cutoffs and a white halter top on the bed, draped the wet towel over a bedpost, and went to her dresser for a fresh pair of panties. She ought to do laundry soon, she thought absently as she snatched up a pair of pink bikini briefs.

A Cheez Doodle fell out.

Jessie recoiled, shuddering. It had been *inside,* she thought wildly, it had been inside the briefs. The powdery cheese had left a yellow stain on the fabric. The Cheez Doodle lay where it had fallen, in the open drawer on top of her underwear. Something like terror took hold of her. She balled the bikini briefs up in her fist and tossed them away with revulsion. She grabbed another pair of panties, shook them, and another Cheez Doodle leapt out. And then another. Another. She began to make a thin, hysterical sound, but she kept on. Five pairs, six, nine, that was all, but that was enough. Someone had opened her drawer and taken out every pair of panties and carefully wrapped a Cheez Doodle in each and put them all back.

It was a ghastly joke, she thought. Angela, it had to be Angela who'd done it, maybe she and Donald together. They thought this whole thing about the Pear-shaped Man was a big laugh, so they decided to see if they could really freak her out.

Except it hadn't been Angela. She knew it hadn't been Angela.

Jessie began to sob uncontrollably. She threw her balled-up panties to the floor and ran from the room, crushing Cheez Doodles into the carpet.

Out in the living room, she didn't know where to turn. She couldn't go back to her bedroom, *couldn't,* not just now, not until Angela got back, and she didn't want to go to the windows, even with the drapes closed. He was out there, Jessie could feel it, could feel him staring up at the windows. She grew suddenly aware of her nakedness and covered herself with her hands. She backed away from the windows, step by uncertain step, and retreated to her studio.

Inside she found a big square package leaning up against the door, with a note from Angela taped to it. "Jess, this came for you last evening," signed with Angie's big winged A. Jessie stared at the package, uncomprehending. It was from Pirouette. It was her painting, the cover she'd rushed to redo for them. Adrian had sent it back. Why?

She didn't want to know. She had to know.

Wildly, Jessie ripped at the brown paper wrappings, tore them away in long, ragged strips, baring the cover she'd painted. Adrian had written on the mat; she recognized his hand. "Not funny, kid," he'd scrawled. "Forget it."

"No," Jessie whimpered, backing off.

There it was, her painting, the familiar background, the trite embrace, the period costumes researched so carefully, but no, she hadn't done that, someone had changed it, it wasn't her work, the woman was her, her, her, slender and strong with sandy blond hair and green eyes full of rapture, and he was crushing her to him, to *him,* the wet lips and white skin, and he had a blue ink stain on his ruffled lace shirtfront and dandruff on his velvet jacket and his head was pointed and his hair was greasy and the fingers wrapped in her locks were stained yellow, and he was smiling thinly and pulling her to him and her mouth was open and her eyes half closed and it was him and it was her, and there was her own signature, there, down at the bottom.

"No," she said again. She backed away, tripped over an easel, and fell. She curled up into a little ball on the floor and lay there sobbing, and that was how Angela found her, hours later.

———————

ANGELA LAID HER OUT ON THE COUCH AND MADE A COLD COMPRESS and pressed it to her forehead. Donald stood in the doorway between the living room and the studio, frowning, glancing first at Jessie and then in at the painting and then at Jessie again. Angela said soothing things and held Jessie's hand and got her a cup of tea; little by little her hysteria began to ebb. Donald crossed his arms and scowled. Finally, when Jessie had dried the last of her tears, he said, "This obsession of yours has gone too far."

"Don, don't," Angela said. "She's terrified."

"I can see that," Donald said. "That's why something has to be done. She's doing it to herself, honey."

Jessie had a hot cup of Morning Thunder halfway to her mouth. She stopped dead still. "I'm doing it to myself?" she repeated incredulously.

"Certainly," Donald said.

The complacency in his tone made Jessie suddenly, blazingly angry. "You stupid, ignorant, callous son of a bitch," she roared. "I'm doing it to myself, *I'm* doing it, *I'm* doing it, how *dare* you say that *I'm* doing it." She flung the teacup across the room, aiming for his fat head. Donald ducked; the cup shattered and the tea sent three long brown fingers running down the off-white wall.

"Go on, let out your anger," he said. "I know you're upset. When you calm down, we can discuss this rationally, maybe get to the root of your problem."

Angela took her arm, but Jessie shook off the grip and stood, her hands balled into fists. "Go into my bedroom, you jerk, go in there right now and look around and come back and tell me what you see."

"If you'd like," Donald said. He walked over to the bedroom door, vanished, reemerged several moments later. "All right," he said patiently.

"Well?" Jessie demanded.

Donald shrugged. "It's a mess," he said. "Underpants all over the floor, lots of crushed cheese curls. Tell me what you think it means."

"He broke in here!" Jessie said.

"The Pear-shaped Man?" Donald queried pleasantly.

"*Of course* it was the Pear-shaped Man," Jessie screamed. "He snuck in here while we were all gone and he went into my bedroom and pawed through all my things and put Cheez Doodles in my underwear. He was *here!* He was touching my stuff."

Donald wore an expression of patient, compassionate wisdom. "Jessie, dear, I want you to think about what you just told us."

"There's nothing to think about!"

"Of course there is," he said. "Let's think it through together. The Pear-shaped Man was here, you think?"

"Yes."

"Why?"

"To do . . . to do what he did. It's disgusting. He's disgusting."

"Hmmm," Don said. "How, then? The locks were changed, remember? He can't even get in the building. He's never had a key to this apartment. There was no sign of forced entry. How did he get in with his bag of cheese curls?"

Jessie had him there. "Angela left the living room windows open," she said.

Angela looked stricken. "I did," she admitted. "Oh, Jessie, honey, I'm so sorry. It was hot. I just wanted to get a breeze, I didn't mean . . ."

"The windows are too high to reach from the sidewalk," Donald pointed out. "He'd have needed a ladder or something to stand on. He'd have needed to do it in broad daylight, from a busy street, with people coming and going all the time. He'd have had to have left the same way. There's the problem of the screens. He doesn't look like a very athletic sort, either."

"He did it," Jessie insisted. "He was here, wasn't he?"

"I know you think so, and I'm not trying to deny your feelings, just explore them. Has this Pear-shaped Man ever been invited into the apartment?"

"Of course not!" Jessie said. "What are you suggesting?"

"Nothing, Jess. Just consider. He climbs in through the windows with these cheese curls he intends to secret in your drawers. Fine. How does he know which room is yours?"

Jessie frowned. "He . . . I don't know . . . he searched around, I guess."

"And found what clue? You've got three bedrooms here, one a studio, two full of women's clothing. How'd he pick the right one?"

"Maybe he did it in both."

"Angela, would you go check your bedroom, please?" Donald asked.

Angela rose hesitantly. "Well," she said, "okay." Jessie and Donald stared at each other until she returned a minute or so later. "All clean," she said.

"I don't know how he figured out which damned room was mine," Jessie said. "All I know is that he did. He had to. How else can you explain what happened, huh? Do you think I did it *myself?*"

Donald shrugged. "I don't know," he said calmly. He glanced over his shoulder into the studio. "Funny, though. That painting in there, him and you, he must have done that some other time, after you finished it but before you sent it to Pirouette. It's good work, too. Almost as good as yours."

Jessie had been trying very hard not to think about the painting. She opened her mouth to throw something back at him, but nothing flew out. She closed her mouth. Tears began to gather in the corners of her eyes. She suddenly felt weary, confused, and very alone. Angela had walked over to stand beside Donald. They were both looking at her. Jessie looked down at her hands helplessly and said, "What am I going to do? God. What am I going to *do?*"

God did not answer; Donald did. "Only one thing *to* do," he said briskly. "Face up to your fears. Exorcise them. Go down there and talk to the man, get to know him. By the time you come back up, you may pity him or have contempt for him or dislike him, but you won't fear him any longer; you'll see that he's only a human being and a rather sad one."

"Are you sure, Don?" Angela asked him.

"Completely. Confront this obsession of yours, Jessie. That's the only way you'll ever be free of it. Go down to the basement and visit with the Pear-shaped Man."

"There's nothing to be afraid of," Angela told her again.

"That's easy for you to say."

"Look, Jess, the minute you're inside, Don and I will come out and sit on the stoop. We'll be just an earshot away. All you'll have to do is let out the teeniest little yell and we'll come rushing right down. So you won't be alone, not really. And you've still got that knife in your purse, right?"

Jessie nodded.

"Come on, then, remember the time that purse snatcher tried to grab your shoulder bag? You decked him good. If this Pear-shaped Man tries anything, you're quick enough. Stab him. Run away. Yell for us. You'll be perfectly safe."

"I suppose you're right," Jessie said with a small sigh. They *were* right. She knew it. It didn't make any sense. He was a dirty, foul-smelling, unattractive man, maybe a little retarded, but nothing she couldn't handle, nothing she had to be afraid of, she didn't want to be crazy, she was letting this ridiculous obsession eat her alive and it had to end now, Donald was perfectly correct, she'd been doing it to herself all along and now she was going to take hold of it and stop it, certainly, it all made perfect sense and there was nothing to worry about, nothing to be afraid of, what could the Pear-shaped Man do to her, after all, what could he possibly *do* to her that was so terrifying? Nothing. Nothing.

Angela patted her on the back. Jessie took a deep breath, took the doorknob firmly in hand, and stepped out of the building into the hot, damp evening air. Everything was under control.

So why was she so scared?

Night was falling, but down under the stairs it had fallen already. Down under the stairs it was always night. The stoop cut off the morning sun, and the building itself blocked the afternoon light. It was dark, so dark. She stumbled over a crack in the cement, and her foot rang off the side of a metal garbage can. Jessie shuddered, imagining flies and maggots and other, worse things moving and breeding back there where the sun never shone. *No, mustn't think about that, it was* only garbage, rotting and festering in the warm, humid dark, mustn't dwell on it. She was at the door.

She raised her hand to knock, and then the fear took hold of her again. She could not move. *Nothing to be frightened of,* she told herself, *nothing at all.* What could he possibly *do* to her? Yet still she could not bring herself to knock. She stood before his door with her hand raised, her breath raw in her throat. It was so hot, so suffocatingly hot. She had to breathe. She had to get out from under the stoop, get back to where she could breathe.

A thin vertical crack of yellow light split the darkness. *No,* Jessie thought, *oh, please no.*

The door was opening.

Why did it have to open so slowly? Slowly, like in her dreams. Why did it have to open at all?

The light was so bright in there. As the door opened, Jessie found herself squinting.

The Pear-shaped Man stood smiling at her.

"I," Jessie began, "I, uh, I . . ."

"*There* she is," the Pear-shaped Man said in his tinny little squeak.

"What do you want from me?" Jessie blurted.

"I knew she'd come," he said, as though she wasn't there. "I knew she'd come for my things."

"No," Jessie said. She wanted to run away, but her feet would not move.

"You can come in," he said. He raised his hand, moved it toward her face. He touched her. Five fat white maggots crawled across her cheek and wriggled through her hair. His fingers smelled like cheese curls. His pinkie touched her ear and tried to burrow inside. She hadn't seen his other hand move until she felt it grip her upper arm, pulling, pulling. His flesh felt damp and cold. Jessie whimpered.

"Come in and see my things," he said. "You have to. You know you have to." And somehow she was inside then, and the door was closing behind her, and she was there, inside, alone with the Pear-shaped Man.

Jessie tried to get a grip on herself. *Nothing to be afraid of,* she repeated to herself, a litany, a charm, a chant, *nothing to be afraid of, what could he do to you, what could he do?* The room was L-shaped, low ceilinged, filthy. The sickly sweet smell was overwhelming. Four naked lightbulbs burned in the fixture above, and along one wall was a row of old lamps without shades, bare bulbs blazing away. A three-legged card table stood against the opposite wall, its fourth corner propped up by a broken TV set with wires dangling through the shattered glass of its picture tube. On top of the card table was a big bowl of Cheez Doodles. Jessie looked away, feeling sick. She tried to step backward, and her foot hit an empty plastic Coke bottle. She almost fell. But the Pear-shaped Man caught her in his soft, damp grip and held her upright.

Jessie yanked herself free of him and backed away. Her hand went into her purse and closed around the knife. It made her feel better, stronger. She moved close to the boarded-up window. Outside she could make out Donald and Angela talking. The sound of their voices, so close at hand—that helped, too. She tried to summon up all of her strength. "How do you live like this?" she asked him. "Do you need help cleaning up the place? Are you sick?" It was so hard to force out the words.

"Sick," the Pear-shaped Man repeated. "Did they tell you I was sick? They lie about me. They lie about me all the time. Somebody should make them stop." If only he would stop smiling. His lips were so wet. But he never stopped smiling. "I knew you would come. Here. This is for you." He pulled it from a pocket, held it out.

"No," said Jessie. "I'm not hungry. Really." But she was hungry, she realized. She was famished. She found herself staring at the thick orange twist between his fingers, and suddenly she wanted it desperately. "No," she said again, but her voice was weaker now, barely more than a whisper, and the cheese curl was very close.

Her mouth sagged open. She felt it on her tongue, the roughness of the powdery cheese, the sweetness of it. It crunched softly between her teeth. She swallowed and licked the last orange flakes from her lower lip. She wanted more.

"I knew it was you," said the Pear-shaped Man. "Now your things are mine." Jessie stared at him. It was like in her nightmare. The Pear-shaped Man reached up and began to undo the little white plastic buttons on his shirt. She struggled to find her voice. He shrugged out of the shirt. His undershirt was yellow, with huge damp circles under his arms. He peeled it off, dropped it. He moved closer, and heavy white breasts flopped against his chest. The right one was covered by a wide blue smear. A dark little tongue slid between his lips. Fat white fingers worked at his belt like a team of dancing slugs. "These are for you," he said.

Jessie's knuckles were white around the hilt of the knife. "Stop," she said in a hoarse whisper.

His pants settled to the floor.

She couldn't take it. No more, no more. She pulled the knife free of her bag, raised it over her head. *"Stop!"*

"Ahh," said the Pear-shaped Man, "there it is."

She stabbed him.

The blade went in right to the hilt, plunged deep into his soft, white skin. She wrenched it down and out. The skin parted, a huge, meaty gash. The Pear-shaped Man was smiling his little smile. There was no blood, no blood at all. His flesh was soft and thick, all pale dead meat.

He moved closer, and Jessie stabbed him again. This time he reached up and knocked her hand away. The knife was embedded in his neck. The hilt wobbled back and forth as he padded toward her. His dead, white arms reached out and she pushed against him and her hand sank into his body like he was made of wet, rotten bread. "Oh," he said, "oh, oh, oh." Jessie opened her mouth to scream, and the Pear-shaped Man pressed those heavy wet lips to her own and swallowed at her sound. His pale eyes sucked at her. She felt his tongue darting forward, and it was round and black and oily, and then it was snaking down inside her, touching, tasting, feeling all her things. She was drowning in a sea of soft, damp flesh.

SHE WOKE TO THE SOUND OF THE DOOR CLOSING. IT WAS ONLY A SMALL click, a latch sliding into place, but it was enough. Her eyes opened, and she pulled herself up. It was so hard to move. She felt heavy, tired. Outside they were laughing. They were laughing at her. It was dim and far-off, that laughter, but she knew it was meant for her.

Her hand was resting on her thigh. She stared at it and blinked. She wiggled her fingers, and they moved like five fat maggots. She had something soft and yellow under her nails and deep, dirty yellow stains up near her fingertips.

She closed her eyes, ran her hand over her body, the soft heavy curves, the thicknesses, the strange hills and valleys. She pushed, and the flesh gave and gave and gave. She stood up weakly. There were her clothes, scattered on the floor. Piece by piece she pulled them on, and then she moved across the room. Her briefcase was down beside the door; she gathered it up, tucked it under her arm, she might need something, yes, it was good to have the briefcase. She pushed open the door and emerged into the warm night. She heard the voices above her: ". . . were right all along," a woman was saying, "I couldn't believe I'd been so silly. There's nothing sinister about him, really, he's just pathetic. Donald, I don't know how to thank you."

She came out from under the stoop and stood there. Her feet hurt so. She shifted her weight from one to the other and back again. They had stopped talking, and they were staring at her, Angela and Donald and a slender, pretty woman in blue jeans and work shirt. "Come back," she said, and her voice was thin and high. "Give them back. You took them, you took my things. You have to give them back."

The woman's laugh was like ice cubes tinkling in a glass of Coke.

"I think you've bothered Jessie quite enough," Donald said.

"She has my things," she said. "Please."

"I saw her come out, and she didn't have anything of yours," Donald said.

"She took all my things," she said.

Donald frowned. The woman with the sandy hair and the green eyes laughed again and put a hand on his arm. "Don't look so serious, Don. He's not all there."

They were all against her, she knew, looking at their faces. She clutched her briefcase to his chest. They'd taken her things, he couldn't remember exactly what, but they wouldn't get her case, he had stuff in there and they wouldn't get it. She turned away from them. He was hungry, she realized. She wanted something to eat. He had half a bag of Cheez Doodles left, she remembered. Downstairs. Down under the stoop.

As she descended, the Pear-shaped Man heard them talking about her. He opened the door and went inside to stay. The room smelled like home. He sat down, laid his case across his knees, and began to eat. He stuffed the cheese curls into his mouth in big handfuls and washed them down with sips from a glass of warm Coke straight from the bottle he'd opened that morning, or maybe yesterday. It was good. Nobody knew how good it was. They laughed at him, but they didn't know, they didn't know about all the nice things he had. No one knew. No one. Only someday he'd see somebody different, somebody to give his things to, somebody who would give him all their things. Yes. He'd like that. He'd know her when he saw her.

He'd know just what to say.

PHOTO: © KAROLINA WEBB

GEORGE R. R. MARTIN is the #1 *New York Times* bestselling author of many novels, including the acclaimed series A Song of Ice and Fire—*A Game of Thrones, A Clash of Kings, A Storm of Swords, A Feast for Crows,* and *A Dance with Dragons.* As a writer-producer, he has worked on *The Twilight Zone, Beauty and the Beast,* and various feature films and pilots that were never made. He lives with the lovely Parris in Santa Fe, New Mexico.

www.georgerrmartin.com

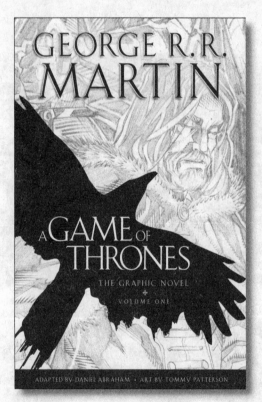

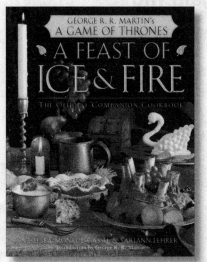

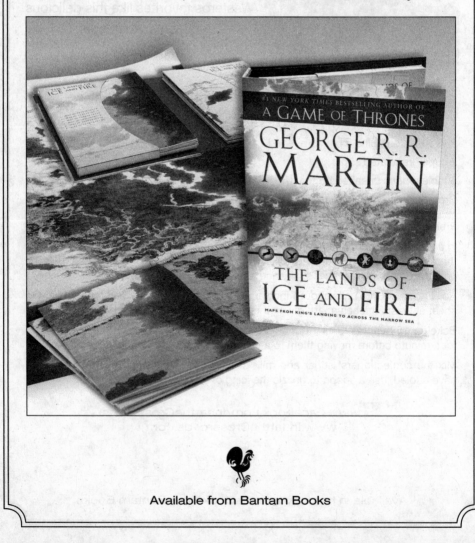

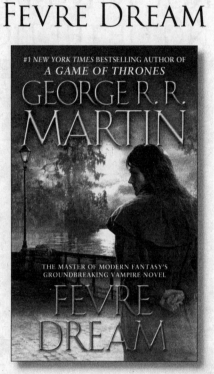

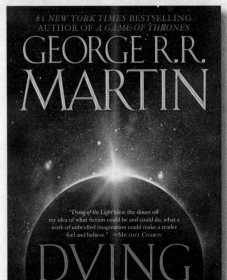

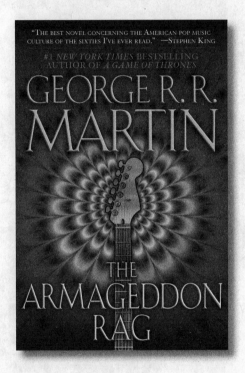

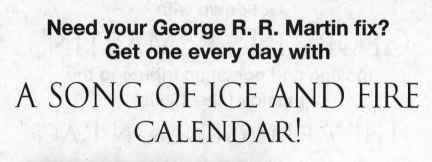